THE DEVIL TO PAY

IN THE BACKLANDS

THE DEVIL
TO PAY IN
THE BACKLANDS

"The Devil in the Street,
in the Middle of the Whirlwind"

BY JOÃO GUIMARÃES ROSA

Translated from the Portuguese by
JAMES L. TAYLOR *and* HARRIET DE ONÍS

1 9 7 1
New York   *Alfred·A·Knopf*

L. C. catalog card number: 65–12544

❁❁❁❁❁❁❁❁❁

THIS IS A BORZOI BOOK
PUBLISHED BY ALFRED A. KNOPF, INC.

❁❁❁❁❁❁❁❁❁

Published April 15, 1963
Second Printing, January 1971

Originally published in Portuguese
by Livraria José Olympio Editôra as
Grande Sertão: Veredas in 1956.

TO

Aracy, my wife, Ara,

THIS BOOK BELONGS

The Place of Guimarães Rosa
in Brazilian Literature

I CAN RECALL only one instance of a greater impact on contemporary Brazilian literature than that produced by the books of Guimarães Rosa: the publication of Gilberto Freyre's *Casa Grande e Senzala* (*The Masters and the Slaves*) in 1933. The repercussion of the Pernambucan sociologist's book was felt throughout Brazil. Moreover, it became the point of departure for a group of novelists who found their inspiration in the drama of the people and the land of Brazil: José Lins do Rego, Graciliano Ramos, Erico Verissimo, Rachel de Queiroz, José Americo de Almeida, Lucio Cardoso, Otavio de Faria, José Geraldo Vieira, to mention only the most outstanding.

Guimarães Rosa made his appearance on the literary scene ten years later with a book of short stories, *Sagarana*. He and his fellow trail-blazers represent the second generation, whose themes reflect that upsurge in their country's development set off by the Revolution of 1930, an upsurge which has been in the nature of an ascending spiral. These are novelists and short-story writers such as Dalcidio Jurandir, Herberto Sales, James Amado, Josué Montello, Hernani-Donato, Adonias Filho, José Conde. The movement was characterized by a determined and highly controversial effort to give new forms to the literary language (still unpolished and rough in the first generation of writers, who were engaged in the task of transforming the vernacular of Brazil into an instrument of artistic creation). The new literature divided critics and public; some became enthusiastic supporters, others violent opponents.

The critics were more divided than the public, as though they were exclusively concerned with and saw only the formal, stylistic aspect of Guimarães Rosa's work through which he was attempting to create, in keeping with the subject matter, a new narrative instrument. The outward cloak of this formal aspect seemed to conceal and hide from certain critics that heaving universe, brutal and tender, violent and gentle, of landscapes, beings, dramas, battles, wild backlands, the cruel, at times ludicrous sorrows which comprise the vast, unique world of Guimarães Rosa, Brazilian and universal at one and the same time.

What the public saw, over and above everything else, was the material out of which the work had been created, its content; that is to say, the lived and living flesh-and-blood life that so powerfully imbued it, at times came gushing from it. The public read and applauded the writer despite the fact that for many the formal expression was often more of a barrier to understanding than an avenue of approach. While the critics were arguing the validity of the experiment, quoting Joyce and showing off their erudition, the public realized that a unique figure, a creator of exceptional gifts had emerged on the Brazilian literary scene, whose revealed and revealing world was the sort that helps to build a nation and the awareness of a nation.

It is odd that Guimarães Rosa should be a *Mineiro*. In the cautious and, for the most part, conservative state of Minas Gerais, landlocked and astute, literature is as a rule well-mannered, fiction even more so than poetry (the poets Carlos Drummond de Andrade and Murilo Mendes are the opposite of well-mannered). Its fiction has not yet freed itself from the apron strings of Machado de Assis, and goes on recreating the unimaginative, mediocre life of the middle class, eschewing startling innovations, experiments with language, a veritable model of polite phrasing. Nothing could be further removed from this than *Corpo de Baile* or *Grande Sertão: Veredas* (*The*

Devil to Pay in the Backlands). For me, Guimarães Rosa is a
novelist of Bahía rather than Minas Gerais, and I think my position in this matter is perfectly tenable. There is a part of
Minas Gerais, that which forms the setting of *The Devil to Pay
in the Backlands,* which is a prolongation of the backlands of
Bahía in its customs, its language, the make-up and character
of its people. And this backland of Bahía—that of the great
bandits, the leaders of outlaws, the indomitable backlanders—
is Guimarães Rosa territory, the clay with which he works, into
which he plunges his hands in the act of creation. All this he
bears within himself, as though this distinguished diplomat
—nobody could be a greater gentleman or more refined—went
invisibly shod in rope sandals, wearing the leather jerkin of the
backlander over his soul, and armed with blunderbuss and violence. He carries this within himself, and returns it to his people in a work of dimensions rarely achieved in literature (I have
deliberately said "literature" and not "Brazilian literature").

I believe I was among the first to grasp and call attention to
the importance of Guimarães Rosa's achievement as a novelist
and to foresee the rapid universalization of his work. Not so
much or even because of its formal aspect, more limited to our
national frontiers, as because of the world revealed, re-created,
and given enduring life through the extraordinarily achieved
beings, through the Brazil that breathes in its every page.

Guimarães Rosa's case is, in my opinion, completely different
from that of Mario de Andrade, the Mario of *Macunaíma,* and
other Brazilian "modernistas." Mario drew mainly on books for
his material, saw Brazil through a veil of erudition, and for that
reason failed to reach the people. Guimarães Rosa had so much
to narrate, to reveal, to bring forth that he had to create an instrument of control—his language—to keep the spate, the flood
within bounds, and bring order to his creation. But what will
insure his greatness in the judgment of foreign readers, and
equate his name with those of the great contemporary writers
of fiction, is his creative power, the Brazilian authenticity of his
characters, the pulsating life that animates his every page.

On the occasion of the publication in English of *The Devil to
Pay in the Backlands* by Alfred A. Knopf, a friend of literature

and a friend of Brazil, thus bringing our master novelist to the knowledge of a new public, and adding new readers to those Guimarães Rosa already has abroad, it makes me happy to have this opportunity to pay tribute to the great writer to whose formation my generation, which immediately preceded his, contributed and for whom we cleared the way. The English-reading public will make the acquaintance of one of the greatest books our literature has produced, brutal, tender, cordial, savage, vast as Brazil itself, the image of Brazil drawn by a writer with a consummate mastery of his craft. Led by the hand of Guimarães Rosa, the turbulent men and women from the heart of the backlands enter upon that immortality which art alone can give them. *The Devil to Pay in the Backlands* bears witness—certainly as much as the great industrial establishments of São Paulo—to the maturity Brazil and its people have reached.

JORGE AMADO

Rio de Janeiro, September 1962

THE DEVIL TO PAY

IN THE BACKLANDS

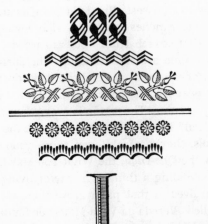

IT'S NOTHING.

Those shots you heard were not men fighting, God be praised. It was just me there in the back yard, target-shooting down by the creek, to keep in practice. I do it every day, because I enjoy it; have ever since I was a boy. Afterwards, they came to me about a calf, a stray white one, with the queerest eyes, and a muzzle like a dog. They told me about it but I didn't want to see it. On account of the deformity it was born with, with lips drawn back, it looked like somebody laughing. Man-face or dog-face: that settled it for them; it was the devil. Foolish folk. They killed it. Don't know who it belonged to. They came to borrow my gun and I let them have it.

You are smiling, amused-like. Listen, when it is a real gun-fight, all the dogs start barking, immediately —then when it's over you go to see if anybody got killed. You will have to excuse it, sir, but this is the sertão.* Some say it's not—that the real

* A glossary of Brazilian terms will be found at the end of the book.

sertão is way out yonder, on the high plains, beyond the Urucúia
River. Nonsense. For those of Corinto and Curvelo, then, isn't
right here the sertão? Ah, but there's more to it than that! The
sertão describes itself: it is where the grazing lands have no
fences; where you can keep going ten, fifteen leagues without
coming upon a single house; where a criminal can safely hide
out, beyond the reach of the authorities. The Urucúia rises in
the mountains to the west. But today, on its banks, you find
everything: huge ranches bordering rich lowlands, the flood
plains; farms that stretch from woods to woods; thick trees in
virgin forests—some are still standing. The surrounding lands
are the gerais. These gerais are endless. Anyway, the gentleman
knows how it is: each one believes what he likes: hog, pig, or
swine, it's as you opine. The sertão is everywhere.

About the devil? I have nothing to say. Ask the others around
here. Like fools, they're afraid even to mention his name; instead they say the *Que-Diga,* the What-You-May-Call-Him. Bah!
Not me. Over-avoiding a thing is a way of living with it. Take
Aristides, who lives in that palm grove there on the right, on
the creek called Vereda-da-Vaca-Mansa-de-Santa-Rita. Everybody believes what he says: that there are certain places, three
of them, that he can't go near without hearing a faint crying
behind him, and a little voice saying: "I'm coming! I'm coming!"
It's the Whoosis, the What-You-May-Call-Him. And then take
Jisé Simplício. Anybody here will swear to you that he keeps a
captive demon in his house—a little imp who is obliged to help
him in his shady dealings, which is why Simplício is on his way
to getting rich. They say this is also the reason Simplício's horse
shivers and shies when Simplício tries to mount. Superstition.
Jisé Simplício and Aristides are prospering, imp or no imp. Now
listen to this: there are people who insist that the devil himself
stopped off at Andrequicé while passing through there recently.
It seems that a certain young man, a stranger, showed up and
boasted that he could get from there here in only twenty minutes—it takes a full day and a half on horseback—because he
would go around the headwaters of the Rio do Chico.* Perhaps,
who knows—no offense intended—it could have been you your-

* A nickname for the São Francisco River.

self when you passed through there, just joking for the fun of it? Don't hold it against me—I know you didn't. I meant no harm. It is just that sometimes a question at the right time clears the air. But, you understand, sir, if there was such a young man, he just wanted to pull somebody's leg. Because, to circle the headwaters he would have to go deep into this state of ours and then double back, a trip of some three months. Well, then? The Whoosis? Nonsense. Imagination. And then this business of politely calling the devil by other names—that's practically inviting him to appear in person, in the flesh! Me, I have just about lost all my belief in him, thanks to God; and that's the honest truth I'm telling you, though I know he is taken for a fact and the Holy Gospels are full of him. Once I was talking with a young seminarian, very amiable he was, turning the pages and reading in his prayer book. He had on his vestments and bore a wand of chaste-tree in his hand. He said he was going to help the priest drive the Whoosis out of an old woman of Cachoeira-dos-Bois. I don't believe a word of it. My compadre Quelemém claims that it's the lower spirits that cause these manifestations, the third-class ones, milling about in the pitch darkness, seeking contact with the living, and that sometimes they will give a man real support. My compadre Quelemém is the one who eases my mind—Quelemém de Góis is his full name. But he lives so far from here—at Jijujá, on the Vereda do Buriti Pardo. But tell me, when it comes to being possessed of a devil, or helped by one, you too must have known of cases—men—women? Isn't that so? As for me, I've seen so many that I learned to spot them: Rincha-Mãe, Sangue-d'outro, Muitos-Beiços, Rasga-em-Baixo, Faca-Fria, Fancho-Bode, a certain Treciziano, Azinhavre, Hermógenes—a whole herd of them. If I could only forget so many names . . . I'm not a horse wrangler. And besides, anyone who fools around with the notion of becoming a jagunço, as I did, is already opening the door to the devil. Yes? No?

In my early days, I tried my hand at this and that, but as for thinking, I just didn't. Didn't have time. I was like a live fish on a griddle—when you're hard-pressed you waste no time in daydreams. But now, with time on my hands and no special worries, I can lie in my hammock and speculate. Does the devil exist, or doesn't he? That's what I'd like to know. I give up. Look: there is such a thing as a waterfall, isn't there? Yes, but a waterfall is only a high bank with water tumbling over the edge. Take away the water, or level the bank—what becomes of the waterfall? Living is a very dangerous business . . .

Let me try to explain: when the devil is inside a man, in his guts, the man is either evil or suffers bad luck. But, on his own, a man as such has no devil in him. Not one! Do you agree? Tell me frankly—you'll be doing me a great favor, and I ask it of you from my heart. This matter, however foolish it may seem, is important to me. I wish it wasn't. But don't tell me that a wise and learned person like you, sir, believes in the devil! You don't? I thank you. Your opinion reassures me. I knew you felt that way—I expected you would—I give you credit for it. Ah! when a man is old he needs to rest easy. I thank you again. All right, then, there is no devil. And no spirits. I never saw any. And if anybody was to see one, it should be me, your humble servant. If I was to tell you . . . So, the devil rules his black kingdom, in animals, in men, in women. Even in children, I say. For isn't there a saying: "A child—spawn of the devil?" And in things, in plants, in waters, in the earth, in the wind . . . "The devil in the street, in the middle of the whirlwind."

What? Ah, yes. Just an idea of mine, memories of things worse than bad. It's not that it hurts me to talk about them. It's better, it relieves me. Look here: in the same ground, and with branches and leaves of the same shape, doesn't the sweet cassava, which we eat, grow and the bitter cassava, which kills? Now the strange thing is that the sweet cassava can turn poisonous—why, I don't know. Some say it is from being replanted over and over in the same soil, from cuttings—it grows more and more bitter and then poisonous. But the other, the bitter cassava, sometimes changes too, and for no reason turns sweet and edible. How do you account for that? And have you ever seen the ugliness of glaring hate in the eyes of a rattlesnake? Or a fat hog, happier every day in its brutishness, that would gladly swallow the whole world if it could, for its filthy satisfaction? And some hawks and crows—just the look of them shows their need to slash and tear with that beak honed sharp by evil desire. There are even breeds of twisted, horrible, rocks, that poison the water in a well, if they lie at the bottom of it. The devil sleeps in them. Did you know that? And the devil—which is the only way you can call a malign spirit— by whose orders and by what right does he go around doing as he damn well pleases? Mixed up in everything, he is.

What wears him out, little by little, the devil inside folks, is suffering wisely. Also the joy of love—so says my compadre Quelemém. The family. Is that the thing? It is and it isn't. Everything is and isn't. The most ferocious criminal, of the worst kind, is often a good husband, a good son, a good father, a good friend of his friends. I've known some like that. Only, there is the hereafter—and God too. Many's the cloud I've seen.

But, truly, children do soften one. Listen to this: a certain Aleixo, who lives a league from Passo do Pubo, on the Areia River, used to be one of the most cold-blooded villains you ever heard of. Near his house he had a little pond among the palm trees, and in it he kept some fierce traíras, immense ones, famous for their size. Aleixo used to feed them every day at the same hour, and soon they learned to come out of their hiding places to be fed, just as if they were trained. Well, one day, just for the hell of it, Aleixo killed a little old man who had come around begging. Don't you doubt it, sir, there are people in this hateful world who kill others just to see the faces they make as they die. You can foresee the rest: comes the bat, comes the rat, comes the cat, comes the trap. This Aleixo was a family man, with young children, whom he loved beyond all reason. Now listen to this: less than a year after killing the old man, Aleixo's children took sick. A mild epidemic of measles, it was said, but complications set in; it seemed as though the children would never get well. Finally they got over it. But their eyes became red, terribly inflamed, and nothing seemed to do any good. Then—I don't know whether all at the same time or one by one—they all went blind. Blind, without a glimmer of light. Just think of it—stairsteps, three little boys and a little girl—all blind. Hopelessly blind.

Aleixo did not lose his mind, but he changed; ah, how he changed! Now he lives on God's side, sweating to be good and kind every hour of the day and night. It even seems that he has become happy which he wasn't before—considers himself lucky, he says, because God chose to take pity on him, changing the direction of his soul in that way. When I heard that it made my blood boil! Because of the children. If Aleixo had to be punished, how were the little ones to blame for his sins?

My compadre Quelemém reproved me for my doubts. Said that surely in a former existence the children had been wicked, too, chips off the old block, imps of the same hell that bred him. What do you think, sir? And what about the little old man who was murdered? I know what you are going to say: that he too may have had some hidden crime to atone for. If, as Quelemém says, folks are reincarnated, I suppose a dead enemy could return as the child of his enemy. Listen to this one: there is a fellow, Pedro Pindó, who lives six leagues from here, a good man in every way, he and his wife both good people, well thought of. They have a son about ten years old, called Valtêi —one of those fancy names that folks around here go in for nowadays. Well, this little shaver, from the moment he had a glimmer of intelligence, began to show his real nature—mean and cruel as all get-out, fond of evil to the depth of his soul. Every little creature or insect that he could catch he would slowly torture to death. Once he saw a colored woman lying dead drunk, and took a piece of broken bottle and slashed her leg in three places. What made that kid drool with pleasure was to see a chicken bled or a hog butchered. "I like to kill," this little monster said to me once. It gave me a turn, for when a fledgling leans out of the nest it is getting ready to fly.

Now the father, Pedro Pindó, to correct this, and the mother too, have been beating the boy half to death; they deny him food; they tie him to a tree, naked as the day he was born, even in the cold of June; they work his little body over with strap and thong until the blood runs, then they wash off the blood with a gourdful of brine. Folks know about it and watch, horrified. The boy has grown thinner and thinner, hollow-eyed, his bony little face like a death's-head, and he has got consumption—coughs all the time—the kind of dry cough that tears the lungs. It is plain to see that beating the boy has now grown to be a habit with Pindó and his wife, and little by little they have come to find an ugly pleasure in it—setting the beatings at convenient times, and even calling people in to witness the good example. I don't think the boy will last much longer, not even till next Lent; he is teetering on the brink now.

Well? If what my compadre Quelemén says isn't true, how do you explain a situation like that? At one time that boy must have been a man—one with a debit of terrible deeds, and a soul black as pitch. It showed. Now he is paying. Ah, but it so happens that when he is crying and moaning, he is suffering just as though he were a good child. Lord, what haven't I seen in this world! I've even seen a horse with the hiccups—and that's a rare sight.

Well and good, but, you will probably say, in the beginning —the sins and evil-doing of people—how did it all get so balled up at the start? That's what stumps everyone. My compadre Quelemém included. I am only a backlander, and I lose my bearings among such notions. My greatest envy is of men like yourself, sir, full of reading and learning. Not that I can't read and write. I learned to read in a year and a half, by dint of primer, memory, and the ferule. I had a teacher: Master Lucas, at Curralinho. I memorized grammar, the multiplication tables, the rule-of-three, even geography and our nation's history. On large sheets of paper I drew pretty maps with careful strokes. Ah, not meaning to brag, but right from the start they found me very quick-witted. And thought I ought to be sent to study Latin at the Royal School—they said that, too. The good old days! Even now I enjoy a good book, taking it easy. At Limãozinho, the ranch that belongs to my friend Vito Soziano, they subscribe to a fat yearly almanac, full of puzzles, riddles, all sorts of different things. I give first place to more worthwhile reading—the lives of saints, their virtues and example—shrewd missionaries outwitting the Indians, or Saint Francis of Assisi, Saint Anthony, Saint Gerald. I am very fond of morality. To reason with others, exhort them to follow

the right path, to give wise counsel. My wife, as you know,
watches out for me: she prays a lot. She is a saint. My compadre Quelemém always says that I have nothing to worry
about, that with my good backing, powerful spirits protect me.
Yessir! That suits me fine! And I help out with wanting to
believe. But I am not always able to. I want you to know: all
my life I have thought for myself. I was born different. I am
what I am. I know almost nothing—but I have my doubts about
many things. At ranging far afield, I am like a well-trained
hunting dog. You turn loose any idea in my head and I'll track
it down in the deepest woods. Look: what we ought to have is a
meeting of scholars, statesmen, high authorities, to settle the
matter, proclaim once for all, in joint assembly, that there is
no devil, he doesn't exist, he can't. Give it the force of law!
Only thus would people have peace of mind. Why doesn't the
government do something about it?

Ah, I know it's not possible. Don't take me for a fool. It's one
thing to put forth good ideas, and another to deal with a country
of people, of flesh and blood, and their thousand and one
problems. So many people—it's frightening to think of—and
none satisfied, all being born, growing up, getting married,
wanting a job, food, health, wealth, recognition, rain, good
business. So you have to choose: either to join in the rat race,
or give yourself up to religion and nothing else. I could have
been a priest or a jagunço chief: I was born for one or the
other. But I missed out on both counts. Now old age has caught
up with me. And rheumatism. As one might say, I'll soon be
eating grass by the roots.

What I firmly believe, declare, and set forth, is this: the
whole world is crazy. You, sir, I, we, everybody. That's the main
reason we need religion: to become unmaddened, regain our
sanity. Praying is what cures madness. Usually. It is the
salvation of the soul. Lots of religion, young man. As for me, I
never miss a chance. I take advantage of all of them. I drink
water from any river. In my opinion just one religion isn't
enough. I pray the Christian, Catholic prayers, and I take
refuge in what is certain. I also accept the prayers of my
compadre Quelemém, according to his doctrine, that of Kardec.

But when I can I go to Mindubim, where there is one Mathias, a Protestant, a Methodist: they reproach themselves for their sins, read the Bible out loud, and pray, and sing their beautiful hymns. It all calms me down, allays my worries. Any shade refreshes me. But only for the time being. I would like to pray—all the time. Many persons do not agree with me; they say that the true religion is only one—exclusive. That's an idea I detest.

There is a colored woman, Maria Leôncia, who lives not far from here, whose prayers are famous for their potency. I pay her, every month, to say a chaplet for me every blessed day, and a rosary on Sundays. It is worth it, it really is. My wife sees no harm in it. And I've already sent word to another one to come to see me, a certain Isma Calanga, of Vau-Vau, whose prayers too, it is said, are of great merit and profit. I'm going to make the same kind of deal with her. I want to have several such on my side, defending me before God. By the wounds of Christ!

Living is a dangerous business. Longing too ardently for something good can be in some ways like wishing for something bad. Those men! All were grabbing at the world for themselves, to set it aright. But each saw and understood things only in his own way. At the top of the list, ahead of all the others, the one of greatest integrity, was Medeiro Vaz. What a man, like those of old! Joãozinho Bem-Bem, the fiercest of all, nobody could ever figure out what he was really like inside. Joca Ramiro—a prince of a man—was a politico. Zé Bebelo wanted to be a politico, but he was both lucky and unlucky—a fox that dilly-dallied. Sô Candelário turned mean as the devil because he thought he had an incurable disease. Titão Passos depended on his friends for everything: only through them, through their friendship, was it that he rose so high among the jagunços. Antônio Dó—a mean bandit. But only one half of him, albeit the greater half. Andalécio, at bottom a man of good will, but a madman in dealing out punishment. Ricardão even—all he wanted was to be rich and at peace; that was what he was fighting for. Hermógenes was the only one who was born a tiger and a murderer. And Urutú-Branco, the White

Rattler? Ah, don't speak to me of him. That unhappy, unruly one—that poor ill-fated boy . . .

So far, so good. You heard what I was saying: evil against evil, they end up breaking each other's back. God waits for this to happen. Man! God is patience itself! Just the opposite of the devil. You whet two knives together and they wear one another down. Even the stones in a river bed, rubbing against each other, grow smooth and rounded as the water rolls them along. Now, what I think is that everything in the world is there because it deserves to be and needs to be. Let me make myself clear. God doesn't appear with a policeman's sabre in his hand; he doesn't impose the letter of the law. Why should he? He leaves them alone: one fool against another; one day one of them cracks and learns his lesson, gets smart. Though, at times, to help things along, God will scatter a pinch of pepper between them.

Isn't it so? Well, for example: some time ago I went by train to Sete-Lagoas to see a doctor who had been recommended to me. To avoid being spotted as a former jagunço, I went well-dressed and first-class. As luck would have it, there came and sat facing me, in the opposite seat, a chap called Jazevedão, a police deputy, returning from the wild North. He was accompanied by one of his henchmen, a secret agent, and one was as mean as the other. To tell the truth, my first impulse was to get away, to change seats. But my better judgment told me to stay where I was. So I stayed and I watched. And, I'll tell you, I never saw a man's face stamped with greater brutality and meanness. He was short and heavy-set, with a cruel glint in his piggish eyes. His jaw jutted out like a stone, and his brows were drawn in a heavy frown; he did not make any sign of greeting. He didn't smile, not even once, but whether talking or silent, you could always see one of his eye teeth, long and sharp like the fang of a wild dog. Muttering and puffing, he talked in low, short grunts, in angry half-words. He was looking over some papers, studying case histories, one by one, sheets with pictures and black fingerprints of outlaws, thieves, and killers. His zeal for work of that nature stirred my anger. The secret agent, a bootlicker, seated close beside him, was being eagerly

helpful, and as ingratiating as a dog. It gave me a feeling of
dread, but only in the foolish part of my body, not in my guts.
At a given moment, one of those reports fell to the floor and I
quickly picked it up and handed it to him. I don't know why I
did it—I certainly didn't want to, just wasn't thinking—I still
feel ashamed when I recall it. I tell you, it made me furious to
have done that, but it was done. The fellow didn't even glance
at me, didn't utter a word of thanks. Even the soles of his
shoes—if you could have seen them—double thick, hard soles,
enormous, looking as if they were made of cast iron. One thing
I knew already: that this Jazevedão, when he went to arrest
anyone, the first thing he did as he came in, without saying a
word, pretending to be in a great hurry, was to step on the
poor devil's bare toes. And when this happened he would let
out a guffaw, yes he would. How I loathed him! I handed him
the paper and got up and left, to keep myself from shooting him
to death there and then. That gross flesh. And he had the
makings of a big belly around his navel that made me feel like
. . . In my own gentle way, I could gladly have killed him.
Your heart isn't calloused enough to listen to me tell the
horrors that this police officer committed. He drew tears of
blood from many a man and woman in this simple little world
of ours here. The sertão. You know, sir, the sertão is where the
strong and the shrewd call the tune. God himself, when he
comes here, had better come armed!

What I'm trying to say: Jazevedão—is there any need for the
likes of him? Yes, there is. Tough hides call for a sharp goad.
And besides in this world or the next, each Jazevedão, when he
has finished what he has to do, stumbles into his time of
penance until he has paid in full what he owes—my compadre
Quelemém will bear me out. You know, sir, what a risky
thing living is. But only in that way, through an ugly instrument like him, were the jagunço bands broken up. Do you think
for a moment that Antônio Dó or Olivino Oliviano would ever
turn good of their own accord, or be moved by their victims'
pleas for mercy, or converted by listening to priests' sermons?
Not a chance!

Honest-to-God jagunços who repented in the midst of their

banditry, I know of only one: his name was Joé Cazuzo. It happened in the thick of a gunfight, above a place called Serra-Nova, in the district of Rio-Pardo, along the Traçadal creek. We were badly outnumbered, and were being hard-pressed by the men of a certain Colonel Adalvino, a big-shot politico, with many uniformed soldiers under the command of Lieutenant Reis Leme who was later made captain. We stood our ground hour after hour, until we were almost surrounded. Then all of a sudden, that Joé Cazuzo—a very brave man—flopped down on his knees, and lifting his arms like the limbs of a dry locust tree, started shouting, hoarsely at times, loud and clear at others: "I saw Our Virgin, in the glory of Heaven, surrounded by her children the Angels!" He kept on shouting without a let-up: "I saw the Virgin!" We started to scatter. I made a dash for my horse. I managed to find him, jumped clumsily on his back, and, madly fumbling, I don't know how, undid the halter rope fastened to a tree. I flew out of there. Bullets whizzing past. The place was in an uproar. In the woods, a person's fear comes out in full force, a fear with purpose behind it. I kicked my horse with my heels, like a wild mule—thud, thud. Two or three bullets buried themselves in the cantle of my saddle, tearing out much of the floss padding. My horse shivered even as he galloped; I know, he is afraid for his master, I thought. I could not have made myself smaller. The leather bag on my back, with my few things in it, was hit too. And another bullet from a rifle, ricocheted off my thigh, searing it without wounding me and, would you believe it, buried itself between me and the saddle flap! My horse stumbled and fell—killed perhaps— and I was thrown over his head, grabbing at the thick foliage, branches and vines, that held and stung me, and for a moment it was like hanging in a big spider web. Where to now? I kept going. Throughly scared, I drove my body through those woods, not knowing where I was headed—and suddenly I started falling and rolling down a steep incline into a hollow place covered over with thick vegetation, which I grabbed at but kept on rolling just the same. Then—later—when I looked at my hands, the parts that weren't blood-covered, were smeared green from the leaves that I had clutched and crushed on my way down. I

landed on some grass at the bottom, and a dark animal
jumped out, with a snort, crazy with fear, too. It was a weasel
that I barely caught a glimpse of, because when it comes to
flight he has no match. I let my weariness overpower me and
stretched out full length. The thought flashed through my mind
that if that weasel had lain here, there were no snakes about. So
I took its place. There was no snake. I could relax. I was utterly
limp but the pounding in my heart didn't stop. I was panting. I
kept thinking that they were coming, that they would kill me.
It didn't matter, I didn't care. For a few minutes, anyway, I had
a respite in which to rest. I began to think of Diadorim. All I
thought about was him. A joão-congo was singing. I wanted to
die thinking about my friend Diadorim, brother, my brother,
who was on the Serra do Pau-d'Arco, almost on the frontier of
Bahia, with the other half of Sô Candelário's men. I clasped
my friend Diadorim to my heart, my thoughts flew straight to
him. But I'm not keeping to any kind of order. I am rambling,
telling things all mixed up. Don't I trust you? Of course I do, of
course. By my guardian angel. But, to get back to my story: we
learned afterwards that even the Lieutenant's soldiers and
Colonel Adalvino's ruffians had been moved to respect the
apocalyptic crying out of that Joé Cazuzo, who wound up as the
most peaceable man in the world, a presser of palm oil and a
sacristan to boot, at São Domingos Branco. What times!

I keep thinking about all this. I enjoy it. The best way for
thoughts to unfold themselves is when one is traveling by
train. If I could, that's all I would do, ride up and down. What
I'd like to know: even in Heaven, when it's all over, how does a
soul manage to forget so much suffering and evil, both given
and received? How? You know, sir, there are some things just
too awful, yes there are. Suffering of the body and suffering
of the mind leave their imprint as strongly as all-out love and
the anger of hatred. Take, for example, the case of Firmiano,
nicknamed Piolho-de-Cobra. He contracted elephantiasis—his
leg swollen monstrous thick and shapeless—the kind for which
there is no cure; and besides, he was almost blind, his eyes
whitened over with cataracts. Years before he had had to give
up the jagunço business. Well, on one occasion, a fellow visited

him at his place at Alto Jequitaí—told about it afterwards; they
got to talking, first of one thing and then another, and Firmiano
said: "What I long for is to catch me a soldier or someone, and
skin him alive with a dull knife. But first, to geld him." Can
you imagine such a thing? The ones who have the biggest dose
of devil in them are the Indians, any kind. You see tribes of
them, deep in the gerais of Goiás, where there are great slow
rivers, of water that is always clear, flowing over beds of pink
quartz. Piolho-de-Cobra prided himself on his Indian blood.
You'll say to me: he was shooting off his mouth—it was his
way of making out that he wasn't a broken-down old man—
talking big, wanting to be respected. They all put on the same
act: they brag about how mean they are to keep up their
prestige, because those around them are as hard as rocks. But
the worst of it is that there comes a day when for that very
reason they have to make good their boasts. The cruelty I have
seen! It doesn't pay to talk about suffering—if I get started I
won't stop. All that makes me sick, nauseates me. What makes
me glad is that nowadays men are good-hearted. In small matters, that is. Evil madness and perverseness, there is always
some, but less. In my own generation it hadn't yet become so.
Ah, there will come a time when men no longer kill each other.
Me, I'm already old.

Well, as I was saying, the thing that preys on my mind . . .
Ah, I put that question to my compadre Quelemém. He answered me that as we near Heaven, we become cleansed and
all our ugly past fades into nothingness, like the misbehaviour
of childhood, the naughtiness. Like there is no need to feel
remorse for what we may have divulged during the turmoil of a
nightmare. So—we become clean and bright! Maybe that is
why they say getting to Heaven is so slow. I check these
matters, you understand, with my compadre Quelemém, because of the belief he holds: that one day we pay to the last
penny for every evil deed we have committed. A fellow who
believes that would rather get up before daybreak three days in
a row than make the slightest misstep. Compadre Quelemém
never talks for the sake of talking, he means what he says. Only,

I'm not going to tell him this: one must never swallow whole everything others tell us—that is an unbreakable rule!

Look; the most important and nicest thing in the world is this: that people aren't always the same, they are not all of a piece and finished but keep on changing. They are in tune or out of tune. This is a great truth. It is what life has taught me. It makes me mighty happy. And another thing: the devil is all hammer-and-tongs, but God is wily! Ah, beautifully wily. His power, when he wants to use it—man! It scares me to think about it. God moves in—nobody sees anything. He does things softly and quietly—that's the miracle of it. And God attacks smoothly, amusing himself, sparing himself. For example, one day, at a tannery, a little knife that I had with me fell into a tank full of tanbark liquid. "Tomorrow I'll get it out," I said to myself. Because it was night, and I wasn't going to try in the dark. Next day, early, the knife, the blade of it, had been eaten halfway through by that dark, quiet water. I left the knife there, just to see what would happen. And by cracky! You know what? That same afternoon, all that was left of the knife was the handle. The handle, because it was not made of cold metal but of deer horn. There you have it. God . . . Well, sir, you heard me, what you heard you know, what you know you understand.

Only, don't think that religion makes a man weak. On the contrary. To be sure, in those days, I used to raise hell. I sowed my wild oats. Youth! But to undo what one does in his youth is a task for later on. Besides, if I had indulged in too much speculation on such matters, I could not have kept up my end with the others when things got hot. And even now, though I have reasoned at length and thought things out, I don't misprize what I could do in a clash of fire and steel. Just let them start warring against me, with evil schemings, with different laws, or prying into things that don't concern them, and I'll still go out and set this zone on fire—ho, ho, will I! With guns blazing and banging away. And don't think I'd be alone, I should say not. Just in case, I have my people settled all around here. Take a look, sir: right next to me, downstream, is Paspe—my sharecropper—who is one of mine. A league

farther on, if that, there is Acauã, and my compadre Ciril, he
and his three boys, I know they could be counted on. Over on
this side, Alaripe: if you only knew how that fellow from Ceará
handles a gun or a knife in a fight! Farther on: João Nonato,
Quipes, and Pacamã-de-Prêsas. And then there is Fafafa—he got
in some mighty blows alongside me, in the old fight at Tamanduá-tão, where we rid the air of those who had no right to breathe
it. Fafafa keeps a herd of brood mares. He raises good horses. A
little beyond, in the foothills, some former members of my outfit: Sesfrêdo, Jesualdo, Nelson, and João Concliz. And some others. Like Triol. I share my land with them, what's mine is theirs
too, we are as close as brothers. Why should I want to accumulate
wealth? There they are, their weapons ready for action. If an
enemy shows up, we pass the word along and gather together:
then we put on a mock gunfight—let them see what a real one
would be like. I tell you this in confidence. Furthermore, don't
get us wrong. What we want is to work, to live in peace. Me, I
live for my wife—who deserves nothing but the best—and for
religion. My wife's affection is what helped me, and her
prayers. Love inspires love. I tell you it's so. I think of Diadorim,
too—but Diadorim is like a soft haze.

Well now, I didn't want to get on the subject again—about
Old Nick—that's enough of that. But, there is just one more
point. I ask you, do you believe—do you find a shred of truth in
this talk—that you can make a pact with the devil? You don't,
do you? I know there is nothing to it. I was talking nonsense.
But I like to be reassured. To sell one's soul—a cock-and-bull
business! And the soul, what is it? The soul must be a
supreme something within us, deeper than we realize: oh,
supreme soul! The decision to sell one's soul is a piece of
bravado, a spur-of-the-moment gesture, not legally binding.
Can I sell those good lands there, inside the Veredas-Quatro,
that belong to a Senhor Almirante, who lives in the federal
capital? I certainly cannot! And, if a child is a child, and for
that reason not permitted to make a deal . . . And, this I
know, at times we are nothing but children. The evil that I
opened the door to in my life was during a kind of dream childhood—everything happens so fast. Does one really have a sense

of responsibility? One dreams, and it is done. So. If there is a soul, and there is, it belongs to God, whether one so likes it or not. It is not subject to sale. Don't you agree? Answer me frankly, please. Ah, I thank you. It is plain, sir, that you have much natural wisdom, besides your learning. I thank you. Your company gives me great pleasure.

As a matter of fact, I wish you lived here, or near here; it would be a help. Here we have no one from whom we can learn. Sertão. You know, sir, it is in the sertão that one's thoughts have to rise above the power of the place. Living is a dangerous business.

Eh, you are leaving? Right now? Oh, no. Not today. Nor tomorrow. I won't let you. Forgive me, sir, and take it as a pledge of my friendship: you must stay. Then, on Thursday morning early, if you want to leave, leave, even though I will miss you afterwards. But, today or tomorrow, no. A visit here, in my house, with me, lasts three days!

But, are you seriously planning to launch out on this sea of territory, to find out what it contains? You must have your reasons. But you have come late. The old days are gone, habits have changed. Of the real things of the past, few or none are left. The bands of bad men have been broken up; many a former jagunço is having a tough time of it, goes about begging. The herdsmen nowadays are reluctant to come to market in their leather garments—they think a leather jacket is ugly and countrified. Even the cattle in the scrubland are becoming less wild, better behaved. Crossed now with zebu, they look strange beside what is left of the old domestic breeds. So, to discover out-of-the-ordinary things, I advise you to undertake a more extensive journey. If it wasn't for my ailments, my stomach upsets and rheumatism, I would go with you. I would show you everything.

I would show you the bright heights of the Almas range: the river pouring down, all eagerness, foaming and boiling: every waterfall a cataract. The black jaguar female in heat in the Serra do Tatú—have you ever heard the rutting scream of a jungle cat? The bright fog over Serra dos Confins, in the early morning when the sky grows light—a kind of fine mist they call xererém. The person who taught me to appreciate all this beauty owned by nobody was Diadorim. The Serra da Raizama, where even the birds reckon the phases of the moon—so it is said—and the huge panther roams. A golden moon from which to mint money. When you dream, sir, dream on these things. The smell of flowered fields, strong, in April: the purple little gypsy, and the yellow nhiíca and the broom. This, in the Saririnhém. The cicadas shrill their music. Ho, and the cold! The hoarfrost collects even on the backs of the cattle, and on the housetops. Or on the Meãomeão—beyond there the earth is almost blue, not like the sky, but a vivid blue, like that of a partridge egg. Winds that don't let the dew settle. A gust of hot wind passing between the fronds of a palm tree. I remember, I disremember. Or, you will be moving in sloppy weather, from shower to shower. You see a stream that is hard to cross, or an angry mud-laden river. In Buriti-Mirim, Angical, Extrema-de-Santa-Maria. Do you like to hunt, sir? There are more partridge there than in Chapadão das Vertentes. To hunt tapir in Cabeça-de-Negro or Buriti-Comprido, the kind that eat a different variety of grass and gnaw the bark of many kinds of trees: their delicious meat is different. Through all these faraway places I went, with someone of my own by my side, and we loving each other. Do you understand? Have you ever felt the numb pain of yearning? They say there is a yearning of the mind and a yearning of the heart. They say the government is going to open up a good highway from Pirapora to Paracatú, up that way.

    In the Serra do Cafundó you hear such peals and reverberations of thunder that you stop your ears; you may even shed tears in fear of you know not what, as when you were a child. You see cows calving in the storm. Then on and on, up the Urucúia River—the fiercely rushing Urucúia. The sierra is so high that the moon is hidden. The sierra runs crooked. The sierra comes to a point. At one place, on the slope, a sulphurous vapor pours from the ground with a big noise and the cattle flee in fright. The same as the ranges of Estrondo and of Roncador where rumblings are heard from time to time. Eh? Did you say something? Look: the Carinhanha River is black,

the Paracatú, brown; for me, the beautiful one is the Urucúia
—the peace of its waters. That's the life! Beyond the Pôrto das
Onças there is a little plantation. We stayed there several weeks,
resting. We needed to—we had been travelling on foot to spare
the horses that were saddle-galled. In places like that, away
from fighting, what Medeiro Vaz liked best was to sleep in a
nightshirt and nightcap. Before lying down, he would kneel and
recite a chaplet. Those were the days for me. We hunted, each
forgot what he wanted to forget, there was no shortage of grub,
we fished in the streams. Just you go there, you'll see. The
places are all still there to bear me out.

Clear streams, springs, shade and sun. The Fazenda Boi-
Prêto belonging to a certain Eleuterio Lopes, this side of
Campo-Azulado, in the direction of Queimadão. It was in
January or February, when the corn is in tassel, the field-
captain vine, silver-pointed, running over the land; the giant
fennel bedecking the thickets; and the dejaniras covered with
their little flowers. The marmelade-grass shoots up quickly, it
comes in doubly thick—so sea-green—born of the slightest
rain. In any patch of woods, around the slightest foliage,
butterflies of every color swirl. You don't see them like that
anywhere else. For, in these plateaus, the same kinds which
are normal elsewhere grow much larger and more brilliant,
you know. I think it must be the dryness of the air, the clear-
ness, the dazzling sunlight. Along the banks of the upper
Urucúia, the little purple-throated tanagra pipes shrilly. And
there was the oriole that chirped in the early morning, and the
swamp cuckoo, the crazy-little-one, the little seesaw, the
warm-weather cuckoo, the cow ground-dove, and the bemtevi
flycatcher whose cry is "Yes, I saw you," and hoarse macaws.
It was good to hear the mooing of the cows waiting to be
milked. And the little manakin bird whose chirp at daybreak is
like a question which it asks and pretends to answer. Then, in
the afternoon, the flycatcher darting all about, up and down,
catching every little insect on the wing—a smart bird. It
looked like rain was coming. But if the trees were filled with
cicadas whirring, in the early afternoon, it wouldn't rain.
Songsters that close the day: the banana oriole, the bluebird,

the wren, the tyrant bird, the thrush, the coco-palm finch. I
was with Diadorim most of the time.

Diadorim and I, the two of us. We used to go for walks together. In this we differed from the others, for jagunços aren't
much given to long talks nor to close friendships; even though
they come together and separate, at random, each one keeps
himself to himself. About us two together, nobody ever said
anything. Let someone say something, joking—he might have
got himself killed. They got used to seeing us paired off. They
no longer thought evil of it. And we were having a talk beside
the creek—the millstream of the old plantation, where the
watercress blooms. One of those twilights, starting to turn
dark. Diadorim lighted a little fire and I went to look for corncobs. Moths were flying thick about our faces, and big bettles
would blunder against us and fall to the ground. A little breeze
started up. The rustling of the wind carried with it a smell of
threatening rain. And the chirping of crickets all about welded
the spaces into one. By myself, alone, I would not be able to
remember all these details—I am not much given to paying
attention to trifles—but my yearning recalls them to me.
Diadorim left traces of himself on these delights of Nature forever. Diadorim, grave, so handsome, in the glow of the embers.
We hardly spoke; but there was something outside ourselves
that drew me to him. In a sort of daze, I kept quiet in keeping
with his own silence. Nearly always it was like that: we would
come to a place; he would tell me to sit down; I would sit down.
I don't like to remain standing, anyway. Then, afterward, he
would come and sit down too. Always a little way off. I didn't
have the nerve to move closer. It was only of me that Diadorim
seemed at times to have a trace of mistrust—of me, who was
his friend! But on this occasion he was there, closer than usual,
within reach of my hand. And I, barely able to resist but not
allowing myself to make any of the overtures that are thought
wrong—I began to forget everything, and in happy lassitude
stopped thinking. But I began to feel an uneasiness, a vague
discontent. I studied it from every angle. It was simply that my
heart asked for more. The body does not speak, but it knows a
lot, and divines what it does not understand. How pleasant

there by the water. You could hear, over by the river, little
sucking whistles of an otter. "Damn it, but I want that day to
come!" said Diadorim. "There is no happiness for me, even my
life is not my own, until those two monsters have been done
away with." And he sighed with hate, as it might have been
with love. So great was his hate that it could not be increased;
it had settled into one of those deep, quiet hatreds. Hate with
patience; you know the kind, don't you?

And that overpowering thing that he felt was taking hold of
me too—but not as hatred; in me it was turning into sadness.
As long as those two monsters remained alive, Diadorim
simply could not live. Until the day came that he could avenge
his father, Diadorim would be beside himself. While we were
like this, not on the move, taking time out for rest, when what
I wanted was closer friendship, Diadorim talked of nothing but
the end of the affair. To kill, to kill, blood cries for blood. Thus
the two of us waited there, in the night hours, side by side.
Without talking. I remember, ah. The frogs. They blew up the
sac of their voices, like gecko lizards, old ones. I looked along
the bank of the creek. The foliage of the watercress—you have
seen it—at certain times gives off a light in the darkness: leaf
by leaf, a phosphorescence, like electricity. And I felt fear.
Fear in my soul.

I did not answer. It would have done no good. Diadorim
wanted the showdown. It was for this that we were headed.
After that rest, we would move out from there, under the
command of Medeiro Vaz, and go after those others—after
them! There was no lack of ammunition. We numbered sixty
men—all cabras of the very best. Our Chief, Medeiro Vaz, never
lost a fight. Medeiro Vaz was a man of good judgment, who
knew the ropes, who did not waste words. He never revealed his
plans beforehand, nor what direction our marches would take
the next morning. Furthermore, everything about him in-
spired trust and obedience. Heavy-boned, with a thick neck, his
big head thrust forward, he was master of the day and of the
night. He hardly ever slept any more: he would get up while the
stars were still out, walk all around the camp, slowly, with
quiet steps, shod in his stout old-fashioned boots of wild-pig

skin. If in his considered judgment he felt it was the right thing to do, Medeiro Vaz was capable of solemnly putting his rosary in his pocket, crossing himself, and firmly giving orders to kill a thousand persons one by one. Right from the beginning, I esteemed that fortress of a man. His secret was of stone.

Ah, I am reliving the past. I recall things out of the order of their happening. I led a free life. Sertão: its wide empty spaces. Go there. Some things you will still find. Cow punchers? As in the old days, you will find them on the tablelands of the Urucúia, where so many cattle bellow. Or farther on: the herds-men of Brejo-Verde and of Córrego do Quebra-Quináus: their horses converse with them in whispers—so 'tis said—to give them wise counsel, when there is no one within earshot. I believe it and I don't. Between here and there are the sources of the Carinhanha and of the Piratinga, a tributary of the Urucúia. The two turn their backs on each other. They rise in the same marshes, enormous groves of burití palms. There the anaconda loops and coils. The thick kind that throw themselves upon a deer and wrap themselves around it, crush it—thirty handspans long! All around is a sticky mud, that holds fast even the hooves of mules, pulls the shoes off one by one. In fear of the mother-snake, you see many animals waiting prudently for the time they can come and drink, keeping hidden behind clumps of palm. The sassafras trees provide shelter around the pool, and give off a good smell. The alligator roars once, twice, three times, a hoarse roar. The alligator lies in wait—bulging eyes, wrinkled with mud, looking evilly at you. Eh, he knows how to fatten himself. On the ponds not a single winged thing alights, because of the hunger of the alligator and the saw-toothed piranha. Then little by little the marshes start turning into rivers. Groves of butití palms come down with them, and follow on and on. To move to another basin you must climb, up slopes as steep as the side of a table, until you suddenly come upon the plateau, a vast unchanging plateau. There is no water there at all, only what you bring with you. Those endless plateaus, alive with biting mutuca flies. The sun beats down, in hot waves, ceaselessly, so much light it hurts. The horses sweat salt and lather. Many times we followed trails through the jungle, tapir trails—coming and going. At night, if it was clear, the sky was filled with balls of brilliance. You almost hit them with your head. How beautiful is the sky, thick with stars, about the middle of February. But, when there is no moon, when it is dark, it is a darkness that grasps and shackles you. The total darkness of the sertão always disturbed me. Not so Diadorim: he never let go the icy fire of his obsession, and he never had doubts about himself. But I always longed for the dawn. Hot days, cold nights. We would gather laurel branches to light a fire. If we had something to eat and drink, I would soon drop off to sleep. I would dream. I only dream, good dreams or bad, when I am free of danger. When day broke through its prison bars, I listened to other birds: the spine-tail, the black grackle, the sniffing dove, the white-breasted dove, and the red dove of the virgin woods. But always the bemtevi flycatcher. Behind and ahead of me, all around, it was like there was but a single bemtevi. "Darn it! Doesn't it sound to you as if there was only one, the same one all the time?" I asked Diadorim. He did not answer, and there was a far-away look on his face. And I was left wondering if maybe it really was the same bemtevi, with its cry of "Yes, I saw you!", pursuing me and accusing me of misdeeds I had not yet committed. Even today it affects me that way.

When you leave there, you should visit the settlements of the Negroes: they pan for gold in the backwoods hollow of Vargem-da-Cria where gold has been found. Of low grade, I think. Blacks who can still sing defiant songs in the language of the Gold Coast. On the uplands, the natives all live shiftlessly, in idleness. Such poverty. The plateau, dun-colored, is all the same, the same. It depresses many persons; but I was born liking it. The rains are less frequent now.

As I was saying: another month, another distant place—we made a halt at Aroeirinha. There, in a doorway, I saw a young woman dressed in red, laughing. "Hey, young fellow with the clean shaved face," she said. When she laughed she showed all her front teeth, the whole row of them. She was so pretty, and alone. I got off my horse and tied him to a fence post. My legs ached from the three days we had been pushing ahead: some-

thing like thirty leagues. Diadorim wasn't near, to hold me
back. Suddenly some of our men galloped by, shouting, and
driving a black steer they were going to butcher and skin down
by the river. I had not even started talking with the girl, when
the heavy dust they raised enveloped us both in a reddish cloud.
Then I went in, drank a cup of coffee brewed by a woman's
hand, and had a cool drink, of wild pear juice. Her name was
Nhorinhá. She accepted my caresses of her satiny skin—
joyous it was, like marriage, an espousal. Ah, the best fruit of
the mangaba is the one you find on the ground, under the tree.
Nhorinhá. Afterward she made me a present of an alligator
tooth, to stick in my hat, to ward off snake bites; and had me
kiss the picture of a saint supposed to be miracle-working. It
was, very.

Her mother arrived, a pop-eyed old woman by the name of
Ana Duzuza, said to be of gypsy parents, who could rightly
foretell a person's good or bad fortune; in those backwoods she
enjoyed great prestige. She knew that her daughter was a harlot, and—as long as they were men from the outside, jagunços
or cattle drovers—she didn't care; even gave the matter her
blessing. We ate some manioc meal with brown sugar. And
Ana Duzuza told me, letting me in on a big secret, that Medeiro
Vaz was going to try to cross the Sussuarão desert from one
side to the other. She was just back from Medeiro Vaz's headquarters; he had sent for her, wanting her to read his fortune.
Was she crazy? What was she up to? I didn't believe her. I
knew moreover that we were turning toward the Araras sierra
—back toward those sparse settlements in the wild country
beyond, the favorite hideout of every unemployed bandit—
where we would have an opportunity to pick up some more
good men. And besides, not a living soul could get through the
Sussuarão desert. It was the worst waste there was, a wilderness in hell. Is there such a place? Ah, is there! Eh? Like the
Vão-do-Buraco? Ah, no, that is something different—beyond the
divide between the sources of the Prêto and Pardo rivers. It is
deathly hot there, too, but different. There you claw your way
up cliffs. What about the Tabuleiro? So you know it? It

stretches from Vereda-da-Vaca-Preta to the Córrego Catolé, down this way, and from the source of the Peruassú to the Cochá river, which flows out of the Ema marshes. Beyond the forests of mangabeira trees.

Nothing times nothing equals the devil. This one, the Sussuarão desert, is the farthest off, way, way, over there, in the wilds. It is endless. Water, there is none. Believe me when you come upon it, it is the end of the world; one should turn back, always. Nobody will go any further; they just take one look, just one. To see the moonlight shining, and to listen to the howling of the wind that knows it is alone, on the bed of that desert . . . There is no dung. There are no birds.

Whereupon I pressed that Ana Duzuza and she could not withstand the rage in my eyes. "It was himself, Medeiro Vaz, who told me," she had to say. Dammit. It was not possible.

Diadorim was waiting for me. He had washed my clothes: two shirts, and a jacket and pair of pants, and another shirt, a new striped one. Sometimes I would wash our clothes, but nearly always it was Diadorim who did it, because, for me this was the worst chore of all, and besides, Diadorim could do it better, he was more skilled. He didn't ask me where I had been, and I lied saying I had gone in there only because of old Ana Duzuza, to get her to tell my fortune. Diadorim didn't say anything to that, either; he liked silences. When he had his sleeves rolled up, I would look at his arms, such attractive, white arms, well-formed, and his face and hands, red and swollen from horsefly bites. Suddenly it dawned on me that I could have asked Ana Duzuza to tell me something of my future fate. Also I could have asked her about an inner secret, that I guarded carefully. Something that I didn't have the courage even to think about. And what if old Duzuza really did have powers of divination, and could look behind the curtain of destiny? I regretted not having asked for for a forecast. Ah, it was a repetition of what has so often happened to me on other occasions. I go through an experience, and in the very midst of it I am blind. I can see only the beginning and the end. You know how it is: a person wants to swim across a river and does, but comes out on the other side at a point lower down, not at all where he expected. Isn't life really a dangerous business?

I repeated to Diadorim what I had picked up: that it was Medeiro Vaz's plan to lead us to the Sussuarão desert, plunge in and straight across to the other side. "That's right, that's right," replied Diadorim, surprising me by the fact that he already knew about it but hadn't given me the slightest hint.

I had been struggling with myself for so long to keep from openly loving Diadorim more than is fitting for a friend but now, at that moment, I felt no shame at the bitter jealousy that came over me, though I knew that Medeiro Vaz reposed much greater trust in Diadorim than in any of the rest of us, and talked things over with him. Why did this difference of treatment upset me now? Medeiro Vaz was a man of another age, he went through the world with loyal hand, he never equivocated, never weakened. I knew that he venerated the memory of one friend alone: Joca Ramiro. Joca Ramiro had been the great admiration of his life. God in heaven and Joca Ramiro on the other bank of the river. All as it should be. But jealousy is harder to repress than love. The human heart—the heart of darkness.

Whereupon Diadorim told me the rest. On the other side of the Sussuarão, inside the state of Bahia, one of the two traitors had his biggest plantation, with many cattle, cultivated fields, and there he lived with his legitimate family, wife and children. Let us manage to cross the desert unnoticed, arrive there unexpectedly, take them by stark surprise—and that would be the end of them! Who would ever think for a moment that the Sussuarão desert could be used as an approach? Ah, they were living fat on their plantation turned into a bronze fortress, which could not be approached from any other direction, for they undoubtedly had lookouts, munitions, and gangs of men stationed at all points of access, in every grotto and bayou. The trick was for us to burst upon them suddenly, from the impossible side, and overwhelm them without warning. I listened, and even shuddered a little. But Diadorim, suddenly sombre, said harshly: "That old witch of Ana Duzuza can cause us trouble, she's no good. From the questions Medeiro Vaz put to her, she guessed his plans and she should have kept her mouth shut. She needs to die, to keep her from blabbing."

Bad words to hear. I broke out in a cold sweat. Diadorim was like that: one killed to be on the safe side. Was someone a traitor? Give him the knife. That had to be our way. Didn't I know that? I am not one to be caught napping, nor am I chicken-hearted. But I couldn't help feeling sorry for that Ana Duzuza, with her pop eyes—you could take hold of them with your fingers. Telling me all those stories. That toothless old hag, with her mouth caved in like a squash. She scraped a chunk of rapadura with an old knife, letting the sticky crumbs of it collect in the palm of her hand; or else, she would hold the piece, licking and sucking on it. It made my stomach heave. Why then did I feel such pity for her? I did not have the cunning to contradict Diadorim. My will was in his keeping. His motives seemed to have spite in it. The only thing I feared was that he would tell me to go back there, and finish Ana Duzuza off myself. I was finding it hard to control my feelings. For some time I had not looked Diadorim in the face.

But then I thought: if they kill old Duzuza, to protect the secret, then they are liable to kill the daughter too—Nhorinhá. That would be murder! Ah, that decided it for me, and I flung open seven windows: "What you've just said, I disagree with! To take the life of that woman would bring us bad luck." It was as far as I got. Diadorim read my thoughts: "I already know that you were with that girl her daughter," he replied curtly, almost in a hiss. Thereupon I grasped the truth: that Diadorim loved me too. So much that his jealousy of me spilled over. After a sudden satisfaction, that other shame arose in me, a strange revulsion.

And I almost screamed: "Is that a warning? Well, if you do it, I'll leave you all for good. You'll never see me again!" Diadorim put his hand on my arm. It made me tremble inside, but I repressed my surge of tenderness. He gave me his hand, and I gave him mine. But it was as though there were a sharp stone between the two palms. "Do you then hold Joca Ramiro in such low esteem? Because of an old witch of a fortune-teller, and her slut of a daughter, here in this backside of the uplands?" he exclaimed softly. It made me mad. "Does the whole world, then, everybody, have to live in veneration of that Joca Ramiro, as if he were Christ Our Lord himself?" I answered him. By that time I had smoked two cigarettes. To be my own master definitely, that's what I wanted more than anything. But Diadorim knew this, and it seemed that he would not let me.

"Riobaldo, listen to me then: Joca Ramiro was my father," he said. I don't know if he was very pale, but afterwards he turned red. Because of this he lowered his face, coming closer to me.

My breathing quieted down. The surprise left me speechless. I felt as if I were hanging in empty space. And I believed what he said so firmly, so quickly, that it seemed as though I had always known it. I said nothing. I watched Diadorim out of the corner of my eye, his head held high, so handsome, so serious. And I let my memory go back to Joca Ramiro: his proud bearing, his quick step, his boots of Russian leather, his laugh, his mustache, his kindly, commanding eye, his broad forehead, his head covered with gleaming black curls. All of him seemed to glow. For that is how Joca Ramiro affected other men, he had an inner light, he was a king by nature. That Diadorim should be his son, now both pleased and frightened me. I wanted to say to him: "I take it back, Diadorim. I am with you, all the way, in everything, and with the memory of your father." But it was not what I said. I wonder why. A human being, without doubt, is like a three-ply rope, all inter-woven. What I said instead was: "Well, as for me or anyone else believing what you have said, old Ana Duzuza might as well turn out to be my mother," and in conclusion, I nearly shouted: "For my part, you can try to bamboozle me all you like: I am not going! I am against these barbarous acts!"

My mind was in a whirl. I waited to see what he would do. In a flash of revelation I knew about myself: what influenced my state of mind was that I was crazy about Diadorim, and at the same time, underlying this, was a dull rage at it not being possible for me to love him as I wanted to, honorably and completely. And I felt even greater loathing for that Ana

Duzuza, who might come between us and break up our friendship. I was almost fascinated by the thought that if it became
necessary to liquidate the old woman, I would go there and do
it myself—only I could not harm Nhorinhá, whom I liked,
liked a lot. Could it be that I was not in my right mind, dammit? I don't know, I don't know. I should not be recalling this,
relating in this way the dark side of things. All this rigmarole.
I really shouldn't. You are an outsider, my friend, but also a
stranger to me. Perhaps that is the very reason why I do it. To
talk like this with a stranger, who listens well and soon goes
far away, has a second advantage: it is as though I were talking
to myself. Stop and think: whatever is bad within people, they
always distort and rationalize to rid themselves of it. Would
that be why people talk so much?

And your thoughtful ideas give me peace. Principally the
assurance that the So-and-So doesn't exist; isn't that true? The
Renegade, the Hound, the Goshawk, the Duck-foot, the Dirty
One, the Sooty One, the Gimpy One, the No-good, the Black-
foot, the Lefthanded One, the Young Fellow, the Messire, the
Doleful One, the What-You-May-Call-Him, the One-Who-Never-
Laughs . . . So, he does not exist! And, if he does not exist,
how can one make a pact with him? The idea keeps coming
back to me. Here is a confused notion, please clear it up for me:
could it be that everything comes from a remote, deeper, more
persistent past, and that when one gets the idea of selling his
soul, it is because he has already sold it, unawares? And all
the person is doing is confirming an old deal, that he sold himself little by little, long ago? God forbid; God who runs everything! Tell me what you think about it, tell me. Who knows,
perhaps mankind is still so vile, that sometimes God can
handle men only by giving his orders through the devil. Or
that the native baseness of man can glimpse God's presence
only in the figure of that other one? What is it that we really
have forebodings about? I wondered for ten years. Let the earth
spin! I have my back protected, thanks to my prayers. I remember Diadorim. My wife must not hear me. Young man: all
longing for the past is a kind of old age.

But, as I was telling you, when I blurted out that angry

defiance, Diadorim answered in a way that I did not expect:
"There is no disagreement, friend Riobaldo, calm yourself.
There is no need to take the precaution of killing this Ana
Duzuza. Nor are we going with Medeiro Vaz to commit atrocities against the wife and little children of the worst of the two
traitors, just because he and his kind are in the habit of doing
such things. All we want is to kidnap his family as hostages,
then he will come out, and how! And he will come out obliged
to fight. But, if some day you should not come with me, I swear
to this: I will die of sadness." That was what he said. He had
placed his hand again in mine when he began to talk, and then
he withdrew it; then he stood away from me. But, because of
his voice, a voice filled with tenderness, I never felt him better
and nearer. Love, in itself, is a kind of penitence. I embraced
Diadorim, as with the wings of birds. For the sake of his father's
name, Joca Ramiro, I would now kill and die, if need be.

But Diadorim added nothing more nor explained further.
And, perhaps to change the conversation, he asked me:
"Riobaldo, do you remember your mother well? Tell me what
she was like, her goodness."

At that moment, I may tell you, I didn't like the question. I
always withdraw, like taking shelter, when anyone asks me a
direct question about what pertains to me alone. But I put this
aside immediately, seeing that only Diadorim could have
touched this sensitive spot without hurting, because of his
delicate friendship. And I understood. It was as it should be.
Every mother's life is kindness, but each one has a special kind
of goodness which is hers alone. I had never thought about it
this way before. To me my mother was my mother, and that
was that. Now I realized. The special goodness of my mother
had been that of a love that went hand in hand with justice,
which as a boy I needed. A goodness that, even as it punished
my excesses, rejoiced in my happiness. The recollection of her
filled my fancy, burst into music for an instant, like a great
hymn, like the moment between daybreak and sunrise. Diadorim went on to say: "I never knew mine." He said it with
stark simplicity, as one would say: sandbar—riverbank—
headwaters. As though he had been blind from birth.

As for me, what I thought was: I never had a father; by this I mean, I never knew for sure what his name was. I am not ashamed of being of obscure birth. Children of unknown fathers and without legal papers, those are the orphans one sees most often in these backlands. A man comes through, spends the night, moves on; he changes places and women; some child is left behind. The poor man develops few ties; there is a constant moving about in the wastes of the uplands, like birds on rivers and lakes. Take Zé-Zim, my best share-cropper here, cheerful and capable. I asked him: "Zé-Zim, why don't you raise guinea hens, like everybody else?"

"I don't want to raise nuthin'," he replied. "I like to move around." There he is, with a young half-breed woman in the house, and two children by her already. One fine day, he'll take off. And so it goes. Nobody thinks it wrong. I'd say as much myself in the circumstances. I look after them. I, that is to say, God, in humble ways. My mother did not lack this either, when I was a child, in my little neck of the backwoods below the end of the Serra das Maravilhas, between it and the Serra dos Alegres: a tumbledown shack on the ranch called Sítio do Caramujo, behind the sources of the Verde, the Verde that empties into the Paracatú. Near there is a large village formerly called Alegres; you should go see it. Today, it has a different name. All the names are being changed. Like passwords. São Romão, wasn't it first called Vila Risonha? And Cedro and Bagre, didn't they cease to exist? And Tabuleiro-Grande? How can they do away with names like that? Do you agree? The name of a place where someone is born should be sacred. Suppose, for instance, that someone were to repudiate the name of Bethlehem, of our Lord Jesus Christ in the manger, with Our Lady and Saint Joseph! We need to hold to things more firmly. You know, sir: God exists, definitely; the devil is His opposite. As I was saying, as you have seen, I have no lack of memory, I recall everything about my childhood. Good, it was. I recall it with pleasure, but without longing. There is no peace in looking back. You know, sir, the first thing I can remember of my early childhood was the hatred I felt for a man called Gramacêdo . . . The best people in that place

were all of the Guedes family, Jidião Guedes; when they left
there, they took us with them, my mother and me. We went to
live in the bottom lands of the Sirga, on the other side, where
the Janeiro flows into the São Francisco, you know where I
mean. I was then around thirteen or fourteen.

Well, to get back to what I was telling you: we spent one
night there, and everyone had slept, soundly. I would say it was
in April, at the beginning. To carry out his plans, Medeiro Vaz
had wanted to wait until after the last rains of March—St.
Joseph's day and its seasonal floods—to catch perfect weather,
with the fields still growing green, because first we were going
to cross some marshy meadows, and from there advance as I
told you, back of beyond. We struck out, stopping two days on
the Vespê. There we had some good, well rested horses under
the care of a friendly settler, Jõe Engrácio by name. There was
still a lot of yesterday's mud on the trails. "To set out on a
journey on horseback without roads—only someone crazy
would do that, or jagunços—" that Jõe Engrácio said. He was a
serious, hardworking man, though a bit of a fool, given to
laughing loudly at his own jokes. But he was wrong, because
Medeiro Vaz always knew the right route to follow, unerringly.
At the same time, Jõe Engrácio noticed the quantity of food
and supplies we had gathered, and all those pack mules. All
that abundance was excessive—the meat and flour, the rapadura, plenty of salt, coffee. Everything. And he, seeing what he
saw, asked where we were going, saying he wanted to go along
with us. "Haven't you just talked out of turn?" was all that
Medeiro Vaz said in refusal. "Yes, chief, I goofed. Please
excuse it," said Jõe Engrácio, bowing his head.
Medeiro Vaz was not a surly man. It was just that he was
wiser, a solid fellow. Sometimes he would talk under his
breath, muttering to himself. With him, nobody took liberties.
He would always accept good and just counsel. But he did not
like chatter. Was everyone talking at the same time? Then,
Medeiro Vaz was not present. Do you know his earlier history?
As a young man, of rich family, he had inherited a large
plantation. He could have managed it and lived in ease and

comfort. But came the wars and the depredations of jagunços
—nothing but killing and robbery, and misusing of women,
wives and maids; any kind of peace was impossible ever since
that foul madness had climbed the sierras and spread into the
uplands. Then Medeiro Vaz, after much thought, recognized
his duty: he cast aside everything, got rid of all he owned in
lands and cattle, renounced everything as though he wished to
return to the state when he came naked into the world. He had
no mouths to feed, no heirs at law. The last thing, he set fire
with his own hands to the fine old plantation home that had
belonged to his father, grandfather, and great-grandfather. He
stood watching until all was in ashes; today the place is overgrown with weeds. Then he went to where his mother was
buried—a little fenced-in graveyard in one corner of the pasture
—tore down the fence, scattered the stones. Now no one could
discover where the bones of his forebears lay to profane them.
Then, divested of everything, completely his own master, he
mounted his horse, draped with arms, gathered a bunch of
brave followers, young fellows from the surrounding country,
and set out to impose justice. For years, he was on the move.
They say he became more and more strange as time went by.
When he got acquainted with Joca Ramiro, he found new hope:
to him, Joca Ramiro was the only man, a man among men, who
was capable of taking control of this sertão of ours, ruling it in
keeping with the law. The fact was that Joca Ramiro, too, had
taken up arms in the cause of justice and honest government,
but only on behalf of friends who were persecuted; and he had
always kept his considerable possessions. But Medeiro Vaz
belonged to a breed of men you don't see any more; I still did.
His mien was so commanding that in his presence, even the
man of learning, the priest, the rich man, deferred to him. He
could bless or curse, and the youngest man, however valiant,
was not ashamed to kiss his hand. For that reason we all
obeyed. We carried out our orders, in tears or laughter, through
thick and thin. Lieutenant of the uplands—that's what he was.
We, his men, were the Medeiro-Vazes.

For all these reasons we cheerfully accepted it when Medeiro
Vaz told us in few words that we were going to cross the

Sussuarão desert, and seek out combat in the depths of Bahia!
Whereupon a tumult of rejoicing and celebration broke loose.
What nobody had done before, we felt ourselves able to do.

This is how we went: we set out from Vespê, descending
gullies and ravines. Then we climbed. The hills become more
heavily wooded as you approach the headwaters. A wild bull
may dash out of the scrub, enraged, because it has never seen
people before—it's worse than a jaguar. We saw such large
flocks of macaws in the sky that they resembled a blue or red
cloth spread out on the back of the hot wind. From there we
descended again, and suddenly came to a lowland, delightful to look at, with a fine pond surrounded by the tallest buriti
palms: slender, green-clad, swaying beauties. And there were
the ruins of a house that was being destroyed by time; a clump
of bamboo, planted long since; and a shack. The place was
known as Bambual do Boi. There we would spend the night
and make our final preparations.

I was standing watch, a quarter-league away, on a high
hummock. From there I could see the activity below: the men,
looking the size of boys, in happy turmoil like a swarm of
bees around a guava in bloom, pulling off their clothes and
running to bathe in the blue circle of the pond, from which all
the birds rose in fright: herons, storks, teals, and flocks of
black ducks. It was as though, realizing what was waiting for
them on the morrow, the men now wanted only to cavort, to
laugh, and to enjoy themselves all they could. But some ten
had always to be on duty, with rifles and shotguns, ready for
action, for these were Medeiro Vaz's orders. In the late afternoon, when the breeze sprang up, there was a continuous
rustling in the buritís, as their fronds brushed against each
other. And in the bamboos, almost the same. Like the good
sound of rain. Meanwhile, Diadorim came to keep me company. I was a bit uneasy. Perhaps the one who dreaded most
what was going to happen was I myself. I admit it. I am not
naturally brave; that is, my bravery has its ups and downs. Ah,
in those days I didn't know it, but today I do: for a person to
change himself into a coward or a brave man, all he needs is
look at himself in a mirror for a half a minute—putting on an

expression of daring or one of cowardice. My ability was bought at a high price; it developed as I grew older. And I'll tell you, sir, the very thing we dread to do when God commands it, afterward when the devil asks for it, we do it. The Damned One! But Diadorim was in a gentle mood: "Listen, Riobaldo," he said "our destiny is one of glory. Whenever you feel disheartened, think about your mother; I think about my father." "Don't speak of them, Diadorim. To remain silent is the way to speak of the dead." I lacked the courage to tell him what I was thinking— that my desire was to place my fingers lightly, so lightly, over his soft eyes, hiding them, to keep from having to endure their fascination. How much their green beauty was hurting me; so impossible.

We all slept well. In the morning early—flights of fowl and birds, chirps and songs—everybody running about, busy, helping with last-minute readying. The leather water bags were filled at the springs, and fastened on the little donkeys' backs. We had brought along donkeys, just to pack our supplies. The horses were still nibbling the grama grass, which came up over their hoofs. Everybody filled up his water gourd, and put in his knapsack his food ration for the day: ground nuts and manioc meal. Medeiro Vaz, who up to now had said nothing, gave marching orders. First, in front, a detachment of five men, the advance patrol. Along with us at all times there were three good scouts—Suzarte, Joaquim Beijú, and Tipote. This Tipote knew how to find water holes and ravines with water; Suzarte had the nose of a bloodhound; and Joaquim Beijú knew every foot of the uplands, by day or night, spelled out, and had he wanted to he could have laid out a map of the whole region. We set out under a full head of steam. Six fat yearlings were being driven along, to supply us with meat on the way. Suddenly, as we drew away, all the birds came back from the sky, dropping straight to their places on the cool edges of the pond—ah, the chattering in the palms, their fronds like fans. Now the sun, in an upward leap, far in our rear, breaks over the woods, in all its grandeur. Day had arrived.

We started moving deeper and deeper into a scrub of mangaba trees, and kept going straight ahead until close to lunch time. But the terrain was getting shiftier, and the trees smaller, raising their skirts from the ground. The only animal to come this far would be an occasional armadillo, in search of honey and mangaba plums. Then, the big and little mangaba trees disappeared, and only the land spread out before us. The vultures in the sky became fewer. The pastures of timothy and paspalum grass gave way to stiff, silvery tufts. The brush growth began to peter out, in those brownish stretches. Coming upon it thus, little by little, we had a strange feeling as of a world grown old in these bleak lands. The wild satintail grass of the plains was no more to be seen. We looked back. The dazzling sun made it impossible for us to see our trail. The light was cruel. A swallow-tailed kite was the last bird we saw. There we were in that appalling thing: a weird, Godforsaken waste, shifting under foot. It was a different world, crazy, an ocean of sand. Where lay the end of it, the boundary? The sun poured down on the earth, which sparkled like salt. At long intervals, patches of dead grass; and some dry tufts of plants, like hair without a head. Up ahead, in the distance, a yellow vapor was rising and spreading. And flames began to enter into our burning chests with the air.

Let me tell you, sir, that the suffering we were to undergo was already being revealed to us at the start; from there on it only increased. And what was to be. I swear, the moment we moved into the desert, one of the fellows, a certain João Bugre, said to me or to the man at my side:

"That Hermógenes has a pact. He came to an understanding with the Capiroto."

That was too much for me. A pact! They say—well, you know, nonsense—that the person goes at midnight to a crossroads, and calls loudly on the Aforesaid—and waits. If it is done right, there comes a gust of wind, for no good reason, and then, by cracky, a sow appears followed by a brood of chicks, or a hen leading a litter of piglets. Can you imagine such a thing? You keep still, and out of the ground comes a smell of burning brimstone. And the Aforesaid—the Gimpy One—assumes shape, takes form. You have to keep up your nerve. You sign the pact. You sign it with your blood. The price is your soul. Much later.

Have you ever seen such stupid superstition? Crazy! "That Hermógenes has a pact." I heard it and believed. Nobody could cope with him. Hermógenes—devil. Yes, that was it. He was the devil himself.

People came from hell—all of us—so says my compadre Quelemém. From some lower depths so monstrous-terrifying that Christ himself was able, thanks only to his radiant strength, to descend for a quick glance, in the darkness of the eve of the Third Day. Do you believe it? That in that place the normal pleasure of each one is to abuse and torment the others; that the heat and cold afflict them sorely; and in order to digest what they eat, they have to strain in the middle, with awful pangs; even to breathe hurts; and there is no rest. Do I believe it? It's hard to say. I think back on the campaign of Macaúba da Jaíba, what I saw for myself and what I heard; and other things—the atrocities which they committed as a matter of course in so many poor little settlements: shooting, stabbing, gutting, putting out eyes, cutting off tongues and ears, not even sparing little children, firing on the innocent cattle, burning persons still half alive in a welter of blood. Did not such things come from hell? Of course. It is plain to see that they came up from there ahead of their time, to punish the others, as a reminder to us never to forget what is raging down there. Nevertheless, many persons land down there with a crash, as soon as they die. Living is a very dangerous business.

But, we too had to undergo infernal suffering. I tell you. Or something like it. The rains were now a memory, and the evil core of the sertão was right there, all empty space and the sun. We would advance a few rods and sink deep in the sand—a sand that slithered out from under us, without body, pulling the horses' hoofs backwards. Later, we had to work our way crisscross through a patchwork of spiny bromelias, hard and tough, the dark green color of snakes. There was no road. Then this changed to a hard pink or gray terrain, rough and full of cracks. Not familiar with it, the horses became skittish. Diadorim— his head always high—his smile doubled my uneasiness. For he spoke: "Ho, we are valiant men, bolder than any—and we are going to suffer and die in this." The men of Medeiro Vaz. Was

Medeiro Vaz pushing on with the scouts? Was it possible that
from there we could still turn back? After a while I saw scowls
begin to gather on some faces. My comrades keeping on, just
keeping on. I was afraid of getting light-headed, like the dizziness of being drunk. I think it came from too much mulling over
of ideas, for I had made more arduous journeys than this, afoot
and on horseback, in the broiling sun. Everything I was carrying weighed upon me. After about a league and a half, I took
my first swallow of water from the gourd—I was greedy for it. I
couldn't connect my ideas, I wasn't thinking straight. Finally we
called a halt. In that same terrain without any change whatever,
with not a tree or gully, or anything, we saw the sun slide down
on one side and the night rise up on the other. I did not even
help to care for the steers, or unload the pack mules. Where
could the animals go to graze? The darkness came down all
over, a darkness without a window. I unsaddled, hobbled my
horse, threw myself on the ground and fell asleep. But, just
before dropping off, two things stuck in my mind, athwart each
other: that perhaps Medeiro Vaz was crazy, and that Hermógenes had a pact with the devil! From Diadorim, stretched out
by my side, I heard: "Go to sleep, Riobaldo, everything will
turn out all right." The words stirred in me a tired annoyance;
but his voice was a balm to my body. That night I had a dream:
Diadorim passing under a rainbow.

How am I to find ways of telling you about the continuation
of our martyrdom on the following day, from the time the bars
of night were broken, in the mist of that wan dawn, without
hope of anything, not even a bird to be seen? We got moving. I
lowered my eyes to keep from seeing the horizons which en-
circled us, unchanging. The sun and the rest, you can fill in
with your imagination; what you cannot do is feel what it was
like, to live it. Know this: that the Sussuarão desert conceived
silence and brought forth evil—just like a person! I could not
wipe out those thoughts: to go, and go, keep on going, and that
Medeiro Vaz was mad, had always been mad, only now it was
out in the open—that is what I wanted to cry out. And the
others, my comrades, what did the others think? How should I
know? Probably of naught and nothing—they behaved as usual

—these long-suffering backlanders. A jagunço is a man who has halfway given up already. That blistering heat! And the burning, the baking, the pain of the heat in every part of your body. The horses breathing hard—you heard only their puffing, and their labored steps. Not the least sign of shade. No water. No grass. When we watered the horses in a leather trough, only half full, they stretched their necks to beg for more, and seemed to be looking down at their hoofs as if to show all the effort they had been making, but every drop of water had to be hoarded. The nightmare continued. A real nightmare, of delirium. The horses whimpered their incredulity. They were about done in. And we were lost. There was no water hole to be found. Everybody's eyes had become bloodshot and inflamed, their faces turning purple. The sunlight was murderous. And we wandered about, the scouts sniffing, seeking. There were those who were kissing their holy amulets, praying. As for me, I gave my spirit over to my body, slumped in the saddle, prostrate. My head seemed made of lead. Is valor always good? I thought of old bygones. Or was my mind wandering? The longing that sustained me was for Otacília, a girl who loved me, who lived in the Serras dos Gerais, at a place called Buritís Altos, source of a small stream, on the Fazenda Santa Catarina. I lost myself in my longing, like the memory of a melody, another water that I tasted. Otacília, she wanted to live or die with me, for us to get married. But the yearning didn't last long. Like those verses:

> Buriti, my palm tree,
> There by yonder stream:
> Little house on the left bank,
> Eyes like a wave of the sea . . .

But the green eyes were those of Diadorim. My silver loved one, my golden loved one. My eyes hurt so they would not focus, my sight was blurred, and I could not stop looking at the sky. I felt pity for my horse's neck—slumped, sweating, suffering. Oh, to turn back to the good sierras! If, before cashing in my chips, I could see a bird soaring motionless, the cool earth turned up by a rooting tapir, the swaying trees, the laughing of the

breeze, the blazing colors of a macaw. Do you know the rush of
the wind, with never a thicket or piece of wall to hold it back?

Diadorim did not leave my side. He knit his brow, thinking.
He sensed that I was far from him in my thoughts. "Riobaldo,
we didn't kill Ana Duzuza. Nothing wrong was done," he said.

I didn't answer. What did that matter to me now—evil deeds
and punishments? What I craved was the soft purling of a
brook over stones, the good sound of a stream slipping away
into the depths of a forest. And I thought back to the birds we
had last seen at Bambual do Boi, stirring up the air. They would
scold us, each casting its shadow on a span of water. There is
nothing like water. "If I get out of this alive, I'll give up out-
lawing, and go and marry Otacília," I swore to myself. But that
moment, I didn't care for anybody any more; only about me,
myself. I was a newcomer in this old hell. The day of our end is
fixed in advance—that is why you still see me here. The water
holes couldn't be found. One of the men had already been given
up for dead. Miquím, a sincere, serious chap, a first-class
fighter, pulled up and laughed: "Looks like we're out of luck."
Then, someone up ahead cried out: "I am blind!" And another
fell full length, all twisted, in the path of the horses. Suddenly
one of them growled, muttering a protest. Then another. The
horses were acting crazy. I saw a circle of men's faces. Their
sweaty faces. One was chalk-covered—even his ears were gray
with dust. And another, all blackened, bleeding from the eyelids and from the bags under his eyes. Wasn't Medeiro Vaz noticing anything? I could hear my veins. Then, reaching out, I
was able to grasp the reins of Diadorim's horse and those straps
hurt my hand. "From here, from this spot, I am not going one
step further! Only if dragged, helpless," I added. Diadorim
seemed made of stone, like a dog staring. He looked at me
steadily, with that beauty that nothing changed. "Then let's go
back, Riobaldo, for I see that nothing is turning out well." "It's
about time," I croaked, hoarse as a howling monkey. It was at
that moment that Diadorim's horse stumbled, sprawled on the
ground, and threshed about in its death agony. I got off my own.
Medeiro Vaz was there, with an uncertain air. The men, standing around, were holding their breath, to see what would hap-

pen. "Do we turn back, Chief?" Diadorim asked. He finished speaking, and gestured for us to keep still. His tone was friendly, but it was plain that Medeiro Vaz could want nothing but what Diadorim asked. Medeiro Vaz, then—for the first time —held out his open hands, admitting there was nothing he could do; and his shoulders sagged. That was all I saw, but I understood. I raised my gourd, took a swallow, bitter as gall. But the decision had been made, we would go back. And— would you believe—suddenly I was a new man, well and feeling fine! All the others reacted the same way. Going back is always a pleasure. Diadorim touched my arm. I looked: his eyes were swimming in tears. What I learned later was that the idea of crossing the Sussuarão desert had been Diadorim's. It was he who advised Medeiro Vaz to undertake it.

But why tell you, sir, in detail, all that we endured after that? It is enough to outline it in brief. With the help of God, we managed to get out of there without major disaster. That is to say, some of the men died, and many of the horses. The worst thing that happened was we were left without donkeys; the poor things had run off, and all our supplies, all, along with the rations, were lost. The only thing that kept us from becoming hopelessly lost was the stars by which we guided ourselves. We set out from there just as day was breaking. And in the wrong direction. We could hardly endure any more. Along with our other sufferings, the men were obsessed with hunger—we found no game—until they shot a big monkey, quartered, carved, and began to eat it. I tasted it. Diadorim did not even taste it. But while they were still roasting and eating it, they discovered that the body was not that of a monkey at all, they could find no tail. It was a man, someone called José dos Alves! His mother came to tell us, crying and explaining: he was an innocent, who went about naked for lack of clothing. He would run away to the woods like that, being weak in the head. What a horror! The woman, on her knees, was crying out. Someone said: "Now that he is good and dead, we can eat all but the soul, so the rest of us won't die." Nobody thought this funny. Nor did they eat any more, they couldn't. There was not even manioc meal to go with it. I threw up. Others vomited too. The

woman was pleading. Medeiro Vaz was prostrate with fever, and
several others were limping. "So, we face starvation, do we?"
some of them growled. But others managed to get some information out of the woman: that about a quarter-league away
there was an abandoned field of manioc. "Don't touch it," I
heard several say, sure that the woman had told them about it
out of revenge and that it must be wild manioc and poisonous!
They looked at her with a terrible rage. Meanwhile, Jacaré had
discovered a kind of dirt which they say is fit to eat, and tastes
good. He gave me some, I ate it, finding it tasteless except for a
strange stickiness, but it quieted the stomach. It was better to
eat grass and leaves. But there were some who filled their
knapsacks with lumps of that dirt. Diadorim ate some. The
woman also took some, the poor thing. Afterwards Medeiro
Vaz had a bad spell, others felt pains; it was thought that human flesh was poisonous. Many were ill, bleeding at the gums,
with red splotches on their bodies, and severe pains in their
swollen legs. I was hit by dysentery and was seized with a
loathing for myself. But we managed to reach the banks of the
Bois, and there in Lake Sussuarana we fished. We had brought
the woman along; she was afraid the whole time that we were
going to need another victim and she would be the one. "Anyone
who tries to molest her, will have me to deal with," Diadorim
warned. "Just let him try it," I chimed in, by his side. At last,
we killed a fat capybara. From a ragged plainsman we obtained
some burití-palm meal, which was better than nothing. We followed the stream that flows out of Lake Sussuarana, and which
is joined by the Jenipapo and Vereda-do-Vitorino, then empties
into the Pandeiros River—this one has singing waterfalls, and
its waters are so tinted that parrots flying over it argue, screaming: "It's green! It's blue! It's green! It's green!" Blessed waters, so near now. And it was pretty, as we passed the low-
lying fields, to see the blood-flower milkweed—all red and
orange, brightly swaying. "It is the blood-flower milkweed,"
cried Diadorim excitedly. But Alaripe, who was near us, shook
his head: "Where I come from we call it Lady Joan—but the
milk is poisonous."

Shattered we were, undone by that licking we had taken. But

not downcast. No one complained. I don't think anyone would
have said he had reason for complaint. A jagunço is like that. A
jagunço doesn't become upset by losses and defeats—nearly
everything is as one to him. I never saw one upset. For him, life
is a settled affair: to eat, drink, enjoy women, fight, and then
the end. And doesn't everybody feel about the same? The ranch
owners, too? What they want is thunder storms in October and
the granary full of rice. All that I myself had endured during
that ordeal, I was forgetting. I was beginning to recover faith in
Medeiro Vaz's leadership and no longer spoke disparagingly of
him. Confidence, you know, sir, does not depend on what you
have done or accomplished: it surrounds a person like a warm
aura. I dismissed from my mind the resolve I had made, to
seek out Otacília and ask her to marry me. After being ashes, I
was fire once more. Ah, but to someone—there's the rub—you
must pay allegiance. Listen: God eats in private, but the devil
goes about everywhere, licking his plate. But my love for Diadorim taught me that these uplands are beautiful.

We needed to rest, too, and wait. In one way or another, we
managed to get some saddle horses; we camped for a few days
at a friendly ranch on the Vereda do Alegre. Then we moved
on across the Pardo and the Acarí, and we were kindly received
everywhere. But it took a long time for us to get wind of the
forces of the Judases. But the advantage was ours because all
the people there were on our side. Medeiro Vaz never treated
anyone harshly without just cause, took nothing by force, nor
tolerated abuses by his men. Whenever we stopped at a place,
people would come and give us what they could in the way of
food and other things. But the followers of Hermógenes and
Ricardão robbed and raped, looted every little settlement, hung
around like the plague. At that time, as we learned, Hermógenes was moving across the border of Bahia, and had with him
a whole world of bad men. And Ricardão? Wherever he was,
he could wait. By easy stages, we reached a certain place in
Burití-do-Zé. The owner, Sebastião Vieira, had a corral and a
house. He stored our munitions for us: more than ten thousand
cartridges.

Why didn't we engage in combat, during all those months

that followed? I'll tell you the truth, sir: we were being harassed by government forces. Major Oliveira, Lieutenant Ramiz,
and Captain Melo Franco, they gave us no rest. And Medeiro Vaz
had only one thought: to avoid a show-down, so as not to
squander our strength, for our weapons had but one purpose: to
fulfill a duty. We would slip away, we would elude pursuit. Following the trail of the burití palms, along the brooks, we would
cross the Piratinga, which is deep, either at the Mata or the
Boiada ford; or farther down, the San Domingos River, at the
José Pedro ford. Or we would follow its banks to its headwaters,
in the São Dominguinhos. The important thing we had to figure
out was how to move quickly across the divides, whenever the
military started crowding us. It was necessary to know the
trails going down into Goiás, for the tableland comes to an
abrupt end as it slopes toward Goiás. There are back-breaking
slopes and terrible red hillsides. I saw places where the earth
was burned and the ground made noises. What a strange world!
In the Brejo do Jatobàzinho, in fear of us, a man hanged himself. Continuing to its far end, you reach Jalapão, a broad tableland. There one of the settlers asked me to be his son's godfather. The child received the name of Diadorim. The one who
officiated was the priest of a throng of migrants from Bahia: the
entire population of a small settlement in Bahia on the move to
a new place—men, women, the kids, the old folks, the priest
with his gear and crucifix, and the image from the church—
they even had a little band which came along too, like a group
of merrymakers at carnival time. They were going to look for
diamonds, so far off, as they themselves said: "in the rivers."
Some were driving pack donkeys, others were carrying their
stuff—bags of provisions, bundles of clothes, and jute hammocks slung over their shoulders. It was an orderly procession,
filling the road, raising the dust with the slap-slap of their sandals, the old women repeating their litany, others singing. They
prayed, on their way from poverty to riches. And for the pleasure of sharing the comfort of religion, we accompanied them as
far as Vila da Pedra-de-Amolar. There in the rainy season the
wind blows from the west; in the dry season, the wind comes
from this direction here. The procession of the Bahians had the

appearance of a festival. In the sertão, even a simple burial is a festival.

Sometimes I think: what if persons of faith and standing were to come together at some suitable place, in the middle of the uplands, to spend their lives in solemn prayers, raised loud, praising God and imploring the glory of forgiveness for the sins of the world? Everybody would start coming there. An enormous church would be erected, there would be no more crime, nor greed, and all suffering would be unburdened upon God, at once, until the hour of each one's death. I argued this with my compadre Quelemém, but he shook his head in disagreement. "Riobaldo, the harvest is for everybody, but each must hoe his own weeds," he answered thoughtfully.

My compadre Quelemém is a man who is not like the run of the mill. Go there, sir, to Jijujã. Go now, this month of June. The morning star rises at three o'clock, the dawn is cold as ice. It is the cane harvest season. In the dark you will see a little sugar mill—and there he is, himself, smiling and sweaty, busy with his grinding. Drink a gourd of cane juice and give him my regards. A man of gentle ways, with heart so white and overflowing with goodness that the gayest or saddest person likes to talk to him.

Just the same, my inner desire was for a mighty ranch of God's, set on the highest peak, with incense burning at the head of the fields, the people intoning hymns, even the birds and animals coming to applaud. Can't you see it? Brave, healthy people, seeking only Heaven as their end. Completely different from what you see here and there. Like what happened to a girl, in Barreiro-Novo: she stopped eating one day, and drank only three drops of holy water a day; miracles began to take place around her. But the regional chief of police came, bringing along his soldiers, and ordered the people to disperse. They took the girl to an insane asylum in the capital, and it is said that there they force-fed her through a tube. Did they have the right to do that? Were they justified? In a way, I think it was a good thing. Because, in no time at all, thousands of invalids doomed to die, appeared there, seeking to be cured: lepers, horribly deformed cripples, people covered with sores, the staring blind,

madmen in chains, idiots, consumptives, the dropsical, all
sorts: creatures that stank. If you had seen it, you would have
been depressed. Those who did were filled with disgust. I know:
disgust is an invention of You-Know-Who, to keep us from having pity. And those people screamed, clamoring to be healed at
once, praying aloud, arguing with one another, despairing of
their faith—what they wanted was only to be cured, they had no
interest in Heaven. Seeing all this, you become astounded at
the capacity of the world to hold so much of what we do not
want. It is a good thing that deformities and repellent sights are
scattered all over. Otherwise, we should lose heart. The backlands are filled with them. It is only when you lead a jagunço's
life and are always on the move, on hard marches, that you
don't notice it so much, the law of wretchedness and sickness.

Here's one for you: a couple, in Rio do Bora, a good ways
from here, just because the husband and wife were first cous-
ins, their four children were born with the worst deformity
there is: no arms or legs, just the trunk. Damn it, my mind can't
grasp such a thing! Let me ask you this: another educated man,
a young chap, who was prospecting for tourmalines in the Arassuaí valley was telling me that people's lives incarnate and rein-
carnate of their own accord, and that God doesn't exist. It made
me shudder. How can God not be? With God existing, there is
always hope: a miracle is always possible, and the world will
settle its problems. But, if there is no God, we are lost in the
turmoil, and life is meaningless. There is constant danger, on
great and small occasions, and we must not be negligent—acci-
dents can always happen. Having God, it is not so serious to be a
little careless, for it will all come out right in the end. But, if
there is no God, then we have no leeway at all! Because suffering exists. And man is trapped in a labyrinth: take the wrong
turn, and things happen, like the deformity of those children
without arms and legs. Doesn't pain hurt even in babies and
animals—even in lunatics—doesn't it hurt without our needing
to know why or how? And aren't people always being born?
Ah, the fear I have is not of death, but of birth. Fear or mystery.
Don't you see, sir? What is not of God is of the devil's domain.
God exists even when they say He doesn't. But the devil does

not need to exist to be—when people know that he does not exist, then is when he takes over. Hell is a limitless thing which cannot even be seen. But if people want Heaven it is because they want an end, but an end where they can see everything. If I am talking nonsense, please stop me. That's how I am. I was born different in my ways from anybody else. What I envy, sir, is your education.

From Arassuaí, I brought back a topaz.

Do you know, sir, why I had gone to those places? You needn't ask, I'll tell you. How is it that you can like the true in the false? Friendship with the illusion of disillusionment? I had it easy, but with dreams that left me tired. The sort from which you wake up slowly. Love? A bird that lays iron eggs. It was worse when I started staying awake all night, not able to sleep. Diadorim was one of those inscrutable persons—he never revealed his inner thoughts, nor what he was surmising. I think I was that way too. Did I really want to know him? I did and I didn't. Not even if you bury it in silence can a thing that doesn't make sense be dealt with. I fell back on cold reason. Now, sir, see how a person's fate works out: I brought back the topaz stone to give to Diadorim; then I was going to send it as a gift to Otacília; and today it is to be found on my wife's hand!

Am I telling things badly? I'll start again.

We were camped at the edge of some marshes, at the end of a meadow. It was easy there to keep the horses from scattering, for there was a kind of natural chute into which to drive them, and also corral traps for catching wild cattle. Pretty country, and tender grass. I can see everything just as it was day by day. Diadorim remained quiet for awhile, with a drinking gourd in his two hands, and I was looking at it: "Come what may, Riobaldo, we shall soon push ahead. This time, we'll fight," he said, leisurely, as always on the eve of action. He shook the gourd: it had something in it, a piece of iron, which annoyed me; a bit of old iron, good for nothing except to irritate me. "Throw that thing out, Diadorim," I said. He didn't say anything, and looked at me in a hesitant sort of way, as if I had asked something impossible. Meanwhile, he put the piece of iron in his pocket. And he continued holding the gourd in his hands; it was from

Bahia, with a fancy design, but it had now become a source of annoyance. And, as I felt thirsty, I took my engraved horn cup —they never break—and we went to get water at a pool that he told me about. It was in the shelter of a palm—a kind I don't know the name of—low, but thick, and with full fronds, which arched upward and then down, until their tips touched the ground. All the fronds, so smooth, so close together, formed a shelter, like an Indian thatched hut. It must have been from seeing something like this that the Indians got the idea of building their huts. There we bent down, lifted the foliage, and went in. The pool was almost round, or oval. As in the depths of a forest, inside the light had a greenish hue. Still, the water itself was blue, but of an impossible blue, which soon changed to purple. At first, my heart was strong. I wondered: what if Diadorim were to hold me with his eyes, and speak out from his heart in clear words? My reaction would be to repulse him. I do that? Ridiculous! Diadorim stood still, looking at everything indifferently. He gave no sign of having a secret, and I had a feeling of disappointment because of his sensible silence. I bent over to get some water. But there was an animal, a dark, ugly frog, blowing bubbles which rose in clusters to the surface. We both drew back at the same time. Diadorim changed the subject, and went off somewhere. He had a strange way of disappearing at times and reappearing, again without a word. Ah, when a person does that, is it not because he is and knows himself to be guilty?

Then I came upon a group of our fellows who were shooting dice to while away their time. The fact is that lately the men in our outfit had been boring me to death; I thought them all ignorant, coarse ruffians. But at that moment I wanted their dull company—Tom, Dick, and Harry—ordinary people. So even though I wasn't hungry, I got myself a mess of manioc mush, to eat alone. I wanted to think about life, and even asked myself: "Do I think?" But at that very moment they all raised their heads: there was a commotion over at the foot of the slope, where some of the others were calling and motioning us to come, something special. We went quickly to see what it was, clambering up the slippery stones.

It was a mule train going by, coming from São Romão and carrying salt to Goiás. The boss driver was telling a sad story, one of those things that happen. "Was he tall, long-faced, with big teeth?" Medeiro Vaz kept asking. "Well, yes," the driver replied, "and, before he died, he gave his name: said it was Santos-Reis. But he could say no more, for with that he died. Captain, believe me, we felt very sorry." Our men, standing around, looked at one another in consternation. Those muleteers had found Santos-Reis on the Cururú, at the point of death; they had lighted candles, and buried him. Fevers? At any rate, may his soul rest in peace. We took off our hats, and we all crossed ourselves. Santos-Reis, of all men, was the one we needed most —he had been on his way to us with a message and plan of operation from Sô Candelário and Titão Passos, chiefs who were supporting us, on the far side of the São Francisco.

"Now someone has to go—" Medeiro Vaz decided, looking about him. "Amen!" we all said. I stole a glance at Diadorim, who was standing just in front of me, holding an ox goad. I sensed he was planning some wanton revenge. I looked away. Stepping forward, I spoke up: "If that is an order, Chief, I would like to go." Medeiro Vaz cleared his throat. I was putting myself forward partly to show off, doubtful that he would consent to my going. Being the good shot I was, far and away the best, they needed me, and so would they be wanting to send me off as a scout, a message bearer? And then it happened: Medeiro Vaz agreed! "But you will have to take a companion," he added. At that point should I not have kept quiet, and left to another the choice of the second man, which was not my affair? What throes! I did not want what I most wanted, and which I could have brought about at once. The wish to bring matters to a head made me blurt out: "If those are your orders, Chief, Sesfrêdo will go with me."

I did not even look at Diadorim. Medeiro Vaz gave his approval. He looked at me hard, and decreed gruffly: "Go, then, and don't die on the way!" In those days Medeiro Vaz was already showing signs of the sickness that was to be the end of him in his labored breathing and drawn features. He was a resin yellow, unable to stand erect, and they say that he groaned when he passed water. Ah, but I have never known another like him. I would like to see a man to match him! Medeiro Vaz —the King of the Gerais!

Why was I behaving in this silly manner? Sir, do I know? See if you can figure it out. Had I but guessed then what I later came to know, after many bolts from the blue . . . One is always in the dark; only at the last minute the lights come on. I mean, the truth is not in the setting out nor in the arriving: it comes to us in the middle of the journey. I was really very stupid! Nowadays, I don't complain about anything. I don't cry for the moon. But neither am I one to be bowed down with remorse. There is only one thing. And in this case, what I feel is fear. As long as one is afraid, I don't believe it is possible to suffer real remorse. My life has not been one of good works. But I have confessed to seven priests, and I have received seven absolutions. In the middle of the night I wake up and try to pray. I can do it, and as long as I can, my sweat will not run cold! You must forgive my talking so much.

Just see what people are like: hardly a minute later, I was saddling my horse and packing my gear, and already I was beginning to feel very sad. Diadorim was watching me from a distance, pretending a kind of unconcern. When I went to say goodbye, I had to whisper to him: "It is for the sake of your father that I go, my friend, my brother. To avenge Joca Ramiro." It was weakness on my part, fawning. Diadorim replied: "Have a good trip, Riobaldo. And good luck."

Galloping off with Sesfrêdo, I left that place of Burití das Três Fileiras behind. Regrets began to arise in me. And then I understood my sudden impulse in choosing Sesfrêdo to come with me. He had left behind, so he told, long years back, in the lands of the Jequitinhonha, a golden-haired girl with whom he was wildly in love. "Sesfrêdo, tell me, tell me what happened," I said to him before we had gone a hundred yards. It was as if I had to pursue the shadow of a love. "Aren't you ever going back there, Sesfrêdo? Can you stand living if you don't?" I asked. "I hold on to that just to have longings, sometimes. Hell's bells! Longings, that's all," and he nearly split his sides laughing. I saw then that his story about the girl was not true. It takes all sorts of people to make the world.

I had to cross many lands and counties, as we travelled this northern country, mostly prairie. That is how I know the provinces of the State; there is no place I haven't been. We felt our way through Extrema de Santa Maria, Barreiro Claro, Cabeça de Negro, Córrego Pedra do Gervásio, Acarí, Vieira, and Fundo, trying to come out on the São Francisco. We had no trouble. We crossed, on a barge. Now we had only to keep heading east, straight towards Tremedal, known today as Monte-Azul. We knew that some of our people were on the move in that area, in Jaíba as far as Serra Branca, wild, empty lands of Rio Verde Grande. At dawn, knocking at his window we woke up a little old man, the owner of a banana grove. He was a friend and carried out the errand we sent him on. Five daybreaks later we returned. Someone was to meet us there, and the one who came was João Goanhá, himself. The reports he gave us could hardly have been worse. Sô Candelário? He had been killed in an exchange of gunfire; machine guns had cut him in two slantwise, above the belt. Alípio, taken prisoner, had been carted off to jail somewhere. Titão Passos? Ah, chased by some soldiers, he had had to escape into Bahia, to the protection of Colonel Horácio de Matos. João Goanhá himself was the only one of the leaders left. He was in command of the few remaining men. But courage and munitions were not lacking. "What about the two Judases?" I asked, Why was it, I wondered sadly, that the soldiers gave us no peace, while they did not bother those two at all? "It is said that they have protection," João Goanhá enlightened me; "that Hermógenes made a pact. And it is the long-tailed devil who looks out for him." Everybody believed this, and because of my fear-born weakness and the strength of my hatred, I think I was the first.

João Goanhá told us furthermore that we had no time to lose. Because he knew that the Judases, with reinforcements, had decided to cross the river at two points, and fall upon Medeiro Vaz, to finish him off once and for all, in his own territory. Where the danger lay, there Medeiro Vaz needed us.

But we couldn't reach him. We had no more than got started toward Cachoeira do Salto than we ran into a detachment of soldiers under Lieutenant Plínio. They opened fire. We fled. Fire on the Jacaré Grande—Lieutenant Rosalvo. Fire on the Jatobá Torto—Sergeant Leandro. We circled around. About that time I was feeling more out of luck than a flea between two fingers. I was neither a hero nor a coward. I was just an average fellow. To tell the truth, I didn't think that I had been born to be a jagunço forever; I didn't like it. How is it then that a person tries to do what he is not cut out for? Anything can happen. I think, I believe, it is the influences about you, and the times. Just as there is a given moment for crossing, a season, the dry months and the rainy ones. Might it not be so? Many other's experience was the same as mine, they neither feeling nor thinking. If not, why those improvised verses that we always sang, as we traveled in bands along the roads, with feigned joy in our hearts?

> *Tra-la-la, my Bahiana,*
> *I was going but now I'm not;*
> *I pretend*
> *I am going*
> *Over there, oh Bahiana,*
> *But halfway there I turn back.*

João Goanhá, a brave man and true, did not have to flaunt his pride. A very loyal and spirited person. He said to me: "Now I don't see what's going to become of us. For a full-scale war, I think that only Joca Ramiro could have handled it." Ah, but João Goanhá also held some high cards. A man with a big voice. And, though ignorant and illiterate, he would suddenly fish out, God knows from where, terrible little ideas, and cause several deaths. And so we tried this and that, feigning flight. There are high plains there too. Steep slopes. And God, the quicksands; have you ever seen any? The surface is dry and hard, deceptively normal in appearance; but anyone who doesn't know the rest, comes, sets foot on it, advances, soldiers on horseback, cavalry. Then, without warning, when they are halfway across, it gives way: it begins to heave, to rumble, to tremble and slip, like an egg yolk in a frying pan. For under the dry crust there lies concealed a deep bed of engulfing morass. Well, João Goanhá ordered us to hide ourselves around this trap—three groups of us—and lie in wait for the enemy. In the morning, the first to pass were Sergeant Leandro and his men; these were the fewest in number, and they had a paid guide to lead them over solid ground. But after they had gone by, we moved in and quickly scattered the green branches which they had laid down to mark the way. Afterwards, came the Lieutenant's men. Lieutenant, you're asking for it! They went straight in. Some of ours, over on the other side, fired some shots, as a feint. As bait! The mounted soldiers dashed forward. And then, God help us, all of a sudden it happened: the crust of the earth shook and, with a loud noise, cracked crisscross for a distance of many meters—and gave way. It was like upsetting a shelf of dishes. The fallen horses, the soldiers crying out, clinging to their sinking mounts, or grabbing at the air, some wildly firing off their guns! Deeper and deeper they sank, never to be seen again. Some of ours went on aiming and shooting at them. The things I saw, saw, saw—ugh. I did not fire a shot. I couldn't bring myself to.

As a result, from then on they hounded us worse than ever, thirsting for revenge. From plains and woods, meadows and caves, everywhere, behind, on our flanks, and in front of us, there were only soldiers, masses of them, growing in numbers. Furado-do-Meio. Serra do Deus-Me-Livre. Passagem da Limeira. Chapada do Cavão. Solón Nelson was killed. Arduininho was killed. And Figueiró, Batata-Roxa, Dávila Manhoso, Campêlo, Clange, Deovídio, Pescoço-Prêto, Toquim, Sucivre, Elisiano, Pedro Bernardo—I think those were all. Then Chapada do Sumidouro. Córrego do Poldro. About six more killed. I'm wrong: some were taken prisoner—it was said they, too, were put to death. We went crazy. The entrances to Bahia were closely guarded. They hit upon the scheme of using any poor devil of a backlander to get back at us. Ah, at times they paid dear for it. Gerais da Pedra. There, Eleutério left us and went off on foot, about two hundred yards, and knocked on the door of a shack,

to ask for information. The backlander came out, told him
something, deliberately wrong. Eleutério thanked him, turned
to leave and took a few steps. Then the backlander called out to
him. Eleutério turned around to hear what he had to say, and
got a load of bird shot full in the face and chest. Blinded, he
wheeled, stumbling, stretching out his arms, covered with red
spots that were spreading. His hair stood on end. And the soldiers began firing from ambush in the woods by the creek, and
from the edge of the clearing, on the other side. The backlander
took cover behind the outdoor mud oven, taking aim from there
with his gun, while bullets tore up the dirt around him, like a
big dog scratching. Inside the shack there were other soldiers
who went to settle their accounts with God. Ataliba, with his
big knife, nailed the backlander to the wall of the hut; he died
quietly, like a saint. There he remained, spitted. We, well—we
got away all right, and managed to reach a spot where we
could stop and talk things over in safety.

Serra Escura. We had neither ammunition nor food left, so
we had to separate, each to take his chances and try to make
good his escape. Goanhá's men scattered. Each for himself, and
let all who survive meet on this side of the Rio: at the junction
of Vereda Saco dos Bois with the Ribeirão Santa Fé. Or go
straight to wherever Medeiro Vaz might be. Or, if the enemy got
too close, to Burití-da-Vida, São Simão do Bá, or still farther up,
where the Ribeirão Gado Bravo is fordable. These were João
Goanhá's orders. Time was of the essence. The air of the countryside reeked of gunpowder and soldiers. In front of me, one
Cunha Branco, an experienced, crafty old fighter, was taking
forever to lace up his leather jacket, his tongue hanging out of
his open mouth. And my fear mounted. We said goodbye. Slipping away without fixed destination, I left, and Sesfrêdo came
with me. By the grace of God, we got through the danger zone.
We reached Córrego Cansanção, not far from the Arassuaí. For
a while, we needed to have a job; anything to keep alive. As for
our arms and some of our clothes, we found a safe spot and left
them hidden there. Then we got work with that doctor I've already mentioned to you who was engaged in mining.

Why didn't we stay on there? I know and I don't. Sesfrêdo

looked to me for all decisions. A certain remorse at not keeping
our promise to return, at being deserters? No, not at all. Being
with another makes it easier to deceive yourself, and the idea of
treason arouses no qualms, nor does any other crime chafe the
conscience. Only if there is talk of shameful behavior among
survivors, then, yes, the disgrace of having turned coward ran-
kles. But I could see an advantage in turning back to the big
plantation of Selorico Mendes, and demanding my rightful
place on the São Gregório ranch. Would they fear that! Or I
could turn up without a care in Buritís Altos, for Otacília's sake,
and resume our love affair. I did not want to. Was I sweating
out a yearning for Diadorim? Certainly not to the point of putting it in words, or even feeling it. It was like the sky and the
clouds there behind a passing swallow. I think, too, that perhaps a lively curiosity had been reborn in me: I wanted very
much to be mixed up once again with the men of Medeiro Vaz,
to see how it was all going to end. The Arassuaí was not my
stamping grounds. Living is continually taking chances. Then,
the nights were changing with the approach of the rains, days
of bad weather. I finally spoke out. "Time to go. Shall we get
going, Sesfrêdo?" "Let's go, its high time," Sesfrêdo answered
me.

Ah, but hold on, wait a minute: I'm getting off the track. I was
about to forget Vupes! My story would be neither accurate nor
complete if I left out Vupes, for he comes very much into the
picture. He was a foreigner, a German, you know—blond, well-
built, with blue eyes, tall, red-haired—a real man for you. A
good person. A methodical man, wholesome, with a kind of solemn gaiety. Hah, with all the political turmoil and fighting going on thereabouts, he took no part in any of it; he traveled
without fuss and went about his business in the backlands,
which consisted of bringing in and selling a lot of different
things to the ranchers: plows, hoes, corn shellers, big steel
knives, fine tools and cheap ones, cans of ant poison, arsenic,
and carbolic acid; even windmills to pump water, complete with
towers, which he would contract to set up. He maintained such
a different mode of conduct that everyone respected him. They
say he is in the capital, still alive and wealthy, and that he owns

a large business, a store, where he made his money. Oh, so you knew him? What a little goat pill of a world! And how is it you pronounce his name—Wusp? That's it. Mr. Emílio Wuspes—Wúpsis—Vupses. Well, this Vupes turned up there, and right away he recognized me—remembered that he had known me in Curralinho. He looked me over slowly, every detail. A shrewd customer! "I am delighted. You are well? Delighted." And I liked that manner of greeting. I always like to meet again in friendship any old acquaintance, and depending on whether the person smiles, we find ourselves recalling the past, but only the pleasant incidents, the agreeable ones, it seems. With the German Vupes there, I remembered those girls—Miosótis and Rosa'uarda—the ones who, in Curralinho, I had looked upon as my sweethearts.

"Mr. Vupes, I, too, am delighted. Are you in good health, too? Delighted," I answered, politely. He smoked cigars. He said to me: "I know that you are brave man, very brave. I needing brave man like that, to traveling with me, fifteen days, backlands here now muchly confused, wild men, everything." I burst out laughing just hearing him.

But it made me proud, it gave me pride in my profession. Ah, the good life of a jagunço. That is what you call carefree living, skimming over life's surface. While leading the life of a jagunço you neither see nor notice the poverty around you. You know, sir, such widespread poverty, people having a hard time and feeling sunk. The poor have to have a sad love for honesty. They are trees that gather dust. Sometimes when we were on the move, a hundred, two hundred men on horseback, arms jangling and tinkling, it would happen that out of some corner there would appear a gaunt, yellowed creature, in rags, cringing in fear, holding out a tarnished copper in the hollow of his hand: he wanted to buy a handful of grub. Married, and the father of a famished family. Things without connection, random thoughts. I thought for awhile, and then asked: "In what direction are you heading?" And Vupes answered:

"I, straight, city of São Francisco, I go forth." When he spoke he never gestured with even so much as the tip of his finger. Well—it was my direction, too—I accepted. Fate! Whereupon I

spoke to Sesfrêdo, who was willing, too; Sesfrêdo never had
an opinion of his own; he did not have the capacity for it.

The roads were never-ending, and through those boundaries
of Grão-Mogol, Brejo das Almas, and Brasília,* without any disturbing encounters, we brought Mr. Vupes. Thanks to him, I
learned a lot. This Vupes was meticulous and methodical in his
way of living, and he never lost his poise. Imagine this: it
seemed as if there was nothing to eat, but he would pick up
something here, another little something there, and still more
yonder—a few berries, a couple of eggs, some bamboo shoots, a
handful of greens—and then, when we came to a halfway decent house, he would order and pay for a dinner or a lunch, of
several dishes, a royal feast; he himself would show how the
things should be cooked, and everything would turn out delicious. So off there in the backlands, he managed to have his
comforts, whatever he wanted. I'll say! We left him at his destination; and I took good care of him, for he had showed his trust
in me.

We reached the River, and crossed. And there the longing for
Diadorim sprang up in me again, after such a long time, hard to
endure, and full of hope. I was eager to arrive, to arrive, and be
near him. A horse that loves his master even breathes in
rhythm with him. Beautiful is the moon, lovely moon, when it
emerges from the clouds, round and clear. We came along the
Urucúia. The river of my love is the Urucúia. The big tableland
where so many cattle bellow. After that, the plains, with the
grass growing green. It is there that the herder shouts at his
straying herds. The air has a sting in its movement, the approach of the rains, the thunder rolling. All the herders herding. The cattle restless. The news was bad about the gangs of
the Judases which kept growing, the dirty mob!

"About how many?" I would ask. "A great many! A whole
kingdom of them," the herders would reply.

But Medeiro Vaz, our people, were not to be found; nobody
knew anything for sure. We kept going, to wherever the world
might end. We just kept wandering. We camped on a broad

* *Brasília:* not the new Federal Capital but a small town of the same
name in northern Minas Gerais.

savannah, a sheltered spot, between the Garapa and Jibóia
rivers, where there are three lakes that form one, of four colors; they say the water is poisonous. Water, waters. You will see
a creek that empties in the Canabrava—the one which empties
in the Taboca, which in turn empties in the Rio Prêto, the first
Prêto of the Rio Paracatú—well, the water of that stream is
salt, a strong brine, and turns blue; those who know it say it is
exactly like sea water; the cattle won't drink it. I am doing all
this explaining because many of the rivers and streams all
through this part of the country have the same names. Until
you have learned this, you get mixed up, and it makes you mad.
In Prêtos alone, I have wet my hands about ten different times,
and as many in Verdes. Some five Pacaris, many Pontes. Bois,
or Vacas, many also. Seven by the name of Formoso. São
Pedro, Tamboril, Santa Catarina. The sertão is as big as the
world.

Now, around here, as you have seen, by River we mean only
the São Francisco—the Chico. The small ones are veredas. And
an occasional broad stream. And now I happen to remember:
on the Ribeirão Entre-Ribeiros—you should go see the old plantation; underneath the house they had a room almost the size
of the house itself, dug in the ground where they tortured slaves
and others, slowly putting them to death. But, to tell you the
truth, I don't believe it. A hiding place for gold, treasure and
arms, munitions, or counterfeit money, that yes. You should be
forewarned: people here are greatly given to foolishness. Out of
a donkey's fart they make a typhoon. They love excitement.
They just have to invent tall tales, and they wind up fearing
and believing them.

For example, there is a marimbú—a killer of a bog—on the
Riacho Ciz, where practically a whole herd was swallowed up,
and rotted there. Afterwards, at night, flickering in the wind, a
million blue flames could be seen, will-o'-the-wisps. People who
didn't know about it, when they saw it, ran like crazy to get
away. Well, this story spread everywhere, traveled more, you
may be sure, than you or I. They said it was a bad omen, that
the world was coming to an end at that place because, long ago,
a priest had been castrated there, about twenty leagues away,

for having refused to marry a son to his own mother. They even made up songs about it: the Blue-Fire-of-the-End-of-the-World.

Now, the gallows, that I did see—a modern gallows, built to scale, made of good brown hardwood, sucupira. It was set on a knoll, beyond São Simão do Bã, near the right-hand side of the Piripitinga. It was built at that particular place because they had no jail there; it was hard to have to make a trip to escort a criminal, and took people away from their work. So that is why they used it. Sometimes, from the surrounding country, they would even bring in a condemned man, on horseback, to be hanged publicly. A poor man came to live near there, almost underneath the gallows; whenever there was a hanging he would pass his hat for alms, after which he would dig a grave and bury the body, with a cross to mark the spot. Nothing more.

Something different happened, however, when a man—Rudugério de Freitas, of the red-headed Freitases of Água-Alimpado—ordered one of his sons to kill the other, seek him out and kill him, saying that he had stolen the golden pyx from the abbey's church. Whereupon the brother, instead of doing as he had been ordered, connived with the other and the two of them went and killed their old father, cutting him up with their brush knives. But first they decorated the brush knives with strands of fibers and different flowers. And they draped the father's body atop the house—a good little house, with a tile roof, the best one around there. Then they rounded up the cattle, which they were going to take a long way off and sell. But they were soon caught. We helped capture them, and they became our prisoners. We tried them. If it had been Medeiro Vaz, he would so reasonably have had the two hanged at once. But our chief at that time, as I would have you know, was Zé Bebelo!

With Zé Bebelo, now, nothing was hard and fast, things took a different turn every time. Rumbling in his throat he inquired: "Now—why did you first decorate your brush knives?" The two brothers responded that they had done that in honor of the Virgin, so that Our Lady would forgive them beforehand for the sin they were going to commit. For all of Zé Bebelo's stiff seriousness and lofty attitude, without a frown on his forehead,

I very soon saw that he was laughing inside. "Most Holy Virgin,"
he said, whereupon all the men removed their hats, in deep respect. "Whether she forgives you or not, I do not know. But in
her name, the Most Pure, Our Mother, I pardon you," Zé Bebelo
declared. "Didn't the father wish for murder? Well, then, he
himself was killed—tit for tat. I find reasons for this decision,
which admits of no repeal or revocation, legal and loyal, in con-
formity with the law." And Zé Bebelo went on, delighting in his
own words: "To forgive is always just and right"—and so on,
and so on. But, as the two brothers were deserving of some punishment, he confiscated that fat herd, which we in turn
promptly sold, pocketing the money. And this episode also gave
rise to a fine song for the guitar. But I bear witness that Zé
Bebelo acted as he did on that occasion only to set an example
of decent conduct. Normally, when we encountered a herd being driven along, he would levy a tax of merely one or two
head, just to keep us supplied with meat. He maintained that it
was meet to respect the work of others, and to encourage per-
severance and order in our benighted backlands.

Zé Bebelo—ah! If you did not know this man, you missed
acquaintanceship with a kind of mind that nature sometimes
bestows, once in a long while. He wanted to know everything,
to decide everything, to be all-powerful, to change everything.
He never stood still. He surely must have been born that way,
headstrong, excitable, a child of confusion. He could switch
suddenly from being the most honest to the most wicked of
men, depending on circumstances. He spoke loudly, artfully,
with an authority all his own, on the spur of the moment. On
one occasion, completely unarmed, he approached Leôncio
Dú, who had stood everybody off and was flourishing a huge
knife, and shouted at him: "Are you looking for blood? Hell, I'll
split you wide open!" Whereupon, Leôncio Dú decided to drop
his knife, and gave himself up. Did you ever hear anything like
it? Zé Bebelo was both intelligent and brave. A man can fool
others about anything, except when it comes to being intelligent
and brave. And Zé Bebelo could size people up at a glance. One
time a certain wild ruffian came to us from Zagaia, highly rec-

ommended. "Your shadow pricks me, thorn tree," Zé Bebelo greeted him, with an animal's instinct. And he had the fellow tied up and given a rawhide lashing. The bandit then confessed: he had come for the express purpose of double-crossing him. Zé Bebelo pointed his Mauser pistol at the bandit's curly head: there was a shattering report and his brains spattered far and near and stuck like glue. We began to sing the *Moda-do-Boi*.

Zé Bebelo fished, hunted, danced dances, harangued his people, inquired about everything, roped steers or managed them with a goad, knew all about horses, played the guitar, whistled tunefully; only he never shot dice nor played cards, stating that he was afraid of becoming too fond of the habit and risks of gambling. Aside from this, he was heartily in favor of everything, no matter what: if it rained, he praised the rain; a second later, he praised the sun. Above all things he loved to give advice. He felt in some way responsible for the progress of the whole of Brazil, and all its territories, and he talked hour after hour. "I have come back for good," he said, when he returned from Goiás. The past, for him, was really past, and didn't count. And he never admitted a mistake, never. One day, trotting along a brand new road, he exclaimed: "Hey, at times these sierras move around a lot." What had happened was that he was lost, having taken the wrong direction, ha, ha. Ah, with him, even the hardships of war had their gaiety, afforded some amusement. When a fight was over, he would set out at a gallop, his pistol still in hand, chasing anyone he came across, and bellowing: "Long live the law! Long live the law!" and firing away. Or, "Peace! Peace!" he would cry, and off would go two more shots. "Long live the law!"—sure, sure, but what law? Did anyone know? With all that, his reputation grew. I'll give you an example: once he was galloping on horseback, for exercise, and a farmer seeing him got scared, fell to his knees in the road, and pleaded: "Please, Mr. Zebebel, for the love of God, for the sake of your soul, don't inflict the 'Long-live-the-law' on me!" Zé Bebelo threw the poor devil a bill, and shouted: "Get up here, brother, behind me, on the crupper," and he brought him

back to eat with us. That's the way he was. He was a man. My
fond memories of Zé Bebelo are ever green. As a friend, he was
one of the persons I have most esteemed in my life.

Well now, at long last I will pick up where I left off and get
back to what I was telling you. From meadows to plains, over
hills, sand dunes and swamps, Sesfrêdo and I finally reached
Marcavão. Before we got there, the weather changed to rain.
The kind of rain that washes bare the roots of trees, cloud-
bursts, downpours that devour the earth before your very eyes.
The rivers began to rise. We dismounted in Marcavão, on the
banks of the Rio-do-Sono. There Medeiro Vaz died, in that
out-of-the-way place. We had arrived in time.

When we met up with the outfit at this place, Medeiro Vaz
was already in a bad way; perhaps because of this we could not
express our joy at meeting, and Diadorim neither embraced me
nor uttered a word of welcome. I became downcast. Sadness
and the sorrowful vigil weighed upon us. "That's not the worst
of it," Alaripe said to me, "the enemy is close by, stalking us."
The rain fell heavily at night, the trees dripped. There was a
damp, chilly wind. In order to shelter Medeiro Vaz, they had
raised a steer's hide—you know, sir: a single hide fixed to a
stake to shelter a person from the direction in which the wind is
blowing. We were camped under some big trees. The sound of
the river was like a continuous murmur. Medeiro Vaz was lying
on a white goat skin—his shirt open over his chest covered with
graying hair. His belly was greatly swollen, but it was not from
dropsy. It was from the sickness. When he caught sight of me,
he tried to raise himself up, struggling to see me. The whites
of his eyes were like the inside of an ant hill. But he gave way,
his arms dropped, and he fell back on the ground. "He's about
ready to cash in his checks," I said to myself. Ah, his face—
yellow as all get-out: like straw! In this state he lasted almost
all the rest of the day.

The afternoon was darkening. Finally Diadorim called me
aside; he was trying to hold back the tears. "In friendship, Riobaldo, I thought of you the whole time" and he squeezed my
hand. I was taken aback, feeling somewhat awkward. Then

they called us: "Hurry, the Chief is about to go!" Medeiro Vaz, gasping, approaching the end. His jaw quivered without let up; terrible moments. So long drawn-out! And there came a downpour, a heavy beating rain, as if on purpose. Night had closed in. Kneeling in a circle around him, we held up some hides, to protect him in his dying moments. Medeiro Vaz—King of the Gerais—how could a man like him come to an end? The water fell in torrents, and ran down our faces in rivulets. Bending under the hides, we could see the soul taking leave of the body. And Medeiro Vaz, pulling himself together in his death agonies, with great effort overcame the wheeze that was rattling the phlegm in his throat, and stammered: "Who will take my place? Who will be the leader?" With the pelting of the rain, few heard him. He could speak only broken words. But I saw that his glance stayed on me, and that he was choosing me. Were his eyes turning red? Yes, with the death rattle they were glazing over. I felt a tightening of my heart. I didn't want to be the chief! "Who will be the leader?" I saw my name in his flickering eyes. He tried to raise his hand to point to me. The veins on his hand . . . By what light was I seeing that? But he couldn't. Death was the more powerful. His eyes rolled up; his breath was rattling in his throat. He went to sleep in a white hammock. He breathed his last.

His day was a busy one. When the rain let up, we searched for something to light. All we could find was the stub of a candle of carnaúba wax, and a torch. I had had a bad fright. Now, in the midst of my dizziness, a strange impulse to sing those verses, like someone singing in a chorus, came over me:

> *My runaway black bull,*
> *A tree to tie you to?*
> *A palm that does not bend:*
> *A buriti that does not twist.*

The bells in all the churches should ring out!

We covered the body with young buriti leaves, cut while still wet. We stood watch, all of us, until the break of day. The frogs were croaking, throbbing. A bullfrog rasped raucously. A tapir whistled, a whistle shriller than the whinny of a colt. At dawn, we dug a deep grave. The earth of the uplands is good.

We had our morning coffee, and Diadorim said to me, emphatically: "Riobaldo, you are in command. Medeiro Vaz chose you with his last orders."

They were all there, the tough ones, looking at me—so many dark pupils glinting hard, pellet by pellet—it was as if I were receiving a charge of thousands of buckshot or hail stones. They approved. They wanted me as leader. I shivered inwardly, and the words froze in my mouth. I did not want to, did not want to. I saw it as something far beyond my capabilities. What a misfortune that João Goanhá had not come! Definitely, I had no wish for laurels, nor for the power to command. I swallowed hard. Finally stepping forward, I stammered: "I can't—I'm not fit."

"Riobaldo, old man, you can do it."

I turned stubborn. A dirty word rose to my lips. Let them think what they would, but nobody was going to push me around just for the fun of it.

"Riobaldo, old man: you think you aren't deserving of it, but we know your worth," Diadorim repeated, his hand raised. Whereupon all the others nodded their agreement.

"Tatarana! Tatarana!" Some called out, Tatarana being a nickname I had.

I was scared. The situation was growing serious. Who gave Diadorim the right to do that to me? I, being the way I am, rebelled:

"I can't, I don't want to! That's final! I can act and carry out orders, but not give them."

There was a moment's pause. All stood waiting breathlessly. Do you know what it's like to be in the midst of a band of jagunços standing around you, when danger threatens, like so many wolves? The worst part is the ominous silence, the lowering gravity. It's not that they kill one another, you understand, but that the least little thing can rob you of their respect, and leave you discredited forever. Everyone was growling. At this point, Diadorim squared his shoulders and took a step forward.

He stopped staring at me, and sized up the attitudes of the others. He was a master at this; he could take in a situation with a quick glance—he was a wonder at counting cattle. Quick-wittedly he said:

"Very well, then, I'm taking over the leadership. I am not the best one, men, but I stick to what I want and value, like all of you. The rules of Medeiro Vaz will be followed, to the letter. But if any one of you doesn't think that this is right, we'll settle it by arms."

Hot damn! Oh, Diadorim, fiercely beautiful! Ah, he knew his way around. Between jagunço and jagunço, it is the stark power of the person that counts. Many of those present would have given their lives to be chief—but they hadn't had time to collect their wits. And the others were glad and applauded:

"Reinaldo! Reinaldo!" They cried in approval. Ah.

At this, suddenly and clearly, there sprang up within me a powerful protest! No. Not Diadorim. I could never agree to that: not so much because I was his devoted friend, and felt for him that troubling affection that was gnawing at me, like a sinful secret love, but, if for no other reason, because I simply could not accept that transformation, the business of always taking orders from him, the fact that Diadorim was my chief. I would have nothing like that thrust upon me.

"No," I sang out, like the clang of a bell, "I'm against it!"

Did all eyes turn toward me? I did not see, I did not quiver. Only Diadorim was visible to me—his outline and the hint of his movements—his hands and eyes watching. I made a quick mental count of how many bullets I had for a point-blank gun fight—plus the bullet that was already in position in my automatic—ah, I had plenty of corn in my saddlebag. Meanwhile, the men, the others, did not move; they just waited; certainly they had developed a strong dislike for me, upsetting their decisions one after another, when I no longer had any right to pass opinions, inasmuch as I had already rejected the leadership. Who knows, perhaps they would have found pleasure in seeing the two of us, Diadorim and me, who until then had been like brothers, slash each other to ribbons. I felt an urge to kill someone—anyone—to relieve my feelings, but not Diadorim, not him. Beyond doubt they sensed this in me. The silent ones. Only Sesfrêdo, unexpectedly, spoke up: "I'm against it, too!" Because he respected me, he backed me up. And Alaripe, a serious man, chimed in: "He's got a right to. Let Riobaldo state his reasons." I straightened up my horns, and announced:

"As I see it, Marcelino Pampa is the one who has to take over the command. In the first place, he is the oldest, and besides being the oldest, he is brave and known for his good sense."

Marcelino Pampa's face was a study. I could see by the expression of agreement on the faces of the others that I had cleverly scored a hit. But, what about Diadorim? We looked each other straight in the eye—we two. At that moment my very great regard for Diadorim was raised even higher, but just the same, just the same, I would have upheld my challenge, had he assailed me in anger, or drawn his gun. At such a moment one has to push a mountain aside to get past. In the end it was Diadorim who lowered his eyes. I was stronger than he! He smiled, after I did. And spoke up firmly: "Gladly. Better than Marcelino Pampa there is none. I did not aspire to power."

He spoke bravely.

And: "Now is the time to drop all differences, to be united without disputes," Alaripe counseled.

"Amen," everyone voiced his approval. Whereupon Marcelino began and spoke thus:

"Because of our need, I accept that which is my duty. Until the coming of one of the right ones: Joao Goanhá, Alípio Mota, Titão Passos. Meanwhile, I need the good counsel of all who have it to give. Now that we are agreed . . ."

He had more to say, but unimportant, without ideas, for Marcelino Pampa was a man of limited ability. I thought only that he was taking on a heavy burden in a spirit of sacrifice. In better times, he would have liked to be captain, but under those circumstances when we were in such desperate straits, who wouldn't have disliked this responsibility? Ha, but then I noticed how from that moment Marcelino Pampa assumed another air, one of ponderous wisdom and supreme satisfaction! To be chief—outwardly, a little reluctant, but all rosy inside!

I felt relieved. Diadorim came close to me, spoke his admiration, his loyal affection. I listened, listened, drinking it in,
sweetest of honey. It was what I needed. There are times when
I think that what we need is to awaken, suddenly, from some
kind of spell. People and things are not real! And what is it
that we frequently experience vague longings for? Can it be
that all of us have already sold our souls? Foolishness on my
part. For how could such a thing be possible?

Listen, I'll tell you something, sir. They say that in Antônio
Dó's outfit there was a big-shot jagunço, well-fixed he was—
Davidão was his name. Well, one day—one of those things that
sometimes happen—this Davidão began to be afraid of dying.
Shamelessly, he thought up a deal which he proposed to a
penniless poor devil called Faustino: Davidão would give him
ten thousand milreis, and by the law of witchcraft, should it
fall to Davidão's lot to be the first to die in combat, then
Faustino would die in his stead. Faustino agreed, took the
money, and closed the bargain. It seems that, as a matter of
fact, he did not take much stock in the binding power of the
contract. Shortly after, they were in a hot fight against the
soldiers of Major Alcides do Amaral, who were strongly in-
trenched in São Francisco. When the battle ended, both of
them were still alive, Davidão and Faustino. What did this
mean? That the day and the hour had not struck for either.
And so they went on for months, safe and sound; nothing
changed; they weren't even scratched. What do you think of
that, sir? Well, now listen: I told this story to a young man,
very intelligent, who had come with others from the big city, in
a truck, to go fishing in the River. Do you know what the young
fellow said to me? That it was an interesting subject for a
story in a book, but that it needed a dramatic ending, carefully
worked out. The ending that he thought up was like this: that
one day Faustino, too, would begin to be afraid, and want to
call off the deal. He would return the money. But Davidão
would not accept it, wanted no part of it under any circumstances. The discussion led to a hot argument, and then to
hand-to-hand fighting. Faustino managed to whip out his knife
and rushed at Davidão; the two grappled and fell rolling on the

ground. But in the melee, Faustino with his own hand buried the knife in his own heart and died.

I like this ending very much. How many really fine ideas occur to a well-educated person! In that way they can fill this world with other things, without the mistakes and twistings and turnings of life in its stupid bungling. For example, does life dissemble? I said that to the young fisherman, whom I sincerely admired. And he asked me what had been the final outcome, the real ending, between Davidão and Faustino. The ending? Who knows? All I heard was that Davidão decided to give up his outlawry. He left the outfit, and by holding out certain promises of a few acres of land, and other compensations, he induced Faustino to leave, too, and to come and live near him for good. Beyond this, I know nothing about them. In real life, things end less neatly, or don't end at all. To strive for exactitude makes one blunder. One shouldn't seek it. Living is a very dangerous business.

What I soon saw was that Marcelino Pampa, for all his good will, was not going to measure up. In an attempt to decide correctly on the first steps to be taken, he called me to him, together with João Concliz. "The Judases are close by, about fifteen leagues off, and they know about us. A real attack, they won't launch now, not with all this rain and flooded streams. But they keep closing in on us, getting nearer, because they are many and to spare. As I see it, we have two outs: either we escape to the tablelands, while there is yet time—but that means we give up all hope and suffer humiliation—or, we do our level best to break through them, then cross the River and look for João Goanhá and our other comrades. I can't think of anything else, and I want all the good advice I can get." That is what he, Marcelino Pampa, said. "But, if they should learn that Medeiro Vaz is dead, they are liable to fall on us this very day," was what João Concliz had to say, and he was absolutely right. I could not think what to say; the confusion of the past hours had me bewildered. In the present situation, what would Medeiro Vaz have done? Or Joca Ramiro? Or Sô Candelário? Thus my random thoughts. It was then I realized that a band of men must have a single head. A commander is needed to resolve the worried, conflicting notions. I did not know then, and wonder if I know today, the rule of no compromise. I could have spent my whole life there, racking my brains doing nothing. Finally, after many silences and few words, Marcelino decided that in the afternoon our discussion would be resumed. Bewildered we were, the three of us.

Then I went over to where Diadorim was. "Riobaldo," he said, hesitantly, "you can see that we have no choice." He stopped, thought a moment, his hands clasped. "And you three, what have you decided to do?" he asked. I replied: "This afternoon we'll come to a decision, Diadorim; are you not satisfied?" He straightened up. And he spoke: "I know what I have to do. As far as I'm concerned, all this is not getting us anywhere. I'm burning to get close to one of the Judases, and finish this off." I knew that he was talking about fighting because he thought it was his duty. I was more tired, sadder, than he. "Who knows, if . . . To find a means of getting close to them, it might even be better . . ." he faltered, then relapsed into an attitude of secrecy. From the look in his big eyes, I believed he was scheming to grab control by inciting the band to revolt. He was capable of madness of this sort. But no; he spoke again: "It was you, yourself, Riobaldo, who bossed everything today. You picked Marcelino Pampa, you decided and acted." It was true. I enjoyed hearing it, filling my sails. Ah, but I was pulled up short by a sudden thought, and I felt a sharp fear, a sharp fear. Every hour of every day one discovers a new facet of fear.

But, after the last meal of the day, when we were again together, Marcelino Pampa, and I, and João Concliz—we didn't have a chance even to get started, when we heard a galloping, the arrival, the skidding stop, the quick dismounting, the slap-slap of sandals. It was Feliciano and Quipes, bringing in a young herder who must have been no more than fifteen years old, and his features were twisting with terror. "What happened was that this one went by us, running away, half wild. We nabbed him. He's got something big to tell," and they shoved him forward a little. He tried to avoid our eyes. Finally, he gulped, and sobbed:

"It's a man. That's all I know. It's a man."

"Take it easy, boy. Nothing is going to happen to you here. Where were you going?" Marcelino Pampa asked quietly.

"It's a big fight. It's a man. I was going far from here, to my father's house. Ah, it's a man. He came down the Paracatú River on a raft of burití trunks."

"What else did the man do?" João Concliz then asked.

"He fired. The man, and five others. They came out of the woods, and fired on the others. There were heaps of others, more than about thirty. But they ran away. They left behind three dead, and some wounded. They were driven off. And they on horseback. The man and his five are on foot. A terrible man. He said he is going to change all this! They came to the herders' hut to ask for salt and manioc meal. I let them have some. They had killed a little plains deer, they gave me a piece of the meat."

"What was his name? Speak up! What do the others call him? What was his manner, what did he look like?"

"Him? What is he like? He is more short than tall, he is not old, he is not young. White man. Came from Goiás. What the others call him and adress him as, is Deputy. He came down the Paracatú on a burití raft. 'We were itching for a fight,' he said himself. He and his five were shooting like crazy. They screamed and howled like wild cats. He said he was going to shake up the world! He came down the Paracatú River on a burití raft. They floated down. They don't even have a horse."

"It's him! But it's him! It can only be—" someone spoke out.

"That's right. And so he is on our side!" another added.

"We have to go after him," was the word of Marcelino Pampa, "Where might he be? In Pavoã? Someone has to go there."

"It's him. That's life for you. Who would have thought it? And he is a regular demon of a man, half-crazy."

"He's on our side. And he knows how to fight."

It was so. The rain had started up again, coming down fast and heavy, but nevertheless Quipes and Cavalcânti mounted and set out, heading for Pavoã. They must not have found it easy, because by nightfall they had not returned. But that man, so you will know, that man was—Zé Bebelo! That night in our camp nobody got any sleep. The next morning, at sunup, he arrived. A red letter day.

With his slouch hat, his striding step, he came toward us, accompanied by his five tough ones. From their manners, from their clothes, they were from the upper Urucúia. Peasant types of the plains. Poorly dressed, but loaded with arms, and with cartridge belts full. Marcelino Pampa went forward to meet him; we lined up behind our leader. It was worth seeing, those formalities.

"Peace and health, Chief! How have you been?"

"How are you, brother?"

The two headmen greeted one another. Then Zé Bebelo's eye fell on me:

"Professor, as I live and breathe! Sooner or later, people always meet again." He never forgot a person's name or face. I saw that he felt cordial toward me, not looking on me as a traitor or disloyal. He laughed heartily. Suddenly, he stopped laughing, and took a step backward.

"I have come for good!" he said; he said it almost defiantly.

"You have come at a good time, Chief! That's what all of us here have to say," Marcelino Pampa responded.

"That's good. Hail Medeiro Vaz!"

"God be with him, friend. Medeiro Vaz has earned his rest."

"I heard of it here. Light eternal!" Zé Bebelo took off his hat and crossed himself, pausing solemnly for a moment, as though setting an example, which touched us. Then he said:

"I have come to avenge the death of my friend Joca Ramiro, who once saved my life. And to liquidate those two bandits, who dishonor the name of our fatherland, and of this backland! Sons of mares," and so great was his wrath that everything he said acquired truth.

"Well, then, we are brothers. And these men?"

The five didn't say a word. But Zé Bebelo, including them all in a wave of his hand, loudly declared:

"I have come for order and for disorder. These here are my armies!"

It was a pleasure to hear these words. If there was fighting ahead, that man's leadership alone would add strength to our arms.

It was Marcelino Pampa's turn to speak:

"In that case, friend, why don't we join forces? We are together, let us go together."

"Friendship and association, I accept, old brother. But as for joining forces, that no. I can act only when I am in full charge; I was born that way. I only know how to be leader."

Taken aback, Marcelino Pampa reckoned quickly. He knit his brow, paused for a moment. His eyes moved in turn to each of us, his comrades, his braves. No one spoke a word. But he understood what each wanted. Quickly he gave the decision:

"And leader you shall be. We rest our arms, we await your orders."

He spoke courageously, and looked at us once more.

"I agree," I said, Diadorim said it, João Concliz said it; they all said: "I agree."

Zé Bebelo did not evince the least surprise: it seemed almost as if he had expected that vote. "Full powers? Everyone's loyalty?" he asked, severely. We reaffirmed our agreement. With this, he stood almost on tip-toe, and called to us: "Gather around me, my children. I now take charge!"

It might have been laughable. But no one was laughing. We stood about him, the five men from the Urucúia intermingled with us. Then: "So here we are. We face hard problems, men. But the assassins of Joca Ramiro are going to pay, with six hundred, seven hundred percent interest!," he asserted, taking us in one by one in his glance.

"Assassins! They are the Judases. From now on, that is their name," explained João Concliz.

"Hells bells! Two Judases, we can shout hallelujahs! Hallelujah! Hallelujah! Meat on the board, meal in the gourd!" Zé Bebelo concurred, practically cheering. We responded. That's the way Zé Bebelo was. As when it thundered, one of those loud and prolonged thunderings of the uplands, just before the drops of warm rain; the booming thunder rolls deep, and you feel the ground shake under your feet. It happened like that, a thunderclap to strike you dumb—and Zé Bebelo made a gesture with the back of his hands and said respectfully:

"That's my affair." And he went on: "All told, including that of my men, I didn't have ammunition for half an hour."

We formed an even higher opinion of his courage. Anyone of us knew that might be a lie. Nevertheless, under all that chatter, a man needed to be very brave indeed.

Smoothly, he took over, on that day and hour, and never let go again. He went first to see the site of the grave; and he determined that the arms and other belongings which Medeiro Vaz had left, since the dead man had no relatives, should go to the companions who had been closest to him, as keepsakes: the carbines and revolvers, the automatic, the dagger, the machete, the cloak, the covered canteen, the knapsack and saddlebags, the bandoliers. Someone said that the big dappled bay ought to be his. He refused. He called Marcelino Pampa over and solemnly made the gift of it to him.

"This animal is yours, Marcelino, and rightly so, because I have yet to see another man with such sense and character." He took his hand, in a firm clasp. Marcelino Pampa bowed his head, deeply moved. After that, he would have laid down and died for Zé Bebelo. For himself, Zé Bebelo took only the sheepskin saddle pad, and a scapular made of three pieces of flannel.

Then he went on looking over, inspecting, checking, one thing after another. He learned the men's names, one by one, where each had been born, what he had done, how many combats, his likes and dislikes, his skills. He inspected and counted the cartridge clips and the guns. He looked over the horses, praising the best shod and the tough and wiry ones. "Horseshoes, horseshoes! That's what counts," he kept saying. He divided the men up into four platoons: three of fifteen men, and one of twenty, in each at least one good tracker. "We need four hunter's horns, for warning," he insisted. He himself carried a whistle hung around his neck which could be heard a long way off. As platoon leaders he selected Marcelino Pampa, João Concliz, and Fafafa. He personally took charge of the largest unit, that of twenty, which included the five from Urucúia, and me, Diadorim, Sesfrêdo, Quipes, Joaquim Beijú, Coscorão, Dimas Dôido, Acauã, Mão-de-Lixa, Marruaz, Crédo, Marimbondo, Rasga-em-Baixo, Jiribibe, and Jõe Bexiguento, nicknamed Alparcatas.

After all had been assigned, there were still nine men left over. These made up a separate squad, to look after the pack animals, as well as the gear and supplies. Alaripe, a regular Jack-of-all-trades, was placed in charge. Each of the others was given his fixed duties: Quim Queiroz to be responsible for the boxes of ammunition; Jacaré to be the cook, and keep us posted on what was needed or lacking in the way of food; Doristino, blacksmith and horse doctor; the others, general helpers. And Raymundo Lé, who understood about cures and physics, was charged with keeping on hand a bag of remedies. To be sure, at that moment, there were none. But Zé Bebelo wasn't one to be upset: "Out there somewhere, later on, we'll buy some, we'll find some, my boy. But in the meantime, start collecting leaves and roots, start getting, start filling. What I want to see is the bag handy." Our camp was like a town.

On important matters, Zé Bebelo gave lessons and issued orders. "Work hard to sleep well," he would say. With relish: "After I'm dead, you can rest." Then laughing: "But I'm not going to die." A very clever fellow, you understand, sir: he could untie any knot. And—strange to say—we liked that. He raised our hopes high. In a way, the best thing to do in time of war is to carry on with peacetime duties. The rest of the time we drilled, on horseback, up and down; or lined up in formation while Zé Bebelo reviewed the patrols, blowing his whistle, ordering them this way and that. Only: "Damnit, we have no time to lose, boys! Keep trying to do better." And always, at the end, by way of encouragement, he would raise his arm high: "I still intend to parade on horseback with you fellows through big cities. What I lack here is a flag, a drum, bugles, and other brasses. But I shall have them! Ah, when we get to Carinhanha and Montes Claros, the wine will flow. We will pitch camp in the market place of Diamantina. We are going to Paracatú-do-Príncipe!"

Turning serious, he would call me to his side, and start sending for others: Marcelino Pampa, João Concliz, Diadorim, the Urucuian Pantaleão, and Fafafa, his deputies. We all had to tell what we knew about that region of the Gerais: the distances in leagues and half-leagues, the fords, the depth of the river marshlands and water holes, the hard-to-reach, densely-wooded places in which to hide, the best grazing lands. This was Zé Bebelo's way of seeing ahead, by questioning and listening. Sometimes with the end of a stick he would scratch a rough outline of everything on the ground. He was organizing all that in his head. He was learning. Soon he knew more than all of us put together. I knew Zé Bebelo well, from other stamping grounds! I would have given a lot to be born like him.

Then, he would go out hunting. It's true he liked to hunt, but what he was really doing was examining the hill, checking all its features. The woods and the open country, how the two formed a unit. He came and went, he would imagine situations, he would ask our opinion: "With ten men on that height, and ten others scattered on the slope, we could hold back two hundred riders going through the arroyo. Then, with a few more striking at their rear." Such matters, that's all he thought about, most of the time. Every so often he would send someone out to check on what the Judases were doing, and bring back live news. I'll tell you, sir, I've never in my life seen a happier man than Zé Bebelo was in those days.

Diadorim, too, was keeping me in the dark. He was enjoying a good revenge by not speaking. I'll tell you, sir: to seek revenge is to lick up cold what another cooked too hot. What is the right path for a person? Neither forward nor back! Only up. Or to stand still. As animals do. Well, who knows what? Living . . . You already know that, sir: living is, etcetera. Diadorim was happy, but I was not. I sought the darkness. And in the morning, the bemtevi birds crying "I saw you, I saw you" the whole time. I loved Diadorim, in a way that is frowned upon; I no longer thought about loving him, I just knew that I would love him always.

Suddenly, one day, Zé Bebelo ordered everybody and everything readied for maneuvers, as usual. Just for the exercise. Addressing the herd of donkeys grazing in good grass: "Put on your packsaddles, little fellows, and bring along our ammunition." But then, after he had mounted, he announced: "My name from now on is going to be Zé Bebelo Vaz Ramiro! I have nothing but confidence in you, comrades, my friends: Zé-

Bebelos! The time has come: we are off to war. Let's go, let's go wipe out that bunch of cowards!" We set out, full of cunning.

The moon was not right for our purposes. Who ever heard of starting a troop of horsemen out on slippery, muddy roads, soft and sodden underfoot, the rain still washing them down? It were better to wait until the rains stopped. "The Paracatú River is high," someone said. But Zé Bebelo cut him short: "The São Francisco is higher still." With him, everything was like that, surmountable; and he wanted no idle chatter. We moved out. The rain was coming down steadily. Until the last moment it appeared that we were going to cross the Paracatú. But we didn't. That man had figured out everything. At that point, he sent the patrols forward. Those of us in his platoon moved along the edge, always keeping the Paracatú on our left. It thundered to beat hell. He said: "That's good, I'll surprise them. There's nothing that pays off like a good surprise. What I want is to attack!" We were headed for Buriti-Pintado, about ten, twelve, leagues distant. "When the hour strikes, each one must draw a bead on only one Judas at a time, take careful aim, and fire. The rest is up to God," he was already saying. "Whenever you want to do a job, you can always find the tools. We could do it if we had nothing but these horses, moving quickly from place to place, forward and backward. That I know, but our main encounters are going to be on foot."

On the bank of the Soninho, we rested. The pack animals, the string of mules, were driven into hiding in a wooded ravine. Only three men were left in charge of them. "I am the one who will choose the time and place to attack," said Zé Bebelo. And, at a still water, we crossed the Soninho River in the dark, taking care not to get our guns wet, carrying the bullets in our mouths.

In the morning, we opened fire on them from three directions.

Zé Bebelo had thought it all out like an act, a design. First, João Concliz advanced with his fifteen men pretending to be off-guard. When the others came at them, the rest of us were already well hidden, at strong points. Then, from another direc-

tion Fafafa moved across with his horsemen: they were closely
bunched, because in this way a band of horses or horsemen
gives the appearance of being much more numerous than it
really is. All the horses were sorrels or bays—a light color also
adds greatly to the impression of size. Ah, and they yelled. The
Judases were shooting badly, erratically, and very little at
that. Then, from our high roosts, where we had stationed ourselves, we let loose our punishment on them. Hermógenes's
men. We let them have it, suddenly, without a word. Just steel
bullets. One Judas ran in the wrong direction, toward where
Jiribibe was: poor fellow. "Ow!" was his act of perfect contri-
tion. Another raised his body a little too high. "You! You
think you have a God-and-a-half?" Zé Bebelo said after dropping
him with a low shot, as you would a running partridge. Another was fleeing cunningly. "He's smart in the feet." Those
that I dispatched, I stopped counting, out of pity. Poor devils.
Victory is like that. Or do you think, sir, that it is a kind of evil
joy, like a hunt?

Rest? If anyone spoke of it, he wasn't listened to. "Do you
think I'm going to let that gang quietly lick their wounds? At
them again, men! Let's go after them!" Zé Bebelo was showing off. João Concliz's men had seized the enemy's horses.
"Let's head north: the face of the earth there is more to my
liking." No, the route lay in the opposite direction. We had
to fall on the main body of the Judases. Through rock gullies
and trails, with those trained horses, we rode, we rode. One
road held four abreast. In the Oi-Mãe. There is an outcrop-
ping of rock there, a wide one, where big rocks rise out of the
ground to the surface. We arrived in good shape, without rushing. Zé Bebelo started advising, counselling, as if he were
guarding a sickroom. He even sniffed the air. Cunningly, like a
cat. You could see that he planned and fought everything out in
his head first. Here's an example: there was a big hollow, where
the enemy lay in ambush, dug in on both sides. How did Zé
Bebelo already know this? Making a wide detour, João Concliz
took his men far beyond, to the edge of the field, matching one
trap with another. This gave time for our platoon to crawl up
the heights until we were overlooking the edges of the hollow.

Ah, and then Fafafa came along, carelessly letting himself be seen, with his riders—they approached innocently, like deer, easy to kill. But—ha—then from on top of the hollow we cut loose, yelling and shooting, in a crossfire with those below. "Here's something to keep you busy!" Heh, heh! It was like bees swarming out of a hollow tree: those that were holed up lost their nerve, panicked and started running under a hail of bullets and curses. João Concliz, as you know, sir, was waiting for them. After that the buzzards could circle down—real buzzards.

Then we turned back, recrossing the Soninho River, to where we had left our mules, with our munitions and other gear. We had retreated while pretending not to. It was a pity, to be sure, but we had to keep them fooled in ways like this, for our resources did not permit us to finish off those Judases once and for all. Always, always, to throw dust in their eyes, Zé Bebelo would keep us moving nearly all together for an hour, and then spread out for another hour. One result of these tactics was that we won a hell of a gunfight at the São Serafim Ranch.

In that same direction, but much further down, there is a place. There is a crossroad. The road leads to Veredas Tortas—Dead Streams. I said it, but forget you heard me. Never mention that name. Please. A place like no other. Places like that are harmless-looking—they give no warning. Now, when I went there, was it that my mother had not prayed for me at that moment?

If you will listen, sir, to what follows, you will understand me. There is a place called Paredão. You go there, sir, you will see it. It is a village. Nobody lives there any more. The houses are empty. It even has a two-story house. There is grass growing on the church roof, and any time you go in there, you hear the whir of bats' wings. Cattle come from the fields and rub themselves against those walls. They lie down. They stand in the shade. At nightfall, the vampire bats begin to cover them with little black veils. Funeral black laces. When you fire a shot, the dogs bark loud and long. They do that everywhere. But those dogs today are wild, they have to hunt their food. Dogs that have licked much blood. The place is so silent that the soft rustle of midnight passes over it at nine o'clock. I heard a noise. A large wax candle was burning. Nobody had remained there. I saw only a tame talking parrot, which was tearing away at some thing with its beak. Did it come back now and then, to sleep there? And I did not see Diadorim again. That village has only one street: it is the street of war. The devil in the street, in the middle of the whirlwind. Don't ask me anything, sir. It is not good to ask about such things.

I know that I am telling this badly, just hitting the high spots. I ramble. But it is not to cover up; don't think that. About serious matters, the normal ones, I have told you almost everything. I have no hesitation. You are a man who judges others as you would yourself; you are not one to censure. And my past deeds have been invalidated, proscribed. My respectability is solid. Now I am like a tapir in a pool; nobody can catch me. Little of my life is left to me. I am talking foolishness.

At the market in São João Branco, a man was going around saying: "This country is no good for old people." I disagree. The country belongs mostly to the old. The man was crazy, his fingers full of cheap old rings, from which the stones had been removed; he said all those rings gave an electric shock. No, I'm telling things in this way, because that is my way of telling them. Wars and battles? It's like a game of cards; first one wins, then the other. Afterwards the rebels came through here, Prestes's men, coming from Goiás; they commandeered all the saddle animals. I know that they opened fire near the mouth of the Urucúia, in São Romão, where a Government boat, filled with troops from Bahia, had tied up. Many years from now, a woodsman will go to cut up a log and find bullets embedded in it. What counts are other things. One keeps the memories of his life in different compartments, each with its own symbols and sentiments, and I don't think they mix with one another. You can only relate things straight through, one basted to the other, when they are matters of minor import. In each vital experience that I truly lived, whether of great joy or sorrow, I see today that in every instance I was like another person. Uncontrolled happenings. As I think of them that is how I relate them.

You are very kind to listen to me. There are hours long past
that remain much closer to us than other more recent ones.
You know yourself how it is.

Take this, for example: that girl, the harlot, with the pretty
name of Nhorinhá, the daughter of Ana Duzuza; one day I
received a letter from her, a simple letter, asking for news about
me and sending her regards, written, I think, by another's hand.
That Nhorinhá had a short scarf on her head, like the crest of a
white-headed cockatoo. But it took about eight years for it to
reach me, and when I received it, I was already married. A
letter that wandered from one far end to the other of these
backlands, these plains, through the kindness of so many
hands, in so many pockets and knapsacks. On the outside was
written only: "Riobaldo, who is with Medeiro Vaz." And it came,
carried back and forth by herders and travelers. It could
hardly be read any longer, so soiled and folded, and falling to
pieces. It had even been rolled inside another piece of paper
like a tube, and tied with a piece of black spool thread. Some no
longer remembered from whom they had received it. The last
person, the one who delivered it to me, almost by chance, was
a man who, fearing his herd might pick up the toque disease,
was taking his cattle back from the plains to the scrub lands,
just as soon as the rains started. I was already married. I love
my wife, always did, and today more than ever. When I knew
that Nhorinhá with my eyes and hands, I loved her only for that
trivial moment. When she wrote the letter she was feeling fondness for me, no doubt; and by then she was living far away,
alas, in São Josèzinho da Serra, which is on the way to
Riacho-das-Almas. When I received the letter, it stirred in me a
feeling of love for her, a great flaming love, that covered the
entire period since the brief visit I had with her in Aroeirinha,
and knew her carnally. Nhorinhá, an abiding good taste in my
eyes and my mouth. Eight years had slipped by. They did not
exist. Do you grasp the inner meaning of that? The truth is
that, in my memory, she had grown in beauty. Undoubtedly,
she no longer cared for me; who knows, she might even be
dead. I know that what I am saying is hard to understand,
very involved. But you are ahead of me. I envy the learning that

you have, sir. I would like to decipher the things that matter. And what I am relating is not the life of a backwoodsman, a jagunço though he was, but the relevant matters. I would like to understand about fear and about courage, and about the passions that drive us into doing so many things, that give shape to events. What leads us into strange, evil behavior is that we are so close to that which is ours, by right, and do not know it, do not, do not!

Be that as it may. Crazily I am saying crazy things. But you, sir, are an unexpected visitor, a man of good sense, faithful as a document: listen to me, think and think again, and repeat it, then you will be helping me. This is the way I will tell it. First, I will tell about the things in my past that were the closest to me. I am going to talk to you. Talk to you about the sertão. About what I do not know. The vast sertão! I do not know it. Nobody knows it yet. Only a very few persons, and they only know about these few rivers and little streams. What I thank you for very much is the courtesy of your attention.

It was something that happened one day that started it. The first thing. Afterwards you will see why, and agree with me.

It happened so long ago, you can figure out how long: I must have been about fourteen years old, if that. We had come a distance of five leagues—my mother and I. To the landing on our Janeiro river, as I have told you. Today it belongs to Seo Joãozinho, the storekeeper. Just "Pôrto" they call it, because it has no other name. That is how it is known in the sertão; it is on the edge of a high river bank, with a store, a house, a barnyard, and a storehouse. Grain. It even had a rosebush. Imagine! Go there afterwards, you will see. Well, on that occasion, it was almost the same.

The Janeiro, half a league farther down, empties into the São Francisco, toward which it flows straight, forming a right angle. Anyone who needs to, can cross the Janeiro in a canoe— it is narrow, not more than a couple of hundred feet wide. Anyone wishing to make an easy crossing of the São Francisco, will begin his trip there, too. The landing has to be up on that high bank, where there is no swamp fever. The path down the bank is almost sheer, and nothing can be done about it, because

84   *THE DEVIL TO PAY*

when the river rises it washes everything away. The São
Francisco, when it is high and full, holds back the Janeiro,
sometimes as early as the first rains in November. In December, without fail. There are always boats waiting there, tied by
their chains to the bared root of a copaiba tree. I remember also
there used to be two or three figs growing there. It makes you
feel sorry to see people going down that muddy bank, often
carrying heavy sacks. Life here is very hard, don't you agree?
Imagine, then, what it must have been like in my time.

Well, what happened was that I had just got over a sick spell
and my mother had made a vow for me to fulfill when I got
well. I had to beg alms until I had made up a certain sum—
half to be paid for a mass, to be said in some church, the other
half to be put in a gourd, well sealed and tarred, and thrown in
the São Francisco, to be carried way down into Bahia until it
came to rest at the shrine of Our Lord the Good Jesus of Lapa,
who is all-powerful along the river bank. Now, the place to beg
alms was at the landing. My mother gave me a small pouch. I
went there every day. I would wait around, at that stopping
point, but hardly anybody ever came. But I liked it there, it was
something new and peaceful to watch. I was afraid to go
down the river bank. But I used to look at the gourds used as
fishing floats, hanging on the cabin wall.

The third or fourth day I went there, more people showed
up. Two or three men, outsiders, buying rice. Each sack tied
with a shoot of new palm leaf, green and yellow, split down the
middle. They struggled with those heavy sacks, and crossed in
boats to the other side of the Janeiro. There was high forest
there, as there still is today. But, through the trees, you could
see an oxcart waiting, the oxen chewing their cud with little
slavering, which showed that they had come a long distance. As
you see, sir: so much work just to cross a few meters of gentle
water, all for want of a bridge. Added to which, they had taken
many days to come by oxcart the distance you cover in hours in
your jeep. Even today it is still the same crawling along.

Then, all of a sudden, I saw a boy, leaning against a tree,
puffing on a cigarette. A boy approaching manhood, a little
younger than I, or perhaps about my own age. There he was,

wearing a leather hat, with the chin strap hanging, and smiling at me. He did not move. Rather, it was I who went over to him. Then he started telling me, quite naturally, that that buyer was his uncle, and that they lived at a place called Os-Porcos, a long way off, but that he had not been born there. He went on talking, a handsome boy, fair, with a high forehead and large, green eyes. Much later I learned that that place of Os-Porcos really exists, not very far from here, in the gerais of Lassance.

"Is it nice there?" I asked.

"I'll say," he answered me, and went on to explain: "My uncle grows everything. But he didn't plant rice this year, because he became a widower through the death of my aunt." It was as if he was ashamed that they were there buying that rice, you see, sir.

I looked at that boy with a delight in his company such as I had never felt for anyone before. He seemed to me so different; I liked his delicate features, even his voice, very soft, very agreeable. Because he spoke without putting on airs, without malice, without over-emphasis, his conversation was sort of old-fashioned, like a grown person's. There kept growing in me the wish that he would never go away but stay on for a long time, just the way he was, without idle chattering, without kidding—my unknown friend and pal. When he wasn't looking I rolled up my pouch, for by then I was ashamed to be begging alms, even if it was to fulfill a vow. He was admiring the work of the men, and called my attention to them, in a knowledgeable way. I felt, in my boyish way, that he already liked me too.

Having money of his own, he bought a quarter of a cheese, and a brick of rapadura. Said he was going for a boat ride. He didn't ask his uncle's permission. He asked me if I was coming along. He did everything with such an air of simplicity, so unhurriedly, that a person could only say yes. He gave me his hand to help me down the embankment.

There were several canoes, all long ones, like the ones you still see today, each made from the hollowed trunk of a tree. One was in use, piled high with sacks of rice being ferried across, and we picked out the best of the others, one that had almost no water and no mud in the bottom. I sat myself in it, like a chick in an eggshell. He sat in front of me; we were facing each other. I noticed that the canoe was badly balanced, and rocked with the movement of the river. The boy had given me his hand in climbing down the river bank. It was a graceful hand, soft and warm, and now I was ashamed, perturbed. The rocking of the canoe made me increasingly uneasy. I watched those fine eyes, green-hued, with thick lashes, shining with a sensation of calm that suffused me. I did not know how to swim. The boatman, just a boy too, kept on paddling. It was not pleasant, all that rocking. But I made up my mind to show my mettle. The only enjoyable part was being near the boy. I did not even think about my mother. I was just drifting along.

In case you don't know it, the Janeiro is a stream of clear waters. And it is a river full of turtles. If you looked to one side you would see one of those creatures on top of a rock, basking in the sun, or swimming along the surface in plain view. It was the boy who pointed them out to me. And he called my attention to the forest at the water's edge, straight, like a wall laid out with a ruler. "Look at the flowers," he said admiringly. High up there were many flowers, suddenly red, of the hyacinth bean and other vines, and the purple ones of the velvet bean, for it was the month of May, the time for those who could not plant rice to buy it. A bird sang. A tinamou? And parakeets, whole flocks of them, went flying over us. I have forgotten nothing, as you see, sir. That boy, how could I ever forget him? A red parrot. "Was that a macaw?" he asked me. "What-what-what," the toucanet inquired.

The boy was so different, as I have already said, not like anyone else. A gentleness of being but clean and strong—like a good smell of which you are only vaguely aware, if you know what I mean, sir. Even his clothes had no spots or wrinkles. To tell the truth, he did not talk much. One could see that he was enjoying the good air, silent and knowing, and everything about him bespoke self-confidence. I wanted him to like me.

Well, in a short while we reached the Chico. It looms up suddenly, that terrible expanse of water; an immensity. The biggest fright you can have is to be paddling along in a little stream,

and without warning be plunged into the main body of a large
river. The change alone is bad enough. The greed with which
the São Francisco, churning red mud, sucks and receives into
itself the Janeiro, almost nothing but a little green rivulet . . .
"Are we going to turn back here?" I asked, uneasily. The boy
did not look at me, because he had already been watching me.
"What for?" he asked simply, cool as a cucumber. It was the
boatman, who was standing up poling, who laughed—at me,
no doubt. But then the boy himself smiled, with neither malice
nor condescension. He did not bat an eye. The boatman, without steering a definite course, was poling along the bar at the
junction of the two streams, where the water is not so deep,
trying to come in easily, with the canoe drifting. Then he
slipped into the Chico headed upstream. I began to gaze at the
forest alongside. Banks without beach, sad-like, everything
looking half-rotted, with the mud-covered debris of the last
flood, when the Chico rises its six or eleven meters. The boatman ran the canoe close to some rushes, and leaned over trying
to break off a branch of passionflower. With the awkward
movement, the canoe tilted dangerously; the boy, too was
standing up. I gave a cry. "It's all right," he said, speaking gently.
"Well, then, you fellows sit down," I complained. He sat down.
But then, soberly, with that lovely charm, he gave the boatman a
brief order, curtly but without offense. "Go across." The boatman
obeyed.

I was afraid. You know? That was what it was: I was afraid. I
could make out the bank of the river on the other side. Far, far
off, how long would it take to get there? Fear and shame.
The brutal, treacherous water—the river is full of menace, de-
ceitful ways, and whispers of desolation. My fingers clutched
the sides of the canoe. I did not think about the Caboclo-
d'Água,* I did not think about the danger of the "water jaguar"
—the otter—which they say rise out of the water in bands and
attack people, first surrounding and then overturning the
canoe, deliberately. I didn't think about anything. I was overcome with fear. And all in that bright light of day. The rushing

* Caboclo-d'Água: In Brazilian folklore, a fearsome, manlike creature
whose domain is the waters of the São Francisco river.

of the river, and only that canoe, and the vast hazard of water
from one side to the other. In the middle of the river I closed
my eyes. Until then I had clung to one hope. I had heard it said
that when a canoe overturns, it remains afloat, and a person
needs only to hold on to it, even by one finger, to keep from
going under, and drift along with it until he comes out on dry
land. I said as much. But the boatman contradicted me:

"This is the kind that sinks to the bottom. It is made of
quebracho. Canoes of quebracho and copaiba don't float." A
dizziness came over me. The anger I felt: so many canoes at the
port, good buoyant canoes, of earpod or ape's-earring, or im-
burana, or mimosa, or cedar, and we had to pick that one! It
was a crime even, to make that kind, out of such stupid wood!
Although it had been a lie, I must have opened wide my fear-
crazed eyes. Sitting quiet and calm in front of me, the boy
watched me. "You must be brave," he said. Could he see that I
was on the verge of tears? It hurt me to answer: "I can't swim."
The boy smiled pleasantly. "Neither can I."

Calm, calm. I saw his eyes; they shed a kind of light. "What
does it feel like to be afraid?" he inquired, but he was not
making fun of me; I could not be angry with him. "Have you
never been afraid?" was all it occurred to me to say. He
answered: "Can't say that I have," and, after I had let out a sigh,
"My father told me that one should not be." That left me
astounded. And he added: "My father is the bravest man in
the world."

At this point, the heaving of the waters, the tremendous forward rush of that river, was the greatest I have seen in my life.
You could hear and count the boatman's strokes, wondering if
they would be sufficient. "What about you: have you no fear?"
the boy asked the boatman, meaningfully.

"I'm a river rat!" the little boatman rejoined, with manifest
pride.

This pleased the boy, and he nodded his head in approval. I
did too. The leather hat he was wearing was almost new. His
eyes, as I learned then and as I know even better today, could
take on a harsh darkness. Young as I was at the time, I noticed
that from seeing me thus atremble, the boy derived greater

strength for his own courage. But I met the scorn of his glance.
Then those eyes softened again and recovered their brightness.
He put his hand on mine. His touch did something to me, deep
inside. It was a white hand, with delicate fingers. "You too are
brave," he said. Dawn broke for me. But the shame that I now
felt was of another kind. The boatman started singing, badly,
one of the couplets the river folk sing:

> *My river of São Francisco,*
> *All muddy as you are:*
> *I've come to give you a swallow of water,*
> *And your blessing to implore."*

Then, the promised land. We reached the other shore, the far
side.

The boy ordered the boatman to tie up; we got out alone.
"Don't go away; you stay here and take care of things," he said
to the boatman, who proceeded to carry out instructions, and
tied the chain to a cashew tree. Where did the boy want to go
to? I wondered, but followed along. We went into the meadow,
into the reddish bluestem grass. Finally, we sat down on a little
rocky mound, surrounded by a rough bamboo thicket. And
there we sat, without thought of time, almost without speaking,
alone. The gnats pestered the life out of us. "Friend, would you
like a bite of something to eat? Are you hungry?" he asked. He
gave me the rapadura and the cheese. He himself took only a
few crumbs. He was smoking. When he had finished, he
pulled stems of capybara grass and chewed them; they taste
like green corn; it is the grass the capybara eats. Then, when I
wanted to take a leak and said so, he told me: "Sure, go behind
there, far from me, and do it." We had no further talk, but I
noticed and was ashamed of how shabby my clothes looked
beside his.

Suddenly, without warning, a man's face appeared behind
us! His two hands were pushing aside branches of the under-
growth; it gave me a start. Some trail must have run close by,
and the man had heard us talking. He was a young mulatto,
around eighteen or twenty years old; but tall, strong, coarse

featured. With a nasty leer, he asked: "You two there—what are you up to, huh?" Then tapping one hand against the other closed into a fist, he made an obscene gesture. I looked at the boy. He did not seem in the least startled, but sat there as if he had not heard, with his usual pleasant smile. "How about it? What about me? I want some, too," the mulatto insisted. Whereupon in a loud voice, I answered that we weren't doing anything to be ashamed of, that we were just watching the river and the scenery. But—what I least expected—the boy spoke up in his nice voice: "You, black boy? Sure, come on over here." His words, his expression, were like a woman's. The mulatto, highly pleased, walked over to sit close to him.

Ah, there are some things that happen so fast the eye cannot follow them. The viper strikes or has it already struck? It was like that. The mulatto jumped back with a scream, a howl of pain. He went dashing through the woods, in wild flight. The boy dangled a little knife from his hand, and did not even laugh. He had buried the blade in the mulatto's thigh, the point going in deep. The blade was smeared with ugly blood. The boy didn't budge from the spot. He wiped the blade on the grass, completely at ease. "It's got a good edge" was all he said, as though talking to himself. He put the knife back in its sheath.

My misgivings did not leave me. Suppose the mulatto came back with a brush hook, a gun, with friends he had rounded up, what would become of us? I pointed this out to the boy, pleading that we should leave at once. "You must be brave. You must be very brave," he soothed me, so affably that I remembered what he had said earlier about his father. I inquired: "So, then, you live with your uncle?" Whereupon he got up, saying it was time for us to start back. But he walked slowly, leisurely, in the direction of the canoe. And he didn't look back. He didn't know what it was to be afraid, of the mulatto or anyone.

The little boatman was asleep, stretched out in the canoe, with the gnats swarming about him, and his shirt soaking wet with sweat from the sun. He was happy to get the rest of the rapadura and cheese, and brought us back across the river, singing all the while. I'm not going to describe the return to you—it was all the same, the same. Except once, when I thought we were going too fast. "Are you brave, always?" I asked. The boy was trailing his hands in the reddish water, and did not answer at once. Finally, without looking at me, he said: "I am different from everyone else. My father told me that I had to be different, very different." And then I was no longer afraid. This is the important point—now listen, sir—listen beyond what I am telling you, and listen with an open mind. This is the point of the whole story, the reason I have told it to you: I did not feel anything. Only a transformation, a real one. Many important things have no name.

My mother was there at the landing, waiting for me. I had to leave with her, and did not have a chance to say a proper goodbye to the Boy. From a distance, I looked back, he waved his hand, and I did the same. I did not even know his name. But I didn't need to. I have never forgotten him, after all these years.

Now that you have heard this, I have some questions to ask. Why did I have to meet that Boy? Silly, I know. I grant you. You don't need to answer me. But what kind of unalloyed courage was that of his? Did it come from God, from the devil? This is what I keep asking, trying to find out, but not even my compadre Quelemém can help me. And what did the Boy's father mean? At the time, being so young, I did not ask myself that question. Take this for example: a boy in Nazaré killed a man who insulted him. Killed him and ran home. Do you know what his father said to comfort him? "My son, this is your coming of age. Now I have someone to defend me, to avenge me, in my old age." The sertão has its own criminal code. The sertão is where a man must have a stiff neck and a hard fist. Anyway, there are questions to which any answer is nonsense. Why was it I met that Boy? You did not meet him, my compadre Quelemém did not meet him, millions upon millions of people never met him. Think about it again, think it over carefully: Why did I have to cross the river, sitting facing that Boy? The São Francisco is always there, flowing strong. The high tablelands stretch to the far end of Goiás. The gerais have no notion of time. I think I had to learn to be happy and sad at the same time; in thinking about the Boy afterwards, that's what I thought. But why? What for? There I was at the river landing, with my little pouch in my hand, begging alms for Our Lord, the Good Jesus, to fulfill the vow made by my mother if I recovered from a grave illness. Doesn't it go to show that our lives aren't just neatly laid out? I keep thinking: Zé Bebelo understood somewhat of this, but he knew it without knowing, and he did not want to know; the same as Medeiro Vaz, and Joca Ramiro; my compadre Quelemém, too, who travels a different road. But sooner or later, today or tomorrow, I bet you will give me an answer. By your way of remaining completely silent, I see that you will make it known to me.

What happened after that? I'll tell you. What followed is simple. My mother died—plain Bigrí she was, that's what everybody called her. She died one rainy December, and my sorrow was great. But it was a sorrow that all understood, a sorrow that I was entitled to. Ever since, and even today, at times the memory of my mother moves me. She died, and with that my life entered upon a second phase. I began to grow up. As my inheritance I received a few poor trifles which could give rise to no disputes: I let others have the water jug, the wash basin, the mats, the kettle, the chocolate pot, a lipped saucepan, and a clay bowl; all I kept was my hammock, a wooden image of a saint, a flower-painted mug with a handle, a large fancy buckle, a wool blanket, and my change of clothes. They made a bundle of all this for me, and it filled half a sack. Then a kindly neighbor felt it his duty to take me—on a journey that lasted six days on account of the rains—to the São Gregório ranch of my godfather, Selorico Mendes, alongside the cattle trail, between Curralinho and Bagre, where the sierras fall away. As soon as I arrived, my godfather Selorico Mendes took me in with great kindness. He was rich and close-fisted; he owned three cattle ranches. This one here belonged to him at one time; it was the largest of all.

"For not having known you all these years, I express my regrets," were his first warm words of greeting, after looking me over. I spent days wondering if he was right in his mind. He never mentioned my mother. On matters of business or routine, having to do with cattle, he rarely spoke either. But he liked to converse, to tell stories about the wild doings of the jagunços— he loved those.

"Ah, real life is very different from that of a citizen in the sertão. Politics! Everything is politics, and powerful leaders. This part of the country has now become sluggish with peace, and I am a private citizen. But farther on up there, there are still big ranchers whose word is law—all of them rulers of bold mobs, gangs of henchmen with sawed-off shotguns and carbines. Domingos Touro, in Alambiques, Major Urbano in Macaçá, the Silva Salles in Crondeúba; in Vau-vau, Dona Próspera Blaziana. Dona Adelaide in Campo-Redondo, Simão Avelino in Barra-da-Vaca, Mozar Vieira in São João do Canastrão, Colonel Camucim in Arcanjos, in the district of Rio Pardo; and many, many others. On every ranch there is always a sentinel patrolling the boundary, with his shooting-stick under his arm, as wary as a jaguar feeding on a carcass. Yes, indeed. The same thing is true along the banks of the river, and if you go down the São Francisco, every place is held by a big landowner, with his whole family, his thousand obedient jagunços. Just look at São Francisco da Arrelia, Januária, Carinhanha, Urubú, Pilão Arcado, Chique-Chique, and Sento-Sé."

He talked a lot about having known Neco and remembered the time he subdued Januária and Carinhanha, back in '79: took all the ports—Jatobá, Malhada and Manga—and did what he liked; he set up his armed camp in the village of Jacaré, which was his territory.

"I was there, with a letter signed by Captain Severiano Francisco de Magalhães, who was in cahoots with Neco. The number of men there on a war footing made the place a regular babel. They even had boats, filled with men armed with muskets, going up and down the river, and from side to side. Day and night, you could hear yells and shots. Detachments of jagunços galloping off to their assigned missions. When they entered a town they would start the fun by shooting off giant fire-crackers and other fireworks. They would order the church

bell rung. They would break open the jail and release the
prisoners, they would grab the money in the tax collector's
office, and they would dine in the Town Hall."

My godfather Selorico Mendes was very scary. He would tell
me that in his day he had been brave, boasted about how
tough he was. He wanted me to learn to shoot well, and to
handle a club and a knife. Right off, he gave me a dagger, and a
pistol and shotgun. Later he even gave me a machete that he
had ordered made for himself, almost the size of a sword and
with a blade shaped like a gravatá leaf.

"I sat at table with Neco, drank his wine, lunched with him.
Under his leadership there were some eight hundred wild
ones, who showed him nothing but obedience and respect." My
godfather, Neco's guest; it always made him feel big to tell
about it. On that occasion, everybody of any consequence had
fled from Januária. Deprived of all protection of the law, they
had gone to Pedras-de-Maria-da-Cruz to wait for better days.
"Neco? Ah! He ruled with greater authority than Renovato or
Lióbas, and he raised more hell than João Brandão and the
Filgueiras." And my godfather showed me a paper in Neco's
handwriting—it was a receipt for six kegs of powder and a
quantity of iodine; the signature read: Manoel Tavares de Sá.

But I did not know how to read. Then my godfather made a
decision: he sent me to Curralinho, to study and live in the
house of a friend of his, Nhô Marôto, whose real name was
Gervasio Lé de Ataíde. A good man. I didn't have to do any
work there, because my godfather had arranged with Nhô
Marôto to pay at the end of each year the cost of my board and
keep, even the shoes and clothing I needed. I ate a lot, and the
expenses weren't small, because I always liked everything good
and of the best. If now and then Nhô Marôto wanted me to do
something for him, he would beat about the bush, flattering me
and saying he would esteem it a favor. I never denied him the
services of my feet and hands, and the work didn't amount to
much anyway. Well, things went along, and one day he said to
me: "Baldo,* what you really need is to study and get a diploma,

* Baldo: short for Riobaldo.

because you are not cut out for manual work. You are not clever with your hands."

What he said impressed me, and I put the question right away to Master Lucas. He looked at me for awhile—he was a man of such fairness and of such manifest honesty that he spared no one. There were days when he used the ferule on all of the boys, and yet none of us bore him any ill will. Then Master Lucas replied: "That is so. But the surest thing of all is that you could be a first-rate teacher." And from the beginning of the second year, he had me help him with some of the routine teaching; I would explain the alphabet and multiplication tables to the younger children.

Curralinho was a very good place; I was happy there. I made friends with the boys of my own age. I spent those years there, without yearnings of any kind and without thoughts of the past. There I had my early infatuations—ah, those girls with the names of flowers. Except for Rosa'uarda—a grown girl, older than I, the daughter of a well-do-do trader, Seo Assis Wababa, owner of St. Joseph's Biggest Bargain Center. She was a foreigner, a Syrian; they were all Syrians. A big store, a big house; Seo Assis Wababa dealt in everything. Both out of politeness, and because he was very crafty, he sought to please me; he would say that my godfather Selorico Mendes was a big customer, and he invited me several times to lunch at his table. Which I enjoyed—meat ground with whole wheat, and other dishes, stuffed squash or the stuffing cooked in grape leaves, and that way of cooking okra sour—what swell vittles! The sweets, too! I liked Seo Assis Wataba and his wife Dona Abadia, and the boys too, Rosa'uarda's brothers, though they were considerably younger. The only thing that annoyed me was the guttural talk that went on among themselves in Arabic. Nevertheless I can tell you that Rosa'uarda liked me; she led me into my first sexual experiences, the whole lot of them, which we performed together in a hidden spot at the bottom of the back yard, and which gave me much pleasure. She would always say Syrian endearments to me, and she called me: "My eyes." But hers were the ones that fluttered with excitement;

they were extraordinarily black, of a singular beauty. All my life I have been very fond of foreigners.

Today I realize how much my godfather did for me, he who had developed such a love for his money, and was so close-fisted. He made several trips to Curralinho to visit me—to be sure, he took advantage of the trip to do some cattle trading and other business—and he would bring me boxes of coconut or custard-apple candy, curd cheese, and quince marmelade. Each November, he sent for me. He never scolded me, and gave me everything. But I never asked him for anything. If he had given me ten times as much, it wouldn't have done any good. I did not like him, nor did I dislike him, but the fact is that I never felt at home with him. Finally, for another reason, I ran away from São Gregório, as you shall hear. I never saw my godfather again. But he bore me no ill will on that account; I don't understand it. In fact, he was highly pleased when he got word that I was a jagunço. And he named me his heir in his will: of the three ranches, two were left to me. Only the São Gregório he left to a mulatto woman with whom he had taken up in his old age. I did not mind it. Even what I received, I deserved less than she did. Now, too late, I realize that when he got old he felt remorseful about me, and now that I am old, I am suffering repentance because of him. I think we two really belonged to each other.

Shortly after I came back from Curralinho for good, something happened that I won't keep from you. One morning at daybreak all the dogs on the ranch started barking; someone was knocking. It was the month of May, in the dark of the moon, and it was bitter cold. When I was that young I hated to get up, not because my health wasn't good but because of laziness which had not been corrected. As soon as I got out of bed and went to see who was at the door, my godfather Selorico Mendes, with a lamp in hand, was already ushering some men into the room, about six of them, all wearing broad hats and cloaks or capes, their spurs clinking. There was an ominous air about them, as of something in the wind, that frightened me. I was astonished: so many arms. But they weren't hunters. Then I sensed they were on a war footing.

My godfather told me to go to the back part of the house and get one of the women up to brew some hot coffee. When I returned, one of the men—Alarico Totõe—was talking and explaining. They all stood around without sitting down. Alarico Totõe was a planter from Grão-Mogol, known to my godfather. He and his brother, Aluiz Totõe, were fine, well-to-do persons. I soon took in that they had made a deal for the support of the jagunços about some political question. My godfather listened, nodding his head in approval. But the person his eyes kept turning to, in flustered admiration, was the leader of the jagunços, the chief. And do you know who this was? Joca Ramiro! Just hearing his name left me agape.

Joca Ramiro stood there with folded arms, his hat pushed far back. Even his shadow, which the little lamp threw on the wall, loomed up different, impressive, seemed to grow. And I saw that he was a handsome man, meticulous about everything. I saw that he was a man of breeding. On either side, two big jagunços stood shoulder-to-shoulder with him; I learned later that they were his lieutenants. One was called Ricardão: heavy-set and quiet, with a pleasant smile; he had the air of a wealthy rancher. The other—Hermógenes. He was standing with his back to me, but it was a misshapen back with a high hump which his hat rested on, a round leather hat that sat like a gourd on his head. It made the man look as if he had no neck. His pants were shapelessly wrinkled; they hung on him in folds like a bellows. He stood with his legs spread wide, but when he took a few steps, they dragged—or so it seemed to me— as though he did not want to lift his feet from the ground. I recall all this and I keep wondering: does life give people certain warnings? I always remember him, but not clearly, as if looking through a cloud of smoke. At that moment, I was hoping that he would not turn his face. But he did. The shadow of his hat covered him down to his mouth, darkening his face.

Alarico Totõe wound up by saying that what they needed was a concealed place where the band of riders could lie low that day, as they traveled by night, attacking by surprise and covering their tracks.

"I have a fine hideout," my godfather replied, and he ordered me to guide the men to the pool at Cambaùbal, which is in a dense woods.

But first they had coffee. Joca Ramiro ran his eyes quickly over everything, an open smile on his gallant face, and put his hands in his pockets. Ricardão laughed heartily. That Hermógenes came over to me, along with another man, a light-skinned, sharp-eyed fellow from up north. That one I liked; his name was, and still is today, Alaripe. So, the two of them mounted, and I on foot, we came to where the others were waiting, a short distance away, at the foot of the road.

It was the month of May, as I have said, with the morning star. The dew dripping by the basinful. And the crickets in a steady chirp. Suddenly, the space was filled with that huge mass, which I sensed before I could see what it was. An assemblage of horses. The horsemen. None had dismounted. There must have been close to a hundred. I drew a deep breath: it was like drinking the smell—the smell of manes and switching tails, of hides soaked in stale sweat stained with the dusts of the backlands. There is muted movement whispered by a troop like this, made up of a myriad of little noises, like those on the surface of a big river. Strictly speaking, you would have said all those men were completely quiet. But a saddle creaks of its own accord, or a spur or stirrup jingles, or the rings of a bit tinkle when a horse licks and chomps on it. Leather rubs against leather, the horses twitch their ears, or stamp their feet. Here, there, a snort, a light wheeze. And one or another of the riders would quietly nudge his mount forward, changing his position in that mass, reining in. I could not hear the men, I was aware only of their horses. But horses under control, mounted. There is a difference. A big one. And gradually men's forms began to emerge, like trees growing side by side. Their hats pulled low, the muzzles of the rifles on their backs pointing upward. Because they did not speak, but just sat there waiting, it made me afraid. Among them there must have been some of the worst bad men of the backlands, astride their well-kept horses, facing this way and that. Was this real or was I dreaming?

Alone, apart from the others, one rider stood out, undoubtedly a sentry. He started toward us; his horse was dark, a light-footed bay.

"Capixúm, it's me and Hermógenes," the northerner spoke up.

"All right, Alaripe," the other answered.

I huddled in the cold, mindful of the dripping dew, the woods full of pleasant smells, the crackling of the stars, the creaking of the crickets, and the massed horses. Day was about to break, the first flush of morning, when the sky grows light. As the air turned gray, the vague outline of those riders could be made out. You must forgive me, sir, for indulging in so many details, but to this day, I can see that hour in my mind's eye, everything so good; and what I feel is a yearning for it.

Together with Capixúm, another came forward, a sub-leader, whom Hermógenes called Marques. Hermógenes had a voice that was neither nasal nor hoarse, yet it came out unevenly, a voice that got out-of-hand. It made you think—his manner of speaking—of a tayra weasel, with its foul smell.

"Aoh, hmmm, you've got somebody there, brother?" inquired that Marques, referring to me.

"It's all right, old brother. A friend who has come to show us where to camp," Hermógenes answered. Another rumble came from his mouth and throat, like a growl.

Without further delay, I set out, walking alongside Hermógenes's horse, drawing them all towards Cambaùbal. Behind us, I could hear the mingled hoofbeats of the big troop steadily advancing. I did not want to turn around and look—they might think I was being nosey. But now they were talking, some of them laughing, making jokes. I supposed they were very glad to be getting some hours of rest, for they had been in the saddle all night. One spoke out louder than the rest—gay and foolish-like: "Siruiz, where is the virgin maid?" We left the roadway, and the wet grass washed my feet. Someone, probably that Siruiz, sang some verses to a tune I had never heard:

> *Urubú is a town high up,*
> *The oldest in the sertão:*

My partron saint, my life—
I came from there, I will not return,
I came from there, will I not return?
I spend my days on these green plains,
My polled and woolly steer:
Buriti palms—blue-hued water,
Carnaúba wax palms—salt of the earth.
Backwater of a river wide,
Guitar of loneliness:
When I go into battle,
I invite my heart to come.

Dawn was breaking. A dewy day in May, as I said. People's memories are like that.

They loaned me a horse, and I went with Alaripe to wait for the arrival of the mule train, up ahead, at the entrance to the bridge. It wasn't long before they showed up. A train of ten mules, and the drivers. But they came with their bells muffled, stuffed with raw cotton; aside from the creaking of their wooden pack frames, they made no sound. We guided the train to Cambaùbal. Then my godfather arrived with Joca Ramiro, Ricardão, and the Totões. My grandfather insisted that I go back to the house with him. By then it was broad daylight. My heart was filled with restlessness.

I did not see their camp again, jingling with spurs. Godfather Selorico Mendes sent me to O-Côcho to find a man called Rozendo Pio, who, my godfather told me, was a scout. He was to come, in the utmost secrecy, to lead Joco Ramiro's outfit over good trails and short cuts through the Trinta Voltas sierra, so as to take only two nights with no more risk than if they took six or seven. Under the circumstances, only I could be trusted to go. I went, against my will. Three leagues, three and a half leagues distant. Besides, I had to lead a spare horse for the man. And this Rozendo Pio turned out to be a knave and a fool. He took a long time getting started, claiming there were some things he had to do first. On the road, coming back, he knew nothing about jagunços or anything: he hardly spoke, wouldn't give any demonstration of his skill. He took no pleasure in it.

It was dark when we arrived, and the band was ready to leave. They broke up into small groups. My godfather had ordered all the dogs on the ranch tied up. They set out. To me it was as if everything had lost its zest, its interest.

During the following weeks, my godfather talked of nothing but the jagunços. He said that Joca Ramiro was a skillful leader—not many like him were born—a glorious one! If lucky, that band of ruffians could straighten out the government. My godfather had spent that whole day among them. He told how carefully they had laid their plans, how everything was worked out, with complete obedience, strict authority. They lacked for nothing: sacks of meal, so and so many kilos of jerked beef, the ammunition carefully guarded, soap enough for everyone to wash his clothes and himself with. They even had a blacksmith, with his equipment and tools: an anvil and tongs, a hand bellows, everything he needed, including a veterinarian's kit with various lancets for bleeding ailing horses. And my godfather described with great pleasure other things which had been freely told him: the combats of the Joca-Ramiros, the skirmishes, the stratagems used to insure victory, a whole bag of stories of every kind of trick and cunning. Listening to my grandfather relate all those things, his enjoyment of them, began to make me sick. It was as if he wanted to be given credit for the daring deeds of the jagunços and that Joca Ramiro was there beside us, taking orders, and that the whole valiant achievement was due to him, Selorico Mendes. My godfather was not a likeable person. Now he was being even less so.

I am not trying to find excuses for my wrongdoings, no, don't think that. What made me happy was to recall that rollicking song that held me in that dawn, ah, yes. I can only tell you that it took possession of my mind. A trifling thing, it soothed me so much that I began to make up verses of that kind in my mind. I made up many, heaps of them. I myself did not sing them because I could never carry a tune, and my lips are not the right shape for whistling. But I repeated them to people and everybody praised them, and many learned them by heart. Now, I draw your attention to one point, and maybe you will agree—

though with what, I can't say as I do not know myself. The point is that I made up those other verses about real things, mine, all mine, all felt by me, of my longings and sadness. Though I prized them at the time, they are now meaningless, finished, have died completely within me, have left no ashes. I do not remember a one of them, not one. What I do remember to the last detail is that dawn: the riders gathered in the darkness, having the appearance of animals and trees, the drip-drip of the dew, the morning star, the little field crickets, the tread of the horses, and Siruiz's singing. Does that have any meaning?

My godfather Selorico Mendes let me live like a lord. At São Gregório I could have anything I wanted, within reason. And as for working, I didn't have to. Whether I did or didn't, my godfather liked me, but he did not praise me. There was only one thing he would not tolerate, and that was for anyone to try to find out just how much money he had. This I never tried to do; I don't pry. I lived high on the hog. What more could anyone wish for?

But, one day someone—I was so eager not to think about the beginning of the matter that I forget who—someone told me that it was no mere chance that I was the spitting image of Selorico Mendes. That he was my father! When I heard that, everything around me began to spin dizzily—the world came tumbling down around me with this great dishonor. It even seemed that in some hidden fashion I had known it all the time. I had heard it from others, in bits and pieces, innuendos and allusions, to which I shut my ears. Should I have asked him? Ah, no, I couldn't. I would ask no one else, either—I had had enough. I couldn't get it out of my head. I gathered up my gear, my arms, I saddled a horse, and fled from there. I first went to the kitchen, put a hunk of meat and some handfuls of meal in my knapsack. If I had found any money lying aroung, I would have taken it; I had no scruples about that. I was leaving for good. I made straight for Curralinho.

For what reason did I do it? I know, or perhaps, I don't. "A" was clear to me, but I don't believe I thought about "B" at all. I had to do something. It was almost an obsession with me, unreasoning, like the pleasure of an evil habit. I whipped up my anger. It was not exactly anger, but a sort of inner vindictiveness; the chagrin that filled me gave me no clue as to what my course should be. Its only effect was to stiffen my neck and to make my head buzz with confusion, turmoil, and despair. I spurred my horse forward, galloping faster. I would not go to Nhô Marôto's house. I would go to that of Seo Assis Wababa— at that moment I wanted only foreign people, very foreign, completely foreign. To see Rosa'uarda, if only for a little while. Did I love her, then? Ah, no. I liked Rosa'uarda well enough, but my thoughts would not stay fixed on the delights of her—for my shame was growing greater. I would go to Master Lucas's school. There, close by the house of Master Lucas, lived a gentleman called Dodó Meirelles, who had a daughter called Miosótis. In a silly, fatuous way, this girl Miosótis had also been a sweetheart of mine, and now, for a while, it comforted me to think of her seeing me and having her know that I, with my deadly weapons, had risen up against my godfather, had left the house with angry shouts, and had ridden my horse wildly through the bush, capable of anything! After that, I would have to explain things to Master Lucas. I did not really care for that Miosótis—she was a little fool—and at São Gregório I hadn't thought about her at all; Rosa'uarda was the one I liked. But Nhô Marôto would soon learn that I had arrived in Curralinho, and my godfather would be promptly informed of it. He would send someone for me. He would come himself. I did not care. Suddenly, I realized: that was just what I wanted; that he should come, that he should beg me to return, promising me everything, ah, even kneeling at my feet. But what if he didn't come? Or took a long time about coming? In that case, I was going to have to find me a way to make a living, put up with all sorts of gibes from everybody, and devote myself to hateful, petty daily tasks. With this my anger rose up anew. More tears came into my rebellious eyes. They overflowed as I thought of my mother, full of love, and I declared out loud that it was all her fault that I was behaving this way; I shouted it. But that was a poor excuse, and my shame only grew. I saw that my horse's coat, as though

begging for mercy, had become dark with sweat. I let up on the
spurs. We came on at a jog. I feared for my life when we
entered Curralinho.

At Seo Assis Wababa's house they received me joyfully. I
ate, laughed, talked. But they surprised me with one blasted
bit of news: that Rosa'uarda was now engaged to marry a
certain Salino Cúri, another Syrian merchant, who had come
there during the last few months. I felt both disappointment
and relief—that love was really not meant for me, for personal
reasons. Dejected though I was, I kept control of myself: I
crossed my legs, assumed an air of reticence—no, sir—yes, sir
—cannily cautious, and inquired about prices. In this way, they
would assume that my trip had to do with some important
matter for my godfather, Selorico Mendes. Seo Assis Wababa
was elated that night with the news that Vupes had brought:
that before long the railroad would be coming there, and that
Curralinho was then sure to become an important commercial
center. Seo Assis Wababa swelled with approval, and brought
out a jug of wine. I remember: I let my imagination take over,
falling into the silly illusion that for me, too, everything would
be settled by modern progress, and I saw myself rich, well-
established. I even saw how good it would be, if it were true.

Well, Vupes was there too, the German, Vupes, whom I told
you about—Seo Emílio Wusp, as you call him. I already knew
him from other times that he had been in Curralinho. An all-
round man. He knew all about handling firearms, but he
traveled about without a gun of any sort. He would say: "Nix!
Entirely unarmed, I thusly, they are all going to respect me
much more, yes indeed, in the backlands."

He once saw me take careful aim, and he praised me for
knowing instinctively to hold my breath at the instant of pressing the trigger. He even said: "You shoot well because with the
spirit you shoot. It's always the spirit that hits the target." It
sounded as if he were saying: it's always the spirit that kills.
Suddenly the idea came to me that what would solve my problem would be to go to work for Vupes, travel through the
country selling tools and cotton gins. I didn't even stop to think
it over, but spoke out: "Mr. Vupes, wouldn't you like to hire me

to work for you?" It was stupid of me. "Nix!" he replied, using a favorite expression. I had no sooner got the words out of my mouth than I regretted them. A new thought had struck me: that even a friendly and courteous person, once he becomes your boss, turns harsh and fault-finding. I bit my lips, but I had already spoken. I wanted to remedy my slip and try to pass it off as a joke, but Seo Assis Wababa and Vupes were eying me with suspicion, and I felt even more humiliated. Everything was against me; the very timing of events was all wrong. I left shortly thereafter, taking my leave politely. Where to now? The only thing to do was to go see Master Lucas. I walked along, full of despair. I remember that as I was walking I began to think about Rosa'uarda, her beautiful, plump legs, her nainsook dress, how she would never be mine to enjoy. I recalled long afterwards that I felt then like the song that goes:

> *If your father were rich,*
> *And had a good business,*
> *I would marry you*
> *And what fun we'd have.*

That's exactly how I felt, at times.

Now, I ask you, sir: in your life, has it been like that? In my life—I see it now—everything important that happened to me, came about by merest chance, in the twinkling of an eye, the luck of the moment, by a hair, by a strand from a horse's mane. Ah, if it had not been that way, hit-or-miss, what would have been my fate? It's an idle question to which there is no answer. There are times when this thought scares me. You will see what I mean. I got to Master Lucas's house, and he greeted me quite naturally. I too found everything natural; but I was so tired. And when Master Lucas asked me if I had come on a pleasure jaunt, or on some business for the ranch, I explained to him that no, I had been granted leave by my godfather to begin my own life in Curralinho or beyond, for the purpose of going on with my studies and acquiring the refinements of city life. I would have sworn that Master Lucas wasn't going to believe me, but he did, completely. Do you know why? It was because on that very day he was involved in a matter which prepared the ground for him to believe me. As I say, he listened to me and then said:

"Riobaldo, you have come at just the right moment."

And then he went on to explain that a gentleman in Palhão, on the Nhanva fazenda, way up on the Jequitaí River, was looking for a teacher of all subjects. Urgently. He was a man of substance, and would pay well. What he wanted was for Master Lucas himself to go, and leave someone in his place in the school at Curralinho for a while; but that was out of the question. Did I want to go?

"Do you think I can do it?" I inquired, for I almost never had the courage to tackle something new on my own.

"Why, sure you can," Master Lucas declared.

He had already begun to stow in a bag all the books, geography, arithmetic, speller, grammar and everything I would need—eraser, pencil, ruler, inkpot. I accepted. The enthusiasm we both felt bucked me up. And the best part of it was, there would be no delay because two of the rancher's hired hands were there in Curralinho, waiting for an answer, and now they could take me back with them. Master Lucas's wife, Dona Dindinha, embraced me when it was time to leave, with a few kindly tears: "There are so many bad people in the world, my son. And you so young, so attractive." I didn't even get to see that Miosótis girl. I did see Rosa'uarda, from a distance.

The two ranch hands, I soon realized, were their employer's henchmen, but well-mannered fellows, not at all swaggering nor overly rough, and they treated me with great respect. We traveled together for four days, almost thirty leagues, much of the time following the Riachão River, in sight of the towering masses of the Serra-do-Cabral on our left. My companions gave me little or no information. They had orders to the contrary. But even before we had reached the Palhão lands, I began to notice strange things which caused me to wonder. Patrols of armed riders; snatches of guarded conversation; a train of pack mules, but among the drivers there were three soldiers. The closer we got, the greater my surprise. The Nhanva fazenda was swarming with men—a milling about as though a fair was going on. It was a fine-looking fazenda, with a two-storied house, big corrals, and a large terrace. I met the owner at once. At first sight, he was odd-looking, dressed in blue crash and wearing yellow boots. He was nervous, thin, a little below average in height, and had arms that seemed too long, what with all his gesticulating. I went toward him, and he came toward me, a big pistol in his belt; a handkerchief fluttering at his neck; his thick hair disheveled, with an upturned forelock. I quickened my pace, and he stopped, with his hands on his hips. He looked me up and down, and gave a laugh—it was plain he did not know who I was. He shouted, in a bantering tone: "Here he comes, walking like a frog, here he comes."

Ah, oh, ah, the humiliation of being made fun of got my goat. I stopped, too. I pretended not to hear. But then he came toward me and greeted me in a circumspect but friendly manner. Mollified, I said: "I am the young man teacher."

His delight at hearing me was amazing. He took hold of my arm, and with many ingratiating words and gestures, escorted me up the stairs and led me to an inside room, quickly, as if he wanted to hide me from everybody. Crazy? Ah, but do you know who he was, this man? Zé Bebelo. As a matter of fact, everything about him was surprising to me.

Did I tell you? I thought I was going to teach the children of some fazendeiro. My mistake. What seemed commonplace matters, where Zé Bebelo was involved, always turned out differently. The student was he, himself, he informed me. He could not wait to see the notebooks, the books, take them in his hands. Reading and writing, and simple arithmetic, he already knew, and he devoured newspapers. He dug the things out and arranged them all on a big table in the room, humming and whistling, happy as a lark. But then he said, speaking earnestly, that all this must be kept a secret, as I could see.

"We'll say that I am working out the plans! And that you are going to be my secretary."

That very same day, we began. That man made me exert myself until I was dizzy, but he sharpened my wits. Such eagerness and thirst, and quickness to understand, I never saw in anyone else. What he wanted was to cram into his head, all at once, all that books give and do not give. What intelligence he had! He was ravenous. He raced from lesson to lesson, asking questions and more questions. It even seemed to make him mad because I knew and he didn't, resentful that he still had more to learn. He would burn two and three candles every night. He even said: "I have stopped looking at the clock. I study and study, until I start stretching and yawning. If I get drowsy, I close the book, lie down, and go to sleep."

With his will power, it was simple. During the day we would be working over the pages, and suddenly he would get up, go to the window, blow a whistle, and start shouting orders: ten, twenty commands at a time. The men ran, carrying them out: it was like a circus, a good show. But, in less than a month, Zé Bebelo had mastered everything, and now he knew much more than I did. With this, his happiness knew no bounds. He would come at me with the book, and ask me point-blank a pile of questions. Often enough I would stall, try to slide over the explanation, make mistakes right and left, cheat. No dice—he would cut me short, show me in the book where I was wrong, correct my mistake, and dress me down. He would burst out laughing, throw out his hands, and give vent to his own ideas on the subject—happy at seeing me in difficulties, me now ignorant, discouraged, and burned up. It was not until then, I tell you, that he became really fond of me. It's the truth. He embraced me, gave me money, and praised me highly.

"Siô Baldo, now I've reached the top! But I can't have you leaving, no sir; I want you to stay on as my secretary. We are going up North, to do great things, and you will not be sorry," he said. "North, bad country." He became high-flown with his own words.

For he had already outlined all his projects to me: how he was assembling and training all those men to set out up-state under his command on a great war. The purpose of it was to fall upon the lawless bands one after the other, make an end of them, liquidate them to the last man, and rid the world of the jagunços. "Only after I have done this, Siô Baldo, will I be wholly free: then I will enter politics right!"

He had already confessed to me that his only ambition, and one that he cherished deeply, was to become a Deputy. He asked me to keep it a secret, which I didn't like, because I knew that everybody was already discussing that bit of foolishness, and behind his back they were already calling him "the Deputy." People are like that. But, even so, the men did not deny him the fullest respect. Because he was all man. Ah, Zé Bebelo was plenty tough—seven daggers with seven blades, all in one sheath! He could handle any firearm and his aim was deadly; he could rope steers and ride the range as well as any cowboy; he could break the wildest animal—mule or horse; he could fight a knife duel with the cunning of a cornered wildcat, on the aggressive every moment; fear, and all the little relatives of fear, he spat upon and despised. They say he would wade right in, and quell any fracas. Rough and tough, a man with guts! And to him, nothing seemed really impossible. For all his ridiculous and contemptible horseplay, God help anyone who dared to give him a sneering look: he was a goner.

"The only man-jagunço I could respect, Siô Baldo, is already dead. Now we have to render this service to our country—the nation comes before all."

The one of whom he spoke, who was already dead, was the notorious Joãozinho Bem-Bem, from Aroeiras, whose life, they say, he had studied in detail and with such devotion that he had given himself a nickname—Zé Bebelo—for his real name, in fact, was José Rebêlo Adro Antunes.

"Must we put up forever with the dirty work of hired henchmen? Just you wait: a few months from now, in this North of ours, we won't be seeing any more political bosses hiring gangs of ruffians for the elections, flouting the law, just to destroy everything civilized and legal!"

He meant what he said, and his anger was justified. People really ought to put a stop to the hiring of armed bands to invade towns, wreck shops, looting right and left, defiling the walls of the district judge's house with human filth, and parading the district attorney mounted backwards on a broken-down nag, with a can tied to its tail, while the pack of thugs shouted curses and set off firecrackers! Didn't they even break open barrels of cachaça in front of the church? And what about exposing priests naked in the middle of the street, and insulting young women and whole families, raping married women, taking turns, one man after another, while the husband was forced to look on?

As Zé Bebelo talked thus, the fire within him would rise so high that he had to stop, and he would rush out on the veranda or to the window, blow his whistle and shout orders. Then, relieved, he would return to me and say: "Ah, I am going, Siô Baldo, I am going. Only I can do what has to be done, for I alone was born for that purpose." Then he would say that once he had done away with organized lawlessness, and had become a Deputy, he would make the North to flourish, building bridges, erecting factories, improving everybody's health, doing away with poverty, opening a thousand schools. Once he got started, he would go on and on, his phrases becoming more high-faluting, reflecting his newspaper learning. I was getting fed up with it, because he always wound up with the same thing.

But my life on his fazenda couldn't have been better. I was like a crown prince. I lived like a lord. I became accustomed to the free and easy life, and made friends with the henchmen. There were always people arriving from the outside, city people, who would talk with Zé Bebelo in private. I learned that one of them was a Deputy, on a mission. And he would introduce me as: "Professor Riobaldo, my secretary." During leisure hours, I would go with the others to Leva, about a league distant, where the women were housed, more than fifty of them. They kept coming, so many of them, that nearly every day they had to cut prices. We did not lack for this agreeable diversion. Zé Bebelo gave his approval: "Where did you ever see a man good for anything, when there are no wenches within easy reach? Where?" He even provided cachaça, in moderation. "Better this way; if not, they'll get hold of it themselves, and then there'll be abuses, fights," he explained. Moreover, there was everything else there, in abundance. Plenty of food, first-rate guns, piles of ammunition, clothes and shoes of the best. And cash for the weekly payroll, for none of those men were there for the fun of it but as a way of earning their living. It was said the money had come from the Government's coffers. It looked that way.

Thus, finally, the day came to set out, everybody, in fighting array, through valleys and over mountains. Oh, what an uproar! The hullabaloo and chattering sounded like a band of macaws in flight—you never saw anything like it, except as described in a storybook. The trappings and equipment were like that of regular soldiers; there were so many horses you wondered if enough pasturage would be found for them, and the men numbered close to a thousand in all. Accompanied by his party leaders—on whom he conferred the rank of lieutenants and officers of his regiment—Zé Bebelo, mounted on a spanking gray and wearing a most magnificent hat, pranced back and forth, everywhere, looking things over. He called me over to him, and I had to keep a thick notebook handy, to take down names, numbers, etcetera, as his clerk. As you see, sir, I was going with them. I was going to my rendezvous with fate. What heartened me was that he had said that when I was no longer satisfied, I had only to say so, and he would give me full permission to leave.

I tell you I went, and I tell you I liked it. At the end of a stiff ride, ready food, a good rest, companionship. Most of the men enjoyed themselves. I was seeing new roads, new lands. We would wake up at one place and spend the night at another, and all that might be stale or unhappy within you was left behind. This was it, at last. This was it.

"Yes, yes, but it's up ahead, when we get into a fight, that all hell will break loose," some would say.

In Zé Bebelo's own good time. He knew what he wanted, that man of foxlike cunning. Already, on setting out from Nhanva, he had divided his people into groups—for each group, a different route. One followed the São Lamberto, on the right; another, the Riacho Fundo and the Córrego do Sanhar; another left us at Só-Aqui, and went along the Ribeirão da Barra; still another kept bearing left, shouldering the São Francisco River; but the rest of us, with Zé Bebelo himself in command, pushed on through the center, following the course of the Córrego Felicidade. We passed close by Vila Inconfidência, and pitched camp in the village of Pedra-Branca, on the bank of the Água-Branca. All was going well. From one battalion to another, runners were sent with orders and messages. We were casting a big net to catch big fish. And so it turned out. I did not see that famous battle—I had stayed behind at Pedra-Branca. Not out of fear, no. But Zé Bebelo had ordered me to. "You be patient and wait," he said, "and as soon as a courier arrives with news of our first victory, call the townspeople together and make them a speech."

It took place as planned. Except that, instead of a courier, Zé Bebelo himself came galloping back. I had been left with a pile of sky rockets to shoot off, and it was a real celebration. Zé Bebelo ordered a board placed across the corner of a fence, as a platform, on to which he climbed and made a long speech. He related what had happened. Over by the Pacú River, in the area of Brasília, they had surrounded a band of jagunços—the one headed by the ruffian Hermógenes—and had completely routed them. More than ten killed, and more than ten of the bandits taken prisoner; unfortunately, however, Hermógenes himself had managed to escape. But he couldn't get far! Whereupon Zé Bebelo praised the law, cried "Long live the Government," and promised many democratic things for the near future. Then he led me forward to make a speech, too. I had no choice. "What you must do is to mention my name often," which I did not do out of modesty. "And talk very patriotically," he whispered to me.

I carried out his instructions. A man like this ought to be a Deputy, I said, emphatically. When I had finished, he embraced me. The people seemed to like what I had said. Then, as we were sitting around after lunch, some of our horsemen arrived, herding the bunch of prisoners. I felt sorry for those poor devils—worn out, scared, nearly all of them dirty with dried blood—you could see they had no decent hopes left. They were to be taken in a body to the jail at Extrema, and from there to other jails, and then, undoubtedly, to the jail in the Capital. Zé Bebelo, looking on, saw me and noticed my softness. "Save your pity. They are the worst kind of thugs."

And so they were. I knew that. But how could I help feeling sorry? What affects a person most is the ugly nature of suffering itself, not the quality of the sufferer.

I thought that now we might have earned a longer rest. What a hope! "On your horses! There is more to be done. There is more—" Zé Bebelo shouted. We struck out. Talking on the way, I asked, I don't know why: "What about Joca Ramiro?" Zé Bebelo shrugged his shoulders, seeming not to want to talk about him. Whereupon I took a kind of mean delight in telling him how wonderful Joca Ramiro's outfit was, how he knew and provided for everything, and that he even took along a man just as a farrier, with his little tent and tools, and everything else having to do with the animals. On hearing that, Zé Bebelo stopped short: "Ah, that's a worthwhile idea, it really is. We have to arrange for the same thing, a good example to profit by," he asserted. And I, who was about to go on to telling other things, about the tactics that my godfather had said Joca Ramiro devised when he fought, suddenly thought better of it and shut my mouth. Observe, sir, how often our impulses in life are guided by hunches, for at that moment it struck me that if I told any more I would be committing an act of treachery. But why treachery? I pursed my lips. One doesn't know, yet one knows. I shut my mouth. We let out the horses.

Between the Condado and the Lontra shooting began. There I saw and I learned. Half of our men dismounted while the rest advanced concealing themselves behind trees. Then suddenly, quickly, they would drop to the ground, crawling and making their way head first. Had they known how to fight from birth? I watched them only for a moment. Following Zé Bebelo, we wheeled back towards the Gameleiras where the fighting was heaviest. It was Ricardão's band, which we surrounded as we neared them. To bring them to bay all we needed were hounds! Hell broke loose as we engaged them. In the midst of woods you can't tell the report of a shot from its echo. I had the impression that many died. We beat them. I did not get off my horse. I did not help nor was I around at the end when the chase got hot, our men pursuing those who fled with Ricardão himself. But we had no luck, for Ricardão got away. Whereupon our men, enraged, wanted to finish off the eight prisoners we had taken.

"Hey, hold on there! Under no circumstances will I tolerate acts of perverse cowardice!" Zé Bebelo roared angrily.

I admired his superiority in this matter of not killing. I also wished that the clean atmosphere of peace would soon prevail and without so much shouting. It had been a rough day. I badly needed rest and quiet, far off somewhere. We got little of it. After the necessary things were done, there was only a brief respite, because our immediate plans had changed and we set out at once for Terra Fôfa, almost on the border of the Grão-Mogol. But I didn't get there. Somewhere along the way, I decided to better my life: I ran away.

All of a sudden I had seen that I could stand it no longer; a feeling of repugnance had come over me. I don't know if it was because I was against all that going with such superiority of men and means, killing and capturing people, in relentless brutality. I watched when they were paying no attention to me and lagged behind, out of sight. Then I slipped away. On the basis of our understanding, I didn't have to do it that way. I could have gone to Zé Bebelo and resigned: "I have changed my mind, I choose to go back to Curralinho." Couldn't I have? But at the very same time that I was making my decision, I began to develop a loathing for Zé Bebelo. Nor did I feel that I could have any confidence in anybody. So I ran away, and thought no more about it. Just like that. You know, sir, how it is: you behave badly, what you do is deplorable, but it lacks narrative substance.

My horse was a good one, I had money in my pocket, and I was well armed. I turned back leisurely. I was undecided about what route to take. I traveled, I kept going, but I don't think I really wanted to get anywhere. After twenty days of loitering along, and with nothing out-of-the-way happening, I headed for Rio das Barras, at a point within sight of the mouth of Córrego Batisterio. There I slept with a woman who pleased me very much—her husband was away somewhere, not far. They had no malaria around there. Early the next morning the woman said to me: "My father lives a quarter of a league from here. Go there, and stay for lunch and supper. At night, if my husband hasn't returned, I'll send for you and let you know."

I said: "You light a bonfire up on that hill, I'll see it and come back." She said: "I can't do that; if someone else saw it they might become suspicious." I said: "Just the same, that's what I want. A bonfire—just a tiny one." She said: "Maybe I will." Both of us serious, neither smiling. Then I left.

But this woman's father was a sharp, wily fellow, with a knack for drawing you out along his own lines. His house— roomy, tile-roofed and whitewashed—was situated on the bank, there where the river was full of low-water sand bars and beaches. His name was Manoel Inácio—Malinácio he was called—and he had good meadows, with a herd of horses grazing, and some cattle. He gave me lunch, and got me to talking. I wanted to be truthful with him. I noticed that when he spoke he looked straight at me, and when he listened, he blinked his eyes; and anyone who looks straight at you when he talks and blinks his eyes when he is listening, doesn't care much for soldiers. Little by little, then, I let him know that I did not want to form part of the Zé-Bebelos, which was the gospel truth. "And what about Joca Ramiro?" he asked. I told him, partly to make myself seem important and to show off, that I had already served Joca Ramiro and had talked with him; that for that very reason, I could not stay with Zé Bebelo, because my attachment was to Joca Ramiro. And I talked about my godfather Selorico Mendes, and about Aluiz and Alarico Totõe, and about how Joca Ramiro had spent the night at our São Gregório ranch. I must have talked about other things too, and that man Malinácio just listened, pretending to be at ease. But I could see that he wasn't. He began to advise me not to linger in that place—that the air was full of malaria. I did not take his hint. I wanted to wait and see if it would be my luck for the bonfire to be lit, for I had taken a fancy to his daughter. For a moment, the crafty fellow was at a loss. But then, when I asked for a place in the shade to stretch my hammock and rest—I said I wasn't feeling too well—it seemed to

please him. He led me to a room which had a bunk and mattress, told me to make myself at home and closed the door. I
fell sound asleep, my arms beside me.

I did not wake up until Malinácio called me for supper. I
entered the dining room and found three other men there. They
said they were pack drivers and their clothes and looks bore
them out. But Malinácio began to comment on and repeat my
conversation with him, which I did not like, because freshly
told secrets are not for everyone's ears. And the driver who
owned the pack—he had a round face, somewhat light-
skinned—asked me many questions. I did not feel comfortable
and began to get suspicious, not because of his persistence—
all pack drivers ask lots of questions—but because of the way
in which the other two were helping him to size me up, keeping
on inquiring about everything. He wanted to know where I
was really going from there. He wanted to know why, if I was
pulling for Joca Ramiro, and was carrying arms, had I not
found a way of trotting North and joining up with the Ramiros?
Suspicion sharpens your wits. Choosing my words, I repeated
what I had said, adding at the same time that I had come this
way as a precaution, and to have the necessary calm to settle
my plans in my own mind. Ah, but, well, while they were
listening to me, another man, a pack driver too, stepped across
the threshold and into the room. I stared at him and felt a
tremor, as of sudden fright. But it was the fright of a heart on
high, and like the greatest joy.

I knew him instantly. The young man, so changed and handsome, was—do you know who, sir, do you know who? It was
the Boy! The Boy, yes sir, that one at the Janeiro river landing,
the one I told you about, the one who crossed the river with me,
in a rocking canoe, it took us a lifetime. He approached, and I
got up from the bench. The green eyes that looked so large, the
unforgettable long lashes, the more than handsome mouth, the
delicate nose, finely cut. Astonishment like that paralyzes,
dumfounds one. I wanted to go toward him, to greet him with
an embrace, but my courage failed me, for at that moment he
faltered, in shy rejection. But it was plain that he recognized
me. Our eyes met and held. The encounter must have been

vivid, because the others noticed something odd—this I perceived despite my confusion. The Boy extended his hand, and what hand says to hand is brief; sometimes the rest can be guessed and understood. And he sort of smiled. I tell you, sir, even today he is smiling at me still. His name was Reinaldo.

Why, in relating something, mention everything, every little detail? That meeting of ours was out-of-the-ordinary, melodramatic, the kind you read of only in newspapers and books. It was not until afterwards that I could put together even what I am telling you now and really understand it—for, when something like this is happening, what you feel mostly is what pertains to the body: the thudding heart.

"Those are one's own hours. The others, those of any time, are everybody's hours," my compadre Quelemém explained to me. It is as though life's trivialities were a pool of water in which we find ourselves submerged, a pool that covers and deadens everything—but once in a rare while we manage to raise our heads out of it, in a sort of miracle: like a little fish begging! Why? I am going to tell you something that is not generally known: always when we begin to love someone, in the normal run of things, love takes root and grows, because, in a way, that is what we want to happen, and so we seek it and help it along in our mind; but when it is predestined, all-embracing, we love completely and fatefully, we have to love, and we come upon one surprise after another. A love of this sort grows first and bursts forth later. I am talking a lot, I know: I am being a bore. But it can't be helped. Well then, tell me: can love like that come from the devil? Can it possibly? Can it come from One-Who-Does-Not-Exist? Your silence indicates agreement. Please don't answer me, or my confusion will grow.

You know, one time on the Tamanduá-tão, in the turmoil of battle, and me winning, I suddenly found myself in the grip of fear—fear only of myself, a self which I no longer recognized. I seemed to be tall, taller than I am; and I was laughing at myself, guffawing. Suddenly I asked myself, but did not answer: "Are you the king of men?" I talked and laughed. I whinnied, like a wild horse. I shot off my gun. The wind was

blowing through all the trees. But my eyes saw only the whirling of the dust. And I'll say no more, not a word! Neither you,
nor I, nor anyone knows.

To go on. Reinaldo—that was his name. He was the Boy of
the river landing, as I have already explained. And from the
moment he appeared in the doorway, more grown-up but otherwise unchanged, I could never again separate myself from his
company of my own accord, for any reason, could I? That is
what I felt within me, as clearly as if in meeting that Boy-
Youth again, I had happened to discover, for always, someone
kith and kin to me. Without substance and without peace, yes,
I know. But, for all that, could love be sent by the Devil? I
say no. Ah—and what about Otacília? Otacília, as you will see,
sir, when I tell you—I knew her under gentle circumstances,
all clear and aboveboard, on a high plane, so to speak; with
angels flying about, almost, almost. At the Santa Catarina
ranch, in Buritís-Altos, headwaters of a stream. Otacília, she
was all harmony, a child of beauty. I'll tell you later; everything has its proper time. My trouble was that I had to weigh, in
one hand and in the other, this love against that one. There
come times when I say: if one of those loves came from God,
then where did the other come from? With me things have no
today or yesterday or tomorrow, but exist always. Torments. I
know that I am outwardly to blame. But when did my fault
begin? For the moment, you do not understand what I am
talking about, and you may not understand me at the end,
either. But life is not understandable. I'll tell you: outside of
these two—and that other girl, Nhorinhá, of Aroeirinha, the
daughter of Ana Duzuza—I never had another love, not one.
And Nhorinhá I stopped loving long ago, with the passage of
time. Looking back on my life, I like everybody, and hold no
one in contempt and dislike except my own old self. Medeiro
Vaz, before going out into the Gerais to impose justice, set fire
to his house; he did not even want to possess the ashes. Later,
houses were burned down through my own shouted orders. I
would stand by listening—the clatter of things breaking and
falling, crackling with muffled sound, abandoned, there inside.
Sertão!

As soon as Reinaldo recognized and greeted me, I had no further trouble in convincing the others about my situation. With hardly another word, he vouched for me to the round-faced fellow who passed for owner of a pack train, and whose name was Titão Passos. As a matter of fact, as I learned, they were not pack drivers, but some of Joca Ramiro's fighters. And the pack train? The one which was about to set out for the North, with three lots of good horses, was to carry munitions. They no longer bothered to keep this from me. That Malinácio was the stores keeper, with the munitions well concealed. Right in front of his house, and above and below, there were three bare shoals in the stream of the river—each with its own name, which everybody knew, given them by the boatmen of the Velhas river. Three shoals and an island. But one of the three shoals, the largest, was a half island; that is, the lower end was soil, with large rocks and trees, overgrown with brush and grass, and lush rosemary trailing its foliage in the water, and bright green clockvine, while the upper end was a pile of bare sand. A sand-bar-with-island, as it is called, Malinácio's crôa-com-llha. The stores were hidden there, and we would go in a canoe and bring back the munitions. The other comrades, disguised as pack drivers, were Triol and João Vaqueiro; also Acrísio and Assunção, posted as sentinels, and Vove, Jenolim and Admeto, who had just finished loading the mules. We all had supper, and were ready to set out on the long journey. I was going with them. We left. I felt no regret at not waiting for the bonfire signal of that married woman, Malinácio's daughter. And she was pretty—strong and shapely. I thought no more about her. The night's march began as though over cotton—cautiously quiet. Those munitions were worth thousands and thousands, and we bore great responsibilities. We did not travel along the bank, but guided ourselves by the river. Titão Passos was in command.

For me to follow along like this, without a hard and fast decision of my own, like a half-starved dog waiting for travelers beside a shack, will perhaps make you think I am a man without will power. I thought so myself. I realized that I was a sham, kicking around the world, without an honest calling of

my own. Everywhere, in those days, whichever way I turned,
people were killing and dying, in a fury of conviction, in a
certainty, and I didn't belong to any side; I neither kept faith
nor formed part of any group. From so much tacking, my
thoughts became confused. The only thing I wanted was not to
change my mind, for with that discouragement always set in
and this was a thing I had already learned to stave off.

Although Reinaldo and I were traveling in the same group,
he did not seek my company nor come near me, not once, nor
show any desire to pursue our friendship. We did not have to
worry about the string of pack animals, patiently following one
another in the darkness of the night, for they could see well
enough. If I had not happened to come upon a certain village,
and a woman there, and made the agreement with that woman
to light a bonfire, would I never again, in this life, have encountered the Boy? I wondered about it. I worried this idea a
lot, sir, but instead of it making me glad that I had been so
lucky, it made me suffer. Luck? What God knows, He knows. I
saw the fog hide the river, and dawn break through on the other
side. Behind us, the crested screamers calling loudly. About
then we arrived at a little farm, and we saw a Negro, a Negro
who was already up and at work, clearing underbrush. The
Negro was one of ours; we made a halt.

Then, while they unsaddled and fed the horses, I said my
morning Hail Mary. Others curried the donkeys and mules, or
unloaded the saddle packs; all the cargo had to be put under
shelter—it filled almost all of the Negro's little house. He was
so miserably poor that we even had to give food to him and
his wife, and their children, lots of them. We could pick up no
news of any sort. At any rate, we were going to spend that day
sleeping; but three men had to stay up, as lookouts. When
Reinaldo volunteered to be one of them, it encouraged me to
speak up and say that I would, too; I was not sleepy; inside I
was all nerves. The river, as we observed, had a shoal of yellow
sand and a wide beach; as it was early morning, the place
was crowded with birds. It was Reinaldo who called my attention to them. There were the usual ones: pure white herons in
a row, jabiru storks, green ducks, crested black-headed ducks,

dancing teals, kingfishers, coots, even a few vultures, in their gloomy rusty black. But the nicest of all—according to Reinaldo—, the prettiest and cutest little bird upstream or down, is the red-legged sandpiper.

Until that time I had never heard of anyone stopping to admire birds just for the pleasure of it, watching their comings and goings, their flight and alighting. That called for picking up a shotgun and taking aim. But Reinaldo liked to. "It's really beautiful," he taught me. On the opposite side there was a meadow and lagoons. Back and forth the flocks of ducks flew. "Just look at them!" I looked, and grew calmer. The sun shone deep in the river, the islands stood out clear. "And those over there—how beautiful!" They were the little sandpipers, always in pairs, running over the smooth sand on their long little red legs, their rumps sticking stiffly out behind, stepping haughtily, full-breasted, fussily picking up their bits of food. A little male and female—at times they touched beaks as though kissing. "You can't help liking them," Reinaldo said. He was right, but the way he said it surprised me. The softness of his voice, the unstudied warmth, the whimsical idea—all this in a fighting man, a tough jagunço—I couldn't understand it! Hearing this from anyone else, I would have thought: softie, here's one whose looks are deceiving. But not of Reinaldo. What happened was that I felt happier on hearing those words. I felt now I could like him even more. I'll always remember. Yes, of all the birds, the little redlegs is the most charming.

Afterwards, we talked about different things, trifles of no importance, and I went on to tell incidents of my life, to talk of this and that, to open up in friendship. Everything was pleasant from then on; I no longer needed to weigh my words.

"Riobaldo—Reinaldo," he said suddenly, "our names, they rhyme."

This discovery gave a fillip to the happiness I already felt; but, on the contrary, it seemed to sadden him. Why was that? At that time I did not know. Reinaldo smoked a lot; I don't know how he managed to keep his teeth so clean and white. To be sure, you had to smoke, because we were pestered every second by dancing clouds of gnats that blanketed the river bottomland,

enough to drive you crazy. I went on telling about my life. I
didn't hide anything. I told how I had gone along with Zé Bebelo, the fireworks I set off and the speech I had made in
Pedra-Branca, the fight on the banks of the Gameleiras, the pitiful prisoners marching past, their shirts and faces dirty with
dried blood. "Riobaldo, you are brave. You are a man's man," he
finally said. I felt my heart fill to overflowing; I felt myself
capable of big things, up to any undertaking.

Please excuse me, sir, I know that I am talking too much, getting away from the subject. I ramble. That's what age does to
you. Besides, what is important and what isn't? Everything.
Well now, do you know why I don't suffer remorse? I think it's
because of my good memory. Reformed sinners light their little
candles in darkness. But I remember everything. There were
many occasions on which I could not have behaved badly, even
if I had wanted to. Why not? God comes, guides us for a league,
then turns us loose. Then everything grows worse than it was
before. This life is an upside-down business; no one can weigh
his losses and harvests. But I will go on with my story. I will
tell it for myself, and I will tell it for you. And whenever you
don't understand me clearly, just wait.

At noon, Reinaldo and I were relieved of sentry duty. We
were not sleepy, and he went off to fetch a pretty bag that he
owned, one with embroidery and three little buttons. What he
kept in it was a pair of scissors, a smaller scissors, comb, mirror, soft soap, shaving brush and a razor. He hung the mirror
on the branch of a wild quince, and trimmed his hair, which
was already cut short. Then he offered to cut mine. He loaned
me the razor and told me to shave, as my beard was heavy. All
this amidst laughter and friendly banter—as when a startled
partridge whirred up before us, or when I jumped to pick a
flower and nearly fell flat on my face, or when we heard the
hee-haw of an ass grazing nearby. Relaxing like this, and with
hair decently cut and smooth-shaven face, gave me a boost.
Ever since that day, for the sake of my morale, I have never
neglected my personal appearance. Reinaldo bought another
razor and brush from someone and gave them to me in that
bag. Sometimes I was ashamed to be seen with that fancy em-

broidered thing, but I prized it just the same. And Reinaldo, on other trips, gave me other presents: a fine striped shirt, a handkerchief and pair of socks, things like that. The result, sir, you see before you: a neat man, to this very day. A clean person thinks clearly. So it seems to me.

Later Reinaldo said I should go take a bath in the river. He was not going with me. It was his habit to bathe alone in the dark, he told me, just before daybreak. I had always known about that superstition, and of the odd behavior of caborjudos, believers in witchcraft whose bodies have been rendered invulnerable. It didn't surprise me. Only just imagine: all that hardship and the discomfort of bumping into branches, feeling your way in the dark, not knowing your right hand from your left, sliding down banks, the slippery rocks and sticky mud, not to mention dangerous spiders and snakes! No, not me. Reinaldo told me to bathe, and left me at the edge of the beach. There was happiness in the air and in my thoughts. I got as far as looking at the waters, the Velhas River flowing full; a river never grows old. I got as far as taking off my clothes. But then it struck me that I was too happy about taking a bath just because Reinaldo had told me to, and it was an empty, disturbing pleasure. "Hell," I thought to myself, and I began to get mad. I got dressed and went back to the Negro's house. It was about time to eat supper and harness up the pack train for the road. Now what I wanted was to ride high in the saddle and far away. I did not even want to catch sight of Reinaldo.

What I am telling you, sir, needs to be explained. It is easy to think evil because life is a mixed-up affair. To live, I think, is to lose your illusions and to see things as they really are. Brazen behavior is so widespread, so easy to fall into, that at first you do not believe in close friendship without evil. That is true, I know. But I give you my word, I was very much of a man, and fond of women, and I was never attracted to unnatural vices. I reject them instinctively. Then—you will ask me—what was that? I shall tell you straight what happened with me, sometimes more, sometimes less, during all that time. That overpowering friendship. I never thought of any developments of an evil nature. But I loved him, day by day I loved him more. Per-

haps you will say it was a kind of spell. That's it. It was like a
spell. Let him be near me and I lacked for nothing. Let him
frown or look sad, and I would lose my peace of mind. Let him
be far from me, and I thought only of him. And did I myself,
then, not understand what this was? I know that I did. But no. I
didn't really want to understand it. That's what I think. That
rough tenderness which he concealed most of the time. And in
me a desire to get as close to him as I could, a craving almost
to inhale the odor of his body, of his arms, which at times I
madly imagined. This temptation made me feel weak, and I up-
braided myself severely. There were many such moments. As,
for example, when I remembered the way his hands touched my
face when he cut my hair. It was always like that. From the
devil, I ask? I will tell you. You just keep on listening. Other
strange doings followed.

And so, in that rapturous state of mine, I had what seemed to
me a good idea: in the next stage of our journey, we would have
to leave the river to one side, cross over the Serra-da-Onça, and
come out at the ford on the Jequitaí, where there might very
well be government troops in ambush. Would it not be smarter
to send just one of us there first, to spy out the situation and
gather other information?

Titão Passos, a simple, judicious man, thought my advice
was good. So did all the others. Those munitions we carried
were urgently needed, but at the same time they were worth
more than gold, than blood, and we could not be too careful of
them. I was praised and called a valuable man, one of good
judgment. I will confess to you, sir, that I was bursting with satisfaction on hearing that—for the fanning of one's vanity is
like feeding fuel to the flames. But afterwards I felt subdued
when I realized that my advice had been nothing but a hidden
wish that we might stay on longer in that place where I was
finding so much enjoyment. I felt a twinge of remorse that with
so much danger threatening, and life such a stern matter anyway, here I was scheming for petty pleasures. I was always like
that: thoughtless, foolish. But my desire was realized, and new
orders issued. To get wind of the situation and see what was
what, Jenolim set out in the direction of Lagoa-Grande, on the

Jequitaí; and for the same purpose Acrísio traveled in disguise as far as Porteiras and Pontal da Barra, keeping his ears and eyes wide open. And we stayed on another five days waiting for them to get back, days full of fun and rest, spent in the house of the Negro Pedro Segundo de Rezende, who was a cattle watcher on the lands of the São Joãozinho Ranch, belonging to a Colonel Juca Sá. To this day, I do not regret it. The days there were different from all the rest in my life. We spent hours wandering through the woods, watching the sun set through the fronds of the macaw palms, and hunting, gathering palm cabbage, and collecting wild honey in pink combs. There were quantities of happy birds, resting on the sand shoals and islands. We even fished in the river. Never again, till the very end, never again did I see Reinaldo so serene, so happy. And it was he who, at the end of the third day, asked me:

"Riobaldo, we are friends, friends for life, aren't we?"

"Reinaldo, I will live and die your friend," I answered.

The sweetness in his eyes reminded me of my mother's in her old age. It was then I saw the colors of the world. In the morning, the rolling river white with mist; and the syagrus palms waving their fronds. Only some good guitar music could make all that live again.

About the others, our companions, there's not much to say. Good, ordinary men, simple-minded henchmen from the poverty-stricken North. I did not mix with them. Not because I was proud, but I find I have always disliked people who are easily content with little. That's the way I am. But Titão Passos, him I did esteem; his saving grace was to have been born with a big heart, capable of deep friendships. He took the North as a matter of course. When we talked, I asked him if Joca Ramiro was a good man. Titão Passos controlled his amazement: it was plain he had never expected a question like this from anybody. I don't believe he had ever asked himself if Joca Ramiro might be good or bad: he was a friend of Joca Ramiro and that was enough. But the Negro de Rezende, who was close by, said, smiling foolishly: "Good? A Messiah!" You know, sir, Negroes, when they are the kind that look you in the face, have a sense of gratitude that knows no bounds.

Reinaldo, hearing Joca Ramiro's name mentioned, came over. It seemed that he did not like to see me in friendly conversation with the others for any length of time; it made him almost sulky. With the passing days I learned, too, that he was not always as even-tempered as I had thought. Ah, he liked to give orders, softly at first, then, if he were not obeyed, harshly. Did I like that strong-mindedness of his? I certainly did not. But I went along with it, perhaps because of a kind of indifference people have at times, for no good reason, about ordinary things, an indifference which strikes me as akin to laziness. And he, Reinaldo, was so trim and handsome, so commanding, a born leader, that it filled me with vanity to think he had picked me as his closest friend, which perhaps I was. But no. No, it was not that. What it was, was that I loved him. I loved him when I closed my eyes. A fondness that came in the breath of my nostrils and the dreams of my nights. You will understand me, sir, though you don't yet.

"You will soon get to know Joca Ramiro, Riobaldo," Reinaldo began, "You will see that he is the bravest man alive!" He looked at me with eyes of tenderness. And he added: "Don't you know that one who is wholly brave, in his heart, cannot help being good, too?"

That's what he said. I remembered it. I thought about it. I kept thinking about it. To me what he had said was not always the whole truth. Take my life. It couldn't be true. But I have kept on thinking about it from time to time. I asked my friend Quelemém: "What are those words worth?" He answered me: "There can be no greater truth." My compadre Quelemém is always right. I keep thinking it over. And at the end you will see that the truth of this only serves to increase my burden of sorrow.

But good things soon end. Acrísio returned: all quiet along the river, no news. Jenolim returned: the Jequitaí was fordable. And so we set out quietly, with no less uneasiness but with no greater fear, up the sierra, along the planned route. Then, after three leagues' journey, I found myself in hot water. Worse than the worst saddle galls. Where I had least feared trouble, there it came. Titão Passos began to question me.

Titão Passos was a simple, good man. He put his questions to me so straight from the shoulder that I did not have the heart to lie or to keep silent. Nor could I if I had wanted to. Up ahead, once we had crossed the Jequitaí, lay nothing but fields of fire and mortal dangers for us. Zé Bebelo's bands of riders were scouring the countryside, hunting down people, intimidating them, constantly on the alert. Among the country folk there were plenty who, distrusting us, would tip them off, for they all wanted to take advantage of the opportunity to be rid of the jagunços for good.

"To die, to die, that is nothing to make a fuss about," said Reinaldo, "but the munitions must get through to Joca Ramiro!"

How could I think calmly about dying there? How could I think about Reinaldo's dying? And what Titão Passos wanted to find out was everything that I might know about Zé Bebelo, the tricks that he employed in fighting, his normal habits, his strength in men and arms. Everything that I could tell him might help. Knowledge for some meant death for others. To give myself time to think, I began to stall, talking in a general way. How was I to bear witness? What could I say? I'd tell all I felt I could. But treachery, no.

No. Nor was it out of a sense of duty or from any principle or noble idea. I just couldn't. Everything inside of me couldn't. I'll never forget what I went through during that hour; my face must have been burning red. Whether I told what I knew, or didn't tell, I would still be in a fix. I simply couldn't, any more than an animal can relinquish eating the food it sees, or a mother animal abandon her little ones in the face of death. Should I? Should I not? Vaguely I saw the approach of nightfall with its emerging shadows. I, who was I? On which side was I? Zé Bebelo's or Joca Ramiro's? Titão Passos—Reinaldo . . . I belonged to none of them. I belonged to myself alone. I, Riobaldo. I did not want to inform.

I talked and went on talking, beating around the bush, and would you believe it, Titão Passos was satisfied with this. He believed all that I told him. I remembered that I still had with me, carefully hidden on me, that notebook of Zé Bebelo's full of names and other things. Was it worth anything? I don't know, I didn't know. As we rode along, I managed to remove it unobserved and tear it to bits, and then throw everything into a fast-flowing brook. Those waters laved me. And everything else I knew about, I made up my mind to forget completely. Later Titão Passos said: "You can be of great help. If we run into any of the Zé Bebelo riffraff, you start talking—say that you are one of them, and that you are conducting this pack train."

This was all right with me. Little by little, I even grew happy at the thought that I could be of help and do my part as a good comrade. To this end, as one of Joca Ramiro's band, I would serve with all my diligence and courage. And it made no difference if I told nothing more about Zé Bebelo, because now, as one of Ramiro's men, I too would suffer and pay for any harm that might result. Thinking on this, I felt a glow of pride and happiness. But it didn't last long. Oh, the muddy waters of the Jequitaí, which flowed past my weakness!

It was that Titão Passos, still thinking, had said to me: "We must be ready for anything. If they have already learned that you ran away, and they meet up with you, they will want to kill you at once, as a deserter."

I was stunned on hearing this, and could not answer. The back of my tongue turned bitter. Fear. Fear that shackled me. I saw myself cornered. A banana plant sways with the wind from any direction. But a man? He is a thing that trembles. My horse was carrying me without any concern. The donkeys and the mules of our pack train—how I envied them. There are several kinds of fear, as you and I know. The worst of all is the one which first leaves you numb and then hollow. Fear that begins with a great weariness. From my temples I learned that my sweat was turning cold. Fear of what can always happen but has not yet occurred. Meanwhile, my imagination ran riot—that suddenly some of Zé Bebelo's armed men would come riding through there and nab me: whatever the reason, there I was, defeated, without hope of rescue, shot down clutching the earth. I could not help remembering other tight spots, and recalling what I knew of those men's bloodthirsty hates, of the cruelties of which they were capable, drawing out their vengeance with all possible tortures. I wasn't thinking clearly, I couldn't. Fear would not let me. My head was in a fog, my brain was spinning. My heart changed its position. And our journey through the night continued. While I suffered the tortures of fear.

And then Reinaldo, when we made a halt, come over beside me. Because of my wretchedness, I knew that he was even fonder of me. Always when I am despondent, others like me more, like my company. I wonder why? I never complain about anything. My despondency is a turning in upon myself, whereas my happiness gushes out. I was unhappy, and Reinaldo drew near. He tried to cheer me up, and jokingly counseled me: "Riobaldo, pull up your donkey's ears." But I was not being sulky. I answered him merely: "My friend—," and said nothing more. For the fact was I needed to be alone. Not even Reinaldo's special company could be of help to me. Being a lone wolf, I need to be alone at trying times—that's what I always seek. With Reinaldo beside me, I would be tempted by my unhappiness to make light of my fear. Unhappiness makes a man like me weak when he is with a friend. I even wished for a measure of desperation.

Quiet desperation is sometimes the best remedy there is. It opens up the world and frees the soul. Fear grips you by the roots. I kept going. Suddenly, suddenly, a golden idea flashed upon me, a nugget of gold! And I realized what help is.

As you listen to me, I will testify. I will tell you. But first I must tell about an important lesson my compadre Quelemém taught me. And then you will see that on that dark night of mine I was hatching great ideas.

Many years later my compadre Quelemém taught me that you can achieve any desire if you have the courage to keep on for seven days in a row, with energy and unflinching patience, doing only that which goes against the grain, which causes repugnance, boredom, and weariness, and rejecting pleasure of any kind. So he says, and I believe it. And he taught me that it is better still, in the end, to cast aside the very desire that motivated you to penance in the first place. And to render all to God, who then suddenly comes with new and finer things, and pays and repays, for the interest He compounds knows no limit. This comes from my compadre Quelemém. A kind of prayer?

Well, as for praying that night, I couldn't. It did not even occur to me. Even when it comes to remembering God, you have to make a habit of it. But it was that spark of an idea that bucked me up, that cleared my mind. A tiny little idea. Just a beginning. It is little by little that we open our eyes; that's what I found out, by myself. This was it: the next day, I would not smoke, no matter how strong the urge was. And I would not sleep, nor rest sitting up or lying down. And I would not seek out Reinaldo's company nor talk with him, which were the things I liked best. I made up my mind to all that, and it made me happy. The fear went out of my breast, out of my legs. The claws of fear grew soft. We were approaching an abandoned house, by the lagoons of the Córrego Mucambo. There we had good pasture. And what I had determined on, I carried out. I did.

Ah, that day I was charged with strength, I tempered the force of other winds. My head held high. This life is full of hidden pathways. If you know, sir, you know; if you don't know, you won't understand me. Here, I'll give you still another example. They say that anyone will turn brave and fearless if he can eat the raw heart of a jaguar. Yes, but the person must kill the jaguar himself, must kill it by hand, with a knife! Well, sometimes you see, as I have, a cowardly fellow who is very much afraid of jaguars but who is determined to become a fearless jagunço. So this fellow sharpens his knife, hides in a cave, and manages perhaps to kill a jaguar, after a fierce struggle; then he eats its heart and is filled with mighty courage! You don't see what I am driving at? I'll tell you. From not smoking, I was assailed by rash impulses that made me grit my teeth, as if I were angry with the whole world. I stood it. I did a lot of walking, taking firm steps: one, two, three, four, back and forth. I felt like having a drink from the bottle. I growled no. I walked some more. I was not at all sleepy, nor was I tired. From within me sprang new life. Great is God's goodness. No more fear? None whatever! Now let them come, Zé-Bebelos's gang or a mob of soldiers—and they would find me, all right! They would find

me—and how! I was ready for any sort of encounter; I would
fall on them, primed for bloodshed, blade for blade. I even
wished they would come, and get it over with for good. Then I
heard footsteps and looked around: it was Reinaldo approaching. He wanted to have a talk with me.

I could not so quickly close my heart to him. He knew that.
I felt it. And he was laboring under a misconception: he thought
that I was put out, and I wasn't. He mistook for ill will my soberness born of self-control. Had he come to bring me comfort? "Riobaldo, my friend—" he said. I was breathing hard,
feeling little patience for trivial matters, and so I barely answered. Ordinarily he would have taken offense. But this time
he did not. "Riobaldo, I never thought you were bad-tempered,"
he chaffed me.

I made no reply, and we stood silent for some moments. We
could hear the sounds of the animals grazing contentedly in the
high grass. Reinaldo came over close to me. The more harshly I
acted toward him, the friendlier he seemed to be, I was thinking, meanly. I think I looked at him with eyes that showed it.
He did not see or notice this. Ah, he was fond of me all right, I
can tell you that.

But now, thank goodness, he said tersely:

"Riobaldo, there is something personal that I must tell you, I
can't hide it any longer. Listen: my name is not really Reinaldo.
That is an assumed name I had to adopt, please don't ask me
why. I have my reasons. People's lives take seven turns, they
say. Life is not even one's own."

He spoke without arrogance and without pride, but rather
hastily, perhaps with a nervous eagerness to get it over with.

"You were a boy, and I was a boy. We crossed the river in a
canoe. We met at that river landing. From that day on we were
friends." This was so, I agreed. Then I heard:

"Well, then, my name, my real one, is Diadorim. Keep this secret, but always, when we are alone, you must call me Diadorim, I beg of you, Riobaldo."

As I listened to him, it seemed so strange. I kept repeating
the name to myself, to get used to it. He held out his hand.
From that hand I received assurances. And from his eyes too.

Eyes that looked at me, so expressive, so large they seemed almost sad. His soul was in his face. I sensed what the two of us
wanted, then I said: "Diadorim—Diadorim!" With deep affection. He smiled gravely. And I liked him, liked him, liked him. I
longed for him to need my protection, for the rest of our lives:
me interceding for him, standing up for him, fighting for him.
What disturbed me were his eyes, but they did not weaken me.
Diadorim.

As the sun was setting, we left and headed for Canabrava and
Barra. That day had been mine, it belonged to me. We were
traveling through level meadows; the moon was coming up. A
bright moon. The sertão was near—that wild Upper North.
These rivers must run swift, I said to myself. The sertão is like
that, you know: everything uncertain, everything certain. The
moon bright as day. Moonlight filling the night.

Reinaldo telling me that Diadorim was his real name—it was
as though he were telling me about some happening in a distant land. It was a name, nothing more. What is a name? A
name does not give; a name receives. I did not feel any curiosity as to the reason for this concealment. Perhaps some crime of
which he had repented, fleeing from some other place; or devotion to a patron saint. But nevertheless, he wanted me alone to
know his true name, and for me alone to pronounce it. I understood the significance of this. He did not want our friendship to be a mere accident, something casual, without meaning. He was giving me his friendship. And friendship given is
love. I was thinking, ready to shout with joy: thinking to make
it last longer. All happiness, even of the moment, creates a longing. Even one like that: illicit happiness, misborn. A little bird
falls in flight, but its wings go on fluttering against the ground.

Nowadays I turn all that over in my mind: I review and compare it. Isn't all love a kind of comparison? And how is it that
love is born? I'm going to tell you about my Otacília. It wasn't
until sometime later that I came to know Otacília well; then
there occured the awful calamity I will tell you about afterwards.
But I'll tell you now about my first meeting with her, although
I'll be jumping ahead of time. This is how it was. Over on this
side we had suffered all kinds of reverses, and we learned that

the Judases had also crossed the São Francisco, so we pushed on, seeking the aid of Medeiro Vaz, our one remaining hope. I had come with Diadorim, with Alaripe, and with João Vaqueiro, in addition to Jesualdo and Fafafa. We headed up a stream towards Buritís-Altos, until we came to the Santa Catarina ranch. We knew that the owner was in sympathy with us, and we were to wait there for a message. As we drew near, the shadows began to lengthen, and by the time we arrived, night had closed in. But the owner, whose name was Sôr Amadeu, wasn't there; no, he wouldn't be back until tomorrow. The man who appeared and spoke to us was a little old man, old enough to be a saint. He talked to us from an upstairs balcony—he seemed to mistrust our looks. He did not ask us to come up, nor did he order any food for us, but he gave us leave to sleep in the shed of the sugar mill. This little old man was Otacília's grandfather, and he was called Nhô Vô Anselmo. But while he was speaking, and in spite of the confusion and the barking of the dogs, I made out by the faint light of a candle there inside, the form of a girl by the window. A girl with a round face framed in long hair. And a certain smile. Waters to quicken my thirst. I said to myself: if Our Lady should appear to me some day in a dream or shadow, she would be like that, that little head, that little face. Ah, youth makes nothing seem impossible! Otacília. Did I deserve a prize like that?

What about Diadorim, you will say—did I not notice any change in his manner of speaking to me, of looking at me, in his fondness for me? No, no I didn't, I can assure you. Other things, perhaps. Do you doubt it? It was that he loved me with his soul. Do you understand me? Reinaldo—I mean, Diadorim. Oh, but he could be terrible when he wanted to. You can't imagine! Have you ever seen a jaguar, her mouth wide open, snarling with rage for her cubs? Have you seen wild bulls fighting in the uplands, or a rattlesnake's seven lightning strikes, or a mad band of peccaries rampaging through the woods? Then you haven't seen Reinaldo in a fight! These things must be seen to be believed. The devil in the street, in the middle of the whirlwind.

Like what happened that time shortly after we had dismounted at Hermógenes's camp. Ah, what a squalid dump that was. A mixed mob of desperadoes, everything about them breathing slovenliness and bandit cunning. They were encamped between Furado-de-São-Roque and Furado-do-Sapo, alongside the Riberão da Macaúba, where the Jaíba woods end. We had arrived there early one afternoon. I soon discovered that the place was a hellhole, but after three days I got used to it.

As I was saying about Reinaldo, I mean, Diadorim: anyone who did not know him, soon got acquainted with him. We had finally caught up, and we were happy to meet up with so many comrades-in-arms; all for one, and one for all. We entered their midst, mixed with them, and built a little fire around which to squat and talk. Nothing special to talk about—you know how it is, sir: around a fire the talk is always about trifling matters. Somebody told about their encounters with Zé Bebelo, and we told our story, everything that had happened on our trip, which wasn't much to tell. But Diadorim was such a handsome chap, with unusually delicate features, that a couple of the men sized him up as lacking in masculinity, and put him down as green at his job. And so before long they began taking digs at him. One of them was a rascal nicknamed Fancho-Bode; the other, a ragged bully, was called Fulorêncio. A bad pair. The smoke from the embers blew into Diadorim's face. "The smoke is bothering the pretty boy," mocked Fancho-Bode. There was deliberate grossness in his tone of voice. We two remained silent. There was no point in starting a fight. But the fellow wouldn't drop the subject. He got up, and began shaking his hips, puckering up his lips as for a kiss, making lascivious movements and snapping his fingers, in a shuffling kind of dance. Diadorim got to his feet and stepped away from the fire. I saw exactly what he was doing: giving himself room. But that Fancho-Bode was bent on trouble, and tried to bump Diadorim belly to belly. And the other, a filthy Negro, on the side line, egged him on in a falsetto voice, singing through his nose:

> *Have fun, have fun, Gaudêncio,*
> *And what about me, Fulorêncio?*

That did it! Suddenly all hell broke loose, but I already knew what was coming. With the rush of a wild steer Diadorim threw himself at Fancho-Bode, drove his fists into his face—one to the jaw, the other under the chin—then kicked him furiously. Fancho-Bode fell to the ground with Diadorim leaning over him, his dagger at the man's gullet, touching a spot just above the Adam's apple, ready to slip it in, the point pricking the skin to remind him what a quick death would feel like. Diadorim had only to lean a little harder and the thing would be done. In the twinkling of an eye, I had my gun out. Hell, I wasn't just warning the others—I was set to kill, if necessary. I think they realized it. The fact is that in a showdown I was never afraid. They scented this, the way a dog does. Nobody made a move. That Fulorêncio instantly stopped his indecent performance, took one look at me, then didn't want to look again. "On your feet, stupid!" Diadorim ordered Fancho to get up and reach for his knife, and they'd see who was the better man. But Fancho-Bode laughed, with a shameless grin, as if it had all been a friendly joke: "By God! You're a real man, pal, old fellow!" It was disgusting to look at him, crestfallen, his face dirty with ugly hair growing all over it. I put my gun away, with slow deliberation. Those two men were not cowards; they just weren't interested in dying so soon. Those two were not well thought of. The other men showed by their friendly attitude that they liked us. And Fulorêncio himself, trying to be friendly, asked me: "Old man, will you buy what I dreamed today?" To which I replied, also in a playful manner: "Only if you will take money from the alligator's mother!" They all laughed, but they weren't laughing at me. Fulorêncio laughed too, but it was a sickly laugh. Quietly, quietly, I thought to myself: "Some day one of us is going to have to eat the other. Or if not, our grandchildren will have to settle the matter, or our children's grandchildren."

Once everything was peaceable again, they offered me a drink of blue-white januária, I took a swallow. That night I slept without waking once.

As I've told you all along, I am a good shot.

Those two men, Fancho-Bode and Fulorêncio, got theirs in our first encounter with one of Zé Bebelo's scouting parties. Because of one thing and another, someone said that I had shot them during an exchange of gunfire. It could have happened, for instance, in the confusion, you know, sir, when bullets think for themselves. Afterwards they even said I did it on purpose, to keep those two from trying later on to get even through some trick or treachery. It is not true. I didn't do it, and I didn't even call down curses on them. They died because their time had come. As a matter of fact, only one of them died. The other was taken to prison—I think—and must have spent a good ten years in jail. In the jail at Montes Claros, perhaps. I am not an assassin. They cooked up that lie about me—you know how people are. Now, I'll agree on one thing: if they had not died when they did, they would have spent the rest of the time lying in wait for me, and Diadorim too, preparing some treachery for us when the right moment came. In stories, in books, doesn't it happen like that? To relate stories full of surprises and deeds of daring may be much more entertaining, but hell, when you are the one who is doing the everyday living, these fancy turns of events don't work. The best thing to do with a treacherous enemy is to get rid of him quickly, with a well-aimed shot, before he can carry out his plan! Also, and I know this for a fact: wherever I went, even though I am orderly and peacable by nature, there were always many people who were afraid of me. They found me strange.

All that I can say is that I am a good shot: I have yet to meet anyone who can match me in marksmanship. Fortunately for me, ever since I was a boy. The German Vupes taught me little. By that time, I was already good. With any kind of firearm: revolver, carbine, shotgun, blunderbuss, army musket, or rifle. I don't brag too much about it, because a natural aim like that is a gift from God. As my compadre Quelemém explained it to me, in another life and incarnation I must have handled a gun a lot. Could it be? Marksmanship, you will agree, is a talent of the mind. Was that Vupes a prophet? On a certain occasion, I went into a poolroom, and my friends wanted me to play, to fill in as a partner. Billiards, I mean. I knew nothing whatever of the game. I had never had a cue in my hand.

"Makes no difference," Advindo said. "You play with me,

since I am an expert. João Nonato and Escopil will play against us."

I accepted. It was agreed that Advindo could coach me and call the shots, with words and advice, but without touching my hand or arm, or laying a finger on the cue. Can you believe that even under those conditions I did not make the least error? Advindo would point out the best play, I would lean over, relax my belly muscles, and drive my cue, aiming at the green: the shot would be perfect, caroms striking and rebounding, backspinning, perfect cushioning, spinning and reverse spinning; but what pleased me most was to hear the clicking of those gleaming, rolling balls.

And so, as I was saying, they respected me for my marksmanship, and tried to give me a nickname: first, Cerzidor,[1] then Tatarana,[2] but they didn't take. Nicknames almost never stuck to me. Would it be because I never remain the same?

Let me tell you what took place, what I saw, in Hermógenes camp!

Ruffians. Toughs. From the start I was repelled by the sight of them. There were more than a hundred and fifty, all wild, hardened outlaws, riffraff, scum. I was apprehensive at first, but kept my eyes and ears open, and soon adjusted myself to the situation. I did so half-heartedly, however. Typical Hermógenes men. There were good ones and bad ones, like everywhere in this world. For every bad one, you soon meet a worse one. The fact is that we were at war. But even so, no one was troubled by the threat of great dangers. Life was one constant rough-housing and joking, to pass the time. They never quieted down. Bunches of men, wandering about aimlessly, loafing, or standing around in groups; some sleeping in the shade, like a steer; others stretched out on the ground but not sleeping—just lying there. They were dressed every which way: one fellow wore a wide sash of red wool around his waist; another sported a beaver hat and a black vest of fine cloth, a regular dude; others had on straw rain capes, even though it wasn't raining; however, nobody wore anything white, for light-colored clothing

---

[1] Cerzidor: dragonfly.
[2] Tatarana: fire caterpillar.

makes you an easy target. But never did any of them go about naked or indecently exposed in front of others, that never. Walking or sitting around, playing games, wrestling, chewing strong tobacco and spitting far, or smoking, crumbling tobacco or shredding it in the palm, leisurely—aside from this, all they did was talk. Sometimes they would swap their trifling possessions, things they no longer wanted, bought cheap. But nobody stole! To steal was to risk death! They sang ditties, and some sang herding songs, without cattle. Or looked after their bellies. The only work they did was to clean their guns—with notches cut on the side of the stock. Whatever else they did was to kill time. For that reason, so it was said, a lot of intrigue and backbiting went on; the bootlickers caused most of it. They even had dogs, running around loose, but each had a master, and it was asking for trouble to mistreat one of them.

After awhile they accepted me, but with reservations. Was this because they were naturally so reserved; or were they standoffish because they found me different from themselves? I knew myself, in fact, to be of a different extraction. For example, it soon became clear to me from something I witnessed that they wanted to be known as one hundred percent jagunços, not alone in deed but in looks as well. I even saw some of the men off in a corner engaged in a strange operation: they were chipping off their own teeth, sharpening them to a point! Can you imagine! The tortures they endured would cause vomiting, the agony was enough to drive you mad. Those working at it were Jesualdo, a likable young fellow, Araruta and Nestor; the ones instructing them were Simião and Acauã. It was the fad to put points on the front teeth, to make them look like the sharp teeth of the ferocious piranha of the São Francisco River. And don't think, sir, that they had suitable tools for the job, a file or rasp. No—they used a knife. Jesualdo did it by himself, squatting on his heels. He would work the cutting edge of the blade along the edge of a tooth and pound the knife handle with a stone. Without a mirror, without being able to see. There he was, his mouth open, slobbering, sometimes drooling blood. At most, he groaned, screwing up his face, for it really hurt him a lot. But he stood it. When it got too much for him, he would rinse out his mouth with water and rum. The other two did the same. Araruta, too, was going it alone, striking the blade with the side of another. But not Nestor—it was Simião who operated on him, using a little hammer to pound with; Nestor no doubt had to pay him something for this. The practice revolted me. "To hell with that!" I said. "Then you don't want me to work on you, too?" Simião asked jokingly. He made a face at me, and would you believe it, sir, he who wielded his blade on others, did not have a single tooth in his gums, as I could see when he opened wide that red toothless mouth to show me. "I don't think one needs to masquerade to be brave," I retorted. Then Acauã, with whom I was already well acquainted, answered curtly: "It's a matter of taste." But another one, coming closer, countered dryly: "Everything in life is a matter of taste, pal. But this isn't one of mine!"

I looked at the man who had backed me up. It was Luís Pajeú, whose dagger-knife had the brand name also of Pajeú, he being from the Pajeú sertão, in the State of Pernambuco. An outspoken fellow, burned dark by the sun, with curly hair, and tremendous courage. Ah, but what was lacking, what he no longer had, was one ear which had been cut off close to his head, like a brand mark. Where could Luís Pajeú have left that ear? "It's not my taste to have my teeth chipped," he said briefly, in his soft, sing-song voice. Someone else spoke up loud and strong: "Hell, where I came from, what they sharpen are bulls' horns!" This was Fafafa, who talked a lot when he'd been drinking, and was a great horseman. I'll have more to say about him later.

There was no shortage of food there as I soon found out. Plenty of staples and good liquor. Where did it all come from, in that poverty-stricken region, and we encamped in a desert almost? And such a stock of munitions that they didn't even need what we had brought, and sent them on ahead to Joca Ramiro's hideout, near the settlement of Bró? And the money to pay that mob of bandits who were there on hire? Ah, robbery was their trade, they even talked of attacking large towns.

Now look, sir: around '96, when the hill men took it into their heads to move in, São Francisco fell without delay or trouble.

But a few years ago, when Andalécio and Antônio Dó thought to
try the same thing, with almost fifteen hundred mounted men,
the people of São Francisco got word of it, banded together, and
received them with gunfire. They say the fight lasted three
hours. They had set up barricades at the entrances to the streets
—piles of sand and rock, cut-down trees—they fought like good
citizens! Afterwards, the bandits returned with redoubled fury
and subdued most of the town, except for Major Alcides Amaral
and some soldiers whom they surrounded in two or three houses
and a yard and who kept on fighting nights and days. Andalécio
was out for revenge, because on some previous occasion Major
Amaral had arrested him and cut off his mustache. I learned
about it from somebody who was there. He recalled with fear
and trembling that during the night-long shooting, Andalécio,
who was in command, would shout furiously: "Come on out,
you dog! Come out and you'll see! A man's mustache is something you don't cut off!" It froze the blood in your veins just to
hear him.

Finally, the Major was rescued by the police commissioner,
Doctor Cantuária Guimarães. He hurried over from Januária
with a big bunch of jagunços hired by ranchers who were supporters of the government. When the attackers had been driven
off, the dead were dug up, in order to make an accurate count.
There were more than sixty of them, some fourteen in one
grave! These things did not occur during my time, because by
then I had given up lawlessness to become a cattleman and a
grower of cotton and cane. But the greatest thing happened just
recently, following the big row in Carinhanha—slaughter, blood
running all over the place, as you know. *"Carinhanha is a pretty
little place"* the riversiders and boatmen on the São Francisco
sing. Carinhanha was always the domain of a man of prestige
and power: Colonel João Duque. I once met Antônio Dó, in
Vargem Bonita. A little fair was being held there, and he showed
up with a few of his henchmen; they stood around in a group,
silent and apart. At one time Andalécio was a good friend of
mine. Ah, the era of jagunços had to come to an end, and towns
will do away with the sertão. Or will they?

I could not figure out at first who was in command over all

of us. It was Hermógenes. But about fifty—among them Acauã, Simião, Luís Pajeú, Jesualdo and Fafafa—were João Goanha's men and took their orders from him. And there was another group of braves belonging to Ricardão. Where was Ricardão, by the way? Recruiting more gun fighters, up near Bahia. Sô Candelário was expected too, with his men. And so was the big chief, who was over all of them—Joca Ramiro. He was said to be in Palmas at the time. I found all that very confusing. Titão Passos, who was in charge of a small group of men, was nevertheless highly respected. The system differed greatly from that of Zé Bebelo. You see, jagunços govern themselves in an invisible sort of way, very difficult for me to explain. It is a kind of subtle understanding, that doesn't call for words, as though there was a tacit and definite agreement among them, somewhat (to use a poor comparison) like that which exists among animals—a band of wild pigs, or a herd of cattle, for example. They made a secret of everything. One day the order was given: round up all the animals, saddle and pack. They were going to be taken for concealment and grazing, between sierras, in Ribeirão Poço Triste, a bottomland. In my opinion, even the location they gave was probably a lie. But I had to hand over my horse, against my will. On foot that way, I felt naked, exposed. And there were little things that annoyed me. While I had my horse I had saddle pouch and saddlebags; I could keep my things in them. At night I would hang the saddle on the branch of a tree, toss my roll of clothes under it, and lie down close by, to sleep in peace. Now I was being put to inconvenience. I couldn't carry my stuff around with me—the weight of my arms, bullets and cartridges, was about all I could manage. I asked a fellow where one put things. "Oh hell, throw it down somewhere. Get rid of it. What have you got in that roll —gold?"

What did they care? All around cooking fires were blazing, smoke smelling of rosemary, pots hanging from trivets made of sticks, the good smell of meat browning and roasting on a spit, and potatoes and cassava roots always hot in the ashes. Manioc and rapadura: heaps of it. Slabs of jerked beef. Even though there was no shortage of dried meat, frequently some of the men would go out and come back driving a steer, which they butchered and divided up. Many laced their manioc water with brandy, pouring a finger of it into their gourd. I had never before seen anyone drink it that way. Different customs! You should have seen Fafafa open a square hole in the ground, fill it with live coals, and lay a big piece of bloody meat right on them; then turn the sizzling meat over with the point of his knife until it was just charred. This I really did not care for. What I missed most was a nice little fricassee of chicken with okra and summer squash, swimming in gravy, or a stew of manioc mush with gumbo. I was homesick for my godfather's ranch at São Gregório—I had lived there like a pig in clover. Diadorim noticed my glumness, and said to cheer me up: "Riobaldo, there are better times ahead. At the moment we are mired down."

To be with Diadorim, and to hear a word from him, was enough to console me. But even so, I did not think it wise for us to spend too much time together, away from the others. I guessed that they were thinking evil, that they had suspicions about the nature of our relationship. Those men were always together, everybody milling around with everybody else. Everything was talked about, openly, by all. It was different and better when we were with Medeiro Vaz. Most of the men there were from the gerais, where people are quieter, more reserved, dwellers in the wide spaces. But, eventually, you get accustomed; that is to say, I got used to it. I had no fear of being relieved of my money, of which I had a good bundle left, for Zé Bebelo had always paid me on the dot and I had no place to spend it. I wanted them to know right from the start how good a shot I was. They enjoyed watching me. "Come on, Tatarana, shoot the pips out of the ten," they would ask me, for fun. At two hundred feet I could put a bullet in the socket of a tin candleholder. Not just once—everytime. In this way I put a stop to the thing that was burning me up, the tittle-tattle. "If anyone says anything bad about me, I don't care. But let them do it behind my back. Anyone who comes to me blabbing and talebearing is a dirty dog, and I'll teach him the name of the whore who bore him." I let them know.

You know, sir, "the name of the whore," and the rest of it, meant—my trigger. Just so they wouldn't unlearn or forget about it, I picked up my rifle—I had a fourteen-shot Winchester repeater—and put on an exhibition. "Drill a line of holes, Tatarana!" they urged me. Did I do it? I never missed, and to clinch it, I repeated the performance with my revolver. "Float a hair up in the air and I'll hit it." I was as good as my word.

I went about pleasant enough, wearing my triple bandolier, which was always filled. Whenever they praised or bragged about me, I took it quietly. About that time there sprang up in me the desire to destroy someone, a certain person. You can laugh, sir: your laughter shows wisdom. I know. But I want you to think my crazy words over. Everything that happens is a warning. If not, why should that pleasant idea have come to me —how jolly it would be to put a bullet low in Hermógenes's forehead?

Hatred for certain creatures takes root in us. Granted that Hermógenes was bad, bad. I have told you, sir, that those people were bandits. Did I expect them to be kind and gentle? Of course not. I was no child, and I was never a fool. I understood what it meant to be a jagunço, even though I was a sailor on my maiden voyage. One day they grabbed a fellow who had come in treacherously to spy on us for the Bebelos. They murdered him. Watch out for men like that. They eat snakes raw. They have to. For that reason, to keep the men from getting soft or faint-hearted, even Sô Candelário, who prided himself on his kindness, even in peace time would order them out on raids, just for practice. It is hard, sometimes, to be always evil; it takes practice in villainy, experience. But as time went by everybody's mind became poisoned. I was afraid they would find me soft-hearted, would learn that I was not made for that sort of existence, that I had pity on all Jesus' creatures. "And what about God, Diadorim?" I asked him one time. He looked at me, with that little silence of his, then said in reply: "Joca Ramiro gave five thousand milreis to the vicar-priest of Espinosa."

But Hermógenes was a hater, by nature, a frozen scourge. He

liked to kill, for his petty pleasure. He did not brag about his deeds; he pretended that he wasn't bad. On one occasion, however, when they brought in an enemy, he ordered: "Keep that one."

I knew what that meant. They took the poor fellow into the woods, and left him there, half dead of fright, tied to a stake. Hermógenes was in no hurry; he sat on for a while, at his ease. You could detect the hideous pleasure in his eyes. After awhile he went there alone, leisurely. He had spent hours sharpening his knife. When it was over, I kept watching Hermógenes: he was very pleased with himself, all cock-a-hoop. He made jokes. But, even while eating or talking or laughing, his mouth opened in a kind of grimace, as though, unconsciously, a mouth of suffering. I did not want to look at him so as not to see that scorpion; it made my flesh crawl. Then I would look at his feet —enormous, bare, covered with scabs, chilblains, sore-infested. I would look at his hands. I came to the conclusion that so much evil must be concentrated in those hands; I looked at them with mounting repugnance. With that hand he ate, with it he shook hands with others. Meanwhile I was comparing him with Zé Bebelo. At that moment I loved Zé Bebelo, almost as a son must love his father. Suddenly I realized that what I wanted was for Zé Bebelo to win, because he was the one who was in the right. Zé Bebelo ought to come, come in strength, and really wipe out that hell of bandits to the last man! There I was, outwardly fulfilling my agreement to the letter, but inwardly, in the depth of my heart, I was a traitor, faithless. I did not want to go crazy thinking. I leaned my back against a tree, and began to talk with Diadorim. How was it that Joca Ramiro, being the great leader he was, so noble in his ways, was willing to have as his subaltern a creature like this Hermógenes, stamped with evil? Diadorim listened to me impatiently, as though doubting that I was right in my mind.

"Riobaldo, what do you use your head for? Hermógenes is tough, but as loyal as they come. Do people cut meat with a knife or a wooden spoon? Would you want nice, well-behaved men for us to fight Zé Bebelo and the Government dogs with?"

After that setback, I kept quiet the rest of the day. Moreover, there was something else I was concealing even from Diadorim: I was already touching bottom in falsity, I was sleeping with treachery. I had lost my guiding star, and melancholy came over me.

Was I, then, so different from all the others there? Yes, I was. Fortunately for me. That gang of ruffians, loafing around day and night, fighting, drinking, forever eating. "Have you eaten, wolf?" And shouting nonsense, even beginning to turn their attention to Diadorim and me. One day one of them said: "Hey, this Reinaldo sure is a good friend. Like when Leopoldo got killed he nearly died, too, he grieved so much."

I purposely paid no attention, but it didn't do any good. All the time I kept brooding over that story, that name of Leopoldo. I took it as a personal offense that Diadorim should have had a bosom friend before me, even though it was a long time ago. Until finally I realized that what I needed was a woman.

And was I like those men? I was. As there were no women there, they talked of bestialities. "Just turn me loose," said one "and no female I meet up with will escape." And they related instances of girls they had corrupted and used for their debauches. "Women are such poor wretches," Diadorim said to me once, after listening to those stories. Those men, in rut, smelled like goats. They found what they wanted somehow. God saved me from becoming addicted to their habits. The first one was a pretty girl, and I had her all to myself. At the beginning she screamed and cursed at me, bit me, clawed me. Finally, when I had overcome her she lay deathly still, her eyes closed; if it had not been for her heart beating against my breast, I would have been afraid. But I could not stop. Then all of a sudden she began to tremble. She opened her eyes, accepted me, gasping out her pleasure—it was a miracle. It was as though I had won her love! If I could, I would have taken that girl with me, and been good to her. Later, at a place near Serra Nova, there was another, a little brown girl, and this one submitted to me, lying utterly cold, as if she was a rock on the ground. Ah, it made me feel like a monster—and, would you believe it, sir— the girl was praying the while she endured me. Hastily I fled from there, leaving her my money, and I even cursed her. I

never again took advantage of a woman. Considering the oppor-
tunities I had, and which I let go by, I hope that God will take it
into account. What I wanted was to see the satisfaction I gave
them. Like Rosa'uarda the daughter of Assis Wababa, who, as
I told you, was a big businessman; all that time he never suspected anything. Like that Nhorinhá, the daughter of Ana Duzuza. You must forgive my telling you things like this which
by rights should not be mentioned. But everything I am telling,
is because I think it really necessary.

Among so many, I fraternized with only a few of those jagunços, trusting to my guardian angels. But only the fairly decent
ones. These were: Capixúm, an even-keeled backwoodsman,
from the plains of São Felipe, who had moved around a lot;
Fonfrêdo, who could chant all the priest's prayers, ate no meat
of any kind, and never said who he was nor where he was
from; the one whose name rhymed with his, Sesfrêdro, I have
already told you about; Testa-em-Pé, a crafty Bahian, who
drank a lot; Paspe, a herdsman from Jaíba, the handiest and
most obliging fellow I ever ran across; good-hearted Dadá
Santa-Cruz, nicknamed Caridoso, who always wanted us to give
our left-over food to the poor people who were too shy to come
asking for it; Carro-de-Boi, who s-s-stuttered. Catôcho, a light
mulatto—a spell was supposed to have made him immune to
bullets. Lindorífico, from the uplands of Minas Novas, with a
passion for hoarding money. Diôlo, a thick-lipped Negro. Ju-
vento, Adalgizo, Sangue-de-Outro. Eh, so many—why did I ever
get started describing them? Dagobé, Eleuterio, Pescoço-Prêto,
José Amigo . . .

What I am telling you, sir, is what I lived: the hard thing is
not to be good and act decently; what is really difficult is to
know clearly what you want, and then to be able to carry it out.
Ezirino killed a comrade, Batatinha, he was called, a poor
skinny half-breed, whose only fault was his damned habit of
contradicting whatever anybody said. Ezirino ran away. Then it
began to be rumored that he had run away to join up with the
Zé Bebelos, for money, and that Batatinha had died only because he knew about this. Everybody was all worked up, seeing
traps and snares everywhere.

We changed camp, moving to a more secluded spot, some seven leagues away, toward the west. I saw plainly that we weren't doing this to make an escape, but that Hermógenes, Titão Passos and João Goanhá had decided it earlier to get into a better position in case Zé Bebelo showed up. Finally, to everyone's satisfaction, ten of Sô Candelário's men arrived. They brought pack animals with more salt, good coffee, and a keg of dried codfish. Delfim was one of them, the driver. And Luzié, from Alagoas. That day I went out with a squad, patrolling the roads on the lookout for Zé Bebelo's men; we rode more than three leagues and returned in the middle of the night.

Early the next morning I learned that there had been dancing the previous evening. "Diadorim, do you dance?" I asked right away. "Dance? Why, he would be at home in a ballroom."

The answer came from Garanço, he of the pig eyes. Garanço was a simple backwoodsman, with merry features, and very pleasant by nature. At times he got ideas like those of a small child. He gave his weapons names: the big knife was torturúm, the revolver, nightingale, the carbine, bleating goat. He was always good for a laugh. More and more, Garanço had taken to seeking our company, mine and Diadorim's; on that occasion, as usual, he came over to us. At times, like this one, he filled me with real anger. Diadorim said nothing; he was lying on his back, on a sheepskin, his head on a sheaf of cut grass. That was how he always slept—Diadorim did not like a hammock. Garanço was from a place called Morpará, on the São Francisco River. Whether you liked it or not, he wanted you to listen while he related long episodes of his life. It became a bore. Afterwards, Diadorim got up and went off somewhere. I rested my eyes for a moment on the beauty of him, so handsomely set-up, always wearing his jacket, which he never took off, and his cowboy pants of buckskin, tanned with peppertree bark. Suddenly, there was something I had to do; I went and lay me down on the sheepskin, in the hollow Diadorim's body had pressed in the grass, my face where his head rested. I paid no attention to Garanço but listened only to a guitarist strumming his guitar. I struggled to keep my mind off Diadorim. Soon I neither saw nor heard anything. I lay there day-dreaming, my thoughts as

unfettered as the drifting air. Did I think about the ranch at
São Gregório? Not about the ranch itself, no; but I felt homesick for the birds there, the pool in the creek, the mill pounding
day and night, the big kitchen and glowing oven, the cool, dark
rooms in the house, the corrals to one side, the balcony from
which to watch the clouds. Do you know what I mean, sir? I'm
not telling it very well because I am stirring the ashes of things
lived long ago, with few embers left, trying to warm my heart
once more on those remembrances. Or I am trying to pick up
the thread, to follow the real course of events, what happened
and what didn't. Sometimes it is not easy. Take my word that it
isn't.

Well, now, in those days, at that time, fairly important things
must have happened that I didn't notice or which did not im-
press me. Even today I cannot figure out what they were. But,
all of a sudden that morning, I recalled a name: Siruiz. I remember that I asked Garanço about that boy Siruiz, who sang
things whose shadow already lay on my heart. What I wanted to
know was not so much about Siruiz himself, as about that virgin maid, that maiden fair, the betrothed, and those verses the
like of which I had never been able to match. Garanço replied:
"Eh, oh, him—Siruiz is dead. He was killed in the shooting between the Morcêgo and Suassuàpara rivers, this side of the
Pacuí."

This news shocked and depressed me. It was as if he had said:
"Siruiz? But wasn't it you people yourselves who killed him?"
Not I. On that occasion I was far away, in Pedra Branca, and
did not even see the fight. How could I have?

Garanço used to take snuff. He was not too bright. He asked if
Siruiz had been a friend of mine, a relative perhaps. "Maybe he
was, "I answered, vaguely. I saw that Garanço didn't like it. It is
always difficult to live close to people, always with their eyes on
you. I did not even wish to inquire further, for I was sure
Garanço knew nothing worth telling. But I remembered sadly
the song Siruiz had sung. So, Siruiz was dead. Then they taught
me the other one, the song which our troop sang as they traveled, sang as they fought, always:

Tra-la-la, my Bahiana,
I was going but now I'm not:
I pretend
I am going
Over there, oh Bahiana,
But halfway there I turn back.

Are you learning it? I can't carry a tune. Not because I have a
mean mouth, as one might say. I am not mean, I am a man
who likes people; when they don't pester me, I am easy-going. I
quarreled with no one there, I accepted the prevailing system
and obeyed its codes. Because of that they made a mistake
about me. That is, one of them made a mistake. A veteran
jagunço called Antenor, from Coração-de-Jesus, I think, began
to try to draw me out, I noticed. He was on close terms with
Hermógenes—that much I knew. He wanted to know what I
thought of Joca Ramiro, Titão Passos, and all the others. Did I
know Sô Candelário, whom they were expecting? Everything I
said, he was weighing my words. I noticed that. And, little by
little, he was trying to sow in me an evil crop: the seeds of
doubt. Always praising and extolling Joca Ramiro, that Antenor
wound up by insinuating to me, a word here, a word there, that
perhaps Joca Ramiro was doing wrong in staying away so long,
that certain low characters were already figuring that he had
deserted his people when they needed him most; that Joca Ramiro was rich, the owner of vast lands, and that he was living
high in the homes of big ranchers and politicos, Sêo Sul de
Oliveira, Colonel Caetano Cordeiro, Doctor Mirabô de Melo,
from whom he received money for munitions and wages. What
did I think?

I listened. Did I answer? Ah, ah. I'm a great one for keeping
a close mouth. I wasn't born yesterday, and I learned early
about men from men. All I said was that doubtless Joca Ramiro
was recruiting men and resources to come to our aid, good jagunços that we were, and that in the meanwhile he had complete trust in Hermógenes, in Titão Passos, João Goanhá, who
had proved their worth and loyalty. I especially lauded Hermóg-

enes and with this Antenor agreed; thus I threw dust in his
eyes. The truth is, he approved everything I had said. But he
kept emphasizing the merits of Hermógenes, and of Ricardão,
too—those two would be first-rate leaders in peace as well as in
war. This fellow Antenor knew how to scratch a snake's chin. A
dangerous character in action, Garanço warned me, with his
shrewd instinct. Action? What I have always seen is that every
act begins with a thought, a thought that persists, spoken or silent, and goes blazing its trail. Antenor had already sowed in
me the shadow of an evil idea, an idea that went sliding down
my back, as insidious as a drop of mist. How can I explain this
to you? As for believing what he had said, I didn't. But in me, to
me, all that was—well, it was like a rank-smelling spot in the
country, some tree perhaps; a fetid place where a skunk had
been brought to bay by the dogs. It was a clear warning I received that day, but less from what I had actually heard than
from what I had already in some way divined. What good was
it? A warning! I think that in nearly every case a warning is not
to ward off punishment but merely to afford solace after the
punishment has come and gone. To hell with it!

I went and found Diadorim. I was feeling a certain uneasiness. I spoke about the present and the past; but I handled it
badly: angrily—unreasonably—right from the start. I think
that because of this, Diadorim did not attach due importance to
my words. Indifferent, sort of. He only showed anger, for a
moment, on hearing that anyone had dared to question Joca
Ramiro's conduct: Joca Ramiro was an emperor, head and
shoulders above anyone else. Joca Ramiro knew what he was
doing, how to rule; nor could his name be bandied about. As for
those two, Hermógenes and Ricardão, without Joca Ramiro they
would collapse in a second, disappear from the face of the
earth—they were worth no more than a flea's hop. Hermógenes?
Sure, a good jagunço, a troop leader, but with no political standing, and no savvy or background. And Ricardão, rich, owner of
ranches, lived only for gain, scheming how to make and put by
money. Of the two, Diadorim liked Ricardão the least:

"He is a money grubbing brute," he said, and snapped his
mouth shut, as if about to spit. Then I said something like this:

"That's all well and good, Diadorim, but to be on the safe side, why don't we get word quietly to Joca Ramiro, just in case?"

I kept talking, concealing my anger the while. Who knows but what Joca Ramiro, with the passage of time, had forgotten how to judge men, failing to sense the changes wrought in them by time? Were Joca Ramiro to come, he could cut out the rotten from the sound, take stock of his braves. He could, he should, get rid of that monster of a Hermógenes. If necessary—well, what of it—we could kill him! Diadorim looked hard at me; I saw in his disapproving astonishment that he did not believe me capable of such evil, even in words. "Like a snake?" he asked. A snake is not malevolent either. What I am is very cautious.

Then cooling off, more friendly toward me, Diadorim began to dissuade me: I hadn't yet had time to understand the customs, I was distrustful of everything and everybody, and he did not know where in the world I got my moon-struck ideas. Sure, Hermógenes had his faults, but he was Joca Ramiro's faithful supporter—he would fight and do battle for him. I should wait a few days longer, and I would see the sun rise. I didn't understand about friendships among the jagunços. Strength and steel, those were the only friends. Was that what he was saying? Ah, no; a friend to me is something different. It is not an arrangement whereby one gives aid to another, and receives it, and the two go abroad the world, swapping help, even though it involves doing injustice to others. A friend, to me, is this: a person with whom you like to talk, as one equal to another, unarmed; someone it gives you pleasure to be near. That—plus any sacrifice. Or, a friend is simply what you are, without needing to define the how or the why of it. Diadorim was my friend; and so were Fafafa, Alaripe, Sesfrêdo. But he didn't want to listen to me. I got over my anger.

I'll tell you, sir: I did not let my thoughts linger even on Diadorim. In those days, then, did I not love him? Yes and no. I did and I didn't. I know, I know that deep inside me I loved him, for always. But one's nature is full of contradictions. There is day and night, inconstancy, in the friendship of love.

What tormented me most of all—this I well recall—was the lack of meaning I found in that environment where I was

trapped among people of that sort. Even after thinking over
Diadorim's words, all I ended up with was that all this was a life
of falsity, of disloyalties. Treachery? The treachery was
mine, call it what you will. Isn't nearly everything one does or
doesn't do, treachery in the end? It has to be, to someone or to
something. It did not take me long to decide what I wanted: I
wanted out. How had I come to this place, and for what reason, and why was I subjecting myself to all that? I would go
away. I had to go away. I was risking my life, throwing away my
youth. Drifting. All I had was Diadorim. What was Diadorim to
me? As I have said, he was not merely someone to be with, to
talk with, to see, but I could not stand to go on living if suddenly I had to be separated from him forever. And my revulsion
for Hermógenes was equally strong. I was rowelled by hate,
which always springs up quickly and sometimes discerns
aright, like the premonition of love. Hermógenes—Beelzebub.
There he was poised in the shadows. I knew it. Never again, not
even afterwards, did I experience this feeling so strongly as at
that time. Hermógenes, a man who derived his pleasure from
others' fear, others' suffering. By God, then was when I really
began to believe that hell was possible. The Eyeless One is remote. Only what one sees in men, what men experience, is possible. And that hell was close to me, it was enveloping me. I saw
and dreamed many dreadful things in the limitless confines of
dreams.

I would leave, run away, at once. What about Diadorim? The
idea did not enter my mind that I could leave Diadorim there.
He was my comrade, he had to go with me. Diadorim did not
understand me. He withdrew into his shell.

I blame myself a lot for this, for not having had the courage
to speak frankly. But if I had said everything, Diadorim would
have stopped me, and in doing so, would not have understood
me. Undoubtedly he would have come out with the name of
Joca Ramiro! Joca Ramiro. You could not form a clear image of
him, he was nothing but a name, a name given him at birth,
with no visible shape or substance, moving in the distance, if he
moved. There was a moment when I wavered. Was it on that occasion? Or some other? It was once; I remember. My body

longed for Diadorim. I put out my hand to touch him; but as I was about to do so, he looked at me—his eyes stopped me. Diadorim, grave, head held high. I felt a chill. Only his eyes denied me. Did I know what was happening to me? My body longed for his body. Terribly. Gloom surrounded us, as when a downpour threatens. I could bury my head in my arms, and stay that way, like a fool, without coming to any decision. What was it I wanted? I didn't want what was hanging over us, so I fetched an idea from afar. I spoke as in a dream: "Diadorim, haven't you, don't you have a sister, Diadorim?"

Do I know if he laughed? Or what he said, what he answered? I know about sadness, sad waters, the grieving heart beside the bank. Neither sister nor brother did he have. "I have only God, Joca Ramiro—and you, Riobaldo," he declared. Ah, fear makes the heart beat wildly in the breast, but with joy it throbs steady and hard against the ribs, it even hurts. "Diadorim, who was that young man, Leopoldo, your friend who died?" I blurted out, without knowing why: I was not even thinking about that. The words were no sooner out of my mouth than I wished them back. "Leopoldo? A friend of mine, Riobaldo, an honorable friendship," and Diadorim let out a soft sigh. "So they have talked to you about him, too, Riobaldo? Leopoldo was Joca Ramiro's youngest brother." That Joca Ramiro's name, overriding, ruling everything, would somehow be brought into this matter, too, I already knew. But I held my tongue. "Let's go away from here, together, Diadorim? Let's go far away, to the landing on the Janeiro River, to the plains of the sertão, to Curralim, São-Gregório, or to that place in the uplands, called Os-Porcos, where your uncle lived." Eagerly, thirstily, the words tumbled out. But soon I began to lower my eyes, feeling Diadorim's gaze riveted on me, in a silence cold and hard as iron. I was amazed at the bitterness of his scorn, doubting my own reason. What I had said was crazy. Diadorim waited. He was unyielding. I left him, wanting to forget quickly what had happened. My face was burning up.

I walked and fretted until I remembered—Garanço. All right, Garanço, he would go with me, follow me in everything; he was a poor stick just waiting for any kindly order. He didn't even

know this himself, but it was so; what he needed was someone's friendship. There he was, bent over, with a big head and
short neck like a cicada. He was cooking souari nuts in a can.
"Well, well, here we are," he said. I struck up a conversation.
He listened to me, nodding his head in agreement, and trying to
look as if he understood. But he didn't, really. A bit more
persuasion on my part, and Garanço would join me in my flight.
At most he might ask: "What about Reinaldo?" because he was
used to seeing Diadorim and me as a pair, and he wanted to be
the third. To that I would answer: "It's a secret, Garanço, you
know, a secret, let's go!" and that Diadorim would come later.
Garanço was different; something in his nature set him apart
from the other jagunços.

But I didn't go so far as to say what was in my mind. I didn't
want to, I didn't tell him anything. What was I going to do with
that simpleton on my hands, fleeing southward or northward, in
the sertão? All he knew was to follow where I led, ruled by my
wishes and my ideas; a companion of that sort did not add to
my safety at all. Did I want a shadow? An echo? A dog? No, I
wouldn't attempt it with him; better to wait; I would stay on a
while longer, whatever happened. Some day, perhaps, Diadorim
would change his mind. Garanço was regaling himself with the
souari nuts, slowly grinding that revolting yellow mass between his teeth. I refused his offer of some. I never eat them;
absent-minded that I am, I was always afraid of the prickles
getting stuck in my tongue. "Well, well, here we are," Garanço
repeated, highly pleased. My friendship overwhelmed him a
little, simple-hearted creature that he was. I'll tell you, sir:
that day I looked down a lonesome road.

Ah, but I am not telling the truth. Do you sense it? Telling
something is a very, very difficult business. Not because of the
years that have gone by, but because certain things of the past
have a way of changing about, switching places. Was what I
have said true? It was. But did it happen? Now I'm not so
sure. So many hours and people, so many things at so many
times, all mixed up together. If I had been a person of more
action and less thought, I would have slipped away quietly
during the night, made ten leagues by morning, hidden out

during the day, then ten more leagues, crossing the São Felipe, the sierras, the Vinte-e-Uma-Lagoas, come out on the São Francisco right opposite Januária, crossed over into settled country, and I would be "home." Suppose I was caught on the road by either Bebelo's or Hermógenes's men, and they killed me? I would have died with the bleat of a sheep or the howl of a hound; but it would have been a different fate and a greater courage. Wasn't it worth it? Anyway, I didn't do it. Who can say if I even thought seriously about Diadorim, or, if I did, that it wasn't by way of an excuse? An excuse for my scruples, perhaps. The lower one has fallen, the greater his need to respect himself. I believe all my own lies. Aren't you the same? We all are. But I was always an evader. I ran away even from the need to run away.

Why didn't I leave? What did I think about? About the terrible difficulties? Certainly, to some degree. How was I going to put distance between me and that Jaíba wilderness, with long detours and hard marches, in danger every minute? I don't think I was afraid of specific dangers; what held me back was the fear of making a mistake, of falling into danger through my own fault. Today I know: dwelling upon fear, that was it. Fear of making a mistake. I have always had it. Fear of making a mistake is my trouble. That's bad. If we could get rid of that fear of making a mistake, we would be saved. Do you follow me, understand my figure of speech? From what I have told you, could it be that I was already falling in with the ways of the jagunços? It could be, I know. Whether I liked it or not, is another story. A person is never entirely himself as long as he is a part of a whole. For instance, Paspe had big needles, thread and an awl: he repaired my sandals. Lindorífico let me have, for practically nothing, an amulet with great powers; and Elisiano's specialty was cutting and peeling a straight guava branch, on which he roasted the most delicious meat, the edges brown, the fat sizzling. Fonfrêdo sang carols you couldn't understand, Duvino made jokes about everything, Delfim played the guitar, Leocádio waltzed about with Diodôlfo; and Geraldo Pedro and Ventarol wanted only to stretch out and sleep the whole time, with Ventarol snoring away. He had a double hammock, of

good cotton, with lacework fringes. Then there were Jenolim
and Acrísio, and João Vaqueiro, who had a special feeling toward me because we had traveled together from Rio das Velhas.
"Hi, there, pardner," they would greet me. We played cards on
an oxhide. And the horse-play around the campfires, the confused noise of many voices as night closed in. There was a kind
of joyousness. Joyousness, that is the word. Each told of fights,
gunplay, dangers overcome, miraculous escapes, great feats of
bravery. Those were men. There I was in their midst, involved
in their affairs. There was no need to plan my life—this was it.
Were I to leave, I would have to make all my own decisions,
with death hovering in the background. Was man made to go it
alone? He was. But I did not know it then. Were I to leave there,
I would have no fixed purpose. With so many others, all in the
same boat, we were fulfilling the main objectives of a plan, and
in the end there would be a gain; how could there fail to be a
general solution? Why was it that they all stayed there, in
peace and in war, and the band did not break up and they didn't
want to go away? Think about that, sir; it is something which
later became abundantly clear to me.

Giving up Diadorim, was that what I was talking about? I say
something, then I unsay it. Perhaps, because of my slipshod
way of narrating, you may be thinking that in the hubbub of
camp life, I saw little of Diadorim and that our friendship
suffered neglect or diminishment. That would be a mistake.
On the contrary, Diadorim and I were always within range of
each other's voice and eyes, never far from one other. From
morning till night, our affection was of one color and of one
piece. Diadorim, always courteous, neat, well-behaved. So sure
of himself, he never felt discouraged. Why, then, do I skip this
part, as I should not, in this sketchy talk of mine? As you can
plainly see, I am rambling. Were I telling you only about
Diadorim and what he meant to me at that time, I would have
to go into endless detail to make my true situation clear to you.
Why, then, do I omit it? It seems to me that a person's spirit is
like a horse that picks its own road: when it is headed for sadness and death it goes along without seeing the beautiful and
the good. Do you suppose so? And that Garanço—listen: what

I said about him, about his kindness and friendliness, was not entirely true. But at the time I did not know it. I only discovered and realized it when I recalled it many years afterwards. That poor devil of a Garanço, he wanted to talk, to tell me things. "I was a mule-driver in Serém. I had three children." But what sort of jagunço recruit could he have been—boyish, rough, good-natured as he was? "Hot damn! And I'll bet you've killed your share of men, eh, Garanço?" I asked him. He giggled and laughed. "Well, well, now. You think maybe I'm a coward? Just you entrust any kind of job to the rifle in my hand, brother! And don't worry, you won't regret it." Garanço, I don't believe he ever had doubts about anything. He just had his likes and dislikes.

I wonder if you will understand something that I don't. Hermógenes was always making up to me; damned if he didn't like me. Always greeting me politely, indulging in pleasantries or kindly remarks, he did not even seem like the boss. Out of courtesy and by the rules, I had to respond. But I did so grudgingly. It made me mad. He made me want to puke, as I have already told you. A deep-seated aversion. I could never look him in the eye. There was an invincible repugnance—an unbridgeable gulf. That man, to me, was not real. And, by God, he never suspected, he never caught on. Whenever he wanted to talk, he would send for me; I had to go—he was the chief. I turned sullen. Diadorim noticed it and counseled me: "Watch that temper of yours, Riobaldo. People aren't as low as you think." "I'm not afraid of him!" I replied.

About then, Hermógenes offered me a present of a horse pistol, and boxes of bullets. I didn't want to take them. I had my own revolver; what did I need a huge, long-barreled thing like that for? But he was so insistent that I accepted it. A gift I would never reciprocate! Why would I be wanting to hobnob with the chiefs? What I always want is to keep as far away as I can from big shots, even from a lot of people I know well. I am a lone wolf. When I like someone, it is for no specific reason, and it's the same when I don't. Nobody can change me with gifts and blarney. That Hermógenes was a killer, a torturer of human beings, a monster. What he said to me went in one

ear and out of the other. My hand had not been made to touch
his. Ah, that Hermógenes—it made me suffer that he should be
alive in this world. When he came to talk with me, in the
silence of my hatred I would even ask the devil to come and
stand between the two of us, to separate me from him. I could
have loaded that very horse pistol and put a couple of bullets
between his eyes. You must overlook and forgive these furious
words of mine, but this was what I felt and suffered. That's
the way I was. I don't know if I still am.

About hate: I think that sometimes hatred of one person
serves to strengthen your love for another. The heart grows in
all directions. The heart is like a brook winding through hills
and lowlands, through woods and meadows. The heart com-
bines loves. Everything fits in it. As when I first met Otacília—
like I told you—in the highlands, at Buritís Altos, on the Santa
Catarina ranch there. When I first glimpsed her, by the faint
light of a lamp, framed in a window, her sweet little face,
smiling mouth, and long hair. But then our party bedded down
for the night in the cellar of the sugar boiler house. There was
me and Diadorim, Alaripe, João Vaqueiro, Jesualdo, and
Fafafa. There we found rest after a hard journey; everybody
was good and tired. But I slept with two guardian angels.

My memories are what I have. I am beginning to recall bygone joys. The Santa Catarina ranch was close to heaven—a
deep blue sky, motionless clouds. It was in May. I love those
months of May, healthfully cool, with their bright sun, the
wildflowers in the fields, and the brisk little May winds. The
front of the ranch, on a hillside, stretched toward the mountain, toward the sky. Between the corrals and the sky there was
only open grassland and a strip of woods, from which white
butterflies fluttered through the fence rails. There you are not
aware of the passing of the hours. And the mourning dove is
heard all day. To this very day, the call of the mourning dove
evokes in me the scent of false nettle leaves. After so much
fighting, I found real enjoyment in sane, everyday things: the
milking of the cows, watching a double-chinned fellow carrying
a big can of swill to the hogs, the guinea hens scratching
furiously in the yellow-flowered wild senna, and the field of

sida plants nibbled down by the cattle and pigs. I imagine that on that occasion I had a brief longing for São Gregório, and a vain wish to be the owner of a piece of land that was mine, mine by right of possession and of hard work, work that strengthens the soul and hardens the hands. I had imagined that these things were bygones, but there I was, once more, in the uplands. The air of the uplands, you know it, sir. We drank a lot of milk. They brought us coffee in little cups. After a chat with the old man, the grandfather, we lazed about, doing nothing. I saw Otacília again later that morning.

She was smiling and pretty as a picture; but meeting her in broad daylight, as you will understand, sir, was not easy, and it made me shy to talk to her. My Otacília, of exquisite charm, in the full bloom of her youth, as dainty as rosemary, her shining presence. I was the one who saw her first. I dipped my hand in honey and dripped it on my tongue! I spoke about the birds that were flying about before the day got hot. It was Diadorim who had taught me to see the birds. But now Diadorim was off somewhere, huffy, in a sulk. The first thing I pointed out was the tame pigeons. A flock of them, at the water trough. And the wild pigeons, flying high over the trees. "Ah, more than twenty of them have passed over," said Otacília, who was counting them. That started our conversation, with occasional intervals of laughter and silences. Every girl is gentle, white and dainty. Otacília most of all.

Beside the porch was a small flower bed, with several kinds of flowers in it. There was one that stood out, a white one—a canna, I thought, or perhaps a lily, tall, very sweet-smelling. It is a flower that has a hidden meaning. Do you know what it is, sir? On a ranch or plantation where there are girls, they plant it beside the door of the big house. It is there for a purpose, to ask a question and demand an answer. But I didn't know that. I asked the name of the flower.

"It is called 'Will-You-Marry-me?' " Otacília answered softly. As she spoke, she looked away, but I caught the tiny tremor in her voice. The name of the flower was that, but only when sweethearts ask the question. Others, loose women, brazen ones, say the name is "Will-you-sleep-with-me?" That is what that beautiful girl, Nhorinhá, daughter of Ana Duzuza, at the edge of the uplands, would have had to say to me; the one who liked me and whom I also liked. Ah, the flower of love has many names. Nhorinhá, prostitute, white pepper, fragrant mouth, with the breath of a little boy. One's life is a muddle; like that Urucúia River of mine winding its way to the sea.

At that moment, impelled by a feeling that was almost distress, I turned to where Diadorim was standing. I called to him—it was a call with remorse in it—and he came over. Then, to have something to say, I said that we had been talking about that flower. Diadorim looked at it and also asked what kind it was, what it was called. "It is called lily-lily," Otacília replied. From her stiff manner, I could see she did not like Diadorim. I tell you, it made me happy. She didn't like Diadorim —and he such a handsome youth, so refined and attractive. That, to me, was like a miracle. She didn't like him? What I saw in her eyes was loathing and antipathy; their eyes never met. And Diadorim? It made me afraid. He was half angry. What is there about a dose of hatred, that it stirs up other hatreds? I remember, I remember him at that hour, on that day, that fateful day. How was it that I had no foreboding? Take yourself: could you have imagined that you would ever see the white, virgin body of a girl, knifed to death, covered with her own blood, her lips bled white, her glazed eyes half open, half closed? And that girl one you had loved, who had been a destiny and blind hope in your life? And so many years have gone by.

From that very first day, Diadorim harbored a hatred for Otacília. And even I could see that it was the lash of jealousy. Please bear with my way of telling. Only by degrees does the obscure become clear. I had known, for a long time, as a matter of fact, that where I was concerned Diadorim was jealous of any woman. Almost from the beginning. And during all those months of close living together, through ups and downs, hardships and dangers, he was not able to hide the gnawing in his heart, though he tried hard. One thing leading to another, he pressed an agreement upon me: that as long as we were on active duty with the band neither of us would touch a woman. When I gave him my word, he said:

"Promise that we will fulfill this, Riobaldo, as though we were swearing it on the Holy Gospels! Lechery and loose living serve only to rob us of the power of courage. Do you cross yourself and swear?"

I swore. If I didn't always keep my promise, the exceptions were vagaries of the body, scapegrace acts. Diadorim cited as an example the iron-clad rule of Joãozinho Bem-Bem, who never took a woman but was as brave as they come. I promised. For a time I abstained from even looking at one. Really. It was hard. Do you know what that means? I held off from a brown girl, who begged for my caresses. And another, many others. One strumpet, one of the high-priced ones, who was passing through, served nearly all our comrades; she was perfumed and pretty, and talked politely about immoral practices. I didn't believe in my oath nor in that story about Sêo Joãozinho Bem-Bem; but Diadorim was watching me. He repaid my sacrifices with his respect and with greater friendship. One day, when I could stand it no longer, he learned about it, he almost caught me at it: I had enjoyed an hour of love with a pretty young thing, a brown girl the color of buriti-nut candy. Diadorim learned what he learned, and wouldn't speak to me after that. In a way, it was I who went several days without speaking, in a mood of unrepentant harshness. Diadorim did not reproach me, but he suffered. I became reconciled to it; I didn't care. What right had a friend to expect such self-denial of me? At times Diadorim would look at me with scorn, as if I were a lost soul, sunk in depravity. It made me mad. I let loose and told him a few things. "I'm no weakling and I'm not cold either. I've got a man's needs!"

I shouted this at him, like an insult. He left me and went off somewhere; I suspect it wouldn't have taken much to make him cry. And should I feel sorry on that account? A man doesn't cry, I thought. What the hell, was I going to leave for the mouths of others that girl who took a fancy to me, the one the color of buriti-nut candy with her beautiful big breasts?

Ah, she was no longer available to me, as we had come a long way from where she lived. But we came to a larger town, modern enough to have a whore house, whose hospitality I enjoyed to the full, yes sirree. Diadorim, I remember, was very sad in that town, and stayed away from the rest of us. I came out of the brothel gaily, to annoy him. Then we went into a store and Fafafa asked if they had mate tea leaves for sale. A man on the street snapped our picture. The name of the place was São João das Altas. The woman was ardent, she had a small waist; it did me good. Please excuse and don't reprove me. With the memories of youth, too many words rush out. Well, my life of friendship with Diadorim went along like that for some time. But it gradually got better, yes. He loved me—it was his destined lot. And I—how can I make clear to you the strength of the love that grew up in me for him? Let my life bear witness to it. Was it love? It was a limitless something. I would have laid down my life for him.

We spent two days at the Santa Catarina ranch. On that first day, I was able to talk some more with Otacília, who to me was becoming more beautiful by the hour. I soon learned that she was a straightforward, strong-minded young woman, prudent yet vivacious. She had no brothers or sisters. Sôr Amadeu ruled big; large herds on thousands of acres. Otacília was not engaged to anyone. Would she fall in love with me? I understood little about family girls. Except, perhaps, Rosa'uarda? I did not want to love Otacília in that way; not, however, that I ever thought the less of Rosa'uarda for it. I don't spit in a plate from which I have eaten well. I went around and around; my thoughts were in a whirl.

I changed my way of talking. I wanted to speak of true hearts and sentimental things, as they do in books, you know what I mean, sir—about beautiful sights, beautiful deeds, beautiful love. How a girl like that can sway one, without need of weapons and combat, but soft and delicate in the shelter of the plantation house, smiling saint-like from a balcony. She wanted to know all about me, and kept asking: "Where are you from, really?" She was smiling, and I didn't hold anything back:

I told her that I was the son of Seô Selorico Mendes, owner of three great ranches; that we lived on the one at São Gregório. And that I was guilty of no crimes or assualts; it was only for sound political reasons that I was leading that party of jagunços, on behalf of Medeiro Vaz, the faithful guardian of all these plains. Those others? Diadorim and the others? Oh, I was not like them.

I stood waiting for what she might say in reply. Did she not believe a word of it? But the expression on her face became serious, and she made no further casual inquiries about my life. Her most beautiful of all eyes were watching the clouds in the sky. I had denied Diadorim, but I swallowed my shame. The afternoon was waning. Sloping towards the back was a yard, and some woods beyond, from which came the harsh chatter of a flock of big macaws perched in an enormous trumpet tree and in some mango trees, their tops made golden by the setting sun. Toward the hills the blue sky was studded with motionless clouds. But in the west, a stray breeze suspended and carried along a blanket of mare's-tails, as though to make with them a fleecy white nest, far, far away, in the solitudes of the plains, where the dark forests and the waters of the Urucúia meet that blue-green sky which soon would bear streaks of red-hot iron and blood. I can tell you this because even now it is all etched on my mind, and I see it as clearly as with my eyes. Do you ask why, my friend? I'll tell you: it is because I had denied and disavowed Diadorim, and for that same reason soon after I came to love him the most.

The night came down, black as a cat. Once again we slept in the boiler-house shed, stretched out on hides and rush mats— there was no room for hanging hammocks. Diadorim lay near me. I did not want to talk, for thinking about all that had happened. I lay there listening to the chirping of the crickets. Just outside, the campfire was dying down, and Alaripe was still there, stirring the embers and smoking a cigarette. Jesualdo, Fafafa, and João Vaqueiro kept on talking, and Alaripe too, about the many good things there at Santa Catarina ranch. What did I think about? About Otacília. I kept wondering about her, half uncertain, not knowing for sure whether she would or wouldn't. We all thought about the same thing; but who knows what each one dreamt of?

"I'll bet there are fish in that pool," said Jesualdo. He must have been referring to her. "Friend, don't mention the name of that girl," I said. Nobody spoke a word; they saw that I was deadly serious; their jaws must have dropped, there in the dark. Off in the distance, a moon-mother, a whippoorwill, uttered its mournful cry: *Floriano, foi, foi, foi.* That meant that somewhere the moon was rising, and that the moon-mother was standing, love-stricken, on a high anthill gazing at it. Lying almost touching me, Diadorim maintained a heavy silence. Then I heard a whisper, and sensed that he was furious. Suddenly:

"Riobaldo, are you in love with that girl?"

Diadorim had risen on his elbow and was leaning over me, his hot breath on my face. I could tell that he was white with rage. His voice hissed through his teeth.

"No, Diadorim, I'm not in love with her," I said, denying her for whom I had disowned him.

"Do you know your destiny, Riobaldo?"

I did not answer. I caught a glimpse of the dagger half-hidden in his hand. I was not afraid to die. I just didn't want the others to see the madness of all that. I did not tremble.

"Do you know your destiny, Riobaldo?" he asked again. He was now kneeling beside me.

"No, I don't know it. The devil knows it," I replied. "Go ask him."

Tell me, sir: at that grave moment, why did I not call upon the name of God? Ah, I don't know. I did not remember the power of the cross, nor any holy invocation. I acted as I had to. I live in the present. Diadorim lowered his arm with the dagger, withdrew from my side and stretched out full-length again. His eyes glittered in the dark. And he must have been biting a leather strap.

Soberly, I wrapped myself in my blanket, but I did not go to sleep. I felt sorry for Diadorim, but my thoughts remained on Otacília. Thus, lying wide awake I wavered between happiness and gloom, filled with new doubts, ideas, hopes. After a time, I arose and went out. I looked up at the Seven Sisters. The stately moon had risen, shedding her blessings all around, in the cold of a night in May. It was at the edge of the field, in the shadow of the surrounding woods, that the moon-mother was giving voice to her so-called song. I stayed a long time, leaning against the cashew tree at the edge of the corral. I kept my gaze on the front of the house, imagining Otacília in her bed, her prayers said, curled up like a white kitten, between the clean, loose sheets; that was the way she dreamed, no doubt. Suddenly, I had the feeling that someone had come up behind me, and was watching me. Diadorim, perhaps? I did not turn my head to look. I felt no fear. I can never be afraid of persons I like. I mean it. I waited awhile; then I started back. But there was no one there, between the light and the shadows. It was an illusion, a fantasy of mine. I drank some water from the brook; in the cold of the night, it tasted warm. I re-entered the shed. Diadorim was there, sprawled in sleep. I could hear his breathing, slow and soft. At that moment, I loved him. If I were not as I am, I said to God, I would embrace and kiss him lying there. Lost in reverie, I must have dropped off to sleep, because I awoke when Diadorim arose quietly and went out without a sound, taking his knapsack; he was going to bathe in a pool at the creek, before daybreak. I went back to sleep soon after that.

Shortly after dawn, Sôr Amadeu arrived, bringing urgent news: that the main body of Medeiro Vaz's band was crossing from Vereda-Funda to Ratragagem, fifteen leagues away, and that we had to go there at once, without delay. Whereupon Nhô Vô Anselmo spoke to me kindly and in a different way, from which I gathered that the old boy knew something, and wouldn't mind if I were to become his grandson. We gulped down some food and mounted. Diadorim, Alaripe, Jesualdo, and João Vaqueiro, started out ahead, followed by Fafafa. But first I screwed up my courage, and asked Otacília to tell me my fate. And she, to my great joy, said that she would love me alone, and that however long it took, she would wait for me until I could rightfully return and arrange our marriage. I left there full of song, with springtime in my heart. It was for a

brief time only—I thought—that I was leaving that blessed
Santa Catarina ranch. Not that I had any burning ambition for
riches; Otacília was really all I wanted; she was my heart's
desire. But, in a mood of longing for peace, for everybody's
friendship, for decent living, I couldn't help thinking about the
wedding ceremony, the clothing, the festivities, the big table
loaded with choice things to eat; and, during the solemnities,
Sôr Amadeu, her father, setting aside a palm grove as a dowry
—for the two of us—as they did in the old days.

I caught up with the others. Diadorim didn't say a word. The
mist-dampened dust of the road clung heavily to us. The tyrant
bird and the half-collared sparrow were singing. The tall ripe
melosal displayed its purple finery. But I was deep in thought,
my heart filled with Otacília. Why couldn't I have stayed there
for good? Why did I have to keep on with Diadorim and the
others, seeking luck and death on these gerais of mine? Destiny.
Diadorim and I had come in flight together. But from that day, a
part of me always stayed back there with Otacília. Fate. I used
to think about her. Sometimes less, sometimes more, as is the
way in life. Sometimes I would forget, sometimes I remembered. The months and the years went by. But Diadorim took
me with him, wherever he wished to go. I am sure that
Diadorim could tell when I was thinking about Otacília—he
divined it and suffered.

These things all happened later. I have got ahead of myself
in my story. You will please excuse this bad habit of mine. It is
ignorance. I hardly ever get to talk with anyone from the outside. I don't know how to tell things straight. I learned a little
with my compadre Quelemém; but he wants to hear about the
facts in the case, the inner meanings, the undertones. Now, on
this day of ours together, with you listening to me so attentively, I am beginning to learn to tell things straight. So I'll go
back to what I was telling you, about me being mixed up with
the Hermógenes outfit.

Zé Bebelo had been spotted: he was on the way. He was
coming against us. We got the news: a league away, in broad
daylight, a large troop of horsemen was headed our way. Not

really a league away—it was more like six leagues. There were
about sixty of them, more or less. I had known all along that
this was our purpose, but just the same it took me by surprise.
I couldn't realize that I was going to open fire on the Bebelos. In
a way, I looked upon Zé Bebelo as a friend, I respected his
cleverness. Zé Bebelo, who always knew what he was doing.
And something blunted my courage. Not fear, but I lost the
wish to be brave. We moved our camp closer, closer.

"This is it! Today is the day!"

Hermógenes gathered the men, all of them. Each was to
take as much ammunition as he could. Where to? Diadorim cut
short my questions with a gesture. To arms! Diadorim was
going into the thing as if we were setting out on a pleasant
jaunt. Ah, one thing I overlooked telling you: during that
period, in the Hermógenes encampment, my friendship with
Diadorim was like clear water flowing over rocks, unroiled by
silt or mud. From the voices of men and the jangle of weapons,
on the eve of violence, you could not help but acquire a measure
of hardness, of greater self-respect, and many a trifle became
even more trivial.

"Zé Bebelo is calculatedly foolhardy, Diadorim. He plays
it safe: somewhere near by there must be another body of
fighters in hiding, ready to attack us in the rear. I am sure of it
—those are his regular tactics. We must warn Hermógenes,
João Goanhá, Titão Passos," I blurted out.

"They know that, Riobaldo. All war is like that," Diadorim
answered.

And I knew that just saying what I had was a betrayal of Zé
Bebelo. But was it? Today I know it wasn't, because I had to
look out for my life and for that of my comrades. Yes, but it
was a betrayal, too—because I thought it was. Now, after all
that happened, was it not?

I grabbed my knapsack, and ate my manioc mush cold.
Everything was being worked out, even what we were to do
afterwards. Then João Goanhá divided the men up into groups
of fifteen or twenty; after the fight was over, each group was to
gather at a certain spot. From that hour on, we were going to

have to fight in small numbers. By the look on the men's faces, I could tell that they were satisfied. Jovially, we all took a swallow.

"Take this amulet, Riobaldo. It was my foster mother who sewed it up for me. I wear two of them."

That was Feijó, a tough old man of eighty; he handled a gun with three barrels. What was the meaning of this demonstration of friendship? I had never even noticed him till then.

"Let's go! Today we do what shouldn't be done," one of the men cried out excitedly. It made me fear God's punishment.

Anyone who wanted to pray had leave to do so; others accompanied them, contritely. Still others were eating. Wolfing down the food, and wiping their mouths with both hands.

"It is not fright, friends, but demands of the body," explained some, as they went off to answer nature's call. The others laughed at them. It was less than a half-hour before sunset. In that wilderness, void of dwellings and cultivated lands, you could hear the lament of the mourning dove, and the penitential howling of a wild dog.

"Give us a hand, will you."

I helped him. It was a fellow from Montes Claros—I have forgotten his name—who was trying to bind his sandals on his feet with strips of cloth. When he had finished, he danced a few loose-jointed steps and whistled. Did that youngster think about anything?

"Riobaldo," Diadorim said to me, "during the fighting change your position whenever you can. And be on your guard every minute: a man could come crawling through the bushes and knife you in the back."

Diadorim was smiling gravely. Someone bumped against me as he passed by. It was Delfim, the guitar player. Where was he going to be able to hide his guitar? I pressed Diadorim's hand; what I wanted was to go off, ride, wear myself out.

Hermógenes came up. His voice, giving out combat orders— have I told you, sir?—was clear and precise; one might even say that it stayed with you. At any rate, he knew where he was going and what he wanted. He outlined his plan. Let all follow orders, let all know what was expected of them! The party of

Zé-Bebelos had taken up a position on Alto dos Angicos, a flat little hilltop. They might have posted sentinels far out, even to the edge of the Dinho creek, or over around on the other side of the hill. But we would soon have the answer to that, because our spies were at work. What we had to do, as soon as it got dark, was to approach the hill and crawl slowly up the slopes during the night. We were going to open fire, by surprise, at the first rays of daybreak. Each from his best position; everything depended on cleverness and cunning; even breathing had best be slowed down by half. If anyone had the bad luck to encounter enemies ahead of time, he was to slip away if he could, or use his knife; guns were forbidden. Guns were to be used, all right, but only after Hermógenes, who was the boss, had fired the first shot. Let each take careful aim, and shoot to kill, because our strategy was to clean them up quickly, before they could bring up reinforcements. Even so, Titão Passos would take some thirty men up to the road on a rocky cliff along which they might come, and lie in ambush to cut them off. Hermógenes explained slowly and repeated everything patiently: it was essential that even the dumbest should understand, and it was made clear that each must get down on his belly and start crawling uphill. But I had understood everything the first time, and every time he repeated the instructions, I would picture the situation. In my mind, things were already taking place, I was there, crawling, getting ready. I began to feel excited. I adjusted my weapons.

I had not expected what happened next. Hermógenes called me over. The straps and cartridge belts, the big knapsack, the rolled-up hammock and a blanket made him look fat.

"Riobaldo, Tatarana, you come with me. Our position is going to be the most dangerous. I need three good men, within sound of my whisper."

Why should I lie to you? For him to pick me out that way, acknowledging my value, gave me a certain pleasure. I liked it. In spite of my aversion for him, which, I tell you, was strong.

I went all out. By dint of will power, which I salvaged from my weakened resistance, I began to be another person. I even felt that I, Riobaldo, had become a jagunço, a man who would kill and die with his boots on. Riobaldo, a man, without father, without mother, without attachments, without belongings. I planted my feet firmly on the ground and clenched my teeth. I was decided, resolute in mind and body. Not that I felt any friendship for that monster of a Hermógenes. At that moment, he did not exist. He was just a name, arousing neither likes nor dislikes; his job was to command. And above him and me was Joca Ramiro. I was like a soldier, I was obeying a higher law, not Hermógenes. The obligation to command was Joca Ramiro's. But Joca Ramiro was far away; he was like a law, a fixed law. I thought only about him, hard. I kept thinking: "Joca Ramiro! Joca Ramiro! Joca Ramiro!" My spirits rose like a surging ocean wave. I no longer needed to hate or to fear. I began losing the urge I had to put a bullet in Hermógenes's liver.

Then Hermógenes told me to choose those who were to come with us. Me? Was he trying me out? I didn't hesitate: "Garanço," I said, "and this one here," I concluded, pointing to the fellow from Montes Claros. I would have liked to have Feijó too; but there were to be only two besides myself. And what about Diadorim, you will ask. Ah, I would not have asked for him, although I was thinking of it the whole time. Strangely enough, I especially did not want Diadorim near me when the fighting started. Why not? I didn't know myself, why not. Was it because I felt I might be hampered in combat if I saw the dangers to which Diadorim was exposed; or was the thought of having him near displeasing to me because it might weaken me, now that I was feeling tough as iron and lion-hearted, in front of Hermógenes? I just don't know. Anyhow, that is how I felt. And so I replied that Garanço and the Montesclarense would go with us.

We set out, in twos or threes or single file. It would be dark any minute. Night in the Jaíba comes down like a curtain, bang. You have to get used to seeing in the dark. We moved in complete silence; not even the shuffling of sandals could be heard. The only sound was the tiny noises made by a million insects in the low growth and scrub all around. The great owl flies there, as quietly as a shadow, but it knows where it's going.

When one suddenly loomed up in the air in front of me, I blinked three times. Hermógenes moved ahead, not saying a word. Nor did Garanço or the Montesclarense speak, either. For which I was grateful. When you're going to kill and be killed, you don't feel like talking. Only the soft-feathered night-born birds do that: the silly goatsuckers, the nighthawk, calling his mate with cackles of laughter. I'll tell you what I was thinking of as I moved along: nothing. There was just one thing in my mind: that I had to keep constantly on the alert, ready for whatever might happen at any moment. I became enormously important to myself.

I said I was telling you everything. What about killing and dying? Nonsense. That's just what I wasn't thinking about. I didn't need to. Here's how it was: I was on my way, following orders: I had to reach a certain spot and cock my gun. Whatever happened after that, would happen; isn't it all a matter of fate? I wanted to remember nothing, nobody. We had gone half a league along a trail. We had to be careful not to brush against the branches, nor crack twigs. To travel at night, in pitch darkness takes instinct—your feet have to guess what you can't see on the ground. You imagine big holes. You expect to hear voices. A few scattered stars; the night was a solid mass. I ask you: does the night belong to death? At certain times, nothing has meaning. You know what I thought about most? About the call of the curiango, the goatsucker. What the curiango cries is: *Curí-angu!*

About two hundred yards from the creek, Hermógenes stopped. We drew together, and felt each other with our hands. From then on, we moved almost treading on one another's heels. Hermógenes, in the lead, did our seeing for us. What eyes he had! He could peel the darkness off of anything, better than a barn owl. With daggers in hand, we crossed the creek, jumping from stone to stone; we knew of a shallow crossing farther downstream, but were afraid they might have posted sentinels there. Here was the worst spot: a shiver went over me; I felt a prickle in the back of my neck. In the dark, anything can happen. On the other side, Hermógenes whispered instructions. We lay down. I was behind a tree, a gum tree. At my back was the creek, flowing over its stones. We had to wait there for hours, allowing time for the others to reach their positions. Near the water like that, the mosquitoes swarm. The smell of sweat on your face attracts them, and they won't leave you in peace. You couldn't light a cigarette and smoke. Night can last a long time. How the mosquitoes pestered us! Maybe it was for this very reason, that Hermógenes had picked that spot: so that the mosquitoes wouldn't let anyone fall asleep. But it wouldn't be me who could fall asleep so close to that man, that prince of evil. What I wanted was for something to happen, and come what might, that the waiting would end.

"Here, take it," I heard.

It was Hermógenes, handing me a plug of tobacco which he had just soaked in strong cachaça, to rub on my face and hands. I took it. Had it been something to eat, I wouldn't have. I said nothing; not even thanks. That was a part of combat procedure. I rubbed it on, good. Then the mosquitoes stopped stinging me. After that, I amused myself picking bark off the tree, and feeling the sticky resin. During that time, my thoughts were aimless; I can't even describe them: memories of various people, snatches of foolish talk, vague things about trips I had made. The night went on.

Shall I tell you what it was like to crawl up the slope to the spot where we were to lie in ambush? It is always the same. A man gets down on his belly, in the grass, on the ground, and starts moving, wriggling like a snake, as stealthy as a cat stalking a bird. You have to relax the weight of the body, as in swimming; you pull and push yourself forward with your elbows and knees. Everything in painfully slow motion; it is irritating but there's no other way. It's no use jerking forward in a hurry; you have to lie stretched out as flat as you can. Your joints crack; you can hear them. Your shin begins to itch; you try to scratch it with the heel of your other foot, but if you have on leggings, it's no use. Now and again, you turn over on your side: you look, you listen. Any careless noise you make means danger. A bird perching in a bush, and flying out suddenly, serves to tip off the enemy. The worst ones are the nesting birds—sometimes they fly about you, screaming. When it's glow worm time, there are thousands of them over everything; you no sooner disturb them than they start glowing and scattering; the grass around you looks like a mat of greenish fire— that is a sure giveaway. What we were doing was sheer madness, conceivable only in war. Holding the dagger in your mouth, without meaning to, you snort. Every bush seems to hold the threat of a hidden enemy about to jump out. Treacherous-looking whitish tree trunks. You flatten thorns and twigs with your belly; you have to know when to bear down heavily on a thorn—it's the best way to keep it from sticking in you. The smell of the ground forebodes evil. Sharp-edged grass stems cut your face. And a grasshopper jumps with a little clicking noise —*tclick*. I imagined it was the prankish stars letting their little droppings fall on my back. Now you claw your way. The grass is sodden with the night mist. Ah, and snakes? To think that at any moment your hand can press down on a rattler's thick coil—it is sure death. The worst is the bushmaster, a monster viper that goes abroad at night; the fastest thing in the world! I uttered a short prayer to Saint Benedict. I was wet from the night damp on the weeds and leaves. I was not finding it pleasant. All of a sudden, the tall grass in front of me waved, and I quickly lowered my head. It was only an armadillo entering his hole, sniffing; I could hear the rubbing of his horny plates. It was a peba armadillo, and I was down on a level with it. Hermógenes was forging ahead, crawling to my right; I could hear his hard breathing, and see that prone bulk of him, within arm's reach. Garanço and the Montesclarense were sometimes ahead of us, sometimes behind. Then, when I least expected it, Hermógenes stopped me. He spoke in a whisper, his hand cupped to his mouth:

"Right here is the place," he announced.

Where were the first stars, and the soft night birds, I wondered. I had closed my eyes. The smell of a white guava perfumed the air. I relaxed.

Until day broke, what did I do with my time, with the passing hours? I could measure the hours by the wheeling stars, sliding down the eastern sky. But, I'll tell you, I did not look at the sky. I didn't want to. I couldn't. Stretched out that way, on the

rough ground, you feel the night chill, and the ground was
growing cold. I thought: what if I get sick? I was already
bothered by a dull toothache. I dozed a bit, but I firmly refused
to fall asleep. With Hermógenes there by my side, silent, just
the thought of him kept me awake. Those deaths, soon to take
place, were already in his mind. I had nothing to do with it,
myself—wasn't I just taking orders? Well, wasn't I? Now,
about my first shot as a sniper. The worst part is till you get
used to it. There is a feeling of repugnance that you have to
drive out of your mind: I was there for the purpose of killing
others—was that not a sin? It was not, it was not, I kept thinking. I dozed awhile, I think; without meaning to. Did I even
fall sound asleep? I wasn't the leader. Did Joca Ramiro want
this? And Hermógenes, the next in authority, as his lieutenant?
I was going to kill human beings. In a short while, the sky
would grow light, and I would have to see the day coming.

What was Hermógenes like? How am I going to tell you?
Well, to describe him in a roundabout way, he was a cross between a horse and a boa constrictor. Or like a big dog. I had
to obey him, do what he said. He ordered me to kill. My wishes
did not enter into the matter. I didn't even know the enemy, I
felt no hatred for them. Zé Bebelo's men, recruited along the
Jequitaí, seeking only to earn a little money, like regular paid
soldiers. How many were going to die by my hand? Meanwhile,
a breeze arose, taking with it the chirp of crickets and of the
many other wandering insects. Night still prevailed, with red
shadows. The good thing about that kind of death is that it
happens so quickly, so neatly. The things I didn't want to think
of, but which I thought about all the more, were about to
happen. Geraldo Pedro had a habit of saying:

"That fellow? He doesn't exist any longer, he turned into a
ghost. I killed him." And Catôcho, would say: "There are some
orphans of mine, there. I had to kill their father."

Why did they talk about such perversities? Why did they
talk? Why was it that I had to obey Hermógenes? There was
still time left: if I wished, I could jerk out my revolver, shoot
one quick, well-aimed bullet, start running downhill, dodging
from side to side, and find me a way to disappear into the wide

world. Ah, no, that would never do, for it would set off heavy firing from all directions, many people would be killed, and the first of all to die would be me. There was really no way out. I was under Hermógenes's control. What do you want—he was the stronger! I thought about Diadorim. What I most wanted was that we should both come through this alive, that the wars would end, that we would both give up this lawless life and go away to the high uplands where we would live a long time together. Now, those others, on the opposite side, didn't they also have the power to kill me? More foolish fantasy: I would go riding along a white sandy road, very early some morning, in Burití-do-A, alongside the stream, accompanied by some kindly little backwoodsman or some other companion; we would laugh, talk about all manner of trivial things, without malice; we would smoke, and I would be taking half a sack of corn on the crupper to a mill, or to a ranch, to trade for cornmeal . . . Pipe dreams. After all, hadn't those Zé-Bebelos invaded the North to kill people? Well, then! What had to be, had to be. Not even Hermógenes was to blame; it was a state of law, not his law, which I obeyed, which all obeyed.

"I'm going to the Gerais! I'm going to the Gerais!" I kept saying to myself. I felt a cramp in one of my legs. Then I worked my fingers, to take out the stiffness. Let's see, Diadorim and I going along, we two, on horseback; the field smelled sweet, the ground was covered with flowers all around. Why should I feel sorry for the others? Were any of them feeling sorry for me? Men are witless, I kept thinking. What we really ought to do was bring the war to a quick end, wipe out those Zé-Bebelos. Thinking about Diadorim brought me the sanity of peace. Ah, I tell you: that's one night I'll never forget. How could I? Little by little, I became dull and indifferent, neither good nor bad. To kill, to kill, what did I care? I cannot forget that night. In the east it began to drizzle.

When daylight comes, the darkness in the sky is pulled away in jerks. We had our backs to the dawn. I remember what I remember: Hermógenes crossing in front of us, flat on the ground, his belly scraping softly against it. That man was as fierce as a tiger; he was whispering close to Garanço's ear, then to the Montesclarense, assigning them their places. Dammit, he then came back near me, this time from the left side. He said: "Be careful, Riobaldo."

I saw when Garanço started to creep, moving, moving, until he took cover behind a big ant hill, about five meters in front of me, a little to the left. Not far off, I could make out the Montesclarense. I changed my own position by a few steps, taking advantage of a tree, a guava with thick foliage. Hermógenes didn't take his eyes off me for a second. That first bit of daylight was actually painful. The pressure was mounting. Why didn't we charge, once and for all, like madmen? Ah, no, we couldn't. At the very first clash with the Bebelos, we four would be killed, skewered on their long, thin knives. About our other companions, we knew nothing. We knew only that the main body of the Bebelos was about an hour's distance from these who were now surrounded. Everything called for patience. A little breeze shook the leaves. So many men in ambush, just watching and waiting to kill, I thought. Now, I even found it pleasing. Little birds began flying about, happy with the coming of the first rays of light, which enabled them to hunt and eat. I looked a short distance ahead to where the enemy was; among some small trees, in the filtered light, the outline of a man could be discerned. He was about to start a fire. Gradually others, too, could be seen, getting up. Soon, perhaps, some would start for the little brook to fetch water, if they were needing any. I wondered, idly, if they had used up a lot of water. Does fear cause one to lose heart? I wasn't hunting for death. I'll tell you one thing: I was glad that Hermógenes was there with us. "Riobaldo, Tatarana! Now," he commanded me, all of a sudden. I brought my hand up to the trigger; I had already taken aim mentally. One thing gave me comfort: that tall man could not be Zé Bebelo. I did not tremble, and I listened to my shot and that of Hermógenes: the tall man fell dead and rolled in the dust. I was seized with fury against him, against all of them. Then everywhere, from every direction, gunfire broke out.

The thunder roared. Rifles were speaking and the others, too: muskets, blunderbusses and carbines. The carnival of death.

Shall I tell you more? I did my share of shooting. Then I took
a breathing spell. Have you ever seen a battle? Without thinking, you stop and wait; you wait for their answer. You want a
lot of answers, for you feel very much alone, in the middle of
nothing. Death? The thing was only a whish and a bullet. At
any rate, you had no choice in the matter. You could only yell
out your hatred, if you wanted to; and the air was poisoned,
crisscrossed by whistling slugs. I tell you, it was something.
Time after time I loaded my rifle and brought it up to my
shoulder. Those enemy fellows were wasting a lot of ammunition, shooting nervously. They didn't want to die by our hand,
they really didn't. I started laughing like hell, and Hermógenes
called out to me in astonishment. He thought I had gone crazy.
But I had suddenly started thinking about my godfather,
Selorico Mendes.

"Now, it's your turn to get it! Don't you want it?" was what I
wanted to shout at Hermógenes. The dirty dog. I laughed some
more. A lone man, with his gun in his hands. Hermógenes was
just another man, like me, only he was a worse shot. And those
Bebelos had got up at daybreak only to be fired upon. I got
hold of myself.

If everybody would take up arms, I thought, and begin shooting everybody else, the world would soon end. Just idle
thoughts that wandered through my mind. I started counting
the shots. The way things were going, the fight would last a
long time. It was now broad daylight, and I could make out the
Montesclarense behind a tree, in a small thicket. Why am I
telling you all this? I am dragging it out. If you have seen it,
you know what it's like; and if you don't know, how can you?
There are things which words can't describe.

We were not crawling from one position to another. This is
almost never done except when you are outnumbered: so the
others will think there are more of you than there really are.
Otherwise it is better to stick to one good place, and not get
careless. A shot from the other side called for a return shot
from us, back and forth. Whenever I fired it was because I had
seen something move, someone's carelessness. My field of fire
was less than three hundred yards away. That was close enough

for a blunderbuss, even. And from what I know and what I saw, I accounted for more than one. But only those whose number was up anyway.

At one stage, the shooting became hotter and was concentrated on a single target. They wanted a duel. The hours were endless. The sun was pouring down on the back of our necks. The sun, the burning sun, under which I sweated; my hair was wet, and the inside of my clothing, and I had an itch in the middle of my back; parts of my body were numb. I kept on shooting. Weren't we going to advance? No. The others were shooting plenty hard, without letup. The dogs! To curse them out loud would serve only to give them a better target. I could see Garanço's back, almost in front of me. He had laid his knapsack and blanket on the ground; his jacket was off, and he had on only his checked shirt. I saw the sweat staining his shirt in the back, between the shoulders, a dark spot that kept growing round and big. When Garanço fired, the kick of his gun shook his body. He was a friend of mine, every inch of him brave; the kind of fellow you like, a man you could count on. Then I, too, would fire. "Bullets and lead," I began to say, "bullets and lead, bullets and lead." I felt a tightness around my heart— I was fleshy and the heat was cruel. "What happened? What is it?" Hermógenes asked me. "Nothing!" I answered, "bullets and lead, lead and bullets." Hells bells! Then all of a sudden, some of our men well to the left of us jumped out shouting, and rushed toward the enemy!

There were two, three. "The devil!" growled Hermógenes, "They have gone loco, goddamit!" They kept right on, waving their guns and knives over their heads. We held our fire, and our breath. Then Hermógenes called my attention to the Montesclarense—poor devil! He too had started to advance and they had put a bullet in him. He fell, clutching the ground. Poor fellow. Did he go crazy, too? Our other men, storming the Bebelos's wasp nest and howling through their dust, they undoubtedly ended up slashed to pieces, like rabbits by a pack of hounds. Let's hope they got some of the others first!

As soon as the thing quieted down, our people began pouring it on—that was what you call shooting! Hermógenes slowed me down. "Take it easy, Tatarana, it's no use overheating your gun and wasting ammunition. Fewer shots but better-placed. Make every one count." That man was cold as ice, like a dark slug. I was thirsty but my water gourd was dry. I quit spitting.

Wasn't it ever going to end, this fighting that you don't know how to stop? They stepped up their fire. A thousand bullets must have whistled over and around the spot where we were.

At the height of the shooting, something came over me, a kind of fear that one doesn't confess: I trembled like a green twig. But if I died, I would find rest. All my worries would be over. I began to see that our attack was not going to serve any purpose, and I needed to see the others, to know what the score was, how many had died or were in bad shape. I wanted to know about their men and about ours. Senseless combat! Just gunfire repeating itself. A thought struck me: what if Hermógenes went into a frenzy and became possessed of the Devil? What if he ordered an advance, an attack with knives, would we all have to advance? In that case, I was there like a slave condemned to death, with no will of my own, a man in name only, being kicked around! Could I not turn just a little, place my gun against Hermógenes's body, and press the trigger? No, I couldn't, I saw that right away. There is a point beyond which you cannot turn back. Everything had steered me in only one direction, my courage had driven me always forward, always forward; and Hermógenes lying there close beside me—it was the same with him as with me. Ah, and he was right there every minute, all the time. He said to me: "Here, Tatarana, have some, and give your body a little treat." Damned if he wasn't holding out his knapsack to me, with meat and manioc meal in it. Here and there, the shooting had died down almost completely. I had my own rations in my haversack, along with my supply of cartridges. What the hell, I didn't need anything of his. Why then, did I accept, and chew that meat, when I wasn't really hungry, and swallow that manioc? And I even asked for water. "Drink this, old man, it's got a kick to it," he laughed. What he gave me from his gourd, was water and cachaça. I took a drink, and wiped my lips. I leaned my rifle against a bush. I was looking at that heavy sweat on Garanço's back. He would shoot, then I would shoot. Life was like that, like heart beats. I even began to feel lazy.

Then it happened. Over on the far side—on the rocky cliff, where Titão Passos and our men were lying in wait—we heard heavy firing, in volleys. Ah, then it must be another party of Zé-Bebelos coming up, a bunch of them on horseback. Hermógenes stretched his neck, listening hard. The firing began to sound different. "I don't like it," said Hermógenes, and added, "something has gone wrong." Alert he was, like a dog. "Maybe they had advance information, or a hunch. It looks like our plan has backfired, for the moment." I was listening and looking. I looked at Garanço's back—the sweat stain was turning another color. Red sweat. It was blood! Blood that was soaking Garanço's back—and I understood what it was, only too well. Garanço was standing still, the front of his body against the termite mound, as if he were hugging it. Death is always a visitor who arrives unexpected. Nausea rose like a lump in my throat, which sometimes turns to tears in the eyes.

"You, Tatarana, Riobaldo: we are in hot water!" warned Hermógenes. "The devil!" I replied, but he didn't catch my meaning. He whispered:

"Be very careful. We've got to retreat in good order—those who are on their way are coming to encircle us, and try to take us from the rear." And so it was. That cursed one knew everything, and he could guess what was coming next—that Hermógenes, the double-crosser! But I still had my self-respect. I hurriedly crawled the few meters across to Garanço—I had to see if he could be helped. "Come back, brother. Be careful!" I heard Hermógenes's hoarse whisper, warning me not to take a chance. But you can't leave a friend bleeding on the grass in a thicket like a piece of trash, or like a wild pig in a hunt. I took hold of him in my arms; it was no use—he was a corpse, one of the kind that don't close their mouth—a corpse with a bad cold. His gore smelled stale. Blood-sucking mosquitoes were flying about, and green flies hovered near, without a sound. Because of the firing, there was no time to light a candle for Garanço, not even for a few seconds.

"Come on, hurry, we are in a tight spot," called Hermógenes, angrily. I turned back. Danger blots out all sorrow. And now Hermógenes filled his lungs, and let out a loud hee-haw, like an old jackass at the edge of a field. Three times. It was the signal to retreat. The signal was repeated by others, and then by others farther on. "Now, fire away to beat hell!" Hermógenes ordered me. I started shooting. Others joined in. Soon all our men were banging away. Although the signal to retreat was being given, the enemy did not know what it was: we needed to make them think we were about to launch a final attack. Is that what they thought? Who knows? They returned bullet for bullet. But, in the interval, we broke out of the growth, here and there, and rushed headlong downhill, getting away as fast as we could. To scatter that way is almost worse than to advance. From one cover to another, jumping the open distance between trees, I kept up with Hermógenes. At one point I got ahead of him, but I turned and waited, because in the turmoil of the hour, it was in Hermógenes alone that I saw safety for my hounded body. Who says that everything we do in life is by choice? Punishment is also fulfillment of something. I kept going. On the down slopes I could see other men running, like myself, and sometimes leaping out of the low scrub like quail flushed by a dog. We kept on until we crossed the Dinho creek and followed the bank of a small pond into some dense growth. "Have you got everything, Tatarana? Ammunition, your weapons?" Hermógenes inquired. "Sure I have," I replied, firmly. And he to me, "Then we're all right." Now he was talking big, being the head man; he was that way. We traveled some five leagues, in a northwesterly direction, toward Cansação, the place where a handful of our men were supposed to gather, effacing our tracks as we went. For awhile we waded up the creek, then stepped from stone to stone; we wiped out our footprints with branches, and making many twists and turns, we moved ahead.

I won't talk about everything. I have no intention of relating every detail of my life. What would be the use? What I want is to bring out a certain fact, and then to ask your advice. For that reason, I want you to listen carefully to these passages in the life of Riobaldo, the jagunço. I have told you in detail about

that day and that night, which I will never find a way of forgetting. The jagunço Riobaldo. Was that me? It was and it
wasn't. It was not! I am not a jagunço, and I don't want to be
one. God help us!

Having said that, I'll continue. When we reached our rendezvous, in a little ravine, we found several of our companions,
come from the fighting, who had arrived one by one, happy to
have escaped with their lives. One of them was Feijó. I wondered if anyone knew whether Reinaldo was out of danger.
Casually, I dropped the question, for Diadorim was all I thought
about. Yes, Feijó had noticed that Diadorim got away all right,
and that he had then stayed behind at a water hole in a small
valley. "He had blood on one of his pants legs. It looked to me
like it was nothing, just a scratch." So Diadorim was wounded.
Then I, too, stayed behind. We were trudging along the Jio
brook, and I wanted to wash my feet, which were hurting
badly. I also had a splitting headache probably from weariness.
I bathed my temples. If only Diadorim were there: it was all I
needed to make me happy. I would not want to talk about the
shooting and fighting; his silent presence would have been
sufficient. In a way, I didn't understand myself just what was
wrong with me. It was pity. Pity for the men I had probably
killed, or for that tall early riser—maybe the poor fellow had
been their cook—who had fallen at the first shot fired? I don't
think so. The pity that I felt was for Garanço and the Montesclarense. Almost like a weight, I felt the blame on me, for it was
I who had chosen them to come with us, and then it all happened. Therefore they—you know what I mean, sir, you follow
me? Self-reproach? Well, yes and no. Look: a couple of leagues
from here, downstream, a cougar clawed and ruined the leg of
a man called Sizino Ló; he had been one of the São Francisco
rivermen, a fireman on one of the boats; later he inherited a
few acres around here. They bought him a good wooden leg.
But because he had been scared out of his wits, perhaps, he
never wants to go out of the house; he hardly ever gets up from
his cot, and keeps repeating over and over: "Oh, when you have
two, you have one, and when you have one, you have none."
Everybody laughs. His sorrow was not remorse. And neither

was my own, for the loss I mourned came from obeying orders.
Pity for a friend is a simple little suffering, but mine was more
than that. I finally arrived at Cansanção-Velho, which is also
called Jio.

There were about a dozen of us there. Some of those who
were supposed to meet there were missing, but they would no
doubt show up later. One thing pleased me: how come hardly
anybody gets killed in warfare? And even at the worst times,
something good happens: the day before, Braz had gone to Jio
and brought back two donkeys loaded with rice and beans, and
pork fat for cracklings; also some pots and tin plates; so we
cooked a meal. I ate a lot, and lay down. What did I have to
think about except that in the deaths of Garanço and the
Montesclarense I had nothing to reproach myself for; and that
Diadorim was on his way and would join us not later than
daybreak? I went to sleep. But I awoke shortly, my hand on
my rifle, as if something was happening. But there was nothing,
no shape, no noise. The others lay about, heavy in sleep, each in
his place, filling the hammocks hung between trees.

I saw just one man up—Jõe Bexiguento, nicknamed Alpercatas. As everyone said and you could see, he was a strange
man in many of his ways. Jõe Bexiguento seemed not to
want to go to sleep; he had remained beside the fire, stirring
the embers; you could see his face in the red glow. And he was
smoking. Gently I replaced my rifle, and turned over on my
other side. Once more I dropped off, but in a few minutes I
started up again, vaguely apprehensive. This happened three
times, one after another. Jõe Bexiguento noticed my restlessness, and came over and sat on the ground at the foot of my
hammock. "At this hour, in other places, the roosters are
crowing," he said. I don't know whether I said anything in
reply. Now I was uneasy.

Was there some danger nearby, of which I was having a
premonition? It's true, isn't it, that many people feel forebodings? I had heard tell of jagunços who acquired this magic
power of sensing things about to happen, and that is how they
managed to escape in good time. Hermógenes and João
Goanhá, more than any others, were given to these hunches,

these warnings of the heart. Was this happening to me, too? Perhaps the Bebelos were heading our way; who knows, maybe they were already crawling close by. I often thought about Zé Bebelo, and how life is full of surprises. Back in Nhanva, I was giving him lessons in writing and reading, and rates of interest. Afterwards, at night, in the big room, we sat at the big table and ate hominy mixed with milk, cheese, coconut, peanuts, sugar, cinnamon, and butter. "I'm getting ready, Siô Baldo, and in due time I'll wipe out those filthy bands of jagunços," he would say, furiously and gaily, while drinking his gourdful of mate tea, scalding hot. Now, however, I was a jagunço, and Zé Bebelo was coming, commanding armed troops, and what he had sworn on that occasion meant that I would be included, my life ended. But I respected Zé Bebelo; my liking for a person is for good and without reservations; I was always like that. If it were not for him personally, if he were not mixed up in all this, everything would be different: I could put my heart and soul into the fighting. But to fight, risking death, against Zé Bebelo—this, I realized, was responsible for that certain repugnance I felt. I got out of my hammock, and asked Jôe Bexiguento to put more wood on the fire. But he said: "Best not to. At times like this it's best not to light even a black candle." I rolled me a cigarette.

I told Jôe that I had a strange feeling; was it, I wondered, a foreboding? He soothed me, saying that warning from heaven did not come that way, but more like a certainty that slipped quietly into a person's mind, for no good reason; that I was undergoing a nervous reaction, caused by the intense heat I had suffered during the hours of gunfighting. "It's the same with me, after every hot fight. It is an itching in the mind, to make a poor comparison. For about six years now I have been at this work, and I don't know what it is to be afraid of war; but at night, after every encounter, I can't get rid of this feeling, this restlessness that comes over me."

For that reason, he told me, he had not been able to sleep a wink, during the whole of that long night, and he didn't even try to. Jôe Bexiguento thought he no longer had what it took to be a jagunço; for some months, he said, he had been in poor health, suffering from erysipelas and asthma. "I learned early how to live alone. I'll go to Riachão, and clear me a piece of ground." It was a plan that he talked about from time to time. "To work with the hands—that is something a backwoodsman can do, even with old age coming on."

"Were you a friend of Garanço's, Jóe?" I asked softly.

"Just a casual friend. What happened to him? Did he really cash in, for good? I think he was always sort of unlucky. He knew it himself."

As I said the words, I realized that I had asked about Garanço just so I could then ask about Diadorim; I mean, Reinaldo. But I didn't have the nerve. I couldn't think of an excuse. So I changed the subject.

"Can bad luck be cured, Jóe? Do you know any useful prayers?" I asked him something like that; just a silly notion that occurred to me.

"Where would we be, if bad luck could not be cured? Everybody has it, at times," he answered me, "but I never wanted to learn any of those spells. The memory God gave me was not for learning mumbo-jumbo in order to act contrary to His wishes."

Sins, remission of sins. But, were we with God? Could a jagunço be? A jagunço—a creature paid to commit crimes, bringing suffering down upon quiet communities, killing and pillaging? How could he be forgiven? I queried Jóe on this and that point, at random, out of pure cussedness. What wise answer could I expect from Jóe, that yokel from Riachão do Jequitinhonha? By what right could we, jagunços that we were, expect to enjoy God's forgiveness and protection, I asked, heatedly. "Well, gosh! We're alive, aren't we?" was his answer.

But I wouldn't have it that way. I did not agree. I argued with him, doubting, rejecting, for I was not sleepy, not thirsty, not hungry, not wanting anything, and without the patience to enjoy a good comparison. Nor at that hour did I wish for the richness the body craves—the rosy whiteness of a girl during the honeymoon. I argued loudly. Someone whose hammock was close by was awakened by my voice and he grumbled and shushed me. I lowered my voice but went on raising objections.

The thing I have always insisted on, you know, sir, is that what is good must be good and what is bad, bad; that black be on one side and white on the other; that ugliness be well apart from beauty, and happiness far from sadness. I want all the pastures clearly staked out. Life is ungrateful at heart, but brings us hope out of the very bitterness of despair. This is a very mixed-up world.

But Jõe Bexiguento didn't care. He was a tough jagunço on the inside, and narrow-minded; he never changed. "I was born here. My father decided my fate. I live, I am a jagunço," he said.

Everything was as simple as that. Well, then, I thought, why could I not be like that, too; like Jõe? Because—I want you to see what I saw—for Jõe Bexiguento, there was no confusion of ideas in this world; all things were well divided, separated. "Of God? Of the devil?" was his reply. "God one respects, but the devil one exorcises and casts out."

By that time I had calmed down and I laughed and laughed —he was really funny. Moreover, I was not so strict and precise in these matters then. Jõe related actual cases. He told about something that had happened in the sertão, in the village of São João Leão, near where he came from. The case of Maria Mutema and Father Ponte.

A woman called Maria Mutema lived there; just a plain woman, with nothing to distinguish her from all the others. One night, her husband took sick; when morning came, he was dead. Maria Mutema called for help; all the neighbors gathered. The village was small, and they all came in to see. There was no visible cause; he had been in good health up till then, and so it was said that he could have died only from a heart attack. And the afternoon of that same day, the husband was properly buried.

Maria Mutema was a woman who had had her share of hardships, a woman of the plains. If she grieved, she kept it to herself; if she suffered much, she didn't talk about it, but mourned her loss without showing it. But that is the rule there, and from what people say, there was nothing anybody could see out of the ordinary. What did attract notice was something else: her

religiousness. She began going to church every single day, and
to confession every three days. She had become very pious—it
was said—concerned only with the salvation of her soul. She
dressed all in black, as was the custom; a woman who never
laughed, a wooden statue. And when she was in church, she
never took her eyes off the priest.

The priest, Padre Ponte, was a good-natured, middle-aged
man, very fat, very easy-going and well thought-of by everybody. Meaning no disrespect, but only to tell the truth, he had
one fault: he used to wander from the paths of righteousness.
He had had three sons by a simple-minded, well-built woman,
who ran his house and cooked for him, whose name was also
Maria, and who went by the nickname of Maria do Padre. But
don't you go making a big scandal out of this situation, because
in the old days these things were tolerated, nobody thought
anything of it. The sons were well-mannered, good-looking
children, and were known as "Maria do Padre's boys." In every
other way, Father Ponte was a fine priest, active and kind,
preaching his sermons with great virtue and answering the
call to minister the comfort of the Lord's consecrated wafer and
of the holy oils to the country folk at any hour of the day or the
night.

But something soon became evident and aroused comment
and it had two sides to it: one, that Maria Mutema was such a
great sinner that she had to make confession of sin and sorrow
every three days, and the other, that Padre Ponte visibly disliked being her father-confessor in that sacrament, where whatever passes between the two must be kept an iron-clad secret.
It was said even that the first few times people noticed that the
priest scolded her terribly in the confessional. But Maria
Mutema would rise from her knees and come out with lowered
eyes, with such humble serenity, that she seemed more like a
suffering saint. Then, three days later, back she would go. And
it was plain to be seen that Padre Ponte's face was one of true
suffering and dread every time he had to listen to Maria
Mutema, and be alone with her. He went because a plea for
confession cannot be denied.

Then, as time went by, Padre Ponte grew ill, of a deathly

illness, as one could see right away. From day to day, he grew thinner, became irritable, had pains, and finally succumbed, yellow as an old corn husk; it made your heart bleed. He died sad. And from that time on, even after another priest had come to São João Leão, that woman Maria Mutema never set foot inside the church, neither to pray nor to enter.

Finally, however, after years had passed, there came the time for a mission, and the missionaries arrived in the village. They were two foreign priests, robust and red-faced, thundering powerful sermons with mighty faith. From morning till night they were always at the church, preaching, hearing confessions, offering prayers and counseling, and setting such enthusiastic examples that they lined the people up on the strait and narrow. Their religion was unadulterated and forceful, all health and virtue; and you didn't fool around with them, because they had some hidden power from God, as you will see in a moment.

It happened on the last day, that is, on the eve, because on the next day, which was Easter Sunday, there was to be the celebration of general communion and blessed glory. It was at night, after the benediction, that one of the missionaries went up into the pulpit to deliver the sermon, and got down on his knees and started reciting the Hail Mary. At that moment Maria Mutema entered. It had been so long since she appeared in church; why had she taken it into her head to come then?

But that missionary had a different set of rules. Maria Mutema continued up the aisle, and he stopped suddenly. Everyone was startled, because the Hail Mary is a devotion which cannot be interrupted in the middle; once you kneel and begin it, it must be said to the very end. But the missionary resumed his praying, only with a change in his voice that was apparent. And no sooner had the amen been uttered, than he rose to the edge of the pulpit, his face flushed, and leaning over, struck his chest a blow; he was like a mad bull. And he shouted:

"The person who last came in, must leave! Out, out, immediately, with that woman!"

Everyone, appalled, tried to catch sight of Maria Mutema.

"Let her leave, with her evil secrets, in the name of Jesus and of the Cross! If she is still capable of repentance, she can wait for me, right away, and I will hear her confession. But she must make it at the gate of the cemetery! Let her go wait for me there, at the gate of the cemetery, where two corpses lie buried!"

That is what the missionary ordered; and those who were in the church heard the rustling of the hosts of God that labor in the depths and on high. Everyone was horror-stricken. Women screamed, and children too, while others swooned to the ground; everyone fell on his knees. Many, many people were weeping.

And Maria Mutema, standing alone, twisted and thin in her black dress, cried out, with tears streaming down her face, as if her body had been pierced by a knife. She pleaded for forgiveness! For mighty forgiveness, the forgiveness of fire, that from God's unfailing mercy it might descend upon her now, before the hour of her death. The words rushed out of her, and between sobs she said she was confessing right there, to obtain everybody's forgiveness. She started out by saying that she, a monstrous wildcat, had killed her husband—that she was a snake, a filthy beast, rotten excrement. That she had killed her husband that night for no reason, he had done her no wrong, given her no cause—why she had done it, she didn't know. She had killed him while he slept—with a funnel she had poured a stream of molten lead in his ear. The husband passed, as they say, from the cave to the cavern—from sleep to death—and nobody took a look at the injury to his ear, it wasn't noticed. And later, when she took a dislike to Padre Ponte, again for no reason, she lied meanly to him in the confessional, saying she had killed her husband because of him, Padre Ponte, for she was madly in love with him and wanted to be his concubine. It was all a lie, because she neither wanted him nor loved him. But it gave her pleasure to see the priest justly angry; it was a foul enjoyment, which became greater each time, and he, poor fellow, being a gentle man and a priest, had no way of defending himself. She would come to the church all the time, repeating her lies and telling others—piling evil on evil. She kept it up until Padre Ponte sickened with distress and died in silent despair. All these crimes, she had committed! And now she implored God's forgiveness, shrieking, tearing her hair, twisting her hands, and then raising her arms.

But the missionary, in the pulpit still, intoned the benediction, and even as he did so, motioned for all the women to leave the church, only the man remaining, because the last preachment each night was always for men only.

The next day, Easter Sunday, the village was decorated with arches and strings of flags, and there were festive sounds, many fireworks, a high mass, a procession—but everybody thought only of one thing. Maria Mutema, jailed for the time being in the school house, would not eat, would not calm down, on her knees the whole time, clamoring her remorse, begging forgiveness and punishment, and that everyone should come spit in her face and rain blows on her, crying out that she deserved all of this. In the mean time, they dug up the husband's bones from the grave, and they say that if you shook the skull you could hear the lead plug rattling around inside—that it even tinkled! So much for the handiwork of Maria Mutema. She remained in São João Leão more than a week after the missionaries had left. Came the authorities, a commissioner and policemen, and took her to the jail at Arassuaí for trial before a jury. Only, during the days before she left, the people forgave her; they came bringing her words of comfort, and prayed with her. They brought the Padre's Maria, and the children of the Padre's Maria, to forgive her too; so many actions like this brought well-being and edification. So great was Maria Mutema's humble repentance, and so evident her suffering, that some even said she was turning into a saint. That was what Jõe Bexiguento related to me, and in a way it entertained me. But just as he finished, we heard the whistle of one of our men, and we answered it: it was Paspe, appearing softly out of the dark, in his noiseless sandals, his rifle slung across his back. A river of a man was that Paspe, fearless and untiring. He had been in Titão Passos's ambush party, and now he had come to bring news about the others, who were gathered at the gap of Covão, and to ask for instructions. He reported that the trap which they had thought to set had proved a wash-out, because the Bebelos had got wind of it, or had smelled a rat. Thus, instead of approaching head on, the enemy had flanked them and had opened up on them first, with heavy gunfire—two of Titão Passos's men, good companions, had been killed, and three severely wounded.

"Ah, and was Zé Bebelo there, in command, in person?" I asked.

"Sure he was! And how!" Paspe replied, and asked if anyone had a drop of cachaça.

After that, I must have asked about Diadorim—just to be asking, without really expecting to get any news of him. Besides, I was afraid it might be bad news. But as luck would have it, Paspe answered me:

"I saw him, he passed by me, and even gave me a message— gosh! it was for you yourself. 'Tell Reinaldo Tatarana for me that I have a job to attend to, and that I'll be back in a few days' —that's what he said. Then he went on by me, on horseback. I wonder where he got that mount? He must have got hold of one of the Bebelos' own horses, left over after the gunfight."

I heard but I didn't believe. He, Diadorim? Wherever was he going, without me? It couldn't be him, it was not like him. I questioned Paspe again, asked for exact details. It was him, all right. But then, was it not true that he had been wounded in the leg?

As to that, he couldn't say yes or no—but he thought "no" more than "yes." He hadn't noticed, in the flash of the moment. He saw only that the saddle had a high bow and cantle and was almost new, and that the horse was tall, scrawny, but full of fire and slid to a stop on all fours; a dark roan.

Ah me, a kind of pain in my soul, you know, sir. I began to imagine nonsense. What did it mean to be faithful; where was my friend? At the worst hour, Diadorim had fled my company. He had certainly run away to be with Joca Ramiro. Ah, he, who knew everything about everything, was now deliberately dropping me without a word from his own mouth, without an embrace, though knowing full well that I had become a jagunço only because of our friendship! I think I must have raved, to

the point that I had such a rush of blood to the head that I felt
my extremities turn cold, and there came over me a heavy
drowsiness, a stupor of sickness, of misfortune. And how I
slept. Like one dead. To awaken me early the next morning
they had to pour water on my head and feet, thinking I had
caught the sleeping fever.

I am going to skip the details of all that happened in the next
few days, from the time I arose from my hammock with the
heaviness of the night in my eyes. I was at low tide. See how
things are: there is normal, regular suffering, and suffering
mixed with remorse, just as there is casual robbery and planned
robbery. Do you understand me? Eleven were the days that I
counted. Meanwhile the war continued. We had a moderate
flurry of gunfire, a small skirmish, and a half-battle. I'll describe
it detail by detail, if you wish. But it's hardly worth it. What I
tell you is what I know and you don't know, but the main things
I want to talk about are those which I do not know if I know,
but which you perhaps do. Now, if you really want me to, I am
ready to give you the complete story—the outcome and everything else—of thirty encounters. I have the memory for it.
How long each one lasted, and even an estimate of the number
of bullets fired. What is there to tell? Of the wild firing that
we stood up under and returned with first-rate shooting, from
the midst of a poor farm, or razorlike cane brake, or green
field, or cornfield whose dry stalks we trampled and broke? Of
the time when the rifles cracked so often, made so much noise,
that you cupped your hand behind your ear, without knowing
why, as if hoping for the miracle of some different noise, any
noise but that deafening racket? Of when a cloudburst fell
upon us, putting a stop to the fighting, leaving everyone sopping
wet and our weapons out of commission? Of unsuspectingly
looking at the blank side of a hill in front of you, and suddenly
having it erupt in gunfire? Of entering a pool to ford it, with
the water almost up to your chest, and having to turn and fire?
Of how, in the space of a single hour, I found myself raising my
rifle and firing, hard-pressed, from the edge of a wood and field,
from the crest of a hill, descending and climbing a series of
little slopes, from behind a fence, from under a trough, from

the top of a copal tree and a souari nut tree, lying prone on a big, blue, flat rock, rolling in sugar cane bagasse, and bursting into a house? Of a companion drenched in blood and the filth of his guts, clinging to you in agony, only to die cursing every mother and father? Of how, in the midst of the turmoil, fighting in the hottest part of the day, everyone on both sides is suddenly siezed with a frenzy of fury, yelling, bellowing, howling —to the point almost of throwing away their firearms and rushing at each other's throats, to finish or be finished by the knife? That is that. Much too much. Would you want to hear more? No? I knew you wouldn't.

We kept going. I pushed ahead during those days, changing my longing for Diadorim into false anger. I was assailed by bitterness, to see myself cast aside like a fruit skin, this being a figure of speech for disdain and whatever else one feels at a time like that, as you no doubt know. But the worst was what I really felt—as if the main prop had been knocked out from under me. And as always happens when one feels he has been treated like a dog, and despised, I got ideas. I remembered Antenor's scheming whispers, and I agreed with his suspicions: who knows, perhaps Joca Ramiro really did intend to leave us to our fate there in the wild plains. And Diadorim knowing this, being in on the plot, had gone to join Joca Ramiro—the only person he really cared about. My world had fallen apart. But I spit hard on the ground three times, and put Diadorim out of my mind. A man like myself is incapable of retaining any semblance of love, once he receives repeated signs of contempt. The only thing is that afterwards one is soul-sick. I thought of having a talk with Antenor. But I didn't do it. I wasn't going to share my doubts with strangers. I have never liked schemers, and I don't begin a conversation with them. I neither tittle nor tattle. So much so that one day Hermógenes called out to me, joking: "You're a hot one, Tatarana! I like that spirit of yours."

"At your orders, sir," was all I said. Because from his manner I saw right away that he was going to offer me a favor, or give some good news. Persons like him, on certain occasions, take a different tack; they pick any little opportunity to talk down to you, like a kind boss or an indulgent father. And I wasn't mistaken. What Hermógenes wanted to promise me was that all that hard work and fighting would soon come to an end, with the Bebelos wiped out, and then we would be free for better undertakings, raiding good places, in the service of political bigwigs. And that when the time came, he would pick me to command a part of his men, to be a platoon leader.

Despite all his praise, I was unmoved, he could not reach me. I declined with thanks. To try him out, however, I took the opportunity to drop a little hint: "Joca Ramiro," I said, with a sneaky little laugh, which between the two of us could have meant anything. Then I waited. But Hermógenes limited himself to saying, gravely, confidently, that Joca Ramiro was a bold, brave captain, beyond the shadow of a doubt. Was Hermógenes being cunning? No, sir. I know and saw that he was sincere. Why was it that everybody paid such high honors to Joca Ramiro, unstinted, spontaneous praise? It left me somewhat confused. But as regards Hermógenes, I was forever harassed by that dread of him, which I had to lash into anger. And for that reason, I said to myself: "I will deny him water, even at the jug's mouth." To exorcise him quietly in this manner brought me tranquillity. Which I needed. Much as I did not want to think about Hermógenes, I could not get him out of my mind, he always in the leading role, I his captive audience. I thought of him often as a hangman, considering all I had heard of him as a past master of atrocities. At first, the mere thought gave me chills of horror, and my mind refused to accept it. But, little by little, I began to want to know how everything that I imagined could be possible. I'll tell you, sir: if the devil existed, and you saw him, ah, you should not look, it is not fitting that you watch him, not even for a second—you can't, you mustn't!

In my efforts to forget Diadorim, a feeling of sadness came over me, and a deep fatigue. But I did not dwell on the past, nor fall into lassitude. If that was a sorrowful passage—well, then, it had to be. Like flowing water in a river. How ever many days it would last, let it; months, even. Now I no longer cared. But today, you know, sir, I think that our feelings circle about in certain ways, turning back on themselves, following a pattern. Pleasure often turns to fear, fear turns to hate; does hate then turn into these despairs? Despair is good if it turns into a greater sadness, and then into love, full of longings—then hope comes anew. But the little embers of it all are only the same coals. A fancy that came to me. Ah, what wouldn't I give to have your learning, and be able to study these things.

After that I sought ways to relax and amuse myself with the others. Talking with Catôcho, with Jõe Bexiguento, with Vove, with Feijó—the serious one, and with Umbelino—the cat-faced one. We laughed, and except for the combat chores, we loafed a lot. And so I went along, under that influence. If there was an order we would first gather into a large band, and then break up into small groups and scatter. The war was the same, but there we felt to a greater degree the lacks and the imperfections which occur everywhere. Is not the São Francisco always muddy? Most of the talk was about women. Everyone wanted them, that's all they thought of. A girl of one's own to enjoy, or else a gay street full of them . . . A friend of mine, Umbelino, used to say: since there were no women around, you had a lot to think about. He was from Rio Sirubim, a place back of the waterfalls. He was a good comrade and skilled fighter. Though he was small, he was good. He recalled: "Once I had a woman all my own, on Alecrim Street, in São Ramão, and still another on Fogo Street." This kind of talk in that heat! Everybody told stories about wenches who had been theirs alone; shameful episodes. But at night—would you believe it?—there were those who sought any kind of disgusting relief. And they were wild and hardened fighters, who knew no other life. During the day songs and singing; nobody knew any verses straight or didn't want to teach them; they made them up as they went along, singing through their noses. Or they would tell jokes and poke fun, cutting up like so many kids. Because of this loafing, we ate more than ever, almost as a diversion. Some would go off to gather palm cabbage, or dig manioc roots in some abandoned patch whose owner had fled. I gorged myself on honey locust, Barbados cherries, bumelia berries, and jack fruit. Fonfrêdo had a cup-and-ball toy with which we used to play, for low stakes. There were some sharp ones who bet even their neck amulets. And they made a business of selling these charms; some even got up fake scapularies. Does God forgive that sort of thing? If you inquired you would learn that to a jagunço God was a capricious master who at times gave His help, but at others, for no reason at all, turned His back, His protection ended, and bang! the blows would fall! And so they prayed. Jõe Bexiguento wanted several to take part in a novena, to a saint of his special devotion, which he did not have the patience to complete within the prescribed time.

And what about Hermógenes? He would come around, laughing and kidding with the others, without arrogance, but sly as a fox. In those days, he walked barefoot, in a pair of shrunken pants tight around the shins, and a filthy shirt. With his growth of beard, he looked like a beggar. He strode about, moving on the balls of his feet, coming and going with a stupid grin, and snooping everywhere. If I didn't actually think of him any longer as a bully, it did seem to me the whole time that he was up to some trick.

I wondered about something. What was that man really like inside? Someone had said that he had a wife and children. How was it possible? I kept thinking, trying to understand his real nature, so different from others. Hermógenes in a home somewhere, with his wife, caressing his little children, giving them lessons. Then he would go out. In the form of a werewolf? You had better cross yourself, my friend. I arrived at the conviction that hell, or some hell, really existed; had to be. And that the devil was wholly insane, completely mad—hopelessly so.

Ah, was I crazy? Hermógenes was queer, different. A desire came over me to get close to him, observe all that he did, listen to his remarks. Hermógenes—he instilled compassion and fear. But I came to realize that you can have no pity for the devil, none at all, and the reason is plain. The devil pulls up and dismounts quietly, making believe he is on foot, looking mournful, and you go near him—then he starts jumping and whirling as in a dance, talking big, trying to embrace you and making ugly faces, his mouth stretched wide. Because he is—

he is incurably insane. Utterly dangerous. During those days I
was also very much confused.

"Do you suppose Hermógenes likes women, too?", I asked,
needing to know. "Hell, he doesn't even ask the price. Only
when he doesn't like them . . ." someone answered. "Nah. I
think the only thing he really likes is himself," another cut in.
Was he really like that?—I wondered out loud, and all the companions agreed that he was. And did they think that in such
circumstances the act was possible and natural? Of course—
why not? And as long as we were on the subject, someone else
spoke up: "The Brejinho flat is six leagues from here—they
have a public park there. And there are women . . ."

Dute said this, I believe, or maybe it was someone else. But
Catôcho denied it: said he had been there and had not seen a
single public woman, just a little country store and an old
woman smoking a pipe, seated at the door, and weaving sieves.
That they wanted women principally for one purpose, was
understandable; I did too. I wanted them with the urgency of
my body, but also with a feeling of tenderness and regard—to
those dispensers of delights I always gave the tribute of my
gratitude. I do not repudiate that which is of sweet use to me;
thank God, all my life I have had consideration for every
prostitute, women who are more than sisters, whom we need
more, their delightful bounty. Then Lindorífico recalled a
carousal in some village down there somewhere: the drum-
beating, the wheezing of accordions, lots of liquor; women
dancing around, bumping men belly to belly; women taking
off their clothes; men taking women into the bushes in the
pitch dark; others trying to start a fight. What for? Why not
enjoy everything, but with good manners, without roughhous-
ing? It made me sad to hear about it. There are some things
which are not bad in themselves, but which cause evil, because
they become changed into something which they are not. Like
cane juice which turns sour.

I don't remember much else, but I know that at that time I
was feeling very wretched. What was there that I could find
pleasure in? In the morning, when I awoke, I was always full

of anger. One fellow told me that I was looking green, like I was sick, that it must be my liver. Perhaps it was. Paspe, who did the cooking, brewed teas for me, camomile, anise, and wormwood. Pain, I really had none. I just felt out of sorts.

Then I learned something that stood me in good stead later on: I discovered that when I felt that way in the morning, angry with someone, all I had to do was to start thinking of someone else, and I became instantly and equally as angry with that one, too. Everybody, one after another, who entered my mind, I would begin to feel hatred toward them in the same way, even though they were my friends and I had neither grievance nor complaint against them. But the sediment in my thought roiled my memories, and I would conclude that what someone had said to me one day had been meant to offend me, and I would put a wrong interpretation on all conversations and actions. Would you believe it? And it was then that I hit upon the real truth: that the anger which burned within me was mine and mine alone, something unrestrained and blind. A person could not be held to blame if I chose to parade him in my thoughts. Nowadays, when I meditate more deeply on this hidden phase of life, I keep asking myself: can the same thing be true, too, of the intoxication of love? Nonsense. You must forgive me again. But, on that occasion, I remembered a bit of advice which Zé Bebelo had given me one day, at Nhanva, which was that while at times it was necessary to pretend that one is angry, one must never give way to anger itself, because when one harbors anger against another, it is the same as permitting that person to control our thoughts and emotions, which obviously is a surrender of sovereignty, and great foolishness as well. Zé Bebelo always talked straight to the point, real intelligent. I understood and I obeyed. I mean, I became stubborn and put my foot down, determined to stop giving way to anger. I remember also that on that morning the heat was less intense, and the air pleasant. I felt at peace—with joy in my heart—as if I were thankful for having received a warning. I loitered for a long time, alone, by the side of the water, listening to the notes of a bird—a robin or a cuckoo. Suddenly, I sensed something and looked up: it was Diadorim approaching, he was already at my side. Smiling warmly, he greeted me:

"How have you been, Riobaldo? Aren't you glad to see me?"

Diadorim's arrival was like a white miracle, a complete surprise. My heart beat fast. But a doubt remained, a doubt that overcast my satisfaction. I was the one to whom something was due, not him. I therefore remained aloof; I displayed no emotion. I waited before replying; finally, I cleared my throat and said:

"Sure. Where have you been, if I may ask?"

With his friendship for me, for all time, showing in his big eyes, he exclaimed:

"You are not in good health, Riobaldo, I can see it. Have you not been well lately?"

"Just taking things as they come."

Whereupon Diadorim gave me his hand, which I barely accepted. And then he began telling me that he had spent those days alone, hidden in the woods, treating himself for a bullet wound which had caught him in the leg near the knee, that it was only a scratch. That left me even more puzzled. If he had really been hurt, why had he not joined us, to receive help and better treatment? A sick person doesn't run off to some hiding place in the woods, all by himself, like an animal. Was he perhaps not telling the truth? At that point, it seems to me, I became suspicious: where had Diadorim gone, and for what evil purpose, and now this cock-and-bull story? He talked so kindly, so sincerely; and his eyes, in which I could see his affection, could hold no pretense. He was thin, wasted, very pale, and still limped a little. What a cruel time he must have had of it, all those days, without help from anyone, treating his injury with poultices of roots and leaves, and eating God knows what. He must have suffered hunger and all sorts of privations. And suddenly I found myself loving him beyond all reason, loving him even more than before. With my heart at his feet, to be trampled upon. I had been loving him the whole time.

It was a time of serene emotion, a thing life most begrudges. Life brooks no delay in anything. Shortly thereafter we turned again to fighting, furiously. I had somewhat lost my understanding of all those procedures and movements, and of the reasons for the orders we carried out. But I soon toughened up, doing my job as a jagunço; I became good at it. Now I had Diadorim close to me, which meant even more in the midst of those perils. I saw too that luck was on our side—that death is for those who die. I wonder?

So, with João Goanhá as leader, we set out, about fifty of us, to capture a pack train of the Bebelos, who were approaching all unsuspecting by night, on the Bento-Pedro, in a stretch of marshland, a rice field. It proved easy to surprise them. The sentinels panicked, without giving one shout of alarm—we just ran them off. That cargo was enormous, a rich haul; it contained everything, even tax-paid cachaça, in cases of forty-eight bottles. Then we drove the pack animals and hid them in Capão dos Ossos, where there is scrub and trails among the stunted growth, and pools drying up, fringed by green vegetation. Then, at Poço-Triste, we got orders to reload the animals. That was a period of fun: the trotting train, the clouds of dust, the neighing of the horses. Huge old spider webs hung from tree to tree. It seemed as if the war had come to a good end. "At last," someone said, "now to enjoy life." "But," I asked, "what about Zé Bebelo?" One Federico Xexéu, who had come with a message, threw cold water on us: "Yeh! Zé Bebel'? He's on the way, with a cloud of men."

Leagues away, fighting was going on. Reports of it reached us. Then a large body of horsemen, rushing headlong, burning up the ground, could be seen galloping toward us. "Wow! Is this it?" No, it wasn't. It was only Sô Candelário, arriving suddenly. He showed up with all those men.

His horse stopped so short that its body doubled up. Sô Candelário. He was tall, deeply tanned, almost black, with a yellowish mustache. He was a commander who commanded. When the fighting started, he would jump in the lead, shouting at the top of his lungs. He took over; compared to him Hermógenes looked like a poor slob. Sô Candelário was the one to take on Zé Bebelo. He dismounted, and stood for awhile with his back toward us.

I greeted Fafafa, who was one of Sô Candelário's men, and with whom both he and Alaripe had reappeared. Fafafa, who later said something to me, on a terrible occasion . . . Ah, but there's something I haven't told you—it's about the prisoner. It happened once that we were well hidden around the house of a settler, in Timba-Tuvaca; the house was whitewashed and had a tile roof. Some of us were in gullies, some high up in trees; some were even in the pigsty, in the muck of the pigs. Then came the Bebelos—about thirty of them. We started shooting as soon as they halted, and killed a number of them; the rest got away. One was taken prisoner. He was entirely unharmed. "What are they going to do with him?" I asked, "Are they going to kill him?" "Probably. Listen, friend, have we any way of guarding live prisoners? You cut their throats from right to left," Fafafa replied. He was right in what he was saying. But who would be the one to do it? I rubbed my eyes, wanting and not wanting to know. I didn't even know his name, what he was called, the young man doomed to die that way, for if we turned him loose he would rejoin the others and report on us. I went to the edge of the creek. I saw them taking the boy, and noticed how he walked normally, heading for his end on his own two feet. Two others afterwards went by, doubtless on their way to do the killing; I did not see Hermógenes. One was a certain Adílcio, who prided himself on being capable of anything. Luís Pajeú was the other. I imagined they were going to kill the man at the edge of a nearby clump of trees. Overcome with pity, I felt a knot in my throat, I was burning up. If that was only a dream, then I was only dreaming; but, if it was not, then I needed some link to reality. I knelt by the creek and leaned over, and with my face against the water, I sucked it up like a dog or a horse. My thirst would not be quenched, and my belly must have swelled up, like a frog's. About two hundred feet upstream, where the creek ran through the woods, they were knifing the boy, and as I gazed at the water, which I could not stop drinking, I expected to see it turn red with his blood. I think I was burning up with fever.

A hullabaloo broke out, fit to make you shiver. Diadorim pulled me along. Sô Candelário in his saddle, hurriedly shouting orders: he wanted a detachment of men in a hurry, to go with him at once to É-Já, beyond the Bró. "Let's go, Riobaldo! We are going to meet Joca Ramiro!" Diadorim pushed me. I mounted. I put my foot in one stirrup but couldn't find the other. "Hurry, Riobaldo!" Diadorim kept after me. That other thing was still going around in my head—but, wait, who was that I just saw? It was the boy, the prisoner, alive and whole. And mounted on a horse. Then they told me: no, he wasn't going to die; no, they weren't going to kill him. Sô Candelário had decided to pardon him because of his youth. "He is a Bahian, and back he goes to Bahia. We will take him with us part way, and turn him loose up there."

In my happiness I saw stars. The others explained further that there was no longer any danger that the prisoner would rejoin the other Bebelos and take up arms against us again, for it had been arranged for an incantation to be said over him that would take away all taste for fighting. But what about Luís Pajeu and Adílcio, the way I had seen them, carrying their knives unsheathed? They had been going to help butcher a hog, there were lots of them there, and cut it up into meat and bacon. Ah, I had drunk all that water for nothing.

We galloped off. It seemed to me that from there on, everything was going to be sheer madness. Sô Candelário galloped ahead of everybody, like the king of the winds.

The place where we halted, É-Já, was a short distance beyond the wooden bridge. As it was full of holes, we forded the rocky stream farther down, at a bad spot, where the water ran fast and the stones were loose and slippery. There was no one there. I felt let-down. All around us lay bright green grass, watering places and good pasture lands. I put the question: "Where's Joca Ramiro?" rudely. Diadorim went on as though he had not heard me: "This is the place, Riobaldo; if the enemy shows up, we die, but not a single Bebelo will get past this point." Diadorim was so boastful, that I mocked him: "What the hell do I care! Is this what you call seeing Joca Ramiro? Well, I'm seeing him." "Don't complain, Riobaldo. At this very moment,

Joca Ramiro must be falling upon them and slashing them to pieces," was his reply. This got my dander up: "You know everything, don't you. Big secrets." But, in exchanges like that, Diadorim always got the better of me. He reproved me, saying: "I know nothing. I know only what you, too, can know, Riobaldo. But I know Joca Ramiro, who alone plans the moves. And I know Sô Candelário, who shows up right where he is told."

And that's the way it was. During the days that we had to mount guard among the large flat rocks, I came to know something of that man. Sô Candelário—how can I describe him to you? He was unique. I don't think he ever slept, he ate almost nothing, and that, hurriedly, and smoked all the time. He scanned the horizons impatiently, seeming to thirst for war, war, much war. Where was he from, where had he come from? From the wastelands of Bahia, they told me. He would pass by without looking at me. On one occasion Diadorim introduced me: "Chief, this is my friend, Riobaldo." Then, for the first time, Sô Candelário really saw me. As for laughing or smiling, he didn't know how, but for an instant a look of kindly soberness would come into his eyes, shutting out their fierceness, and that was supposed to be a smile. I saw at once that he knew Diadorim and thought highly of him. "Riobaldo—Tatarana —I know," he said, "You are a good shot, a skilled marksman," and kept on walking. He couldn't stand still. And in some way that I couldn't quite make out, there was something about him that reminded me of Zé Bebelo himself.

But it was Alaripe who told me something that everyone knew and talked about—that what Sô Candelário sought was death itself. He drank his strong cachaça almost constantly. Why? I'll tell you—he was afraid he had leprosy. His father had had it, and his brothers too. Leprosy—there is nothing more to say: then is when a man comes to know the curse of punishment. Punishment, for what? Because of this, no doubt, Sô Candelário was possessed of hatred. He lived with his mind on fire. Leprosy takes time, it lies quietly in the body, then breaks out suddenly; it can appear at any hour, early or late. Sô Candelário had a fixed habit: he was always lifting his shirt, looking at his arms, at the tip of his elbows, and scratching his skin until he bled. He carried a little pocket mirror in which he stole glances at himself. We knew that he took certain remedies; he was the first up every morning, before daybreak, swallowed a dose of theriac, and went to wash his body in the pool; he walked toward the edge of the creek naked, naked as the leg of a stork. Today I think that of all people, Sô Candelário is the one I understand best. He courted death because of his fear of leprosy, and at the same time, with the same tenacity, he strove to heal himself. Crazy, was he? And who isn't, even I or you, sir? But, I esteemed that man, because he at least knew what he wanted.

The enemy was delaying so long in showing up, that we began to get on edge. Some, no. That Luzié, for instance, who sang without a worry, like a cicada between showers. Sometimes I asked him to sing those verses, which I never forgot, from the song of Siruiz. When I heard them, I felt like trying to sing them myself. My mother was the one who could have sung them for me. Gentleness makes one forget many things— the stupid things we spend our lives doing, like prisoners, only because we have to, without nobility. At times when he thought he was alone, Diadorim used to sing to himself, and he had a good voice. But when anyone was around, he never would. Come to find out, the others didn't see in those verses of Siruiz the same beauty that I did. Not even Diadorim. "Have you a longing for your boyhood days, Riobaldo?" he asked, when I was trying to explain my feelings to him. I had no such longing. What I would have liked, if it were possible, was to be a boy, right then, at that very hour. Ever since that time, I have thought that people's lives, for want of common sense and zest, flow aimlessly, like a story without head or tail. Life should be lived as on a stage, each one playing his part with great gusto. That is what I thought, it is what I think still.

As for Sô Candelário's behavior, it varied. "Goddamit, we haven't any news. I don't know. Information is something we have to go after, go right out and get!" Sô Candelário almost shouted. He ordered three men to mount and advance up the road for a distance of one league, to gather what information they could and spy on the enemy scouts. He sent me, too. To tell the truth, I more or less volunteered. I stepped forward and looked at him long and hard. "You, Tatarana, go too." When he called me Tatarana, I knew that he was recognizing my skill as a marksman. I mounted and went off at a fast trot. Diadorim and Caçanje had gone ahead, about four hundred yards. As soon as they saw that I was coming, they turned in their saddles. Diadorim lifted his arm and waved. I wanted to catch up quickly, and tried to spur my horse into a half-gallop, but just then he got other ideas: he jumped and shied to the left side of the road, and I came near falling off. What had startled him was a dry flying leaf carried by the wind that was whirling around us that had lodged against his eye and ear. Swirling eddies—you know, winds fighting. When one meets another and they whirl together, it is a crazy sight. The dust rises high, in a dark cloud full of flying leaves and broken twigs, with whistling sounds, spinning and jumping like a top. Diadorim and Caçanje had stopped, waiting for me to catch up. "The dust devil!" said Caçanje, cursing. "There is a cross wind blowing from the direction of the ocean," said Diadorim. But Caçanje would not have it that way: the whirlwind was His, the devil's. The devil was there, he travelled inside it. I started laughing. What I thought was: "The devil in the street, in the middle of the whirlwind." I think the most terrible time in my life is summed up in those words, which you must never repeat. But, bear with me. We'll get to it. Even Caçanje and Diadorim laughed, too. Then we got going.

We were going as far as the joining of the two creeks, where there is a broken waterfall. I thought no more of the whirlwind, nor of its alleged owner, who lives and travels in it—the Dirty One—the one who takes our evil words and thoughts, and brings them all to pass; the one who can be seen in a black mirror; the Hider. So, we reached the junction of the two little creeks at the waterfall, and stayed there until the sun went down. How were we going to take any information back to Sô Candelário? Is news something you get by wishing for it on a star? The coatis were climbing down, sniffing, after their day's sleep in the trees, and the guans were flying from tree to tree, getting ready to roost for the night, fussing like a lot of chickens. I was oppressed by a sense of ominous foreboding. If I could only live in a large city. But I didn't know any really large city. I stood looking off in the distance where there was still a little light from the day's end. I remember the lapse of time, and the thoughts that came into my head. The stream licking everything it saw, like a dog. The palm tree whispering to itself. When night fell, we left. The first owl flew; I could have shot it down.

But Sô Candelário's calculations were not foolish. The very next day we had news, plenty of it! From here and there, it began coming in, in bits and pieces. One Sucívre galloped up, out of breath, and reported: "Nho Ricardão opened fire, at Ribeirão do Veado. Titão Passos got thirty or more of them, in a hot fight at the spur of the sierra."

The Bebelos had scattered, half-crazy, in the face of hard facts and a hail of bullets. We became jubilant. Sô Candelário climbed up on the platform of branches—which he had ordered made, and on which he slept without resting—and stood there a long time, looking off in the distance, like an eagle poised for flight. Now it was war, at last; the shouts and hallelujahs were no doubt resounding, way yonder. Then came Adalgizo: "Seô Hermógenes went by, about six leagues from here on his way to join the fight."

Our time was close, for the retreating Bebelos would have to pass us there, at É-Já. Sô Candelário approached, and with tears in his eyes cried out that he had never led a body of men as brave as we were, or so capable. And he wanted the enemy to come quickly, quickly. We were on the alert every minute, and we slept that night with one eye open, hugging our weapons. The number of sentinels between nightfall and sunup was doubled. Fighting erupts like a bolt of lightning. The least strange noise or incident was like a shout of alarm: someone would suddenly kick away a burning stick, throw a handful of dirt on the camp fire to put it out, and let out a warning whistle. One time, shots were fired, but it wasn't anything— just a hungry and sleepless steer which had come there alone to graze in the lush grass, and showed its long face at an odd

hour. "Everything crazy happens in war. Damn it to hell!"
someone grumbled, but there were those who laughed about it
until nearly daybreak. I enjoyed everything that went on; each
day I liked it more. Gradually I learned to see the humorous
side of the turmoil. I felt that I could display courage whenever it was called for—a feeling that grows steadily in the
midst of easy laughter, with swigs of cachaça and sleeping
alongside one's gun. What is needed is that easy companionship with everyone, like brothers. Diadorim and I, we formed a
single shadow. Everything was fine just as it was. Sô Candelário was a chief to my liking, my idea of what a chief should
be. And what about Joca Ramiro?

An unusual restlessness among the herd of horses tipped us
off that something was about to happen. Suddenly, a large
body of men loomed up out of the vastness of the North, heading our way. Cries of "Joca Ramiro! Joca Ramiro!" Sô Candelário jumped into his saddle, like a steel spring, and galloped
to meet them. At first, we were all stunned. I saw such a burning brightness of joy in Diadorim's eyes that it annoyed me.
Was I jealous? "Riobaldo, you are going to see what he is like!"
Diadorim exclaimed, embracing me. He seemed like a child in
his excitement. How could I get mad about that? Then, in a
rush, the whole troop, preceded by an advance guard, drew
near, the horses' iron-shod hooves pounding the gravel. There
were about two hundred men, nearly all seasoned campaigners
from Bahia, and some recruits. They hailed us and shouted
their greetings. And Joca Ramiro. There he was on a white
horse, a horse that haughtily looked down at me. A tooled-
leather saddle, from Jequié, with ornate black-and-white designs. Beautiful, heavy reins. He was a big-shouldered man,
with a large, red face, and compelling eyes. How can I describe him to you? Curly, black hair? A good-looking hat? He
was all man. Handsome. You looked at him but without staring.
You were almost afraid to hurt, to injure, that man among men,
with your roughness that came from living in the sertão. And,
after he had gone, the thing that remained, above all others,
was the memory of his voice—a voice without a trace of doubt
or of sadness in it—a voice you could not forget.

In the midst of all that hubbub, I didn't find out as much as I would have liked to. The chiefs had dismounted, and all the men, too, in noisy but orderly fashion. Sô Candelário didn't leave Joca Ramiro's side, explaining everything with wide gestures, so excited he could hardly talk. The delay was short. The troop had to push on at top speed—they had chosen the place and hour of combat—so we learned. They had time only for coffee. But Joca Ramiro walked around, with wide, slow strides—he wanted to inspect the camp, and greet this fellow or that one, if only with a word of appreciation and pleasure. His manner of walking—I studied it well—was majestic and imposing, like nobody else's. Diadorim kept looking at him, and tears came to his eyes. Impulsively, he walked up to Joca Ramiro and took his hand and kissed it. Joca Ramiro looked at him hard, for just an instant, but so fondly, with a different degree of friendship. How he loved Diadorim! He put his arms around him in an embrace. Then he came toward us, to where we were. And I did as Diadorim had done—I don't know why: I took that man's hand and kissed it. Then all the others—the young ones—kissed it also. The older ones were ashamed to.

"This one here is Riobaldo, you know, sir? My friend. Some call him by his nickname of Tatarana," so spoke Diadorim. Slowly, Joca Ramiro turned to look at me, and said: "Tatarana, a fire caterpillar with stinging hairs. My son, you have the earmarks of a true brave. Riobaldo. Riobaldo. Wait," he said, "I think I have something for you."

He sent one of his men named João Frio to the pack animals for whatever it was. It was a government rifle, a cavalry musket. And Joca Ramiro was making me a present of it! I tell you, sir, my satisfaction knew no bounds. Would the others be jealous of me—and how! Diadorim was looking at me, greatly pleased. He called me aside. I observed that as he was so much liked and singled out by Joca Ramiro, he purposely kept his distance so that no one could complain of favoritism. "Isn't he really the chief of them all? Isn't he really the boss?" Diadorim asked me. There was no doubt that he was. But I had not noticed how quickly the time had passed. They were already leaving. Mounted on his white horse, Joca Ramiro waved a farewell. I saw him take a last look at Diadorim. Sô Candelário shouted: "Hail to Jesus, in routs and victories!" And in an uproar, they set spurs to their horses and dashed away, stirring up a cloud of dust that hung long in the air. It was like the sound of music.

From the moment Joca Ramiro stopped in our midst, we talked of nothing else. He was going straight into combat—it would be the end of the war! "Sô Candelário wanted to go too, but he was ordered to stay behind," said Diadorim, and explained that because of his passionate eagerness to advance and keep advancing, Sô Candelário might upset the carefully laid plans.

Joca Ramiro had also ordered that our group be split up into three or four patrols to keep a close watch on the fording places and the roads leading to them. Diadorim and I were assigned to one of these patrols, about fifteen men, led by João Curiol. We went to the Umbuzeiros flat, an ugly place, covered with dusty bromelias and some high rocks. On the other side of the ford there is a small plain, called Plain-of-the-Crested-Screamer, almost purposely, it seemed, for it was there, in effect, that the enemy showed up. It was terrible. I'll tell you all about it right now.

It was terrible because of the suddenness with which it happened. There are always surprises, you know, sir, even when you're expecting something, the thing happens, and you can hardly realize it. You don't believe your own eyes—it comes so suddenly. A good breeze was blowing from their direction, so that we soon heard their galloping. We readied our arms. They dashed through the creek so fast that the water splashed high. It looked real pretty in the sunlight. We opened fire.

I saw many a man knocked off his horse. We let riderless horses escape, but we picked off the men on the ground, one by one. The horses, no. But there was one which panicked and started to rear and plunge. The rider could not control him and they came close to us. Both died suddenly. My friend, it was utter destruction. But those were men! They halted as quickly as they could, the survivors dismounted and started crawling, answering our fire. Ah, they were able to hide behind some rocks, and then we couldn't get at them. There must have been about ten left, or maybe only eight. They yelled curses, in a fever of hate, and called us everything. We did the same. We poured on the fire whenever a man gave sign of himself. The bullets splattered against the rocks, chipping them. One man showed himself, and fell at once. They were short of ammunition. As for fleeing, they couldn't. We kept on shooting, until about six—a half dozen—were left.

"Say, do you know who is in command over there?" the scout Roque asked me. "Do you know?"

Ah, I knew, all right. I had known from the first moment. It was the one I did not want it to be. It was Zé Bebelo! And I was condemned to kill him!

"Shoot them! Let daylight through them!" yelled João Curiol. Sooner or later, we would have to go after them with our knives.

"Scum! Take that, you dog! You filth! You gelding!" It was the voice of Zé Bebelo.

I did not yell. Diadorim, too, was shooting silently. Their ammunition was almost gone. There must have been about four of them left, maybe three. The barrel of my rifle was getting too hot.

"You gelding! Take. . . !" Freitas, one of our men, yelled and fell, badly hurt. The bullet had come from Zé Bebelo. We returned a barrage. They responded. But their response was weak. I tell you, sir, I liked Zé Bebelo. I'll tell you more: that I was shooting less than I thought. How could I have a hand in his death? A man of that kind, with his body, his mind, all that he knew and understood? I thought about that. You always had to think about Zé Bebelo. A man, a weak thing in himself, soft even, skipping between life and death among the hard rocks. I felt it in my throat. Could I live with that on my conscience? Suddenly I cried out:

"Joca Ramiro wants that man alive! Joca Ramiro insists on it!"

I don't know where I got the sudden impulse to say that—a

pure invention. Boldly, I shouted and repeated it. The others accepted it and also shouted, even João Curiol:

"Joca Ramiro wants that man alive!"

"It is an order of Joca Ramiro's!"

There was no further shooting from the other side, just an occasional bullet.

"How about it, Chief? Shall we go after him with knives?" asked Sangue-de-Outro.

João Curiol said no—that they must be hoarding their ammunition for a last stand.

"It is Joca Ramiro's orders to take the man alive," I repeated.

I had saved Zé Bebelo. They had all approved. Now, you are not going to understand me. See how strange things are. They had all agreed, and then, amazingly, I felt shocked at what I had done. Had I failed to think the matter through? What was I doing, why did I want them to catch Zé Bebelo alive, flesh and bone, so he could later be tortured and killed in a worse way? I became enraged with myself. I was overcome with remorse and bitterness. It would all be my fault, forever. So I called upon my rifle and cartridge holders for all they had. I kept firing and firing. I wanted, at all costs, to reach Zé Bebelo with a bullet, to finish him off once and for all, to save him from martyrdom.

"Are you crazy, Riobaldo?" yelled Diadorim, crawling over to me and grabbing me by the arm.

"Joca Ramiro wants the man alive! Joca Ramiro wants it that way, he ordered it!" they were all shouting at me now.

Now they were all against me. What could I say? I didn't see clearly what happened next. Suddenly Zé Bebelo showed himself, cocky as a bantam rooster. In one hand, he had his dagger; in the other, a large, center-fire pistol. He unloaded the pistol by shooting it into the ground, near his own feet. The bullets kicked up the dust. When the dust had settled, there he stood, straight, taut, full of fight. He flashed the dagger and waited. He himself wanted to die gallantly, quickly. I looked and looked. I lacked the courage to shoot him. Then one of our men—I don't know who—threw his lasso. Zé Bebelo had hardly put out one leg to steady himself, when he fell, crying out, as he was dragged along: "Riffraff! Vermin!" But they all fell on him and took away his knife. I stood still, perplexed, awkward. I did not want, oh, I did not want him to recognize me.

A loud clatter of hoofs filled the air—it was Joca Ramiro with all his men. Clouds of golden dust billowed up, filling nose and eyes. I huddled in the same place, behind a large rock. The trouble was, I was ashamed. The din was frightful. More groups of our people kept arriving; I heard Sô Candelário's shouts. The ring of horsemen continued to grow. Someone blew on a steer's horn. They were going to the camp. But Diadorim was looking for me, and for João Curiol, too, among our dead and wounded, and also because he must have lost some belongings of his there.

"A terrific man," I heard someone say. My eyes were fixed on the ground, and I saw that I was trembling. "Zé Bebelo, I'll tell you, won his spurs! He is a killer!"

"Is he?" I said, and at that moment Diadorim appeared, beaming with happiness, almost dancing: "We have won, Riobaldo! The war is over. Furthermore, Joca Ramiro was very glad that we had taken the man alive." That gave me little comfort. Afterwards, what? "What for, Diadorim? Will they kill him now? Are they going to kill him?" I was barely able to ask. But João Curiol turned and said: "No, not kill him. They are going to try him."

"A trial?" I did not smile, nor did I understand.

"I'll bet I know. It was he himself who asked for it. The crazy man! Prisoner though he was, in that hopeless situation, when he came face to face with Joca Ramiro, he shouted angrily: 'Go ahead! Either you kill me here and now, or I demand a full and legal trial!' Whereupon Joca Ramiro agreed and promised an immediate trial." At least that was how João Curiol explained it to me.

I was thankful for that much. We left, taking João Concliz with us, to go out into the surrounding territory and pass the word along. It was a general round-up. We had heard that Titão Passos's and Hermógenes's bands were on their way. Ricardão would arrive any minute. I did not want to return right away with the others; I thought it better not to see Zé Bebelo. We mounted and vanished amidst those plains, among those souari nut trees.

"A funny, crazy man!" Diadorim mused. "Do you know what he said, what happened?" And he told me.

Joca Ramiro had arrived, regal on his tall white horse, and faced Zé Bebelo, who was on foot, ragged and dirty, without a hat, his hands tied behind him, and held by two men. But even so, Zé Bebelo lifted his chin, and looked the other man over, from top to bottom. Then he said:

"Show me respect, Chief. You, the great horseman, are look- ing down on me, but I am your equal. Show me respect!"

"Calm down, sir. You are a prisoner," replied Joca Ramiro, without raising his voice.

Then, to everyone's surprise, Zé Bebelo also changed his tone, and tauntingly made a bold but witty remark:

"A prisoner? Ah yes, a prisoner. So I am, as well I know. But then, what you are seeing is not what you see, old man: it is what you will see."

"I see a brave man, prisoner," Joca Ramiro then said, and he spoke considerately.

"That's right. I am a prisoner, but there's something else."

"What, old brother?"

"It is, it is the world beyond control." Thus Zé Bebelo capped his remarks, and all who heard him laughed.

Was it all foolishness? Not at all, for I could not see Zé Be- belo a prisoner. He was not one you could hold in, something you could lay your hands on. Like quicksilver he was. And there would be a trial.

So, we returned; early the following morning we lined up there in camp. What would the trial be like? I said right off that nobody knew for sure. Hermógenes heard me and agreed:

"That's right, that's right. We'll see, we'll see something that isn't usually done" were his words. "So now we have trials!" many said jokingly. I listened to what the others had to say. "That's true, that's right. Joca Ramiro knows what he's doing" Titão Passos spoke up. "It's better this way. We have to get rid of those skunks for good!" said Ricardão. And Sô Candelário, who wouldn't get off his horse, shouted as he came by: "A trial!

That's the thing! They have to learn who gives the orders, who's the boss!"

Finally everybody was gathered together; we were at the camp at É-Já, which could barely hold such a crowd. There were bunches of donkeys, horses grazing, jagunços of all breeds and brands milling about, eating, drinking, jabbering away. Sô Candelário had sent two men all the way to São José Prêto, just to buy sky rockets to be shot off at the end of the trial.

And where was Zé Bebelo? He was being kept out of sight in a canvas tent, the only one we had because Joca Ramiro himself had got out of the habit of sleeping in a tent on account of the heat. You couldn't see the prisoner inside there, under guard. They said he accepted food and water, and was lying on a cow hide, smoking and thinking. I liked that. What I wanted was to avoid his setting eyes on me.

"Where are we going? Where will the trial be held?" I asked Diadorim, when I saw preparations being made for departure. "Man, I don't know." Diadorim knew nothing about the matter. It was only later that the word got around. We were going to the Sempre-Verde ranch, beyond the Brejinho-do-Brejo ranch, the one that belongs to Dr. Mirabô de Melo.

What was the reason for taking that man such a distance? Was it necessary? Diadorim didn't answer. But from what he said and didn't say, I surmised what lay behind it: Joca Ramiro was deliberately traveling three leagues, accompanied by all the jagunços and group leaders and chiefs, with the prisoner mounted on a black horse, and all the troops and munitions, booty, and food supplies, heading north—all for show. The trial, too. Was this right?

We set out, in noisy tumult, horses and riders of every kind and description. Zé Bebelo was up front, surrounded by a guard of horsemen, Titão Passos's men. He had his hands tied, as is customary. There was no need to tie his hands. I didn't want to see it. It left me with a bad taste, made me feel depressed. I kept hanging back. It depressed me so much so that I made the whole journey at the tail end of the line, alongside the gentle band of big-eared donkeys that brought up the rear. But I kept thinking: whether he was good or bad, could they do away with

Zé Bebelo? Who had the right to put Zé Bebelo on trial?

In due time, we passed Brejinho-do-Brejo. We were approaching the Sempre-Verde ranch. Something came over me, suddenly. I spurred and galloped to the front, all stirred up, on the rebound from those anxieties. I suddenly wanted to be near, to see with my own eyes all that happened next. I no longer cared if Zé Bebelo saw me. I passed on ahead of nearly all the others. They thought I had arrived with a message. "What happened, Riobaldo, what happened?" Diadorim shouted at me. I gave no answer. No one there would understand. Only Zé Bebelo.

The house of the Sempre-Verde ranch was enormous. We turned off the road and entered the approaches to the barnyard corrals, with that large body of men. It looked like a funeral procession. Before I reached it, the big gate creaked open and we started filling the corrals with our horses. The Big House was closed. "It must not be opened. It must not be opened." The order was repeated from one to another. Hell, it wouldn't do to break in—it belonged to a friend, Dr. Mirabô de Melo, who was away. We gathered on the large, flat terrace. They had taken Zé Bebelo down off his horse. His hands were tied, all right, but in front of his body, as if he were handcuffed. "Tie his feet too!" some hothead shouted. Another came forward with a strong thong of capybara leather. What were those men thinking of? What did they want? They were all crazy.

Joca Ramiro, Sô Candelário, Hermógenes, Ricardão, Titão Passos, and João Goanhá were in a huddle, holding a confab in the middle of the terrace. But Zé Bebelo was not cast down. He straightened up and threw out his chest—like a turkey when it gobbles—and marched forward. Little though he was, he was mighty. Every inch a man. He kept going. "Well, I'll be—" said someone in amazement. A three-legged stool, with a leather seat, had been brought and placed in front of Joca Ramiro, in the center of the terrace. Quickly, Zé Bebelo sat himself on it. "Did you ever!" some were saying. The horde of jagunços closed in around them, like at a round-up, with Zé Bebelo seated, and Joca Ramiro standing, Ricardão standing, Sô Candelário standing, João Goanhá, Titão Passos, all of them. That was a piece of boldness, or else, sheer madness. He alone was seated, on the stool, in the midst of all. Then, he crossed his legs, and spoke:

"Sit down. Sit down, gentlemen. Make yourselves at home," he said with a mock air of apology, bobbing his head and gesturing with his elbows at the ground around him.

Such queer behavior had never been seen. And seeing it, the others frowned, their eyes glinted. I think they were getting ready to kill him—they weren't going to be insulted in that manner—they weren't going to put up with that mockery. There was a dead silence. We were ordered to stand back to make more room.

Then, suddenly, Joca Ramiro, shrewd as they come, accepted the crazy invitation to be seated, and smiling lightly sat down on the ground in front of Zé Bebelo. The two looked at each other. It had all taken place very quickly and through the crowd there ran an enthusiastic murmur of approval. Ah, Joca Ramiro had an answer for everything—Joca Ramiro was a great man.

Then Zé Bebelo—do you know what he did? He stood up, kicked the footstool aside, and clumsily seated himself on the ground, too, in front of Joca Ramiro. A babble broke out; everyone was pleased by the incident. Who doesn't like a plucky gesture like that? And even the other chiefs, all of them, one by one, changed their stance: they didn't sit down but began to slouch and squat, so as to be on a level and avoid a position of deference. Whereupon the rank and file of jagunços pressed in closer, without letting go their weapons, anxious to see and hear all that took place. A shiver of excitement ran through that throng every so often, like the wink of a parrot's eye. I watched Hermógenes, I knew the worst would come from him. Then, all waited still and silent. Was Joca Ramiro going to speak the customary words, without further ado?

"You asked for a trial," he said, in a full voice, beautiful in its repose.

"I am on trial every hour," replied Zé Bebelo.

Did that make sense? But he was neither crazy nor worried, nor ready for hanging. Even when a capybara sits, it does so to think, not to lose heart. Lifting his head, he looked about him, scanning the faces of all those men. He took a deep breath and raised his chin, bolder and bolder. A man like that divines everything, lightning-fast, in a person's eyes. I had full confidence in him.

"I warn you: you may be shot, once and for all. You lost the war, you are our prisoner," Joca Ramiro declared.

"Really! In that case, then, why all these formalities?" Zé Bebelo quickly came back at him.

I smiled at his nerve. He himself had invented this demand for a trial, and now he was twisting the reason: as if at the end of a trial no one could rightfully be shot. He was no fool, but he was playing with death. All that was needed was for Joca Ramiro to lose a little of his patience, just a bit. Only, luckily, Joca Ramiro never lost his patience. He taunted him, nothing more:

"What good is it to want to know so much? You knew plenty already—so I was told. But, all of a sudden, you showed up here in the sertão, and you saw a lot of things you had never seen before. The knowledge you gained was no help at all. What was the use?"

"It is always useful, Chief: I lost—I recognize that I lost. You won. But let me ask you something. What have you gained by it?"

Pure nonsense, and lots of impudence. The jagunços did not understand what they had heard, and some made signs to indicate that Zé Bebelo was cracked in the head; others kept an ominous silence. One said: "We won't get anywhere this way." Joca Ramiro did not answer at once. He pulled at his eyebrows. Then:

"You came to sow confusion, to turn the people of the sertão from their old ways."

"That which is old has already lost its bearings. The old was good when it was new."

"You are not of the sertão. Not of the land."

"Am I of fire? Am I of air? The worm a hen finds and eats is of the land, which she scratches!"

You should have seen those men—the look on their faces. All those many men, on this side and on that, encircling the open space in the middle, their gun butts grounded, how they shook their heads under their pulled-down hats. Joca Ramiro had power over them. Joca Ramiro was the one who ruled. He needed only to speak briefly and give an order. Or show that charming smile under his mustache, and speak, as he did always, in a gentle and very effective way. "My boys. My sons." They quieted down, as was expected of them. But don't you ever trust that stillness. At the least thing they could instantly erupt into angry buzzing, like so many hornets. They were listening without understanding, as when hearing mass. Each by himself, understood nothing, but all of them together understood everything. The ones I studied were the chieftains.

If you had looked at that moment, what would you have seen? Nothing, really. You don't know these people of the sertão. In everything they like to take their time. I saw that by keeping quiet that way, the bandits were hoping to have some fun. But the chieftains were not in the same mood—they were showing traces of annoyance. Each had his own ideas on how to proceed, and was scheming accordingly. Some disagreed with others, subtly. They were thinking. As I saw it, Sô Candelário was on the side of Joca Ramiro, with Titão Passos and João Goanhá; Ricardão was on the other, with Hermógenes. Zé Bebelo had begun a lengthy speech, talking sixteen to the dozen, as was his wont, whereat Ricardão gave a yawn, and Titão Passos arose from his squatting position, putting one hand to his shoulder—it must have been injured. Hermógenes pursed his lips. João Goanhá had that hidden, almost vacant look of cunning on his face. Hermógenes was darting glances, swift dark glances, at a face here and there. Sô Candelário, standing up, was working the stiffness out of his legs.

Joca Ramiro must have sensed those cross-currents, for he turned to Sô Candelário and inquired:

"My friend, what do you think?"

Sô Candelário mumbled and made those awkward movements of his, trying to unbend, but he couldn't. How tall, thin and tough that man was! Yellow eyes like a hawk. He couldn't find the words to express himself, just said:

"We'll have to see! I am with you, my friend and chief."

Joca Ramiro agreed, nodding his head, as if Sô Candelário had made some profound remark. Zé Bebelo opened his mouth wide and let out a snort, as if on purpose. Some laughed at him. Joca Ramiro waited a moment, and then:

"We can begin the accusation."

Everybody, all, approved. Even Zé Bebelo himself. Then Joca Ramiro spoke again, in his usual manner, sure of himself, saying what he had already made up his mind to say. He said that they had before them an enemy conquered in combat, who was now going to learn the fate that awaited him. The trial would begin at once. He himself, Joca Ramiro, as provided by law, would reserve his decision until the end, and pass sentence. Now, whoever wished, could charge Zé Bebelo with crimes, acts, and motives, and recommend punishment.

Who would be the first to speak? Hermógenes cleared his throat. Right from the start, I knew he would be the one—that Hermógenes thirsted for revenge.

He was a fellow born of swamps, rocks and waterfalls, a mongrel of a man. Men like him, whatever they can't control, they fear and hate. I watched him closely. You don't ever want to miss the habitual expressions of a man's face, the look in his eyes. Coolly I thought: what if I pulled out my revolver, and shot him point-blank? That would be the end of a certain Hermógenes—one moment safe and sound, and the next in a welter of blood, on his way back to hell. What would happen to me? Would they all fall on me? That would be all right with me. I wasn't afraid. It was a good idea that held me for a moment, and vanished as quickly as it came. What I really wanted was to hear and see what was going to happen. It was apparent that it would be something sensational. About then, Diadorim worked his way through the crowd and came and stood next to me, so close that even without talking, I was aware of his sweet-smelling breath.

Here it came! Hermógenes had got to his feet and started speaking:

"The recommendation I make is that we tie this scum up like

a pig—and bleed him. Or else, stretch him out on the ground and everybody ride their horses over him until there is no life left in him!"

"Yeh?" Zé Bebelo taunted, stretching his neck and moving his head forwards and backwards several times, like a woodpecker working on a tree. But Hermógenes didn't catch on, and continued:

"Dog that he is, he is ready for the knife. Nobody provoked him, he wasn't our enemy, nobody bothered him. But he came of his own accord, to kill, to lay waste, with a huge gang of bandits. Does this North country belong to him? He came paid by the Government. He is more of a dog than the soldiers even. He doesn't deserve to live. That is what I recommend, a charge of death. The devil, the dirty dog!"

"Wow! Gosh!" cried Zé Bebelo, twisting his features and making ugly faces in mock fear of Hermógenes.

"That's what I think! That's what I think!" Hermógenes almost screamed, in conclusion. "He is nothing but riff-raff."

"May I answer him, Chief?" inquired Zé Bebelo, seriously, of Joca Ramiro.

Joca Ramiro assented.

"But, in order to talk, I need to have my hands free."

Since there was no reason not to, Joca Ramiro gave the order to loose him. João Frio, who had stuck near the prisoner, came around and cut and unwound the thong binding his wrists. What would Zé Bebelo do now? Just this:

"Come in closer, come in closer, next to these elbows!" he said, impudently clapping his hands, and whistling and grimacing like a monkey. Instead of being cautious, he seemed to be trying to get his accuser's goat. I saw it was all put on, but it could turn out badly. Hermógenes jumped forward, and started to draw his knife. If he controlled himself, it was only from strong habit. And also because Joca Ramiro had intervened with a word:

"Take it easy, friend, old man. Don't you see, he is still muddled."

"Hold on! Begging your pardon, Chief, I disagree completely!" exclaimed Zé Bebelo. "I claim that my mind is clear

and able to reason. My reaction is one of protest, because an
accusation has to be made in judicious words, not with affronts
and insults!" He looked hard at Hermógenes. "A man does not
abuse another man! He doesn't raise his voice!"

But Hermógenes, bristling with anger, and twitching all over
as if he had a terrible itch, spoke to Joca Ramiro, and to all of
us there, in a cracked voice, in a crooked, twisted voice:

"Filthy rag, despicable dog, he has offended me! He has offended me, even while he stands here, beaten and our prisoner!
It is my right to do away with him, Chief!"

I saw the hand of danger. Many of the men surrounding the
spot, gathered in rings of ten or twenty, muttered their approval.
Standing close by, those of Hermógenes's band went so far as
to speak out loud and harsh. There was danger in their voices.
Even the chieftains whispered among themselves. But Joca
Ramiro knew how to keep things from getting out of hand.
Joca Ramiro was really the headman, the big boss. He merely
observed:

"But he didn't call you a son-of-a-bitch, friend."

And that was the truth. Only for "son-of-a-bitch" or "thief"
was there no forgiveness, these being unpardonable offenses.
After Joca Ramiro had put it that way, there was not a jagunço
but accepted the reasonableness of the reminder. Hermógenes
himself was shaken by the sudden setback, and had to give in.
He said nothing, but his mouth was twisted like someone who
has tasted rock salt. And Zé Bebelo also took advantage of the
break to change his tactics. You could see that back of his bluff
he was feeling his way step by step; his mind was working under high pressure for a way to save his life.

Quickly, Joca Ramiro called on Sô Candelário, thus leaving
no opportunity for further disturbance:

"And what about you, friend? What charge have you to
make?"

At that, Sô Candelário jumped forward, his jacket unbut-
toned. He was dying to talk:

"Sure enough! Sure enough!" he said, his voice growing
stronger as he continued: "I just want to ask a question:
whether he will agree for the two of us to settle this by the

knife! I'm asking for a duel. That's what I think! There's no need for further discussion. Zé Bebelo and me—us two—by the knife!"

Sô Candelário could not express himself beyond that; he just kept repeating the challenge, fidgeting all the while like someone with Saint Vitus dance. He showed almost no anger, I noticed, but no patience either. Sô Candelário was like that. But Joca Ramiro stepped in, resolutely, and said, hiding a smile:

"The decision and sentence, we leave for the last, friend. Wait awhile and you will see. Now we are presenting the charges. What crimes does my friend impute to this man?"

"Crime? I don't know of any crime. That's what I think, and what I say—I am not swayed by the opinions of others. What crime? He came to make war, the same as us. He lost, that's all! Aren't we all jagunços? All right—jagunço against jagunço—hand-to-hand, face-to-face. Is that a crime? He lost, and there he is, like a hog-plum tree nibbled down by cattle. But he fought bravely, you've got to hand him that. The only crimes I know are treachery, or to be a horse or cattle thief, or not to keep your word."

"I always keep my given word!" shouted Zé Bebelo from the other side.

Sô Candelário looked at him quickly, as if not realizing that he had been there all along, three paces off. Only then did he continue: "Well, in that case, what I think is that we should turn the man loose, on his promise to get his people together and come back here from the North, so that the war can continue, bigger and better than ever."

The men, when they heard this, were startled and here and there you heard grunts of satisfaction: courage is always gratifying. Diadorim grabbed my arm, and whispered: "It's madness, Riobaldo. Sô Candelário is stark crazy."

It could be. But I had noticed, while he was talking, a glint of hate when he looked at Hermógenes, and it came to me: Sô Candelário did not like Hermógenes! It was possible he didn't know it himself, was not fully aware of his dislike, but it was there, all right. Just because of this, I admired his outburst all the more. Sô Candelário stopped talking, drained dry. He could only puff and huff, amazed at himself.

"What have you to say, friend Ricardão?" Joca Ramiro asked next.

That one took so long to start speaking that I thought he was going to remain silent for good. He was the famous Ricardão, the man from the banks of the Verde Pequeno. The bosom friend of important politicos, and owner of many holdings. He was a heavy man, broadly built. If he wasn't exactly fat, it was only because in the sertão you never see a fat man, but you couldn't help but be surprised at so much corpulence, like a zebu steer. The flesh piled upon itself—it seemed that he must have eaten much more than anybody, more beans, more corn meal, more rice and manioc, all compressed into him, sacks and sacks of it. Finally, he began to speak:

"Friend Joca Ramiro, you are the Chief. What we see, you see; what we know, you know. There was no need for each to give his opinion, but since you wish to let all have their say, we accept this favor. And we duly thank you for it. Now, I go along with the reasoning of my friend Hermógenes: this man Zé Bebelo came looking for us in the North sertão, a tool of politicos and of the Government, for pay even, so it is said. As for losing, he lost all right, but he caused a lot of trouble and damage. We were exposed to serious dangers, as you well know, friend Chief. I remind you of our companions who were killed, whom he killed. Can they ever be replaced? And the many, many who were disabled by wounds. Their blood and sufferings cry out. Now that we have won, the hour for vengeance has struck. Look at it this way: if he had won instead of us, where would we be at this hour? Dead, every one of us, or prisoners, sent in chains to the military headquarters at Diamantina, to different jails, to the state capital. All of us, perhaps even you, sir. I beg your pardon, Chief. We have no jail, nor any other way of disposing of this fellow—just one: a straight bullet, at short range, and the thing is finished and settled. Isn't that what we did with the others? The law of the jagunço is swift, without frills. I am reminded also that we have a burden of responsibility with re-

spect to Seo Sul de Oliveira, Doctor Mirabô de Melo, old man
Nico Estácio, friend Nhô Lajes, and Colonel Caetano Cordeiro.
These are being harassed by the Government, they had to leave
their lands and plantations, which resulted in big losses to
them, and everything is still in great disorder. Therefore, in
their name, too, I am of this opinion. Let sentence be passed
without further delay. Zé Bebelo, even though crazy and irre-
sponsible, could turn dangerous. The one sentence that means
anything is a bullet from a gun. That, Chief, is my vote!"

Obviously delighted with what he had been saying, the rank
and file of the jagunços praised and agreed with Ricardão.
Judging by those who applauded the most, I guessed how many
were Ricardão's own men. Zé Bebelo has had it, I thought;
whatever chance of salvation he might have had was definitely
oozing away. The worst of it all was that I myself had to agree
with Ricardão's arguments and recognized the truth of the
words he had spoken. That is the way I felt, but it saddened me.
Why? From the standpoint of justice, it was right. But in another way—I'm not sure which—it wasn't. It was right as far as
what Zé Bebelo had done, but wrong as regards what Zé Bebelo
was or was not. Who knows for sure what a person really is?
Then, if no one knows, a judgment is always faulty, because
what one judges is the past. Well and good. But, in the book-
keeping of life, judgments cannot be dispensed with, can they?
Only, there are some fish that swim upstream all the way
from the mouth to the headwaters.

Meanwhile, Joca Ramiro had called on Titão Passos to speak.
He was like a son of Joca Ramiro's; they shared their thoughts
like true friends. I pricked up my ears. Something told me it
would be worth listening to what he had to say.

"I, too, appreciate, Chief, the distinction which is mine on
this occasion, to cast my vote. I am not against the reasons
given by any of the companions, nor will I argue against them.
But I know in my conscience that I have a responsibility. I
know that it is as if I were under oath: I know because I served
as a juror once, on the jury at Januária. Without wanting to
offend anyone, I will state my view. What I believe is the following: this man is guilty of no recognized crime. He may be a

criminal in the eyes of the Government, police commissioners and district judges, army officers. But are we or are we not people of the sertão? He wanted to make war and so he came—and found warriors! Are we not people who make war? Now, he gambled and lost, and here he is, on trial. If at the time of his capture, in the heat of the moment, we had shot and killed him, it would have been all right, it would have been done and over with. But the fighting has all ended. Is this, then, a slaughterhouse where he is to be butchered? Ah, not me. No killing. Begging your pardon."

With Titão Passos's words, I took heart again. He was what you call a man, the kind I admire. I smiled at him and gave him an approving nod: I don't know if he saw me. And there was no further commotion. But I saw that a fuse had been lit—the men were changing sides again. Now they were getting more anxious to know what the big bosses would decide. Titão Passos's own men were the smallest band of all—but they were very brave people. Brave like their good chieftain. "To which band do I belong?" I thought to myself. I realized that I belonged to none. But from then on, I wanted to be under Titão Passos's direct orders. "He is my friend," Diadorim said in my ear. "He is a great-grandson of Pedro Cardoso, and great-great grandson of Maria da Cruz!" But I didn't have a chance to ask Diadorim what he was thinking of. Joca Ramiro now wanted the vote of João Goanhá, the last speaker.

João Goanhá made as if to rise, but remained squatting. It took him a little while to get started, and all he could say was:

"Me, boss, I go for whatever the boss decides."

"But that's not exactly the way, friend João. Each of you has a vote. You must give yours," Joca Ramiro explained.

Whereupon João Goanhá got to his feet, fiddling at his nose with his fingers. Then, he tugged at each of his sleeves, and adjusted his belt with its weapons, with a resolute air. I heard a clink, and moved my eyes.

"Well then," he said in a strong voice, "my vote is the same as that of friend Sô Candelário, and of my friend Titão Passos. He has committed no crime. He should not be killed. Hell no."

I swear, when he spoke like that, that hairy backlander, my

happiness knew no bounds. He spoke out, powerfully, as if it
were a challenge to war. I sneaked a glance at Hermógenes: he
was black with rage. Ricardão was nodding, as if dozing, the big
frog-face. Ricardão was really the one who bossed Hermógenes. I knew he was only pretending to be asleep. And now?
What else was there to do? Wasn't everything finished and well
finished?

Ah, no, sir. Joca Ramiro was not a man to be hurried. He was
fanning himself with his hat. In a sovereign but not domineering manner, he ran his eyes over the men ringed about, then he
said loudly:

"If any of my sons wishes to speak for the defense or the
prosecution, he may do so!"

Was there anyone? There was nobody. They were all looking
at each other, puzzled, peeping from behind their saddles, as
they say. They weren't there to talk. Nobody had expected such
a thing.

Joca Ramiro repeated the question:

"Among you, my stalwarts, is there one who would like to
bring a charge against Zé Bebelo, or say a word in his defense?
If so, he may speak up without embarrassment."

Would anyone wish to speak? I doubted it. I'll tell you, sir:
there were more than five hundred men ringed about, if I am
not mistaken. They all kept silent. That silence was worse than
an uproar. Why weren't they shouting, why weren't they all
saying, each in his turn, that Zé Bebelo should be set free? I lost
heart. Have courage, I thought, struggling with myself. At that
moment, my friend, I toyed with the idea of how good it must
be sometimes to be powerful enough to dictate to everybody, to
make the world spin and carry out our every wish. I believe my
forehead was sweating. Or else, I thought, why not engage in a
fight right there: half the men on that side, the other half over
here, some fighting to uphold justice, the others wrapped in the
coils of the devil's tail! But let there be knives and bullets, and
hand combat, until there were piles of dead and the purity of
peace. I kept gulping saliva as if I had eaten salt.

Once more Joca Ramiro repeated the question:

"If there is anyone—," and so on, all over again.

I felt a sudden urge. I straightened up. I was going to speak. Ah, but I wasn't quick enough, another beat me to it. A certain Gú, a river man, squat but with a long face. He began:

"With your permission, Chief, I will give my honest opinion, which is, that if you order the release of this Zé Bebelo, good will come from it. A favor done, that one does, stands one in good stead later on, in case of need. I am not speaking for my own benefit, but I speak in behalf of you chieftains yourselves, with your permission. The rest of us are just bearers of arms, running the risks of every day, and whatever may befall. But if on some later occasion, which God forbid, a chieftain of ours should fall prisoner in the hands of some lieutenant of Government dog-catchers, he, too, will receive better treatment, without having to suffer indignities and cruelties. In this way, the war will become one of good manners, of good behavior."

That was reasonable enough. It had been so easy, and Joca Ramiro had even helped Gú along, in spots, with encouraging gestures. Once more I opened my mouth. But another got ahead of me again, and raised his hand to speak. He was a fellow called Dôsno, or Dôsmo, a backwoodsman from the lands of the Cateriangongo river—between Ribeirão Formoso and Serra Escura—and he had shifty, crossed eyes. What could a man like that have to say, a backwoodsman typical of all the backwoodsmen here in my North? I listened.

"Me too, I beg leave, Chief, sir, trusting my boldness will not be taken amiss. It's just that, it's just that, well, what I think would be best, before loosing or finishing off this man, well, we ought to make him say where his fortune is hidden, his loot. On account they say he has lots of money salted away. That's all I have to say, that's all, begging your pardon. Begging your pardon."

Some laughed; why did they laugh? Let them. I took a step forward, raised my hand and snapped my fingers, like a schoolboy. I began to speak. Diadorim tried to hold me back, startled no doubt: "Wait, Riobaldo," he whispered in my ear. But I had already begun. I think what I said was something like this:

"By your leave, our great Chief, Joca Ramiro, by your leave! What I have is a mighty truth to tell, and I cannot remain silent."

I'll tell you, sir: I noticed myself that I was talking too loud, but there was nothing I could do—I had already started. My heart was pounding inside of me. I felt my face on fire, aware that everyone was staring at me. I refused to look at anyone, for the one I did not want to see was Hermógenes. I did not want to lay eyes on him nor even think of him—let there be no Hermógenes in this world, neither for me nor for himself! And so I let my eyes rest on one man only, just one of the crowd, through no choice of mine but only because he was standing right in front of me, a brown boy. Poor fellow, embarrassed at being looked at so much, he hung his head. Meanwhile I went on talking:

"I know this man well, this Zé Bebelo. I was with him at one time, I never lied about it, everyone here knows it. I left him more or less as a fugitive. I left him because I wanted to, and I came here to fight, under famous chieftains, you yourselves. It has been on your side that I have fought, and I have given loyal service with my gun and trigger. But now I declare: Zé Bebelo is a brave and worthy man, an incorruptible one, who keeps his word to the last jot! And he is a jagunço chief of the first order, who stands for no atrocities, nor the killing of enemies taken prisoner, nor for their mistreatment. This I swear! I saw it. I witnessed it. Therefore, I say, he deserves full acquittal, and does not deserve to be killed for any reason. And I say this because I had to say it, like a bounden duty, and in compliance with the permission granted by our great chief, Joca Ramiro, and by my subchief, Titão Passos!"

I got my second wind, I was throbbing. I did not know myself. I kept right on.

"The war was a big one, it lasted a long time, it filled this sertão. Everybody is going to talk about it, throughout the North, in Minas and the whole of Bahia, and elsewhere, for years to come. They are going to make up songs about the many deeds. Well then, comrades, is it to be said that the chiefs of all the bands, with all their men, and full equipment, gathered here at Sempre-Verde, under the general leadership of Joca Ramiro, for just one purpose: to do away with one lone little man—to condemn Zé Bebelo to be slaughtered as if he were a beef steer? Is such a thing an honor? Or is it a disgrace?"

"To me, it is a disgrace," I heard, rejoicing, and the one who spoke was Titão Passos.

"A disgrace! What do you mean, a disgrace! A damned disgrace!" And the one who yelled this, and more, was Sô Candelário.

With everything popping all of a sudden like firecrackers, I never even finished the chilling thought that had struck me: that I had committed a big blunder which was sure to make matters worse, by saying that Zé Bebelo did not kill prisoners, because, if on our side we did kill them, what I had said would seem like a grave reproof. With Sô Candelário shouting that way, I feared I would lose my opportunity to finish what I had to say. I didn't look at Joca Ramiro—I had decided, too quickly, that he was not approving my outburst. Then, because I had no time to lose, I continued:

"But if our verdict is for acquittal, and we turn this man Zé Bebelo loose, with clean hands, and him punished only by the defeat that he suffered, then, I think, our fame will be great. Fame with glory: that first we conquered, and then we freed!"

By then I had thought through my previous worry and decided that it was foolish. A jagunço, by his very nature, almost never thinks straight; they would find it normal that we should kill the prisoners taken by our side, and at the same time applaud the fact that Zé Bebelo let our comrades he had taken prisoner live. Silly people.

"Fame and glory! All I know . . . By the wounds of Christ!" Sô Candelário resumed his shouting. Then he cut loose! He did a wild clog dance; those near him got out of the way quickly, to give him more room. What did Hermógenes have to say now? Hermógenes was biting his lips. Ricardão made believe he was dozing. Sô Candelário was a man to be feared.

But instead of the angry outburst which we expected and

which no one could have restrained, Sô Candelário looked up, with wonder on his face, and in an oddly quiet way spoke from his heart, in a pleasant voice:

"Let there be fame and glory. Everybody will talk about this for many years and in many places, giving praise to our honor. They will make up verses about it in the market places, and it might even be written up in city newspapers." He was in a transport.

Then did I stop to think, to weigh my words? No. I spoke up. I spoke truly, quickly, on the spur of the moment:

"And what danger is there? If he gives his word never to return to war against us, he will certainly keep it. He probably will not want to return, anyway. It is the right thing to do. Better still would be for him to give his word that he will leave this State, and go far away, not stay in this part of the country nor in Bahia," I said; I said it gently as a mother, softly, smoothly as a snake.

"I have some relatives in Goiás," Zé Bebelo spoke up, suddenly come to life. He spoke unexpectedly, and so eagerly, too, that some laughed heartily. I did not laugh. I took a deep breath, and then I realized that I had finished. That is, I began to be afraid. In an instant, in a second, I was overcome with fear. I looked and saw Joca Ramiro make a gesture—had he been making them?—that he wanted me to shut my mouth; I had no permission to hold forth on matters which were none of my business. I wanted to turn suddenly into a nothing, a nobody, a humble nonentity.

But Titão Passos grabbed the ball, sir. Titão Passos raised his forehead. He, who usually talked so little, how did he acquire the capacity for saying so much now? He said:

"Then, if he goes far away, he is punished, exiled. That is what I vote for as being just. What major crime did he commit? For our comrades who died, or who are wounded and bad off, I feel sorry."

Sô Candelário said:

"But to die in combat is an everyday thing with us; what are we jagunços for? He who goes ahunting, loses what he doesn't find."

Titão Passos said:

"And for so many deaths, no one chief is to blame. I mean it. And moreover, those important friends of ours—Dr. Mirabô de Melo, Colonel Caetano, and others—will certainly agree with whatever decision we reach, provided it is a just one and for the the general good. That's what I think, Chief. At your service."

The silence was all Joca Ramiro's.

Zé Bebelo's and Joca Ramiro's.

No one was noticing me any longer. Only Diadorim, who almost embraced me: "Riobaldo, you spoke well! You are a man with all kinds of guts." But the others, the ones near me, why were they not praising me, too, saying: "It was great! Tatarana! That's the way to tell 'em!" Diadorim told me again that I had spoken well, and added that it had been not so much my words as my forthrightness and fiery manner, revealing a kind of power that came over me. I had not looked at Zé Bebelo. What must he have been thinking of me? And Joca Ramiro? These two were facing each other, eyeing each other, taking each other's measure.

In the interim, there must have been an exchange of words, too low to be heard. There must have, because Zé Bebelo had been told to speak, the permission had been granted him. He began. He started off slowly, talking without saying anything. I saw and understood: he was feeling his way across the ford. Smart fellow. If any murmuring arose, he would catch its meaning in the air—his ears were attuned to it, his head poised. By now he was somewhat dishevelled, but he quietly began:

"I give you my deepest thanks, Chief Joca Ramiro, for this fair trial, this gallant action. I thank you without any fear, and without intention of flattery. I—José—Zé Bebelo—José Rebêlo Adro Antunes—that is my name. My great-grandfather was Francisco Vizeu Antunes, he was a cavalry captain. I am forty-one years old, and the recognized son of José Ribamar Pachêco Antunes and Maria Deolinda Rebêlo. I was born in the quiet country town of Carmo da Confusão."

Saints alive! Why all that rambling nonsense, those pointless statements? He spoke earnestly, however, and without his former antics, protests and quips.

"I thank those who spoke well of me and who stood up for me. I am now going to testify. I came to the North, I did, bringing with me war and destruction, at the head of my men, my own war. I am a full fledged fighter and I wanted to measure arms with other valiant men. Was anything wrong with that? I wanted to follow the example of Joca Ramiro, Joãozinho Bem-Bem, Sô Candelário, and so many other famed chieftains, some here present and others not. I fought with restraint, and perpetrated no injusticies or atrocities; I was never accused of that. I will have no truck with cowards and low behavior! I have little or nothing to do with the Government: I was not born with a love of soldiers. What I wanted was to proclaim another government, but with the help, afterwards, of all of you. I see now that we have been fighting each other mainly because of a misunderstanding. I do not obey orders of political chiefs. If I could have done so, I would have gone into politics myself, but I would have asked the great Joca Ramiro to steer his brave followers into voting for me, for Deputy. Ah, if only this North were left alone by the politicos, then we would see mighty progress, abundance for all, national rejoicing! Though I had the craving for politics myself, I have it no more. We have got to wake up the sertão! But the only way to wake the sertão is to do so from within. This time I lost. I am a prisoner. I lost, that is, because of bad luck. But I don't think so. It was gross carelessness on the part of others. To have been kept alive as a prisoner, and put on trial, is something I can only give praise to, and it greatly pleases me. It proves that you, our jagunços of the North, are really civilized: that you don't kill with a careless wave of the hand every enemy you happen to capture. You don't run things as you would a stable. I am finished with evil disorders. I am grateful. Hurrah for Joca Ramiro and his chieftains, commanders of his troops! And long live his brave jagunços! But, I am a man. Only, I have no fear; I have never had."

He made a fine gesture, and his manner became spirited.

"What the devil, I came to make war, open and aboveboard, with plenty of noise. I did not come under pretext of something else, with guile and trickery. I lost because of carelessness—not because of bad leadership on my part! I should not have tried to go against Joca Ramiro, I should not have. But I confess to no blame or regret, because my rule is that whatever I have done, it was the best course at the time. That is my unvarying rule. Today, I know I should not have done it. It depends, however, on the sentence that I receive in this noble trial. A trial, I say, for which I asked while my weapons were still in my hands, and which this great Joca Ramiro, in his eminent nobility, granted me. A trial—it is something one must always ask for! Why? In order not to be afraid. That is the way it is with me. I needed to have a trial only so you could see that I have no fear. If the verdict goes against me, my courage will sustain me. If I receive a verdict of acquittal, I will thank you with the same courage. But ask for a pardon, that I will not, for I think that one who does so, to save his skin, deserves a half-life and a double death. But I thank you, sincerely. Neither can I offer to serve under the banner of Joca Ramiro—for though it would be an honor, it would look amiss. But if I give my word, I will keep my word a thousand times. Zé Bebelo has never hedged or reneged. And so, having nothing more to say, I await your distinguished verdict. Chief. Chieftains."

I tell you, sir, it was a stirring moment.

Zé Bebelo, having finished speaking, just sat there, small, tiny even, huddled up. He was just a little ball of a person. But he ended his discourse a man. I looked and I looked. You could barely hear the low whispering of all those present, but it was favorable—I knew it was:

"What a man! Wow!"

"He's crazy as hell but he's got guts. Bet he could geld a yearling with his fingernails."

Diadorim wasn't saying anything but he looked pale. Then I stole a glance at the chieftains. They stood in a little circle, talking hurriedly. Hermógenes and Ricardão—Joca Ramiro smiled at them, his comrades. Ricardão and Hermógenes—they were hand in glove. Sô Candelário, aggressive, he was made that way, Joca Ramiro smiled at Sô Candelário. João Goanhá—short, fat and strong. Titão Passos, a man so good, so honest, was alone, looking on quietly, his hands clasped over his belly—just waiting for something to happen, whatever it might be.

Joca Ramiro was about to decide! Hermógenes started to lean over to say something in his ear, but Joca Ramiro cut him short with a gesture. The hour had struck. He looked straight at Zé Bebelo, and said:

"The judgment is mine, and the sentence I give holds good throughout the North. My people honor me. I am a friend of those I support politically, but I am neither their servant nor their henchman. The sentence will be upheld. The verdict. Do you accept it?"

"I accept it," Zé Bebelo stated, his voice firm, though he was now more dishevelled than before. He even repeated it three times: "I accept it. I accept it! I accept it."

"Very well, if I consent to your going away to Goiás, will you give your word, and go?"

Zé Bebelo delayed answering, but only for a second:

"I give my word and I will go, Chief. I ask only that you grant that my departure take place in a proper and fitting manner."

"Meaning what?"

"That if any of my men are still alive and being held prisoner, that they too be released, or given permission to come with me."

"Agreed. Agreed," broke in Joca Ramiro.

"And if there is none, that I be permitted to leave without patrol or guard, but you to furnish me with a horse and saddle, and my own weapons, or other good ones, some ammunition, and food for three days."

Again, Joca Ramiro said three times: "Agreed. Agreed. Agreed!"

"In that case, I go with honor. But now, by your leave, I ask a question: for how long a time am I bound not to return to this State nor to Bahia? Two or three years?"

"For as long as I live, or until I countermand the order," Joca Ramiro said with finality. Then he stood up suddenly.

Ah, when he stood up, he seemed to pull everything else with him—the people, the ground, the scattered trees. Everybody else stood up at the same instant. The meeting broke up. A buzz of rejoicing arose; everybody was tired of the trial, and feeling hungry.

Diadorim called me over, and we started talking in the midst of that din. I could see that Hermógenes was bitter, swallowing hard with his mouth tight shut. "Diadorim," I said, "that Hermógenes is eaten up by envy." But Diadorim must not have heard me, for he started to speak. "Praise God!" he said, but I could not help worrying.

The men were having a time. The caretaker of the Sempre-Verde ranch had opened up the kitchen: big pots and kettles, cooking everything available. Someone was pounding corn with a pestle.

I don't say it idly but because it was a fact: the memory of Hermógenes during the trial was burning in my eyes. At first he had been taciturn, withdrawn—just stood there with his legs spread wide, holding his big knife—but afterwards he showed cunning mixed with frustration, like a snarling dog. And Ricardão? There was a veil of dullness over his face, but when he stopped dozing, those thick eyes, blinking as if festered, boded no good. The business was all over, settled, finished. But was it? I had asked Diadorim to wait for me by the irrigation ditch, saying I wanted to take care of my horse, to unsaddle and curry him. I ran into Hermógenes. Rather, I spotted where he was, and I stopped awhile near him. I was on the point of going back to where he was and listening. But I did overhear him say:

"A put-up job." What did he mean? Hermógenes was not fool enough to sneer at Joca Ramiro's decision. A put-up job? I heard nothing further, at least I don't remember.

In a little while Zé Bebelo was saying goodbye. They had decided to let him take a carbine and his other arms, and a bandolier filled with bullets. By then he had eaten. He had other rations in his knapsack. He got up on the paint horse and into the good Minas-Velhas saddle he had been provided with, then off he went. He started down the road, without looking back, into the setting sun. He was accompanied by Triol for a distance of one league only, as it was restricted territory. I felt a certain sadness. But this was outweighed by my satisfaction.

After that we were all grabbing something to eat, out of the great abundance that was there. Mush and collard greens,

boiled strawberry squash, cracklings, and slabs of meat roasting over every fire. If anyone wanted soup, he had only to go to
the kitchen door and help himself. There was a shortage of
plates, however. Plenty of cachaça was on hand, for Joca Ramiro had ordered drinks all around—it was extra good. You
would have enjoyed seeing that crowd of men, the things they
said and did, the way they laughed, indulging their idleness, all
well-fed, crammed full. Then it grew dark. Men were lying on
the ground everywhere, sprawled out where the grazing horses
could almost pee on them. I was feeling stuffed, and in need of
a good sleep. I went with Diadorim in the direction of some
fruit trees, following the irrigation ditch. With the coming of
night the flowing water sings coldly, and the smell of the moss
on the trees is good. Zé Bebelo had gone away, forever, on his
paint horse; he had raised little dust. And there we were loll-
ing about, filling the hammocks. Will I ever forget that? No, I
will not. Though we were unsheltered, we were happy as boys.

I had come there, to the sertão of the North, as everyone does
sooner or later. I had come almost without noticing that I was
doing so, compelled by the need to find a better way of life. Suppose they expelled me now, the way they had driven Zé Bebelo
back? I had not forgotten those words of his: that the world
now was beyond control.

I said so to Diadorim. But Diadorim did not answer me.
After awhile he spoke: "Riobaldo, would you like to go live at
Os-Porcos, where it is always so beautiful, and the stars so
bright?" I said yes. How could I say otherwise, for was not Os-
Porcos Diadorim's own part of the country, the place where he
had grown up? But even while he was speaking, I thought Diadorim might have answered something like: "World beyond
control? But, Riobaldo, that's the way the world has always
been." Foolishness, I know. I was talking and thinking about
one thing, but Diadorim kept bringing up others. "Zé Bebelo,
Diadorim: what did you think of that man?" I inquired. "For
him, now, there is neither day nor night: he is on his way, making his trip. He was lucky that he came up against someone as
generous as Joca Ramiro," was Diadorim's reply. We both remained quiet, thinking. Then, after I had smoked my cigarette

down to the butt, I asked him: "Let's see, who was it saved Zé
Bebelo from death?" Diadorim wanted to make his reply in such
secrecy that he pulled the edge of my hammock over to his, so
that we might talk almost face to face. "You want to know who
saved Zé Bebelo from death? Next to Joca Ramiro, it was Zé
Bebelo himself, at the start. Then, at one point, Sô Candelário
came to the fore—a queer fellow and very sure of himself, but
absolutely loyal, even though he commands more than three
hundred henchmen who at a sign from him would advance and
kill and kill." I had hoped he would explain the fact in a different way, but he went on: "You saw Hermógenes and Ricardão,
the two of them overcome with impotent fury—they make me
afraid, frighten me. I hope to God. . . ." Then he finished by
saying: "As long as Joca Ramiro may have need of us, you
promised me yourself, Riobaldo, you'll stay." I repeated my
promise, confirming it. After that, lying in the open night air,
we talked no more that I remember.

I could tell by his voice that Diadorim was heavy-hearted. So
was I. Why, you will want to know. Because Zé Bebelo had gone
away—was that the reason? Beyond the Paracatú lies the
world. Zé Bebelo's going for some reason, I don't quite know
why, had left me unable to think straight, and besides, my stomach was too full, too much food and drink. The only thing that
made me feel good was that the trial had been held, and that
Zé Bebelo's life and reputation had been saved. The trial? I tell
you, for me it was a very important thing, and it was for this
very reason that I have made a point of telling you all about it
in such detail.

You may say it wasn't a genuine trial at all: just an absurd
and disorderly performance, a senseless piece of madness
that took place in the middle of the sertão. By that same token,
Zé Bebelo was not a real criminal! Ah, but in the middle of the
sertão, madness may at times be the best of good sense and
judgment! From that hour forward, I believed in Joca Ramiro.
On account of Zé Bebelo. Because Zé Bebelo, in that hour, on
that occasion, was more than just a person. I liked him in the
same way that I now like my compadre Quelemém; I liked him
because I understood him intuitively. For that reason, the trial

had brought peace to my mind—better still, to my heart. I went to sleep, saying goodbye to all that. How could I know of the terrible things that were to come afterwards, as you will see, and which I shall tell you about right away?

Briefly: after one more day there at Sempre-Verde, we broke up. Normally, there is no advantage to keeping a large body of jagunços together; all it does is attract the soldiery, besides causing delay and unreasonable expense. It was rumored that João Goanhá would head for Bahia, and that Antenor would follow the banks of the Ramalhada, with a handful of Hermógenes's men. New orders, so many orders. Alaripe was to go with Titão Passos. Titão Passos called Diadorim and me, and told us our route would be to follow the São Francisco as closely as possible to the other side of the Jequitaí, and beyond. What was that for? Weren't we going to accompany Joca Ramiro, and stand by in case he needed our help? But we found out that our task was highly important: we were to bivouac at certain places, and wait for the arrival of shipments, and also keep our eyes skinned for detachments of soldiers that might be moving into the North. We saddled up, mounted, and departed. Joca Ramiro was leaving, too, at that same moment, headed back to São João do Paraíso. There he was, on his white charger, flanked by Sô Candelário and Ricardão: they all galloped off together. All the other chieftains were leaving too, their bands slowly separating, with much milling about and shouting. Diadorim looked and crossed himself. "In this manner, he gave me his blessing—" was all he said.

It always makes one kind of sad when a great crowd breaks up. But, on this same day, we covered nine leagues on our good horses.

Nine leagues. Ten more brought us to Amargoso Lake. Another seven, to a waterfall on the Gorutuba. Ten more, and we bivouacked between Quem-Quem and Solidão; and kept pushing ahead, always in the sertão. The sertão is like that: you think you have left it behind you, and suddenly it surrounds you again on all sides. The sertão is where you least expect it. We kept on and on, and we climbed, until one fine day we halted in a soft and pleasant land, with many waters. My memory went back to those birds—the teals, the swamp cuckoo, the water hens, the gulls. And the little red-legs! Diadorim and I together. The herons in flight. The lazy, free-flowing river. And there we stopped for a time, in a lonely field, in the midst of open meadows, with many cattle grazing.

The place was near Guararavacã do Guaicuí. It was called Tapera Nhã. Was it good there? It was peaceful. But there are times when I ask myself if it wouldn't be better if one never had to leave the sertão. It was a nice place, all right. There were no dangers to guard against, and we had no work to do. There were twenty-three men all told. Titão Passos gave instructions for a small squad, headed by Alaripe, to go to the other side of the hill, the lowland proper of the Guararavacã, just in case anything should happen. The rest of us stayed where we were.

Our lot, in the beginning, was one of happy days. A slow, lazy awakening at daybreak, listening to the calls of the huge flocks of iridescent black rice grackles. They roosted at night in a patch of woods, and in the morning would fly over us aimlessly. And the bunches of steers and cows getting up from their sleeping places, raising their bodies noiselessly, in the half darkness. When there was no wind, the sun came down strong. We ate good fresh fish every day—they were easily caught—curimatã or dourado. The cook was Paspe; he made plenty of manioc mush, and passed out rations of fine white cachaça. We also did some hunting. Everybody took turns standing watch, and there was plenty of time left over for loafing. I took long naps during the day. The hawks shrilled their cries until the day got hot. Then strings of cattle would amble to the river bank and stand there on the strand, or cool themselves off in the water. Sometimes they would swim over to a long island, where the grass was a lush green. Whatever is peaceful grows of its own accord. From hearing the cattle bellowing at will, the idea came to me that everything is merely the past projected into the future. I imagined things like that. I remembered what I did not know. And I had no news about anybody, nor about anything in the world outside—you can see how it was. I wanted a woman, any woman. There are times in life when one becomes so languid that even the rekindling of evil desire is good.

One day, without a word to anybody, I got on my horse and left, headed for nowhere, free. I wanted to see other people, different people. I rode two leagues. The world was empty except for cattle and more cattle. Cattle and cattle and plains. I followed the cow trails. I crossed a green stream at a point where ingá and umbú trees hung over the edge—it was a cattle ford. I thought to myself: the farther I go looking for people, the deeper I seem to sink into loneliness. And then I began to accuse myself. I was to blame for everything in my life, there was no other answer. A feeling of dejection of the worst kind came over me: that without reason. Then I noticed that I had a headache, and thought perhaps my mood of sadness came from that. This diagnosis gave me comfort. I no longer knew what I was after, nor where I was going. So much so that when I came to a small stream—just a little white brook—it looked at me and said: "No," and I had to obey it. It told me not to go any farther. The little brook was asking for my blessing. I dismounted. Life is worth-while to a horse when he sees grass and can eat it. I lay down and covered my face with my hat. I was exhausted. I went to sleep, lying on my saddle pad. When you sleep, you turn into all kinds of things: you become stone, you become flowers. Try as I will, I cannot convey my feelings to you, as I dredge up my memories; that is why I indulge in these fantasies. But by going to sleep I was settling my fate. Today, I know it. And I know that at every turn in the plains, and under the shade of every tree, there stands a devil, day and night, motionless, in charge of things. A little imp, a boy-devil, who runs ahead of you, lighting the path of your sleep with a little lantern. I slept in the arms of the winds. When I awoke, I couldn't believe my eyes: all that is beautiful is absurd. Precious as gold and silver, who should be there, two paces from me, watching me, but Diadorim.

Sober, quiet, like himself, just like his living self. He had sensed my urge to run away, had tracked me, and had found me. He did not smile, he said nothing. I did not speak either. The heat of the day was passing. The green in those exquisite eyes of Diadorim's was always changing, like the waters of a river in shady spots. That green, always changing yet always young, was full of years, many years, trying to tell me things that our minds cannot grasp—and this, I think, is the reason we die. Diadorim's coming and standing there, waiting for me to wake up and watching me sleep, was funny, and enough to make us laugh happily. But I did not laugh. I neither could nor wanted to. I felt, instead, something unspoken, like a decree, as if Diadorm were saying: "For the rest of your life, all of it from now on, you must remain mine, Riobaldo, attached to me, forever!" We mounted and started back. And I'll tell you, sir, the manner of my love for Diadorim: it was such that at no time, on no occasion, did I ever want to laugh at him.

The Guararavacã of the Guaicuí: take note of that name. But you won't find it; it exists no longer. Now it is called Caixeiro-pólis, and they say it is fever-ridden. It didn't used to be that way, not that I remember. Anyway, this was the place and the time when my destiny was sealed. Do you suppose there is a fixed point, beyond which there is no turning back? Guararavacã—listen—write it.

That place, the air there. It was there I first realized that I loved Diadorim—real love, poorly disguised as friendship. The full realization of it had come to me suddenly. It did not startle me, I did not think it evil, I did not reproach myself—at the time. I remember it clearly. I was alone, in a corner of a hut, a herdsman's old hut; I was lying on a grass mat. My weapons were close by, well cared-for, their barrels shining. With them I could send death to others from a distance of many yards. Might one, in the same manner, project love? The hut was at the edge of a wood. In the afternoon, which was drawing on, the air was turned cool by the wind that comes from the Espin-haço range, a full-bodied wind. It ruffled the foliage there, and moved ahead to the river bottom where it tossed the tall white tassels of the uva grass. Over there on the banks, I could hear the song of a poor-John, a water lover. It made me long for a buriti-palm grove at the green, grass-covered headwaters of a stream, where the tableland drops off. Longings that are born of the wind; longings for the Gerais. There you can see the wind lashing the leaves of the buriti palms when a storm is brewing. Can one ever forget it? The wind is green. There are moments when you can seize the silence and clasp it to your breast. I am from where I was born. I am from other places, too. But there, at Guararavacã, I was content. My neighbors, the cattle, were still grazing; the smell of cattle always makes for happiness. The blue-headed jays were running about, in pairs, among the cattle, hunting and pecking at the smooth, flat ground. In the trees the woodpeckers were rapping and chattering. I heard the sound, from inside the forest, of a solitary tinamou—always a sly bird. It was a month in which the tinamou still went about alone—male and female unmated, each by itself. The tinamou came toward me, loafing along the way, muttering to itself, and scratching the ground here and there, like a hen. I laughed. "Look at that one, Diadorim!" I said. I thought Diadorim was within earshot, but he wasn't. The tinamou looked at me, its little head raised high. It had come straight toward me, almost to the entrance of the hut. It looked at me, and turned its eyes. What was that bird looking for? It had come to cast a spell over me. I could have shot it easily, but I held back and didn't. I just picked up one of my spurs and threw it near the bird. It became frightened and brought its wings forward as if to cover its head before turning a somersault. Then it walked backward a few steps before fleeing into the forest, where it no doubt went looking for a good roosting place for the night.

The name of Diadorim, which I had called out, stayed with me. I embraced it. The taste of honey clings to the mouth. "Diadorim, my love." How could I say such a thing? I will explain it to you, sir: as if on purpose, to keep me from feeling shame, the image which I held in my mind was different. It was of a singular Diadorim, phantom-like, completely apart from everyday life, distinct from all other people—as when rain falls on distant plains. A Diadorim for me alone. Everything has its mysterious Diadorim. There are some things you can't explain. I must have begun to think of him as no doubt a snake thinks about a bird on which it fixes its gaze. It was like a serpent inside me. That thought was transforming me, filling me with I know not what, that caused both pain and pleasure. If I had been going to die at that moment I would not have cared.

I know now what had happened: during the previous months of tumult and fighting, in the midst of all those jagunços, and almost without recreation of any kind, the feeling which had been in me all along was dulled, latent. My love for Diadorim had been dormant, unperceived by me, in our everyday living. But now it was springing to life, like day breaking, bursting. I lay still a moment, my eyes closed, thrilled and glowing in my new-found joy. Then I got up.

I got up because I had to find out, to learn if it was really true. The thinking we do on our feet—it's the only kind worth anything. I went over to a campfire where Diadorim was seated along with Drumão, Paspe, and Jesualdo. I looked hard at him, the Diadorim of flesh and bone; I had to keep looking until my false image of the other Diadorim had vanished.

"Hey, Riobaldo, so there you are—is there anything you want?" he asked me, startled at seeing me.

I asked for a brand from the fire, and lit a cigarette. Then I returned to the hut, slowly, with lagging feet. If it is true—I thought—I am half lost. I took hold of my thinking: I could not, under any circumstances, admit the truth of it. In the name of peace, decency, and common sense, I would force myself to forget about it. But if I could not, ah, then, I should obliterate it, do away with myself—with one bullet in the side of my head I could put an end to everything in an instant. Or, I would run away—I would wander far, cover great distances, travel all the roads. I dwelt upon this, it gave me comfort. Ah, then I was half saved! I cocked my horse pistol—I just had to fire a shot into the woods, a booming shot.

"What was it?" they shouted at me. They always laughed at aimless shooting.

"I think it was a little monkey, and I think I missed," I explained.

From then on, I made believe that I was looking Diadorim steadily in the face, quietly, and saying: "I deny that I love you in the wrong way. I love you, but only as a friend." I said this to myself often. I made a habit, from then on, of repeating it whenever I was near Diadorim. And I even believed it. Ah, my friend, as if obedience to love were not always the opposite!

Look here, in the distant gerais there are places where, if you put your ear to the ground, you can hear the rumble of big waters rushing along inside the earth. Can you sleep on top of a river?

As I say, our stay at Guararavacá do Guaicuí lasted about two months. A good secluded place. From there we visited the adjacent areas, and covered all the surrounding countryside. We exchanged messages every day with Alaripe's group. No news whatever. The munitions that were supposed to be delivered didn't arrive. On the other side of the river, it was field-burning time; when the wind shifted it brought us the dismal smoke. At night, the side of the hill glowed red, flickering flames and embers interspersed. On this side of the river, about two leagues distant, there was a little farm belonging to a fellow who was still young, a friend of ours. "Ah, if he would only rent me his little wife, I would pay a good price," said Paspe, sighing. But the ones who came were the farmer's sons, mounted on a thin horse, bringing bundles of sugar cane to sell us. Sometimes they would come on two thin horses, five or six boys clinging to one another, some so small you wondered how they made it. These little boys were always asking to see our weapons, and wanting us to fire some shots. Diadorim liked them very much and would take them by the hand—even carrying the smallest ones—and go to watch the birds on the islands in the river. "Look, look at them: the little red-legs have finished moulting."

One day, when we had shot a fat paca, Paspe salted down a quarter of it, wrapped it in leaves, and gave it to the oldest boy: "For you to take as a present to your mother, tell her I was the one who sent it," he said. We all laughed.

The boys were afraid of the cattle, some of which were wild; one day a cow chased them. But with the coming of the dry season, the cattle became so thin and weak they would get bogged down in the mud holes; some even died. When dust filled the air, there were few vultures in the sky. They settled in the pindaiba trees on the edge of the swamp. João Vaqueiro would call us to help pull out as many of the animals as we could. Some were tame: for a handful of salt, they would come

close and lick the ground at our feet. João Vaqueiro knew
everything. He would approach a cow and squeeze her teats.
The grass was so good—would you believe it?—some still
had milk in their udders. "We need to get out and do some
shooting and fighting," someone wisely said; a jagunço grows
soft in idleness.

A good four leagues distant, in a northeasterly direction,
where the scrub begins, there was a country store. They sold
liquor made of bananas and of souari nuts—very strong—,
calf's foot jelly, good tobacco, quince marmalade, salt pork.
Jesualdo was the only one of us ever went there so they
wouldn't get suspicious. We would give him money, and each
ordered what he wanted. Diadorim ordered a whole kilo of
macauba palm oil soap, to wash himself with. The owner of
the store had two daughters, and each time Jesualdo returned
he would spend the day and night telling us what they were
like, how beautiful. "Hey, when the time comes and the war
makes it possible—ah, if that storekeeper is against us—ah, I'll
go there and grab one of the two and turn her from a girl into a
woman," said Vove. "You'll do no such thing," Triol retorted,
"because what I want is the right thing: I'll go there and
politely ask her in marriage, and we'll go on a honeymoon."
And Liduvino and Admeto sang sentimental songs, through
their noses. I asked them—what about that song of Siruiz's?
—but they didn't know it. "I don't know it, I don't like it. Old
stuff," they said.

There came a rumble of thunder. More thunder. The air
was filled with flying ants. The first rains began to fall. We cut
some poles and palm leaves and enlarged the hut. Then some
herdsmen came to look over the cattle at Tapera Nhã; they
took away the heifers that were with calf to renew their stock.
These men were so simple-minded, they thought we were
prospecting for gold.

Days of heavy rain followed one after another. All alike. The
herons sounded their odd notes, the tiger-heron clanging like a
cowbell, the bittern booming staccato. The swampy pindaiba
forest was full of croaking frogs. In the cold spells between
rains, we would laugh at our dismal situation. With the first dry

spell, one of the herdsmen, Bernabé, showed up on his chestnut
horse: he had come to bring us the cheese curds which we had
ordered and paid good money for. "Some day things will change
for the better," we kept saying. Cheese curds are best eaten
with coffee good and hot. That herdsman, Bernabé, returned
several times after that.

One bad day, we saw him coming out of the woods, down the
road toward us, the little chestnut horse running so fast its
head didn't even bob. At least we thought it was him, but it
wasn't. It was one of our men, a brown half-breed, known only
as Gavião-Cujo, arriving from farther north. He had come
through heavy rain, and was covered with mud from bridle bit
to the tops of his boots. The horse's underbelly was caked with
it. He stopped and jumped off all in one movement; you could
see he was bursting with news. What was it? Gavião-Cujo
opened his jaws but no word came out, as he gasped for air,
unable to catch his breath. The news must be either urgent or
overwhelming.

"What is it?" Titão Passos urged. "Did someone call down a
curse on you?"

Gavião-Cujo raised an arm, asking for a moment's time.
Suddenly, he almost screamed:

"They have killed Joca Ramiro."

All hell broke loose—in the midst of it I heard Diadorim's
wild sob. The men were snatching up their arms. Titão Passos
shouted orders. Diadorim had nearly fallen to the ground, but
was caught in time by João Vaqueiro.

He had fainted and lay there, pale as wax, like dead,
wrapped tight in his clothing and leather trappings. I ran to
help. Paspe picked up a water gourd and sprinkled some on my
friend's face. But there was nothing I could do: I had barely put
out my hand to unbutton Diadorim's leather jacket, when he
came to and pushed me away fiercely. He wanted no one's help;
he sat up alone and then stood up. His color came back, his
face red with sudden fury, though his beautiful eyes were full of
tears. Titão Passos ordered Gavião-Cujo to talk. The men were
stupefied. The ground seemed to have fallen out from under
them; the world was coming loose at the seams.

"Repeat what you said, Gavião."

"Oh, Chief! Oh, Chief! they killed Joca Ramiro . . . !"

"Who? Where? Tell us!"

I felt the gooseflesh rise along my arms. My mouth went dry. A pain shot through my belly. I pitied poor Diadorim. Everything had fallen on us, like a bolt of lightning.

"It was Hermógenes who killed him."

"The son-of-a-bitch! The filthy scum! The dirty traitor! He'll pay for this." Everyone gave vent to his feelings. Their hate was building up to the bursting point.

Could Joca Ramiro have died? How could they have killed him? We were there like a black bull, alone in the deserts of Guararavacã, bellowing in the storm. Joca Ramiro was dead. And we raged aloud, trying to hold back fear—and the sad and bitter truth—without knowing why, except that we were all unfortunates together.

"Hermógenes . . . The men of Ricardão . . . Antenor . . . Many others . . ."

"Yes, but where, where?"

"At a place on the Jerara, on lands belonging to Xanxerê, on the bank of the Jerara—there where the Jerara creek runs down the Vôo sloop and enters the Riachão—Riachão da Lapa, that is. They say it happened suddenly, unexpectedly. It was out-and-out treachery. Many of the ones who remained loyal died: João Frio, Bicalho, Leôncio Fino, Luís Pajeú, Cambó, Leite-de-Sapo, Zé Inocêncio, some fifteen altogether. There was a terrible gun battle, but Hermógenes and Ricardão had too many men. As many of the decent ones as could, ran away. Silvino Silva managed to escape with twenty or more companions."

But Titão Passos abruptly cut Gavião-Cujo short and grabbed him by the arms:

"Yes, but are there any left under arms ready to go against Ricardão and Hermógenes and help us fight for vengeance and satisfaction for this outrage? If so, where are they?"

"Ah, yes, Chief. There are all the others: João Goanhá, Sô Candelário, Clorindo Campelo. João Goanhá is in the Quatís range with a bunch of men. He was the one who sent me here. Sô Candelário is still off in the North but the bulk of his bands are in the neighborhood of Lagoa-do-Boi, in Juramento. Another messenger was sent there. A runner was also dispatched to break the news to Medeiro Vaz, in the gerais, on the other side of the river. I know that the sertão will take up arms."

"Ah, thank God! Well, then, it is all right!" Titão Passos answered.

And so it was. It was to be war again. We felt relieved, with an enormous sense of well-being.

"We shall have to go. We shall have to go," said Titão Passos, and all responded eagerly. We had to get moving without delay and head for the Quatís range, to a place called Amoipira, near Grão Mogol.

Meanwhile, Gavião-Cujo kept giving us more details, almost as though afraid to stop talking. Hermógenes and Ricardão had long since cooked up that crime between them. With guile and cunning Hermógenes lured Joca Ramiro away from Sô Candelário and led him into the midst of men who were nearly all with himself and Ricardão. Then they shot him in the back, bullets from three revolvers. Joca Ramiro died without suffering.

"Did they bury his body?" Diadorim asked, struggling with the pain in his voice. He didn't know, Gavião-Cujo answered, but no doubt they had given him a Christian burial, right there on the Jerara, no doubt. Diadorim turned very pale, and asked for cachaça. He drank some. We all drank. Titão Passos was trying to keep back the tears.

"A man of his great goodness just had to run the risk of being killed, sooner or later, living among such evil beings," he said to me, in a way that made it seem that he wasn't a jagunço, which, of course, he was.

So now we had to begin the war all over again. Men and weapons. We would use them to extract the sweetness of vengeance, as you use a can on a stick to dip hot syrup. Joca Ramiro's death was the decree of a new law.

Someone had to carry the news to Alaripe and his band, on the other side of the hill. "Let's us go. Riobaldo!" urged Diadorim. I could see that he was restless because of the momentary delay. We saddled our horses, and up the hill we went.

The wind as we galloped drowned our words. The sky was
overcast, the weather warm and humid. On the down slope,
Diadorim stopped me, and handed me his halter rope. "People
forget everything in this life, Riobaldo. Do you think, then,
that his honor will be soon forgotten?" I must have been slow
in answering, with an expression on my face of not understanding, for Diadorim went on: ". . . his, the glory of the departed,
of the one who died." His tone was a mixture of love and fury,
and in his voice a despair such as I had never known. He dismounted, and wandered off into the woods. I stayed behind,
holding his horse. I supposed he had gone to answer nature's
call. But he took so long about returning, that I decided to go
after him, to see what was the matter. I spurred my horse,
leading his along behind me. And then I saw Diadorim, lying
face downward on the ground. He was sobbing convulsively,
biting the grass in a frenzy. My throat turned dry. "Diadorim!"
I called. Without rising, he turned his face away, his eyes
flooded. I talked and talked, trying to console him, but he only
asked me plaintively to go on alone, and to leave him there
until my return. "Was Joca Ramiro a relative of yours,
Diadorim?" I inquired very gently. "Ah, yes, he was," he
answered, in a very faint voice. "Your uncle, perhaps?" He
nodded affirmatively. I handed him his horse's halter, and
continued on my way. When I came within a certain distance of
them, I stopped and fired into the air a few times, as a signal to
the Alaripes and to avoid delay. By the time I got there, luckily
for me, they had all gathered. It was raining, as the sultry
weather had foretold.

"I bring news of the death of a great man!" I stated, without
dismounting. They all removed their hats, waiting for what I
had to say. "Long live the fame of our Chief, Joca Ramiro!"
I shouted, and from the grief in my voice, they understood.
Nearly all of them wept. "Now we have to avenge his death!" I
went on. They instantly got ready to return with me. "Tatarana,
old man, you know how. You have what it takes to be a chieftain, you have the mettle," Alaripe said to me on the way.
I shook my head. The last thing I wanted was to be a chief.

And so it came about that at dawn the next day we moved

out, Diadorim at my side, sorrowful, very pale, with black circles under his eyes, his mouth drooping. We left that place behind forever—the one I told you was so memorable for me—Guararavacã do Guaicuí.

Out into the wilderness we rode; we were going to invade the sertão, breast the oceans of heat. The streams were muddy. Then every river roared full, the meadows became flooded, the heavy downpours chilled the mountain tops. The terrible news had spread far, and everywhere we went people showered attentions on us and spoke reverently of the dead leader. But we passed through, like an arrow, like a knife, like fire. We cut across all that cattle country. We appeared by day in the villages and settlements, and filled the roads without any attempt at concealment: we wanted the whole world to see our revenge! By the time we reached our destination on the upper Amoipira, our horses were worn out. João Goanhá saw us coming and opened his arms wide. He had his own three hundred fighting men with him, and others were arriving all the time.

"My brother Titão Passos, my brother Titão Passos," he said, coming close, "and all of you, brave ones. Now the big fight will take place!" He said that in three days we would set out under arms. João Goanhá was a man of action: he didn't believe in dilly-dallying.

And Sô Candelário, where was he? Sô Candelário, whose health had worsened, should be in Lençóis any day now, whither a runner had been sent with an urgent message. But even so, João Goanhá did not feel it necessary to await his arrival before attacking the two Judases. We thought this good strategy. Others kept coming, offering their help. Even some we wouldn't have imagined, like Nhão Virassaia, with his thirty-five fighters, famous throughout the Rio-Verde Grande. And old Ludujo Filgueiras, from Montes Claros, with twenty-two gunmen. And the big rancher, Colonel Digno de Abreu, who also sent thirty or more of his henchmen, under the command of his natural son, Luís de Abreuzinho. The cattle on the hoof, to be slaughtered for food, was turning into a herd. Sacks of manioc meal, bags of salt, brown sugar, coffee, even the supplies of corn meal, rice, and beans, came in by the cartload. The only thing we were

short of was munitions. Titão Passos was unhappy that we had
not been able to bring our own supply, for which we had waited
in vain at Guararavacã. After an exchange of messages, there
also arrived from the north, from Lagoa-do-Boi, a good number
of Bahians, under the command of Alípio Mota, Sô Candelário's
brother-in-law. We were going to surround the Judases: there
was no way they could escape. Even if some managed to slip
away to the west and cross the river—ah, they would run into
iron and fire, for there was Medeiro Vaz, the king of the Gerais!

We started out, after them. But I'll tell you, sir, we ran into
nothing but one piece of bad luck after another. The weather
was against us, the timing was bad, and all the rest of it. No
matter how hard we tried, everything went wrong. Should not
God help those who seek righteous vengeance? He should.
Were we not strong in men, our courage high? We were. Ah,
but there is the Other One—the Big Bat, the Duck-footed One,
the Evil-faced One, that one—the One-Who-Doesn't-Exist! That
he does not exist, my soul tells me that he does not, does not.
And I protect myself against the possibility of his existence by
kneeling on sharp stones and by kissing the hem of Our Lady of
Abadia's mantle. Ah, only She avails me, and She prevails
throughout an endless sea—the sertão. If She fixes her saintly
eyes on me, how can the Other One see me? I tell you this, sir,
and I say: peace. But, in those days I did not know any better.
How could I have known that those monsters were the Other
One? And that he operates without any scruples whatever, because his time is short. When he protects someone, he comes
and protects him in person. Perched lightly on Hermógenes's
shoulder, pointing out every route. As tiny as a grape seed, inside Hermógenes's ear, listening to everything. A speck of light
in Hermógenes's eyes, the first to see things. Hermógenes, void
of soul, had more than damned himself unto the end of the
world and the last judgment. We were going against him. Can
one stand up against the devil? Who can? Unluckily miracles
also take place, as when the Judases—Ricardão and Hermógenes—managed to escape through our fingers. For escape they
did. They passed close by us—a league, a quarter-league away
—with their mob of jagunços, and we neither saw nor heard

nor knew about it. We had no means of heading them off. They advanced silently, slipping through the woods, heading west until they reached the São Francisco. They crossed near us, without our being aware of it, as the night crosses the day from morning to twilight, its blackness hidden from sight by the whiteness of the day, I suppose. When we did at last learn about it, they were out of reach. Most discouraging? But wait till you hear what followed. Government soldiers! Soldiers everywhere, large troops of them. They had sprung up on all sides, without warning, clawing at us in their fury, like a pack of hunting dogs. One company of army soldiers under Lieutenant Plínio. Another under Lieutenant Reis Leme. Afterwards, with many more, came a Captain Carvalhais, one of the toughest. This one drank coffee out of a gourd and spit pepper and gun powder. We underwent hardships, and were chased from one place to another. Life is full of injustices like that when the devil is calling the tune. Imagine: that bunch of soldiers had come to the North to avenge Zé Bebelo, and Zé Bebelo was already far away, safe in exile whereupon they turned on us— the partisans of Joca Ramiro, who had saved Zé Bebelo's life from the knives of Hermógenes and Ricardão; and now, by so doing, they were indirectly helping those two marauders. But who could explain all this to them, who had come like an enormous machine to crush and destroy us, with their claws on our throats but their thoughts off in the rattletrap capital of the State?

I will refrain from telling you everything that happened— you are tired of listening, and this thing of war is always the same, over and over. We fought as well as we could. The fighting began at Curral de Vacas, near Morro do Cocoruto, where they caught us off guard. We fled, after much shooting. Afterwards, we engaged them on the Cutica, on the Simão Guedes plateau, but they struck back hard. On the Saudade range, we fell to pieces, but managed to get away all right. And Córrego Estrelinhas, Córrego da Malhada Grande, Ribeirão Traçadal— all were bad for us. Am I just reciting a list of places to you? They are associated in my mind with terror and suffering. I never complained. The soldiers ferreting everywhere kept us

busy all the time. Corn grew in the fields, the thrushes raised
their nestlings, the gameleira figs dropped their little fruits, the
souari nuts ripened on the trees and fell to the ground; came a
warm spell in the winter that matured the cashews and pitanga
cherries. The storms returned, alternating with nights in which
the stars crowded each other. Then the wind grew stronger and
changed its direction, for the wet season was coming to an end.
Lieutenant Reis Leme kept engaging us in skirmishes: he
wanted to wipe us out. We killed a heap of good soldiers. We
were on the Bahia frontier. Five times we went in and out of
Bahia, without laying down our arms.

It looked as if we were going to spend the rest of our lives
fighting the soldiers. But we had more urgent business elsewhere, that struggle to the death against the Judases, our own
private fight. But our strength was not sufficient. Diadorim was
grumbling. Tomorrow is no consolation for today's pain of hate
or love. I was feeling the same. But, one day we received
definite information: that Hermógenes and his gang had set up
a camp where they were living high, on the yonder side of the
Chico, in the headwaters to the right of the Carinhanha, on the
plateau of Antônio Pereira. We discussed the matter, and
talked about everything that should and should not be done.
The upshot was this: that the thing to do was to send reinforcements to Medeiro Vaz—fifty or a hundred men, in small
groups—who would try to slip through or between the danger
spots. Meanwhile, João Goanhá, Alípio Mota, and Titão
Passos, each in his own territory, would first cover their tracks
in the scrub, and then hole up for awhile, on friendly ranches,
until the soldiers vanished.

I set out, with Diadorim, Alaripe, Jesualdo, João Vaqueiro,
and Fafafa. We were headed for the other side, for my gerais,
and I was happy. Our route was as follows: Impirussú, Serra do
Pau-d'Arco, Mingú, Lagoa dos Marruás, Dôminus-Vobíscum,
Cruzeiro-das-Combaúbas, and Detrás-das-Duas-Serras. Then,
Brejo dos Martíres, Cachoerinha Rôxa, Mocó, Fazenda Riacho-
Abaixo, Santa Polônia, and Lagoa da Jaboticaba. After that, by
shortcuts to Córrego Assombrado, Sassapo, Poço d'Anjo, Barreiro do Muquém.

At different places along the way, I made up for lost time. I lay with the best of women. At Malhada, I bought new clothes. But Diadorim would never touch a woman, he was always serious, buried in thought. I was liking him more all the time.

Then, one day, we came to the Lagoa Clara. This was already a part of the waters of the mighty Chico. We could see the ferry landing a little way off. The crossing there might be dangerous, with so many soldiers about. Should we break up? But we had only to call the ferryman: "Hô, boatman! Hô, boatman!" and he would come. Then we had an idea. If the ferryman saw only two men, João Vaqueiro and Fafafa, they could take five of the horses across, saying they were for some hunters. Once on the other side, João Vaqueiro and Fafafa could take the horses to a place called Ôlho-d'Água-das-Outras, on up the Urúcuia. We would all meet there.

Left behind with only one little horse, Alaripe and I, Diadorim, and Jesualdo, walked slowly along the river bank. We waited to see what would happen. A little farther on there was a landing for firewood. "Are you afraid, Riobaldo?" Diadorim asked me. Me, afraid? With him, I would embark in any kind of vessel.

And so, with our rifles out of sight, we signaled to a large boat, one with a wooden bull's head at the prow—it would bring us luck. The boatman blew a blast on his conch, and they drew alongside. We four, plus the horse, were nothing, just a few extra kilos. We boarded the boat, then the boatmaster greeted us, in the name of Our Lord Christ-Jesus, and said: "I am a friend to everybody, in keeping with my calling." Alaripe accepted a swallow of cachaça; we all did.

We were headed upstream, and with very good, hardworking oarsmen. Most of the time, we scudded along, with a sail full of wind—the oarsmen had nothing to do. They asked for news about the sertão. The sertão never makes news. They gave us plenty of jacuba to drink. "Where are you gentlemen from?" the boatmaster inquired. "We came from the Rompe-Dia range," we replied. A harmless lie. We could just as well have said that we had come from the São Felipe range. The boatmaster did not believe us, and shrugged his shoulders. But he

gave us a pleasant trip to the mouth of the Urucúia. Ah, my
Urucúia, whose waters are always clear. We entered and went
up it a league and a half, for which we paid extra. The beautiful
rivers are the ones which flow north, and those that come from
the west—on their way to meet the rising sun. We went ashore
at a landing place where there is no beach but many tall trees
—the purple-flowered caraíba, so typical of the region. And the
broadleaf, the black startree, the bloodwood, the shady paraíba
trumpet-tree. The Urucúia and its borders—there I saw my
gerais!

Those were not just woods—they were forests! We went
straight to Ôlho-d'Água-das-Outras, picked up the others who
were waiting for us, and followed the first small stream down
between slopes, with the wind caught in the buriti palms,
struggling against the barrier of their high leaves; the sassafras
trees, giving off a refreshing odor, like lavender; the ever-
flowing springs; winds from every direction. That air, striking
my body, spoke to me with the voice of freedom. But freedom
—I bet—is still merely the freedom of a poor little path within
the steel walls of a mighty prison. There is one truth which
needs to be revealed, and which no one teaches: the way to
freedom. I am an ignorant man, but tell me, sir, is not life a
terrible thing? Enough of this rigmarole. We kept on and on.

And so it was that we beat our hard-fought way across the
uplands, wading through fields of tall sapé grass or treading
colored sands as hard as cement, and meeting only cattle or a
lone wandering steer. In our weariness, following, I know not
how, God's route across the ranges in the gerais, we kept
climbing until all at once we came upon the Santa Catarina
ranch, in Buritís-Altos, at the headwaters of a stream. It was
the month of May, and we stayed there two days and I got
acquainted with my Otacília. You remember, I told you, how
Otacília and I had liked each other, how we had talked and
agreed to become engaged, and how on the second morning I
said goodbye, while she gave me the light of her eyes, her little
kitten head bright in the high window; then I left, with
Diadorim and the others. And how we had gone looking for
Medeiro Vaz and his band, who fifteen leagues off, were on

their way from Ratragagem to Vereda-Funda, and how, by cutting across, we had joined up with them at a place called Bom-Burití. I remember it well. A beautiful sight: the afternoon sky reddened by the setting sun. Up there the peaks are high. The tanagers like those cold heights—they sing like mad.

What followed, as I have told you, was our meeting with Medeiro Vaz and his stalwarts, in Bom-Burití, in a clearing at the edge of some woods. Medeiro Vaz—bearded, tall and dignified, his big hat pulled low, wise with the wisdom of old age but not himself old. I said to myself: "This is a good man." He kissed Diadorim on the forehead, and Diadorim kissed his hand. Of one like him, you could ask his blessing, and feel proud of yourself. Medeiro Vaz stood taking snuff, and passing out orders through his quartermaster. Climbing into our saddles, we left, full of hope, to invade the sertão—the wild sertão, inhabited only by macaws. Medeiro Vaz's only farewell was: "Hallelujah!" Diadorim had bought a large black handkerchief which he wore hidden over his heart, in token of mourning. The uplands were hard going. Then we forded a river, a river with low banks, with nothing but burití palms growing on them, the silent buritís. The caraíbas were in flower—brilliant purple, a purple that reaches up into the sky. On that part of the trip, I remember Diadorim turning to me, with the look of a little boy on his small face, and saying: "Riobaldo, I feel happy!" I rejoiced with him.

It was thus we began our many hard marches and indecisive battles and sufferings, whose melancholy tale I have told you, if I am not mistaken, up to the point of Zé Bebelo's return, with five men, coming down the Paracatú on a raft of burití palm trunks, and gallantly inheriting the command; and how, under Zé Bebelo, we went on fighting, winning victories. I think I even told you about the hot fight we fought, and won completely, on the São Serafim Ranch.

Is there no more? Ah, sir, what I think is that you already know all there is to be known, for I have told you everything. I could stop here. To learn the end, to find out what happened afterwards, all you need do is to think hard about what I have been telling you, turn it over in your mind, for I have related nothing idly. I don't waste words. Think it over, figure it out. Build your own plot around it. In the meantime, we'll have some more coffee, and smoke a good cigarette. This is the way I spend my time—mulling over the past—seated in this big old lounge chair, which came from Carinhanha. I have a little bag of remembrances. I am an ignorant man—I like to be. Isn't it in the dark that one best perceives a little light?

Urubú? It is a very old place in Bahia, with streets and churches, a place for families to live in. It will do for my thoughts. It will do for what I have to say; I would like to have been remorseful, but I am not.

But there really is no devil. It is God who lets the instrument tune itself as it wishes, until it is time to dance. A crossing, with God in the middle. When did I acquire my guilt? Here we are in Minas, yonder is Bahia. I was in those high old towns and villages. The sertão is secluded. My compadre Quelemém tells me that I am very much of the sertão. The sertão—it is inside of one. Do you accuse me? I told you about Hermógenes's selection of me, and my reluctant yielding. But my patroness is the Virgin through thick and thin. Could I have chosen a middle way? Vampire bats did not elect to be so ugly, so cold—it is enough that they chose to fly in the shades of night and to suck blood. God never goes back on his word. The devil does all the time. I left my beloved gerais. I came back with Diadorim. The moon, the moonlight: I can see those herdsmen driving their cattle at daybreak, with the moon still in the sky, day after day. I ask questions of the burití palm, and I gain courage from its answers. The burití reaches for the whole of the blue sky, but will not leave the water beside which it stands—it must have its mirror. A master is not someone who always teaches but someone who learns swiftly. Why does not everybody unite, to suffer and conquer together, once for all? I would like to found a city based on religion. Yonder at the edge of the plateaus, at the headwaters of the Urucúia. My Urucúia comes down clear, between dark slopes, and empties into the São Francisco, a mighty river. The São Francisco divided my life into two parts. Medeiro Vaz came into power, after burning down his house on the ranch. Medeiro Vaz died on the ground, like a lone bull bel-

lowing his last; as I pictured it to you once before: a black bull
bellowing in the storm. Zé Bebelo enlightened me. Zé Bebelo
came and went, like a flame in the wind, in a flash as quick as
thought—but the waters and the land wanted no part of him.
My compadre Quelemém is also a man without relatives, from
a distant land—the range of Urubú do Indaiá. Joca Ramiro was
a man so different and commanding, that even while he was
still alive he was revered as one dead. Sô Candelário? Sô
Candelário raged in despair. My heart understands and helps
my mind to recall and retrace the past. Joca Ramiro lay until he
disintegrated, buried among the carnauba wax palms, in salty,
sandy soil. Was not Sô Candelário, in a certain way, a relative
of my compadre Quelemém? Diadorim came to me, inde-
pendently of any knowledge or wish of mine. Diadorim—I
wondered about him. Was it a bad dream? And I thought a lot
about Otacília whenever I saw pickerelweed drooping in the
glassy water, club mosses, all the lilies, waterlilies, Easter lilies,
ginger lilies. But Otacília, to me, it was as if she was in the
tabernacle of the Host. Nhorinhá, at Aroeirinhas, the daughter
of Ana Duzuza. Ah, she was not to be spurned. Besides her
generosity and simplicity, Nhorinhá was a whore and beautiful.
The Miosótis girl? No. Rosa'uarda. I remembered her; I wanted
to keep all my memories of her with me. The bygone days
follow one after the other back to the sertão. They return like
horses—like riders at daybreak—strung out behind each other.
Do you remember Siruiz's song? Those sand bars and islands in
the river that one sees and leaves behind. Diadorim lived possessed of only one feeling at a time. It's a strange thing: high
places make me dizzy. Before, I had perceived the beauty of
those birds, on the Velhas River, once and for always. The little
red-legs. Could I give up all this? If I sell my soul, I am selling
the rest too. Horses neigh for no reason; do men know anything
about war? Jagunço and sertão are the same thing. You might
ask: who was he who was the jagunço Riobaldo? But that boy,
Valtêi, while he was being tortured by his father and mother,
would cry out to strangers for help. Even Jazevedão, for all his
brutality, might have succored him, had he been there. We can
live close to another, and come to know him, without risk of

hate, only if we love him. Any portion of love is of itself a
degree of health, a lull in the madness. God knows me.
Reinaldo was Diadorim, but Diadorim was in my heart.
Diadorim and Otacília. Otacília was a quiet force, like those
wide expanses of backwater on the Urucúia, which is itself a
riotous river. Diadorim is far away forever. Alone. On hearing
the music of a guitar I remember him. Just a little tune that
can't even be danced to. Isn't God in everything, as they say?
But everything is stirring and moving too fast. God could really
be glimpsed only if everything were to stop, just once. How can
you keep your mind on the ultimate things—death, judgment,
heaven, hell—if you are bogged down in all these other things?
All that has been is the beginning of what is to be—we are forever at a crossroads. Living is a dangerous business; and yet, it
is not. I don't even know how to explain these things. One
person's emotion differs from that felt by another who shares it.
What I want is to have things in the palm of my hand. Ah,
there was no pact with the devil. A pact? Imagine, sir, if I
were a priest, and one day had to listen to Hermógenes confess
his horrible iniquities. Suppose he had had a pact that one
person would die instead of another—or that one would live
instead of another—what then? But if I wanted to make another pact, with God himself—I wonder if I can?—would this
not wipe out everything that went before? I do have fear, more
or less. However, the fear I feel is for everybody. What is
needed is for God to have greater reality for people, and for the
devil to amuse us with his own non-existence. One thing is
sure, one alone, even though it differs for every person, and
that is: God waits for each of us to act. In this world, there are
all degrees of bad and good persons. But suppose everybody
were bad; would not then everybody be good? Ah, it is only for
the sake of pleasure and happiness that we seek to know everything, to develop a soul, to have a conscience. To suffer, none of
this is needed. Animals suffer pain, and they suffer without
knowing the reason. I tell you, sir: everything is a pact. Every
road is slippery, but falling doesn't hurt too much—one arises,
one climbs up, one returns! Does God slip? Let's see. Am I
afraid? No. I am fighting. One must deny the existence of the

"What-you-may-call-It." I find today that God is joy and courage, I mean, that He is loving-kindness, first of all.

Now, you will hear about those matters in which I was at fault and erred. Let's go back—to Burití-Pintado, to Õi-Mãe, to the Soninho River, to the São Serafim Ranch, to any of the other half-forgotten places. At the foot of slopes, among the swollen streams, or going up and down muddy inclines, drenched by rain and more rain, we toiled and fought bitterly, under Zé Bebelo's extraordinary leadership. Zé Bebelo Vaz Ramiro—long live his name! We were on their track, the Hermógenes, to kill them, to do away with them, to harry them. In the bad weather, Hermógenes kept running away from us, using every trick to give us the slip. But I had already got used to that life. It was both bad and good.

Then, after the wind had swept the sky and the weather got better, we found ourselves in the tall grass, on the nearly flat tableland. We moved in groups of twenty or thirty, with Zé Bebelo setting a furious pace. The landscape flew past. The tableland is just one thing—vastness. The sky so bright you couldn't look at it. The scattered green of the grasslands. The hard sands. The stunted little trees. Bands of screeching macaws flying over from time to time. Hurrying parakeets, too, with their less strident chatter. Does it rain there? It rains— but the rain does not flood the water holes, nor rush down gullies, nor make mud—all of it is sucked deep into the ground in a minute, slipping in like so much light oil. The surface of the ground turns hard early, with the diminishing rains which cease altogether in February. Nothing but tableland, tableland, tableland.

During the day the heat is awful, but at nightfall it cools off, and by morning you shiver with cold—this you know already. To keep away the gnats, we would burn arapavaca leaves. It was pretty, when an ember popped, scattering sparks, and the flames flickered. My happiness lay in Diadorim. We used to blow on the fire together, kneeling facing each other. The smoke would choke us and bring tears to our eyes. It made us laugh. Although February is the smallest month, it is when the burití nuts ripen, and in the sky, after the rains have stopped, all the year's stars are gathered. I laughed then, too. A man asleep, with his head thrown back, two fingers on his chin. It was Pitolô. Pitolô something, a fearless outlaw, with crimes to his name in the manihot rubber country above Januária; but he was born on the riverbank. On the near-black Carinhanha, a long, mighty river, with many settlements on its banks. He used to tell about his love affairs; Diadorim liked to listen to him sometimes. But Diadorim's thoughts were all on making war. As for me, in the intimacy of my thoughts, love would turn to lust. I became cranky. "A swallow that is continually coming and going, needs a good rest in the church towers of Carinhanha," Pitolô would say. I had other sudden desires, to pass my hand slowly over Diadorim's body, which he kept covered. And what about Otacília, didn't I think about her? Yes, now and then. I thought about her, my bespoken wife, and her dowry. One day, I would return to the Santa Catarina, and she and I would stroll in the orange grove there. Otacília, honey of rosemary. Did she pray for me? She did. Today I know it. And it was during those beneficent hours that I would turn over on my right side and sensibly fall asleep on my pallet of dark thoughts.

But I carried my fate with me. The region we were in was not for us: it was a country fit only for the witless. Who wants to listen to hawks crying and flocks of seriemas screeching, and see the big rheas and deer running, even going in and out of old corrals on abandoned cattle camps, left over from the time when the wilderness was more than just wilderness? The tableland is for those pairs of tapirs that weave long trails through the scrub, blowing hard as they go, oblivious to all around them. Here and there, lordly toucans, filled the trees, just a pistol-shot away from me. Or a mother tinamou, clucking to her chicks, scratching the ground and calling them to search with her for worms and insects. Ah, and the gray ouzel is a fine singer. Small streams. Not a living soul. Then whole days, nothing—not a thing—no game, no birds, no partridge. Do you know what it is like to traverse the endless sertão, awaking each morning in a different place? There is nothing to which to accustom the eyes, all substance dissolves.

Zé Bebelo, restless and on the move, was wasting our supplies. That Hermógenes should do nothing but keep running
away—this he could not understand. "Go on digging burrows
—keep it up—you'll see," he muttered irascibly. He was talking
less these days, or, when he spoke, I tried not to hear him. In
moments of ordinary conversation, Zé Bebelo frayed my patience. I'd much rather have a simple talk with Alaripe, or with
Fafafa, who had a brotherly love for horses, understood all
about them, and was expert at training and raising them. Zé
Bebelo interested me only when we were on the threshold of
big doings, making life-or-death decisions, in moments of action, all hell a-popping. At other times, his ranting annoyed me.

On the move, day after day, I did plenty of thinking. I thought
about love. Was Otacília really my promised bride? What I
needed was an all 'round woman—I wanted both the cow and
the milk. As for Diadorim, I should have felt disgust. For myself, or for him? But gradually my thinking became less
disturbed, like awakening from a dream, and I noticed how his
warm smile began first in his eyes, before breaking out on his
lips; how he spoke my name with sincere pleasure; how he held
the reins and the rifle in his fine, white hands. Those tablelands
of flat ranges, awe-inspiring by their size, making you feel tiny.
I felt as if I was wearing a pair of comfortable old slippers, and
what I wanted was a mustard plaster, or hard, unbroken,
army boots.

And what about the others, you will ask. Ah, my friend, warring men also have their weak moments: a male alone without
a mate finds other outlets. I surprised one—Conceição, it was
—lying on the ground, hidden by some heavy brush: something
one sees as rarely as a wild animal defecating. "It is one's
nature," he said, though I had not questioned him. What I
wanted was amusement of some sort, to relieve the monotony.
In that crowd there was no one who sang, no one who had a
guitar or any other instrument. Then I tried hard to amuse
myself thinking where I would have been had the past events
not occurred.

I never left Diadorim's side. I felt an urge to eat and drink his
leftovers; I wanted to touch whatever he had touched. Why? I

remained silent, I remained quiet, I quivered without trembling. Because I did not trust myself. I did not wish to indulge in vile temptations. I said nothing, I lacked the courage. Was I living in hope? For a while, I even stopped thinking about Nhorinhá, Rosa'uarda, and that girl, Miosótis. But everybody was talking, and in me a silly dream was fading, like ground fog in the August cold, swirling and dissolving in the morning sunlight.

There was one night, I admit, when I lay awake, unable to sleep. With a firm hand I curbed my impulses: the effort left me exhausted, depressed. This was followed by a strong desire to wash my body under the white waterfall of some brook, put on a new suit of clothes, abandon everything that I was, and seek a better destiny. I got up and walked away from the camp before the break of day, in the heavy dew. Only birds could be heard, the kind you hear without seeing. The day breaks there with a green-tinted sky. Zé Bebelo could jabber all he wanted to, about how we were going to catch the Hermógenes and smash them, and about the righteousness and future benefits of making war and controlling politics, but what good was all that to me? It made me tired. I kept on to the edge of the stream. The cold was sharp, and I waited for the darkness to pass. When daylight came, I saw that I was near the burití palm grove. There was one burití—an enormous beauty. There I made up some new verses, to add to the old ones, because I was thinking of Siruiz, a man I never knew. These were the verses, as I recall them, and not very good, either:

> *I brought all this money,*
> *All this I brought in my bag:*
> *To buy the end of the world*
> *In the middle of the tableland.*

> *Urucúia, that wild river,*
> *Singing the way I love:*
> *The song of limpid waters*
> *That melts the heart away.*

> *Life is a dangerous business,*
> *Lived because we must:*

Drifting downstream by night,
A well of darkness by day.

But I didn't sing these verses so anyone could hear, didn't
think it worthwhile. Nor did they quiet me down, probably because I had made them up myself. Whatever virtue they may
have had retreated within me, like a steer being driven out of
the corral, which takes sudden fright and dashes back in,
scraping its sides against the narrow gate. I don't much wonder,
for I myself could not get clear what I wanted, and what I did
not want, going round and round in circles. In the living of life,
things get mixed up. Life is like that: first it blows hot, then,
cold; it tightens, then loosens; it soothes, then disquiets. What
life demands of us is courage. What God wants is to see us
learning to make ourselves happier in the midst of happiness,
and happier still in the midst of sadness! And to be able to do so
suddenly, on any occasion, on purpose—through courage. Can
it be? Sometimes I thought so. When day dawned.

The sun was rising, and the comrades, one by one, were
coming around for coffee, all in good humor. If we endured all
that hardship, it was because of that good fellowship, and that
steady activity. I got on well with all, or nearly all, of them, and
had no quarrels. Real men, they were. Among these—listen
carefully—were Zé Bebelo, our Chief, always in front, never
resting nor tiring; Reinaldo, whose other name was Diadorim:
knowing about him, you know my life; Alaripe, made of iron
and gold, and flesh and bones, whom I held in greatest esteem;
Marcelino Pampa, second in command, accomplished in many
things, and a man worthy of respect; João Concliz, who could
imitate bird calls like Sesfrêdo; he never forgot anything;
Quipes, a fast-moving fellow: he could cover fifteen leagues in
a day by horse; Joaquim Beijú, a scout, who knew every corner
of the gerais; Tipote, who could find water like an uplands
steer, or a buriti palm seedling; Suzarte, another scout, like a
trained hunting dog; a good person; Quêque, who was always
yearning for his little old farm; it was his ambition to own a
patch of planting ground again some day; Marimbondo, handy
with a knife, a dangerous man in a quarrel when he had had

too much to drink; Acauã, a queer bird: just looking at him you saw the face of war; Maõ-de-Lixa, a cudgel-wielder: he never let go of a good club, which in his hands was a deadly weapon; Freitas Macho, from Grão-Mogol: he could tell you the biggest cock-and-bull story, and you would end by believing it; Conceição, who carried a bag with every picture of a woman he could find, even clipped them out of calendars and newspapers; José Gervásio, an expert hunter; José Jitirana, from a place called Capelinha-do-Chumbo: he was always saying that he looked very much like an uncle of his called Timóteo; Prêto Mangaba, from Cachoeira-do-Chôro: he was reputed to know all about witchcraft; João Vaqueiro, a true friend, as you already know; Coscorão, who had been a Jack-of-all-trades, though he was left-handed; Jacaré, our cook; Cavalcânti, an able fellow, but very touchy—easily offended by any joke or remark; Feliciano, who had only one eye; Marruaz, strong as an ox—he could hold a colt by two legs; Guima, lucky at all card games; he was from the Abaeté sertão; Jiribibe, little more than a boy, for whom everyone had a fatherly affection; Moçambicão, an enormous Negro: his father and mother had been slaves in the gold fields; Jesualdo, a levelheaded fellow—I still owe him eighteen milreis that I forgot to pay him: Jequitinhão, a onetime mule driver, who expressed himself only in proverbs; Nelson, who used to get me to write letters to his mother; I don't know where she lived; Dimas Dôido, crazy in name only —just foolhardy and hotheaded; Sidurino: everything he said was funny; Pacamã-de-Prêsas, who wanted to fulfill a vow one day, to light candles and kneel in São Bom Jesus da Lapa; Rasga-em-Baixo, one-eyed too, clumsy in his movements: he used to say that he had never known his mother or father; Fafafa, always smelling of horse sweat: when he lay on the ground, his horse would come and smell his face; Jõe Bexiguento, nicknamed "Alparcatas"; I have told you about him; a certain José Quitério: he ate everything, even lizards, grasshoppers, snakes; Treciziano, a poor devil, and José Felix, another; Liberato; Osmundo. And those from Urucúia whom Zé Bebelo had brought with him: that Pantaleão, Salústio João, and the others. And—I was about to forget—Raymundo

Lé, a healer, he knew what to do for any disease; and Quim Queiroz, who took care of the munitions; and Justino, blacksmith and farrier. The rest I can count on my fingers: Pitolô, José Micuim, Zé Onça, Zé Paquera, Pedro Pintado, Pedro Afonso, Zé Vital, João Bugre, Pereirão, Jalapa, Zé Beiçudo, Nestor. And Diodôlfo, Duzentos, João Vereda, Felisberto, Testa-em-Pé, Remigildo, Jósio, Domingos Trançado, Leocádio, Pau-na-Cobra, Simião, Zé Geralista, Trigoso, Cajueiro, Nhô Faísca, Araruta, Durval Foguista, Chico Vosso, Acrísio, and Tuscaninho Caramé. I name them so you can see how well I remember. Aside from one or two I have forgotten—a lot of others, I mean. Many of them died in the end.

The truth of the matter is that I was following Diadorim, we two and all the rest under the command of Zé Bebelo.

"We are going to do it, Professor, my son; we are certainly going to back those goats up against the river and make Hermógenes fight," Zé Bebelo announced, nodding his big head pompously. I didn't express my agreement right away, so he imagined I was being skeptical. "Forget your doubts. I know exactly what I'm doing. I have it all figured out up here," he said tapping his forehead with his finger.

I believed him, all right, but I had no way of knowing how my luck was running. I say this because in a bend of the Ribeirão-do-Galho-da-Vida we had bumped into a small enemy party that had come there on a spying mission. The exchange of gunfire did not last long, but I was hit by a bullet which grazed the fleshy part of my arm and I lost a lot of blood. Raymundo Lé washed the wound with angico bark, and I was better inside of an hour. Diadorim bound it up well with a strip torn from a shirt. I was grateful for his kindness. Actually, everyone was solicitous about me; it was a comfort. But, after a couple of days, my whole arm hurt and became swollen. The swelling made me tire easily, and I was always wanting to stop for a drink of water. "If I have to shoot, what will I do? I can't." This was another of my worries. I was surprised, because José Felix had also been hit, in the thigh and leg, but his blood was good and the wounds healed of their own accord, so you could hardly notice them. Since this was the first time anything had happened to me, I was disturbed. Even my chest hurt, and I couldn't move my fingers. "Ah, my Otacília," I groaned, "perhaps you will never see me again, and in that case you won't even be my widow." Some of the men recommended mountain arnica, and others advised a balsam plaster. Raymundo Lé guaranteed a cure with erva-boa, but where would he find erva-boa?

We reached the Tucanos Ranch and stopped there—it is on the edge of Rapôsa Lake, past the Enxú river. We visited the big old house. There wasn't a living soul to be seen. We weren't far from the Chico River. Why, then, not keep advancing by forced marches, in order to attack? "I know what I'm doing," said Zé Bebelo, without further explanation. Well, I didn't. I found me a folding cot, in a half-darkened room. Nothing mattered to me. "Save your strength, Riobaldo. I'm going to look for a remedy for you, in these woods," said Diadorim.

We spent two days at Tucanos, during which we ate palm cabbage, and set the meat from two steers out in the sun to dry. In the early afternoon of the first day, a drover and his cowhands showed up. They had come from Campo-Capão-Redondo, and were on their way to Morrinhos. Why had they traveled in such a roundabout way? "Will you let us pass in peace, Chief?" the drover asked. "We give you peace, friends," Zé Bebelo answered. Thus assured, the drover decided to give us some news—that we were in the midst of danger. Yes—soldiers! "How many, old man?"

Government soldiers on duty, more than fifty. And where were they? "They are in São Francisco and in Vila Risonha, and more of them are on their way, Chief; that's what I heard tell."

Zé Bebelo was listening, all ears. He kept trying to learn more. Whether this, if that. And did the drover know the name of the District Attorney in Vila Risonha, and of the Judge, the Chief of Police, the Tax Collector, the Vicar. The drover could not say who the commanding officer of the troops was. That drover was an earnest man, whose word could be relied on, and who wanted to be on good terms with everyone. He had a bottle of laxative wine in his baggage, and offered me a swallow,

which did me good. They spent the night there, and left very
early the next morning.

In the meantime, my arm improved and I felt a lot better. I
walked all around the ranch, looking it over. It was huge—took
a lot of walking. At the far end of the inner court were the old
slave quarters, and in the outer court, around the edge, the
cane mill, the harness shed, many workmen's houses, and the
barns. This outside patio was big and rock-paved, and had a
cross set in the center. Grass was growing all over, a sign that
it was deserted. But not completely, for a cat had been left behind. It came to Jacaré, the cook, begging to be fed. Even on
the terrace, there were some tame steers and cows, the kind
that hang around where folks live. João Vaqueiro saw a good
cattle horn, hanging on the wall in the front room; he took it,
went out on the balcony, and blew a blast. The cattle understood, and a few entered the corral and went to the troughs,
hoping for salt.

"There were people living here less than a month ago," declared João Vaqueiro. And it was the truth, for in the pantry we
found a lot of food we could use. It was really nice there, at
Tucanos. The time went by so fast that the two days stretched
into three.

It was still dark when I woke up at dawn, on the morning we
were to leave. Some noise had awakened me—it was Simião
who had slept in the same room and was now up and groping
around. He called me. "We're going to round up the horses.
Aren't you coming?" he said. I didn't like the idea. "I'm sick. Do
you expect me to go? Don't make me laugh," I answered tartly,
and turned over. That leather cot felt good.

Simião left, along with Fafafa and Doristino—they were all
well and the dew in the pasture would do them no harm. Diadorim, who had slept on a mattress against the opposite wall,
had arisen earlier and disappeared from the room. I napped
some more. That house, with its owners gone, seemed to
welcome us. That enormous old echoing house, the big pieces of
furniture, the roominess of the clothes chests, the whitewash on
the old walls, the mildew. The peacefulness of the place was
impressive. I was struck, too, by what seemed so out-of-keeping:

the amount of old dirt and soot on the ceilings. I lay there thinking all sorts of things, until I heard the whistling and shouts, the trample of horses. "Ah, horses at daybreak!" That familiar sound came back to me, I remembered suddenly, from way back, and I ran eagerly to one of the windows. The first streaks of light were visible through the bars of the night. The men were arriving with the horses, which were filling the corral. Lively, they were. It was good to breathe deep, to take in all the smells, to inhale the soul of those fields and places. Then I heard a shot.

It was a rifle shot, in the distance. I knew what it was. I always know when a shot is a shot—that is, when there are going to be more. Many shots followed. I tightened my belt. I tightened my belt, and the next thing I knew, my weapons were strapped on. I had been hungry. But now suddenly I was ready for action and had forgotten my hunger.

I wish you could have been there and seen it! Confusion but without confusion. I left the window, a man running bumped into me, others were shouting. Not others, just Zé Bebelo— shouting orders. Where? What? Were the others quicker than I? But I heard someone say: "They killed Simião." Simião? "And what about Doristino?" I asked. "Huh? I don't know," someone answered, "but besides Simião they killed Aduvaldo, too." "Don't tell me any more!" I cried out, but on the instant, I turned and asked: "Ah, and Fafafa?" "No, not Fafafa—he is doing some killing himself!" And so the war had come: like a bolt out of the blue, our terrible enemy had fallen upon us. "It is they, Riobaldo, the Hermógenes!" said Diadorim, suddenly appearing before me.

They let loose one heavy volley after another against us. They shot up the sides of the house. Diadorim smiled grimly and shrugged his shoulders. I looked and looked at him until his image turned dark in my eyes. I felt like someone else. I breathed heavily. "Now," I thought, "we are hopelessly lost." Then I immediately said to myself: "Who ever heard of being trapped in ambush—it's ridiculous." Meanwhile my outer ear was catching noises around me: the heavy tread of feet running in the hallway; the whine of bullets, rattling as they

struck like so much corn pouring out of a sack. A steady
spitting and spitting. I felt as if I myself were being struck by
the bullets defacing that ancestral home. I had no fear, there
had been no time for it—it was something else. For the moment, I had the notion that Diadorim, his brows knit, was about
to tell me to buck up! But he said nothing, and I quickly gained
control of myself. "Let's go! This is it!" I exclaimed, placing my
hand on his shoulder. I was breathing quickly. My befuddle-
ment had lasted only a matter of seconds. My mind cleared
and in a flash I regained my usual cool-headedness. I realized
what we were up against: we had been surrounded.

It was a sight to watch João Concliz moving continuously
from one spot to another, hugging the walls, as one does at such
times, deploying his men! "You stay here, and you and you—
you over here—you over there," he ordered. "You, Riobaldo,
take charge of this window. Don't leave here, don't get careless,
under any circumstances." Down below, off to one side, I could
see Marcelino Pampa making for the slave huts, with five or six
companions, Freitas Macho and some others running to the
granary, and others still, with Jõe Bexiguento, alias Alpercatas,
heading for the cane mill. My heart was beating double-time, in
all that uproar. I kept my rifle at the ready, my clean weapon,
my mistress. I spotted Dimas Dôido and Acauã, lying behind the
big cross in the patio. One of the Urucúians, and then another,
could be seen dragging a huge basket of cotton. Other men
were bringing up sacks filled with corncobs; they were after
more sacks, and brought a box, too. They were collecting everything they could lay their hands on to barricade the outside
patio: boards, stools, gear and harness, a carpenter's bench.
Preparations for war, as I then saw, are always carried on in a
different spirit than peacetime work: men eagerly working in
unison with other men, and with such good will that you wonder
if the devil, or even the spirits, had breathed loving kindness
into them! Someone mumbled something and nudged me. It
was Prêto Mangaba, who had been sent to reinforce the position with me. He was offering, friendly-like, to share a piece of
coconut sweet cake with me. Only then did I remember that I
was hungry. Quim Queiroz, along with some other men, was

bringing us more ammunition heaped in a hide which they were dragging along the hall floor. I looked through the window at the other end of the room and saw the world's indifference, the distant spaces. Once again they were blasting away at us, at the sides of the house. Not a single one of the enemy could be seen. I wondered how I was going to manage, with my arm the way it was. I lifted my hand to scratch my forehead, but crossed myself instead.

I fired away, and they fired back.

Where could Diadorim be? I learned that he was at another spot, filling the post assigned to him. Along with Fafafa, Marruaz, Guima, and Cavalcânti, he was holding down the end of the veranda. Soon João Concliz returned, bringing Alaripe, José Quitério and Rasga-em-Baixo with him. "Wait!" he said. Pitolô and Moçambicão came back, too, dragging some cow-hides with them. These hides were to be nailed to the lintels over the upstairs windows and left hanging like loose curtains. Afterwards, Pacamã-de-Presas and Conceiço punched some holes in the walls to shoot through. Was the war going to last all our lives?

Then, suddenly, Zé Bebelo appeared and came over close beside me. "Riobaldo, Tatarana, come with me," he said, in a low, deep tone, but the voice was more conspiratorial than commanding. I wondered what he wanted of me. For me to move to a more advanced position, to a place where it would be easier to kill and get killed? I went with him, remembering that with Zé Bebelo everything had to be done in a hurry. Where he took me was to another room. It was a small room, without a bed in it, and all you saw was a table, a stout table of an aromatic red wood. I didn't understand. In that room, the war seemed shut out, but Zé Bebelo's thinking process—as I well knew—was something that crackled and blazed, full of ideas.

"First, set your rifle down over there," he said. Let go of my rifle? Instead, I placed it carefully across one corner of the table, on which there were paper and ink. "Sit down, brother." He offered me a chair, one with a high wooden back. If it was a matter of sitting down, I chose to sit on the edge of the table. Zé Bebelo had his pistol in his hand, but was not pointing it at

me; it was his symbol of command, which he carried constantly during the turmoil of battle. Without even looking at
me, he said:

"Write."

I was astounded. He wanted me to write, at a time like that?
But he told me what to say and I began to write, since it is
easier to obey than to understand. Was it? I am not a log, a
dumb object. There is nothing I resent more than being forced
to knuckle under. "Ah, it's what I don't understand that is
likely to kill me." I remembered those words, words which Zé
Bebelo himself had spoken on another occasion.

"Write."

The steady gunfire was keeping me from thinking straight.
Wasn't that Zé Bebelo's job, to think for all of us? It looked as
if there wasn't going to be enough paper for what he wanted.
There must be some more around there, we had to look for it.
In the meantime, I should keep on writing as best I could.

Suddenly, a cry of pain, followed by occasional groans of
entreaty.

"What happened?" "One of our boys has been hit—Leocádio,"
we heard. Zé Bebelo dashed out to see. Without conscious
decision to do so, I followed him. The man—the first to be
wounded—was sitting on the floor, his back to the wall and his
legs sticking out in front of him. He was supporting his forehead with his left hand, but in his right he still held his rifle,
for he hadn't let the damn thing drop. Some of the men were
returning with cans of water which Raymundo Lé had already
sent them to the kitchen to fetch. He washed Leocádio's
bloody face. Leocádio had been hit in the jaw, a bullet had
broken the bone, and the blood was oozing and dripping red.
"My son, can you still fight?" Zé Bebelo wanted to know.
Leocádio grimaced and swore that he could. "Sure I can. In the
name of God and of my fighting Saint Sebastian, I can!" His
features contorted, for it was difficult and agonizing for him to
speak. "And of the Law. And in the name of the law, too. Ah,
then, let's go, my boy, get revenge, get revenge!" Zé Bebelo
urged.

Zé Bebelo was like one possessed. He took me by the arm,

under a compulsion to get back to the table and resume his dictation, with me as his amanuensis. As he went on, pistol in hand, at times I got the notion that he was threatening me. "Now we'll see. Once I've got some army troops, they will protect my rear," he said. He urged me to speed up my writing. They were missives addressed to the Comanding Officer of Military Forces, to the Most Excellent Judge of the District of São Francisco, another of the President of the City Council of Vila Risonha, another to the District Attorney. "Finish them up," he said, "their length alone will carry weight."

I caught his meaning and I wrote. The theme was the same in all the letters: simply, that if the soldiers would come immediately, by forced marches, without wasting a minute's time, here at the Tucanos Ranch, they could bag big game—wolves and wildcats together—the biggest bunch of jagunços gathered in one place in the whole of the backlands. At the bottom, a proper and formal ending: "Order and Progress. Long live Peace and the Constitution. Signed: José Rebêlo Adro Antunes, Citizen and Candidate."

For a second my mind snapped, and I stopped. But then I was able to understand the reason for my sudden suspicion. The terrible thought that assailed me was: could this be treason? I stole a glance at Zé Bebelos's eyes. It all seemed clear to me now. He had been in the pay of the Government all along, and now he was delivering us up to the Government troops. And what about us, all of us? What about Diadorim and me, our sad and happy ups and downs, Medeiro Vaz's celebrated death, the vengeance in the name of Joca Ramiro? Nor did I know for sure, after so many months, what Zé Bebelo had been up to, what he had really done, besides just keeping his promise to go to Goiás. I did know, however—worse luck— that by his very job and nature, he could not stop thinking, he could not keep from planning ahead all the time. And as we were under his command there was no escape for us, none whatever. He had led the band here to the São Francisco, and had wanted to spend those three days on this vulnerable ranch. Who knows, then, but what he himself had already, some time previously, sent word to the soldiers to come? The idea filled

me with fright, as when the wildcat springs, or the canoe overturns, or the rattler uncoils. Could it be? On the way to hell—
for good! I had to regain my nerve. The firing doubled in
intensity. What I was hearing was the sound of war.

No doubt I was exaggerating. Rather, Zé Bebelo was the man
of the hour, relentlessly capable. Nor was he disturbed. "Have
they no shortage of ammunition, that they can waste it?" he
said scornfully, as the firing increased, the bullets whining and
thudding. They were breaking the roof tiles, and all the walls
were being peppered. Chunks of plaster were falling from the
top. "Hurry, Tatarana, for we both have to shoot, too!" He said
it gaily. In the window there, where one of the cowhides had
been hung, a bullet would strike and knock the hide inward,
then, fall to the floor, its force spent. With the impact of each
bullet, the hide would billow in, then swing slowly back into
place, with only a scar on it, not a hole. In this way the bullets
were rendered harmless—that was what the cowhides were for.
Treason? I didn't want to think about it. It is not the uproar
and the zinging of the bullets on that day that I shall never
forget, but the black cowhide swinging suddenly in, then gently
back.

Someone brought me more paper which they had found by
rummaging in drawers in the other rooms; paper with writing
in ink on it, but parts of which, or the reverse side, could be
used. What was written on those old papers? One was a letter of
bygone days, dated February 11th of a year in which we still
had an Emperor, whose name was spoken with respect, an-
nouncing the arrival of a shipment of tools, drugs, and dyed
cotton thread. A receipted bill for the purchase of slaves, by
Nicolau Serapião da Rocha. "Write quickly, my son, hurry."
What about the betrayal, then? I could hear the men's loud
cries and curses rising above the noise of the shooting. Duzentos
and Rasga-em-Baixo, standing there beside the window, would
occasionally aim and fire and jump back out of sight. I couldn't
go on and once more I stopped writing—and looked Zé Bebelo
full in the face.

"What is it? What's the matter?" he asked. He must have
read in my eyes that I knew something was wrong.

"Well—why don't you sign yourself Zé Bebelo Vaz Ramiro, as you once said you would?" I asked in turn, in reply to his question.

He gave me a look of startled surprise that seemed to say I had caught on to him. Sometimes a person will betray himself unknowingly. But he had not perceived the real meaning of my question, the reason for my suspicion. Shrugging his shoulders with affectation, but pleased with himself, he thought to deceive me by saying:

"Ah, yes—I had thought of that, too. I thought of it, but it wouldn't do. My devotion to Medeiro Vaz and Joca Ramiro is very high and sincere, but the formalities don't permit it; the formalities are very exacting."

After that, I went on writing. I just went on, that's all—because life is a miserable thing. My handwriting was slow and shaky. My other arm was hurting again. "Treachery"—without meaning to, I wrote the word down, but then I scratched it out. A bullet knocked up the cowhide, and while it was up in the air, another bullet followed the first through the window, hit the wall opposite, ricocheted, and fell near us, still hot. On the wall, there was a cow's horn on which to hang clothes. All through that house they had horns instead of hooks on which to hang the hammocks. I kept wishing that another bullet would come whizzing in. I don't know why. Zé Bebelo's heavy silence disturbed me. But, leaning over my shoulder, he said.

"What is it? What mistake did you make?" He couldn't see, because I had already scratched it. But then he started talking a lot, explaining his plan. At night, when it got real dark, he would send two men, two of the smartest, to slip through the enemy line encircling us, each with a package of identical letters. Then, with God's help, if they, or one of them, managed to get through, it was a sure thing that the soldiers would come in a hurry. They would suddenly appear and trap and destroy the Hermógenes!

"And what about us?" I asked.

"Huh? What about us? You must not have understood me. In the confusion and hullabaloo, we'll find a way of escaping."

"Yes, but it would be awfully hard," I commented.

"Ah, yes, my son, difficult it would be. But I'll risk it—it's our only salvation. If not, what chance have we?" Zé Bebelo was pleased with his reply.

Then I said, respectfully, that we could try to do that now: blast our way out through the Hermógenes, fighting and killing. That's what I said, but I had forgotten that I was dealing with Zé Bebelo. Who could match wits with that man, get the better of him?

"Is that so, Tatarana? Well, listen, think—those Hermógenes are no braver than we are, nor is their number greater, but the fact is, they slipped up on us, surrounded us, and occupied all the best positions. They are sitting pretty. For us, at this moment, to force an escape—well, we might be lucky, but even so, many of us would be killed. There would be no way of off-setting our losses, not a chance of killing a good bunch of the enemy. Do you understand? But, if the soldiers were to come, they would have to open up fire on the Hermógenes first, and do them a lot of damage. While that was going on, we could try only to escape. At least, we will have had that advantage. Ah, don't you get the idea? Well, that's what you want, too, isn't it?"

He was being reasonable not in what he was doing but in the way he was talking about it. He laughed. Laugh, did he? He drank me like I was water, he stepped on me like I was grass, he blew on me like I was ashes. Ah, no! What did he think—that I was squatting there on the floor? A rush of blood burned my face, and the pounding of my heart filled my ears like a cataract. I pushed my foot into my sandal and pressed down hard on the board floor. I forgot everything for the moment, seized by a strong resolve. What I decided to do—and my decision was as solid as a rock—was that when the soldiers arrived I would stick close to Zé Bebelo, and if he made the least move of treachery I would raise my rifle and let him have it. I would kill him outright. And then . . . And then I would take over the command—I myself! I disliked being a leader, and dreaded its burden of responsibility, but I would do it. Until the moment arrived, I would not breathe a word to anyone, not even to Diadorim. But I'd do it, all right. A feeling of something strong and true came over me, filling me with joy.

I was Riobaldo, Riobaldo, Riobaldo! I nearly shouted my name, my heart crying it out loud. Then, after I had gritted my teeth and finished writing the last note, I felt calm and whole, and so fully resolved that I think that must have been the turning point in my life. I handed the papers to Zé Bebelo; my hand did not tremble in the slightest. I was filled with boldness and the urge to speak out.

"You, sir, you are a friend of the Government soldiers," I said, laughing scornfully. I laughed to assure myself that I was not afraid of any man or chief. He was startled and amazed.

He said: "I have no friend, and soldiers have no friends."

I said: "I am listening."

He said: "What I have is the Law. And soldiers have the law."

I said: "Then, you are together."

He said: "But now my law and theirs is not the same: they are opposed to each other."

I said: "Well we, who are only poor jagunços, have none of that, we have nothing."

He said: "My law, do you know what it is, Tatarana? It is the welfare of the brave men I am leading."

I said: "Yes. But if you come to terms with the soldiers, the Government will honor and reward you. You are in politics. Is that not so? You want to be a deputy."

Ah, I laughed ugly, because it was the way I felt. I thought sure he would try to kill me. I was pushing my luck that day. But nothing happened. Zé Bebelo only frowned darkly. He closed his mouth tightly and thought hard. Finally he said:

"Listen, Riobaldo, Tatarana, I hold you as a friend, and I esteem you, because I detected your true worth. Now, if I knew for sure that you doubt my loyalty, or that you are suggesting a dirty deal of some sort for your benefit and mine. . . . Look, if I knew this for sure . . ."

I said: "Chief, a man only dies once."

I coughed. He coughed.

Diodôlfo came running up and reported: "Jósio is dying, with a bullet in his neck."

Alaripe came in and said: "They are trying to take the pigsty and the corncrib. They are swarming!"

I said: "Give your orders, Chief!"

I said it deliberately, not perfunctorily. Zé Bebelo smiled, relieved. He put his hand on my shoulder, that of my injured arm. "Let's go, let's go, with monkeys and bananas! Here, in the dining room, my boy," he urged. I crouched at the window and rested my rifle, a fine one, on the sill. Now to go to work. Were those fellows crazy?

The head of one, round as a coconut, appeared above the palm-leaf thatch of a cow hand's hut. I fired and saw the skull fly into pieces. The pain in my arm was so intense I had to bite my lips to bear it. But I carried on. I soon downed another one with a bullet in the chest, two bullets. By God, they were fearless! Meanwhile I was groaning and aiming. One by one, they continued falling, yielding to the deadly force I was directing at them. I kept count: there were six that I know of, up to lunchtime—half a dozen. I don't like to relate these things; one should not remember them. But to you, now, it is all right. I can tell when a man only appears to have been killed, when he doubles up from a wound, or when he falls because he has really been slaughtered. Did I feel pity? Is one going to feel sorry for a wildcat, or have compassion for a scorpion? I might have regretted missing a shot, only I never missed one. Let one of them show as much as an inch of his body, and my bullet would find its mark. My arm was throbbing and paining me terribly, like a raging fire. I could feel the pain even in my belly. Each shot I fired made me screw up my face and whimper. Afterwards, I would laugh. "Tie up this part of my anatomy with a cloth or something, pal," I pleaded. Alaripe, always helpful, tore up a bedspread, and bandaged me tightly with some strips of it. It hurt, but what of it? When he had finished, I knocked over another one, close by. That one is ready for the vultures, that one was dashing to one corner of the fence, that one jumped high in the air, that one let out a scream—little though I wanted to use men as targets, as if I were being paid so much a head. But I saved the life of many a one, too—their fear of my aim kept them from showing themselves. We fired one murderous volley after another. Then they started pulling back, and soon the fighting stopped altogether. A good thing, too, for it was time to eat. Just then something happened that made me and everyone laugh: a gorgeous butterfly which had flown in through the window with the bullets, as they were kicking up the cowhide, was now flitting around the room, without finding whatever it was looking for. It was one of those swallowtails with spotted greenish-blue wings. "Hello, welcome. Good-luck Mary!" cried Jiribibe, so loudly she might have understood. She was almost peace itself. They brought me my food where I was. Everyone praised my markmanship. You can't imagine with what zest I downed that food: beans, jerked beef, rice, greens, and manioc mush. I drank water, lots of it, mixed with cachaça. It is my favorite "coffee."

Zé Bebelo came over and congratulated me: "You are a wonder, Riobaldo, Tatarana—a flying serpent." He offered me more cachaça, and drank some himself, to our health. Was he only trying to cover up, because of an uneasy conscience? A man reveals himself by what he tries to hide. "Ah, Urutú Branco —the White Rattler—that is the name for you. We are friends. One day, you will see, we will enter the city of Januária together in triumph," he said. I don't know what I said in reply. A friend? I was there, on the side of Zé Bebelo, but Zé Bebelo was on nobody's side. A friend? Yes, I was. That man knew me, he understood my feelings, but only in part—he did not know about the sequel, the showdown to come. I thought to myself: if I saw him in the act of double-crossing, he would die. He would die at the hands of a friend. I swore it, silently. And then my mind leaped ahead to the big city of Januária, where I would like to go, but without fame as a fighter, and alone. I remembered that in the hotel and in the homes in Januária, you use a small towel to dry your feet with; and there is good talk. I wanted to be among decent people, home-loving people, and to know them, at work and at rest. I wanted to see pretty girls strolling arm in arm with one another, some of them with their black hair shining and smelling of umbu oil, adorned with gay flowers. I would go to Januária with Diadorim, and join the crowd waiting to hear the river boat's whistle and see it tie up at the slip. I would visit the distillery, where the men run the stills so skillfully, and where the cachaça—the aro-

matic "26" brand—acquires its taste and caramel color in great
vats of umbarana wood.

After a while I stood up and went to the porch to see how
Diadorim was getting on. I reserved the right to move about as
I pleased, for it had been my straight-shooting rifle that kept
the pigsty and corncrib from being taken, and after them perhaps the house itself. Diadorim was fighting and enjoying himself, without letting up, and not wanting to be interfered with.
So far, God, who had saved me, was also shielding my friend
against every danger. The bullets were flying thick and fast.
There was a man lying in an awkward position. I thought he
was trying to get a little rest. "Let's take him to the chapel,"
Zé Bebelo ordered. It was Acrísio—shot through. He must have
died without suffering. Weren't they going to look for a candle
to light for him? "Who has a rosary?" But at that moment
Cavalcânti exclaimed:

"Look, they are killing the horses!"

Damned if they weren't. The corral filled with our good
horses, the poor things imprisoned there, all so healthy, they
were not to blame, and those dogs, with neither fear of God nor
justice in their hearts, were firing right and left into that living
mass, to torture and sear our souls! What an appalling sight.
Realizing without understanding that the devil was at work,
the frantic horses galloped around, rearing and pawing and
coming down with their front hoofs on the backs of others,
stumbling, colliding, their heads and necks stretched, their
manes stiffly flying: they were just a lot of writhing curves!
They were whinnying, too—high, brief whinnies of anger, and
whinnies of fear, short, hoarse, as when a wildcat snarls
through wide-open nostrils. Round and around they went,
bumping into the fence, kicking, scattering, panic-stricken.
They began falling, sprawled on the ground, spreading their
legs, only their jaws or foreheads held upright, trembling. They
were falling, nearly all, then all of them. Those slow to die
were crying in pain—a high snorting groan, some as if they
were talking, others whickering through their teeth, struggling
with their last breath, gasping, dying.

"Those devils from hell! The damned wretches!"

Fafafa was weeping. João Vaqueiro was weeping. We all had tears in our eyes. There was nothing we could do to put a stop to that cruelty, there was no help for it. They, the Hermógenes, were killing wantonly, wreaking havoc. They were even shooting the loose steers and cows, the tame ones, which when we first arrived had approached the house, seeking its protection. Wherever we looked the animals were piling up, dead and dying, like our horses. The fence was a high one, they had no way of escape. Only one, a big light bay, that belonged to Mão-de-Lixa and was called Safirento: he stood on his hind feet and hung over the top rail, balancing there like a heavy weight, his thick rump turned in our direction; then he fell over on the other side, and we could no longer see what happened. Utter depravity. We swore vengeance. Not a single horse could be seen moving—they had all been shot down!

That innocent blood cried out for God to appear, incarnate, His eyes all-seeing. We called down curses. Ah, but faith is blind to the disorder all about. I think that God does not wish to repair anything except on His own terms. The hardest thing to endure was to have to listen to those awful sounds of suffering, those frightful screams of dying horses, like a sword through the heart. What was needed was for someone to go and blot out their pain with a compassionate bullet, one by one, ring down the curtain on that heart-rending drama. But we were powerless to do it. You understand what it was like: the horses, covered with blood and red foam, dead and dying, lying on the ground against one another, the sound of their voices one long, drawn-out wail like that of human beings in mortal terror—it made your hair stand on end. In their frantic suffering, the horses could not comprehend their pain. They were begging for mercy.

"Dammit, I'm going out there, I'm going out there and put the poor things out of their misery," yelled Fafafa. But we didn't let him, because it would have been utter madness. Before he could take two steps he would be riddled with bullets. We grabbed him and held him back. We were forced to stay inside that house, fighting the best we could, while that horrendous crime took place. You don't know, sir: the cry of an agonizing horse suddenly becomes deep, filled with hollows, and sometimes they give out grunts like a hog, or their voices turn high-pitched and quavering. You think that some curse has turned them into another kind of beast. And when you hear a lot of animals suffering martyrdom together, you wonder if the world isn't coming to an end. What had the animals done, for what transgression were they paying? To think that these had been our backlands ponies—so handsome, so good they were—and now they had been slaughtered in that manner, while we did nothing to save them. We had been helpless! And what were those Hermógenes after? It must be that they intended to keep those awful cries alive in our ears day and night, until we could stand it no longer and sooner or later be forced to rush out into hell. You should have seen Zé Bebelo: he was thinking with his whole being—like a team of oxen straining to drag their cart out of a mudhole. Suddenly he ordered: "Start shooting! Aim low." Guns blazed, here, there, in angry compassion. It did no good—just a waste of ammunition—for at that distance from the corral we could not reach the horses. To discharge volleys against the hidden enemy would do no good either. We had to face the hard fact that our hands were tied. At this point I rose above reality: I prayed! Do you know how I prayed? It was this way: God is all powerful—and I would wait, wait, wait, like stones wait. "Those are not horses whimpering, it is not horses that are whimpering—the one who is whimpering in misery is Hermógenes, inside his skin, in the crevices of his body, in the grinding of his organs, as one day it shall come to pass, by my design. From this day forward it must always be so: he, Hermógenes, mine to kill—I the hunter, he the hunted." Occasional cries could still be heard. The horses were sweating out their final agony.

We had grabbed hold of Fafafa, as I told you. But now suddenly Marruaz shouted: "Look! Look over there!" What was it? The Hermógenes themselves—who would have believed it?—were shooting the still-living horses to end their suffering, to give them peace. "God be praised!" exclaimed Zé Bebelo, brightening with relief, like a good man. "Ah, it's great," said Alaripe, too. But Fafafa said nothing, he couldn't speak; he just sat himself on the floor, with his hands pressed against the

sides of his face, and cried, cried like a child. We felt only
respect for his unabashed tears.

Then we waited. We rested our rifles for a while, without
firing a single shot. We wanted to give them a truce during
which to finish off our poor ponies. Even after the last whimper
had died on the air, we remained appalled and quiet for a long
time, until the sounds and the silence, and the remembrance of
that suffering should begin to recede in the distance. After that,
everything started up all over again, even more fiercely. And
in what I am telling, we see the desolation of the world. God
exists, yes, slowly or suddenly. He acts, all right—but almost
wholly through the medium of persons, good and bad. The
awesome things of this world! The backlands are a powerful
weapon. Is God a trigger?

But I am telling less than what happened; no more than
half, just enough to give you the idea. Even I, who, as you have
seen, review the past with a highly polished mirror, and retain
everything—big and little—even I could not describe all that
took place, all that we underwent, while besieged in that house
at Tucanos by Hermógenes's bandits. I don't recall how many
days and nights It was. If I say six, I think I am lying, but if I
say five or four, I may be lying even more. I just know it was
a long time. At times it felt like years, and at other times,
because of a different feeling, it seemed to have passed in a
whirr and a flash—like the fight of two hummingbirds. Now
that I am older, and the more remote it becomes, the memory
of it changes, is transformed, and turns into a kind of beautiful
passage of events. I have learned the right way to think: I think
like a flowing river—I barely discern the trees on the banks.

Those days and nights went by in sluggish confusion, directed toward one single terrible objective. Time took on a
different rhythm. We inhabited a roofed and walled target. Do
you know what it is to be holed up like that? I don't know how
many thousands of rounds were fired—my ears were filled with
the dizzying noise, the constant whining, popping, cracking.
The plastered walls, the beams and tiles of the big old house,
these were our shield. One could say—and I want you to believe
me—that the entire house felt outraged, creaking complaints,

and smoldering with rage in its dark corners. As for me, I
thought it was just a matter of time before the whole thing
would be razed and nothing left but the bare ground. But it did
not happen that way, as you will soon see. Because you are
going to hear the entire story.

The next to die was Berósio. Then Cajueiro. Moçambicão
and Quim Queiroz kept dragging up quantities of ammunition
for us to help ourselves. Zé Bebelo moved about everywhere,
telling us to shoot sparingly and effectively. "Ah, that's it, my
boys, don't waste. Kill only live people!" he said hotly, "train
your sights carefully, and bang! The dead will never bother us
again." We shouted words of encouragement to each other, to
keep fear at bay. And we cursed the Judases. To keep from
being afraid? One often resorts to rage to keep from being
afraid. The pain from the feverish swelling in my arm kept
getting worse. Alaripe thoughtfully put a pan of cold water near
me. When there was a lull in the firing, I would wet a cloth
and let the cool water drip over my arm. One of the comrades
helped me all he could, for which I was grateful. He was a
Urucúian, one of the five Zé Bebelo had brought with him. It
struck me as strange, at the moment. I suddenly noticed that
the man had not left my side for a long time, and was always
following me around.

It made me somewhat suspicious. That fellow always at my
side—was it by mere chance? His name was Salústio. He had
tiny eyes in a round face, a slack mouth, and seven long
whiskers on his chin. It annoyed me and I said to him: "What's
the idea? Have you taken a fancy to me? Stay in your own
burrow, armadillo." He laughed half seriously. A Urucúian of
few words, with green eyes—a very ugly fellow. He still said
nothing—just rubbed his belly with his knuckles—a Urucúian
gesture. I struck my right hand over the left, which was holding
my rifle, and kept it there—a jagunço gesture. I pressed him:
"What do you want of me?" Then he answered: "I like to watch
you, your skill. You are some marksman! It is from those who
know that one learns to do better!" This was his way of praising me. He laughed, very sincerely. I thought to myself: those
Hermógenes were people just like us, and until recently they

had been our companions—brothers, as they say; and now they were engaged in a struggle against us, trying to do us in. But, why? Was the world so crazy and senseless?

I quieted down. I shouldn't be having so many ideas. That kind of thinking was bad—it was opening the door to fear. It separated me from the group, left me out in the cold alone. For my own good, I had to be like the others, our united strength was suckled by the twin of rage—blind hate. Hatred of Hermógenes and Ricardão? I never even thought of them. Rather, I thought again about the Urucúian's suspicious ways. I felt sure he had been ordered by Zé Bebelo to spy on me.

It was further proof that Zé Bebelo was preparing treachery. I could feel it in the air. Could it be Salústio's assignment to bump me off at my first false move? Hardly, I decided. Zé Bebelo wanted me watched to keep me from telling the others the truth. As a matter of fact, some of the companions had seen me writing those notes—a strange thing to be doing in the midst of gunfire, but no doubt they thought that the letters were to friendly ranchers, who had squads of henchmen, appealing to them to come with reinforcements for our rear. Now Zé Bebelo was afraid that I would gossip. So he had sent the Urucúian to be my shadow. But Zé Bebelo would need me as long as the seige lasted. Double-crosser though he might be, did I not need him, too—his head for straight thinking? For at that time I had not learned to think clearly. Was I learning? I did not know how to think clearly—because of that, I killed. I was here, the others over there. The hell they poured on us, the bullets from countless rifles, bullets that tore into doors and ceilings—ah, this was a witless calamity, an evil without an evildoer, almost like a hailstorm, like the blind rage of thunder and lightning. How was I to feel hatred for men I could not even see? I had plenty for those I killed. But even so it wasn't quite hatred; it was only the acceptance of a fact.

The afternoon waned and the sun started to go down. We had lost track of the exact time of day. There was only anxiety-filled activity, then afterwards, a feeling of weariness. As night closed in, the danger might increase. Would not the Hermógenes attack, under cover of darkness, for a final showdown

inside the house, with gun butts and knives? Quiabo died.
Others had been wounded. As we had to occupy the chapel, the
dead were placed in a small, windowless room, next to the hall
stairs. Alaripe found a candle, which he stuck in a bottle and
lit. One lone candle for the lot. Zé Bebelo called me over to
where he was standing in the light of a small wall lamp. He
had also sent for Joaquim Beijú and Quipes, for secret confab.

It was now decided that those two would slip out and start
crawling as fate led them, each taking one of the packets of
letters. One would go in one direction, and the other in another,
and whichever met with God's approval would reach his destination. They agreed and asked no questions. Everything in
secrecy. Well then, if Zé Bebelo's intentions were honest, why
didn't he then and there tell everybody about his plan? I continued to wait. But—you will say—why didn't I myself reveal
the scheme, at least to Diadorim and Alaripe? I don't rightly
know. But one thing I did know for sure: I would watch Zé
Bebelo like a hawk. One false move and I would kill him. Zé
Bebelo had his own way of doing things; was he being loyal
or a traitor? This I would wait and see. I would wait and see
whether at the crucial moment he would try to save his own
skin at our expense.

Before leaving, Joaquim Beijú and Quipes went to the kitchen
to get some food to take with them. Jacaré, our cook, when he
wasn't cooking, also took part in the fighting; he would join
Mijafogo at the corner of a window. The night was dark as
pitch; it would stay that way until about ten o'clock when a
piece of the moon would rise. Little by little, both sides stopped
firing and a heavy silence fell over the scene. We were careful
not to make noise of any kind, so as not to reveal our exact
positions. A flash of gun powder at night always betrays the
gunner. "The dark is for surprises; the night is when the animal
springs," whispered Alaripe. That good Cearense: he was always
the same; with him, your worries disappeared; fighting became
a natural obligation, a man's bounden duty. For fellows like him
I would do anything; for their sake I myself would have to be
completely loyal. This meant that I would have to get hold of
Zé Bebelo and give it to him straight. He had to know where I

stood so that he would not ruin himself without being forewarned. For our own good, too—because if Zé Bebelo was to be
our downfall, he alone could also be our salvation. All right,
then, I would speak to him and challenge him quietly. Would
it do any good? Suppose it didn't. In that case, I would have to
seize power. I would have to fill Zé Bebelo's pockets with fear.
This alone would be effective.

Meanwhile, he was carrying on, issuing sensible instructions,
and neglecting none of the customary practices. He chose those
who were to take turns sleeping and standing guard. For each
who slept, another was to remain awake near by. Others would
make the rounds. Did Zé Bebelo himself never sleep? That was
his secret. He had the air of one who wanted to know and
manage everything himself. Which he just about did. Our water
for house use came from a ditch which ran down alongside the
kitchen and passed under the shed in such a way that we
could fill our cans without danger. "What they are going to do,"
said Zé Bebelo, "is to block the ditch up there and leave us
without a drop." He ordered every can and vessel that could be
found to be filled and stored. This was done. But as for the
stream in the ditch being diverted, it never happened. Right up
to the last, there was plenty of fresh, gurgling water all the
time. Suppose they were to poison the water? A foolish idea.
Where would they get enough poison to poison running water?

God keeps records in ledgers only. That night, Zé Bebelo
crept out into the dark, dressed in black garments which he
had collected from different people. He must have gone far,
moving like a rat in a corncrib fearful of being spotted by an
owl. He wanted to size up the situation with his own eyes. When
he came back he gave new orders: that we should all take
advantage of the dark of the moon to perform our natural
needs outside, at some sheltered places over by the old slave
huts. Then he turned to me: "The enemy's strength is the same
or smaller than ours. That is why they can't get up enough
courage to make an assault; also because they don't know the
inside of this house." Why did he choose me to whisper secrets
to? Did he look upon me as his stooge? "The numskulls, they
are not foemen worthy of me!" he sneered, showing his dis-

appointment. By now I had lost almost all my belief in Zé Bebelo. I had already set aside my friendship for him—seeing that he might yet have to die by my hand. It was clear to me now. I had written those notes and letters, on slips of paper, as his amanuensis. I therefore shared his guilt. It was the ruse of a power-mad opportunist. "Riobaldo," he added, "you come with me, you are a sharpshooter, you will be my general staff." I saw through it all. Now was the time. Now was the time for me to do and say what I have told you, for I was convinced that I was right. So I retorted:

"Yes. I go with you and the Urucúian comes with me. I go with you and that Urucúian, Salústio, comes with me, but when the hour strikes . . . When the hour strikes, I'll be right there close by, looking—looking at what goes on, at what's going to happen—at what's going to be or not to be." My speech bogged down and I was stammering. Do you know why? Only because he gazed at me, suddenly, intently, and I got stuck in the middle, addled, squelched. Foolish? I'm not sure. But I was not afraid. It was only that my excess of courage subsided, as a flame is lowered. I felt awkward and couldn't go on speaking.

Zé Bebelo blazed out:

"Silence, Riobaldo Tatarana! Am I not the Chief?"

With my head in a whirl—as they say—I sensed my danger. With my eyes closed, I glimpsed it. My legs began to quake and give way. Was I not going to defy Zé Bebelo's authority?

All right, now was the time. There was no other way out, now. But then, somehow, I was no longer returning Zé Bebelo's stare. "There is no Zé Bebelo in the world. There was once but he exists no longer. He never really existed. There is no such Chief. There is no person or ghost like him, nor any bearing his name—," I kept reassuring myself. I did not look him in the eye, but fixed my gaze on a little spot on his chest, a dot of a spot, a tiny little spot, where one could drive a bullet straight into the big vein of his heart. This alone flashed through my mind. Nothing else. I was not afraid. Just that mortal little target. I looked at it intently, softly. Then, I heard myself cough, and my voice saying:

"You are right, Chief. And I am nobody, nobody, nobody. I

am nothing at all, nothing whatever, nothing. I am not the least little thing, you know? I am not the least little thing, nothing whatever, the least of all. Do you understand, sir? Nothing. Nothing. Nothing."

That's what I said, but why? Zé Bebelo heard me through, astonished. He thrust out his lip. He nodded his head three times. Was he not afraid? He was worried. I soon knew it. So I had been right. Then Zé Bebelo laughed indulgently, and spoke: "Not at all, Tatarana. You are worth more than anybody. You are my man!" I murmured something, not even in words. "All right," he said in conclusion, putting on a show, "let us go and encourage our boys." Then we parted; I went to the kitchen and he to the veranda. What had I done? I had scored —not through knowledge but only through intention. Now he was going to think about me very carefully. So I believed. Now he was not going to find it so easy to commit treason, but would have to watch his step and think twice before doing a double-cross. There was even something a little funny about this awkward situation. I was holding good cards.

That night, I slept my share. At daybreak, the firing started up again. But only an occasional shot, to keep from wasting ammunition and to make every shot count. The other side was doing the same. A neat, careful war, like embroidery work in a frame. I went to look at the dawn. The eastern sky was bright with the first rays of the rising sun. But the sky over the corral was already black with vultures. When the wind veered, a stench came from that direction. But, God forgive me, it was even worse inside the house, really awful—our dead companions. We latched the door and stuffed all the cracks with raw cotton and sacking. But the smell came through just the same. After a while we heard a cat meowing. "Dammit! the cat is inside there!" someone yelled. Ah, yes, it was the cat. We let it out and it slunk off to hide under a cot in another room. We gave it something to eat, for it brings good luck to be kind to cats. In the outside room, I again took up my post as sharpshooter. The vultures were no longer frightened by the gunfire but dropped to the ground in the corral and began tearing big chunks of flesh with their beaks. Afterwards, they lined up

close together on the fence. Whenever they beat their wings to
take off, it stirred up the stink. As the day went on, the smell
grew worse. I couldn't stand the taste of salt, so I chewed dry
manioc with a handful of brown sugar. In the whole house not
a speck of lime or cupful of creolin was to be found to kill that
vile odor. When Quim Pidão died, we laid his body on a bench
in the parlor for the time being—no one had the courage to
open the room with the other corpses. The day advanced. I
sneaked a visit to Diadorim, just to see him; we talked hardly
at all. I wondered how long we could hold out there, under
siege. At the end, we might have to eat the cowhides, like that
one-eyed devil of a Dutra Cunha, who resisted the siege of his
place at Canindé by Cosme de Andrade and Olivino Oliviano.
Zé Bebelo knew his story well. Now I was laughing at Zé Bebelo.
A lot of other things could happen between daybreak and nightfall. Nobody mentioned Joaquim Beijú and Quipes. By this
time they had either been nabbed by the enemy, or were
beating their way to the towns. Perhaps, when it grew late or
dark, they were galloping ahead on horses they had rustled up
on the plain, thereby gaining time for us. Would the soldiers
really come? The next day, Acerêjo died. The smell of old death
hung heavy in the air. "That stink is going to end by poisoning
us," someone kept saying. It permeated even the drinking water
and left a bad taste in our mouths. The House of the Tucanos
was withstanding the battle—that vast, big house, with ten
windows on each side, and its foundations resting deep on
solid rock. I think the House had a way of talking back, of
answering the whines of bullets on their way from rifle to
target. The bullets coming in a stream drew a whistle of air
after them. Let them knock off splinters! The men laughed at
the least thing, they were not going to add gloom to their
troubles. When someone laughed out loud, the others farther
away would send to find out the reason for it, or would shout
the question while the firing went on. Another thing happened:
Zé Vital had a fit, a real ugly attack which began after he had
complained of his nose being hot. He knew it was coming on:
he squealed like a pig and fell flat on the floor, stiff as a gun
barrel, his eyes protruding, and foaming at the mouth, but

beating his arms and legs all the while, trying desperately for something or someone to hold on to. Someone said: "This is an old sickness, it is not the result of war." The fit turned into a state of semi-death, and they laid Zé Vital in a sort of leather basket. The day was getting on. The House was filling with flies, the kind that appear at funerals. A few at first, then a black swarm buzzing about, trying to find the source of the stench. The worst things cannot be kept out by closing doors. I stayed away from Diadorim—to avoid seeing him feverishly aiming and firing, neglectful of his own safety, concerned only with revenge. His true self was hardly recognizable in his ashy face, his bloodshot, sunken eyes. That was the work of war. Why? Because Joca Ramiro was said to have been murdered? The usual reason for anything is not the true one, it doesn't fit. My home was far from there, in another part of the world. The sertão has no places in it. Bigrí, my mother, had not placed a curse on me.

Late morning, the same thing all over again: the rifles cracking, the awful smell of dead men and horses, and the flies, swarming every where. Though all my desire was for peace and quiet, there I was—against my will, actually—in the midst of all manner of absurdities, with death on my left and right hand, with new death in front of me, and I sure of nothing—without Otacília, who was to be my bride, who was to become the mistress of great farm lands and lush pasture lands, lands bathed by springs and palm-fringed streams. How is it that life's disorders are always more powerful than we? I did not want to have to accept that, being plunged in all that hell. I wanted to live my life in my own way. I felt sorry for Diadorim: his deadly hate, crying for vengeance, was like that of old people living in the past. Diadorim thirsted for Hermógenes's and Ricardão's blood, as the solution. Two different rivers—that is what we two were—crossing. I stayed at Diadorim's side a few minutes, while he fired away. We could never see the enemy, not even a glimpse, in the puff of smoke which followed each of their shots. A trick of some sort; no doubt they were camouflaged with green branches and foliage, and this made it almost impossible for us to spot them. Ah, but it didn't

keep their bullets from whizzing toward us, and knocking off
pieces of the roof tiles. Mother death. Did the one who most
deserved to die, get killed? "Help, folks! They got me—I am
passing out—I am going blind," cried Evaristo Caitité, who had
carelessly shown himself and got hit square in the side. His
body lay motionless, and his legs were turning cold. He was
smiling as he died, his eyes wide open. "What is he seeing? He
sees our victory!" said Zé Bebelo, rising to his full height. The
victory was to the vultures gorging themselves on my little
gray pony which I would never ride again. The men's uneasiness became alarming. They no longer tried to sleep, they
were so jumpy. The situation called for a firm hand at the
controls. Some wanted to break out and attack in a rush—one
of those sudden crazy notions that destroy a fighting unit.
"Steady, my sons. We must hold on and be patient—just keep
loading and reloading and crooking your finger," said Zé Bebelo
encouragingly. Now we had nothing left but the hope of some
miraculous relief. Was there no way by which we might safely
escape? Our only chance lay with Zé Bebelo—this I pondered
over and over, and I believed it—Zé Bebelo, who always liked to
first let things get worse and more complicated. A swig of
cachaça gave me good counsel. Unless the soldiers came—if
they were coming—we were lost, weren't we? And Zé Bebelo
was the one who had sent for the soldiers, wasn't he? Yes, but
now Zé Bebelo would no longer try to double-cross us, thanks
to me. What Zé Bebelo needed was to be curbed by someone
with a strong will who could take charge and guide him. That
was what I was doing. I knew it. Zé Bebelo made believe that
he was unaware that I was watching him. But I had him
trapped, and he knew it. Now he was being forced to sharpen
his wits and dream up some other and better way of achieving
final victory for us all—without treason or madness. I really
believed this. I knew that Zé Bebelo was very capable. "Well,"
I said to myself, "I'll go see if I can pick off at least one more of
those Hermógenes before dark." But I didn't. I couldn't. What
happened was that Zé Bebelo grabbed me by the shoulder. He
changed his position and cocked his ear at the window. "There,
can you hear it, Tatarana Riobaldo, can you hear it?" he said

with a brilliant smile which revealed neither evil nor goodness. It must have been around three o'clock in the afternoon, judging by the sun. Yes, I heard it!

Could it be that the military had been contacted and the soldiers were actually arriving? Yes. Yes! This created wild excitement among our men because they did not know what had gone on before; they knew nothing of Zé Bebelo's plan. The soldiers? The sudden volley in their rear took the Hermógenes by complete surprise. The machine gun poured out a steady stream of bullets, chattering away: rat-tat-tat-tat—tat-tat-tat—tat-tat-tat—rat-tat-tat—swinging from side to side like the wind. It was damaging the House, too. "That's all right, boys, it doesn't matter. It's to our advantage to keep quiet," Zé Bebelo cautioned. He was riding high. He had no doubts. He would win! It is hard for one who is winning not to have a fiendish look on his face.

I stayed close to him, observing the attention and order he had called for. Was it my rifle barrel that was keeping him in line? Up to this point, I could not question any of his orders nor what he said. But thinking of what was in store robbed me of my strength. Against my will, but because my knowledge was greater than the others, I was second in command. Supposing Zé Bebelo got killed or turncoated, would I have to take over the leadership, and give orders and commands? Let someone else do it—not me; Jesus help me! It would be bad, the men would not obey me; they were not even capable of understanding me. The only one capable of understanding and obeying me was Zé Bebelo himself. By rights—I thought—only Zé Bebelo could be my second in command. It was funny but it was necessary, though I myself didn't just know why. But it was necessary, even if I didn't fully understand the reason. If I tried to find it out, it would be worse. What is a person really like, behind his eyeballs and the holes in his ears? My legs were unsteady. I was filled with anxiety. Fear leads a life of its own. The only thing that bucked me up was knowing that I was being all that I was meant to be at that time. My hand and my rifle.

Now, what were we waiting for? Only Zé Bebelo could say for

sure, but he gave no clue as to his next move. Everything
remained the same. By that time the day was drawing to a close,
the sunset coloring the sky. Some red-rumped orioles flew by.
There was hardly any firing from the soldiers and the Judases,
just an occasional shot here and there, as if they scarcely
wanted to fight. We waited, as wary as wildcats. They must be
maneuvering under cover behind us and on the sides, seeking
protected positions from which to encircle the others and
launch a final assault.

"All a soldier wants is a safe spot and double pay," someone
said. The moment could hardly have been more perilous. A
jagunço is like that—you can bet on it. A place to rest his rifle
and a full cartridge-belt—that's all he asks for. None of the
men were jittery or showed fear. Nobody was talking, wondering how we would escape from there alive, from the Tucanos
ranch. The arrival of the military, which might mean our doom,
aroused their merriment. Some yelled like male macaws. What
characters! Like so many boys. It made me sure of one thing:
that I was different from all of them. If I was not a complete
jagunço, then my being there in their midst was a mistake. I
feared everything. They did not think. Zé Bebelo was thinking
the whole time but about practical matters. And I? I saw death
with many faces. I was all alone—you know what I mean. Then
something completely unexpected took place. At the edge of the
woods, someone suddenly raised a white rag on a pole, over the
top of some lobolobo bushes.

We had no right to open fire on that white target. Were we
going to agree to negotiate with the Judases? To me, they were
forever branded with the mark of Cain, and all they could
bring us was disaster. But Zé Bebelo, quick to act, tied a large
white handkerchief to the end of a rifle and told Mão-de-Lixa to
hold it out and wave it in the air.

"Rules are rules," said Zé Bebelo, "you must always consent
to receive an emissary, even from heretics, even from savages."
The others approved, said he was right. I think what they
wanted was news, to find out what was happening. I was also
surprised to see that the ceremony of those white cloths, on

their side and ours, took time. As with other things in this life, it had to be done right.

Finally, a fellow appeared in the tall grass and came toward us. He must have crawled through a hole in the fence. When he reached a certain point on the terrace, one of our men recognized him: "Ah, it is Rodrigues Peludo, who's hand in glove with Ricardão." It was he, all right, the others agreed. Right behind him, half crouching, appeared another. "It's Lacrau!" Then Rodrigues Peludo turned around and said something to him. He seemed to be telling Lacrau to go back. But Lacrau insisted on accompanying him. "Where in hell did that Lacrau show up from? It's been a long time since anybody heard a word about him." They said he was from Gerais do Bolor, in the Jequitinhonha River country, and a fellow not to be taken lightly. A light-skinned caboclo. On one occasion, when he was being tried for some crime, he had knifed the prosecuting attorney in the courtroom. I found it very strange, under the circumstances, to see those two men standing in front of us at the top of the stairs. Rodrigues Peludo lifted his eyes, as if we were in heaven, said something by way of greeting, and then:

"Chief, sir. . . ."

"Turn around, fellow," ordered Zé Bebelo. As a matter of course they both obeyed. But they were heavily armed. During those few moments, I felt admiration for the cool courage of those two, who might easily have been killed on their way there by some soldier in hiding, just for the hell of it, because the soldiers were not a party to the cease-fire.

Zé Bebelo demanded to know what errand had brought them there. Diodôlfo, standing near me, was sucking his teeth, as was his habit, and José Gervásio whispered: "It's a trick." But Zé Bebelo was running the show, his hand on his pistol. For a man to repeat his message, with his back turned, in the midst of enemies and so many threatening weapons, took a lot of doing. Rodrigues Peludo spoke out, without the least tremor in his voice:

"With your permission, Chief, sir, I am bringing these words that I was sent to repeat to you: that, in view of these soldiers, and the other circumstances that are unfavorable to us all, would it not be more advantageous to both our sides to declare a truce, for a while. It was to make this offer that I came, under orders, and to ask whether you are willing to consider it. And whether you agree to it or not, to give me the answer that you wish me to take back to my chiefs."

"Which chiefs?" Zé Bebelo inquired, with no hint of sarcasm in his voice.

Rodrigues Peludo hesitated a moment and started to turn but stopped in time.

"Nhô Ricardão. And Seu Hermógenes," he answered.

"And so, they are asking for peace?"

"They are proposing a straightforward agreement."

A good distance away, a rifle shot rang out from the woods in the hollow. And then others, a lot of them. It seemed to me a lack of respect, even though the shots were not directed against us. Nevertheless, Zé Bebelo said:

"Men, you can relax now."

Rodrigues Peludo, still with his back turned, squatted and laid his rifle on the floor. Lacrau remained half-kneeling.

Our men gathered in a tight circle, exuding the smell of good cachaça. Marruaz traced a Solomon's seal over his heart with one finger. In changing places Prêto Mangaba bumped into me —this I remember because it hurt my arm. Diodôlfo spit hard— something he had belched up. And Fafafa asked bitterly: "And who is going to bring our horses back to life?" Then Moçambicão, standing behind me, breathed heavily on me, like a steer nuzzling my back. Of its own accord, my hand took hold of Diadorim's. I didn't even turn my face. That hand was enough. I sensed its gentleness, its soft warmth. But then I stole a glance at Diadorim, and he suddenly realized where his hand was and jerked it away, almost with a gesture of repugnance. He was grim, his eyes glowering with old hates, his hair dishevelled. "Double talk," Diadorim hissed between his teeth. Diadorim wanted blood pouring out of veins. Alaripe dug into his knapsack; he was refilling his cartridge belt. But all this that I am telling you, sir, lasted only a few seconds, and took place without interruption, because Zé Bebelo, with his hand on his belt, was being cold and precise, like a snake.

"What else, man?" he said.

"I have already told you everything, Chief, sir. Now I ask for your reply to take back. And in case of an agreement, an honorable one, I have orders to close the deal under oath." This was Rodrigues Peludo's answer, spoken in the clear voice of one who is carrying out orders though somewhat reluctantly.

"Well and good," Zé Bebelo replied, "but who is doing the surrounding, and marauding, and attacking?"

"Well—it's us. That is . . ." Rodrigues Peludo admitted.

"Ah, so it is. Well, then?"

"I came to make a deal. For the salvation and benefit of all parties. Both sides. In case you agree, sir."

Not even his tone revealed any loss of aplomb. I retain the impression that in spite of everything, Rodrigues Peludo, too, had his loyalties. Thus, as an enemy, he would remain an enemy, though a brave one; but strictly as a man, one could not fault him. So, it would seem that those over there—the Judases —were not all mad dogs but some, like ourselves, were merely jagunços working at their trade. Looking at it in another way: were we now, to avenge the killing of Joca Ramiro, terrible as it was, going to spend our whole time in wars and more wars, dying, killing, five, six, ten at a time, all the bravest men in the sertão? A dust of doubt powdered my mind, a dust of the finest sand there is, such as the Urucúia River rolls in its broad waters when the winter rains come. There, of my companions, so many lay dead. Chance had made us companions, and now all that was left of them was memories, and that heavy, nauseous stench which grew worse by the hour, even though they were stacked in that dark room, with the door cracks stuffed, and on the outside we were burning pieces of leather mixed with leaves. By the all-pervading stench, Rodrigues Peludo and Lacrau could certainly make a good estimate of the number of our dead, not counting the slight and seriously wounded. But Zé Bebelo had cannily called together Marcelino Pampa, João Concliz, and many others, so that packed shoulder to shoulder we

gave the impression of a strong and numerous band. You hide
the dead with the living. Those dead ones: Jósio, all twisted,
with clots of blood hanging from his ears and nose; Acrísio, re-
posing quietly, something he never did in life; Quim Pidão,
honest about every little thing, who had never seen a train and
who now and then would ask what one was like; Evaristo Caitité, with his dead eyes bulging; he had always been the jolly
one. Whose the blame for all this? For the hapless ones of the
sertão? Did no one there have a mother? Did the blame rest on
that Rodrigues Peludo, for example? I denied it. Diadorim's
hatred was being vented against something that did not exist.
At that moment only mine was the kind of hate that stirs one to
just action, but at the time I did not know the difference.
When I thought of Hermógenes at all, it was casually, and only
because I needed to compare myself with someone. For I could
no longer compare myself with Zé Bebelo.

For it was I—I myself—who was sitting in judgment on Zé
Bebelo. Suppose he knew that? Ah, but in that big head of
his, Zé Bebelo was thinking only of the practical, the business
in hand, and of haste. He spoke curtly, putting an end to the
matter:

"I have made my decision. If this is an honest offer, I accept
a truce at arms for a period of three days. Three days, remember! Now go, take it to your chief, whoever he may be."

"I go," promised Rodrigues Peludo.

"If it is an honest offer, then have someone fire three times, to
close the deal. The truce will begin tonight, at the moment the
first little star appears."

"I go."

Rodrigues Peludo hitched up his bandolier and raised his
hand in a parting salute. No one said a word, either of doubt or
approval, for we did not know whether Zé Bebelo's decision had
been right or wrong. Rodrigues Peludo put his rifle under his
arm and started down the steps in a crouch. The will of one
strong man had prevailed, one who knew his own mind. Zé
Bebelo was in command; his eyes were hard with thinking. The
rest of us abided by his wishes. All except me, that is; I still had
my misgivings.

Then, of a sudden, Lacrau, who up to that moment had remained as quiet as one hearing mass near the altar, whirled abruptly and exploded like a firecracker:

"As for me, here I stay, my Chief! That is what I came for. I am the man I always was: on the side of Joca Ramiro—he who was always in the right. Now, Chief, I offer you my arm, for whatever comes, if you will take me."

The forthrightness of it, the strong, outspoken word! We were so taken by surprise that we were struck speechless. When he had finished speaking, Lacrau raised himself up straight. By his silence then, he renewed his previous question, his stirring appeal. It was an imposing sight. Just imagine, just imagine, sir, the lift to our spirits! Lacrau did not seem to be acting on the spur of the moment, looking for closer friendships, greater personal safety, but as though he had come on purpose to be one of us, besieged though we were. Was everybody flabbergasted? Not Zé Bebelo.

"That's fine—I accept you, my boy."

War has things like that which don't seem plausible when you tell them afterwards. But he lies little who tells the whole truth. In the meantime, Rodrigues Peludo had paused for an instant but stiffened his neck to keep from turning and looking at Lacrau, who thereupon, half raising his rifle, said to him: "I'm playing the game my way, brother, boss of my own actions, against whomsoever. As for the gun, it has always belonged to me, no employer gave it to me. And I've still got my balls." Nobody said a word. Rodrigues Peludo made no attempt to interfere, and slouched off.

We stood around waiting until three shots were fired by the others, over the brow of a slope, in confirmation of the agreement. We answered with three shots. Then Zé Bebelo turned to us and said: "Do you think I am crazy? Those others aren't capable of living up to their word, which isn't worth anything, anyway. What I did was to set things up for our next move. And I accepted our victory!"

Whether or not they understood what he was talking about, they gave their approval. Even Diadorim. The world is like a stage: one in the royal box, the others trained to keep quiet. In

any case, Zé Bebelo glanced at me occasionally, with misgiving
and respect. Of all those there, I alone, aside from him, was the
only one who was juggling ideas. I alone knew what I was waiting for, and this gave me status. What would Zé Bebelo do now,
in the twilight hours? Could he drop what he had first conceived and set in motion—a plan to betray us—and now find
some way of salvation? I won't deny that, for his own sake even,
I hoped he would and thereby redeem himself. My reasoning
thus was both because I liked and admired him, and for the
sake of our own skins. I thought it would be monstrous and
strange if it turned out that I had to kill Zé Bebelo after all.

"Friends, I praise and am proud of you all, each one better
than the other. Now let us go back to our stations and turn on
the heat, good and heavy, until it gets dark!" Zé Bebelo ordered
in his practical way. At this point, he said, as we had ample
ammunition, we should concentrate our fire first on the low
growth in the pastures and low spots, and then on the overgrown hummocks, where there were some gullies. And, in keeping with the plan, Marcelino Pampa would return to the slave
huts, Freitas Macho to the granary, and Jõe Bexiguento, nicknamed "Alpercatas," to the sugar mill. As for me and Alaripe,
Zé Bebelo chose for us to remain with him while he put some
questions to Lacrau.

But Lacrau had little to tell us, though he gave straight answers to the questions. He said the enemy numbered about one
hundred but a fair number of them were unseasoned jagunços,
not much account; that they were awaiting the arrival of others
as reinforcements, but it was not likely they would show up
very soon, with the soldiers around. He could tell us nothing
about Hermógenes and Ricardão themselves, nor their plans,
nor anything concerning the death of Joca Ramiro, beyond what
everybody already knew. Afterwards, when Zé Bebelo and Alaripe had stepped out into the hall, Lacrau, relief showing in his
face, said with a grin: "That Zebebéo chief of ours is one smart
man! I never knew another like him to scare you to death and
make you want to come clean."

We left the room and I went to the corner of a window and
started shooting. Weren't those the instructions, Zé Bebelo's

plans? Every time I pressed the trigger, I remembered what Lacrau had said about Zé Bebelo being the kind of creature whose
presence alone was enough to milk you dry of fear. What about
Diadorim himself, who was of the bravest, did he know that?
Fear is something that grows inside a person, something
planted there; at times it stirs and shakes, and we think it is for
some reason, because of this or that, when these things are only
holding a mirror up to ourselves. The purpose of life is to destroy these bitter dregs of fear. A jagunço knows that. Others
explain it with different words.

Jacaré came around, saying it was time to eat. I ate nothing
but manioc meal. "What about the soldiers?" everyone was
asking. The shooting had died down on both sides. Day was
practically over; the hour agreed upon had almost arrived.
"Diadorim," I said to him, "tonight, when the time comes, you
stay near me and help me." But Diadorim did not accept my
suggestion and wanted to know the meaning of my strange behavior of late. Then I thought of Alaripe and imagined what he
would say if I spoke to him. "Nothing doing, friend. That's a hot
one." Alaripe thought me funny. Now, which one could I call on
for help? Acauã, or Mão-de-Lixa, or Diodôlfo? They were all
following their usual habits; a new pattern would bewilder
them. A fine pickle I was in! Was I there as a sort of nest egg?
I had no notions of how to govern; I lacked the master touch; I
did not have the confidence of the others, nor a backlog of
power, the power of bending men to one's will. Even my injured
arm, which had been improving by itself, began hurting again
while all this was going on. Meanwhile, the wind had veered and
I could smell the stench of our horses, their stinking bones—
the pity of it. Was it foreordained that I should suspect people?
Ah, in those brief moments, I was not going to try to explain to
them my vague suspicious, which might turn out to have no
foundation anyway—for, to tell you the truth, sir, I was beginning to doubt them myself. If I had to keep a close watch on
Zé Bebelo, and upset his plans if it came to that, how was I
going to face him? See how he had managed to turn the tables at
his trial on the Sempre-Verde—and had got off scotfree. But
could Zé Bebelo, by himself alone, with no over-powering mo-

tivation, win out over the sertão? "I don't care . . . I don't give
a damn . . ." I kept saying to myself. In my position I ran no
risk. Who was going to address me as "Lord and master"? I was
nothing, a nobody. Am I talking too much? I just kept waiting
for Zé Bebelo—to see what he would do, filled as he was with
self-importance and pride in his schemes.

He came up to me. "Riobaldo, Tatarana . . ." He looked me
in the face, his shrewd eyes half-closed. He understood me, all
right. Did he also fear me? "Riobaldo, Tatarana, come with me,
I want your unbiased opinion." He took me to a window in the
kitchen, from which we could see the wood-covered hill in the
distance. Zé Bebelo took the drinking cup and filled it from the
water pot. I also took a drink, and listened as he spoke, assum-
ing a friendly air.

"Son, you are one who accepts killing or dying on equal terms.
I know. There are no bounds to your courage—the best kind,
the kind you build yourself."

I kept my back turned; I may have said something.

"So far, so good; what are they going to do now, our opponents?" he inquired of me.

"That I can't say. What I would like to know is about us—
what are we going to do now?" I answered in reply to his question. Then I added: "I am sure and yet I am in doubt; I am puzzled."

Zé Bebelo chose not to hear me, and kept right on:

"Just put yourself in their place. What they are doing at this
very minute is heading for that hill, which the soldiers have not
surrounded completely. Once over it, they will strike south over
a crooked road, and by daybreak I'll bet they'll have reached
Burití-Alegre. And the soldiers? They are guarding the surrounding positions, except the base of the hill and the spots
near it—the dry wash which skirts it—because it is reasonable to assume they would want to avoid shooting each other.
Oh, that's it, all right!"

I didn't say a word.

"Very well, and now, about us?" Zé Bebelo asked.

I made no answer, but I was taking it all in.

"Ah, it's time to go! We, Riobaldo, my boy, are going straight through that wash—and without delay, because later on the moon will come up full."

The moment had arrived. Night had fallen. High in the dark sky a single star appeared. A little star, twinkling. Who had come out ahead? Zé Bebelo or I? Which of us had won out? I left it to Fate to decide.

The noise of many feet. Soon all the men were gathering in the corridor, readying themselves—the restless lines extended all the way from the front room to the kitchen, the silence broken only by their brisk movements. Now and then, Zé Bebelo would explain further what was to be done. One or two small lamps lit up the pale faces. Now we were going to go it on foot, without our gear. What hurt was the quantity of munitions we were abandoning there. We filled everything we could with clips and boxes of bullets—bags, haversacks, cartridge belts— but it wasn't enough. Somebody had the idea of rolling up a quantity of cartridges in a pillow case, and tying it over one shoulder like a bandolier. Many others did the same, and soon there wasn't a case left. A quantity of food was also being taken along. When all was ready, we would step out through a door, into the dense black of night. João Concliz, Moçambicão, and Suzarte were sent forward to feel out the way we were to follow. Our few wounded uttered no complaint, not even Nicolau, who had to support himself on his rifle. Only the dead would remain in the House. They had no need of our farewell prayers. Let the soldiers who would come on the morrow bury them. We split up into groups; five, I think. Diadorim and I fell into the last one, under the personal command of Zé Bebelo, and so did Acauã, Fafafa, Alaripe and Sesfrêdo. Those in the first group started out, each following the one ahead—like a stream seeking its level, or one dog trailing another. We stood waiting our turn. We were leaving a lot of stuff behind in that big kitchen. I counted our companions by the sound of their breathing. Steadily they moved ahead. Not a sound came from those in front. Every moment I expected to hear a shot and a cry of "Halt! Who goes there?" But it was just nervous excitement.

I admired Zé Bebelo. Our turn arrived. We would have to accustom our eyes to the darkness. We bent low and stepped out, too.
We were on our way.

Saved! In the dark, with the greatest of good luck, we
slipped through and beyond. We walked for a long time, in complete silence, breathing deep to keep cool, until we were sure we
were out of danger, and joyfully safe from being spotted or attacked. We halted a few moments for a breather.

"You know, we left the cat," someone said laughingly.

"Ah, more than that," said another, "we left the House, too."

That death-ridden big ranch at Tucanos. The good smell of
foliage and field grasses that I was now inhaling made me think
of the stench of death which no longer filled my nostrils. And
Zé Bebelo, coming close, took my hand and whispered, looking
back in the direction from which we had come: "Riobaldo, listen: I have just thrown away my last opportunity to get rich
with the Government and to pick political plums." It was the
truth, and it wiped the slate clean: we were now on the same
side of the fence. It began to grow light—the rim of the fat full
moon came into view. We started up again. You know something, sir? Bathed by that moonlight, I remembered Our Lady.

We plunged ahead, bearing left toward the north. Later, we
turned due west. Daybreak found us once more in open country,
and presently we forded Vereda-Grande at Vau-dos-Macacos.
With the coming of full daylight, we arrived at the place of one
Dodó Ferreira, where we drank milk and my eyes gamboled in
the trees. There, in truth, I was myself again—like an ox which
stretches its body with pleasure after the yoke has been taken
off. And in the joy and brightness of the new day, I surged
again with love of Diadorim. Such is freedom. Though on foot
and heavily loaded, the march had seemed to tire me little.
Diadorim—his name will stay with me forever. But the paths
go in all directions, criss-crossing one another, for all the world
like the wiles of the devil. Listen to me and you'll understand.

At this place of Dodó Ferreira's, we left Nicolau and Leocádio; they would stay in hiding until they had fully recovered. But not us. From there, with our rifles on our backs, we
headed straight for Currais-do-Padre, to outfit ourselves again,

for there we had a good herd of horses in reserve. Our feet became swollen, our legs leaden. You couldn't call it a march—it
was a drive, as of a band of captives. The road was terrible, all
rocks, for leagues on end. What's the use of going into detail—
aren't you glad you weren't along? We made headway by dint of
slogging and pushing on. By sheer will power, we drove ourselves up slopes I can scarcely remember. The climb up to a
flat top is very tough—worse than a trail through the dry scrub.
Over much of the terrain, shoes were not as good as hemp sandals. The wind came up. Hawks and kites passed overhead, ut-
tering their cries—you should have heard the little sparrow
hawks! And there you could have observed the shifting flocks of
parrots. At every stream to which we descended, we greeted the
burití palms and drank our fill. Though we ran out of rations,
we didn't go hungry; we killed us a steer. And besides, there
were still ripe custard apples in the woods. But to shoot a wild
steer took luck and skill, for they are a shy and wary breed.
When one of us had used up the tobacco in his pouch, the others
would share theirs with him. The wind had the smell of rain,
and the rain came. We took shelter under the pequí trees, while
it poured. We slept as best we could in the cold mud. In the
morning, there were footprints of roaming jaguars. Once again
we headed out through the tall grass, our spirits low. That land
was not made for travel; there is no hope there to keep one
company. Well I know it. A poor devil, without his horse, is entirely on his own. The plains devour a man on foot.

Diadorim stayed by me constantly. He seemed to me morose,
low-spirited. But it was not at all what I thought and mistakenly believed for nearly two days. Only afterwards did I realize
that the dejection was my own, a yearning for friendship.
Diadorim marched steadily, with his typical short steps, which
he strove hard to make brisk. I took it for granted that he, too,
was tired and aching. Even so, his rare smiles and the warmth
of his eyes conveyed to me his esteem. Sometimes I had the
feeling that it hurt him to walk. But this idea arose out of my
fondness for him. Had it been possible, I would have gladly carried him on my back. I enjoyed letting my fancy play with the
notion that in some manner—I don't know how—he was aware

of my concern, and was inwardly grateful for it. Such vagaries of the heart arose in me time after time, giving me a subtle satisfaction. Nor did they disturb me, for each of us kept his emotions to himself, giving no thought to anything which might trouble his conscience; moreover, we ourselves were not aware of the true depth and nature of that affection. That is what I think today. However, at one point, I said:

"Diadorim, I have a gift that I have been keeping for you and which I have never mentioned." It was the sapphire pebble which I had brought from Arassuarí, and which I had been carefully guarding for a suitable occasion. I kept it rolled up in a bit of cotton, inside a little bag like an amulet, sewed in the lining of the side pocket of my knapsack.

From the time I spoke of it, Diadorim was very curious to know what the gift was and kept asking me questions, which I put off answering until the afternoon, when we made a halt. The spot—as I well remember—was beside an unknown and nameless stream, just a shallow brook of very clear water. There, when no one was looking, I took the knapsack, picked out the stitches with the point of a knife, and handed him the present, without saying a word.

Diadorim drew his head back quickly, greatly surprised, and with lips parted, his eyes intently examined the gem in the hollow of his hand. Then, he caught himself, turned serious, pressed his lips together, and for no reason that I could see, handed the stone back to me, saying only:

"From my heart I thank you, Riobaldo, but I cannot accept a gift like this, now. Put it back and keep it for awhile—until we have achieved vengeance for Joca Ramiro. Then, on that day, I will accept it."

I could see that he was holding back something from me. I noticed it even before he had finished speaking, as the color rose in his naturally pale face. I held the stone, given and returned, in my hand. Then I said:

"Listen, Diadorim: let us give up this bandit life, for it is later than we think, and the living must live their own lives. Vengeance is not a promise to God, nor a sacrament. Are not our own dead, and the Judases we killed, enough to balance accounts for Joca Ramiro?"

At this, he stiffened, his attitude hard as bones. An angry retort arose in his throat and his eyes flashed. But this lasted just a second and with a sigh he controlled his temper; however, he mocked me:

"Riobaldo, are you scared?"

I took it without offense. But I was unshaken in the decision I had made back at the Tucanos ranch. I was only waiting until we reached Currais-do-Padre to carry it out in orderly fashion, as is my wont in such matters.

"You know damn well I am not scared! You do as you like. Me, I'm getting out!" I snapped back, returning evil for evil. I had good reason to. Chagrined, I put the stone in my pocket, and then for greater safety moved it to the pocket in my belt. Diadorim was breathing hard. He said in reply:

"Riobaldo, think carefully: you swore vengeance and you are loyal. And I never imagined that our friendship would end like this." He stepped forward. "Riobaldo, listen closely to what I am asking: stay! There is something I haven't said to you before, but which I have felt for some time: you have ability as a leader —but you hold yourself back; whenever you decide to assert yourself, the war will take on a new complexion."

"You're wasting your breath, Diadorim. That is out of my line."

So, he was trying to tempt me. With soft soap and blarney, he thought to change my stand. Did he think I would fall for it? Didn't he know me better than that? With my inborn reserve, devoid of smooth talk or the power of swaying others, I was the opposite of a commander. Was I now to try to instigate a general mobilization against Hermógenes and Ricardão? To stir up the sertão, as if I were its master? But the sertão is not to be subdued by force; on the contrary, little by little, it does the subduing. All who ride high and handsome in the sertão hold the reins for a short time only: they find they are riding a tiger. I knew this, I had seen it. I had said: not me! I had rejected the very thought. My only talent was being a first class marksman with any kind of firearm. As soon as I opened my mouth people thought I was a fool or impostor or half-crazy. In fact, I could not keep up my end of a conversation. Conversation about things that seemed important to me, annoyed and bored other persons. I was never certain of anything.

Diadorim said: "Now wait a minute! Courage breeds courage."

And I said: "What am I supposed to be—a Captain-General?"

I saw through all his subtlety, trying to cajole me into staying on, caught up in the web of war without beginning or end, without front or back, and which I hated. I shrugged my shoulders. He placed his hand kindly, lightly, on mine. I was afraid I might weaken. So I answered harshly, with another shrug:

"I am going to leave—that's for sure. I am going along only as far as Currais-do-Padre. There I'll get me a good horse, and head out into the world."

That was my avowed purpose, as I have said. I was not being obstinate. And because of that, Diadorim did not persist in his counsel; but finally he said jestingly, with a trace of derision in his voice:

"All right, then, since you really want to leave, go ahead. Riobaldo, I know where you are going; you want to see that girl again, the fair one with the broad face, the daughter of the owner of that big fazenda in the Serra uplands, at Santa Catarina. Go ahead and marry her. You two make a nice couple, you will get along well together."

I had said nothing about that. I hadn't even thought of Otacília. Nor did I swear at Diadorim and tell him to shut up. Instead, he went on:

"Go ahead, take that gem with you and give it to her as an engagement present."

Slowly I rolled a cigarette. We were at the edge of some woods where the slope begins, under a paratudo, a tree whose lonely sisters could be found growing far away on the banks of the Urucúia. Here was one of the head-streams. When the weather cools off and the air freshens, the buriti palms lift their fronds high. Close by, we could hear the hubbub of our companions.

Just looking at him, I felt sorry for Diadorim on these hard daily marches. It was getting late afternoon. A tardy macaw was flying to roost.

"Or who knows, you might think better of it and decide to send it as a gift to that special young woman at Rama-de-Ouro, the daughter of that hag. She is all right, Riobaldo, she gives joy to the world, she gives sugar and salt to every passerby."

She wasn't at Rama-de-Ouro but at Aroeirinha. But why was he speaking now of Nhorinhá, remembering her so clearly? One would think that he knew even better than I what I held hidden and forgotten in my heart. Nhorinhá—a little yellow ground flower which says: "I am pretty!" Everything around us could be beautiful, but Diadorim had opted for hatred. Was this why, at heart, I was fond of him? Not at all: it was destiny that had decided this, from the very beginning, with all its joys and suffering. I was also fond of Nhorinhá, the whore, who did not know the meaning of pettiness, beautiful for all, in her lemon-yellow skirt. Only, I did not know then that I was fond of Nhorinhá, the daughter of Ana Duzuza. Think this over, sir: the burití grows on the bank and drops its seeds in the stream— the current carries them and plants them along the edges; and thus you have the palm groves which line both sides all the way down, almost as if by design.

"Marry her, Riobaldo, the girl at Santa Catarina. You two will get married, I just know you will. She is beautiful, I admit, refined and graceful. I pray God she will always love you dearly. I can see you two together, close together, she with a jasmine flower in her hair. Ah, the clothing women wear: a white chemise all trimmed with lace. The bride, in her white net veil . . ."

Diadorim was saying this with tenderness in his voice, like nectar in a flower. I felt enchanted—he was teaching me to love my Otacília. Now he spoke slowly, almost to himself, as if he were dreaming, as if he were telling himself a story. As if I were not there at his feet. He talked about Otacília. About her daily life. Otacília combing her long hair and perfuming it with oil of jasmine, so I would find greater pleasure in passing my hands over it. Otacília taking care of the house, and of the chil-

dren we would surely have. Otacília in the bedroom, on her
knees praying in front of the image, ready for bed in her night-
gown of fine batiste. Otacília on my arm going to festivities
in the city, proud and happy, in a new dress. He went on in this
fanciful vein. I forgot all about what had given rise to our discussion. Now I merely listened, in a sort of trance, my heart
beating fast, like that of a pigeon. But I remember that in Diadorim's sudden abandon there was something strange, something that he tried to hide even from himself and which I could
not make out. I sensed a gentle but definite sadness in him,
which was not connected with me in any way. About then João
Concliz, Sidurino, and João Vaqueiro appeared with some of
the other men; they gathered wood and built a fire beneath the
paratudo tree. The leaping flames spashed their colors on the
leaves and branches overhead, turning them gold, red and
orange, and making them glow more splendidly than all the
stones of Arassuaí, of Jequitinhonha, and of Diamantina. That
was the picture when darkness fell. We only know well that
which we do not understand.

I wish nowadays that I could recall many more things about
Diadorim, both strange and commonplace, but I can't. Things I
have long since forgotten, and which are now beyond recall. I
think it is because he was always too close to me, and I was too
fond of him.

The following morning we set out on the last leg of our journey. At one point, Zé Bebelo called me to him. Even though he
had won this round, Zé Bebelo must have been fuming. My
guess is that the victory he had contrived had turned to ashes in
his mouth: the thought that our enemies, wherever they might
have got to by now, had carried off loads of our gear and munitions with them, and were well supplied with everything they
needed.

"Hermógenes wants to make himself the boss of the sertão," I
took the liberty of saying. I kept on needling him, just to be
mean. Zé Bebelo did not reply to me directly; he was thinking a
thousand things. In the midst of his reflections, he would whistle softly to himself and bob his head, with its floppy-brimmed
hat, from left to right; and sometimes he would puff though not

because he was tired of marching. When he could contain himself no longer, he started talking: "I still don't understand it. I still don't understand it. Up to now, I'll admit, he has been lucky—the fat-bellied frog without a neck. But just wait till we go and come—he will pay for his eggs by the dozen!" I was sorry to hear him say that Hermógenes had had good luck. It disappointed me. I did not want to exasperate Zé Bebelo, but, in my opinion, he was very much mistaken: it was because of all those moves and detours we had made, and from which he derived so much pleasure, that we had failed to trap Hermógenes for a final showdown. That was what I thought, looking up at the sky shared by clouds and buzzards. What did it all matter to me now. It was water over the dam. Finally, we reached Currais-do-Padre.

There were no corrals there, nor a padre—just a palm grove, with one hut in it. But all about there were large pastures of lush grass—mostly the rich, oily meloso grass, with patches of blue santa-luzia and duro-do-brejo in the low places, and jasmim-da-serra on the high, stony ground. There they came: our fat, rested horses, that is, those that had belonged to Medeiro Vaz and which we now inherited. I chose one, a handsome animal, a chestnut sorrel, with white eyebrows, that looked good to me, but I made a mistake, for he was tricky and hard to handle. I named him "Padrim Selorico." The owner of the place could neither read not write, but even so he had a leather-bound book, called "Senclér das Ilhas," which I asked him for, to pore over during rest periods. It was the first book of its kind I had even seen—a novel—because until then I had known only school books. I found new and extraordinary things in it.

I kept putting off making decisions about my next moves. The following morning the sky was dark and overcast. Diadorim avoided me; he was hurt and apprehensive, or so I thought. The high rain which threatened chased the buzzards home. The horses were grazing hurriedly. Never, in all my days, have I seen the winter rains so long in coming. We should have waited. But Zé Bebelo ordered us to get started. Since nearly all of us were riding bareback, we had to push on to Curral Caetano, where we had a large quantity of riding equipment

stored. Then, from there, to Virgem-Mãe for munitions. We lost
no time. The roads were full of holes filled with sticky mud, like
black sugar that had melted. Time and again, our horses slipped
and fell in the mud and we with them, feeling like laughing or
crying. You know what the trouble was? Our horses were un-
shod.

Where to after that? Ah, to the good uplands: the Urucúia
tableland, abounding in bellowing steers. But we never reached
Virgem-Mãe even. As I remember, I had felt right at the start
that we were headed in the wrong direction. I had no idea
where we were. After many days, during which the sierra had
come toward us as we approached it, suddenly, far in the distance, we noticed a tremor on the horizon which turned into a
fine black line, then gray, then blue, with the passing leagues.
After that, a wall of hills. We took the first road we could find
to get through, then down the other side. The streams were
muddy and boiling. What we needed was the help of Joaquim
Beijú, the Scout, but he was not with us. Zé Bebelo, upset and
confused, kept moving his fingers up and down the reins, as if
telling his beads. We were lost. Later we learned that our guide
had got the names confused: instead of Virgem-Mãe, he understood he was to take us to Virgem-da-Laje, another place altogether, on a stream much farther south, where there is a grist
mill. But it was too late.

The thunder boomed, the wind blew. And my tongue licked
up the rain. But when the weather cleared for good, I don't
know if it was any better, for a terrible hot spell beat down on
the gerais from one end to the other. Those who went through it
and didn't die, still remember it. The air during those months
was unbearable. Sickness and sickness. Our men, many of
them, developed sores. I'll tell you about that later. As long as
you have listened to me this far, just hold on, for the moment
is arriving when I shall tell you many strange things.

We traveled on that way, through places whose names we
didn't even know. On and on. The road was all elbows. The
sertão, they say, you never find by looking for it. Suddenly,
when you least expect it, the sertão appears. And where we
were, there was the sertão, its own vile self. Our misgivings

grew, our doubts increased. We went down ravines between steep hills and their ancient trees, following the stream until it opened out into a river. It was not the Abaeté, though it looked like it: a broad river with yellow banks. The river made a wide sweep around a clearing, and some coconut palms could be seen in the distance. It was a far-off and inviting spot which seemed to beckon to me. But we did not go toward it, for our route lay in another direction and we moved steadily away. The terrain grew more sterile. Rarely did we meet a human being. A man away off, hoeing or chopping wood, or a little woman in the doorway of a palm frond hut, spinning tow on her distaff or weaving on her wooden loom. One man tried to sell me a tame macaw who could repeat any word with an "a" in it. Another old woman, smoking a clay pipe, covered her face with her shawl, to hide her eyes. The cattle, too, grew scarce: only by chance did we see an occasional unbranded steer or cow, wandering about in the wilderness. Deer, yes, I saw many: sometimes leaping and running across the fields, one, three, twenty in a herd—pampas deer and brockets. But the stillness of silence was lacking, as was all sound of human speech. It disturbed and haunted me. Later, after three days' journey, there was not a soul to be seen.

This brought us to the foot of the hills. We were deep in the wilderness, facing the upward slopes. On our way up, we came upon an obstacle in the road—a pile of branches placed there as a warning not to pass. But this warning was no doubt a private one directed at someone other than ourselves. In any case, we paid no attention to it and kept going. As we were about to cross a stretch of gravelly ground, we came upon another heap of branches, which we also ignored. I was up front, with Acauã and Nelson, leading the way. We had already gathered up our reins to start another climb, when we heard dogs barking. And we saw a man up ahead a ways—several men. They all had guns.

These strange-looking men were waving to us to turn back. They could not have known who we were, and they figured that three lone horsemen did not pose much of a threat. One of them, I saw, was giving orders: a wild-looking backwoodsman whose pants and spurs were dragging. But the others were miserable tatterdemalions with hardly a rag to cover their nakedness. One had not even that—not even a ragged loincloth—and in place of a shirt he had a kind of vest made from otter skin. They numbered ten or fifteen. I saw that they were cocking their guns, and I could not make out why they were threatening us. Did they want us to pay toll? Were they trying to pick a fight as an excuse to kill us? It wouldn't be wise to start attacking them, just like that; on the other hand, it might seem cowardly to turn back, so we advanced slowly and stopped when we were almost upon them. We were going to wait for the rest of our people, but in the meantime, those men facing us offered no explanation. One said only:

"You mustn't. You mustn't."

The poor fellow shook his head from side to side as he spoke, in a tone of voice peculiar to that part of the country; and the others shook their heads, too, as they muttered dismally: "Ah, you mustn't—you mustn't."

That is the way it must have been in olden times.

Such strange people, I had never seen or heard of before in my life. The one with the spurs went off and got on a donkey— it was the only riding animal they had. I think he felt the need to mount in order to command our greater respect. He came back, slapping the donkey's rump with his hand. I looked at each of them. One had a coal black beard, lighted up only by his eyes. Though the day was unbearably hot, another was dressed in a long gown of red baize—probably the only garment he had. Perhaps he would turn out to be their priest!

"Man, these people are covered with lice," said Nelson, under his breath.

They all had some sort of weapon: long, small-bore shotguns, old-fashioned blunderbusses, muzzle-loading pistols, muskets and flintlocks—arms of other ages. Nearly all were dark-complexioned, deeply tanned but with a sallow overcast from eating almost nothing but burití pulp, and I could have sworn they were drunk on burití palm wine. One, a big-chested Negro-Indian, held only a short cudgel, but he must have wielded it with a bone-shattering arm. He was so ugly it was pitiful, with his nose smashed flat and his big misshapen mouth. Another had a bush hook on a long handle, and a gourd tied across his chest. He was carrying on a serious confab with the others: some kind of sorcery. At times he let out howls like the devil himself. He answered to the name of Constantino. Though all they had was their little bags of bullets and powder horns, and their miserable firearms, even so they did not display too much fear of our rifles. To our way of thinking, they were all crazy. How could such castoffs choose to become highwaymen? Ah, but they weren't. What happened was that these wretched souls, buried in those forgotten corners of the earth, in the wilds of the backlands, were simply the inhabitants of that region. Acauã knew about them and explained it to us—that they lived in the hollows, in this God-forsaken fashion. They never left their haunts, and it struck me that their young must be born in burrows, like animals. But no doubt they had huts around there somewhere, and women and children. Shacks erected on stony hillsides, or on the lowlands at the edge of a swamp. There they planted their little patches of ground; often they had neither fat nor salt. I felt pity for them, great pity. How could they possibly have the look of brave men? They made their own powder by grating saltpeter from the rocks and mixing it in pans. It was a stinking, black powder, that made a loud noise and filled the air with smoke. Sometimes this coarse powder caused their weapons to explode, burning and killing the shooter. How could they possibly fight? How could they even live?

Finally, our companions came into view and climbed the first slope. They were a sight—that large band of fighters. I almost wanted to laugh at the scare it threw into the backlanders. But it didn't, really, for they never budged; just stood there silently, looking at the ground, this being their way of expressing their astonishment. The one on the donkey, Teofrásio, who acted as their captain, said something to the one with the bush hook, who was called Dos-Anjos, and who was the spokesman; the latter came forward to greet Zé Bebelo and explain matters:

"Begging your pardon, master, we just here . . . Begging your pardon . . ."

He was all bones and jaw, and the voice which rumbled from

the depths of his chest had the chanting tone of a litany to the saints, or a requiem for the dead.

"Begging your pardon, master. . . . We are not accustomed. . . . We are not accustomed. . . . We are guarding these roads, to keep away anybody from over there—people of Sucruiú—they have got the sickness that takes everybody. You are a big chief, and it pleases you. Should I address you as Your Lordship? A plague of the black pox. . . . Our settlement is at Pubo, on the other side of the swamp—you and yours passed near there, about half a league distant. The women stayed behind, taking care, taking care. . . . We came straight here. Three days ago. To barricade the roads. The people in Sucruiú —they say—are no longer burying their dead, even. Someone might want to come, with a message, bringing the sickness, that is why. . . . One came, wanting to get help, and gave us a crazy, mixed-up story. But he had to go back, and go back he did, for we did not let him pass. They are under an awful curse. A punishment from God Jesus! The people of Sucruiú, a bad lot. Begging your pardon, master, you had better change your route to avoid Sucruiú. The black pox!"

The fellow had laid his bush hook on the ground, and put his foot on it; he spread his arms, then brought the palms of his hands together, keeping his eyes closed, as if invoking some sort of spell. He was thin, so thin he hardly filled one's view. The others had slowly gathered closer. To keep from laughing, Zé Bebelo assumed a severe look, which they mistook for annoyance, because one of them—an old fellow whose straw hat was frayed all around the edges—came forward with a coin in the palm of his hand, which he held out to Zé Bebelo as if offering to pay for his forgiveness. The coin was a silver doubloon, from the days of the old empire, one of those of 960 reis, but which is worth two thousand reis in Januária, and in the capital they might give you ten for it. But Zé Bebelo very politely refused the money; the old man, however, did not understand him and stood there with his hand extended. The others were saying nothing, just staring at Zé Bebelo and at the coin, and revealing their intense envy. They had a way of trembling all over at times, but that was something natural to them, not from fear, for when they were afraid they seemed to grow darker and breathed with a low growl, without moving. I thought to myself: those men are not even tame beasts; most of the time they are in fear of everything around them.

I wish you could have seen those backwoodsmen laugh! The one with the bush hook picked it up, the one on the donkey held his hat in his hand, to show respect, and the old dotard slipped the silver coin back in his pocket. All of the others laughed, opening their mouths wide, in which hardly a tooth was to be seen. They laughed for no special reason, just trying to keep in our good graces. More sure of himself, the one with the bush hook inquired:

"Meaning no offense, sir, but where have you come from, citizen chief, with all these followers and equipment?"

"From Brazil, friend!" Zé Bebelo sang out, in high good humor. "I have come to bring order and justice—a new law—to every corner, every foot of this sertão."

The old one made a gesture; he wanted to say something in reply, but Zé Bebelo, who had heard and seen all he wanted to, waved "no" with his hand and started up, and off we all went with him. I took a last look at those poor faces, filled with wonderment at us and longing to ask the hundred and one questions which they had held back for fear of seeming rude. Only about our rifles, one had asked: "Is that a modern bird shotgun?" The one on the donkey shouted his parting counsel: that we detour at the palm grove of a little lake on the right-hand side to avoid passing through Sucruiú; and that after we had picked up the road again, on the left, at a ford close by the virgin forest, we would have to continue only another seven leagues to reach the place of a certain Abrão, who was very hospitable. That man shouted all this advice, not to be helpful to us, as I easily perceived from his tone and manner, but solely to show the others that he, too, had the courage to speak out in the presence of so many jagunços, bearers of mighty arms. But Zé Bebelo, refusing to be intimidated by what they had said about the village where there was an epidemic of smallpox, gave orders for us to continue straight ahead.

It was laughable to think that for all their poverty and afflictions, those backlanders had their headmen, whose actions were mere imitations of things they did not understand. Poor creatures.

But I didn't laugh. Ah, since then, I have never laughed whole-heartedly again in all my life. It struck me that to have come across those backlanders, and talked with them, and then disobeyed their warning could bring bad luck. I had a presentiment that it was the beginning of much trouble. Those were men of a different breed, crude in their ways and habits. In even small matters, they had an almost effortless capacity for deep and far-reaching hatred. Just the fact of having run into them was cause enough for gloom. It cast an evil spell. All the more so because, unable to get the better of us in any other way, they had surely called down a curse on us. Thinking about this made me quake inside, to the bottom of my soul. Those men had big ears, they were governed by the phases of the moon, and they sniffed in their sleep. And they had great powers of evil. I learned about it from old-timers. They could blow hot hatred on the leaves of a tree and dry it up; or mutter words into a hole which they made in the ground and then covered up: the road would then wait for someone to come by and do him harm. Or they would hold a handful of dirt in their closed fist three days and nights, without opening the hand or losing any of the dirt; then, when they threw the dirt down somewhere, three months later there would be a grave on that spot. Always fear a man who has no power and no money! I'll say more: it is best never to mix with people too different from ourselves. Even when they have no avowed evil intentions, their lives are bounded about by their habits, and being an outsider, you run subtle dangers. There are many places and many kinds of people. I learned about it from old-timers. The wise thing is to flee from everything to which we do not belong. Keep the good far from the bad, the healthy far from the sick, the living far from the dead, the cold far from the hot, the rich far from the poor. Don't neglect this rule, and hold on to the reins with both hands. Put gold in one hand and silver in the other, then close them tight so no one will see. Those were my thoughts. With those backlanders calling down curses, how could I keep from thinking about them? If they had caught me alone and I had been forced to dismount, they surely would have killed me for my weapons, clothes and other things. They would have done me in without scruples, for they had none, me being an outsider and a stranger. Were I sick, or wounded and bleeding, would one of them be capable of giving me a drop of water from a gourd? I doubted it very much. I mistrusted the snares of the world. Why did there have to be so many different kinds of people in the world—some of upright sentiments and behavior, exemplary in their life, alongside others who don't know their own minds nor the brute reasons behind what they do or don't do? Why? In order to inspire fear, eternal wariness, or by way of punishment? Suddenly those men could become a crowd, then a multitude of thousands and hundreds of thousands, emerging from the wilds, filling the roads and invading the towns. How could they know, even if they wanted to, that they had the power of being good, in keeping with a framework of rules and obedience? They would not believe themselves capable of it. They would want to gulp down all the good things they saw, looting and yelling. Ah, and they would drink, they would soon drink up every drop of rum in Januária. And they would seize the women, and fill the streets, and soon there would be no more streets, or children's clothing, or houses. The church bells would be set pealing, imploring God's help. Would it do any good? And where would the inhabitants find holes and caves to hide in—let God tell me that.

These were the thoughts that troubled me for almost an hour in that punishing heat, mounted on that devilish pony called Padrim Selorico, as we crossed those desolate wastes until we neared the village of Sucruiú where the horrible plague raged amidst the greatest poverty. Was it nonsense on my part? Not one of my companions, in the routine of their daily living, gave a thought to such matters. Was I then the only one? I was. I, who had been put under an evil spell by those poor creatures of the sertão. Of the depths of the sertão. The sertão: you know what it is, sir.

But then I turned my thoughts to Zé Bebelo, and from him I derived hope and light. I came to my senses. Zé Bebelo, at the

head, a chief of chiefs, one who ordered our lives; the presence
of a rock-solid man like that bore its own good tidings. My admiration for him grew, and my respect, based on esteem and
confidence. I could see that our entire safety and protection lay
in his person, in that big head of his, for Zé Bebelo had long
planned to come here, deep in the dark sertão, and all he
thought of, wanted, and demanded now was to attack it, as one
would an enemy, and push it back! This then was what we were
going to do. To me, he was like a master canoeist, with paddle in
hand, crossing the wild waters of a swollen river. "You must be
brave. You must be very brave." I remembered those words. I
had been brave. Diadorim, the rosy-faced boy who had spoken
them, was now by my side, tested by every hardship but still
steadfast; storm-tossed but unshaken. I know that he loved me,
did he not? The others, our other companions, were like poor
infants who had been cast away, and whom we now had to care
for. Zé Bebelo on my right hand, and Diadorim on my left: but
I, what was I? I wasn't anything yet. We kept on and on. Zé Bebelo's dove-gray horse was the finest, the biggest of all.

Now that we were nearing Sucruiú, according to the leagues
which our horses' hoofs had checked off, it remained to be seen
what Zé Bebelo would order: whether to go straight on or detour. Ah, straight ahead it was. But none of us took alarm. What
was to be, would be. That stricken place must be yonder, on the
high ground in the plain. About a rifle-shot distant. And they
must be doing a lot of cooking, on a lot of stoves, for the clouds
of smoke rising into the sky were like those of pastures being
burned over out of season. The weather was hot as an oven. But
in the little brook that trickled between banks˙ of black earth,
frisky as a squirrel's tail, and which we crossed at the bottom of
the hill, only the horses quenched their thirst, for we ourselves
were wary even of running water. Where does the plague come
from? The very air seemed full of it. Dust and poverty. The sky
a shabby faded blue, without lustre. The sun looking old before
its time—the beginning of June seemed like the end of August.
It did not look as if there would be any cold weather that
winter. What had been the good of all that rain? That immen-

sity of backlands was lost, I said to myself. Now we were approaching Sucruiú, which we would pass through. All we could see were huts enveloped in smoke. Shacks, they were. People? None in sight. And we certainly felt no greater fear. Rather, everyone wanted to get a closer look as we passed through, and see what was really there. Of course, we had faith in our amulets and veronicas. And suddenly the word spread that Jõe Bexiguento and Pacamã-de-Prêsas knew prayers to Saint Sebastian and Saint Camilo de Lélis, who free one from all vague evils. How to get hold of them and learn them? There was no time. But then came a message; turning in his saddle, each man repeated it to the one behind: there was no need to learn the prayers, for those two were going to say them for all of us, and it would be sufficient if each of us at the same time would recite many Hail Marys and Our Fathers. And that we did.

Some day after today, I hope to forget that episode. The road —fairly wide at this point—ran through two rows of houses but they barely could be seen. Praying and looking at the same time, I approached. Houses—something human. What they were burning in front of all of them were heaps of dry cow dung; the grayish-greenish smoke was rising and filling the air, and the clouds of dust that we kicked up mixed with it, turning the atmosphere dark and gloomy. It made me cough and spit between prayers. We heard no voice nor cry, nor any other sound, as if every creature, even the dogs, had been put to death. But there were people there, all right: through the dust and green smoke their figures could be glimpsed, their sad, white faces like masks. The strange and silent men and women were feeding dry cow chips to the fires—the smoke their only remedy. They paid us no heed—didn't move from where they were, didn't hail us. They were tragically aware of their danger from the accursed pestilence. They were living in hopes of not dying. I wondered where the stricken ones lay groaning. And the dead ones? The dead ones, who then became the evil ones, condemning others to death? I prayed with renewed fervor. Our passage took only a minute but it seemed endless. Even our horses moved more slowly, as in a procession when their riders are praying to themselves. Not a word was spoken. Finally, we emerged from the clouds of dust and dung smoke, shot through by an occasional flame, in that humid heat. May God take care of them, of Sucruiú and its afflicted people.

I looked up at the clear sky. It gave me a sense of freedom, of escape from horrendous possibilities. I glanced at everyone around me and at Diadorim, who was kindliness itself. I did not look backward, to avoid seeing those houses in their vaporous bluish-brown mantles. What I craved most was some way of urgent salvation: I wanted to get out of there quickly, to go I knew not where, away from drowning in uncertainies, away from that dismal expanse. I would take Diadorim with me. At first, I did not realize that I would also want to take Otacília, and that girl Nhorinhá, the daughter of Ana Duzuza, and even old Ana Duzuza herself, and Zé Bebelo, Alaripe, all of my companions. Then, the other persons of my acquaintance, and those I hardly knew, in addition to the fond and lovely Rosa'uarda, young Miosótis, my teacher Lucas, dona Dindinha, the merchant Assis Wababa, the German Vupes—Vúsps. All of them, and my godfather Selorico Mendes. All of them—it would take me hours to remember them all. I would also take, ah yes, those people in Sucruiú, and now, those from Pubo—the dark backwoodsmen. And to the new land I would take the horses, the steers, the dogs, the birds, the places: I concluded by wishing to take even those sad plains which we were crossing. Everybody? No. There was one I would not take, I could not take: Hermógenes!

It was then I remembered him: how I hated that Hermógenes! It was a kind of loathing. Nor, in my mind, did this loathing call for explanation or require a cause—it just was. It came from the depths of my being. What kind of hatred is it that needs no reason for being? To give you an answer, this is what I think: one forgives a past offense; but how can one remit enmity or injury which lies in the future and of which he has no knowledge? But I had a presentiment of it. That I can swear to.

Was I afraid? Only of the future, with its uncertainties. As long as there is one fearful soul in the world, or a frightened child, everyone is in danger—fear is contagious. No one has the right to instill fear in another, no one. My greatest right, the one I cherish most, is that no one is entitled to make me afraid!

I felt tired. Probing ahead, we moved rapidly after crossing the ford at the edge of the forest. The sun was setting: the sky blazed with reds and purples. We gathered at the foot of a slope, in the yellowing grass. An occasional patch of tilled ground. Soon, there we were, at Abrão's place, where the plain opens out. It was a good house. But suddenly, some men inside dashed out through the doors and started running, like rats abandoning the rind of a jackfruit.

Zé Bebelo, riding as usual at the head of the column, charged us not to chase those men, nor to shoot at them. It was plain we had caught them stealing, for they even had sacks to carry their plunder in. I guessed instantly who they might be, and I guessed right. One of them, in the wild scramble to get away, had lost his bearings and dashed almost under our horses' feet. He was a small Negro.

A gangling, jet black lad; just a boy, you might say. Bare from the waist up. His ragged pants were nearly falling down; he kept his legs close together. He was panting and blowing, like someone who has swallowed a mouthful of scalding coffee. A carbuncled calf makes a noise like that sometimes. To keep from losing his pants altogether, I think, the boy dropped to the ground on his knees and bent over. "Your blessing!" he asked. Then he thought quickly, and before you knew it, he had taken the things out of his sack and thrown them as far away as he could: a single sandal, a tiny lamp, of the kind that come from Bahia, a kitchen skimmer, a shiny something of black leather, resembling a gun sling. Then, showing us the empty sack, he said:

"I didn't take anything, nothing at all. I haven't anything . . . nothing."

All this took place quickly, like a toad's squirt; and so innocently, in a way, that anyone seeing it would have laughed. A crazy statement like that, you almost believe it, it is so absurd.

"Where did you fellows come from, where?" demanded Zé Bebelo.

"We want to go back home. Yessir, we are from Sucruiú, yes-sir."

As if taking advantage of the opportunity, he tightened the belt of fiber cord that held up his rags. He shrunk up and grinned to hide his fear. What might his name be?

"Guirigó, that's my name. I am the son of Zé Câncio, your servant, yessir."

So skinny and pitiable, so neglected, that boy must have known every kind of suffering. His eyes bulged, the black pupils surrounded by an expanse of white the color of peeled manioc root. His dark skin twitched now and then, as if it too were afraid of something. And as he watched us, his lips parted, re-vealing a thick tongue, glued to the bottom of his mouth, and looking as if it were too big to fit inside. You sometimes see that in a diseased calf. A strange kid. A thoughtless jagunço seeing someone like that might easily shoot him out of kindness, to put him out of his misery.

"Guirigó, what did you fellows come here after? Speak up!"

"What did we come after, yessir? They came, and I came with them—to look for something to eat."

"That's a good one, boy! I'd like to see you eat the stuff you hid in that bag."

The little Negro cowering on the ground shook his head in vigorous denial: "But there wasn't any food." He would doubt-less deny everything and stick to it: that he had had a mother, even; or that he was born of her; or that the raging plague was killing the people of Sucruiú, and all his relatives. We wanted that hapless boy to feel sorry for himself, and to shed a tear in his wretchedness, just one little tear. Ah, if he would only do that, we would feel genuinely sorry for him, and would be satis-fied. But no, the black boy persisted in his denials. His effron-tery was tantamount to claiming that he did not exist, that he was bound by no rules, that he was not there at our horses' hoofs. All he wanted was to save his skin, to escape. He would grasp at any straw. Nothing else mattered to him.

"All right, you can go now!" Zé Bebelo consented. And he even threw him a chunk of rapadura, which the boy caught easily, as a dog catches a morsel in midair. "For you to sweeten your little black guts with!" cried Zé Bebelo. Without another word, nor looking back, the boy sprang sprily away, and disappeared. He hadn't looked as small as he really was.

"Poor little devil, his teeth were so white," said Diadorim.

"What? What?" exclaimed Zé Bebelo. "What I demand is that the children of the sertão be educated and cared for!"

I started to cross myself, in mockery, but my hand did not get that far because it seemed an unkind thing to do, thinking of the little black boy.

Following our usual procedure, we first stationed sentinels on all four sides, and then located a well-enclosed and handy pasture. After that, we sized up the place and entered the house, to look it over and start a fire in the big kitchen, to cook dinner. Holy Virgin! I'll tell you, sir, the inside was pitiful. I never saw any place so stripped and pillaged. Everything you usually find in a house, that could be carried off by hand, or in boxes or bundles, was gone. We did not find a single garment, a single tin lamp, a single wall calendar, a single hammock hook, a single grater, a single halter hanging on a peg, a single floor mat, not one thing you could lay your hand on. Only the tables, the cots, and the benches were left. They had picked the bones clean. Where could the owner be? We learned, however, that his real name was not Abrão, but Habão. According to a cere-moniously drawn-up document I spotted on the floor, in a cor-ner, this Habão was a properly titled Captain in the National Guard. This place we were at was called Valado. In another few days, the crew from Sucruiú would have torn down the house itself, for its struts and beams. Not to mention that there was not even a vestige left of the cattle, chickens, pigs, dogs and all the rest. Only the wild birds remained, which, as they do everywhere, chirped briefly at day's end, cheerful in the midst of that desolation.

On the wall in one of the more secluded and now darkening rooms inside the house, was a little shrine, containing a few images and the stub of a candle. This they had not disturbed, out of respect. We, then, went into the room, one after another, and kissed the largest saint, which was Our Lady Mother-of-All, looking like a beautiful doll in her mantle. Afterwards, we ate and went to sleep.

No lying abed the next morning, I assure you. Each day is another day. And the weather had cooled off. Sad is the life of a jagunço, you will say. It makes me laugh. Don't tell me that. Because of a false idea, we get the notion that "Life" is a continuous something. Each day is a day by itself. Zé Bebelo had already given certain orders to be carried out before the coming of dawn. And we learned then that Suzarte and Tipote, and others, along with João Vaqueiro, were out scouting in all directions, taking the measure of the world by sight and by scent. In a very few hours, they made their report. The ground, in places, bore the footprints of a great many cattle, all headed in the same direction. Those tracks had been made in the mud after the last rain. From the condition of the grass, from the look of the washes, and from the height of the debris left on their banks by flooded streams, since receded, they determined the amount of rainfall. They learned much, also, from the land grazed over by the cattle. And from the footprints of horses and dogs. The people of the house had traveled west. But the cattle, after having been abandoned, choosing their own way and without being driven, had turned northward toward the salt licks. The trackers deciphered many things, reading pages which to others looked blank. They could even describe the ways and habits of the people who had been living there, tell you whether that Habão was thin or fat, close-fisted or open-handed, a rascal or an upright man. Of the hundreds and thousands of bits of trackers' lore that seem like magic, you could fill a book with what Tipote and Suzarte alone could tell you. And before midday, they had found and butchered two fat yearlings, which provided us with some fine meat. A good tracker is invaluable.

That place—Valado—I liked it. It would have suited me fine to stay there for awhile. It seemed to be a part of my destiny. But Zé Bebelo was undecided. Suddenly, however, he made up his mind that we should move on.

Zé Bebelo had begun to be afraid! Why? There comes a day

when fear creeps in. His fear was of the smallpox, of the danger of sickness and death: perhaps those men from Sucruiú had brought their poisoned air here, and besides, we were still too near Sucruiú itself. I couldn't help laughing. But I laughed to myself; outwardly I remained as grave as a dead tree on a plain. Even so, I erred, though I did not realize it at the time. But the sum total of life is a mingling of the lives of all, and life follows a pattern, with little variation. When anyone near you, for example, is afraid, his fear reaches out to touch you; but if you stand firm and refuse to be afraid under any conditions, your courage amazingly doubles and redoubles.

Well, Zé Bebelo, who was always so sure of himself, with everything under control, was now wobbling. And I began to waver, too.

We traveled about five leagues. That fellow Habão, too, must have left because of fear. Need we have done so? It would have been good if we could have had at least a week of well-earned rest, for none of us was any longer completely well. Those men from Sucruiú, hedged in on the other side by the backwoodsmen, could find space only over here, on the side where we were. I know that one can easily upset himself without order or purpose, and that fatigue encourages despondency. What I really wanted was to be convalescing from a long illness, sipping my thick soup, and, on cold, wet winter days, warming myself by the fire, with a cock crowing off somewhere in the early morning. The order was to leave? Let's go!

We headed down a stream to which we gave the name of Porcupine Creek because we spotted one of those animals on the way. Low tablelands with easy slopes. Then a thickly-wooded plateau. We came to a halt at last at a sheltered but ugly place, ugly as all get out. But I consoled myself with the thought that it was all part of the great plains country. There was a man with a hatchet in his hand and a gourd hanging from his neck, who was extracting wild honey from a tree branch. He answered all our questions and told us where we were: at Coruja, an abandoned ranch.

I had a presentment about the place from the start. I felt at once that it was marked by fate as the starting point of great suffering and terrible wickedness. I should never have come there, and there I should not have stayed. It is what I said to myself in passing, as I looked around and saw the age and condition of the house. It's name suited it. It really was like an owl, the big, horned kind, with its chilling laughter, not the little barn owl which is so beautiful, with mottled plumage over white silken stripes. The place had nothing to dispel its gloom. A sad little stream wandered slowly through it. The burití palms along its banks were themselves prisoners. Half a league away there was another small stream, the colorless water moving slowly over its bed of black earth. These were two separate streams, but soon they spread out and joined to form a dismal swamp, thick with tangled growth, dark and rotting, and soft, bottomless mud. They both had the same name: Veredas-Mortas—Dead Creeks. Remember that name. In the middle of the scrub, in the middle of the scrub, there was a crossroad, dividing the way of those who went there, by one road or the other. An augury? I believe in the malefice of certain places. There are places where, if you place your hand palm-down on the ground, your hand will shiver and draw back or the ground will tremble and sink under it. You throw a handful of that dirt down your back, and it gets hot: that ground would like to devour you, and it smells as if it had already devoured others. A crossroad! Just be patient. Remember: Veredas-Mortas. There I came to a dead end.

I won't say much about the bad days, the wretchedness of the whole time we spent at Coruja. Any narration of this sort bears false witness, because the full extent of all that was endured escapes the memory. And you were not there. You did not hear the lugubrious song of the whippoorwill at nightfall. You cannot form an adequate idea of the extent of my sadness. Even the birds become very different, in keeping with their surroundings. Or is it the times through which we pass?

It turned intensely cold. Nearly all the men had fallen sick. Not of the smallpox, no, but of other things. Fevers. Somewhere back there we must have camped in a malarial spot. Now most of the men quaked with intermittent chills. We had no medicine that would do any good. The men got weaker by the day, and their spirits fell. There was also an epidemic of colds, which I caught, too. I got nothing worse, but I know about myself. Formerly, everyone considered me normal, as in fact I was, and now, suddenly, I was changing from day to day. I was jittery, and easily angered by everything around me.

"It's your liver," they would say. I slept hardly at all. During the hours of the night, as I lay awake, my head was full of ideas. I went over and over them in my mind, like a jay bird pecking in cow manure. Everything that occurred to me, I fitted into a sort of plan. Like something copied from a dream, I laid it all out—something which in the beginning seemed pure fantasy, but which, as the days went by, took on reality and began to possess my mind: a project that had to be carried out. What it was, I won't tell you just yet. Something which had been driven into me. I dwelt upon it, uneasily, as the water at the edges of a river swirls backwards; or calmly, as threads of slobber fall from a steer's mouth.

Ah, but hair-raising as it was, I had to go through with it. I had to! By very astute means that I had learned, I fully understood what was involved and how I had to go about it. How had I done that? Little by little, asking questions of some, listening to others, and recalling old stories I had heard. For a long time almost without consciously knowing what I was working toward and striving for. Doing it was no worse than not doing it. All that was needed was the heat of a cold fury with gritted teeth, a surge of great courage. It was something, therefore, which had to be kept in the heart of darkness: the most frightful of responsibilities—a step which only rarely is anyone willing to undertake, in the whole of the sertão.

The day came when I was willing. Up to then, I had kept putting it off and putting it off. I had wanted it more or less, but had avoided facing the steps I had to take and my motives. I had merely been feeling my way. But now I started. There was a definite procedure. The first step: neither to eat nor drink anything but cachaça. A swallow of it was like fire let loose in your gullet and insides. It does not break the demon's fast. I was confident that I was ready to go ahead with my plans of stealth and darkness. But I was mistaken. While waiting for the hour to strike, I must not let the slightest normal idea creep into my mind. But I did. Just for an instant: Diadorim came near me, surrounded by his aura of gentleness. He started to talk and I accepted his company. I weakened in my purpose. I went after food. I ate a lot, wolfing it down, and my body was grateful. Diadorim, with his long lashes and youthful eyes. After that, I didn't want to think about those other things, and I laughed, chattered and went to sleep. Life was really very normal, and all right the way it was.

A big mistake. Three days later, full of remorse I renewed all my earlier plans. I dreamed some very bad things. It was worse now because I had slipped shamefully, not having had the guts to finish what I had started. And I was plagued by my old doubts. So much had happened, I thought, and what did I amount to? A common jagunço sharpshooter, prowling the sertão like a dog. There were other things that I might have been capable of tackling with success, of being, of doing; but I had not even attempted them. Just going on living in the open, wandering about, ranging the wilderness. But, why?—I asked myself. Ah, then I found the answer: because I had got accustomed to it, and because of the others. The others, my companions, who lived aimlessly, and without restraint; they lived too close to me, forever distracting my attention, disturbing my composure and self-assurance, and frustrating my hopes of a higher destiny. Because of this, I hated myself, and I was mistrustful of everybody. Of Zé Bebelo, more than anyone.

Zé Bebelo was not sick. Him, sick? Such a thing was not possible in one like him; not unless he was out of his mind. What he was, was hexed. I knew it right away. That was the reason for the mess we were in, our sorry plight. In my opinion, Zé Bebelo had thrown away our advantages. Zé Bebelo had wilted and his color changed; he was no longer full of fire; nothing he said resembled his former wild exaggerations and boasts. All he could say was we had to wait right there until the sick got well. He saw only the impossibilities. And meantime, we were having nothing but bad luck. I don't say this because of Zé Vital who had another of his fits: the foaming, mouth-twisting kind, throwing his arms and legs about which were as stiff as wood. But Gregoriano was bitten by a rattlesnake, crawling in the grass and fallen leaves: a little one, not more than four handspans long, but with killing venom, and Gregoriano died after a few hours of agony. And I will tell you also what happened to one Felisberto. He seemed to be in good health in spite of having been shot in the head some years before. A pistol bullet—a copper one, they said— was buried deep inside his skull, at a point where no doctor's instrument could dig it out. Now, a few months back, suddenly, and for no understandable reason, this Felisberto's face started to turn green, even his teeth became covered with verdigris, and he felt very bad. His eyes became swollen and each one turned into a large, green spot. His nose became stuffed up and swollen. He hawked a lot, and the green stuff he spit out was horrible to look at. Then, like a calathea flower in the midday sun, he would turn blue in the afternoons. He coughed like a consumptive calf. He said he had lost his sight, couldn't see a thing. His greatest boon was not knowing who had shot him; it kept him from wondering where that person was, and from bearing him undying hatred.

Meanwhile, all discipline gone, we went on frittering away the days there at Coruja, as if our sole purpose was to take advantage of the fresh meat and jerked beef to be had by tracking down cattle in that wilderness. There was no let-up in Zé Bebelo's chatter about his shallow plans, a kind of make-believe. A millstone keeps on grinding even when there is no grain falling on it; it just grinds and grinds. Would our sick companions ever get well? It didn't look like it. Those who hadn't caught malaria, had other things: dropsy, bronchitis, stomach pains; one even fell into a stupor. I got something, too. I felt as if I had eaten the meat of a capybara in heat. My liver seemed to hurt, but I didn't check it: it always makes me feel worse to have to be thinking about my body. Raymundo Lé made me some urumbeba tea.

It was an attempt to relieve my pain, and it was done out of kindness. And that is just what I said to Raymundo Lé, in gratitude. Alaripe began to praise the virtues of other roots and leaves. "Even these here, I don't doubt, could be used as medicine of some kind, only we don't know what for," he said, pointing to a thicket of prickly cordia, and to some water hyacinths growing near by. There, at that moment, it was brought home to me how normal it was for one to value these comrades. Diadorim—who, thanks to God, was entirely well— offered me all sorts of wise counsel. And Sidurino said: "What we need now is a real shooting fray, to keep from getting rusty. We ought to raise hell in some village, hereabouts and then do some loafing." We agreed heartily—we were all in accord with the idea. I, too, approved of it. But, I had no sooner said so, than I was shaken by an arpeggio of doubts, as though a viper had bit me. Those fellows there were really a gang of kind friends who helped each other at every turn, and who did not balk at sacrifices to that end. But the fact remained that, in support of some political feud, they would not hesitate to shoot up a village of helpless people, people like ourselves, with mothers and god- mothers. And they found it quite natural to go out and do the same thing for the sake of health and exercise. I was horror- stricken—you know what I mean? I was afraid of the race of men.

I had instantly grasped and seen through to the heart of that particular suggestion; but how many other outrageous ideas might not be controlling our lives without my recognizing them all at once! Then, it appeared to me—I have no hesitancy in saying this to you—it appeared to me that I alone had any sense of responsibility; I no longer placed confidence in anyone. Ah, I thanked God that He had blessed me with good marks- manship, because they respected me for it. But I kept wonder- ing: suppose mine were some other fate, that of being just a poor villager somewhere, subject to the whims of jagunços? In that case, then, those who now were my comrades, could show up there, hell-bent on evil, and do me great harm. If such a thing was possible, how could they now be my friends? You will excuse me for dwelling on the point, but those were the thoughts which ran through my mind. Ah, I only wish I had been born in the city, as you were, so that I might have been educated and intelligent! I am telling you everything, as I said.

I don't like to forget anything. To me, forgetting is almost like losing money.

Deep in thought, I said out loud, without meaning to: "Only the devil . . ." "Wha-a-at?" one of them said, startled. Then I persisted and went on: "Only the One-Who-Doesn't-Talk, the One-Who-Doesn't-Laugh, the Somber-One—the greatest dog!" They thought it funny. Some crossed themselves. I did so myself. But Diadorim, who held on to an idea like a pup to a root, spoke up: "The enemy is Hermógenes." He looked at me after he had said it. Perhaps he did it to soothe my spirit.

I replied firmly: "Why, of course! the enemy is Hermógenes!"

I watched Diadorim; he raised his face. I saw the power eyes have. Diadorim had a light burning inside him. By then, night was drawing on, it was getting dark; the darkness was blotting out the others. But the way Diadorim glowed, I shall remember as long as God lasts. Between us, without anyone's knowledge, and not fully aware of it ourselves, what we had just done, in our souls, was to pass the death sentence on Hermógenes.

Hermógenes Saranhó Rodrigue Felipes—to give him his full name. Today, in the sertão, everybody knows it; his name appeared in newspapers, even. But the one who told me, at the time, was Lacrau, the one who at the risk of great danger had come over to our side, at Tucanos, as I have already related. I asked him a lot of things about that fiend, and he answered me readily. Was it true, what they said? Yes, it was—Lacrau assured me—Hermógenes positively had a pact with the devil. It had been known all along. Nobody knew where he had come from, but it was said that he had cattle and ranches beyond Alto Carinhanha, and at Rio do Borá, and at Rio das Fêmeas, in the gerais of Bahia. And by what signs could you tell that he was being so greatly aided by the Evil One? Ah, because he never suffered nor got tired, he never lost anything nor got sick; and whatever he wanted, he always got, everything; in a tight spot, something always happened at the last minute to get him out of it. And what was the price of this secret? "Ah, these things are for a time only. He signed over his soul in payment. What

good is the soul, anyway? What can you do with it?" Lacrau
laughed, only to make his point. He told me that Hermógenes's
nature had undergone a change which made it impossible for
him to have pity on anyone, or to respect honesty or virtue. "He
was always ready to kill. So they say. It was because the
What-You-May-Call-Him had rebaptized his head with fresh
blood: the blood of a just and upright man who was bled to
death for no reason." His good luck was fantastic beyond all
reason—much greater than could come from any magician's
prayer, greater even than from the ceremony of "sealing the
body." He had a compact, all right, that put him ahead of
everybody.

"You, Lacrau, who attach no value to the soul, would you be
capable of making such a pact?" I inquired.

"Ah, no, brother, I want no part of those shady deals. My
courage is the kind to match itself against other men made like
myself; this business of waiting at a crossroad at midnight to
meet the Figure is not for me." Silently, I thought to myself, this
fellow Lacrau made sense out of nonsense. He told me other
things. Are you like me? Without believing, I believed.

The fear Hermógenes sooner or later aroused in everyone
was what generated these stories and built up his renown. Facts
created more facts. But, among all the people of the sertão, was
there not a man to be found who was more of a man, so to
speak, than this one? The others were children compared to
him. Hermógenes was unique: treacherous, domineering, fearless. Evil, but wholly so, genuinely so, unquestionably so, pure
malignity. He was capable of anything; he had even killed
Joca Ramiro, when the moment came. I was being completely
impartial. I recognized fully that Hermógenes stood head and
shoulders above all the rest, like that peak of the Itambé range
high above the clouds in the distance, when you approach it
from the side of Mãe-dos-Homens. He might even have been
my friend; a man's man. But Diadorim was right: what we had
to do was put an end to Hermógenes. I remembered Diadorim,
Reinaldo then, as a boy, in his new clothes and new leather hat,
bolstering my nerve to cross the Rio do Chico with him, in a
leaky canoe. That boy and I were the ones destined to do away

with the Son of the Devil, the Devil's Partner! It was the right
thing to do, we had to do it. That was the upshot of my thinking.

But meanwhile, in my eagerness to tell you everything, I
haven't mentioned Otacília's name. I wanted to think about her,
on occasion; but it was no use, it became harder all the time to
do so. My memory of her was becoming clouded, her beauty
forgotten. Our words of love, spoken in faraway Santa Catarina,
seemed no more than a story heard from someone else. I
know that I would have liked to feel a longing for her, and for
this I prayed to all Our Ladies of the Sertão. But then I cast
those prayers aside, on the fine waters and the air of the winds.
It was as if they were false, for they gave me no response—only
the vexatious reminder that because of my origin and what I
was, her father would certainly never consent to the marriage,
nor tolerate my brand as a jagunço, steeped in wickedness and
without honor. And besides, the large dowry! You understand,
sir, what I am telling you is only a summary, for in real life we
analyze our affairs carefully, and one day is filled with hope
and the next with despair. But then I hit upon the possible
cause, the reason. The one major reason. Don't you want—
aren't you wanting—to know what it was?

That thing, which I had not yet been capable of doing. That
thing, even if it were only to prove my judgement. "Ah, one of
these days, one of these hours . . ." was the way I set the time.
Some day, some night. Some midnight. Just to strengthen my
decision, or rather, my weakness. Was there any substance to
the thing? I did not really believe in the existence of the
Renegade, the famed apparition. Not a bit. And now, with this I
have said, do you understand what it was? That thing? It was
that I would go to the crossroad at midnight to await the Evil
One—to close the deal, to make the compact!

I see you haven't laughed, even though you may have
wanted to. I felt like it myself. Ah, today, ah—I wish I could! To
laugh too quickly makes one choke. And I was taking the matter
seriously. I needed only one thing: to gather my strength, as
when one jumps a wide ditch, or whips out his knife.

There came a morning, when there was nothing on the slate,
and I decided within myself: today is the day. But again I put

it off. For no special reason. I just postponed it. Not that I was afraid. Nor did I believe that when I actually took the step, a vision would appear. To me, it was merely a test of courage, requiring only a small first step. If others had done it, why not I? All the other stuff was a lie: about the Gloomy One appearing at a crossroad to negotiate in blackness, in the small hours of the night, in the form of some dark-skinned animal, its little whimpers alternating with dead silences, then suddenly, rising before you, changed into the Devil—thick-lipped, teetering on his goat's feet, a plumed red cap perched atop his head—horrendous, as he demanded a document signed with living blood, then disappearing in a puff of sulphurous smoke. I did not believe it, even as I shivered.

Time dragged on our hands—as well it might. Because of Zé Bebelo's arbitrariness we had been holed up on that deserted Coruja ranch for more than a month. Diadorim never gave up hope for a moment. There was no change in my affection for him, only, I never told him so. During that period I hardly ever opened my mouth in conversation.

One day, two men showed up unexpectedly; you could see one was the master, and the other some cow hand in his employ. We soon learned that the first was the owner of those places, principally of the one at Valado, and, as I have said, he was named Habão. When I first saw him, he had already dismounted, but was bent over, holding the bridle in his left hand. He was a middle-aged man, dressed in heavy, dark blue duck, and wearing knee boots. When he lifted his face, I liked his looks. But his horse—I fell in love with it: a big sorrel, proud and spirited, with a flowing tail—later you will see what he really was like—a horse with a head held high and soft muzzle, a horse that knew how to arch his neck, and when he drank he splashed water on his forehead. He knew how to look at people around him, with liking or disdain, and he could fill his lungs with all the air he wanted, through his big nostrils. Well, I'll tell you later.

Seô Habão was talking with Zé Bebelo. I liked what I saw. He was sensibly calm and steady, and reserved in his gestures. His eye didn't miss a thing, as he looked about, sizing up the situation. The glance of a proprietor—you know what I mean. He was telling Zé Bebelo that he was carrying no money with him at the moment, but that if we would give him the pleasure of accompanying him to his main fazenda, on the watershed of the Roncador, some twenty leagues distant, he would be glad to help us out with a small contribution. And he said it in such a sincere way that we sensed deeply the value he attached to money. From this I saw that he was being both foresighted and clever.

But Zé Bebelo, acting the warrior, cut him short with a gallant gesture:

"Ah, no, my countryman and friend, not that, absolutely not! We are not bandits. As a matter of fact, we are in your debt already—for our stay here on your property and for several head of your cattle that we had to slaughter for food."

The man said quickly that he was pleased, that his herds were at our disposal; but, nevertheless, through force of habit, he inquired how many head, more or less, we had consumed. Thus, he was taking stock, inquiring, observing everything; a man had to attend to business. I thought to myself: as long as that man is alive, the world will not come to an end. And was he from the sertão? To my surprise, he was.

I kept on watching. I saw how Zé Bebelo, little by little, began to boast, trying to make a big impression about his prowess as a famous jagunço chieftain, and I saw through it as a subtle desire on his part to find favor with the other man who was slow, preoccupied with more serious matters. Seô Habão listened respectfully, and bit by bit began asking questions related to farming, and telling about the losses he had suffered that year on account of the unseasonable rains and the blistering heat, and the epidemics. All of which gave me an uneasy feeling, for I recognized that a big rancher is a part of the land, but a jagunço is nothing but a fly-by-night.

After awhile Zé Bebelo began to tire of showing off. Seô Habão, mild and placid, with no vain-glory whatever, was like a tree stump, unmovable, always in its place. He knew only about commonplace matters, but he was mindful of them with the slow, relentless force of a draft ox. And he never even listened, despite his courteous and respectful attitude, when the talk turned to tales about Joca Ramiro, about Hermógenes, about Ricardão, about shooting frays with the soldiers, and about the great capture, by five hundred riders, of the beautiful City of São Francisco—the one the River loves most. And so it came to pass that, without noticing it even, Zé Bebelo found himself talking about cattle diseases, good bottom lands, the bean crop, the ripening rice fields, in which God's little birds turn into an evil pest. I said to myself: this fellow Seô Habão is the kind you don't want to have around, or else you get rid of him as soon as you can, for there was no possible way of our getting along with him. He was of such a persistent nature, so opposed to ours, that his mere presence was a judgement, reckoning, and reproof.

Nevertheless, because of some morbid need, perhaps, to see for myself if what I thought was true, I did not rest until I was able to strike up a conversation with him. This was not hard to do, for he spent many hours there with us, almost the whole day. I strolled over to him casually, as if not meaning to, and began to talk. Seô Habão looked at me in a way I was so unaccustomed to that I became conscious of my pretense—and forgot the first words that I had planned to address to him.

"Seô Captain Habão," I said, and instantly realized that I, too, was trying to be agreeable to him. So, what I told him was that I knew of his captain's rank from having read the diploma in the house at Valado, which the people from Sucruiú had looted. And I told him that I had picked the document up from the floor and had hidden it behind the images inside the little shrine on the wall.

He displayed no interest in the matter, nor thanked me nor asked any question. He said only:

"The smallpox at Sucruiú is over. I know about those who died: there were eighteen of them." Then he inquired if I knew whether much damage had been done to the cane fields. "Between what they left standing, and what the wild pigs and raccoons did not chew up, there are bound to be some wagonloads left, enough to grind." His eyes had a vague, faraway look, as he thought on those matters. He said he was going to put the people at Sucruiú to work cutting the cane and making rapadura. He would then sell the rapadura to those same people, who would have to pay for it by working twice as much. Hearing him say that, in the same unfeeling tone of voice, suddenly filled me with irritation. As if those people at Sucruiú were yokes of oxen, creatures entitled to no pity or protection! But in spite of that I felt no hatred for Seô Habão, I assure you, for I did not find him obnoxious. What I felt was a sort of resentment that I would have to meditate on.

"Next year, God willing, I will plant many fields at Valado and here. Beans, corn, lots of rice." He reiterated what wonderful things could be done there in the way of farming development. He glanced at me with those dull eyes—and then I caught on to what he was driving at: that we, Zé Bebelo, I, Diadorim, and all the companions could pitch in and weed and hoe, and harvest, as if we were his farm hands. It made me sick. Here we were, fighting jagunços, risking our lives, and that Seô Habão was looking at us like an alligator in the rushes: he coveted us as slaves! I don't know if he realized it himself. I don't think his mind worked that clearly. But his nature wanted, needed, everybody as slaves. And I still maintain that I felt no hatred for that Seô Habão. Because there was such a gulf between us. One does not hate a boa, for though a boa squeezes it has no poison. And Habão was only fulfilling his destiny, to get what he could out of everything. If he could, he would have saved on sunshine and on rain. He was shredding a piece of rope tobacco with a knife, letting the crumbs fall in the hollow of his hand, and I'll swear to you, sir, that he didn't waste the tiniest scrap. His happiness lay in going over and over the figures: twenty, thirty wagonloads of corn, ah, and a thousand alqueires of rice. If Zé Bebelo had been listening to these plans, he probably would have been filled with enthusiasm and start exclaiming that this was the way, all right, to transform the whole of that sertão with improvements, with good government, for the benefit of this Brazil! What a hope! Seô Habão was not one to allow himself to be carried away like that. He dreamed only of ox carts loaded with cane. And he was a giver of orders; dull and routine orders, no doubt, very dif-

ferent from those of jagunços. Every person, every animal,
every thing obeyed. We would find ourselves turning into
hoers. We? Never! I would sooner have all the Hermógenes
burst upon us, galloping headlong and yelling, their rifles
blazing, and let him who could stand the racket and see the
blood flow. We would show them up for what they were: pil-
lagers! Then, to get even with him, I hitched up my gun belt,
and said:

"I wonder, Seô Habão, if you know my father, the fazendeiro
Senhor Colonel Selorico Mendes, of São Gregório?"

I thought he wasn't going to believe me. But, I'll swear to
you, sir, he looked at me with very different eyes. I met his
gaze, feeling at ease. Seô Habão nodded yes with his head,
surprised but attentive.

"I've heard of him—I've heard of him," he said, almost
regretfully.

I don't know if he was aware of my godfather Selorico
Mendes's renown and wealth, which were known even here in
the backlands. I rejoiced, but my rejoicing was not complete,
for I saw that a man of the stripe of that Seô Habão, if you took
from him, suddenly, everything he owned, would whimper like
a motherless child and would grope all his life, like a blind man
trying to find his cane on the ground. I almost felt sorry for him.
A person's nature does not fit into a mold. Seeing the man in
front of me grow big, then diminish—all this in my mind—I
don't even know which opinion of him I was forgetting and
which I was remembering. After a little, with the setting of the
sun, he mounted his handsome sorrel once more, and off he
dashed on the twisting road to Valado.

Meanwhile, some exciting news had spread among our men,
a thing which I have been slow in telling, because even a clever
storyteller cannot find a way of relating everything at the same
time. What happened was, that that cow hand who had come
along with Seô Habão, chatting with one or two others, had
casually mentioned that a band of about ten men, jagunços like
ourselves, judging from their talk and appearance, were idling
away their time at Fazendão Felício, as if waiting for some-

thing. This fazenda is to one side of the main road which
opens up the western ranges, and leads to the old boat landing
at Remeira, on the Paracatú, where everybody shows up one
day, sooner or later. They quickly reported the matter to Zé
Bebelo, and he at once recognized who the men were from their
description:

"By the wounds of Christ! It is they. I've been asleep. It can
only be João Goanhá and the others." He instantly sent off two
messengers with instructions to hurry there and bring back
our friends and comrades. It made us all happy to hear this,
for it was something new for a change.

Except me. I had found myself. I had made my final decision,
in all seriousness. That thing. Ah, now I was going to do it!
Someone had to be on my side: the Father of Evil, the *Tendeiro,*
the *Manfarro.* The one who doesn't exist, the *Sôlto-Eu,* Him.
And why now? Was this occasion different from the previous
ones? I'll tell you what it was: the hour had struck. I would do it
—because I knew that if it was not done that night I would
never again have the courage to act. I felt it as a challenge, as
much because of the little things that were pestering me, as
because of the bigger ones that were due to befall any day now.
I thought about the coming of João Goanhá, and that we would
have to start out all over again, battling the land and the
enemy. Did I look on that Seô Habão as a source of trouble? I
don't really know. But these things were struggling inside me
as though demanding that I not depart that place without ac-
complishing my purpose. Veredas-Mortas!

Shadow by shadow, the afternoon wore on; twilight set in.
Was I feeling dauntless, self-assured? My hairy hand never
shook. It had been a long time since I had felt so full of daring.
Indeed, never so much as at that hour and on that day. It is only
when in high spirits that we carry things out well—even the
unpleasant ones. I withdrew from everyone. From Zé Bebelo
most of all: he might become suspicious and say all manner of
crazy things. I fled from Diadorim. Ah, let the brook in the
grotto purl on undisturbed. For, deep in my heart I loved
Diadorim so much that I had a scruple: I wanted him to stay

far from all tumult and danger. I hope that with this gentle reminder of my action, Our Lady may yet give me credit for it. God save me!

I left and went out into the open country at nightfall—at the hour when the capybara awakens and comes out of its hiding place to forage. God is very contradictory. God permitted me to go, on foot, of my own volition, as I did.

I walked toward Veredas-Mortas. I crossed the dry scrub, then there was a stretch of cleared land. A worn road ran through it. Then came the dense woods; I kept going. Dark objects in silent flight: owls. I watched everything as I went. My destination was the cross road. The night grew darker. Then chilly. I had to select a waiting-place. A good spot would be under a tree fern. Better still, a capa-rosa, because it is underneath such a tree that the Careca dances, leaving a circle of bare ground where not a blade of grass will grow. But there was none. The cross road is devoid of such vegetation. I arrived in total darkness. The moon remained hidden. Fear? A banana plant trembles in every frond. But from inside my tremor, I dragged the horrendous words. I was like a brand new man. Was not mine a will of iron? I could, if I wished, hang myself to death from those branches with a piece of liana tied about my neck: who could stop me? I was not going to be afraid. What I was feeling was the fear that he was having of me! Who was the Demon, the Unsmiling One, the Father of Lies? He had no flesh grown from food, no blood that could be shed. If he should come, he would come to obey me. An agreement? But an agreement between equals. First, I was the one to give orders. And was he coming to steal the lightning from my spirit? How could he? It was I—I, a thousand times over—who was there, willing and ready to confront so monstrous a sight, to let my eyes rest on a heap of nothing.

I had it in my power to wait for what I had come in search of. But there was no sign of it. Even with the darkness and things of night, everything around there should have been still, watching, waiting. The animal noises. Who can imitate the screeching hoot of an owl? It makes your hair stand on end.

I felt neither relaxation nor fatigue.

If he existed he had to come. At that moment, to me, he existed. He had to appear, sooner or later. But, in what form? The ground of a cross road belongs to him, where pack animals stretch and roll in the dust. Suddenly, with a loud clap, or in a moment of dead silence, he could appear before me. Looking like the Black Goat? The Big Bat? The Xú? And from somewhere—so far and yet so close to me, out of the depths of hell —he must be watching me, a dog picking up my scent. How is it possible for one to find himself in a black hole, helpless and at the mercy of whatever another might wish to do, and yet keep hold of himself? Everything called for fear, and yet more fear; ah, but that is just the point. This was why I did not have the right to lose control of myself, I did not have the freedom of the air. My will did not falter. Nor did I think of another course. Nor did I wish to remember other persons and things. I had in fact already forgotten nearly everything, even the reason which had brought me there in the first place. And what was it that I wanted? Ah, from wanting so much of everything, I don't think I really wanted anything. Just one thing: I wanted only this—to be myself!

And so the hours went. "It's past midnight," I wanted to say. I felt the cold gripping me. I coughed a little. "Am I getting hoarse? Somewhat," I whispered to myself. To be strong is to remain quiet; to endure. I guessed at the time, looking up at the sky; not even the Seven Sisters nor Orion's Sword were to be seen; they had set, but the Southern Cross still shone just above the horizon. Standing next to me, almost touching me, was a tree with sparse foliage, the litter from its branches under my feet.

I was waiting for a sudden strong gust and him enthroned, seated on a high-backed throne in the center. That is what I wanted now! I wanted to be more than myself. Ah, I wanted to, and I could. I had to. "God or the Devil?" came the old thought. But, how did I want it, in what manner, how? Like the drawing of my breath, like the essence of my being: otherwise I should deem it better to die once and for all, if that were not now granted me. And in exchange, I would pledge my all, my soul —lock, stock and barrel. God and the Devil! "To do away with Hermógenes! To get rid of that man!" This I specified more because I needed some formal reason on which to rest my case. As for Hermógenes himself, in person, I barely thought of him, as though he were an unruly child, soiling and wetting itself, or an ant on the path, between one's foot and the ground. I was getting impatient, peering here and there, clenching my fists. But He—the Damned One—yes, let him stand up to me— I was stronger than He, than fear of Him—I would make him lick the ground and obey my orders. I sized the matter up. Does a snake feel hatred before striking? There is not a moment to spare. A snake strikes and it is over with, finished. As long as I was there, I wanted to stay, I could and I would. Like Him. We two, whirling in a gust of wind—turning, spinning, throughout the world, a funnel of whirlwind: ". . . the Devil, in the street, in the middle of the whirlwind." Ah, I laughed, but not he—I, I, I! "God or the Devil—for the jagunço Riobaldo!" Feet firmly planted, I was waiting! From deep inside, from the wide world outside, I climbed to the very pinnacle, filled with strength. The kind we draw, when necessary, from seventy and seventy fathoms, out of our own depths.

I stamped my feet, then was surprised that not a hint of anything happened. The hour was passing in vain. Well, did he not wish to exist? Let him exist. Let him come! Let him come, for the final issue. I'll tell you the truth: I was drunk with myself! Ah, this life, at one time or another, is terribly beautiful; in a horrible way, life is great. I filled my lungs:

"Lucifer! Lucifer!" I called out, at the top of my voice.

Nothing. The voice of the night is as that of a single being: it begins with cricket chirps and the booming of a bullfrog; it ends with the plaintive cheeps of little birds in their nests, awakened from a sound sleep.

"Lucifer! Satan!"

Only another silence. Do you know what silence is? Silence is only ourselves.

"Hey, Lucifer! Satan of my Hells!"

It was then I knew—he does not exist. He neither appeared nor answered—just a figment of the imagination. But I was satisfied that he had heard me. He heard me—as if he had taken in all my words, and closed the deal. Whereupon I received in return, all of a sudden, a fluttering, a paroxysm of pleasure, then calm—like a blow. In that instant I endured the labor pains of my new power.

I tarried there, lingering on in the stupid place, feeling as if I had been turned inside out, drained of my essence. "And still the night continues." I stayed on, too dispirited, in effect, to take myself away; nor could I make up my mind to anything. What time was it? And that cold, making me numb. Why did the night have to be to me like the body of a mother who no longer speaks, having just borne a child, or, if she speaks, her words are unintelligible? Dawn. The night had seemed never-ending.

At the bottom of the slope ahead, great white billows of morning fog were rising from the mud flats of the Veredas-Mortas. I left, I came away, following no defined path. Though very cold, I had a burning thirst. On the way back, I stopped by the edge of the buriti palms, where there was a sheet of water. Its smooth surface reflected the few remaining stars. It was a watering hole for deer and jaguars. I bent down and drank my fill. The water did not taste the way it does in winter: my tongue did not feel in it the slight warmth which it should have when really cold weather prevails. It was my body that was feeling its own cold, inside and out, making me rigid. I had never in my life felt the solitude of cold like that—as if I were frozen and would never thaw.

The dew had drenched everything. The desolation of the place was becoming visible, with streaks of light in the sky, the morning star waning, the day breaking. I lay face down on the ground, the ordinary strength of my body exhausted. Near the water, my numbness from the cold grew. I curled up at the foot of a tree, a resin tree. A tapir had broken off branches and left its dung there. "Can I hide me from myself?" I stayed there for I don't know how long, as though drugged, deaf to the birds' early morning calls. I lay in the leaves, as enervated as if my blood had been sucked by a vampire bat. Hunger finally drove me to get up. I remember spotting an aratim beehive in the lower trunk of a pau-de-vaca tree. The fragrant honey was oozing out and running down on to the ground into weeds and dry leaves, like a seepage of water.

I got back to the camp just as Jacaré was finishing making the coffee. "You're shivering—did you catch malaria?" someone asked me. "The hell with it," I replied. And even though the sun was coming out warm, I hunted up a blanket and hammock. After all, nothing had happened to me, and I wanted to rid my memory quickly of the madness of that night. I lay there, unable to sleep, brooding. I got to thinking that a jagunço's existence has no meaning, no purpose. We do a lot of living, and sometimes a lot of thinking. But no dreaming. The devil is the End, the Austere One, the Great Severe One.

From then on I never daydreamed again; the easy habit by which I used to foretaste my days and nights was lost to me forever. Was it a sign—that the term had begun? What I was doing was thinking without volition, thinking on new things. Everything now shone clearly, filling my thoughts. I found myself remembering many different things in the past, long-forgotten things, and I saw them in a new light, without express desire on my part to do so. I even tried to avoid it, but I went on just the same, thinking like this the whole time, almost without stopping.

It seemed very strange at first, but as time went on I began to accept it as right and normal. And I noticed that little by little I was experiencing sheer joy, glad to be alive, but with a feeling of urgency. However, I didn't dare to believe too wholeheartedly in this new-found happiness for fear the old unhappiness would return. Ah, but it didn't; for the time being, it didn't.

"How come, Tatarana, you're being so talkative? What a change!" they said. Alaripe questioned me. Perhaps they were teasing me.

As a matter of fact, I had been telling them, with embellishments, certain incidents of my past, and then, for fun, I had described the benefits that the big shots in the Government could bring about by repairing their neglect of the sertão. In my talk, I repeated some of the set phrases that Zé Bebelo used so often in his discourses, and at the same time, as a joke, I tried to imitate his gestures and mannerisms. At first the men did not understand, but as soon as they caught on, they began laughing. They laughed till it hurt.

"Boy, have you got it down pat," said Alaripe.

"You sure have, brother," another—Rasga-em-Baixo—added.

I didn't like the way he said it—that cross-eyed Rasga-em-Baixo, who kept his head tilted to one side, breathing heavily in and out, snorting and snuffling through his nose. I made believe I didn't know what he meant and countered by saying:

"What are you sure of, in this life? I don't even call anybody a son of this or that, for fear it may be really true."

And while they were laughing and enjoying my remarks, I followed this up with a story about a young fellow who had slowly gone crazy, at Aiáis, not very far from Vereda-da-Aldeia: he didn't want to fall asleep because he was afraid that some night he might forget how to wake up again, and would remain imprisoned in his own slumber.

After a number of such vagaries I suddenly switched to what we really needed to do:

"First of all, we've got to send a messenger to some place where there is a pharmacy, to buy strong medicine—for there is such—to get rid of the malaria, for good!"

As soon as I had said this, they all approved, and Zé Bebelo agreed immediately, too. A messenger was sent off at once.

I was disgusted with all the dawdling, and I spoke to Zé Bebelo:

"Chief, what we have to do is send one of our men who will be clever enough to worm his way into the band of the Judases, find out what is going on, and get word back to us and leave clues for us. He might even find a way to liquidate Hermógenes by his own hand—feeding him poison, for example."

"What you're proposing is madness, Tatarana," Zé Bebelo objected.

"A crazy idea is one that doesn't work. But you don't know it's crazy until you've tried it," I retorted, curtly, because at that moment I thought Zé Bebelo inferior, and because it made me angry when anyone spoke out in opposition to me.

Zé Bebelo hesitated. Looking at me, he finally said:

"The man for such a daring exploit . . ."

"The sun picks out the sharp steel points," I interrupted, without half thinking. Meanwhile, Zé Bebelo was completing his statement:

". . . would be only me—or you, yourself, Tatarana. But we are branded steers."

But then, having understood me, he closed by saying:

"Riobaldo, you're a man with real guts."

He said it sincerely, and it touched me. As a matter of fact, everyone who came face to face with me had to be sincere, for in their eyes alone I searched for their inner hearts. In their eyes alone.

José Vereda was smoking his pipe, seated near his belongings. Balsamão was with him—a rough-mannered, scowling sort of fellow. Lately, the two had become close friends, especially as they came from the same part of the country—from the high grasslands. I had an evil impulse to say, and I did: "Can't you fellows find anything to talk about? Watch out, in case one of you has a young and pretty wife, when you get back home. . . ."

That could have been enough to start a fight. Was I looking for trouble? I can assure you, that had never been my habit. But now, I seemed bent only on needling others and making disagreeable remarks. Once, when some of the men wanted to hold prayers, it being Sunday, I couldn't resist saying: "Pray, then raise hell." Some laughed. Pretty soon they dropped that pious farrago.

By then Diadorim himself thought my ways strange. He told me so, and I let him have it with both barrels: I wouldn't stand being reproved and contradicted. I bore down hard. But Diadorim kept on with such a guileless look in his wide open eyes, that in an instant I was overwhelmed by a wave of tenderness. Love is like that: a little mouse comes out of its hole, turns into a huge rat, then into a lion! That same morning, as we were talking, he had said to me:

"Riobaldo, I wish you had been born a relative of mine."

This made me both happy and sad. A relative of his? He

wanted certainty in place of uncertainty, something that had meaning. A relative is not chosen—he is branded. But it is because she is captive in her bit of ground that a tree holds out so many arms. Diadorim had a different destiny. I had come, and I had chosen for my love the love of Otacília. Otacília—when I thought of her it was as if I were writing her a letter. Diadorim—do you know what a wild river is like? All its life, from far and afar, its waters flow, from here, from there, fleeing into the wilderness. One time he himself said: "We two, Riobaldo, just us, you and I. Why is separation so heavy a duty?" His words were like lead. Diadorim thought of love, but he felt hate. One name was ever-present: Joca Ramiro—José Otávio Ramiro Bettancourt Marins, the Chief, his father. A mandate of hatred. As I thought of it, I could not resist a stinging remark:

"That one must be somewhere between the Urucúia and Pardo rivers, about now, Hermógenes, I mean."

His face turned ashen. He trembled, and tears rose to his eyes. I saw that as Reinaldo he was gallant and terrible as a warrior. As Diadorim, however, there was something feminine about him, but fierce just the same, and it made me glad to see him that way now. This was the way he was: the only man whose courage never faltered, and, because of this, the only one whose total courage I sometimes envied. It was made of lead and iron.

Looking beyond, I felt like telling the men about all the mistakes we were paying for and which, I craftily deduced, were the result of recent mismanagement. Politely, I spoke to Zé Bebelo himself, saying:

"Meaning no discredit or offense, Chief, but I doubt if we have done right, all of us staying here, waiting to get well. Would it not have been smarter to have sent off half a dozen men, of the healthy ones, to go and bring back munitions from Virgem-Mãe? The munitions would have been here by now, and we would be safer."

Zé Bebelo took it hard—he threw up his head and clenched his jaw. Then, quickly, he explained to me, in a low voice, that our blunder had been even more complete, for instead of Virgem-Mãe, we had taken the wrong road and headed towards

Virgem-da-Laje. I listened without a word. At another time, a
piece of news like that would have upset me. But on this occasion it amused me. What I mean is: whatever happened after
that would strike me as new and funny, and would call for
more action. In such light-hearted fashion, my life went on.

Afterwards, all the horses were rounded up and driven in. The
morning sun was high, and they were milling about in a field—
a troop of them, kicking up the dust with their nervous hoofs. I
had done nothing to startle them, but I'll confess to you what it
was: they were frightened of me. As soon as they saw me approach, they got panicky. What do horses know, anyway? Some
were whinnying with fear; horses are always high-strung. They
were letting out those shrill little whickers; and as they
couldn't escape far, some were sweating, and some frothing
and trembling, their ears pointing forward. They stayed like
that, but shrinking and obedient when in a moment of sudden
anger I sprang into their midst: "Beelzebub! Quiet, you fools!"
I yelled. They understood me. I even put my hand on the back
of one, who shrank at my touch, drawing himself in and lowering his head, while he shook his mane and snorted.

I saw that the men had noticed the horses' strange behavior
and my handling of them. Only, they were laughing, taking
things lightly in the usual jagunço fashion. "Beelzebub!" It was
as if my self-assurance came from the Dark One. I stood there in
the midst of the horses, who quieted down and accepted my
presence.

"Are you a horse-breaker and wrangler?" asked Ragásio,
jokingly. But I turned around, for other hoof-beats could be
heard: it was that Seô Habão coming back. Three men were
jogging along with him—three ranch hands. His animal—the
handsome sorrel—stopped in front of me, and as soon as Seô
Habão had got off him, he reared back with his tail touching the
ground; the halter rope flew out of his master's hand, high into
the air. "Beelzebub!" I scolded. The horse meekly dropped to
the ground, and thrust his front legs forward, at the same time
pushing his body backwards, like a female jaguar in heat. He
was obeying me. This, I swear to you, sir, is a true fact.

Seô Habáo saw it all but pretended not to understand what

had taken place. He turned red. But I think men who are concerned only with buying and selling are sometimes the first to catch the essence of things, with subtle quickness. Without a stammer, he said to me:

"If this horse is to your liking, sir—if he pleases you—I gladly give him to you, as a token of friendship. Just as he is, young man, he is yours."

I didn't believe him, you ask? I assure you, sir, I had not the least doubt. I thanked him warmly, and took the end of the halter rope. Now, from that hour, the big horse, with his spots and streaks, was mine—ah, how he trod the ground, how impressive he was! I ran my hand over his face, and along the side of his neck and shoulder. The animal was mine, by right of possession, outfitted as he was, with a good saddle of high bow and cantle, and broad wooden stirrups. But just the same, I asked myself: why had Seô Habão suddenly seen fit to present me with so valuable a gift—I, who was neither friend nor relative of his, someone he hardly knew? What was in the back of his mind, what powers did he suppose me to have? Was he afraid of me? I became aware of my companions' astonishment, the stir around me. Sure, they must be envious! Let them be! The first thing a person who wants to rise in life must learn is to override the envy of others. Because of that horse, if for no other reason, my prestige had shot up and I knew it. They weren't laughing at me now.

"What an animal! So big, strong, and well-cared for."

"That's the way luck is—deserve it and you have it."

They could talk of nothing else. I concealed my pleasure, and talked of other things I planned—like how I wanted my horse outfitted in gaucho style, with a breastband studded with silver crescents, and all the metal parts silverplated.

"Say, Tatarana, is it really true what I heard: that you are going to call him Beelzebub?" someone laughingly asked me.

"No, wise guy! Don't be alarmed! The name that I'm giving him right now and that he'll be called from now on—learn it if you can—is Siruiz!" I gave this answer without a moment's thought, then I mounted.

Ah, the important things in life slip up on us, thief-like, for

Zé Bebelo had come on the scene and I quickly realized something I had overlooked: that for me to be offered a present like that under those conditions and to accept it, was a gross affront to Zé Bebelo. Such a gift had to be for the Chief. I realized it, but I didn't back down, nor did I dismount. This shows that inwardly I must already have been regarding Zé Bebelo with a kind of contempt. Whatever was to be would be and I didn't care. Any other jagunço chieftain would have been tempted to settle the matter once and for all, then and there. I waited. Could that have been Seô Habão's purpose: to sow dissension among us? I thought about it for a moment. And my mind was on my weapons.

But Zé Bebelo, on learning what had taken place, merely looked at me with a little smile.

"It suits you, Professor, to be mounted so handsomely. It will be good to see you looking smart, fighting the good fight, when the time comes!" This was what he said, though I know he wasn't happy about it. Ah, that man was all intelligence, that's what he was. I dismounted.

Deliberately, though as if on the spur of the moment, I handed the halter rope to Fafafa and said: "Unsaddle, feed and curry him—take care of him." I did this because Fafafa just naturally liked horses and was the best one to care for an animal, even one that was not his. But I had given an order, and thereby regained my position. Seô Habão had also brought a quantity of medicine, bitter pills, for the malaria. Everybody took some.

I walked away a few steps, my back to Zé Bebelo. He could kill me in an instant, shooting me from behind—of this I was aware. Nevertheless, I stopped walking and just stood there. I felt no fear whatever: I was free, gloriously secure—who could muster up the courage to shoot me? His courage would falter and fail, his hands drop, inert. I could turn my back on everyone. Whatever the Drão—the devil—had said to me, he had said it; could that be all there was to it? I looked up at the sky: at the clouds caught in a field of blue. I was charged with power and I stood there, on fire. I felt light, light enough to run around the earth. I'm telling you just how it was, on that otherwise ordinary day.

How could I ever forget such fateful events? That day was a prelude.

Seô Habão shared our evening meal with us. Raymuno Lé doled out the pills to those who needed them. Diadorim was in a friendly mood. Zé Bebelo called me aside and told me in detail about several changes he intended to make. Alaripe engaged me in conversation, and I want to tell you about it. With me drawing him out, we talked a lot about prayers for healing bullet wounds, and about scapularies that seal the body against all harm. Alaripe then told this story about a case that happened in the wilds of the sertão a long time ago.

A certain José Misuso was teaching one Etelvino, for a fee of forty milreis, how to make an enemy miss his target when he shoots at you and this was his precept: "All you need is to have the coolness of faith and at the critical moment look at him and cry out mentally: 'You are going to miss me, you will miss, you will miss, the bullet will pass to one side, you won't hit me, you will miss, you will miss, you son of a bitch!'" This was the way Misuso was instructing Etelvino. But then Etelvino objected: "Hell, if that is all there is to it, just that little bit, I already knew that much myself, without anybody teaching me—I have done it just that way lots of times." "And did you do it exactly like I told you?" inquired Misuso doubtfully. "Exactly like that. Except only at the end, the insult I thought of was: 'you son of a whore,'" Etelvino answered. "Ah, then," Misuso interrupted, "in that case you only need to pay me twenty milreis."

We all laughed a lot. It was an hour of contentment and happiness to spare. We joked, we drank, someone sang funny songs. Gently as a mother, the night enveloped us. I slept with my face in the moonlight.

I awoke. The moon was still shining, I remember, when I was awakened by the noise of riders approaching at an easy gait and then reining in their horses for a quick halt. I guessed there were some ten of them and I was right. I jumped out of my hammock, wondering who they could be. All the others had picked up their rifles. I had heard no sentinels' warning. The dawn was bright with moonlight, as you see only in the sertão.

"That's our João Goanhá with his men," said Diadorim,

whose hammock was hung a few feet from mine. And so it was. João Goanhá, Paspe, Drumão, Ciril, Bobadela, Isidoro. To meet up again with companions like those, that makes life worth-while. João Goanhá: fat, strong, bearded. His beard was very heavy, very black. He had come through the moonlight, feeling fine. Everybody was talking, embracing one another. Soon the fire was lit, coffee was put on and something to eat. Meanwhile, Zé Bebelo, standing as straight and as imposing as he could, was questioning the newcomers.

Such were the ordinary things that took place. I had just been aroused and wasn't yet fully awake. Diadorim, however, was especially gay: he must have taken a drink. I remember check-ing the bullets in my pistol. I wanted lots of movement and change. Like rivers, which never sleep. A river does not want to go anywhere; what it wants is to grow bigger and deeper. I walked forward. Then—oh, man—I took one more step: now anything could happen.

Don't think I did it on purpose. No one was startled. I neither raised my voice nor challenged anyone. I simply spoke:

"Ah, and now who is the Chief?" I merely asked the question. Do I know why I did? Only because I wanted to know, and per-haps also because of my recently acquired mania for saying crazy things, talking wildly. Under no circumstance did I wish to offend anyone. In fact, I was feeling lazy. The truth, how-ever, was that one of them had to be the Chief—Zé Bebelo or João Goanhá. They looked at one another.

"Now, who is the Chief?"

Was I the only one not taken by surprise? Zé Bebelo—the thinker, proud and opinionated. João Goanhá—a tough, simple man, come from beyond the river, despite hardships and dis-tance, to be with us, needing our company, for without it he was at a loss. I took charge of the situation with my eyes.

"Who is the Chief?" I repeated.

They looked at me. They did not know and they could not answer—because it was neither of them. Was Zé Bebelo no longer Chief? His face was gray. And João Goanhá: I saw him stir quietly, hot and cold. Under my gaze his bones and every-

thing about him seemed to diminish: gestures, speech, looks
and presence. Neither of them. I myself was the Chief! They
looked at me.

"Who is . . ."

By then all the men had gathered in a ring around us. I was
master of the situation. Didn't they understand me? Some of
them growled. And it was that Rasga-em-Baixo, the ring-leader
among them and a secret enemy of mine, as he now revealed,
who reached for his weapons. In a sudden frenzy, he raised his
knife to strike me. My gun spoke true and Rasga-em-Baixo
sprawled on the ground, without moving, lifeless. Then his
brother, José Felix, staggered and fell sideways; he had no
further need for air; I had shot him too.

". . . the Chief?"

Everyone stood in stunned silence. Ah, I, my name was
Tatarana! Then Diadorim, tense as a jaguar, sprang to my side,
striking fear in those around us with his look and posture. He
was superb. They saw it, they felt it, and they must have guessed
it from the attitude assumed by the two of us; and also because
we were shortly joined by Alaripe, Acauã, Fafafa, Nelson,
Sidurino, Compadre Ciril, Pacamã-de-Prêsas—and many, many
others—who came and stood by our side. I have got to be the
chief!—I said to myself, for I had wanted it and thought of it.
I demanded it, no less. João Goanhá smiled at me. Zé Bebelo
shrugged his shoulders.

It had to be there and then. I confronted Zé Bebelo, our faces
almost touching. Zé Bebelo knew no fear. He was ready for anything—blood-letting or come what may. And I was not going to
have much talk about it, either.

"Who is the Chief?" I wanted to know.

I asked the question calmly enough. Zé Bebelo hesitated. I
was friendly, relaxed. I knew he was thinking and sparring for
time.

"Who is?" I pressed him, mildly.

I was aware of everybody's breathing. If the situation lasted
much longer, I would drop it, for it was already beginning to
bore me. I had a crazy impulse to gloss over the incident: Zé

Bebelo, old friend, excuse me—but I kept silent. Zé Bebelo
shrank a little, but his eyes were steady:

"You are, Riobaldo! You are the chief, Chief. You are the
Chief from now on! More power to you!" he said stoutly, trying
to be gay and enthusiastic. But I was afraid he was going to
cry. I had never seen so much unhappiness on the face of any
man or jagunço.

"It's up to you, men," I said to those about me.

Many, many men held up their rifles, shouting their acceptance and approval of me. I was now Chief Riobaldo, and they
swore their allegiance solemnly and sincerely. It had all taken
place peaceably, except for those two accursed brothers lying
there at my feet. It would not do to bury them for it would show
want of respect for me. Everything had been handed over to me.
Now, just see how things are: you try to tell about how quickly
a thing happened, and nobody believes you. They think you are
making it up. Now me, I know: things that happen, it's because
they had been made ready elsewhere and their time had come,
so in effect every occurrence is a spontaneous one. That was the
way I became Chief. That's exactly the way it was—I'll swear
it to you—though some tell it differently.

At the end, after João Goanhá had shown his approval of me,
I looked up Zé Bebelo—to have an understanding with him.

"Now you, sir—" I started to say, but he cut me off.

"No, Riobaldo. I have to go away. I don't know how to be third
or even second. My reputation as a jagunço is ended." Then he
laughed and said politely, even: "But you are another man, you
will turn the sertão upside down. You are formidable, like an
urutú-branco, a white rattlesnake."

He was giving me a new nickname. The others all heard him
and broke out laughing. Soon they were shouting, full of
enthusiasm:

"The Urutú-Branco! Hey, the Urutú-Branco!"

You will see from this that for all their crudeness they had a
quick understanding, because it would no longer do for them,
now that I was Chief, to call me simply Riobaldo, or by my other
nickname, Tatarana.

There had been a fleeting moment when I felt I might have to

take Zé Bebelo's life so there would be no question in the future
as to who was chief; and now I was almost unhappy, sorry to
see him leave. But it really would have been ludicrous to take
Zé Bebelo along as my subaltern through all that lay ahead. Ah,
one does not kill a man like him. And a man like him is not
given to obedience. I ordered that he be furnished another
horse and a pack animal—with provisions and what-not, and
better ammunition. Within an hour he set out. Headed south.
I watched as he said good-by to the others and left—followed
by everyone's good will and respect—and it reminded me of
that other time when he had started out alone for Goiás, after
being tried and expelled from the sertão. It was all being repeated. But this time it was he himself who had passed judgment and sentence. And now the time had come when all hell
was going to break loose.

After Zé Bebelo had left I stopped for awhile, to catch my
breath. I noticed that the men were already obeying me, and
had set to work ahead of time. They were bustling about,
making ready for departure, shaking out the saddle cloths and
saddling the horses. There were so many men, but I knew all
their names and each one's worst fault, as well as their strength
and courage and rifles. Now I was the boss. Now I was free,
relieved of my past unhappiness. Now the decisions were mine.
I felt as if that whole vast part of the country belonged to me.
The greater the dangers that lay ahead, the greater my rejoicing. By God, when I gave an order, it would be carried out
—or else. "I swear it," I said to myself and mounted, full of
self-confidence. According to the established practice, this was
the signal for departure. I took to the road. I did not even look
back. Would the others follow me? A trinca-ferro was singing.
A macaw gave a loud squawk—and almost got shot. Behind me,
the men were shouting hurrahs. They were coming, they were
coming. Joyfully, I listened to the clatter of their horses'
hoofs.

I gave my horse the rein. We rode into Valado again, as we
were going back that way. At a gallop, as I have said. We were
surrounded at once by the people there, children, farm hands.
That Seô Habão was there too, very much dismayed. We dis-

mounted for a halt. What I needed was a few moments alone, to collect my thoughts. This was the first trip under the new leadership, and I had to do something unusual, for all to see and admire. I saw a smooth rock peak, and climbed up it. I told the men to wait below with the others. I did not want my personal influence and prestige to become diluted by too close association with a lot of people. I looked down from the top: they didn't even need to have names—what they were good for was to live or to die, as I wished it. They had placed the world in my hand as a toy.

I stayed up there for awhile. When I came down, I had made certain decisions. Where were we going? Looking for Hermógenes? Ah, no. First, to the Urucúia tablelands, where you can hear many a bull bellowing. They were to follow me there. But not this way. That is what I thought but did not say: not this way.

Seô Habão appeared before me, ahead of any of the others: smooth, bustling, prepared to make a deal. What a man! He wanted to make me an offer of money, and to aid me in other ways. Ah, no! He was the one who would have to receive, to accept, from me. I took hold of the cord with all the medals on it, that I wore around my neck, and broke it. I had worn some of those medals since I was a boy. I made a gesture and dropped the string in Seô Habão's hand. You would have enjoyed seeing the look on his face, forced to accept payment in coins that were not of the king's mint but tokens of gratitude to the saints. He became all tremors—as do men who are not ashamed to show fear. I'll tell you, sir: he kissed my hand. He must have been thinking that I had lost my mind. He thanked me profusely, nevertheless, and put the medals carefully in his pocket; actually, there was nothing else he could do. To kill that man would have been senseless. As a first step toward setting matters right in the world, what good would that have been? We might have taken everything he owned, and then turned him loose in some far away part of the country where he was absolutely unknown: then he would have to beg alms. I thought of it for a moment. But no, that was no good either: even as a beggar, in utter dejection, he would be driven by his nature to garner crumbs until the day of his death.

The medals and prayers, he could sell or hoard for hell. I kept only the scapular—the one I have mentioned before, which held some flower petals sewed up in a piece of altar cloth with a petition to Our Lady of Abadia. Later that same afternoon I hung it around my neck once more, on an oiled and braided cord. This one I would not throw away; ah, no, I could never give it up, not even if it condemned me day after day for my trespasses, not even if it burned the skin on my breast, underneath which the flesh was writhing like a piece severed from a deadly viper.

In a reversal of judgment, I began thinking what I might do for him, for Seô Habão, as a sort of reward, for, as a matter of fact, he deserved it, and I was in his debt: he had recognized my power ahead of any of the others, and my handsome horse, Siruiz, on which I was mounted, had been and was a princely gift from him.

Then, I remembered something that it would be suitable to entrust him with and in keeping with his character: the stone, the valuable stone—so beautiful it was—that I had brought back from Arassuarí a long time back. I removed the little package from my belt pocket and handed it to him. I said:

"Seô Habão, listen and do what I tell you: take this gem and guard it with all the fingers on both your hands. I want you to get on a good horse and strike out at once for Buritis Altos and the Fazenda Santa Catarina there, at the head waters of a stream."

I told him he was to deliver the gift from me to the girl of the house there, whose name was Otacília, to whom I was engaged to marry. But for him not to refer to me by high-sounding titles, nor mention my leadership of jagunços. Only to praise me to her as Riobaldo who with my men was bringing glory and justice to all the territory of the great rivers flowing from west to east since the world began and for as long as God endures!

Ah, no: he was not to speak of God. Seô Habão listened carefully, then he weighed my words which had upset and sobered

him. He repeated what he was to say, turning over the words as
if they were coins. Is being rich some kind of affliction? It annoyed me that anyone could be so cautious as he was. Who was
he? For the first time, I noticed that he had large ears, enormous ones; even without meaning to, I reached up to feel the
size of my own. Would it be better to take this fellow with me,
so that I could keep a close watch on him at all times? No, the
best thing would be to destroy his image by keeping him far
away, out of sight. I don't want to have to look at your chest,
your nose, your hard soft eyes, I thought to myself. But he also
had a kind of commanding presence. I turned away a few steps
and there was Diadorim. "What I tolerate but do not understand about this man is why I can feel neither aversion nor
pity for him," I said. But I saw a dark shadow cross my friend's
face, filled with unhappiness, fighting back the tears. I saw that
it was because of the topaz. I had not considered Diadorim's
feelings. "Never mind, Diadorim, there is time, there is time,"
I thought, half aloud. I was completely certain of Diadorim's
friendship, and didn't let the matter upset me. Early in the
morning, do you stop to think that night is already on the way?
And I had been engrossed in other matters. True enough,
lately I had not thought much about Otacília, nor longed for
her. Otacília was becoming a vague something, belonging to the
past. I would wait and see what the future would bring.

But Seô Habão wasn't through yet: there was something else
he wanted to settle. I gave him permission to speak. He inquired, artfully, if I wouldn't also like to send a message
through him to the gentleman, my father, Selorico Mendes,
owner of the São Gregorio and other good and rich fazendas? I
found the suggestion amusing and nodded: yes, he should go
and extend my greetings. Then it was that Seô Habão lifted his
face, reassured at last, and smiled. Then at once, in order to put
matters back on a serious footing, I said to him: "I want you to
go now, quickly, by the most direct route, and I don't want you
to bring back any answer." I smiled to myself to see how
speedily he obeyed me, with no need of a will of his own.

I had no sooner got rid of him than I promptly shouted for
the others and ordered them to go out and round up all the men.

Which men? Any and all they could find. Anyone with a musical instrument—have him come playing it! Any who like to dance—so much the better. To get things ready, bring the women, too. It all had to be made to look like a social gathering, in order to quiet fears, for was it not I—the Urutú-Branco, the White Rattlesnake—who was giving the orders, pleasing himself and commanding? A fiesta? Ah, no. I had already decided on the opposite: it was my purpose to gather up all those men and make fighters of them. To take them with us. Would my plan work? The others had not expressed themselves: they probably had no thoughts one way or the other. Moreover, all my men wanted was to please me; and besides, the job I had assigned them was fun. Out they went on their hunt, scattering in all directions, laughing and joking.

But they brought in the people. They brought all they could find, herding them in. From Sucruiú, a few, some with the smallpox pustules still drying on their pitted faces; others with smooth skin, the few who had escaped the disease. Those who pretended not to be afraid of me, also pretended to have come of their own accord; they were laughing uneasily. I directed that everyone be given a swallow of cachaça. Those people showed signs of having suffered the greatest poverty and misfortune. They had to be forced gently into coming with us. Would that be a wicked thing to do? It was the farthest from my intention; what I wanted was to rescue all of them from their misery. And that is what I did. Most of them were those backlanders, those from Pubo. They were all talking at once, and you can't imagine the crazy confusion they were creating. I think from having been rounded up and brought in like that, they were preparing themselves for the worst. Then, when I gave a shout, they began to fall into line, craftily trying to make out that they were soldiers. Would they behave that well in a pinch, would they be any good as fighters, could they be included in a fighting unit? Everybody thought the whole thing so ludicrous that my jagunços wanted to turn it into horseplay. Ah, the backlanders would do all right—as replacements.

They were bewildered and understood nothing; they eyed me fearfully when I shouted:

"Sons of . . . !"

All of a sudden, I felt confidence in those poor devils, with their ancient, outmoded weapons, gourds hanging from their necks, and flashpans of black powder that gave off a stinking, blinding smoke. I could see that they respected me and beheld in me a glorious vision. Did they not have longings? Their skin and rags were filthy. Were they not hanging their heads, like criminals?

"The world, my sons, is far from here," I explained. Did they want to come, too?—I inquired. A hubbub arose: a confusion of many voices from which you could grasp nothing. It was easier to understand them if they kept still. I let out a roar. I put the question to one of them. He could barely muster the courage to answer me. He was a young fellow, wearing a high hat. He replied that his name was Sinfrônio, and pointed to another— his father. The father said his name was Assunciano—and pointed to still another. But I did not let them go further. There was the one with the donkey—he was astride the donkey, a little brown donkey turned sideways. His name was Teofrásio; he did not get off the donkey, for I had previously ordered him not to. He said to me:

"Praise be. In everything, Chief, we will obey you," and the donkey turned his little white muzzle toward me. The man cleared his throat, but respectfully. "Whatever may be your pleasure, Chief. We ask your blessing."

And I permitted Teofrásio, who was a kind of chieftain of theirs, and the owner of the donkey, to bring it along. But then there was a hitch. One of the others, looking depressed and awkward, spoke up: "Who is going to take care of our families, with all of us gone? Who will work our little patches of ground?" What he said for himself, he was saying for all. "The digging? The planting?" Then another with his hands placed together as in prayer, started whining: "I have my wife and three children to feed, under my thatched roof." He was a tall gaunt man, in rags and tatters. "What is your name, you?" I asked. His name was Pedro Comprido—Long Peter. By then I had decided. "All right! Your families will do the hoeing and gather the crops, while you are covering yourselves with glory, fighting to bring peace to the whole of this sertão, and to wreak vengeance for the treacherous death of Joca Ramiro!" "Virgin Mary! Imagine us, sons of Christ, turned into jagunços!" I heard one say. Then I went on: "We are going out into the world, taking money from those who have it, and belongings and valuables of every kind. And we are only going to quit when every man has plenty, and has enjoyed two or three women, strong young ones, in his bed or hammock!" Approval glowed on the faces of all or nearly all. Even my men, too. I made a gesture to show my pleasure. I was going to transform the way of doing things. I called everybody to arms. "What about Borromeu? What about Borromeu?" they asked. Who was this Borromeu? I sent for him. He was blind. "Tell me, old man: what do you do?" "I am here in my corner, sir, getting ready for the little moment of my death." "Are you devout?" "I am the worst sinner. A sinner with nothing to do, who begs from Negroes and priests alike." He pointed with his finger, the way blind men do, at random. I raised my eyes but saw nothing. He was pointing to the North. "Ah, sir, what I know is how to beg many alms." Well, then, let Borromeu come with us too, let him come. I ordered that he be placed on a gentle horse, and that he ride alongside me on my right. Some laughed. They laughed because they did not know that a blind beggar such as this one, riding beside you, divines the approach of curses that others call down on you and wards off their evil power—as I had learned from the old timers. And then, suddenly, for no special reason, I remembered the little black boy whom we had surprised stealing in the house at Valado, with his sack in which he put whatever he could find. I had them go look for him. He had been hiding the whole time in the manioc patch, lying face down. When they caught him, he cursed, bit and kicked. His name was Guirigó. He had big, very bright eyes. "Guirigó, are you coming clothed or naked?" For of course he was coming. They got a horse ready for him, which was to stay abreast of mine, on my left. Let us be off, my people! We started. There were not enough horses for all, but as we moved ahead we would run across others that we could lasso or catch by hand. Among the many who followed on foot were those backlanders, still somewhat wary. They were wondering what next. I wanted to reach the plains. We stopped for the night after a march of ten leagues. My head was buzzing with plans and ideas, and I couldn't get to sleep; tired as I was, I didn't close my eyes all night. I walked around, talking unexpectedly with those who were posted as sentinels, and had them light little fires for roasting manioc roots and bonfires for illumination. Ah, we were going to fill the empty spaces in the world ahead of us.

Where were we headed, we jagunços? To the uplands, to the uplands. I wanted to be everywhere at once. But first we would steer north, to the uplands of the Urucúia, where you can hear many a bull bellowing. I wanted to see my river again—drink a handful of water at its edge. Ah, and those white roads that make the stars stand out more clearly. I thought of all that and longed for it. And what about Hermógenes, the Judases? Well now, enemy, you take one step in any direction and you will find woe waiting for you. Did I not have plenty of time? The prospects were bright and I was riding high. Even while lying down, I felt that I was traveling, galloping. When the dawn came, I was already buckling on my spurs. I'll say again: there is such a thing as new boots that are comfortable and old slippers that pinch. Judging by the fringes of the sky, the day would be one of airy beauty. We lined our stomachs, and left, moving along with the morning through the still dripping dew. I could see over the tops of the forest and beyond! Traveling along, I pondered all things, and none cast a shadow over me. No trace of fear was lurking coldly behind my eyes, and because of that I was chief to all, even in lonely silence. In due time, we reached the Barbaranha fazenda, at Pé-da-Pedra. Close to seven leagues distant. And I'm going to tell you what happened there.

But first: I was amused that no one sought to give me advice —not Alaripe, or João Goanhá, or Marcelino Pampa, or João Concliz, not even Diadorim, nor any of the older men. It was my privilege to disregard all the rules of the previous chief; the only policy that suited me was one of quick adjustment, free improvisation. There was only enough manioc and jerky left for three days? Nonsense. Every steer grazes daily as long as it lives. Common sense and beans can be replenished every day.

Let there be no shortage of courage and there would be plenty of burití pulp and wild steer meat. League after league I went, and they following. "Are you seeing how big the world is, Guirigó? What do you think is the prettiest thing of all?" I asked that little gnome, shiny black all over, except for his big white eyes which he never took off me as he rode perched on his high horse at my left. And brazenly he replied: "Of all things, the prettiest one is that little knife you carry in a sheath at your belt." So, he had fallen in love with my silver-handled dagger. "All right: the first time we get in a gunfight, if you don't get scared and start bawling like a baby, the knife is yours," I promised. Because of a shortage of rations, was I going to rein in and slow down? More nonsense. Another customary procedure that I discarded was that of dividing the men up into groups as a precaution. Nothing doing. If I were to get cautious, I would develop fear right at the start. Courage comes from other practices. You have to believe in the impossible— just that. "Seo Borromeu, how are you liking these plains, eh, Seo Borromeu?" I inquired cheerily of the blind man on my other side. "Ah, Chief: it is always like the coming of morning, and everything here is pleasant—the breeze never stops blowing, but it is a breeze that comes from a good direction," he answered. "I owe nothing for what I can't see—since I don't take it in," he continued. He liked to talk, but he often lapsed into silences. He jogged along, astride his horse's saddle, in a different world. "This business of being a jagunço, my chief: it's a nice pursuit, for the live ones." I took his remark as something to laugh about. But as for dividing up my people, I would hate to do it, at least for the time being, because the thing that gave me the most pleasure was to see the big body of them strung out behind, like a squadron.

I stood off to one side and watched them go by, our whole force, and listened to the steady clatter of hoofs. Horses and horsemen! A procession moving across the wilderness, through the hollows, over the heights, a long mounted line forging ahead, with my men high in the saddle, their leather hats nearly all shined with tallow and cream, their rifles slung across their chests, the barrels pointing upward. What came next? All that we had in view was to keep moving until the appearance of the evening star, with a halt then to rest and eat. In the meantime, when one said something, another would laugh as soon as he heard it, then others would talk about what the first were laughing at. They bragged and kidded. I also enjoyed hearing the creak of leather and the sound of moving flesh and bones. The sharp dust was red and white by turns; it stung our faces in the wind. A body of armed men on horseback. Anyone seeing us, watching with hidden eyes from the woods alongside, would be filled with fear and run away. Even the bush animals, which hear everything from far and near, soon learned to be still and wait in hiding, and none could be seen or found. The birds, too, always flew away at our approach. Ah, no, I had been born to be a jagunço, all right. That life was for me, and even today the tug of it is strong, as of something that lies in my future. As we ambled along, what I wished was that we were entering a large city somewhere, just as we were.

Only, at times, in sudden apprehension, I would glance about me—I was still haunted by thoughts of Zé Bebelo. I would slow down my horse and ponder. But then, loosing the reins, I shrugged off the habit, and Zé Bebelo was no more. Only my men. I listened and looked at them—there they were: the ones who would yet raise a lot of hell and kill a lot of bad people. By the tens and score, I remember them all, I assure you. They pass and pass again through my memory, and I call them by their names as they go by.

Looking at the troop of jagunços, I was struck by the same-ness of their pace: their mounts all moved their haunches alike, heads low, unable to hide their thinness. The men, all sons of different places, were now welded into one in their undivided respect for me and my firm leadership. Even the backlanders were falling into the pattern; some mounted, the rest hustling along on foot, they were beginning to catch on. The backlander Teofrásio, too, on his donkey, which like the worthy donkey it was, was jogging along in fine style now that it had the company of other animals. And Guirigó and Borromeu, on either side of me, always within reach of my hand. But there was one who stood out alone: Diadorim, riding a Bahia saddle, with short stirrups and thick reins held close, on his prancing, white-footed pony: a frisky critter, with eyes black as night—Diadorim, who had been the Boy, and who was also Reinaldo. And I. I? Iron stirrups, iron bit, a strong girth—and a pair of holsters!

The men began to sing:

> *Tra-la-la, my Bahiana,*
> *I was going but now I'm not:*
> *I pretend*
> *I am going*
> *Over there, oh Bahiana,*
> *But halfway there I turn back.*

I listened a long time, smiling to myself.

Well, we were going along in this fashion, winding our way down between two rises, seeking the river road, when we came upon a ranch, the Barbaranha, in a round and unpretentious place at Pé-da-Pedra. I have already mentioned it to you. But I will add that the present owner was a Seo Ornelas—Josafá Jumiro Ornelas was his full name.

"About three days ago was Saint John's day, and tomorrow is Saint Peter's," someone said.

This Seo Ornelas was a man of good family, and owned lots of land. Formerly, he had wielded much power and was mixed up in many fights because of politics. And he still had influence, crony that he was of Colonel Rotílio Manduca of Fazenda Baluarte.

"Is it true that he is a man of great courage?" I asked.

"They talk of sixty or eighty known dead to his credit," vowed Marcelino Pampa, "and he still hasn't cooled off."

We arrived in orderly fashion; the sky above was very serene. In front of the patio at the ranch, they had raised a flag pole honoring Saint Peter. I saw people moving about. Some women at the mouth of a smoking oven were sweeping it out with besoms of green twigs and bringing the black baking pans. Those delightful smells of baking and of the newly-swept hot oven of themselves were enough to comfort my stomach. I dismounted and tied my horse's halter to the flagpole that had been raised in honor of the saint.

But I did nothing overbearing or high-handed, nor acted rough in any way. I had no wish to bully anyone. And the fazendeiro, the master there, came out to greet me and offer his hospitality; he gave me a big welcome. I admired his dignified bearing, his white hair, his quiet manner. A good man. In deference to him, I removed my hat and spoke slowly.

"A peaceable friend? Come in, my chief, and make yourself comfortable: this old house is yours," was his reply.

I said I would. But to avoid any later diffidence or awkwardness, I also said:

"You have my fullest respect, sir—but we are going to need some horses." I said this right at the start before we got too deep into relaxed and pleasant conversation which would make our business embarrassing.

The man did not bat an eye. With neither frown nor smile, he replied:

"You, my chief, have only to ask and I will give with pleasure. I think I have some five or seven animals in fair shape."

I entered the big house with him, and in a loud voice asked the protection of Jesus on it. Then I was offered all the usual courtesies and regaled with food. There in the big dining room, seated at table, we supped off chicken, pork, farofa and several choice dishes. Diadorim, I, João Goanhá, Marcelino Pampa, João Concliz, Alaripe and some others, and the little Negro, Guirigó, as well as the blind man, Borromeu. Everyone thought the presence of these two very amusing and entertaining.

The rancher's wife was a woman beyond the age of allurement, but she had three or four daughters, and some other women relatives, both married and single, who were luscious indeed. I quieted their fears, however, and neither indulged in nor permitted any lack of consideration, for it gave me pleasure to see those women and girls move about freely in our midst, exchanging courtesies, their honor and persons safe from harm. Supper was beginning, and I talked only about serious matters, such as politics and the business of farming and cattle-raising. The only thing missing was a good bottle of beer and someone reading aloud from a newspaper, so that we could discuss all the news.

Seo Ornelas had me sit at the head of the table. "Here is where Medeiro Vaz used to sit, when he passed through," were his words. Medeiro Vaz had in fact ruled in these parts. Was he telling me the truth? That old fazendeiro had everything. He had been a semi-jagunço, as well as a hospitable friend and the owner of much property. Because of his family background, he had the poise and manners of a man from the city. This was something it would take me a long time to acquire, even if I worked at it constantly. That's a fact—and because of this I began to feel unsure° of myself. A kind of fear? Like fear, anyway; it was a sneaky misgiving that soon began to infiltrate other areas. Little by little, I began to lose my desire to eat my fill.

"The sertão is good. Everything is lost here, and everything is found here," Seo Ornelas was saying. "The sertão is a confusion which has become bogged down in too much peace."

The remark pleased me. But I shrugged my shoulders. Sometimes, as a defense measure, I would pretend I had not heard. Or start talking about something else. I threw chicken bones to the dogs that stood waiting near the table with their eyes fixed on me. They never missed; each dog would catch the bone in mid air, throwing up its head so fast its ears almost snapped. The others at the table, showing me the greatest deference and liking, were passing me bones to throw to the dogs. It made me laugh, and we all laughed together.

The boy Guirigó had eaten too much and was nodding, slumped in his chair, but he woke up with the laughter. He had already asked if some day he couldn't have some clothes made, and a leather hat to fit his head—which, incidentally, was not a small one—and a cartridge belt, too. "You've got plenty of brass, Guirigó. You go right after whatever you want," I teased. Then, jokingly, to the others: "If you doubt it, just give him a big sack, and a window to jump in and out of, and he'll swipe everything he can lay his hands on in a fazenda house as large as this one." I had grown fond of the little rascal. And the women folk talked and played with him; he was the only one with whom they lost their shyness, since he was only a child, after all. But Seo Ornelas remained grave, and I think purposely pretended not to notice the boy. I gathered from his manner that he did not approve of my bringing such company to the table: the boy and the blind man, Borromeu, with his blank eyes.

"The crops . . ." Seo Ornelas was saying. A methodical man, set in his ways. His orderly way of life, his strictness in dealing with the dogs, everything he did, recalled the old-fashioned habits of some faraway land. He ate almost nothing. Now and then he would toss a handful of dry manioc meal into his mouth. "Let us hope that you will go and return. The sertão needs a strong, fast-moving man. Come back whenever you wish, and may God bring you to this house."

It vexed me not to know the proper answer to make in such circumstances—one which would exactly fit, as in a well per-formed play. It was almost as if I had nothing to say. To tell the truth, that is how I felt: as if I were trapped in ignorance—not for want of schooling or intelligence but because of lack of status. This was foolishness: I cleared my throat and assumed a different expression, while he continued:

"My friend Medeiro Vaz once fought a battle at Conta-Boi, about two leagues from here. Against the forces of one Tolomeu Guilherme. My late friend Medeiro Vaz, may God rest his soul. He was in front, leading, setting the example. We bury the best men."

"I know," I said, not really intending to say anything. What was he thinking of me, that stubborn old man? "And I want you to know, sir, that it was Medeiro Vaz himself who chose me among all the others, as his eyes were closing in death, he picked me to lead and rule. Tolomeu Guilherme, whom I know, must be at this moment loading goods for us at the river port of Pirapora. But in my own right, I am Urutú-Branco—Riobaldo —formerly Tatarana—perhaps you have heard of me? The sertão has yet to see its master and its savior!" I spoke some-what angrily.

"I am honored all the more, my Chief: for only men of high courage and integrity of character have sat in the master's

place, at the head of this poor table," he answered, giving no
sign of being disturbed. I turned my back and snapped my
fingers at the dogs. In this way he would be made to feel the
danger of my displeasure: he would fear receiving from me—
as the saying goes—what you get when a mule turns its rump!

At that instant, I caught Diadorim's eyes going from me to
one of the young women who were waiting on us: the best looking of all. She had on a black skirt and a little white blouse, and
a red bandanna around her head—which seems to me the most
becoming way for a woman to dress. She was standing still, in
the midst of the others, almost touching the wall. Diadorim's
glance was pointing her out to me, directing my admiration
toward her. Enchanted, I called her over: "Young lady, miss,
do me the kindness to come closer." Her face flushed red, but
she came; I noticed her pretty, perfect hands, hands for weaving my hammock. I asked her name.

"She is my granddaughter," spoke up Seo Ornelas. I could
barely hear the name she gave me in reply. She was shy and
embarrassed, and I enjoyed seeing how she strove to remain
still, though she was trembling like a dish of jelly.

But in the old man's tone of voice I had detected a trace of
fear, a slight trepidation. That satisfied me. Dignified and
stately he was in everything, but when it came to the women-
folk of his house, his family, he did not hide his feelings. I
sized up Diadorim, too, and saw jealousy in his staring eyes.
I'll say this: love breeds fear, but also courage.

No one spoke. A long pause ensued, as when the anteater
sticks out its tongue, or someone kneels waiting for communion. I was strongly tempted by the girl standing before me in
water-like stillness; her beauty had set my flesh on fire. She
was in great danger. No, she was not, for in that instant I
found tucked away in my mind a higher sentiment: the un-
written code of the truly brave. That delicate beauty, that
sweetness, would remain unsullied, as safe from harm as
though she were my own daughter. Suddenly, a wave of tender
affection for the girl came over me; I wanted to protect her.
Diadorim had no way of knowing this. His eyes were not
reproaching me—they were imploring pity. Seo Ornelas had

turned pale. There was no doubt that in a flash quick as light-ning—had I so wanted—Ornelas would have dropped dead with a bullet between his eyes, before he was even aware that I was reaching for my gun. Diadorim, if I had to, I would have dis-armed; and my men would all have stood there shoulder to shoulder, a solid wall against the world. The girl, whom I could have seized in my arms, would have been just a choice morsel, kicking and screaming. But I did not want it so! I'll show you, sir, just how much I did not want it, and God Him-self will nod His head in agreement. Ah, he was being a very different man, that Jagunço Riobaldo—for what I now wanted was to offer her my guarantee of her safety, forever. I struggled with the turmoil in my head; I took myself by the horns, and thus restrained, I quieted down—and felt better, as if, after being boiled in the oil of my own blood, I was now being cooled by the strong, fresh breeze of loving-kindness.

"My girl, when the time is ripe, you shall have a proper husband, one who is handsome and industrious, as you deserve and I pray. I will not be here on that day to share in the festivities, but if ever the need arises, you and he can send for my protection, for it is yours for the asking, just as though I had been the best man at your wedding!"

I felt high-flown after I had spoken. The girl again took fright and turned redder than before, unable to speak or move. But I received my reward from the joy in Diadorim's eyes. Could it be, perhaps, that I had done what I did just to please him? Or possibly even for the sake of that old man, Ornelas himself, who was now saying:

"Thank this great chief for his words, my daughter, he who is now our avowed and cherished friend before the world, in all the vicissitudes that lie ahead!"

Thereupon I turned back to him. After that, I was eager for further talk with him, and I esteemed the friendship of that man of bygone days of the sertão. I asked him many questions. I accepted orange-leaf tea, which I had always liked, in a large bowl decorated with an intricate design. My men listened to our talk.

"Have you, sir, any idea who Zé Bebelo is?" I inquired at one point, to establish myself.

"Zé Bebelo? It might be, I'm not sure. . . . But I don't believe I have ever heard that name, no sir," he replied.

Was such a thing possible? But it was a fact, that he simply knew nothing about Zé Bebelo, nor about Ricardão, nor about Hermógenes. In that case, everything in that part of the gerais was but an illusion of law and order. That part of the country had to begin all over again. "I have little to do with politics," he said. "I gave it up." He did not mention the name of his own chief—as if I didn't already know it. The latter was renowned, too, and you may have met him yourself, for he made frequent trips to Rio de Janeiro, though he was notorious as a hirer of armed outlaws for his political maneuvers. Slight and skinny, he was well-dressed, with small hands and feet, and he always had a startled air. They say he himself was responsible for some two hundred killings. Did you know him, sir? Colonel Rotílio Manduca, in his Fazenda Baluarte, on the banks of the São Francisco. Now there is peace.

To change the subject, I asked Seo Ornelas about Seô Habão. This was the answer he gave me:

"He is a relative of my wife's, and a distant one of mine, too. But it's been over ten years since we broke with him."

I dropped the subject, as was proper under the circumstances, for the reminder of an enemy is always unpleasant. Seo Ornelas then told us about several incidents. The one I remember, because it was so unusual, was this one that I am going to repeat for you. It took place on the outskirts of the city of Januária.

Seo Ornelas, on that occasion, was friendly with the congressman, Dr. Hilário, a very civil, well-educated young man, of ready wit, and such an engaging talker that it was a pleasure to be in his company. "I learned half a thousand things from him. His was a courage tempered by politeness and ease of manner. It was only after a dangerous quarrel was over that you realized how he had played the part of a man."

Well, one afternoon, Seo Ornelas—as he told it—was at a

spot near the entrance to town, chatting with Dr. Hilário and two or three others, and a military orderly who was in civilian clothes at the time. Suddenly, they saw a man coming, a wayfarer: a backlander on foot, with nothing remarkable about him. He carried a long stick on his shoulder, and an almost empty sack hanging from the end of the stick. "It looked as if he was coming from Queimada Grande or Sambaíba. He did not look like a criminal nor one having evil intentions. There was nothing unusual about his poverty-stricken appearance." Seo Ornelas wasted few words on descriptions. "Well, then, this man appeared, with his half-filled sack on the end of a stick, and came over to our group seeking information: 'Which one of you gen'men, excuse the question please, is the Honorable Mr. Congressman?' he inquired. But, before anyone else could answer, Dr. Hilário himself pointed to one Aduarte Antoniano who was there—a bad fellow, greedy and grasping, and said to be very treacherous. 'This one, my friend,' Dr. Hilário said as a joke. No sooner had he said this than, quick as a flash, the man loosed the sack from the stick, and brought it down hard on Aduarte Antoniano's head—as if he wanted to maim or kill him. There was an uproar; the stranger was soon subdued and arrested, and first aid given to Aduarte Antoniano, who had blood oozing from a cut in his scalp but no serious injury. Seeing what had happened, Dr. Hilário, who was fond of moralizing, said only: 'You live a little but you see a lot.' I asked him what he meant. 'Another can take our place, but we should never take the place of another: it's not wise,' was his answer. I think this was one of the most instructive and amusing incidents I have ever witnessed."

Seo Ornelas told this and other stories, one after the other. I let him run on the whole evening, though at times I had my doubts; I wondered whether, being a chief, I should tolerate another's dominating the conversation. Then, as it was getting late, we got up from the table, and I persisted in my refusal of the offer of a bed indoors and went outside to be with my men. I hung my hammock between a cashew and a genip tree, near the corrals, and after my first sleep, I moved it to a couple of faveiras inside a fenced-off place. But that boy Guirigó had fallen asleep at the table, so I allowed the women to pick up the poor little devil, though he weighed almost as much as a grown man, and put him to bed between sheets on a mattress some-where. Life is full of surprises! You start something, without knowing why, and then you lose control; life is like a stew, stirred and seasoned by everybody. I had brought the little black Guirigó, from Sucruiú, and here he was being carried to a soft, clean bed, in the arms of damsels. Only, being sound asleep, he neither knew nor appreciated what was happening to him. "Well, a good night to you, Chief, and a pleasant awaken-ing," were Seo Ornela's parting words, to which I politely replied in almost the same words.

I am telling in detail everything that happened and did not happen there at Barbaranha, not because I want to drag out the story nor monopolize your time, but only because my crony Quelemém holds that what happened there was of considerable significance in my life, beginning with the incident related by Seo Ornelas and its artful lesson pointed out by Dr. Hilário. Please bear with me.

The next morning, I awoke with a bittersweet taste in my mouth; this day did not belong to the previous night. We rounded up as many horses as we could, about ten all told, including the donkeys and mules. Seo Ornelas approved of our action, and moreover, wanted all of us, to stay for the day's festivities, but I thought it better to leave right away. Sincerely thanking our host, we got into our saddles and rode off through the dawn's fast-disappearing shadows. Our departure was en-livened by sky rockets—a good half-dozen of them—which Seo Ornelas ordered set off. Our people shouted farewells and hailed the saint atop the flagpole. Then, with spur, reins and knees, I urged my horse forward.

We covered about two leagues of very sandy roads. But I was feeling irked. The things in this world that change the quickest are the direction of the wind, the trail of the tapir in September and October, and a person's feelings. So it was that suddenly I felt I had been diminished by that conversation with Seo Ornelas. Little by little, in the ease of his presence, under his roof, I had neglected keeping the upper hand. Other persons' opinions radiate from them and stealthily mix with and influence our own, without our realizing it. In the case of a serious matter, therefore, one had to set one's jaw, close one's ears, and shut one's eyes. Something of another's person infects us, like a contagious disease. To be apart from everyone else: that was the way for me, in matters big and small. My worst fault was my habitual indiscretion of the heart. This taking a too-quick liking to others was a mistake that clouded my judgment of them; with the result that later on I became disillusioned with them; all of a sudden, they seemed to be going crazy. Riding along, thoughts like these made my throat tighten up, and my mouth fill with saliva, salty as a saddle blanket. Then, I remember, I saw Alaripe a short distance from me; restrained in everything, he had the easy sway in the saddle of a cattle driver. I called him over to me.

"The old man handed over the horses, eh Alaripe? His blood turned to water," I boasted. "He came through without an argument. Tell me, Alaripe, doesn't all this peace make you sick?"

"Well, that's the way it affects some."

"But isn't peace a good thing? How come, then, that it can be distasteful, too?"

"It's a person's nature, contradictory-like."

"You see everything, Alaripe. I think the distaste for peace may also be a kind of fear of war."

"Could be."

"But it is only fear of war that turns into valor."

"I don't quite understand, my chief, but you must be right."

"Well, isn't it? It is only when the river is deep, or has deep holes in it, that you build a bridge across it."

I invented other things to talk about, for I needed to get my bearings, to feel my mastery. The steer craves the taste of salt in its mouth—the salt of the red salt lick. I was calling up courage within myself.

We kept on our way, a long line of horses and riders. We crossed a shallow and narrow stream, less than six fathoms wide. Streams like that which come to a dead end are called Jordan River. Everyone crossed ahead of me while I stood to one

side on my horse, watching. We did not rest a single day. We
had now reached the marshes along the Paracatú. By this time
I had managed to fill myself with great purposes. How I would
achieve them all, I did not see, though I was determined. But I
could not even tell the others what it was I wanted. All I could
do was put it into some verses which had come to me, like
these:

> *I took up arms, I made a pact*
> *In the Veredas, with the Hound.*
> *I follow love to its destiny*
> *Whether it leads up or down.*
> *When it comes round-up time*
> *Every steer is wild:*
> *The panicked cattle stampede*
> *The King of the Sertão rides high.*
> *Crossing the great Gerais*
> *All with arms in hand.*
> *The Sertão is my shadow,*
> *Its king is the Captain.*

I sang as the verses came to me, but full of feeling. Then
the others chimed in, though they did not understand me; they
begged me to repeat the words and then sang them, over and
over, full of fun and swagger. I saw less of Diadorim than of
anyone: he was keeping to himself. He was unhappy; how
could I ignore that unhappiness? At first, I tried to brush it
aside. Then, of a sudden, I didn't want to. Ever since I had become Chief, the distance between Diadorim and me had grown.
Quiet, he was; one beckons to love very quietly, just as things
beckon to us in silence. We were now in front of the Paracatú,
which was low and sluggish. I neither stopped nor tried to see
what lay ahead but plunged my horse into the water. The
others followed, and thus we crossed.

We kept on and on. The days followed one after another like
waves. I don't know how many steep slopes we climbed, almost
straight up. The sky over the high tableland was iron-gray.
There was a new moon. Big white rocks that turned cold at
night. The caraíbas were in bloom. My body measured the force

and sweep of the far winds. We encountered a lone cattle driver in his leather outfit, hailed him and said: "Friend, oh friend, where are we?" To which he replied: "Here, sir, you gentlemen are on the tablelands above the Urucúia." The high plains. I felt it. It is here the stars delight in shining their brightest. How far, far off you can see in the distance—your eyes never reach the end. Here I entered my freedom. Only I knew how to breathe here. My heart overflowed. Even now, my heart beats are an echo of that time; and any strand of hair that you pull from my white head will declare the reality of it. There I stood before open doors—free to go as far as the day is wide.

But someone stopped me. Or was it that it just had to be so? Buzzards flying very high, headed west. Diadorim called me and took me by the arm. He had seen those changes in me and was worried: he feared for my salvation and for my perdition. Or was it Our Lady of Abadia who ordered that it had to be like this? But Diadorim removed the sting from my actions and purposely pulled and held me back. In those heights, the meaning of something came to me that I will tell you about later. It is only in the blue of twilight that the tablelands end.

It happened as we descended some slopes around a deep wash. Diadorim said:

"Here I am; I see you, Riobaldo."

"Do you?" I answered.

"I want to say one thing to you, Riobaldo."

"All right, say it."

"It is because I care for you, that I speak, Riobaldo." His voice was like a whisper, as when the afternoon breeze runs its fingers gently through the buriti palm leaves down by the stream.

I said: "Keep on talking!"

His forehead was covered with big beads of sweat as if they were frozen there. Did he fear me? Was there a warning that he wished to give me?

Then, suddenly, I did not want to hear it, whatever it was, I did not want to, and I made believe I was provoked. Did not my own men have to give me their full approval? Around me there would be obedience. The ruler must know how to rule. I realized, of course, that these plains were poor territory for banditry: the poverty of the land, nothing but poverty, the melancholy lives of its few inhabitants, the great distances between settlements, the dearth of water, the wild cattle roaming mournfully in search of it. What my men would like would be for us to cross the Chico, and go looking for towns and villages where we could levy tribute and have some fun. The best places would be where political battles and elections were going on. I knew this. I was no fool. A chief has to know without asking questions. I had my own nostalgic longings too.

I would have found joy in returning some day to the Velhas River country, with its patches of open pasture dotting the forest, the groves of tall macaw palms on the hills, the big, low-flying screamers, and the dainty little bird that shows one how to caress: the red-legged stilt. Diadorim—did I love him? There are many seasons of love.

"The time has come for fighting," I said to Alaripe, Pacamã-de-Prêsas, Acauã and Fafafa, my group leaders. I could drive my battle flag deep into the ground anywhere, could I not? First, then, we would cruise these purple sands right here, to get the feel of the air. But you will say, what about Hermógenes? Was not the war directed against him and the other Judas? Yes, I know. But in our goings we were bound to meet them in their comings. Knowing this kept me in the seat of my saddle, soaking it with my sweat, keeping on and on, through the dense brush and over hills, the sands glinting under our feet. The world grew quiet in the afternoons; only the tinamous calling to one another. At other times, the silence was so complete, so all-encompassing, that you could catch the toll of a distant bell. Did Diadorim not understand me? Or did he?

If I had been full of meanness, Diadorim would have understood me. But I was not. For example: we met a herd of cattle, rocking steadily along. The cowboys, their coiled lassos hanging from their saddles, were singing out to their charges, just for the pleasure of it. I enjoyed seeing the little ways in which they disguised the fear they must have felt of me. The herd was headed for the mouth of the Paracatú, unless they changed

their route. We were going in the opposite direction. We
slaughtered only two head, for food. We roasted the meat the
way the plains people do: on a green stick, holding it over the
coals until it was good and brown. The delicious smell filled
the air and set our mouths to watering. We gave the boy,
Guirigó, and the blind man, Borromeu, cachaça to make them
talk and say funny, crazy things. Was there any advice or
warning for me in the things they said? No more than the
dwarf cashews and custard apples which grew in profusion
thereabouts—as you will mention in your writings—could give
me. For, I tell you, sir, my star had risen and was shining bright
on everything, as events will show.

Then, there was the case of the woman. They sent for me:
she was having a hard time bringing her baby into the world.
It was a moonlight night, and this woman was in labor in a
poor hut. Not even a hut—just a miserable shelter. I pushed
aside the cowhide or palm-leaf screen, I forget which, that
stood in the doorway—for the place had a doorway—and
entered. The woman was destitute: too poor to buy even a box
of matches. And the town had in it only proud, pretentious
persons. The woman saw me from the mat on which she was
lying on the dirt floor, her eyes filled with terror. I took a bill
from my pocket, and said: "Here, daughter of Christ, madam:
buy some warm clothing for the little one who is about to be
born safe and sound, and whom you will name Riobaldo."
Thereupon, I tell you, sir, the babe was born. With tears in her
eyes, the woman kissed my hand repeatedly. In taking my
leave, I said aloud: "My lady, madam: a boy has been born—the
world has begun again!" and stepped out into the moonlight.

Those good deeds, then, had Diadorim not seen them? Ah,
the advice of a friend is welcome only when it is gentle, like an
afternoon breeze riffling the water. But love turns its back on
all reproof. And that was what Diadorim was bitterly offering
me now.

"It hurts me, Riobaldo, that you are turning into an altogether
different person. You want turmoil and disorder." (I stirred the
saliva in my mouth.) "I speak with good intention, Riobaldo,

don't be angry any longer. What is changing in you is the pattern of your soul—and not because of your authority as chief."

Diadorim spoke, and his voice held me like a cry; the sincerity of it. Was I going to accept this reproach? Ah, never. And, unexpectedly, I hit upon another motive to oppose to his: the snatch of conversation that Diadorim had held, on the quiet, with the driver of a pack train. I asked him:

"The secret talk you held with the old pack driver, Diadorim —was it something about me?"

This train, which we had met a few days before, was headed for Abaeté, with a load of tobacco, sheets of crude rubber, jaguar and otter skins, and palm wax—nothing important. They were going to cross the river at a landing, then they would go on through country familiar to me, in the smaller sertões. Now, I wanted to know.

"He took a message of mine. I instructed the man to take a message."

"A message, about me? Well, what? Have I done something wrong?"

"A message. Don't ask me any more, Riobaldo, what it was about."

With this, Diadorim drew away from me, determined to remain silent. I had closed my ears to him. I did not want to hear the rest at that time.

Diadorim had mentioned my soul. Regardless of anything he might know or not know, he had no inkling whatever of my having gone in the dead of night to the cross roads at Veredas-Mortas to make a deal with the Occult One. Was not that my secret? And any way, nothing had happened that night. No pact, no deal was made. Proof that the Devil himself knows that he is not, that he has no being. And I was free and clear of any guilty contract, and could wear an amulet—praise the Lord!

As time went by, other things came to pass, but they happened naturally, and no one could say the contrary. I was the chief. It was my turn to give orders and to be the top man.

Zé Bebelo had disappeared completely. What we needed now was to get hold of more munitions. Everyone was duty-bound to obey me completely. Only, I did not want to abuse my authority. Why not? Well, I was still having doubts. It was on this account that I shuddered slightly at the mention of certain things, as though something were threatening me from afar, like rain clouds piling up in the distance. In spite of everything, could the devil still put his brand on me? If not, why had Diadorim reproached me in those words?

Something Diadorim had found strange was the way I handled a fellow who called himself Nhô Constâncio Alves, whom we had encountered at Chapéu-do-Boi. Also, the incident of the poor devil and his mare and little dog, that took place three leagues after the first one. Minor matters of no consequence.

What was Nhô Constâncio Alves to me? He had spoken up right away to say that he was born at the foot of the Alegres range, which was my birthplace, too. We treated him well. But he said it could be that he had known me when I was a boy. That's what that Nhô Constâncio Alves said—was he expecting me to reward him? At first, I did not dislike chatting with the old-timer, my fellow-countryman; he was cleanly dressed and friendly. We drank coffee together, then he began making himself at home and enlarging upon his answers; I even encouraged and led him on.

Then, at a certain moment, the little Negro Guirigó slipped up behind me and babbled something in my ear. Sometimes he acted queerly and his words didn't make sense. The devil—did he say something about the devil? Or perhaps, just from seeing and hearing the boy, I had thought of the devil. Anyway, there was something that had to do with the devil. And suddenly, at that moment, my other self took control. The man had a sum of money with him: he had a bad conscience and cash in his pocket, that was the way I sized him up. He deserved punishment by death, I saw at once. How? By the light of Lucifer? All I know is what happened. I was seized with an overwhelming urge to kill the man, to slaughter him. The money had nothing to do with it, for in that case all I had to do was demand it and he would have turned it over to me. No: the urge was simply to kill, to murder, for the hell of it. I rubbed my hands together and was about to reach for my weapons. Then, I almost had to laugh: to think that Nhô Constâncio Alves did not know that his life had less than a tiny part of a minute to go.

But then, from somewhere deep inside me a little voice, so weak it was strong,—and I am not even sure it was my own— spoke in a whisper. In that brief moment, the little voice gave me a warning. Ah yes, there is a secret place, little backwaters, through which the devil cannot slip into my great palaces. My heart, that's what I mean. The little voice was saying: "Watch out, Riobaldo, take heed, for it is the devil who is behind this!" I heard it like one in the vanguard who is struck by an arrow, and I pulled up hard. But how? Is, then, restraint possible? It is, it was. I resisted at once. Without a second's delay. That is the way. How well I know.

But, that urge to evil needed a collaborater—and it had none. Was I, then, myself the devil? I almost went out of my mind. Would I kill this nobody by myself? Would I not kill him, on my own alone? I tried hard to bear in mind the injunction of that little voice. I bit my lips—I thought I'd burst. I saw that I would end by having to kill, that that was what I myself wanted. It seemed as though the entire tablelands were filled with thousands upon thousands of imps, shoulder to shoulder, playing upon beautiful guitars—to drown out whatever I might say to myself and whatever I might strive to do for myself against what the head demon had willed. I want you to know, sir, that at the end I was hardly able to resist. And from this you will have to see, sir, who that jagunço Riobaldo really was, and what he was like! For, in the flash of an instant I had discovered the sweetness of God, and I cried out on the Virgin! I clung blindly in the dark, but I knew it was Our Lady! The perfume of the Virgin's name lingers a long time; sometimes for a whole lifetime.

Quickly, then, I discovered an out, a crack through which I might escape, carrying the hapless Nhô Constâncio Alves to

safety with me. This is what it was: I would ask him a question:
if he answered wrong, he would die; if not, he would go free.
This was the question:

"Being as you are from my part of the country: did you know
a man called Gramacêdo? Might you be some kin to him?"

I waited. Let him say he had known him, and he would die
then and there, for in that case I could not not-kill; meanwhile,
his salvation flickered like the dying flame of a candle.

But Nhô Constâncio Alves was fated to win, for his answer
was:

"Gramacêdo? I am sorry to say, but him I never saw nor
heard spoken of. I am not related to anyone by that name."

My hand was already resting gently on my pistol. Nhô
Constâncio Alves sensed the danger he was in. In his confusion,
he shrank even smaller; his knees must have opened, from the
trembling of his legs. For a fleeting second, the treacherous
thought came to me that perhaps he was thinking that he
deserved to die. Ah, but no! I had decided. Every creature is
worthy of life's struggle and this man deserved to live—because of an immense beauty which I suddenly became aware
of in the world. Did an angel fly over at that moment? I had
resisted a third time. Now Nhô Constâncio Alves was delivered
from danger. I only said roughly:

"Have you your money with you?"

With a new lease on life, the man quickly picked up and
opened his little bag: it was full of bills rolled up and wrapped
in cloth, which he handed to me, as you would a gift. I looked
at his pitiful throat—it was moving as if he were swallowing
all the beads of a chaplet.

I took the money. Him—Nhô Constâncio Alves—I let him
leave. I didn't even look—to keep from seeing his back. But,
then, in order to appease myself and hold off the Other One, I
said out loud:

"I acquitted that one, but the first one we meet on the road
will pay for it!"

I said it. Would I fulfill it?

Shortly afterwards, the first one came along. We had gone
almost three leagues. There was a meadow, in which a few

cattle were grazing. We met this fellow; he looked like a wanderer. He was riding a chestnut mare. The harness was so old it was almost falling apart. One of the reins was of leather, the other of braided horsehair. Furthermore, the mare had a limp. The man's face looked like an animal's muzzle; the bones pushed his mouth forward; he had no chin. To judge from his looks, what could he expect of life? This was a miserable creature. Why waste pity on him—he would be better off dead, I thought. Following along behind him was a little dog.

They stopped. The little dog started barking, under the compulsion nearly every dog feels to be bravely defiant. The man wilted in his saddle; he was terror-stricken. He turned three colors at once. Turning to the little Negro Guirigó, I asked:

"This one here, shall I kill him?"

"Will you kill him? Are you going to kill him?" The boy's eyes almost stood out from his head.

I heard the man's jaws and teeth chattering. He was utterly abject, unable to speak or to beseech mercy. What he didn't know, he guessed. Did he foresee that he was going to die merely to pay for another's pardon, merely to take the place of Nhô Constâncio Alves?

But now—the urge to kill had left me! I know and I knew then: the devil was concealing his intentions, for he suspected that I would not want to carry them out. That is the way he is, sir: he always bides his time. He knew, furthermore, that this time it was no use trying to incite me to anger. He knew that I even felt sick about the pitiful state of that man on the mare, and that it would be a pleasure for me to let him depart, free from harm. But the devil also knew that I was under strict obligation to kill: that I could not go back on my spoken word, which my followers had heard and talked about. Ah, the devil knew me well enough! He must have been somewhere close by, astutely watching me like an overseer, making fun of me, wanting to see me do a good job as I performed my criminal duty.

The man on the mare looked at everything without seeing anything; he tried to make himself as small as possible, and he groaned in silence. Where was his guardian angel? He had to

die. He had to die because the devil—in his sly way—had roped
me in the noose of obligation, and because there was no other
alternative. The little dog understood this, and barked, whined
and howled; it knew how to moan even better than its owner.
But I was thinking hard.

How was I going to kill that poverty-stricken fellow, and kill
him in place of a fat-bellied, rich one? Was there justice in
that? Come to think of it, he probably didn't know Nhô
Constâncio Alves, or even know who he was. Was that being
just? Was such a thing possible? What would Zé Bebelo have
come up with, faced with such a quandary?

The others stood around, waiting to see what would happen.
Not one showed pity for the man on the mare. They were intent
only on seeing what I would do. It annoyed me that I had got
myself into a position where I had to take immediate action. It
was then—to delay matters a few moments—that I inquired
of Borromeu:

"What will it be, old man? Is this it?"

I spoke hurriedly, because to ask the advice of a blind man, in
public like that, exposed my uncertainty.

"Is it, Chief, is it? Is this what you proposed, hm? Do you
want such a one to be killed?" The blind man answered,
rambling. I saw I had brought him along for no good reason.

"Are you going to kill him yourself, sir?" the boy Guirigó
asked in a fluty voice.

"Shut up, you little devil! Get away from here," I scolded.
It made everybody laugh.

Meanwhile, the condemned man, still mounted on his mare,
was crying bitterly to himself; he was regretting, no doubt,
ever having grown out of his remote childhood. I did not even
ask his name, nor where he was from. A person in his fix had
want or need of nothing. In his anguish, his face lost its shape
and color—he was no longer recognizable. Then Acauã—at a
warning gesture from me—began keeping a close watch on
him, because sometimes a terrified man will suddenly go ber-
serk and start shooting. He just sat there on the mare, shrunken
and huddling—the poor devil.

"Get away from here!" I yelled again at the boy.

I had to come to a decision. The quicker the better, so my men would not think me a fool. Or the devil. The devil? He was lurking around there, all right, present but invisible; and he was laughing at me in my predicament.

Was I feeling sorry for the man? The little bitch was barking. But, how could I shoot a hapless person like that, whose shoulders drooped as though he were battling a heavy storm? The little bitch was upsetting the horses. I had to act, for I had given my word. Or was I also in fear of the Tranjão, the Tibes, the What-You-May-Call-Him, whom I myself had sought as my protector? The mare was becoming restive, because when a riding animal senses human terror it feels obliged to demonstrate its contempt for the rider. Just then, everybody began laughing. "Oh, oh, he is shitting himself!" someone exclaimed. Had the man really voided in the saddle, soiling it and himself? Laughing and joking, the men crowded around him on their horses, to have a look, whereupon the little dog attacked them in defense of its master. Its barking and snarling made some of the horses shy and rear. The man himself was doubled up, fear-crazed, saying nothing. Zé Bebelo!—I suddenly remembered him and former days. The horses rearing like that, their riders shouting: it reminded me of him. Only Zé Bebelo knew how to handle a situation like this. Where was he, I wondered? And then it burst upon me: a great idea! Pulling my horse up and making him rear and paw the air like the others, I spoke— I shouted—full of heat and enthusiasm, as Zé Bebelo himself used to do, in the midst of an uproar of prancing, rearing horses and flying manes.

"Damn it to hell! I don't have to kill this poor bastard, because my pledged word does not apply to him: the one I saw first was this little dog!"

A moment of stunned silence. Then they broke out in cheers. They all understood and admired me. That much I know. Now, let me tell you, it was my turn; for the moment it was I who laughed at the devil!

"All right, boys, tie up the dog!" I ordered. In a trice, the little bitch was caught, fighting. Since they could not use a hobble, lasso or halter for the purpose, Pacamã-de-Prêsas and Jiribibe got a piece of thin rope and tied the little animal to an assa-leitão tree. "Don't let her howl, don't let her howl" said the blind Borromeu; he seemed afraid of the howling of a dog. "The best way to do with a dog: you hang it," the boy Guirigó had the brass to suggest. I ordered him to be taken away. They slapped his horse on the rump, and João Vaqueiro led them off out of sight and hearing.

"A dog—when you hang it—it sheds tears; its eyes behave just like people's," said Alaripe, simply. After all, I thought, why kill that little bitch? I couldn't do it if I had to. Meanwhile, she was being as plucky as ever, barking her head off. Ah, no! I would not kill her. Besides, I had grown skilled in artfulness. Once again, I countermanded:

"Hold on! It wasn't the bitch, either. It was the mare that I sighted first!"

Actually, I was changing my plan—and I wanted it so under-stood. I am sure they approved. They were all cheerful; who was going to contradict me? I was the master; whatever I said went. I didn't give the devil a passing thought. I now had a more pressing concern. "Get that man down off his horse—send him on his way—tell him to get going!" I ordered at once, for he was unaware of what was going on around him, benumbed, motionless. I was afraid he might drop dead, struck down by terror.

Then, ah then, my ultimate destination would be fixed: it could only be the lowest reaches of hell. Gingerly and with aversion, some of my men carried out my command and dis-mounted the man, who was barely able to stand up. "All right, now, beat it," I said. "Go away!" I had to yell. Then he under-stood and started walking. For a moment, I thought he was going to run. But he stopped, without looking back. At last he had broken down crying, sobbing aloud like a small child. It didn't make sense and it bothered me. Exasperated, my men yelled at him and he started running, followed by their shouts. Once again he stopped: he must have been weeping, the way his shoulders were heaving. I grew tense. Abruptly, there swelled up in me a strange feeling that I was going to cry, too.

I did not want to, nor could I. My eyes saw only the darkness,
not the anguish inside me. I became disgusted with myself.
Ah, at the last, the one who laughed best was the devil himself.
The Sooty One! Because of the prolonged torment to which I
myself had subjected the man by stalling for time in order to
save his life. It would have been better to have killed him in the
first place. But how was it possible to treat an unfortunate like
that with such utter contempt? How was it possible? The man
had not glanced backward to see about his little dog, which
remained there, tied and undaunted. She was no longer barking
and everyone had forgotten her. A feeling of discouragement
came over me. Perhaps, on account of that man and my callous
behavior—who knows—I might later on be liable to severe
punishment.

Some time elapsed, during which they unsaddled the mare
and hung the saddle and blanket on the branch of a tree by the
roadside. There was that scrawny animal, with Fafafa holding
her by the halter. They were waiting for me to finish her off, or
order someone else to do it, in keeping with my promise. The
little bitch, I thought, I would give to Diadorim, who had stayed
close by the whole time, without saying a word. The time had
arrived for me to make good. I had begun the disastrous affair
and I had to wind it up. All I had to do was pull out my pistol
and drill the mare through the forehead for her to topple over
dead. Why didn't I?

Just then, Fafafa, who could keep silent no longer, turned to
me and said: "Our Chief, with your permission, I ask if you will
let me pay in money the price of this innocent animal, so it
may be spared? She's not a bad little mare."

The others all seconded his request. My first reaction was almost one of anger, because even Fafafa had crossed me. The
others, it was plain to see, were reproving my decision to kill
the mare. Were they being rebellious? Ah, no; in fact, I myself
now agreed with them. I rejoiced to hear my people protest that
cold-blooded business. They were disagreeing with the devil! A
good gang, smart fellows. Only, the way they wanted it, was not
in keeping with my own. As for selling the mare to Fafafa, that

I would not do. Ah, no. I made up a speech on the spur of the moment. This is what I said:

"I confirm what I said: the first one I sighted was the mare. Therefore, she was doomed to die. But the mare is not a person, not a human being. In that case, it is not fitting that the mare be killed, because my pledge was to kill a man! So, I will not execute her. The pledge is not binding and hence void—as I have just made clear. Therefore, I declare the subject closed and the matter ended."

Everybody expressed approval, truly happy over the outcome. Or perhaps they were only admiring the cleverness of my solutions, little suspecting that these wiles of mine were to balk those of the Tempter. I was therefore rather pleased but at the same time unhappy with myself, for in a way these things were cutting the ground out from under me. However, I rubbed my hands together.

"Hurry, somebody, and go after that man again," I said. "Bring him here so we can give him money, and something to eat and coffee, and return what is his."

I was referring to the mare. Suzarte, José Gervásio and Jiribibe set off at a gallop to fetch the man. We had loosed the mare and she was browsing on tufts of grass. As long as we had already halted and were waiting, and there was good water in a stream near by, Jacaré set up his trivet and made coffee. I sat in the shade of a pau-doce, and around me I could hear voices singing my praises, foretelling bigger things to come.

"Man for man, the Chief comes up with smarter tricks than Zé Bebelo himself," said one.

"I'll swear, he decides with as much justice as Medeiro Vaz," another said, more flatteringly.

This, I confess, lulled my anxiety. At that moment, I was proud of my men—let them enjoy themselves, let them talk. But, to stress my role as leader and to enhance their respect, I ordered them to quiet down—that I was going to seize the opportunity to take a nap. I enjoyed listening to the breeze across the tablelands and its gentle rustling of the leaves of the batecaixa. The little dog—still tied up—was no longer barking: I guessed someone was feeding her bits of jerky. I remember that I could still relax in that brief span of Sunday-like tranquillity. The best—ah, the best thing of all!—would be if the Old Nick would just not appear, if he would not come around arguing all the time; the smartest thing would be for him not even to try, since he had no reality.

I soon got over my drowsiness. Suzarte, Jiribibe and José Gervásio had returned empty-handed, they had had no luck at all. "The fellow has vanished from the earth, taking his tracks with him; he must have been scared out of his mind. Not a single trace did we find." What could we do about it? We would resume our march, without further delay. We would turn the mare loose there, in case the man came back some day, or someone gave him word of her. We mounted. And the little bitch? "Reinaldo, do you want her?" I asked Diadorim. Without replying directly, he said: "The only thing to do is untie the poor thing, and she is sure to find her master, wherever he may be." And he himself untied her. You should have seen the little dog streak off like a thunderbolt; without a second's delay, she sped away, barking joyfully, as if she knew exactly where to go, as if she had wings! She disappeared in the distance and we set out in the opposite direction. The mare stayed behind, grazing; and the man's saddle gear hung like a scarecrow on the branch of a tree; the flies were already swarming over it.

After all that had occurred I felt relieved. I trotted ahead. I was going along, holding the reins loosely, not worrying, not thinking. Do you suppose—I ask you, sir—that I cruised the sertão with the Other One as my partner? Don't even think it! But I have no way of understanding why Diadorim found me strange. It was on that account that we fell into conversation, motivated by what I have just related to you in detail.

I was upset by what I had said to Diadorim and by his last remark, ashamed of my evasion. But what to do? I wanted to hear him out and yet I didn't. The rest of his answer, no matter what it was, had to be an accusation. But I wanted to hear it. Whatever came over me, I don't know, but I was forced to ask him:

"The message you sent, Diadorim, tell me what it was. It is your loyal duty to speak plainly, and I insist on it—you owe it to me!"

"I am your friend. The message I asked the pack driver to take, Riobaldo, was to a woman."

"Ah, then it was to a young woman, the daughter of the rancher at Santa Catarina—Otacília, who is to be my bride—is that right?"

"Yes, Riobaldo, it was. Do you find anything wrong with that?"

With an oath, I jerked the bridle. Even my horse was startled. If life can spring such surprises from one hour to the next, then what security does one have? Diadorim was looking at me. Diadorim waited, all serenity. His love for me was of pure gold: he was no longer tongue-tied, either by jealousy or fear. He continued:

"I asked her to pray for you, Riobaldo. Not to stop praying the whole time, the way she always does, for the sake of whatever hopes and longings for you she might have."

With a strange feeling of bitterness, I realized, even before he spoke, that I already knew what he had not avoided telling me. Nevertheless, I asked him, harshly:

"So! You think I have need of her prayers on my behalf, Diadorim?"

"I do, from morning to night, Riobaldo. Very much so. I sometimes wonder if someone has put an evil spell on you. Your mother herself, if she were alive, would think so too."

Man, oh man, the blood rushed to my face and ears, and my lip hurt from biting it to keep from insulting Diadorim in the most offensive words. With a slap of the reins, I turned my horse's head away from him.

"You mind your own business. What I need is less familiarity," I said angrily, pulling away. I thought to myself: that's a good one! Prayers against what? You are using bird shot to hunt a tapir. And I laughed maliciously. What was there in our talk that had upset me so, in the space of a minute?

Soon after, when we halted for the night, I made it plain that I didn't want to talk to or see anyone, that I was busy planning, and that I was angry. Actually, I was miserable. We had reached the far end of the tablelands, way to the west, the direction in which we had been heading since I took over. I reflected on many grave matters in the cool of the late afternoon.

I would be lying if I did not tell you that I was full of doubt. You know what I was speculating about, and whom. Does he exist? Has he any power? Even yet I suffer torture at times to know the answer; I used to more than I do now that age has brought a degree of tranquillity. Does the devil exist? Only if he exists in his own way, unbounded, without proper being—like a stretch of backwater. What about me, then? I went to the crossroads at Veredas-Mortas at midnight. Did I meet my phantom? The more I think of it, the less I know. The deal to be made, if one was made—but it wasn't. How could it be, if the What-You-May-Call-Him did not even appear, though I waited and called him? Did I sell my soul to someone? Did I sell my soul to someone who does not exist? That would be even worse. Ah, no: I say I did not. I strayed from the road but I found it again. Don't you feel sure I did? I tripped but the ground did not hold me down. When I think about it now, I absolve myself. And I pray. God turns His back on my prayers but He cocks an ear. I keep on praying. I still want to see a big church with a bell high in its white towers reigning over the tablelands. Why shouldn't some saint yet arise from the banks of my beloved Urucúia? There is no devil! None whatever. It is what I say constantly. I did not sell my soul. I signed no contract. Diadorim knew nothing. Diadorim was merely puzzled by my behavior. I can hear his clear infrequent laughter; that is, I remember it. My crony Quelemém gives me comforting counsel. He always says: "Think of the present and the future." I know.

I always knew, really. Only, what I wanted all the time, what I strove to find, was just one thing—the whole of something whose significance I see I always partially grasped: that there exists a formula, a norm for a right and narrow path for every person to live by, only we don't ordinarily know how to find it. How is one to go about discovering it by himself? Never doubt that there is such a lodestar. There has to be. If not, everyone's life would always remain the crazy confusion which it is. Every

day, at every hour, there can be only one possible step which is
the right one. What it is lies hidden; but apart from it, everything that I do, that you do, that everybody does or does not do,
is wrong and mistaken. Ah, because the first is the law—obey-
able but hard of discovery—of true living. For every person, for
his continued existence, a part has been planned for him to
play, as for actors on the stage, whose parts are thought out beforehand and written down on paper.

Now look. Can sinning be corrected with more sin? Certainly
not! My compadre Quelemém agrees with me on this, I think. I
wanted to find the right road, I tried hard; only, I tried too hard,
or maybe in the wrong way. But my soul must be from God; if
not, how could it be mine? Pray with me, sir. Any prayer. Look:
all that is not prayer is madness. Well, then, don't I know if I
sold my soul? That is what I am afraid of. Doesn't everyone sell
his soul? I tell you, sir: the devil does not exist, there is no
devil, yet I sold him my soul. That is what I am afraid of. To
whom did I sell it? That is what I am afraid of, my dear sir: we
sell our souls, only there is no buyer.

I am laying myself bare. These are the things I thought
about; but I thought about them only briefly. It was like snatching a respite in the midst of my confusion, to do some clear
thinking—for as long as it takes to repeat the Creed three times.
The rest was already on its way. You will see. But farther on.

In the Tatú sierra, it gets so cold that before morning you
need three blankets. In the Confins sierra, in the middle of July,
the winter winds of August are already buffeting and whipping
across the land, blowing down trees. Wherever I might be
headed, everyone accepted it as natural. The Chief is the chief.
Do you suppose they did not know that I did not know where I
was going? In a way, that is, in a way. They might not know the
beginning and the ending. In some way, I was going and knowing. I wonder how the owl learned to fly without making the
slightest sound? I harbored no resentment or hard feelings
against Diadorim. The tactless things he had said and done, and
that unpleasant conversation of ours, left no cloud behind;
better still, they fled from my memory altogether.

My first inclination was to go as far as Serra do Meio and

cross at the Urucúia falls. But then I decided against it, and turned straight north and crossed at Lagamar instead. But I am forgetting to tell you that before that, at Lugar-do-Touro, we had replenished our munitions. And that even a few days before that, we had a happy surprise. Quipes showed up!

After all those months, Quipes was rejoining us. He had been missing ever since that time we were surrounded at the Tucanos fazenda—you remember?—and he was sent out to get aid from the military. He was happy and full of confidence. Seeing a companion reappear like that, after a long absence, made us all feel younger.

Quipes was alert and well-dressed, mounted on a good yellow horse; he was smoking factory-made cigarettes and had a pocketful of money. He was leading two spare mules, and he had bought some things: a trivet, some pans, and real sugar and powdered chocolate. He was quite pleased with himself, and bold, even.

"Well, look who's here! How have you been? And where did you hear about us?" I asked him as a starter.

"It was like this, Tatarana: not having any news, I started scratching for myself. I have been in Ingàzeiras, in Barra-da-vaca, in Ôi-Mãe, in Morrinhas. Isn't the Urucúia the center of the world?" he said boastfully.

What he was saying was not altogether true. The fact is, he was newly-arrived. And he had addressed me as Tatarana. Perhaps he had spent the time in solitary wandering, keeping off the buzzards, so he arrived in our midst without having learned that it was I who was Chief now. He inquired about Zé Bebelo, about whom he had not heard either. Nor did he know the whereabouts of Hermógenes, nor have any clue of Joaquim Beijú, or other news of any kind to give. Only, in conclusion, he boasted of having had two offers of employment as a jagunço: one from Dona Adelaide, at Capão Redondo, and another from Colonel Rotílio Manduca, on his Fazenda Baluarte.

"Ah, I even entered the cities of Januária and São Francisco, enjoying myself as a man of peace," he boasted further. This was no doubt true. Just as it was probably also true that he had stolen the mules and other stuff, or the money to buy them with, in some prosperous locality. What he said was: "I bought all this, at José Vassol's store." A reckless spendthrift, that Quipes.

Hearing how little Quipes had to say, left me crestfallen. Here I was, invading the world, in command, and yet I was unheard of. I—Urutú-Branco—the White Rattler! Being a jagunço chief meant nothing. It carried no distinction—anybody could be one. Does not the sertão put up with everything? I was nothing, Zé Bebelo's glory was nothing. Whatever brings fame, brings scorn. I should not let it annoy me. What I needed was a fight, our first fight, to flaunt my courage before my followers. Or were they perhaps already settling down to being wanderers? Am I a gypsy? I thought to myself, angrily. There lay the north, waiting for us. I gave orders. We changed our course abruptly, raising a big cloud of dust. Straight ahead we went, following the Ribeirão da Areia. What did I intend doing? You wait and see.

I have told you that I did not hold any resentment against Diadorim for what he had done; I mean that message he had sent to Otacília. Nevertheless, I was somewhat upset by his action, which I naturally thought strange, it was so absurd. Of one thing I was sure: Diadorim would not lie to me. When love lies, it is only to tell a greater truth. But to take it on himself to send my Otacília that message—it was because he knew in his heart that she cared for me. And did he know as much about me? I soothed my thoughts by picturing Otacília, true and tender, waiting for me in her home. Now I was traveling away from her, from the fazenda at Santa Catarina, but my longing for her was returning with a rush.

Then, for a split second, my mind reeled. Supposing Otacília, out of love for me—for beyond what I deserved—and in the belief that I was facing great dangers, were to be so sweetly mad as to run away from home and go venturing through the sertão in search of me? I pictured her on a handsome mount, appearing suddenly, and asking for me by name. And I, with her in full view there by my side, proclaiming her royal greatness before the vast body of my men. . . . In a manner quite out of the ordinary, my life was taking on new and greater meanings. This flight of imagination, which could not properly be called thinking, stirred in my mind. It could hardly have been a dream, either. I had a sudden misgiving: that I might have received foreknowledge of something that was going to happen, a kind of prophecy.

Otacília. I remembered the honey-like luster in the slow glances of her eyes; her hands, that no one had to tell me were made for caressing; her graceful figure, with clearly defined breasts and waist, the first sight of which etched itself on the mind. And the melodiousness of her voice; afterwards you could travel and keep on traveling, throughout leagues of tablelands, and never once lose the sound of cool, rippling waters. Well, then, was not all this love? Of course it was. And because it was, I was afraid that Diadorim might have lied to me after all about the message he had sent Otacília; perhaps he had told her to come at once, that I needed her badly. I simply mention this, though it was most unlikely. But if you believe, sir, that any human thing is altogether impossible, then you could never be a jagunço chieftain, not for the least part of one little day, nor in your wildest dreams. Indeed not! If Otacília were to arrive in our midst, what would happen next?

Foolish thoughts. Otacília was safe at home with her father and mother, with her family, in the big house on Fazenda Santa Catarina, the best place in the world for me but the farthest away. Meanwhile, without rhyme or reason, I was pushing ahead in the opposite direction, day by day widening the distance between us. Each day farther from Otacília—but with Diadorim. I would have you know, sir, about Diadorim. All it took was for him to look at me with his dreamy green eyes, and though I was ashamed to admit it even to myself, I was roused by the smell of him, by his very existence, by the warmth that passed from his hand to mine. You will see. Was I two different persons? At that time I did not know something I still do not understand.

The most I remember is that during a waning moon we were camped at the headwaters of a small stream, a place of limitless grazing lands, where the horses could enjoy a good rest. We halted and stayed there several days. And I remember I wanted to write a letter.

This letter of mine: I could detail a man, one who could really cover the ground, to deliver it to Otacília, my intended bride, and return with her reply. What I thought of writing was very simple: I would say I was well, then inquire how she and her family were getting on, and close with regards. I am surprised that I thought it natural not to say anything, for the time being, about my being chief. Why mention it? I wanted to write some verses too, but the occasion was not propitious. I found the letter very hard to write. I wrote only half.

But how could I tell it was only half if I hadn't written all of the letter to measure by? Ah, you see! I said that just for fun, for a laugh, but also to state an important fact: that it was almost a year before I finished that letter and sent it off. Shall I tell you why? Simply because I couldn't finish it sooner. Remember this, sir, I absolutely could not. But, on the other hand, remember too: day follows night—that is what sets the little birds to singing.

I speak with twisted words. I narrate my life, which I did not understand. You are a very clever man, of learning and good sense. But don't get impatient, don't expect rain during the month of August. I'll soon tell you, I'm coming to the subject that you are waiting for.

Did the Evil One exist?

Sometimes, I think. Isn't a scarecrow dressed in an old coat and torn hat, with a stick for arms, standing in a rice field, a devil? The blackbirds see it and stay away, other birds chirp from a distance. It seems to them a man. Never take too much stock in the devil. The sertão is known by many names: here it is the gerais, there the chapadão, way yonder the caatinga. Who understands the nature of the devil? There are times when that which does not visibly exist has great power nonetheles How could I say to an emptiness like him: "Stop looking over m shoulder!?" Because what I was going to put in that letter was almost a plea, an exact repetition of Diadorim's message: that she pray for me; Otacília, say prayers for me. Ah, but then it happened. My hand weakened before my heart: I couldn't do it. Some fiendishly irrational compulsion intervened—I simply couldn't do it. Then I suddenly felt ashamed, and it annoyed me that I should be trying to write that letter. I stopped and put what I had written in my knapsack. Ah, no. Of Otacília, I was not worthy. Diadorim was an impossibility. I dismissed the whole thing.

The devil: did I hate him? Did I think about him? At times. Not with the part of me that was brave; but when I did think, what worried me was becoming entangled with him. I would think about this in the cool of the afternoon, when the sun was going down but while it was still day. Or, better yet, at dawn, at the instant of waking but before my eyes were open. During those few brief moments there in my hammock everything seemed clear and explicit, and I would say to myself: "Take care, Riobaldo, not to let the devil get his saddle on you." Then I wished I could devise a plan by which I might elude him, the Temba, whom I had mistakenly called up. Was he lurking about, my master? If he could rule me, then I was not the White Rattler, I was not chief of anything, I was nothing! I had to find a way, some clever scheme for beating the Dirty One at his own game, and freeing myself from a calamitous end. But how?

The interval between sleep and waking was too short, it flashed by. It left me nothing to take hold of, and the clarity of my insight soon vanished. The stirrings of the others about me served to blot out those warnings and designs, as if they had dried up. And the rest of the time, I was against my own self. Was I not? I was obeyed and held in greater esteem each day by everyone. Gradually, I got into the habit of jumping out of my hammock at once, as if to avoid that beneficent bit of intelligence which seemed to tell me that it was coming from the center of my heart. With a sudden motion, I would extinguish it, that momentary blaze—like the flash of a hummingbird which is here and gone—and then at once I would find myself immersed in everyday affairs, in half-happiness: good and evil mixed fifty fifty. I would arise, catch and saddle my Siruiz—a horse made for the dawn—and set out alone.

To ride out into the darkness, you know how it is, sir: the tree branches striking against your head. I always went a good distance, and when I got back I would find the men up and about, the coffee made, the horses rounded up. On one occasion, I went farther than usual. And I met a leper.

He looked as if he were lying in wait, hiding in the top of a tree, like an ararambóia snake. It gave me a start. He was covered with disgusting sores, a real leper, about done for. Not to see things like that, I'd throw away my eyes! I reached for my revolver. The man shrank suddenly, trembling, and his trembling was so violent that the branches of the tree shook as if from a strong wind. He did not cry out nor say anything. I wonder if he had any voice left. I had to destroy that inhuman thing.

At that moment I recalled something I had been told, about the time Medeiro Vaz spotted a leper like this one in a guava tree. The man had gone there to lick the ripe guavas on the tree, one by one, in order to pass his disease on to the persons who would later eat the fruit. Some do that. Medeiro Vaz, who was a just and upright man, took the leper's life. This was echoing in my ears now. The leper filled me with revulsion and loathing: he probably stank, and wherever he was or wherever he went, he left a slimy trail, like a big snail, and contaminated everything he touched with his cursed disease. The guavas of every guava tree would turn into poisoned fruit. And as for my pulling the trigger, there was the example of Medeiro Vaz.

"You filthy thing!" I yelled at him. And I called him dirty names. I wonder if I was insulting him in order to put off doing my duty? He did not answer. But his eyes were fastened on me: ah, he had two eyes, staring through the foliage. He was a pitiable creature, I assure you. But then I saw and recoiled from that something which constitutes the hatred of a leper! I took aim at the head that held those two eyes.

At that instant I heard hoof beats. I waited. I wouldn't want it said that I had shot the leper stealthily, to avoid being seen. Who was coming? In the clear light of early morning, I recognized him from a distance: Diadorim! I put away my pistol, for no reason. Was Diadorim pursuing me? "Look, Diadorim: are you looking for him?" I would ask, pointing to the hidden leper. "I am here, Riobaldo, looking for you," he would say. "Take heed, Riobaldo."

This imaginary conversation passed through my mind like a
live coal hissing in a pan of water. It made me tremble. Because, the very breath of my foolish notion bore the accusation: "You have the Renegade with you." I and he—the devil?
Then it struck me: could it be that he was really trying to take
charge of me? "Ah, that, never, never!" I growled, smiling. I
came alive in my saddle, like a dog springing up from a doze. I
could hear Diadorim coming closer. But I turned away and with
a shout spurred my mount; he responded with a leap and galloped forward full tilt.

"Ho, devil! Demon! Eh, demon! Devil!"

We rocketed straight ahead for almost a quarter of a league,
at breakneck speed. We three? That's what I thought. Then I
pulled up; my horse shook his mane. I looked all about, shading
my eyes with my hand. I did not see the devil. My spirit was in
fearful turmoil. How was I going to cope with this miasma that
seemed to have invaded me, pressing heavily on my stomach
and interfering with my breathing? I had to refuse it room.
Deny it. I would do it! Would I?

I looked back and saw that Diadorim had stopped near the
tree with the man in it. He had no doubt spied the creature,
and was puzzled about my mad flight. I gazed at him from that
distance. Stiffly upright in the saddle, he looked taller, and from
what I could see he sat unmoving. And the leper? Ah, he had
better look sharp, he had better flee, if he wanted to stay alive.
What did it matter that at that hour the birds were singing in
the newly awakened sertão? As long as a leper like that existed
in the world, even far away, everyone would be in danger of the
disease, for that man hated all mankind. From every indication,
that wreck of a man was accursed of the devil—his guilt
showed on his body! If not, why did he not rid himself of the
evil, or let the evil do away with him? He was dead already. No
matter what Diadorim might say: that that leper was my
brother, a fellow-being I would deny it. Knowing of the existence of a leper like that, how could I enjoy my love for Diadorim, for Otacília? And was I not the White Rattler? A chief's
function is not to reap praise but to redress wrongs. I turned
my horse and spurred him forward. "I do not belong to the

devil and I do not belong to God!" I thought savagely, as if I
had uttered the words; but the utterance would have had to be
spoken in two voices, one very different from the other. Now
my mind was made up. I took out my revolver once more. And
I told myself what Diadorim would no doubt say to me:
"Riobaldo, kill the poor fellow if you must, but at least do not
scorn him: rather, kill him with your own hand plunging in the
knife. You will see that under the rotten flesh, the blood that
spurts from his heart is healthy and warm." Should I drive the
point of my silver-handled knife in him? "Here, take that!
Now fall to the ground, you!" Galloping with these thoughts rac-
ing through my mind, I threw my revolver away. I threw it away
—or it may have been that the branch of a thorny bumelia
reached out and snatched it from my hand as I flew past. I rode
up and stopped short. My horse—so handsome he was—
stamped and pawed the ground; he gave a snort like a mule. I
saw Diadorim. But the leper had got away, thanks to my not
having seen him come out of the tree; he must have climbed
down fast and managed to scramble away in the brush. By this
time I was feeling completely fed up with the whole business;
perhaps it was because I did not know whether I would have
killed him or not, if he had been there—the leper, I mean.

In the face of Diadorim, halted there in front of me, a beauty
greater than I had ever seen shone forth, and of an altogether
different kind. His eyes—which seemed to grow under my gaze
—were of a green like no other, greener than any grassland.
And all of him seemed nimbused with goodness and kindness. I
swear to you, sir, that for one fleeting instant I saw in Diadorim's person the beauteous image of Our Lady of Abadia!

But I repulsed it all as a giddy vision. It was as though I were
separated from him by a deep valley, by the width of an enormous river in flood. How was it possible that I could love a man,
another being of my same nature, a male like myself in attire
and weapons, rough and ready in his actions? I frowned. Was
he to blame? Was I to blame? I was the Chief. The sertão has
neither windows nor doors. And this is the law: either you are
lucky and rule the sertão, or the accursed sertão rules you. Had
I rejected the vision?

I had to do something before Diadorim could open his mouth
to smile or speak to me. Half in anguish, half shrewdly, half
angrily—where did I get the idea, the gesture, and how did I remember what I did? I don't know. But I pushed my hand between my weapons and cartridge belts and the straps of my
knapsack, and opened wide my jacket and shirt. Then I took
hold of the cord with the scapulary of the Virgin—I finally had
to cut it for I couldn't break it—and threw the object to Diadorim who caught it in his hand. He started to say something
but I did not let him, for it was his voice that affected me the
most. So, I spoke first. "Let's go back—they're all waiting for
me!" I said at last. I was still breathing much too fast.

In this way I was giving an order, as was fitting. I was not
going to lower the barrier. For me, at that moment, a span
could become three fathoms. I pressed my knees, but my horse
did not even need that: as soon as I moved a foot he would take
off like the wind. Free at last! But instead of following me at
once, Diadorim rode away in the opposite direction. I pulled up
my Siruiz so I could take a look, as I was curious. Diadorim
was going along looking for the revolver which had fallen out of
my hand. In a quiet little corner of my heart, I silently thanked
his friendship for this kindness. Then I took off again, always
far ahead because my superb steed would not let the other horse
catch up. Then I started singing. Even though badly, I sang, for
I saw that by those long silences, Diadorim gained a stronger
hold on my affections, discussion of which was impossible.

When we arrived back at the camp it was to be confronted
by a strange new situation. With the Urucuians. You remember: those five taciturn fellows, backlanders from the headwaters country of the Urucúia. Those who had showed up with Zé
Bebelo, after floating down the Paracatú on a raft of burití palm
trunks. They were quiet, dependable, well-behaved, close-
mouthed men, and because of this, we had never given them
much thought. Now they wanted to talk to me alone, away from
the others. One Diodato was their leader. He stood in front of
the others and started the parley.

I liked those men. Their bravery went hand-in-hand with
great seriousness. People say that a Urucuian can charm fish

into taking the hook by talking to them. Nonsense, of course.
Just as they say that the dwellers on the plains of Goiás salt
their food with horse sweat. I don't know about that. A place
gets a reputation from the stories told about it; people, too. But
those five suited me fine. I was surprised to see that they were
still unmounted, and that they had bundles and blanket rolls
strapped on their backs as if they were setting out on a journey
on foot. Their taciturnity seemed to have grown. I listened to
what the head man, Diodato, had to say.

"Meaning no disrespect, Chief, we-uns have decided. . . .
We-uns is leaving. With your permission," the man said, just
like that, glum but serene. I took a good look at his features; a
face like his had to be studied in detail.

I understood what he said but asked him to repeat it. His
eyes were like those of a wooden image. He had a big, drooping
nose. His beard consisted of a few wisps of hair, like those on a
horse's chin.

The man did not scratch his head. He spoke firmly. They
wanted to leave, once and for all; they had to. They knew the
rule, all right: a jagunço may leave the band whenever he
wishes—he has only to declare his intention and return whatever belongs to the chief or employer. They did not return their
arms because they were their own, but as they had arrived on
foot, they were leaving the horses behind. They were taking a
few rations: a bit of manioc meal and jerky, and some rapadura
—barely enough for three days. Even so, I thought they were
crazy. It was madness for them to attempt to wander straight
out into the high wilderness and distant woods. Why were they
leaving, without even waiting for me to win my first fight?

"This is the way it is, Chief—we sort of feel the need to,
meaning no disrespect, sir, yessir," the man answered, very sincerely. I looked at the hat on his head: it was made of deerskin
with a floppy brim. His face had a trustworthy, prudent look, in
spite of being splotched with traces of some former disease that
looked like cashew juice stains.

"Your full name is Diodato what?" I inquired.

"Diodato the Nose—it's a nickname," he said, turning white
as he said it. I recognized that I had never paid the slightest at-

tention to those men and what they were worth. They had been baptized Pantaleão, Salústio João, João Tatu, and O-Bispo. Only at that hour did I become aware of them. I never heard of them again after that. Now I'm sorry. At the moment, I was trying to find a way to hold them. I questioned them further. Where were they from?

"From different creeks—from Buriti-Comprido, Tamboril, Cambaúba, Virgens, Mata-Cachorro, the Cobras. From beyond Barra-da-Vaca, Arinos." They are all in the sertão, those places. And what good was it for me to know where they lived? What I wanted to find out was where they fell in with Zé Bebelo, when he was returning from Goiás.

"Ah, yessir, way up there—on some farms on the São Marcos River, yessir, on the Esparramado, on the fazenda of Dona Mogiana." Were they her henchmen? They were. They had been. But only as farm hands. What crimes had they committed to start off their careers? Did they pay off well? And why had they joined up with Zé Bebelo? I wanted to ask them these things, but instead, I suddenly said:

"Just why is it that you have become disheartened about staying on with the rest of us?" As soon as I had spoken I regretted it, for when negotiating it is a mistake to ask questions or to brag. But the man Diodato was stumped by my question, and hesitated a long time, ill-at-ease and snuffling. He had no agreement with me but neither did he want to offend me without reason. He finally looked at his companions, who nodded their heads slowly in a silly sort of way so that you couldn't tell whether they were for or against his unspoken query to them, a habit common to people of their kind.

"Well, sir, yessir," he spoke at last, "before it was different— we lost our understanding." He was almost shamefaced.

I said: "What do you mean?"

"Don't you see, Chief, with all respect, things have changed. We came with Siu Zé Bebel'. Then, when he left, we lost our understanding."

"You mean, what Zé Bebelo told you when he enlisted you?"

"That's it. When he enlisted us, yessir."

"Did he promise you benefits?"

"Not exactly. He sent for us. He talked mixed-up. Then we came with him."

"And just what did he say?"

"We don't know any more, now. He talked very reasonable— he talked very reasonable. Now, begging your pardon, we have forgotten, we have lost our understanding. But he talked very reasonable."

"Well, then, why didn't you leave right away with Zé Bebelo, when Zé Bebelo left?" I asked irritatedly.

"It was none of our business. We're not complaining—we're not complaining."

I studied him and saw what I had already sensed. That man was pulling out because he had noticed something which made him suspicious of me. Those other men, straight out of the backlands and the woods, sniffing with their wide nostrils like dogs: what did they think about me? I thought for a moment: ah! To size up their misgivings, I would put them to a test. Suddenly and unexpectedly, I said in a loud voice:

"Praise be the name of Our Lord Jesus Christ!"

You should have seen the start it gave him, how he stared at me, not believing his own ears, and what a long time he took to answer, in a low voice: "Forever. Amen."

With that I dismissed them, they could leave.

But no. That was silly. If in fact he had found it strange, it was only because of the tone of my voice. If it was because of my voice, then it was because in my eagerness to utter the sacred name with complete sincerity, I had mumbled—nervousness, you know.

Well, they were leaving, as I had given up trying to hold them longer. In the circumstances, what good would they be to me? A fighter's contract of courage is not made with a bailiff's staff, nor with gifts and offers. Besides, those men were not mine; they were Zé Bebelo's.

Life is a motley confusion. Write it in your notebook, sir: seven pages. Those Urucuians were not going to look for Zé Bebelo. They were returning to their neck of the woods. You can plant a patch of manioc anywhere; and if you cut down and burn some woods and clear a bit of ground, you can plant corn and beans, too. They left; I let them take their horses. I also divided up some money among them, which made their eyes open wide with pleasure—money is always a friend in need. If I had insisted on holding them, then they could only have served me disloyally. They were men so different from me, so set in their ways, that—well, to tell you what I thought: that I should have asked them to remember me constantly in their prayers. Was it some sort of augury, their deserting me that way? I don't know. How can I tell? I had faith in myself alone. The only thing I can swear to, that I know, is that a toucan has a craw!

I wondered if I should have asked them to. On the road, in the days ahead, I wavered between wanting and not wanting them to pray for me, by request and for pay. Good, simple prayers of others would help me the most—little Ave Marias and novenas. They would be like the message which Diadorim had sent my Otacília by the driver of a pack train. I struggled to settle my mind at rest on this point, and then I myself would unsettle it. Sometimes I thought the best prayers would be those I knew nothing about, offered up by people far away. I remembered a man I knew when I was a boy, from the other side of the river. He had a prayer that was so mixed-up and obscure that I don't think even a priest could understand it, or would sanction it. Well, it would suit me fine. Or the woman who gave birth to her baby back there on the floor of that hovel; she owed me her gratitude—well, then, couldn't she send God a little prayer on my behalf? "What if the pack driver just keeps on going after he reaches Santa Catarina?" I asked Diadorim. I wanted his opinion. I wanted to think about that in the afternoons, during halts. Sitting down. But soon that quiet peace would leave me. Can a cowboy lasso the air? I went around and around, struggling against my aid-giver. Today I know, and I know why. I am satisfied my mind was sound. It was only that I was lost in a maze. Much later I came to understand more than my eyes took in, after the horrifying events that I am going to tell you about. Only afterward, when it was all over. It was then I put an end to these queer imaginings.

What did Diadorim say in reply to a question I had not asked? "Great courage, Riobaldo. One must be very brave." Ah,

I knew that. To talk of courage to me! Who could outdo me in that, who could withstand my presence, like a towering mountain? We were going forward together, Diadorim and I, we two. Only if their courage is very great, can men walk hand-in-hand with one another. It seemed as if we two had been riding side by side all our lives. Courage is what makes the heart beat; without it, the beat is not true.

There was only the sun, in all its brightness. It made the world as clean as shimmering water. The sertão was made to be like that always: bright and happy! We kept moving. Desolate lands, abandoned by their owners, reddish plains. There was a new road there. A cattle trail.

Then I hit on my plan.

I'll tell you how it was: pleasure itself makes you light-headed, giddy. Because living is a dangerous business. Diadorim's face was fresh and his mouth lovely, but his pride revealed a trace of unhappiness. Was it because I had felt myself disconcerted, and for that reason unhappy, too? I was already in my glory. Nor did Diadorim have any doubts about the route I was following, or that my purpose was to meet up with Hermóg- enes. At this time we were descending some sandy, rocky slopes with chasms on either side, and so steep that there was danger of our saddle straps breaking. In working their way down hill, the horses almost sat on their rumps, stretching their necks far out at the same time. And piles of rocks rolled down the sides. It made me laugh. Diadorim believed all the more in my determination to go after Hermógenes. These steep grades were delaying me. Afterwards, I would be in a great hurry.

Now I want you to know what my plan was: I was going to cross the Sussuarão Desert!

Even now the thought of it amazes me. What was driving me? Now that I am old I see it: when I think it over, when I recol- lect, I recognize that at that time I was acting rashly, vain- gloriously. God let me. God is persistent but in no hurry. The sertão is His. Whatever you want to know, I'll tell you, because you are thinking a lot out loud. About the devil? Whether he is like an owl that flies, from silence to silence, catching rats which it carries off in its curved claws? I thought of nothing like that; how could I? I had just one idea, which occupied every minute of my thinking: to cross the Sussuarão Desert. I was going to do it. As we went along, I became highly elated.

As we took another way around, by-passing Vespê and Bambual-do-Boi, none of my men got an inkling of my purpose. They were going to be astounded. Some began to wonder why we were where we were. Barely five leagues away, behind the mountains, lay the boundless enormous raso. We kept the Vão-do-Ôco and Vão-do-Cúio on our left: two precipitous valleys big enough to hold the ocean, with great forests growing on their sides. The river that flows way down at the bottom is hidden by black trees, so old that their branches have matted together. This is called a vão. And I would caution you, sir, against going exploring in one of these valleys, even if there should be good trails on the woody slopes among the clumps of tree ferns. It is a sure thing that at the bottom there are jaguars that go there to whelp and raise their young in dens; and tapirs that live there permanently, safe from hunters' guns. But the real reason is because of the malaria—the worst kind. The fever there in the hollow is really bad. You catch the tertian malaria, the malignant variety, and you can be dead inside of a week.

I was giving no thought to my fate. It was Diadorim, in the shadow of love, who asked me:

"Riobaldo, do you believe that a thing badly begun can some day have a happy ending?"

Somewhat nettled, I retorted:

"Brother, oh brother, I don't recognize you! Am I not the White Rattler? In this that I am doing most of all!"

Diadorim fell silent, and withdrew into his fine self. To my sorrow, I did not know that we were at cross purposes. Today I know it; that is, I suffered for it. I thought his was an odd remark, brought on by misgivings. Here he was wanting to tell me everything and I, too hot-headed to catch on. Man, I don't know. Life has no rhyme or reason.

What I thought at the time was that Diadorim was reminding me that Medeiro Vaz had not succeeded in crossing the desert. But, if so, Diadorim did not fathom my spirit, either, for it was for that very reason that I wanted to do it. To win a victory like no other had ever won! My imagination was on fire. Not I, but my pride, was daring the impossible.

The shadows of approaching darkness fell and rose. We called a halt beside a small stream leading out of a marsh, in a little grove of burití palms. We lighted a fire. I slept poorly, hugging my secret. The first part of my sleep was sound, but the rest was in fits and starts. A pleasurable excitement burned inside me, a satisfying anticipation, as on the eve of a jamboree.

Daybreak found me wide awake.

Ahead of us lay the mangabeira forest. Then, the Sussuarão Desert—at least fifty leagues deep and almost thirty wide. No one could make me turn back from there, beaten. Furthermore, I was not undertaking this aimlessly, but for a very good reason. Was it on account of Hermógenes? Our two bands were at war, marching and countermarching throughout the gerais, like dogs looking for each other. The only trouble was the sertão was too big a hiding place. Therefore, I would cross the desert and attack his fazenda, where his family was. An egg is something that can be smashed. Thoroughly, too. To conquer, you must give no thought to the enemy, just do what you have to do. I was turning my back on the snake and going after its nest. Had that not been Medeiro Vaz's own bold plan?

The day was glorious, exuding sunlight; the wind was still. I saw the ground change in color to gray, and the lizards scurrying lightly under the cuculucage bushes. Wouldn't my men be feeling uneasy? I saw an owl—but just a little burrowing owl; an owl is a bad omen only in the middle of the night, when it starts to hoot. I spat on the milk-white trunk of a maria-brava tree which was in full and fragrant flower. The hour had struck. I pulled up to a quick stop. I called to my men.

"Here, boys. Over here."

Men under my command! With a certain amount of confusion, they all gathered around me to find out what was up. I told them. Did they understand me? Lined up, their faces all had the same expression. Would they follow me? Ah, not one looked as I had thought he would, and as I had for so many days been anticipating. Neither João Goanhá, Marcelino Pampa, João Concliz, nor even Alaripe. Not even Diadorim. Diadorim looked at me, his eyes glistening with courage, with willingness. Yes, he would. But the others? Were they taking the measure of my madness? Thinking I had gone stark crazy?

Because not even Medeiro Vaz himself would have believed what I was demanding. I wanted everything: to invade that treacherous raso, its baked ground, its empty, ghostly waste, without preparations of any kind, neither pack animals loaded with provisions, nor steers for food, nor leather water bags filled to overflowing, nor a herd of donkeys to carry them. Why did I need so much impedimenta? Well, didn't the old-timers themselves know that the day would come when you could lie in your hammock or bed, and the hoes would go out alone to chop weeds, and the scythes to reap by themselves, and the cart to fetch the harvest—that everything that is not man himself belongs to him and is subject to his will? I did not think that— but in my heart I felt it. I was not on the side of security: I was on the side of fate! I did not even send a scout patrol— not even Suzarte, Nelson or Quipes—to feel out the way; nor Tipote as tracker, to read the signs, and see what he could find that might be helpful, some unlikely water hole, perhaps.

If each had pride in his courage, they would all follow me. "We are going to start now, and halt for the night in there," I decided. It was just a matter of getting going. But as soon as the boy Guirigó heard me, he said:

"You mean me, too?"

He was just a boy, after all. Should I not send someone to take Guirigó back and leave him in some safe place? I did not. Why had he come along, if not to share in everything? If the others should not obey me, would I have to turn back, give up my intention? Never. I would go it alone. I would go, even if it meant leaving my bones bleaching there. For an agonizing moment I waited for their answer. Then I gave the command to start! My men. Ah, a jagunço does not ignore one who gives mad orders.

"If my day is tomorrow, I won't see the day after."

"Before a child is born, the hour of his death is fixed."

"When your appointed day arrives, you won't live past midnight."

They were all saying things like that, backing up the group leaders. They were brave and were taking heart. We journeyed as usual until we came to the end of the grass. There we halted, face to face with the Desert. We picked up our reins. We began to move.

The sun was glorious. I thought about Otacília; I thought about her as if I were sending her a kiss. Slackening the reins, I rode into the horizons. I entered the gray sand; everyone followed me. The horses moved slowly ahead, as through the sea.

And so we went. I in front, upheld by the strong arms of angels. Or the Whoosis? With every step the others profited from a share of my wild courage. We pushed our way across the desert, the harsh desert. We went across it, we did, and I can't say it was too difficult. At least, that time it could not have been. Sorcery? Everything conspired to help us, and we even shortened the distance. The stars shone as though they were on fire. In nine days we got across. Everybody; everybody, that is, but one. I'll tell you about that.

How did it happen the desert was not so terrible? Was it through grace that we found everything we needed, without having to search for it even though we traveled an unknown route? From good to better, without major hardships, without getting lost. What was it like there inside the Sussuarão Desert? It was an ugly world, exaggerated in all its features. The ground was bare except for a tuft of dry grass here and there, and it stretched before us as far as our eyes could reach and beyond. It contained everything. There were hard, flat stretches of blue rock against which the horses' hoofs struck sparks. Then, soft, ash-like sand overlying the rock. And even gullies and hillocks. We were fully exposed to the hot sun, but with the good fortune that was ours, the sky clouded over, and this brought us relief and cooler weather. There were some strange places, too, where there were ticks. I wonder what they found to suck for their meagre livelihood? Yes, and we found wild cattle, that had either run away and grown accustomed to the place, or couldn't find their way out of it; at any rate, they were living there and we killed some as we would deer. And we killed two deer also— somehow they had managed to get fat. I heard the hum of bees all the time. The presence of spiders, ants and the wild bees proved there were flowers, too.

All in all, we did not suffer too much from thirst. Because suddenly, as if conjured out of the air, we would come upon oases. And, though you nor anyone else will hardly believe it, oases with plants.

We had adopted a rule, without really knowing whose idea it was in the first place. This was to break up into small groups and travel at a distance from one another, and when one spotted anything unusual, they could give a signal calling everybody together to share the good news.

And the plants were not just rough grass, or the fearful monk's-head cactus, as hairy as a dead possum. Nor the spiny pilocereus, with its snakelike arms, which burst into white flower when the rains come. Nor black cactus, blue cactus, or hedgehog cactus. Ah, no. The horses were treading on low-growing quipá and nettles, but then came the blue-flowered treebine and the yellow sertaneja-assim and maria-zipe, dripping dew, and sinhàzinha whose delicate flowers are so laden with dew they seem about to wither. And herbage. And berry-covered bumelias.

And—we found water. Not just water caught and held in the leaves of gravatá, but water suitable for the horses in a hole in the bed of a dry creek. We rejoiced. There were even some marshy spots, lacking only burití palms. And a muddy pool, whose water was a joy to contemplate, because around its edges —would you believe it?—you could witness the courage of trees, forest trees. Though not very tall, there were simaroubas, laurels, pau-amarante, pombo, and a fig: the gameleira-branca! As we used to sing:

> *For shade, give me a gameleira,*
> *On the bank of a lazy stream* . . .

Thus we found everything; moreover, without great difficulties or disappointments. The respect in which my men held me kept growing. My jagunços, the Riobaldos, the breed of the White Rattler! Forward! But, then, a thought, which came to me only fleetingly now, hit me once more. You know the one I mean. The one it mortifies me to mention so often—the devil! For all the help he had given me, was he going to make me pay in kind? "Don't worry, I'll find a way out in the end," I said to myself. A sad mistake. What I had not remembered or did not know was that his game was just that: to let you go along, little by little, getting in deeper and forgetting.

Just about that time, Diadorim came to me to make up. It grieves me how well I remember. Diadorim, in all his beauty.

"Listen, Riobaldo: let us fall in step with each other again," he said; and he trembled, not out of fear but because of love— today I know it.

"Riobaldo, the hour of our revenge is approaching. Afterward, when everything has been repaid and settled, there is something, a secret, I am going to tell you."

There was love in every word he spoke. I heard him. I heard him, but in vain. I was far from myself and from him. I didn't listen to half of the rest he said. I only know that, although the sun shone all around us, it seemed more like a bright night. It was the way I felt. But in the brilliant sunshine, I was watching something: a little donkey that had turned wild and lived in the scrub, browsing among the nettles.

Did I not have more important matters to attend to? Like Zé Bebelo—whom I recalled at the moment—when he was angry or when he wanted to instill fear in everyone, he would shout: "North of Minas! North of Minas!" And he was right. But Zé Bebelo was a planner. I—I always followed my hunches, using all help that came my way, but always on my guard against the Malign One. His tricks are always new, and so numerous they are like grains of sand in a sand pit. How well I knew it!

I was thinking about that when the fellow snarled at me. Who he was, I'll tell you: he was a barrel-chested, irascible, brown man, from I don't know where. Is there a race of people like that?

Fortunately, I was in full possession of all my faculties. "I'll pay no attention to it," I said; that is, I said it to myself. I did not want to make anything of it, because it smelled of the What-You-May-Call-Him—one of his maneuvers. "Peace," I

said, I said to myself. "I'll pay no attention to it," I promised myself. I was being very wily, keeping all my wits about me, as
though walking on a tightrope. All that went through my mind
in a flash. But I sensed everything that was coming to a head,
as a horse senses the rush of a furious steer.

Then I heard his voice. It quavered nervously, like that of a
young goat; the way he screamed, demanding a fight. Poor
devil. I looked at him.

I already knew who the man was; his name was Treciziano.
A brute; to talk to him you had to use a club. I knew it. It
was not surprising that I suspected the devil. This Treciziano
fellow was very short-tempered; or could it be that he was suffering from thirst more than the others—his nostrils were quiv-
ering—and had gone out of his head? They say he used to get
headaches, and suffered from rashes and ringworm. He was talking and railing at me, and shouted an insult. The man was like
crazy, his eyes burning. I, as I have said, was in complete control of myself. I reflected slowly, like a donkey. My first impulse
was to tolerate him, because the devil was not powerful enough
to order me about and make me angry. I had only to exercise
calmness and tact; then, avoiding a fatal fight, I would give the
rebellious Treciziano fair warning in strong words, reprehend-
ing him by virtue of my authority, but without sticks and stones.
This was one time the devil was not going to catch me.

But some things are easier said than done. You should have
seen what happened, what took place. What I saw. When you
suffer thirst, you swell up, your eyesight goes bad, you can even
go blind. But I saw it. In a flash. Almost absent-mindedly, in half
a second, a person loses his good sense for ten years. I saw him
—the hat brim that would not stay up, the dagger sticking far
out of his belt, the horrendous, altered face. It was the devil,
there in front of me. The Devil! He made an ugly face that
glowed, I know. It was the Devil, mocking me in person!

He came straight at me, trying to ride me down. The devil?
His rush was like that of a wild bull. I rose in my stirrups. "Eh-
hey!" He flashed his knife, sharp as a razor, and screaming with
hate, leaned far forward and made a lunge at me. I grappled
with him. The point of his knife, through some twist, got stuck

for a second in my belt and bandolier. Quick as lightning, I
caught him under the chin with my large bone-handled knife
and ran the sharp edge from ear to ear; the steel grated against
bone, there was a loud whistle from his severed windpipe, and
the blood spurted up in a high arc. He fell from his horse, his
hard eyes blank even before he hit the ground. He died accursed, he died with his gullet gurgling in his throat.

And what did I see? Blood on my knife—shining bright like
satiny varnish. And he: he was lying among the thorns of a
torch thistle, such as he himself had been. But no one ever saw
the devil dead! The body lying there was really that of Treciziano!

His death was deserved. And did it occur because it had to?
Yes, it did, and therefore the devil does not exist! Schemes,
traps. From then on, I never wanted to think of him. Nor of poor
Treciziano, lying there with his throat cut, whom I had . . .
A freezing chill swept over me. I suffered agonies to think that
one's hand is capable of action before thought has time to inter-
vene.

Everyone showered compliments and words of praise on me
because my victory had been won hand-to-hand. If it had been
by shooting, they would not have admired me as much, my
fame with the trigger being what it was; but I had triumphed by
the knife! And from the other group, far off but the closest to us,
on the left-hand side, one of the men who had heard or seen,
came over. It was Jiribibe, young Jiribibe, on a galloping black
horse. Diadorim had fired a shot into the air; from nervousness.
Soon they would all learn about the dead man's mad act. The
gash in his throat had widened: the skin across the upper edge
had receded, and at the lower edge it had fallen away almost to
his nipples, forming a gaping hole of raw flesh.

Then Alaripe exclaimed: "From what I know, this fellow was
from Serra d'Umã." Some were already examining his body—he
did not have a hair on his chest. They wanted to relieve him of
anything of value. Someone said he had a silver trinket, and the
spurs were excellent, of good metal.

I was not upset. The death of that ruffian had been tantamount to suicide. "The way he died—did he go to hell?" the boy

Guirigó asked earnestly. After all, what did I have to do with it, that everyone should praise me? To be sure I was responsible for it, that I know, but tell me, my dear sir, what about the hour, the moment, in which it occurred? The blind man Borromeu began a nasal chanting of tierces and responses. A blind person's fear is not real fear. Diadorim looked at me—as if I were beyond the moon. Only then did I see the blood—the fetid red smears on my clothing. I wiped most of the thick alien blood off my chin; would I, who detested blood, leave the rest as a sign? Never; the mere thought of it filled me with horror. Blood—blood is something that should remain in the viscera, something never to be seen. Perhaps because of this the glory of the consecrated wafer of God is immensely greater when hidden in its immaculate whiteness within the golden pyx—the thing I venerate most.

The body—we would leave it there to the desert air. We quit the place fast and pushed ahead. Traveling along, I gave my spirit its head. Hallelujah!

As I said, that Treciziano had only fulfilled his destiny with his unhappy end as a madman, for we had not gone three leagues when we started moving out of the desert. Almost as if it had been pin-pointed, we came upon a little meadow and the spur of a sierra; of tablelands, I mean. I dismounted and set foot on the blessed soil. We were within sight of the crondeúba plains of Bahia.

Farther on I stopped, peaceably, at the hut of a solitary settler, to ask for a drink of water. He informed us that for ten leagues all about, everything was quiet. We kept going. Earlier, we had crossed the Alto-Carinhanha—where the Devil King paints his face black. We were getting closer to the spot we longed to reach. Another day and a half—just following this route which we had soon learned was the right one—and we would be at the gates of the Hermógenes clan! At this rate we would get there just before dawn, and take them by surprise in a sudden assault, for at that hour Hermógenes was far away, following my old tracks, little dreaming of our daring feat. Here was my counterthrust. Ah, a bird that flies away leaves the nest unguarded.

We had not a minute to lose, for we did not want news of us to get there first. We did not take a single day's rest. Trotting and jogging, we covered a great distance, and by daybreak we had reached our goal. We spread out and surrounded the place, communicating with each other by means of our signals, which were the cry of the acauã hawk and the whistle of a monkey, for there were bound to be sentinels posted, henchmen with carbines. We waited for the first streak of light and the start of a fearsome morning. As was our practice. Then we opened fire.

Ugly things make an ugly story. I know. Because of that, I will not go into all the details. At the end, you can fill them in yourself. But, we had gone a long time without a fight, and we were itching for a free-for-all, with no holds barred.

The fazenda house was a big squarish whitewashed one, sitting on the top of a hillock; there was something odd about its appearance, it seemed crooked, somehow. We went in with all guns blazing—screaming and yelling!

The men who were there were second-rate—they melted under the feet of my host. It was a complete rout! As their wings were already broken, they made no attempt at resistance; I heard only a few shots from them. Some of us burst into the house, plunging, erupting, stumbling through, wreaking havoc like a hurricane. I will refrain from telling you what I did. Did they not all do the same? Coming back out, I was afraid Diadorim would not approve of me; but Diadorim with his own weapons was sharing in the action that went on outside: the killing and destruction of humans and animals—even the tame steers that were licking the dew, even the thin pigs at the edge of the sty.

Evil was king. May God remove it from me, may God redeem me. Once and for all.

Next, we set fire to the house, with dead in every corner. It made a huge blaze; it burned up completely, like a stick of white umburana. We left the place when the fire died down, in the early afternoon. And the following morning we camped at the edge of some quiet water. We were dog-tired and asleep on our feet. But there in our midst, brought with us as prisoner, was the woman we had sought so avidly: Hermógenes's legal wife.

The woman was hard as flint, scornful of whatever might be her fate. She had on a threadbare, faded black dress. When the black cloth which she had wound around her head fell off, being bareheaded did not matter to her. They told her she could sit down, and she sat. She showed no sign of agitation. She must have been pretty in the flower of her youth; she still was. The men gave her some food, and she ate. Something to drink, and she drank. She gave brief answers to two or three questions, and after speaking, she closed her mouth tight, pressing together her straight, thin lips. She spoke almost in a hiss. I don't figure that she chewed tobacco or smoked a pipe, but nevertheless she spat on the ground about her, and did not dry it with her foot, as is the custom. I noticed she was barefooted, probably not out of habit but because of the hour and confusion at the time of her capture. A pair of sandals was found for her. She knew that she did not belong with us. She met my gaze steadily, coldly, resigned in her quiet hatred. If she could, she would have scratched me to death with even her toenails. She wrapped her face in a green shawl; a very pale green. But her image had already fixed itself on my mind; her eyes would remain in my memory. Her fine, pale face was thin, but her eyes were different from all others: suddenly black and hard, dark pools drained of all sweet waters. Her mouth seemed to bear the marks of old sufferings. I never learned her name.

She did not say a word to me, nor I to her. I felt uneasy lest I might even come to take a liking for her as a female. I was half afraid that I would feel a twinge of pity; certainly I did not fear giving her cause for curses. It would have been much better if we had not had to bring her with us. That is what being a chief is, sometimes: you have to carry snakes in your bag without a right to kill them. She remained muffled up like that, her face hidden, her hands open, palms upward, as if to show she had no hidden knife, or because she was begging alms of God. I remember that woman, as I remember my own past sufferings—she, whom we went to Bahia to get.

We did not let the grass grow under our feet, but kept on the move—extorting sums of money as we went, under the jagunço system, but without plundering or killing. I ruled with a hard hand and high spirits. I showed myself in Jalapão, and in all those other gerais. Those districts which in former days had been the domain of the ruffian Volta-Grande. Afterwards, we wandered down into Goiás itself, with its many deserts and poverty-stricken little people. Through the distant lands we went, always by-passing the large towns, for which I held a blind hatred, though I had never been in them. Hatred—because I had not been born and raised in them. I journeyed full of lust. I became tigerish, really a White Rattler.

The only things that sustained me, that touched my heart, were certain memories and incidents, though fleeting and few in number. The songs of Siruiz; Bigrí, my mother, chiding me; the fruit of buriti palms, hanging in bunches; Diadorim; the sprightliness of that gallant little wading bird, the red-legged stilt; the image of Our Lady of Abadia; the small children, more naked than little angels, tagging after their mothers on their way to fetch water at the beach of the São Francisco River, with pots on their heads and no time for big sorrows; and my Otacília.

From this silken string of recollections, I think I panned another kind of goodness. I own that on these occasions I must also have wanted the caresses of that girl, Nhorinhá, again. I wonder why, then, I did not seek her out? Ahead in the vastness lay the direction in which she now lived. Had I known it, I would have hastened to her. But I did not know it then, and we turned away. What my eyes don't see today may be what I will have to suffer the day after tomorrow.

While we were traveling through that desolate country, I began, little by little, to train those backlanders—you remember the ones I mean—in the handling of weapons for hard fighting. They were already showing promise—a mule balks only at the start. I gave my approval when I saw their head man, Teofrásio, point his ancient pistol, both triggers cocked, at a harmless old rascal, but I did not allow him to shoot. Would Zé Bebelo have consented to excesses of that kind? The one who still remembered Zé Bebelo was I, in my wisest hours. If he were still alive, he would surely have had news of what I was doing: that we had the Woman with us, and that with her in our hands, Hermógenes would be forced to give combat.

The woman, astride her horse, remained sunk in silence, her face out of sight behind the green shawl. They had given her an ouricurí palm hat, to fend off the hot Bahian sun. She made no demand or complaint—not a word of any kind. What I could not understand about her was her ferociously quiet calm, her dogged patience. If it was hate alone that gave her this self-control, then hate was a good thing, in the sense that sometimes it is like a hope fulfilled. God deliver me from it!

But the man at whom the backlander Teofrásio had aimed his antiquated weapon, was an old fellow. As I say, I saved his life. He lived in a tiny community, in a solitary shack in a thicket of sempreviva-serrã under the bright leaves of pindoba palms.

I and some of the others had climbed to the top of the hill, where the wind blew in all directions. There my mind could reach out to many horizons. Fifteen leagues to one side was São Josèzinho da Serra, a flourishing place, where Nhorinhá, the daughter of Ana Duzuza, was now living. It was something I did not know at the time, as I said. Afterwards, afterwards. I had not yet received her letter. For me, she was just a longing to be treasured. That's what I think nowadays. Nhorinhá, coquettish, who received all men, was over there; she was pretty, her skin was fair, her eyes so much her own . . . And the men, disputing among themselves, liked to enjoy that something better than innocence. If she was worthless, how could she be of value to so many men?

But, in coming down from the top of the hill—the Tebá, I mean, the Morro dos Ofícios—coming down, we ran into the old man at the door of his hovel. He was a half-crazy type, who talked of the old days under the Good Emperor. He was a Bahian, a Bahian-Goianian, with a beard like piassava palm fiber. He was so poor he didn't have three ears of corn in his corncrib. He was an albino mulatto, sort of. His beard was like dirty grass, and his hair a windstorm. I asked him something, which he pretended not to understand, and the backlander, Teofrásio, wanting to show what a tough jagunço he was, the backlander Teofrásio, roared and jabbed his big old pistol against the man's chest. But he didn't press the trigger. The old man was forbearance itself. The patience of old men is admirable. He talked with me. About what he had learned in his long life. My God, how well that man knew all the practical things of everyday existence, about planting, the forest, everything. But now that he had this fund of knowledge, the infirmities of age had robbed him of the ability to work, and even what he had learned had become out-dated. As he spoke, he squinted his half-closed eyes.

Was he an old fraud? I don't think so. The reason I am telling you about him is because of the strange impression the old fellow made on me. For weapons he had only a small knife, a blunt machete, and a kind of blackjack. This was a club partially hollowed out and refilled with lead—you could kill with it. He limped badly—half of his left foot was missing. It had been amputated because of a snake bite—probably a rattler. Gaining confidence as he talked, he asked me for a good, big handful of salt, and also accepted a chunk of jerky. His ordinary diet consisted of iguanas or possums, which he managed to kill by throwing his club at them. He addressed me as "Big Bandit Chief."

At the end, to show his gratitude, he told me, very confidentially, that he knew for sure about a lot of money, a huge amount, buried deep in the ruins of an abandoned fazenda house. I was to go there, he said, and dig up this well-deserved fortune, for my companions and me. "Where is it, which way?" I asked, to please him. He winked toward the forest. Over that way, thirty-five leagues, at Riacho-das-Almas. Nonsense. Was I going to strike out and start plodding through forests and the trails across the scrublands, just to fall in with an old man's madness? There was no time, with the war I had on my hands. And besides, if he knew about it and it was true, why didn't he go and dig up the gold for himself? I laughed at him to myself. Why does one give advice to others? Chickens like to pick their own place to dust their feathers.

And the old man showed by the way he looked at me and acted, that he was not entirely easy in his mind about me. But— what was it? What was it? I had to find out. And, because it doesn't do for a chief to let others see that he is anxious and un- certain about something, I had to make my inquiry sound casual, almost joking: "Old brother, were you born here, or where are you from? Do you really think the sertão is good?"

He answered me stupid-like, but he answered well:

"The sertão is neither mean nor kind, son; it takes away or gives, it pleases or embitters you, according as you treat it."

He answered in a deranged sort of way, as if he were about to attack me, pointing his finger at my chest. Had he taken offence at my banter? I could not figure out his meaning, plumb his thoughts. But we abandoned the place quickly because the old man blew his nose with his hand in a way that made me sick. We sauntered down the rest of the hill. When we got back to camp, the branches of the trees were darkening with the dust of nightfall.

Does what I know today derive any values from the past? Be- cause, the old man's treasure could have served me as a motive. If I had wanted to go to Riacho-das-Almas, thirty-five leagues away for a look the road passed by São Josèzinho da Serra, a pleasant place, where Nhorinhá was living. A second time with Nhorinhá, I know full well, and my life would have flowed like a stream between other hills, seeking a different outlet. I would have married Nhorinhá, happy as the sky is blue, and moved over there. I think about it many times. What if at a certain moment the road had changed—what if what had happened had not happened? What would my life have been like? Memo- ries without foundation. The past is bones around an owl's nest. From what I say to you, don't misunderstand me. I am happily married—my loving friendship for my kind-hearted wife is pure gold. But—if I had stayed behind in São Josèzinho, and had given up the leadership of the outfit in which I was the White Rattler, how many terrible things the wind clouds would have had to scatter, to keep them from happening! Possible is that which is—possible that which was. The sertão does not call anyone openly, but hides and beckons. But the sertão may suddenly quake beneath one's feet—and even that is possible which was not. What I was saying was because I was really thinking about Nhorinhá. It always hurts to remember now and then any love which might have been, but which one day we spurned. But, like the jagunços that we were, we pressed on, with a string of good new horses for remounts. Over the flat sandy gerais, full of nothing. Over the dead brown sands, without wind-breaking sierras.

We kept moving west, probing our way, riding slowly over the purple plain, an endless tableland. There were only handfuls of grass here and there, sparse and thin. The good thing was that now when anyone sighted our wild column, they were people from far away who did not know the woman and who no longer said: "She is the wife of a certain Hermógenes, whom they are taking to a dungeon."

She herself caused no trouble; the Woman in the green shawl. A woman for whom there was no salvation—that is, she was going to the death of a man, to witness his doom. I was afraid she might get sick. I gave orders that she was to be well treated. I ruled out brutalities in the villages, ordering that no one was to be molested without due cause. Such things would not add to my glory, and I was working for a great purpose. Disorders—assaults and fights—did not tempt me. I had no time for these and other jagunço misdeeds, nor for idle talk. Not because of softness or lack of manhood; ah, no, because during the entire period of my leadership, and even before, I endured every type of hardship. I take that back: I found the cold hard to bear. When there was frost, I slept between two bonfires. Cold weather does not agree with a jagunço. Even as we went along, there on the high tablelands, we loaded up with stalks of canela-de-ema, a good kindling. After daybreak, I would drink jurema tea, which I had saved, and it put new life in me. After that I found it easier to stand the early morning cold. Unlike Diadorim, it had been a long time since I had put a razor to my face. My beard shone big and black, and conferred on me a certain presence, as I could see for myself in the water, whenever my horse Siruiz leaned down to drink from some little stream.

Because of their urgent need for women my men were wanting to bring some along—any they could catch by the roadside
—and they came to me, with much beating around the bush. I
put my foot down on any such idea: we were not yet at the
point where we could indulge ourselves. Furthermore, as there
would not be a woman for every man, their presence would upset our routine and give rise to dissension and strife. What we
did catch and take along, though, was every good horse we
could find. We also had fifty some head of Bahian cattle. There
was no problem with them when we were crossing grassy plains.
Later, it got worse. But other things got better. Seek for your
share of happiness, for even in the solitary sertão it can be
found.

Speaking of women, I'll give you an example. When you are
riding steadily, after awhile the warm saddle begins to speak of
love-making. I was going along at a good clip across the wide
tableland, my mind occupied with pleasant thoughts. The air
there is restful. The Hermógenes were far away. And no platoon
of soldiers would ever come searching for us here. Tranquillity
breeds desires. I was not in favor of wasting time, but I
wanted some simple enjoyment, in a town where there was a
cattle fair in full swing. I wanted to hear a good guitar, and the
stamp of dancing feet. But, at bottom, what I needed was
woman's flesh. So I eased my rule, and passed out instructions
that everybody could amuse himself with women who were
willing, but not to leave them empty-handed, nor commit
atrocities against the women's fathers, brothers, and husbands,
provided the latter behaved sensibly. That was my law. Why
destroy wantonly, for no reason, the life of a healthy working-
man? Zé Bebelo would have done the same. And now I ask:
Where was the devil then, with his persecution? I must say
again that I wanted the delights of a woman, to pleasure a few
hours of life. But I was choosy—I demanded a voluptuous body
and a merry face. The ones I detested were inexperienced girls,
as green as the day they were born, and ugly, housewifely
matrons. But just then, I heard about Verde-Alecrim. I broke
into a gallop and headed my horse that way.

My guide was a young fellow, a Goianian cowboy from the

Uruú. He gave me the details: Verde-Alecrim was only a tiny village, seven houses set among century plants, alongside a clear little stream. Half a dozen of them were just wattle and mud huts, thatched with grass. But there was one large house, with a porch, and isinglass window panes. The house was white-washed and had a real tile roof. It belonged to two good-looking strumpets, who ruled the community, although the other in-habitants were God-fearing families, living their honest lives. I arrived there and soon decided the name of the place ought to be changed to Paradise.

Before that, however, being the chief, I had given thought to the others, that they too might have their share of pleasure. I divided the outfit up into groups, and sent them out ahead along specified routes. Only a few leagues beyond where I was going, they would find two towns, Adroado and São Pedro, and also Barro-Branco, a small village. As for Diadorim, it seemed best to send him off fast, which I did, to take charge of the scouting patrols. When all was ready, I came away, accompanied only by a guard of ten men. What I hadn't told you was that Verde-Alecrim was situated in a pleasant bottom, surrounded by hills. From the top of one you could see it at a glance. I spurred my mount and we galloped down.

I arrived there in fine fettle. I let my men go to the neighbor-ing houses and engage in conversation with the married women and their broods. I dismounted at the house of the two women. When everything is right, there is nothing like a professional's love-making. She knows all the gay practices. She dispenses pleasure and happiness to the passer-by; and as for really liking people, you like them best when you are not too well acquainted with them socially. I arrived at night, and they had the house lit up, to receive me. How promiscuous love-making keeps women young! Take Nhorinhá, for instance, who had many men and awoke every morning fresh as a flower. But it is not fair to use Nhorinhá as an example, because these two could not compare with her; they weren't fit to wash her feet.

But that is not to say that they lacked beauty, either. One of them—Maria-de-Luz—was a brunette, an octoroon. Her hair was incredibly long, black, and thick as that of an animal—it almost covered the face of that little Moorish witch. But her small mouth was soft, with fleshy, pouting lips. The corners curled upward when she smiled, and her chin was fine and pointed. Her eyes were amethyst, with green lights in them, that set me afire. She was very expert. She soon cast her spell over me. She was no simple loose woman. The other, Hortência, of medium size and very cute, was nicknamed Snow White, because her body was so beautifully white, and she needed to be snuggled tight at dawn to keep from freezing. She was unique even to the smell of her armpits. And the groove over her spine meandered down her back like a mountain stream. Because of this, you could never measure its exact length. Lying between both of them I discovered that my own body had hard and soft spots. There, I was like an alligator, that's all I know.

In the middle of the night, I got hungry, but I didn't want to drink cachaça. I lounged awhile and had a dish of very cold clabber. I ate some cake with citron in it. I drank good coffee, sweetened with white sugar. The two girls were rich; they must have had a lot of silver money put away. Their house was an overnight stopping place for wealthy planters, like a high-priced inn. But the two themselves came from very good families. Hortência "Snow White" was the daughter of a big fazendeiro from Paraná, who had died. They owned lands, they had fields of corn and beans in the foothills and up the slopes. Right there in Verde-Alecrim itself, they owned all of the arable soil. Because of this, the inhabitants and their families served them well, with courtesy and respect—all of which I thought very good: a system that should prevail everywhere.

While we were drinking coffee, we heard someone cough outside. It was the man I'd left on guard. It happened to be Felisberto—the one who had a copper bullet in his skull and because of which at times he used to turn green all over, as I have already told you. The girls thought I should let Felisberto come inside and have some coffee, too, because it wasn't right for him to be out there in the cold night air while others were inside enjoying themselves. From which you see, sir, that they were very kind persons.

I gladly agreed, for they were right. Only, being the Chief, it would not do to let Felisberto see me the way I was, completely naked. Maria-da-Luz then brought one of her old dresses to tie around my waist like an apron. I tried it on. Then I saw she was playing a joke on me. I got mad and pushed her away, and untied the thing and threw it far from me. I put on my own clothes, even my jacket. They laughed at me all the more. Was I to be made a fool of? I could have slapped them—if it hadn't been for their beauty and femininity, and their mad mirth, which half charmed me.

Felisberto came in, greeted everyone, ate and drank. On that occasion, he was feeling all right, normal. The only thing was he remained silent. I think it was more because he was wanting to be polite than that he was ill at ease; he was the kind of young man that women find attractive. Looking at him, you would say he was younger than I, more indifferent. He seemed to want no amorous sporting with the women—just a quiet corner to himself. He did not lust after either of them or their caresses. Nor did I notice at the time that Maria-da-Luz had her eye on him. But what she was thinking came out when Felisberto, after he had finished eating and drinking, started to leave, and she turned to me to say that if I had no objection, Felisberto could go into the other room with her, to spend a couple of hours, and that during that brief period I could occupy myself happily with Hortência. Angrily I said no, whereupon she retorted: "You found us here by chance, through good luck. You came and you leave satisfied. Aren't you willing to share what you have?"

If I said no, it was only because the rule could not be broken: no orgies were to be indulged in without a sentinel on guard. I was the chief. Felisberto was the sentinel. That house, the delights it offered—I could find none better in this world, I thought. I wanted to reign there, for my own pleasure. You know: I the chief, the other, the sentinel. This Felisberto, from the looks of things, had so little time to live, it could well be he no longer cared about his job. Then it came to me: I was a sentinel myself! You know, sir. Even under those baneful circumstances I managed to do my own thinking: I was not wearing the hoofs or feet of a goat. Felisberto, poor devil, had

death inside him. The foreign object—the bullet from a gun—
had buried itself deep inside his head, in the recesses of his
mind, and from time to time it drove him to act wildly; one day
it would prove fatal. It could well be that he would like to give
up being a jagunço. That bullet buried inside him, though,
which had not killed him outright but did not reprieve him,
either, bothered me. For all his worth and bravery, I wondered
if I should keep him in my band. The two women, beauties that
they were, dispensing delights . . . I had other ideas. I knew
only one thing: I was a sentinel! But I cannot describe my state
of mind when I realized it; I know only the basis for it.

The morning had dawned bright. Maria-da-Luz was not being
avaricious; this I could see from the endearing way she looked
at Felisberto. Who knows, he might like to stay there for good?
I asked him. Felisberto laughed, so hesitantly happy, that I
saw at once I had guessed right. And they, too. "Leave the
young man—we promise to take good care of him. He will
never want for anything!" Their saying all this altered the whole
situation. Women! And Felisberto, sensibly enough, would remain there, in thrall to those enchantments; what better
medicine could he have as he approached the end of his life?
Thereupon I embraced him, and I embraced the girls, saying
farewell forever and making believe that I had had enough.
Clever women! I heard afterwards that in their leisure time
they even lived together as lovers. When I was already on my
way out, what do you suppose they said to me? "But are you
leaving so soon, lover? Just a short visit, like a doctor's?"

I couldn't help laughing.

I gathered my other men together and we dashed away. There
is no doubt—I felt a certain envy of Felisberto. But then, I esteemed Felisberto as if he were my brother. Just as in heaven
there is splendor, so here there is woman's beauty, for which
we thirst. May God much bless those two!

Once it was over, I wanted to forget all about that spree—
that concession to my maleness. All the more when I saw
Diadorim again, who, as I perceived, had been waiting for me,
with some companions, shooting quail in a grassy field. I went
toward him, somewhat hesitantly. And how right I was. Dia-

dorim already knew about everything. How did he know about
it? Ah, anything I tried to keep from him soon came out.
"Riobaldo, you dallied with those two at Verde-Alecrim. Are
you satisfied?" he asked me frankly to my face. I shrugged and
ran my hand over my chest. But I was surprised that Diadorim
did not seem angry. In fact, he chuckled, and his air was one of
malicious satisfaction.

"Have you given her up?" he inquired finally.

"Her, what her? What do you mean by those tricky words?"
I countered, for I had understood on the instant. He stopped
talking. I had understood at once that the reference was to
Otacília. My fiancée, Otacília, so far away—her beautiful white
face gradually emerging through the mist of my imagination.

All this doesn't make sense to you, my dear sir, it doesn't do
any good. But in repeating so much detail, I am reliving the
past. It is all mixed up, I know. But I am drawn to that which I
have lived and lost, to that which I have forgotten. I wander in
the past.

I will tell you how it was; you stop me when you want to.

We turned back from the point we had reached. To the west
of it lay only desolation. Our new route would take us across
the gerais of Goiás to the gerais of Minas Gerais. Behind us we
left bottom lands, deep ravines, dense forests, where the João-
congo sang its sad song. No, I'm wrong: today it seems sad but
then it was happy. The white-spotted deer would run from us,
with their heads held far back to keep from catching their
antlers in low branches. The white-spotted deer and their does.
One day we killed an anaconda, thirty six spans in length. There
were places at night when you would suddenly reach for your
revolver, or even your rifle; we had to build bigger bonfires, because in the dark some strange animal might come wandering
in our midst: large jaguars roaming about, snarling, or a nighthawk, flying silently as an owl; or, suddenly, from down wind, a
male tapir, whistling loudly, could burst upon us with the
violence of a wild horse. And it was there that Veraldo, who
was from Sêrro-Frio, recognized a plant which, if I am right, is
called guia-tôrto, but which in his part of the country they call

candeia: you light it and set it in the fork of tree, and it burns bright and clear, like a torch.

We crossed broad plains. Bright days of unlimited sky. Many hawks flying. The pastures in Goiás were being burned over, filling the air with smoke and ash, turning the sun a dark red.

I recalled some of our other smoke-filled adventures. Pitolô was killed by a bullet fired accidentally by some one—a thing always liable to happen. At a place called Padre-Peixoto, Freitas Macho also died from great pain in his belly, on the right-hand side. A medicinal brew did him no good. Alaripe got an inflammation of the eyelids. Conceiço dislocated an arm, and it took a lot of effort and pain to put it back in place.

From the rich and well-to-do fazendeiros, we exacted tribute in goodly sums: five, ten, a dozen contos, which they hastened to pay. With it, I filled our money box. They opened kegs of cachaça and served it to us. We were given banquets, with singing afterwards by a chorus. Sometimes, I don't know why, I thought about Zé Bebelo, and made inquiries about him, but no one in those parts knew the man. The one whose fame some had heard of was Medeiro Vaz. Going along, I took a fancy to only one woman, a married woman she was, who shook like a leaf, and who soured me at once when she replied: "Well, if God is willing, if it is what my husband wants. . . ." I cut her short: "Ah, then, I don't want it any more either, my lady. I am not in the mood." And, without meaning to, I cast an evil eye even on a little boy who was standing near.

And so we traveled. But, though I relate these things to you, I don't tell you about all the empty time we spent. And mark this well: it is very hard for a man to hold fast to an idea in a land of such distances. You travel and travel, but whether you will it or not, you can never get your feet free, for they will always be in the sertão. Don't be deceived by the quiet of the air, for at best, the sertão can be known only superficially. And it either helps you, with enormous power, or is treacherously disastrous.

I was feeling more self-assured in my position as chief. Come to think of it, I must have put aside all my doubts about life and was enjoying my physical well-being during those

temperate days under a cloudless sky. The days were so bright
and clear. The harvest flies kept up their shrill and noisy song.
Some hoped it meant that the winter rains would be late in
coming. But it didn't. As for me, I believed and hoped for the
best in everything. And I always treated the older men with
friendly respect, the ones whose daily duties carried serious
responsibilities. These were: João Goanhá, Marcelino Pampa,
João Concliz, Alaripe and some others, deserving in their own
right; and I did not forget the customary practices. Except that
I never asked for advice. There may have been no harm in it,
but to ask for advice is to have no trust in oneself; and that
could be harmful. Neither did I reveal my plans. The Urucúia
flows out of a forest, silently it slips along: it is the sun that
pulsates when they touch.

Diadorim himself misunderstood me. As I remember, it was
at some time during an afternoon, when we were moving across
a long, open saddleback. We two in front, a couple of men; it
was blistering hot; the horses had a league to go over crystal
and mica outcroppings. Limitless deep blue sky. Go to Goiás
and you will see a world inside a world.

And what Diadorim said to me began this way: he asked me,
glancing at me sideways, if I was engaging in that war whole-
heartedly. I took it as a criticism—that he was censuring me
for maneuvering in such a roundabout way instead of heading
straight for a showdown with the enemy.

"Well, Diadorim," I snapped at him, "you are the head man
on this job, aren't you?" Then, half in scorn, I added: "As soon
as I win I am going to be less of a figure-head." I don't think I
am now garbling the words I used.

Diadorim reined up and stopped; with clear, clear eyes, he
contemplated me at length. Slowly he said:

"Riobaldo, nowadays I don't even know what I know, and I
no longer know what it was I knew."

I waited a moment for him to explain what he meant. Then
he said: "I go to avenge the death of Joca Ramiro: I go and I
carry on, as in my duty. Only—and may God see me through
this—I go, not with the heart that beats within me now, but
with the heart of former times. And I say. . . ."

I tell you, I did not understand a word of what he was saying, because at that time our ideas were at cross purposes and we were out of step with one another. And the seriousness of his tone sent my thoughts in other directions: to the Urucúia—to the sunless, ageless forests there. The São Miguel forest is enormous—it shades the world. Could it be that Diadorim was afraid? I wondered. I knew that one day fear rises and makes a dent on the soul of the most valiant. So I said:

"Everything in life obeys that rule."

I was not long left in doubt. Diadorim was not afraid, nor did it embarrass him to say to me:

"Furthermore, I go less to avenge my father Joca Ramiro, which is my duty, than for the purpose of serving you, Riobaldo, in whatever you wish to do."

I didn't stop to think. "That's right, Hermógenes has to be done away with," I said.

Diadorim's eyes started to fill with tears of cheated hope. He was looking at me, and I didn't catch on. Could it be that I had even taken his expression of devotion for granted? I must have. I did not stop to analyze it. But I think, too, that the reason I didn't answer him further then was because of a distraction which occurred at that moment. What happened was, a swarm of tanajuras began their flight, in such vast numbers that it was an amazing sight, such as I had never seen before: rising from their nests in the ground, their hum filling the air, then falling to earth again, as they do, because their backsides are so big and heavy with ripe eggs that they cannot sustain the arc of their flight. Every foot of the ground was being littered with their coppery black bodies, which gave off their characteristic smell like that of a lemon on a hot griddle. The horses were startled, and some began to shy. And the boy Guirigó, eager for a better look, rode up to the front, with shouts and gestures, full of enthusiasm, all of which met my approval because I had brought him along with me from Sucruiú so he could learn about the world. But the heavy rain of ants came falling everywhere, on top of us, like hail, plopping and clinging to the men's shoulders and the horses' skin, much to their annoyance. I myself had to slap many off me, and afterwards shake others

out of the crown of my hat. Flying ants: I've heard it said that
hungry men will sometimes eat the filthy things, fried with
manioc meal. The birds, yes: the little kites went scouring the
plains, looking to fill their craws. No sooner did a tanajura hit
the ground than she knew she had to start burrowing fast,
wherever she chanced to land, and disappear into the hole,
deprived of her wings, like bits of paper, which she herself had
nipped off. But, then, when I looked about me, I saw that
Diadorim had drawn away from me and lost himself among
the others. And to think I had not understood him!

Please be patient, sir. When I spoke as I did it was before
Diadorim had his talk with Hermógenes's wife. I am going to
tell you now what I know about that.

The weather turned very bad—lots of rain. After it had
rained steadily for three days, we decided to take shelter and so
we moved in on the Fazenda Carimã, which belonged to one
Timóteo Regimildiano da Silva, better known as do Zabudo. He
was closely related to the Silvalves, of Paracatú, whose holdings
bordered on his own. Do Zabudo: listen closely if you want to
hear about a cunning fellow.

We met him suddenly as we were crossing a small tableland,
sparsely covered with grass. It had already started to drizzle
and I was thinking that somewhere near there we would come
upon a shed or shelter of some sort. And that is just what happened. There he came on a bay horse, with one of those odd
saddles they use, and wearing very good snake-skin riding
boots, of the kind they used to make. Naturally, it was a shock
to him when he saw us.

He recovered instantly, however. He dismounted hurriedly,
removed his hat with a great flourish, and politely announced:

"Sirs, my cavaliers, you may pass through, without fear and
at your pleasure, for here is a friend."

"A friend of whom?" I challenged.

"Yours, my cavalier, sir. Your friend and servant."

He was hoping to see the back of us. I pressed him: where
did he live?

"Over that way, sir, a poor little farm," he answered, cringing.

I cut in: "Well, then, we'll go there, to get out of the rain. You show us the way." At that, he changed his manner, speaking as if he were very pleased, sincerely so. The fazenda was just there, only a little way. He was already being astute.

Do Zabudo was a miserly fellow, very disgusting but prudent. I demanded a tribute—which I set at seven contos—and he put on an act of desperation, making faces, and kissing the back of his hands, first one then the other, several times. Moaning first that he couldn't pay, then that he would, he begged leave to point out to me how badly things had gone during the last three years, what with the cattle plague, which had struck twice, and the cane disease, which had ruined his sugar harvest. Everything he said, he enlarged upon and repeated, and even wanted to take me out in the rain so that I could see with my own eyes the shape things were in. Because of his pestering, I cut the figure down to three and a half contos; also because I was afraid his bad luck might rub off on me. At the same time, considering all the money we had gathered up in Goiás and still had with us, I had no need to press anyone too hard. We even agreed that he would furnish only one-half of our upkeep free of charge; he accepted this, though grudgingly. The rest I would pay for at a good price, plus extras: several dozen horseshoes, corn for the animals, some flitches of bacon, and ten kegs of cachaça— which, incidentally, was no good. What was good there was the rope tobacco. Things reached a point where I was practically paying him just to keep quiet. In the end, I think, our stay there didn't cost that do Zabudo hardly anything.

As I said, it was raining all over Goiás and we stayed indoors, only going out in the yard to pick and eat jaboticabas. We had cards and played rouba-monte and escôpa, but not truque, which I would not consent to because I felt incapable of joining in the boastful challenging and shouting which the devilish game inspires; and besides, I felt it was beneath my dignity as Chief. While we amused ourselves in this fashion, do Zabudo would come and go, hanging around, trying no doubt to figure more ways and means of hoodwinking and gouging us with his whining rascalities. Then, suddenly, he reported to us—the last thing in the world we would have dreamed of—that the missis—that lady—begged the favor of a private word with the young man called Reinaldo.

That missis was the wife of Hermógenes, whom we were keeping locked up in the oratory. And Diadorim, as you know, was known as "Reinaldo."

You ask if this surprised me? Very much. I was in the dining room, playing cards with João Goanhá, João Concliz, and Marcelino Pampa. Alaripe was sitting in the doorway that opened out on the yard, with a little pan of scouring powder and a rag, cleaning his weapons. He said: "I hope to God Reinaldo doesn't bump the creature off." We doubted that he would. "Hey, do you suppose she performs witchcraft?" João Goanhá suggested, with a laugh. "For a good job of magic, one that really works, they say a Negro woman is best, or even a man." This was Marcelino Pampa's opinion, expressed while he took the seven of diamonds with the seven of clubs. I played, and João Goanhá added six and three on the table, which he took with the jack and won the game. Diadorim had gone to where the Woman was, to hear what it was she wanted to say to him.

It was my turn to shuffle and deal. If it was some request she had to make of him, all right. Then João Goanhá was saying that what the Woman was begging for was her freedom. I changed the subject, first by remarking casually on João Goanhá's fondness for covering his fingers with rings, and then I called attention to the numerous leaks in the ceiling of that big room which made it necessary to set cans at various spots, and even a big bowl on the table, to catch the water. But I had lost all interest in the game; I got up and wandered outside, where I saw some men dozing in the shed, fed up with the steady rainfall.

Diadorim took a long time about coming out of the oratory. And, when he finally appeared, he didn't tell me anything. He just passed it off, saying: "Ah, all she did was complain of her lot." I did not quiz him at the time. And because I had not done so, later it did not seem befitting my dignity to ask him any questions. Diadorim was ill at ease in his silence, for it was not the right thing for him to be withholding information from me.

I was on the point of saying that I didn't like hypocrisy, but I refrained. Could I doubt Diadorim's actions? Was he capable of treachery? Ridiculous! I rejected the thought as beyond belief. But, as I was feeling disgruntled, I decided we would leave that place, and on the instant I gave orders that the horses be fetched and saddled, regardless of the weather—torrents of rain, thick clouds, dark skies and crashing thunder claps. Rain that turned the roads into deep, soft mud.

My orders were carried out, but hardly had the horses come in from the corral when there was a sudden let up in the weather brought on by a change of wind. The sky cleared and the sun came out. Everyone expressed amazement. And I saw that the less they understood me, the more they attributed to me great powers of leadership.

Do Zabudo, I would have you know, sir, was the only one who hung back, without enthusiasm, like the sharper he was. Even so he came to me with a long face and excuses, seeking a further reduction and asking for excessive discounts and long terms of payment. Now, I would have you know about another thing, sir, that he did during the confusion of our departure, to achieve his ends. All of a sudden he brought and offered to Diadorim, as a present, a box of the finest and most expensive Goianian quince marmelade. "You try it, sir, and you will like it the best of all. The Santa Luzia brand isn't a patch on this." By making that gift to Diadorim was he not trying to curry favor with me, for his own benefit? I knew he was. What was in the back of that larcenous mind of his? That sly, scoffing way he eyed me—at the time I couldn't figure it out.

He ended up by not paying a cent, and even came close to getting a loan from me. Even for the horses and mules that he furnished us, he received an equal number of ours in return, and better ones except that they were travel-worn. I even let him keep his own horse, the bay, which he claimed to treasure because it had been left him by his father. Highly pleased with himself, he got into that ludicrous saddle and rode with us for a quarter of a league, to keep us company. You don't often see that. He was so grasping, he had no fear. He kept looking at me slyly and inquisitively. Now, sir, did you follow closely what

I've told you about that devil of a do Zabudo? Tell me, sir: did you suspect any trick, did you sense anything?

We vanished from that place. After five leagues, I saw the mud dry. The fields were turning green. I let our journey proceed unhurriedly, easily. I wanted it that way. My reason was, I wanted to gain time so that my plan could develop in all its details.

To do away with Hermógenes! The way I looked upon Hermógenes he was a mad bull. But, strange as it may seem, I did not, strictly speaking, hate him. Look at it this way: he was like part of a task, a test of my prowess, something standing between me and the high tablelands. A shadowy something, barely glimpsed, wraith-like. And he, he himself, was not he to be my foil? My need to topple him was in order to enhance the greatness of my own exploits! And in this I saw no danger, for I had no doubts. The heyday of youth! Hell, I would just raise my hand and shout a command—and Hermógenes would tumble. Where could he be? I did not know, nor did I have any reliable news, but news that you are going to get tomorrow, betrays itself today. I knew it; I know it. The way a dog knows.

So I knew, though nothing told me so—that is, my heart told me—that before much longer Hermógenes and I were going to meet at some point in the plains of Minas Gerais. I knew it. Why hurry? In fact, the road was impossible, piled high with deep, sticky mud that sucked off horseshoes, even new ones, and made us slide and fall; some of the horses suffered broken legs or necks. The going was slow, for we had to pick our way. We lost time. But I found the delay agreeable. I was on a hunt and enjoying it. We also spent time resting on fazendas and in villages. It was better this way, for then my name would become known in that region, too. Moreover, they showered me with rewards and favors because I was going to rid the world of Hermógenes. Hermógenes—I struggled to remember what he looked like. But I couldn't. Hermógenes: an irrational evil. Had it been in order that I might kill Hermógenes that I had met Diadorim, become fond of him, and undergone all these misadventures?

We tarried. Finally there came a warm, dry spell, and we set

out at a trot. We stopped within leagues of the border, and I
sent out scouts and advance patrols. I checked my men and
their arms. Everything was in order. The river flowed between
high banks. On the Minas Gerais side a forest advanced slowly
toward us.

The weather worsened. We crossed over into Minas and
started the long climb, with the horses straining. There were
showers and gusts of wet wind. The slope was very steep but
we reached the edge of the mesa. Then the wind filled our ears,
a wind whose tune never varied. All was well; this is fine, I said;
the everyday happenings, occasional rain, our steady advance
across the tablelands: it was like a river below, flowing between the legs of my horse.

Ancient sertão of the ages. One sierra calls for another and
it is from these heights that you can discern how the sertão
comes and goes. It is no use turning your back on it. Its border
lies near and in far-distant places. You can hear its sound. The
sertão belongs to the sun and to the birds—buzzards, hawks—
which fly continually over its immense expanse. A journey
through it is dangerous, as is the journey through life. The
sertão rises and descends. But the curves of its plains extend
ever farther. The wind grows old there. And the wild beasts in
the valleys. The thunder crashes and rolls in the hills.

I could turn back from there, couldn't I? Or perhaps I
could not? Do I know or do you know? Who knows: perhaps all
that is written is subject to constant change, but we don't know
the road we are on, whether good or bad, while the changes are
taking place.

My advance scouts returned, bringing news: the Hermógenes, an enormous band of them, were headed in our general
direction, no doubt aware of my own course. This was it. We
trembled with haste. We pressed forward. We caught up with
some plainsmen and others who were herding cattle, or driving
their herds back to the scrub to keep the animals from killing
themselves by grazing on the young grass which in this region
sprouts full of sand. But these men knew nothing whatever.
We cut across in order to be the first to arrive at Nestor's place,
at Vereda-Meã, and then at Coliorano's, beyond the Mujo.

Vãozinho-do-Mujo, I think it was called. Coliorano lived on a palm-fringed lake and manufactured straw hats—the best kind. We had to reach his place, and Nestor's, ahead of Hermógenes because we had a supply of munitions hidden there. We kept detouring. Many marshes and frog ponds had filled up again. The rivers were muddy, and the umbuzeiros in bloom. Every river carried much spume on its surface, a sign that it was being swollen by heavy rains at its headwaters. Even so, we lost no time in arriving and collecting the munitions we were after —the whole lot. The hour had struck. Come, gather around me, all who want to fight!

They all did. And there were times when I regarded all of them with affection as though they were my brothers, the seed of one father, all gestated at the same time in the womb of one mother. My sons. But why recall and tell about them one by one? About Dimas Dôido, who swore at everything—at a branch that brushed his face, even at a little mosquito that bit him? About Diodôlfo, who moved his lips continually: when he wasn't praying softly he was repeating evil about others, talking to himself? About Suzarte, whose eyes took in everything: the ground, the trees, the dust, the winds, that he might store those places in his mind and contemplate them later at his leisure? About Sicrano João, astride his donkey? And about Araruta, completely trustworthy, a man who already had more than a hundred deaths to his credit? About Jiribibe, forever riding up and down the line because of his urge to hear and repeat and know everything? Or Feliciano, who would open wide his one good eye the better to hear what you were saying? Tuscaninho Caramé, singing some sentimental ballad in an agreeable voice? João Concliz, whistling a never-ending tune, like those of the pack drivers in Goiás? Or José do Ponto and Jacaré, prodding the burros loaded with their kitchen gear?

But I am speaking of minor matters—little things that we glimpse at odd moments and which we almost always forget, I am sorry to say. I used to think for an instant about the responsibility that was mine when I saw an older man like Marcelino Pampa—once a chief himself—living and working, by his own choice, on an equal footing with the others, or when he pulled up his horse, and remained still, without turning his head toward me but lowering it a little, while he gave heed to my counsel. Or when one of the older jagunços would caution some young fellow about being careful in handling firearms around others, or with the baskets of ammunition, for they quietly watched out for everything. You felt as if it were some peacetime activity, some detail of housekeeping. Or even when I caught sight of one of those backlanders, all of whom I had brought along, refugees from their own homes. Did they respect me? Yes, I think they did. Or perhaps it was a mixture of admiration and fear. And there were some—as I have told you, I remember everything—like that Assunciano: when the talk was about shooting, he would lean forward, in a half twist; he was thin but egg-shaped because of a protruding belly; and if someone's hat was fancier or newer than his, it would fill him with foolish envy. My sons.

But these pauses did not last long and I would be on fire again, seething with greater and more vaulting plans. I was like that. Am I still? Don't you believe it. I was the White Rattler—the Chief—after having been Tatarana and after having been the jagunço Riobaldo. I gave those things up, and they gave me up, in the long ago. What I want nowadays is faith, and also kindness. The only thing is, I can't understand anyone being satisfied with little or nothing. Me, I am not content just to whiff the dust from a full measure but must heap up the grain with my own hands until it is running over. I was heading for suffering, without knowing it. See for yourself. "War is here!" I proclaimed, "War is here! We will fight tooth and claw!" They all approved and started singing:

> *Tra-la-la, my Bahiana,*
> *I was going but now I'm not:*
> *I pretend*
> *I am going*
> *Over there, oh Bahiana,*
> *But halfway there I turn back.*

That other song—the one you called the song of Siruiz—I alone sang it, silently to myself.

I knew what I wanted, as I have told you: in the end to marry Otacília—sunshine of the rivers. I would marry, but as a king. That is what I wanted. What about Diadorim? Just wait. Is ingratitude the failing which we least recognize in ourselves? Diadorim, he would go one way and I another, like two little streams that rise out of the same bog in the uplands: one flows east and the other west, away from each other forever, but flowing clear in the shadow of the palms on its banks.

At other times, this thought would keep cropping up: that my memory of Otacília was proper and beguiling, and that my feeling for Diadorim was one of love, which was impossible. That's right. Do you understand, sir? Let it go—I'll tell you later. During those days, the thing was to keep on the move, until finally, suddenly, I would meet up with Hermógenes. On the alert, I sniffed every wind. Hermógenes and his outfit— like a long, thick snake gliding noiselessly under the dry leaves. But I was at the ready. At times, I awoke during the middle of the night, and felt as rested as if it were broad day-light. The middle of the night, when the forest noises begin to quiet down. Or when there was moonlight, as in the uplands, with the stars shining. When the moon shone like that, it had to be a very powerful star to show against the blue background.

And we arrived! Where? The place you arrive at is wherever the enemy also wishes to arrive. The devil watches; what the devil wants is to see. All right, then! The place was the plains of Tamanduá-tão. The enemy was approaching at a fast trot. Headed for destruction. The plains of Tamanduá-tão—write about it. On the plains of Tamanduá-tão. It was a great battle. There was no warning. I gave battle. As we had wanted it: law against law, fire against fire.

Tamanduá-tão is a plain that we saw from the top of a hill, and we descended to it through a narrow gorge, almost a fissure, cleft in the slope. More than two thousand head of cattle, or some eight hundred horses and mares, if need be, could have been pastured in that great meadow extending from one wood to another. On one side there was a strip of dark forest. Another strip of forest on the other side. Beyond these woods you would still be inside that enormous meadow, the Tamanduá-tão, be-

cause there was just this one name for everything there: the
Big Woods of the Tamanduá-tão, the Little Woods of the
Tamanduá-tão, and so on. There was even a Fazenda House of
the Tamanduá-tão a time long ago, which had slave quarters
and an upright cane crusher. But it had been forgotten, its roof
caved in and its tumble-down walls enclosing scattered growth
on piles of rock and dirt, everything in ruin. Nevertheless, there
were poor people living in the vicinity—you could see patches
of cultivated ground, and gay little fields of corn and beans. But
of the people themselves we saw almost no one. There was also
a stream called Tamanduá-tão, fringed by tall burití palms,
with its smooth water, pure as a virgin, without one speck of
dirt. They say the fishing is good there—fat piabas. What I
know about it is that a lot of shooting took place over it. There
was a trough on the ground, in a field; the cattle heard the noise
and dashed wildly away. My people galloped to the edge of the
stream—all up and down it—like a frenzied bushmaster looking for a female. And the enemy gave way! They could find no
shelter. That is how we began.

How am I going to give you a good description of all sides of
the place? Only by means of a sketch on a piece of paper. Now,
you take it and draw a cross—four arms, and the end of each
points to one of the places. The one at the top is where we were
coming from, down the gorge. The one to our right, that is, toward the west, points to the Big Woods of the Tamanduá-tão.
In the opposite direction, to the left, the Little Woods of the
Tamanduá-tão. At the bottom—at the end of the plain—there
rose abruptly the ugly, eroded wall of the Sierra of the
Tamanduá-tão. The gray gullies were strange-looking, filled
with rounded rocks and humps resembling the backs of a herd
of animals. Now, put a mark here to show the ruins of the old
fazenda house, halfway more or less, between the Sierra of the
Tamanduá-tão and the Big Woods of the Tamanduá-tão; then
on the other side, between the Sierra and the Little Woods,
mark the places of the few poor settlers. There we have it. The
stream angles across the plain from the head of the Little
Woods toward the fazenda house, and is a cheerful green as it
meanders along in short curves like any snake. And that's

all. The rest, just sky and plain. So vast, as I saw and heard at the end: the tumult, the shouts and neighings, the dust raised in flight, the horses stampeding . . .

But first, there was the beginning. And another beginning before that, which was our own coming. A good coming. Only, we did not expect what happened to happen so soon. We were approaching the end of the sierra called Serra da Chapada. We had only to descend and cross those meadows, the great plain. Of the enemy, we had no notice whatever. Our scouts had given us no word. How could I have known? My innocence was pitiable. And I nourished my happiness in many little ways. For example, once when I wanted to try the mettle of my backlanders. One of them, Dos-Anjos, liked to display the skills he had acquired: how fast he could aim and fire. I was amused at the rattling speed with which he reloaded. But it was a very old, smoothbore gun, one of the poorest, the barrel badly worn. "Let me see your blunderbuss, old brother," I said, taking it from him. He didn't want to let go of it. "It's mine," he bleated sadly. I thought he deserved something better. I ordered that a suitable weapon be found for him: a reinforced rifle or Winchester 27, or any carbine, and lead bullets. At that, Dos-Anjos offered to make me a present of his old firearm, he looked at me shamefaced and sheepishly. Marcelino Pampa—I think it was —when we had finished laughing came up with a good idea: he said that one time Medeiro Vaz had hidden a bunch of soldier's weapons in a cave halfway up to the top of the hill. He said there were five Mauser rifles, well-oiled, in a box hidden deep inside a big hole in the face of the slope. And that outside of monkeys, no animals went there, and that the rifles were no doubt still serviceable. "Why did Medeiro Vaz hide them?" "Because at the time he had no ammunition for them." "And now that we do have, where are they?" "Let's look."

As I have told you, I knew nothing of the enemy, nor he of me, yet we were headed for a meeting. I called a halt before we got to the bottom—we were still high up, and the morning was young. Then we broke ranks and began scrambling up the jagged slope. We found no firearms in the cave, which was very big; only the bats that lived in it. And, because I felt like it, I said I was going to climb higher, to the top. Only a few went with me.

Only a few; I remember Alaripe was one. He went just to be going. We had started back down from the high point, the wind playing on our faces—the beautiful view unrolling before us, as I have described. Even while descending, we had rolled cigarettes but had not had a chance to light them because of the updraft of wind. We stopped. Alaripe struck a spark from his tinderbox, then suddenly bent low and pointed. "Look—over there on the quembembe—" he exclaimed hoarsely. By quembembe, as used in his part of the country, he meant the slope. And sure enough, over across on the Serra do Tamanduá-tão, a rider could be seen coming down the slope. And there were many others.

It was them! But we had already taken cover. "Hold every-thing!" I said. What I felt was not fear, nor stupor, nor disconcertion. I felt nothing, nothing at all; a blank nothing at all, enveloping all my moves.

We would fight as many as came, but a chief must make decisions. I spoke. Afterwards, when I thought about it, I realized I had given the proper orders; everything just right, as you will see. First, that three men were to take the non-combatants to that cave on the slope—the boy Guirigó, the blind man Borromeu, and Hermógenes's wife—and wait there until it was all over. For this purpose I also chose the back-lander Dos-Anjos, and I soon saw I had made a good choice, for the first thing he thought of was the amount of food to be left for them. Next, the precise and very simple fighting tactics: we would split up into three groups and descend the sierra by dif-ferent canyons. I, with my group, would continue the way we had started; João Goanhá would go to the right, and Marcelino Pampa to the left. They were to circle the enemy, then turn back and attack from the rear!

In a matter of moments, the men were ready to leave and on their way; a jagunço never dawdles. Those with João Goanhá and those with Marcelino Pampa set out first since they had farther to go. I, with my men, had more time. It was, in fact, better to wait. I counted the horses. "Arm yourself well,

Diadorim!" I said. "Arm yourself well, brother, my brother!"
Why did I say that? You must agree, sir, that I was not ungrateful and that Diadorim's welfare was ever in my thoughts. Is
that what love is: to love but to hurt the loved one? I firmed
myself in the saddle, which my legs were warming. I grasped
my pistol. Some of the men took advantage of the wait to eat
what they had. One wanted to give me half his loaf of hardtack,
and another had a leather bag full of red and yellow cashews. I
refused, even though my fast had been broken only by a drink of
jacuba. I did not even feel like smoking. Not that I was nervous.
But I knew it was a matter of minutes and not of hours. The one
with the bag of cashews—João Nonato, from Diamantina—
spoke up cheerfully: "Today, Chief, after we have won, will we
celebrate with plenty to drink?" Oh, yes. And of a sudden I
said: "You, son, you come ahead with me. You bring me luck!"
We spurred off.

While descending the gorge, fortunately we were out of sight.
And right at the bottom, at the edge of the plain, tall grass was
growing in the cool moisture of the foothill. The grass was
higher than I—we were completely hidden in it. Through the
green stems I could see butterflies flying about as though
trapped in a labyrinth. Better and better. I also saw that we
could maneuver somewhat to one side. And I chose, in my
mind, a group of men to go out with Fafafa. They were to advance first—as decoys—and upset the enemy's calculations,
when the fight started. We marked time with our breathing,
during those waiting moments. The ends of the grass tickled
our faces and made us want to sneeze. The only sound you
could hear was the horses chomping on their bits. I was in a
hurry for a showdown, but even greater was my patience; if
necessary I would have waited there forever. Hell, yes—but I
could also take an enormous, flying leap, suddenly. I saw that
what fights is the animal in us, not the man. The field of grass
combined the sultriness of the air and the coolness of the gorge
—cold and warmth side by side in the same fine leaves. But the
warmth was climbing up my legs into my body; my feet were
sweating, they were so hot. I could not see the ground but from
the smell of the place it was soft yellow clay. Steady in our

places, we swayed gently in our saddles, from side to side—a kind of release from tension, which our spirits needed. We remained very quiet, however, not to frighten the birds which were feeding on the grass seed, because their sudden flight high in the air would give the enemy a signal.

I now took a foot out of the stirrup and knelt with one knee on the seat of my saddle. Because it was time to look. I looked and I saw the enemy coming—lines of men, a pack of them, more than a hundred. I held everything back, as they were still far off. Fafafa placed two fingers on my knee, as though to receive my silent order. He was waiting for a certain moment in my breathing. My hand played on the bow of the saddle. The jagunços say they do not know themselves if they are afraid, but none of them thought about dying. You curse and swear but it is for the other fellow's blood.

I took another look. I saw that they were coming, and that a few had moved out in front at a fast gallop, sent forward, no doubt, to reconnoitre the gorge and the up-slope passage, as a precaution. I closed my eyes and started counting to ten, but I couldn't stand it and at seven I made my decision. "You are on your own, Fafafa!" I said. And he yelled: "Let's go!" and spurred forward. And I saw the horses dashing after him, trampling down the grass. I let a few more than twenty go with Fafafa—I counted them as they went by, as through a cattle chute. And I had a hard time holding back the others who wanted to go too. Diadorim was one of these. "Me too!" he said. And I said "No!" and caught hold of his horse's rein. Why did I do that? My command would have been sufficient. It was only that I wanted to keep Diadorim with me. We could hear loud shouts and firing: it was Fafafa and his followers destroying the enemy's vanguard. This had begun at the same instant, but even so I had had time in which to feel ashamed of myself, and to realize that Diadorim was not indispensable to me. And that by his mere presence he was not obeying me. I know: one who loves is always a slave, but he never truly obeys.

Then I raised myself again and saw it was the start of the big battle. With Fafafa leading, he and his men were dashing forward, screaming boastful defiance!

At the same time, the others, the Hermógenes, who at first were bunched together, were quickly spreading out, separating themselves from one another, a human grove. In this way, and by shouting and yelling, they gave the impression of being more; they knew their business, all right. Actually, I did not hear many shots, but over the dry flat in the middle of the plain there rose a plumed cloud of dust. I drank drop by drop; what I mean is, I continued to wait, because Fafafa was purposely prolonging his advance with a very deceptive half-gallop—the others might have some trick up their sleeve. To see better, I stood up on my saddle, and my horse took care not to move, for he was a very wise animal. And I want you to know, sir, what I did as I stood there: I respectfully crossed myself! Was this the act of one who had a pact? Of a child of the devil? By God's wounds, no! And I even remember something that came to me, that I believed, absolutely: that the one who belonged to the devil, to the Hound without a muzzle, was him—Hermógenes! But it was courage given of God that I wanted; and I had it, did I not?

The exact moment had arrived. I only called out to João Concliz: "Now is now," and turned my horse's head. "This is it!" My horse plunged forward. All the others followed, in a sudden take-off, a world of them. I shouted defiance at the top of my voice. And my men, yelling fiercely, seemed to have dropped out of the air. I could see less than before. But the fighting had broken out over the whole of the Tamanduá-tão. I escaped to one side, with my good horse, and pulled up. As I did so, I found myself under a spreading tree—a canjoão, I thought it was. I could hear bursts of fire, and see puffs of gunsmoke. Bullets whizzed through the nearby grass. And because I wanted to see it all, the longer it took and the harder it became to fix my eyes on any one thing. The scene resembled a large table which had been luxuriously set and then someone had jerked the tablecloth and jumbled it all up. Who could bring order out of that chaos, and achieve a victorious end? Bullets whined around me. I planted my feet firmly in my stirrups and pressed my legs against the sides of my saddle. I had to command. I was alone! I myself would not engage in the fighting.

Was I Zé Bebelo? I could view everything, coldly, devoid of all
fear. Nor was I full of fury. My rage had abated. And even if I
could see, what good was it with everything so mixed up? I
kept my pistol in my hand but folded my arms. I closed my eyes.
By the pressure of my legs I had trained my horse Siruiz to
stand still. What I held to be my role was to command. In that
case, could I go and get mixed up with all the others? No! I was
in command of the world which they were despoiling. To command is just that: to remain still and have greater courage.

More courage than anyone. Had someone taught me that
for this hour of mine? They should have seen me! The fact is,
courage is something you can always absorb more of—like air:
you can take more and more of it into your lungs, no matter
how full, by breathing deeper. By my faith, that's what I did. I
tell you: if I did not praise God, ah, neither did I attach myself
to the devil. I spoke one name alone, softly but passionately,
and I thought it even more intensely. It was: Urutú Branco!
White Rattler! Urutú Branco! And that was me. I knew what I
wanted.

It was then that the fighting swept closer to me, like a sudden
blaze of fire. A few of the enemy had advanced. Their bullets
were striking and ricocheting around me. Some would graze the
grass and tear up a handful of dirt. Others would clip pieces
from the branches over my head, and seed pods, from which I
recognized the tree as an angico. I remained still. Was I not the
chief? Even when a rifle bullet passed through my cowhide hat,
and another, whining past, grazed my jacket, I did not move a
finger, but scorned the danger. However, had I unfolded my
arms and raised my hand to return the fire with my pistol, I
would have been dead—a larger target for the bullets which
were whizzing by so close I could even feel their heat. Urutú
Branco. I repeated the name to myself, whispering softly, as
when you make love to a girl. I felt exalted in my happiness.
High-flown. And nothing but bullets, for an enormous minute.
But, as for clearing out of there, that I would not do. I might be
killed—the thought barely occurred to me—but if so, I would
die facing forward in my saddle, unflinching, as the bravest
man in the world might do, at the moment of his highest

courage! By my faith, that is how it was. I became like a lake, so calm.

Then, of a sudden, everything changed. The enemy turned their horses, and started scattering in the distance. The reason was that João Goanhá's men had just come around the end of the woods and had begun a howling attack on their main body from the rear. These we had to overtake and defeat. And those Hermógenes who had approached in my direction were fleeing wildly. One of them, on a black horse, lost his head and was ridden down by Paspe, Sesfrêdo, and Suzarte, galloping as one —they made an ugly cloud. When his horse was brought to a sudden stop, his dead body shot straight up in the air and bounced when it hit the ground, like a board. Another panicked —João Vaqueiro, who had dismounted, shot him several times. He hunched over in his saddle, like an armadillo, and fell almost at my feet, badly wounded and groaning. "Disarm him but don't finish him off, old brother," I said to João Vaqueiro. The fallen man was crying out in agony, and trying to bury his nails in the bark of a stick of wood. He lamented bitterly that they had been doomed to defeat because they were riding worn-out horses, and had run head-on into such a disastrous surprise. He bemoaned his luck, cursing softly, three of his ribs shattered. But he begged for water like a Christian. Thirst is a human condition common to all. I leaned down and put my gourd in his hands; it was almost full and as good as a canteen. I closed my eyes to keep from melting with pity at the state he was in. Nor did I listen, for one's ears can be closed, too. The field that it was my duty to command lay before me. My courage filled my whole being; my person, my figure, the shadow of my body on the ground. A thousand times, I craved intensely that we would win; and I was silent in my craving— like a towering tree.

The fusillade was getting hotter.

And then Marcelino Pampa and his men also came on the scene, appearing unexpectedly, to the greater distress of the Hermógenes. It was a slaughter. We caught the enemy in a cross fire. You could hear nothing but the crack of rifle fire. It was hell let loose on the Tamanduá-tão. And, at the very height of the battle I was filled with the certainty that my strategy had proved right and that everything was already won from that moment until the final outcome. There was only ripe fruit left for me to pick. I dashed away at a gallop to where the fighting was thickest. I was shouting. I started shooting and killing with my rifle. Where was Hermógenes? With whoops and yells, we took out after some of the enemy in the direction of the stream. Every palm tree was riddled.

To top it all, the enemy had no way of falling back, since they were losing their horses. It also happened that the flat land at that point offered no woods in which they might make a stand and lie in wait for us. Only a few managed to reach the distant thickets or the tall grass, where we refused to go to drive them out. They must have lain there in fury, with knives in their hands, waiting like snakes. Only with bloodhounds, which we didn't have, trained in hunting down people, could they have been captured. The others were rushing pell-mell in a mad flight to escape our hail of bullets. Not many got away, and we chased hotly after those who did. We swept across a gully, then through a clump of lobeira trees. We were now near the small planted fields. Some low hills; we opened fire. A tumbledown shack, then another; we shot them up. Very few inside escaped. Those who had slipped off to one side were shot down by our flankers.

But one big man, who had jumped off his big horse which had been shot, started running toward a hovel in front of him, which he reached and entered. He would, no doubt, start shooting at us. Then all of us stopped our chasing of the survivors and surrounded the hut, at a prudent distance, seeking such shelter as we could find. It was going to be a terrible contest. And who was that man? "It's Ricardão," someone cried. And I, too, knew it was him. I ordered a volley. The palm hut shivered, twisted and was battered out of shape. If we had kept on firing it would have vanished. But I ordered a cease fire. "I wonder where Hermógenes himself is?" I inquired. No one knew. But they had heard from some wounded and prisoners that Hermógenes was not a member of that particular band, but was traveling with some others far ahead of us, about twenty leagues west. By now nearly all our men had gathered to witness Ricardão's last stand. I gave my orders.

"Seô Ricardão, come on out, sir!" I shouted from my sheltered position.

He did not answer. "Pour it on, men," I said. The hut began to fall apart. But not a single shot came from inside. Was he dead? Was he out of ammunition? I swallowed three times, then I shouted again. "Seô Ricardão, come out, sir." And he, strangely enough, replied: "I'm coming," in a natural voice. I ordered all my men to hold their fire. And to keep quiet. I took a look.

Over there, the shambles of a door was slowly pushed open. The man came out and took a few steps. He came with his hands up, hat on his head, half smiling, even. His eyes betrayed no terror. Was he thinking that he would be given a trial? I believe so. He was not wounded. He took a few more steps. Then—was it just an idea?—ah, no, I saw that Diadorim, in his hatred, was about to go for him with a knife. I settled the matter in a flash: I fired, only once. Ricardão dropped his arms and crumpled up, pierced by my bullet. As he fell, one leg sprawled this way and the other that. He lay where he fell. He lay as if he hadn't known that he was dying, but we could see that he was already dead.

I really think everyone heaved a sigh. I tell you, this right hand of mine had fired almost by itself. What I know is, it returned Adam to dust. That's just my way of talking.

"Don't bury this man," I said.

It was justice. Anyway, how were we going to bury all we had killed that day?

As we returned to the sierra, I looked up now and then at the sky. The first buzzard that I sighted—it was coming in from the direction of Sungado-do-A—was slowly moving its wings up and down, as if waving to me in friendly greeting. Fly on.

But—what was yet to happen! What the next three days were like, I shall no doubt narrate poorly. Alert yourself, sir, for we are rushing; prepare yourself for a terrible, terrible ending.

Could I have foreseen it? Man exists like the tapir: he lives life. A tapir is the most stupid of animals. And I, supremely

confident of my victory! I liked to hear the blind man, Borromeu, who was never downcast, say: "Ah, I haven't smelled
these plains before." But sometimes, when he wanted to know
something, he would ask. He would ask questions about the
natural surroundings of a place. Then he would versify:

> *Star-shaped prickly cactus,*
> *who gave you all those spines?*

I suspect now that blind Borromeu inquired only about things
he already knew. If not, if not, listen to this as closely as you
would to a holy edict; is it not revealing?

> *Said the star-shaped cactus*
> *To the quixaba tree:*
> *I am the one who loves you, my love,*
> *So why don't you love me!*

Behind him, on another horse, rode the boy Guirigó, growing
older. And Hermógenes's wife, mounted, too, very thin, looking
as if she were floating on a cloud. She had unwrapped that green
shawl from around her face, without any embarrassment,
revealing herself from the chin up. Who can understand another's pride, who can understand another's madness? She ate,
she drank; at one time, young and happy, she had married.
When I looked at that woman, I felt only revulsion for life's
terms. She never spoke a word. The day was almost ended. The
woman, the boy, and the blind man came out and set off. At my
orders, they had been brought from the cave in the hillside, and
were being taken under guard to the village of Paredão,
guarded by a company of ten men.

The reason was that Hermógenes might show up, coming
from the west. Let him come! We learned that their numbers
had been swelled by some bandit jagunços. And some of those
who had escaped with their lives from Tamanduá-tão must
have reached him and given him warning. I sent out my scouts
to make sure of the distances. His most likely route from the
west to Paredão would take him through a place called Cererê-
Velho, on a hill. We headed for it.

We hurried forward, at a stiff pace, until the heat of the day had lifted. Then there came thunder and gusts of wind. Everyone said it would soon start raining. At the edge of the forest, on Cererê-Velho, we went to work on branches and lianas with machetes, and put up some shelters. But the weather improved and the rain held off; the wind died down. However, that work of ours was necessary and we could not relax, not even for my daily chat with Diadorim, as I well remember. Night fell. I lay down to sleep, dog-tired. But only for a brief spell, for my spirit rejected sleep. Suddenly, I was wide awake.

Dawn at midnight. The moon was far gone; the hill and the woods blended into each other. I looked about me. The world was asleep. Only the little forest sounds that slip out through the silences, and the doleful *ô-ô-ô* of a nighthawk, high in a tree. Then I heard the long, drawn-out howl of a dog. The men were all sleeping; I alone was awake and on foot. My heart was heavy. Was it because of that dismally howling dog, I wondered. Why had I alone awakened at such an unearthly hour, before all the others? I would have to endure my heavy-heartedness until it passed. Was God punishing me—for there comes a time—or had the devil begun to haggle? I saw that I could choose between letting my feelings go in the direction of unhappiness or of joy—far, far, to the very end, as far as the sertão is vast.

I looked up, I lifted my eyes. Those unfalling stars—Orion's Belt, the Wain, the Southern Cross, the Milky Way. They aroused desires in me. I had to stay wide awake. I was going to wait, doing one thing or another, until the day broke, with sunlight for all. At least I found a way to distill from the chant of the night, from the end of it, a line or two of song:

> *Still backwaters of a wide river*
> *God or the devil, in the sertão*

The daylight and rain came together. The world turned white, jags of lightning. The lightning flashed, the thunder boomed, water poured off us; and everything we thought of or did was deep in mud. My only concern was about the horses, lest they run off. They know how vast the uplands are. In the gerais you see things like that: a still night, then suddenly in the morning, a downpour. Then, before noon, a sudden clearing: a wind sprang up, the sun came out, and we saw how quickly the sand dried. I guessed at the hour. I could see my riders milling about, all mounted, filling and peopling one end of the clearing, like bees in a hollow umburana tree. They were on edge with a knowledge they knew not of what; they were extremely restless.

The returning scouts began to arrive, soaking wet. One said: "They are nowhere near, they are not headed this way. Unless they have been delayed." Where was Hermógenes? The sky began to cloud up again. Another said: "I found no trace of them." Then I sent out still others, more experienced; they were to go and return, they were to beat the farther edges of the world. How was I to sense, to be able to say to myself from the emptiness about me, "The Sertão is coming?" For it was. I gritted my teeth. I bit the hand of fate. For it was the eve, as you will see. But this thing, so alive, so close, was still hidden behind the clouds of the future. Who knows what these rocks about us are sitting on, and what, in a given hour, they may hatch out, like birds, from within their hardness? But that the enemy was near, I knew; you can tell by the fretting of the body, wishing it had more eyes; by the deep-seated gnawing in your breast, in your loins, in your guts. Hermógenes was about to strike, full of rancor, maneuvering in the dark. Was the war destined to be settled by battle there, in Cererê-Velho? My men, a thundering herd of fierce jagunços, which one word from me would loose, were waiting in suspense.

And it was at that moment that Suzarte arrived. After the battle at Tamanduá-tão I had sent him off, to pry and spy, to range far and wide, like a dog following a scent. He came in, galloping on a dying horse. He skidded to a stop. The bay was ready to drop; its front legs buckled pitifully at the knees, and it fell over on the ground, the blood from its burst bowels and lungs gushing out of its mouth and nostrils. But Suzarte had already freed his feet from the stirrups and sprung from the saddle to the ground. "They are there!" he gasped, pointing with his finger.

That cursed Hermógenes! He, they, the Hermógenes, were

coming by a different course than I had calculated. They seemed
to be going around the northern end. Suzarte had spotted their
flanking scouts the day before, and from a distance he had
sized up the main body; from their dust, they were about
eighty. It was Hermógenes, all right. He was circling around,
like a hawk, as if he had no appointment with me; and this was
his right, the wiles of war! Against one evil, set another; but
the danger at that hour was greater than just one of position.
Because they could come at us either then or later. And they
could come straight at us, or even—as we waited there, as in a
hunting blind—switch suddenly toward Paredão, snatch the
Woman from my ten men, do with them as they wished, and
then head back to Cererê-Velho and attack us from the rear. I
saw all of this in a flash. My jagunços were waiting for my
decision: at the moment they were not even looking at me.
"Attention," I cried. I explained briefly. By God, the words I then
spoke were those quickly whispered to me in snatches by the
navel of my mind. It was our plan of action.

I gave orders accordingly. We would split up. Half and half.
Those with João Goanhá and João Concliz would stay there on
the Cererê-Velho, in dauntless vigil, on the alert. I called the
others, with Marcelino Pampa as second-in-command, and we
started for Paredão. Everything went off quickly and smoothly,
as the horses wheeled about. Soon we were out in the open,
soon we were loping ahead. And Diadorim, who was following
a few yards behind—when I turned my face I saw my smile
on his lips. We were riding resolutely ahead, our backs to the
setting sun. I sketched out roughly in my mind the battle that
was to come. Riding thus on horseback was when I did my best
thinking.

From Cererê-Velho to Paredão: six leagues; and I had to
leave at least one man behind every half league, so that messages could be relayed with the speed required by war. This I
did, as I went forward, and I would do the same on the way
ahead. My men were performing splendidly. The happiness of
a jagunço lies in galloping movement. Happiness! Did I say
that? Ah, no, not I. Please, sir, strike that word back into the
recesses of my mouth.

What happened, then?

Fresh news.

We had ridden steadily forward, and had come to within a league of Paredão, when Trigoso appeared. He was returning from scouting the southern end, and was wholly unaware of all that we had learned. Regarding Hermógenes, he knew nothing. But he insisted on making a report anyway. He said a lot of useless things. Did he feel the need to put my spirit in turmoil, to freeze the blood in my veins?

"—on the Saz—a little creek three leagues below here, Chief —I ran across a herder who was passing along a message: that there was a man called Abrão, with a goodly young woman, that they were following the river, and that their stuff was loaded on two pack animals, and that they were accompanied by two hired hands."

He said this and it completely bowled me over. Otacília! Anything can happen in this world, and my mind had at once grasped the real significance of Trigoso's words! I said to myself: "Seô Habão? Make sure whether he has with him a most beautiful girl, or whether he brings only disillusionment." And Trigoso was still talking, telling all he knew. It was she! Otacília. Otacília. I had to hear Trigoso over again, but he really did not know the truth of the matter. My imagination took over. Otacília—coming into the sertão, on my account, to find me and see me again! But she had run into the warfare of all the jagunços of this world blazing in the gerais, far from her father's house, without guarantees of any kind. What protection could this Seô Habão give her, with two timid hired hands, and everything in such a turbulent state? It was a bitter dose to swallow. My men surrounded me, showing by their silence that they understood. I asked again: who knows, if they had stopped at the edge of the river, perhaps they had turned back and were also headed for Paredão?

"Ah, no, Chief. The herder said they were going away from there—out of the frying pan into the fire. And in Paredão itself, no one was left. All the families and inhabitants had fled on foot, panic-stricken, as soon as the fear arrived there. The fear is very great."

I shivered. The hour had struck. Just hearing about the emptiness of Paredão caused my people to gather up their reins, eager to start galloping again. I rubbed my hand over my face. I knew well enough that vacillation is not permitted a chief. But, there I was, in command, my men waiting on me, and over there was Otacília, in need of my protection. And the fighting could break out from one moment to the next, or even sooner. What should I do? In this predicament, with time beyond my control, could I take leave of my men? I had to go. Not for the pleasure of it, ah no. But my Otacília had come, at such an inopportune hour, at the worst possible time. Full of dismay, I could barely formulate this entreaty—to God or to the devil—:

"Only give me what is mine—that is all I want, all I want." I would go to her. Was not Otacília my betrothed, whom I had to cherish as my future wife?

Finally I said that I was going there on a quick journey, that I would return at once. It was a short hop, as they say. There would be time enough to get back and give battle. Let the others go on to Paredão, fast. It was already getting dark.

But many thought that they should accompany me instead, alleging that, whatever the problem was, I, as Chief, should not go alone. I shook my head. Nevertheless, I accepted two of them: Alaripe and Quipes—their company would be enough for me. I was not going to upset our plans nor weaken the strength of our forces by detaching more men. It was time to go. I gave out orders, and urged my horse forward.

But, but—I halted again. I halted, in order to turn back Diadorim, who had started to follow me. "Well, what is it?" I said harshly. If Diadorim had it in mind to accompany me, I was suspicious of his motives. He did not answer me. I read in him a kind of fury, from the way he narrowed his eyes, looking off into the distance. "Aren't you going to Paredão, are you afraid?" I said, to torment him. Diadorim was delaying me. The burning hate in him was because of Otacília. He heard me but said nothing, as he brought his horse alongside mine. He looked down at the ground, and turned red with embarrassment. Now he was offering me the boon of friendship—and I repelled it, I repelled it. But I was half out of my mind, and I felt an urge to be mean, to be harsher still, ungratefully harsh. Diadorim's attitude aroused my perverseness. "Go back, brother. I am the Chief," I ordered. And he, revealing in his voice an affection of enormous innocence, replied simply:

"Riobaldo, you have always been my Chief, always."

I noticed how he rubbed his hand over the bow of his saddle, —a hand so soft in peace, so hard in war. I retorted with an ugly curse. I shouted it, making his remark my pretext. I let out the reins, and in a short gallop caught up with Alaripe and Quipes who were ahead waiting for me. I did not look back to see whether Diadorim had obeyed me, surmising that he had stood there watching until I disappeared from sight. It was unfair. But the day's duty was driving me. And I thought of nothing else, I went forward, to the pounding of my heart. You would say, sir—you will say—that at that moment Diadorim and I had separated from each other—like a little lump of salt and a little lump of sugar, in the same vessel of water. I went on, torn by mixed feelings.

Later I regained my composure, but at first I was unable to. I talked preposterously. "Diadorim is crazy," I said. I caught myself instantly, for "Diadorim" was a secret name between us, which no one else had ever heard. Alaripe, with a blank look on his face, said only: "Huh?" But then I removed the veil that covered the past—I didn't care—and explained: "Diadorim is Reinaldo." Alaripe remained silent, the better to understand me. But Quipes laughed: "Dindurim—it's a good nickname." He spoke the name as if it were that of a bird. I frowned. "Reinaldo is the bravest of the brave, a superb backlander. And a damned good jagunço." I raised my voice. "A damned good one," I repeated. Alaripe, out of respect for me, chimed in: "He's a damned good one, that he is." Why was it not possible for him to talk to me without being deferential?

It had grown completely dark, the moon had not yet come up, and as I could not see to read the effect of my words in his face, they remained hanging in the air. "Otacília is my betrothed, Alaripe. Do you remember her?" After a moment of silence he replied: "I remember. There is a fine big fazenda." Even

Alaripe's zealous way of always going ahead, taking care to part
the foliage and branches of trees to make it easy for me to
follow annoyed me. We were almost on one another's heels. I
stopped trying to talk. The darkness closed our mouths.

Where and why was I going? I had to go, it was my duty, but
my Otacília—that delicate sheltered girl—should not have
chosen just this occasion. So entirely inappropriate, to come
venturing out among killers, without any protection at all.
Alaripe and Quipes did not fail to keep a sharp lookout all
about, on all sides of us, figuring that in time of war and in the
night darkness, some enemy could waylay us when least expected. Where were we headed? Should we go straight up the
Vereda do Saz, or follow the Paracatú? Everything conspired
to make me furious—all on account of that herder's report.
And I wasn't even sure that it was Seô Habão, or if it was
Otacília.

In about half of the sky, stars could be seen through the rain-
laden clouds. The Seven Sisters lay just above the western rim
—it must have been about nine o'clock. At that moment we
heard a loud noise inside the woods, a crashing in the under-
growth. We stopped suddenly, our rifles in our hands. "It is a
tapir" said Quipes, quickly recognizing the sound, "being
stalked by a jaguar, waiting for the moon." Otacília was being
exposed to all that because of my thoughtless message. "Seô
Habão delivered the amethyst to her," I said. I spoke loudly,
and I did not want Alaripe to echo my words: "He delivered the
stone to her." The stone was a topaz—telling about it this way,
I get the two confused. Perhaps it was Diadorim who suffered
most of all because of my gift of that stone. Otacília should not
have come. Now where was I going to find that wayfarer, or
that bastard of a herder, and get the news straight? He would
not stay in one place, following after his Urucuian cattle.
Everybody was fleeing from Paredão and from everywhere,
their bundles on their backs. Just then we saw a little light up
ahead on the plain: it must be some people camped out in the
open, on their way to nowhere, I thought. But it wasn't. It was
only a little bluish light that flitted about and scattered in the
breeze: a will-o'-the-wisp. We had not found what I had thought.

Was I different from all the others? I was. It startled me when
I realized it. Alaripe, Quipes, even their silences, untroubled
by specters, must have been different, with fewer thoughts. I
know that they must have sensed the pervasive forest smells in
some other way, and have heard differently than I the unending
chirp of so many thousands of field crickets. This gave me a
feeling of antipathy, and yet there was a kind of comfort mixed
with it. As when, riding along like that, in the dark of night,
your mind filled with worry, your horse suddenly snorts and
throws up his head—you become aware of his sweaty odor,
and are reminded of his steadfastness, his patient reliability.
Was the night becoming stronger than my decision? I don't
know. In my memory, it is a night in the open, in the dew.

The day was breaking when we stopped for rest at the edge
of a nameless stream. Dawn: the rising sun, and flocks of rice
birds. The sky glowed with color. Many childhood memories
crowded in upon me, memories of bygone days. We missed not
having coffee; but we ate some manioc, and drank water. Quipes
found some ripe custard apples; he was always looking for
fruit in the trees and thickets. And Alaripe gathered sticks and
started a fire, but only for the sake of warmth and out of habit,
for we had nothing to heat up or to cook. I recall how little by
little a larger bird started singing sprightly and rousing others
and still others to their daily tasks, not unlike going to work. It
made me envious to think of the nests they built from bits and
pieces, so small and artful, yet just the right size. And I thought,
too, that although the water in that stream had always been
there, flowing between clumps of sassafras and buriti palms
waving in the breeze, it was on this day, on this precise day,
that I had felt impelled to come there, as though for a meeting
with them. Why was this so? Nonsense. I felt tired and had a
pain in my side.

To relieve the tedium, I started talking. "Listen, Alaripe, what
name do you think this vereda should have, what should it be
called?" Alaripe, who was squatting near, stopped blowing the
fire and turned toward me. "I figure it already has a name, only
we don't know what it is. In case we run across someone who
lives around here, we'll ask him." But I said not to bother. I

picked out a spot on the ground for a doze. We had to stay there
awhile in any case, on account of the horses. They would need
to rest and graze, for the day that lay ahead. As you know, sir,
a healthy horse is indifferent to sleep, he just feeds and feeds,
all the time. Drowsiness overcame me, and I slept soundly for
a couple of hours.

Why do I tell you all this, in so much detail? Ah, just remember what I am going to tell you. I awoke feeling sore and out of
sorts. I had a bitter taste in my mouth. I wondered if I was going
to be sick with the colic. I felt queasy and tired, as if I'd had no
rest at all, insecure, full of doubts, not knowing what I should
do next. I had been awakened by the voices of Alaripe and
Quipes; they were already waiting for me, and were engaged
in their usual trivial conversation, matters of no importance.
Alaripe took a bottle of cachaça out of his knapsack and offered
me the first drink. It was a clear, medium size bottle, like a
medicine flask. Eagerly, I took a nip. But it didn't help me much,
and I felt let down. I wanted to talk about something, anything.
"What do you think about what you know, Alaripe?" He did not
catch my meaning, and began to talk about Paredão, about
Cererê-Velho, about Hermógenes. I cut him off: not that, but
about life, what's it all about? "Man, how do I know? I have
lived roughly for so long that I have worn out any wish to understand anything," he said, and it was well said. But I persisted.
"Not to understand the meaning of life, that's the only way to
be a really good jagunço." Alaripe was on the point of breaking
a dry stick in two, but stopped and looked at me. "If it is only a
matter of understanding, here inside myself I understand. I
understand things and people," he answered, and it was well
said. Did he, then, understand me? I had a crazy idea. I would
sit in a circle, right there, with Alaripe and Quipes, and relate to
them every detail of my life, every foolish thought and feeling,
the most unimportant things, early events and recent ones. I
would tell them everything, and they would have to listen to me.

That is what I thought, and I almost said it. It lasted for just
a second. Would I have? Ah, no, my dear sir. It passed as
quickly as it had come, and that was the end of it. Was I a

jackass, a long-eared fool? I was the Chief, to rule and decide: I was the one who passed judgments! Then I spoke:

"You go on alone, you two, following the river and searching. My duty prevents me from going any further. I am returning to Paredão at once."

Alaripe sparred for time: "But we—maybe we will be needed back there."

But my mind was made up. Since I could not go on myself, I could at least send them. They must go, let them go at once. They must find my Otacília and give her good protection. We mounted, all three. I waited until they left.

I even remember that when the moment came to say goodbye and leave, Alaripe, still reluctant, pointed to the woods upstream and said: "I think I see a horseman riding past, behind those trees." But it wasn't. It wasn't, because Quipes couldn't see it, and Quipes had eyes like a hawk. Then I thought: perhaps Alaripe is getting to be an old man. My friend—and a stranger to me. I still remember that is what I thought.

I headed back, while those two went on. Now a change came over me, and I trembled with excitement at the thought of the fighting to come. I cast aside my misgivings as easily as I had become dejected just before. Now my joy was mine again. Otacília would be well guarded. Then I was startled to find myself thinking about Diadorim. I remembered how Diadorim looked at Cererê-Velho, standing in the rain: he had looked the same as always, as before, in the dry of winter. The rain fell in bright streaks, and ran off his leather jacket in rivulets.

I sped forward. My horse galloped as with ten legs. And I reached Paredão in the late afternoon light.

Diadorim was anxiously waiting for me. I saw the happiness in his face.

Paredão. Picture it. Like a place where a steer had been slaughtered, with fat flies buzzing about. Everything was perfectly quiet. Diadorim—his hat cocked and turned up in front. He displayed complete assurance: in the way he held his head, in the curve of his mouth, the smile in his eyes, his slim waist; the cartridge belts crossed over his chest. The others, readying their weapons, ran their fingers over them, caressing them. I talked with everyone. Here was the war—the war they had wanted. And those backlanders of mine: their faces were becoming like those of demons. The ugliest thing about the devil is his nose and lips.

I checked the sentinels. I went to see where they had put the Woman. She was locked in an upper room of the two-story house. Let her stay there, under guard. The house was about midway the length of the street. But for men under arms, what good was that cluster of empty houses? I decided to leave only a few men there, on guard. All the rest of us went to a rise in the ground, about two hundred yards off, a natural gateway to the town and a good place to make a stand. We made suitable preparations. Had my mother been living and could have seen it, she herself would not have accused me of the slightest negligence.

I looked my men over—some calm, some excited—my band of jagunços. They were all supplying themselves with ammunition, and checking their guns and rifles. The war was everybody's. I would not attempt to give too many orders, prescribing every little thing, for a jagunço has professional pride in his skill and can be easily offended on that score. It was from their manner and attitudes that I could tell whether I was in fact being their Chief. Affably, I would say: "Look, So-and-So: it is all right here, but wouldn't it be better over there?" dreading at the same time that he might reply and explain to me why it wasn't better. I kept thinking to myself that they should be working up greater hatred. Hatred displaces fear, just as fear comes from hatred. I noticed this: no one referred to Hermógenes by name. That was as it should be, for on the eve of battle you don't talk about the enemy. One said only: "He's not a lasso—he's a hoop." And another: "He is crazy." But the rest said nothing. This suited me fine. I was only concerned lest it occur to someone to add: "He has a pact."

Ah. And suppose he did? That did not mean he had special privileges of any kind. Does not the devil belong to everybody? The strongest of feelings came over me that I was certain to be victorious. Hermógenes wouldn't leave that place alive, under any circumstances. Did I hate him? With deep hatred. Only I did not know why. I think my hatred reached back by stages, one deriving from the other, over the entire past, so that you might say the sole purpose of my life, from the time I was a boy, was to put an end to Hermógenes—on that day, in that place. I made an effort to recall his features, and all I could envisage was a man without a face. Black he was, with no face at all, looking as if I myself had shattered and hollowed it out with bullets. The whole thing nauseated me. I had no fear, but I was taut with tension.

I was also hoping that everything would be over fairly soon, so I might then give up my life as a jagunço. At that hour, thanks to God, my Otacília was far from that place, sheltered and protected. As soon as we wound up everything, I would fly to where she was, meet and escort her. Thinking thus, I despised the jagunço business, the sham of being a chief. Do you know who the chiefs are? Only the triggers of firearms and the hands of clocks. The only sensible thing would be for me to get out of the sertão, and go to live on a fazenda near town. I thought about my river, the Urucúia, forever trying to escape from the sertão, twisting and turning, but in the end pouring its clear waters into the São Francisco. I judged that by now Alaripe and Quipes should have found my Otacília, far up on the Paracatú. It seemed like a dream that on the dawn of that very day I myself had been headed that way. Do you know the great sertão? The ones who know it are the vultures, hawks, kites, and birds like that: they are always high up there, feeling the air with lowered feet, sizing up at a glance all joys and sorrows.

Now all was ready—and there was only the waiting. Night was rapidly falling. We lit no bonfires, not to betray our whereabouts, but myriads of fireflies were blinking in the fields. The men were gathered in squatting groups, talking. They needed to joke with one another, kidding about who was going to be scared or lacking in courage. This served to build up greater self-assurance, and I listened with satisfaction to their frivolous banter.

"Little crab, will you go out without plenty of cachaça?"

"Hell, you mean you are the one who won't!"

From their laughter and teasing, I saw that all of them were strongly confident. Before long, each of them would be as dangerous to tangle with as a poison-spitting toad.

"Listen, man: tie up your mule, the load is slipping."

"Don't worry about my load—what I want is to see what I am going to see."

Thus they mocked one another, as they would in a hot game of cards, but without a deck. I wonder why that pleased me? Diadorim was standing near me, silent, but I could feel the vibration of his presence whenever our thoughts met, a kind of love in the dark, a pending caress.

"You can bet the shooting is going to be red-hot! Then is when I will see a certain fellow turn into more of a boy than J'bibe."

"If you don't know it already, you'll find out: I have already earned my reputation."

"Jiribibe? That one, eh: he begs alms of the king."

And many other such gibes. Now that they had become accustomed to the hour and the place, they were ready for whatever might happen. Like a herd of cattle that comes to a new pasture, and wanders about, sniffing and investigating, but soon settles down and begins to graze. Now, yes, now, my men were primed for battle. It would be better for them not to do any napping, so as not to be rudely awakened, feeling alone and in fear of possible death. Did I feel sorry for them? If I said I did, you would be entitled to laugh at me. No one was ever forced to be a jagunço. Look, sir: for people of the sertão, the sertão is just one long wait.

At one point I asked Diadorim: "Has the Woman said anything?" It was not that I wanted to learn of any trivial remarks she might have made, but rather to find out if she had uttered any sort of crazy prophecies. "No," replied Diadorim. But he for his part must have had the weight of another matter on his mind. Instinctively I knew what it was: he was wondering about Otacíla. Then, after a moment of silence: "Alaripe and Quipes, where did you leave them?" I don't know why, but that time this evidence of Diadorim's jealousy gave me no satisfaction. And I fobbed him off with a vague answer: "Out there" I

said, nodding toward the Dog Star. Thousands of fireflies. But
the sky was dark, cloudy. Half sorry for what I had said, I tried
to talk about other things, but Diadorim countered with eva-
sions and sly cutting remarks. I remember it well. It made me
angry. But, gradually, my anger turned into a feeling of strong
affection, which I did not repulse. I tell you, sir, if I harbored
it, without shame, it was because of the hour: the little time
left, bereft of possibilities, before the impending battle. It gave
me a sense of freedom and I let my body desire Diadorim. What
about my soul? I remembered the smell of him. Even there in
the dark I retained his fine features, which I could not see, but
remembered in my mind's fantasy. Diadorim—even the brave
fighter—seemed made for caressing. My sudden impulse was
to kiss the fragrance of his neck, there on the side behind the
hardness of his jaw. Beauty—what is it? Beauty, the shape of
a person's face, a person who may be destined for another, is a
matter which Fate decides. Under the circumstances, I was
obliged to love Diadorim in this repressed manner, and not
utter a word. Were he a woman, no matter how haughty or
disdainful, I would be emboldened to passionate word and
deed—I would seize and subdue her in my arms. But two
fighting men, how could they reveal their love, even in simple
conversation, from behind an array of weapons? They would
sooner kill each other, in a fight. It was all impossible, and so
impossible, that I got careless and said: "My loved one, if only it
were daylight, so I could see the color of your eyes." I said it in
a moment of forgetfulness, as if I were thinking out loud, as
one might recall a line of verse. Diadorim stepped backward,
startled. "Sir, you can't be serious!" he exclaimed indignantly.
He had addressed me as "Sir." He laughed scornfully, I recovered myself instantly, furious at my own folly. "No offense
meant, brother. I know that you are courageous—without looking at your eyes," I said, to disguise my meaning and make
believe I had been joking. Then I stood up and suggested we
go for a walk. I wanted to get some air. Diadorim came with me.

The night was pitch black. A breeze was blowing, an unusual
one for that time of year: first it would blow from the south,
then from the north, as you could tell by striking a match or

throwing a handful of white dust up into the air. We kept on walking. But now my feeling toward Diadorim had changed to one of friendship only, real and strong; in fact, to something more than friendship. It was an affinity which drew and held me, so much so that in all honesty I could have told him of my affection, of the constancy of my esteem.

But I did not speak of it. The reason I did not was because of the danger of the occasion: I thought it might bring bad luck, on the eve of battle, to talk about things like that. Diadorim— I wonder what he was thinking; I did not know and I do not know. It is something I will wonder about until I die. One thing is sure: we talked only of unimportant matters, unhurriedly. The wind changed, now coming straight from the north, as I could tell because only one side of my face felt cool. The sertão began to boom with thunder. It looked as if there would be a heavy rain storm, so we decided to gather up everything and spend the night in the houses of the village, leaving only a few men as sentinels atop the mound. This was done, but it upset and tired me more than the other events of the day. True, I had spent the whole of the previous night traveling under the stars, and most of that day too, except for two or three hours' sleep at dawn. I went and found myself a cot and lay down, saying that, barring an emergency, I was not to be called. I fell dead asleep. That was one night I slept—the White Rattler, the Chief, which is the same as saying: Riobaldo, the jagunço.

I was the last to wake up. The place was flooded with light from the risen sun. By then, only a few flocks of birds were passing over. I could see that the day was going to be fine and clear. It was getting warmer, and the mud puddles and dripping trees were drying quickly—there had been a light rain during the night. I drank some coffee, ate a chunk of fat meat rolled in manioc meal, and munched a piece of rapadura. I observed that my men were in high spirits and confident as before. We returned to the position of the previous day, and each one sought out his sheltered spot. Cavalcânti arrived with a report from Cererê-Velho: nothing new. I sent him back to Cererê-Velho to say I had no news either. This was confirmed by my scouts, who had found nothing to report. For all our being on the alert, the day was one of peace. Everyone noticed it. Peace was in the very air. "Do you suppose they're not coming?" someone grumbled, leaning on his rifle. I wondered myself. It discouraged me to think that they might not come—and that we would have to postpone the final showdown, begin our wanderings all over again in a vain chase through the wilderness. "Ah, no!" I protested. No man would leave his wife a prisoner in the hands of others, and delay attacking. Sooner or later, he was bound to come. Let everyone wait. And I myself did not leave my weapons behind when I stepped down to the river for a moment to take a bath. It was very close by. From there I could see all that took place.

It was my mind—not my eyes—that turned away. Unbuckling my arms and cartridge belts, unhurriedly removing my clothes, then wetting my wrists and slowly starting to enter the water—these actions diverted my thoughts from the realities and provided a quiet surcease. I felt sure of hours of peace. At that moment did the devil speak to me? He did—with gunfire!

The shock it gave me was like a clap of thunder. And the shouting began.

The yells and the shots. I wonder which I heard first? In one leap I was out, pulling on my clothes and arming myself as I ran. I saw a fantastic sight. My people, yelling and shooting but also pouring out of the village like so many angry bees. But why? I could not understand, then all too soon I saw the reason: the enemy had suddenly burst upon us from the rear, whence we never expected them to come, nor was it reasonable to have supposed that they would. There were plenty of them. Boldly, boldly, they kept coming, advancing, as if they were about to take the houses at the end of the street, the village itself. I was appalled at the thought that during my brief absence the world had started to fall apart. Everything was different from the way it had been planned. And I knew the meaning of stupefaction: I had caught up my pants and shirt and stood paralyzed for an endless moment in the act of dressing, the thought numbly beating in my brain: "I won't get there in time—it's no use—I won't get there in time."

I don't know how long this lasted. But I could see my men advancing, too, bravely and steadily, at this end, to keep the village from being taken, for Paredão consisted of only one straight street—like a gun barrel. But all the while I kept telling myself that I was a fool, an ass, a thousandfold idiot, for now my opportunity was hopelessly lost, and the war was raging, out of my control. I finished pulling on my clothes, and heard a voice: "Don't go there, are you crazy? It's no use—stay here and let them fight it out between themselves, because now everything is being done wrong and different, according to no plan, and you have nothing to do with it, for they spoiled the war." That is what I heard, a soft whisper, a little voice lying to me very friendly-like. Was it my own fear? No. Ah no, the hair was bristling all over my body. That loathesome sweetness of voice. I swore at myself. A fellow came running, and I almost shot him. A deserter? Ah, no, it was Sidurino, running for a horse. Good for him! He was going to dash to Cererê-Velho for reinforcements—have them attack the enemy from behind. I hugged my rifle and ran forward. I felt no fear whatever. Fully alive, I joined my companions. My men! I gave orders. Bullets were flying.

It was like a raging fire. The bursts from the enemy's guns were so bright it hurt to look—like looking at the sun, a rising sun, at that! Their bullets splintered and splattered. They could have knocked the bark off all the trees in a forest.

Ah, those jagunços of mine—like flattened armadillos—were burrowing into the ground and finding shelter behind everything. They knew how to fight without being told, as if they had always known, from inside their mothers and fathers. Yelling and bellowing at the top of their lungs. I had arrived and taken up a position. "By the wounds of Christ!" I shouted, and my people shouted other things in response. A rifle in your hands is a stirring thing. We fired from inside the yards, and advanced. We fired from behind the houses. And we held the head of the street. The racket from the shooting was like some kind of machine. Many pressed the trigger at the same instant: five men, five fingers, five hands. We had to crouch low in shallow holes. Even behind shelter, your head turns instinctively, as if to dodge the bullets. But you do not get panicky. I would say: "Here!", and release the hammer against the firing pin. I cautioned Diadorim not to get careless. Diadorim said: "Be careful, Riobaldo." Diadorim became dishevelled—handsomely so—his face was all eyes. Was I in command? You command in the present, not in the past. As the leader, I was Urutú Branco, but here I had to be also Tatarana, the sharpshooter who never missed. If an enemy aimed at me and I at him, and he escaped, it was a miracle—and that I was not killed was a miracle, too. The day of each man's death is decreed in advance. This was my lucky day. I say it but I also deny it, as you shall hear.

Everything there carried a curse, the bullets were seeds of death. To hear one whining past, almost grazing your scalp, made your hair stand on end, and it was even painful, really painful, just as if it had pierced your eye socket—the kind of bone-invading pain that you get sometimes in the roof of your mouth from eating ice cream. It was the pure face of death. Then Marcelino Pampa was hit—it had to be him. He didn't even look at anybody, just doubled up and was about to hit the ground with his forehead, when he sprawled with hands out-stretched and the blood gushed twice from his mouth. His life's blood. He looked as if he had been stepped on by a steer. I fired ten times to the front of me, to avenge his death. Then I looked at him. A man dies more completely than he lives, without sudden fright, and he still has secretion in the corners of his eyes, snot in his nose, spit in his mouth, feces, urine, and undigested food in his guts. But Marcelino Pampa was a man of gold who deserved a woman's tears over him, tremulous fingers to close his eyes. You won't soon see another like him, of such real worth, able and dependable, who looked for no praise. If only there could have been a lighted candle at his feet—just one, if no more—that the flame might have guided his soul's first steps, for they say that only a flame sheds light on both sides of death, the hither and the yon. I pulled the body to one side, so it would not lie in a mud puddle, for there had been rain during the night, and Diadorim picked up Marcelino's leather hat and covered his face with it. May the peace of heaven be with him still, that companion, Marcelino Pampa, who without doubt would have been a great and good man, had he been born in a big city. I turned on the heat. The place was falling apart, shattered by bullets.

But we had managed to tighten our hold—we had taken more than half of the village, of the street. The two-story house remained in our hands. Anxiously, I took a good look at it—that fine house on the right-hand side of the street, its well-built door and window frames painted blue. It was the main dwelling house in Paredão, a queen among the others. Inside it, the Woman was being held in custody, and closely guarded. The boy Guirigó and the blind man Borromeu were also in there, for safekeeping. From the windows above and the doors below, my men were firing from time to time. That big, two-story house stood there, looking serene—it pleased me to see it towering over everything.

Should I go there?

"At present there are two men upstairs—one is José Gervásio. Downstairs, in the shop, there are about four." I was so informed by Jiribibe, who had to shout in my ear to make himself heard, such was the din from the shooting.

"They aren't enough for the job. You join them, Riobaldo." It was Diadorim who said this to me, after a pause. Bullets were whistling past. Some would strike the ground with an angry thud and tear up the dirt.

I went on firing, methodically. Three or four times. I reloaded my rifle.

"My duty is here, Diadorim. Where the danger is greatest," I said briskly. Everything that Diadorim advised, I would turn down, as if I had a foreboding.

"Go, Riobaldo. High up there is where the chief belongs. With your marksmanship, it is your duty. Up there you can reach farther. Besides, this position here is now secure," he said softly, persuasively.

I exchanged my repeating rifle for my Mauser pistol, pressed the trigger and fired. I don't know whether I killed anyone that time. Again, I looked up at and admired the tall house. Was it my post? At the same time I also looked at Diadorim: his attitude was convincing enough, like that of a doe which first shows herself, on purpose, then moves away in a feint to keep you from discovering her fawn, lying hidden in a thicket. That house was like a tower. There in its heights was the place from which to command—overlooking the whole of the battle ground!

"I'm going," I said, and went.

I left João Curiol in my place, a fellow of great merit. I crawled out and took the only path open: through the yards behind the houses. I turned once and looked back. I still wanted to see Diadorim. Love saying farewell with a smile and a sob, in the midst of life and death.

I advanced across the clear spaces and vegetable gardens, with my arms and equipment strapped on. Our people were everywhere, and shouted greetings at me as I passed, as is proper when a leader displays his valor. Jõe Bexiguento, alias Alpercatas, with his men. And João Nonato was there, too, with his cheerful air of good luck. I kept advancing, broke through a little bamboo fence, and went around a piece of wall through which Paspe had knocked some loopholes. And then I realized that Jiribibe had been following me. A good boy. You could see his little eyes only because they were not entirely black. "Do you suppose the riflemen on the other side know how to shoot?" he asked me. I wondered why he said that. Didn't he know that our fight now was to the death? Then he laughed and I saw that he was like a black kitten stretched out on the soft ground under a rose bush, sound asleep, deaf to everything about, its little paws joined in an attitude of prayer. Then, close to me, a pellet of steel buried itself into the trunk of a papaya tree. "Watch out, get down!" I yelled at Jiribibe. You could hear the wild roars of the enemy, in a kind of tuneless chant, according to which all of us were sons of bitches. The dogs! But Jiribibe shouted even greater insults in reply. Then, quickly, we gained some holes behind an outdoor oven, and at once a burst of gunfire and bullets rained about us like hail. A deadly place! We lay waiting. "Let's get out of here, Jiribibe, I figure they must have people shooting at us from the tops of trees," I advised. We started crawling. We had almost reached the back yard of the big house: only a small fence lay between us, a fence covered by a chayote vine, laden with fruit, enormous ones. "Le's go, Chief!" cried Jiribibe—and fell backwards, dead, a bullet in his forehead. I did not cry out, but continued crawling. When I made a final leap to the door of the kitchen, I knocked over a big basin that was leaning against the wall. As I entered, the basin behind me was riddled with bullets and clattered like an old tin can. When I went in, I was hailed by those who saw me: "Howdy, Chief!" and I responded: "Howdy!" At that instant, it seemed to me the war was becoming crazy. But I had no fear. Then I climbed the stairs.

Listen to my heart, sir, and feel my pulse. Look at my white hair. Living is a dangerous business, isn't it? Because we are still ignorant. Because learning-to-live is living itself. The sertão produced me, then it swallowed me, then it spat me from its hot mouth. Do you believe my story?

I climbed the stairs, hearing the wood creaking under my feet, and calling out repeatedly: "It's me coming, boys!" In those half-darkened surroundings, the musty air smelled like an old-fashioned Sunday. Then, I noticed that I was a bit out of breath and that I was thirsty. I imagined there must be a pot of fresh water there somewhere. "It's me, boys," I repeated. Even so, they were startled at first, but then showed their pleasure at seeing me. Those in the big room facing the street were Araruta and José Gervásio, making good use of their weapons, and the boy Guirigó, together with Borromeu, the blind man, seated on a bench against the back wall. The two of them were sitting close together, and trembling a little; they must have been praying.

"Where is the Woman?" I inquired.

The boy wanted to show me: she was locked up in a room. Was she praying, too? An old hallway, with many doors opening on to it; behind one of them they had shut the Woman, in a bedroom. The blind man held the key in his hand. It was a huge key, and he made as if to hand it to me, but I refused it. "Is there a jug of water around here?" I asked, in a great hurry. "They say there is one down there," the boy answered. I gathered he was suffering from thirst, too, and wanted to go with me, because he was afraid to go down the stairs alone. And the blind man also, though he did not answer, moved his mouth softly, softly, and it sounded like someone who had just finished chewing a piece of rapadura. It disgusted me. But he had not eaten anything. I could not contain myself: "Did you hear me, impudent one, did you hear me? Is that the way you show me respect and thank me for having taken care of you and brought you with me everywhere?" That's what I said. He said: "God protect you, Chief, on behalf of all of us. And I beg your forgiveness for everything." Then he knelt. Hearing and seeing this embarrassed me, and I felt a twinge of remorse. For it had been unkind of me to bring this man—without carnal vision, and of no use whatever—away from the place where from the beginning he had been living out his life. Now he must be suffering double terror, imagining that something might happen and we would run away, and leave him behind, in the clutches of the enemy. But these thoughts merely raced through my mind, since they had no foundation. I only remember and repeat them now to confirm the memory of them. Like the vague vision I beheld of Otacília, in that same hour. I went to the window, and in imagination thought to see her in that far-off place, wherever she was. I tell this so you may know how many different things enter a person's thoughts at the very peak of battle. José Gervásio and Araruta were crouched, each at one side of the window, their rifles in their hands, their cartridge belts filled. They were looking at me attentively, as if wanting some signal. Then a high bullet whizzed in, very close, and from its music I recognized it as coming from a comblém. I would have to give those two further training. I went to a window with my rifle, and scanned the area. I—the boss!

Listen, sir: I was high up there, towering over the scene, like a hunter in a blind, lying in wait for a blood-thirsty jaguar. Did I catch sight of something or not? I kept peering. Soon it paid off, the peering. Some of theirs, on a terrace across the way, were firing their deadly weapons at will. I took aim. One of them was a big fellow, a Bahian from the looks of his clothes. On the instant I dropped him with my trigger finger. He fell writhing, and another did the same. There were three of them; the third realized that there is a heaven, and started running and dodging from side to side. Wham! I don't know how many slugs I slammed into his back. Ah, this was great, up where I was. Just then they replied with a heavy volley. I stepped back, but continued observing them without letting myself be seen. It was a good two hours since the battle had started. And it was high noon.

Only cattle bellow for no reason, except cows. This time, the fighting would not come to an end without a show-down. Hermógenes was not the kind of dog to let go once he had sunk his teeth in; moreover, he had come from a distance of fifty leagues! The tune had to have an ending. Is there any way of telling it all correctly—all that took place? The gunfire, screams, echoes, thuds, shouts and shooting, and shatterings. There were even moments of silence, for the volume of sound rose and fell. The noise of mingled blows, rattlings, splinterings, poppings, thunderings and explosions, would first dwindle, then go suddenly dead, or taper off slowly into silence.

I lost track of time. Time? If people had to stop to think— that's another thing: I see time as rising from underneath, quietly, softly, like water in flood. Time is the life of death. Just some of my foolish ramblings—don't pay any attention to me. But all the same, it was on matters like these, I repeat, that I longed to have questioned Diadorim the previous night when we had gone walking together. At that time, I had wanted to ask him:

"Don't you think the whole world is crazy? And that the only time a person leaves off being crazy is when he is completely filled with courage or under the spell of love? Or when he is praying?"

I did not ask the question, but I knew what Diadorim would have said in reply:

"Joca Ramiro was not crazy, Riobaldo; and, him, they killed."

Then I could have said:

"Well, anyway, when all this is over, Diá, Di, then when I get married, you must come live with us, on a fazenda, on the good banks of the Urucúia. On the Urucúia, near the mouth, there are some beautiful sand bars and islands, with green trees leaning over their edge. And there are many birds there, all the nice kinds we saw at Rio das Velhas, jaburú storks, water hens, and white herons, and pink herons flying over in clouds, like a woman's dress. And the little red-legs, which step about and preen themselves so daintily—don't you agree that of all birds they are the prettiest and most loveable?"

I had not been able to say those words of balm to Diadorim; in fact, we talked only of commonplace matters—munitions and equipment, preparation for battle. But now, there, surrounded by death, I thought the matter over; and even if Diadorim had been near me at that moment, what would I have said to him? Even today, I don't know. How could I have known what was in store. There, all around me, I was gently branding men with the iron of death, like a cattleman who burns his brand on a window or door, or on the board of a corral fence or wall of a house, wherever he goes, to make known the brand of his cattle. Like that. I remember I had a headache; it was a bad headache, that didn't let up; it felt like an auger boring in. I sweat it out. Must have been from thirst.

Then it happened: bullets flying about like hummingbirds— some hitting and splitting and splintering the window frames, others falling to the floor, their force spent in ricocheting, and lying there flattened like a piece of lead or looking like hard filberts. They lay, slowly cooling, harmlessly giving up their lethal heat that could have meant someone's death. José Gervásio and Araruta withdrew to the center of the room, and urged me to take cover. But I stayed where I was. I said no, no, no. My hands had begun to shake, but not in fear. My legs did not tremble. But my fingers twisted nervously up and down, as if I were playing the harmonica. Then I yelled: "Dunghills!" They replied with a fusillade—a close volley—the reports and whistling of bullets coming like a driving gust of wind behind the rain. Even so, I remained standing and firing, without leaving the open window or giving way. I did some good shooting, with utter disregard for the missiles flying about. Not that I was courting death, you understand. I wanted to experience the feeling of greatest courage. A male and his rifle, discharging salvos. Was my body supernaturally invulnerable? I'd rather think not; I don't want to think about it. I killed but was not killed. And I saw. Without danger to my person.

It was then that I became momentarily alarmed: down below, the situation was changing. What had happened was that, unexpectedly, a part of Hermógenes's men—there were so many of them, the filthy pack—had succeeded in working themselves into position behind my people at the head of the street, and were attacking them from the rear. Was it possible they were going to win? Ah, no, they could not beat us. Even yet I can see my friend João Vaqueiro: all man, very dark, cursing a blue streak, not even sweating in his all-leather outfit—he kept going forward, attacking as he went, his back exposed. He died, they killed him. After about a hundred yards.

Ah, no! Ours were standing fast, firing streams of bullets. What a fight!

And I, hesitating on my feet, regained my confidence: instantly I knew where my duty lay. Was it to go down into the street and join my men? I could not, should not, do it; I saw that. A man, a chief, had to remain there, in that place on the top floor. But I ordered Araruta and José Gervásio to go, go quickly! They themselves wanted to. They went down the stairs. The din from the gunfire was almost unbelievable. Was it not all-out war? Like a big pot on a trivet boiling over. I waited. When the end was in sight, I was standing in the back of the room, alone, with those two: the boy, Guirigó, who was wringing his hands, trembling, his face twisted and his lips parted, as if in pain, grimacing. He was just a boy. And Borromeu, the blind man, with his eyes closed.

I felt sorry for them. I could hear nothing, and I said: "Really?" Then I said: "You must have patience, my sons. The world is mine, though not just yet." I assured them that the more blows, the greater the noise, was a sign that we were winning—we were winning—winning! I slapped the smooth stock of my rifle hard. Victory! Ah, victory—and I in the midst of it, as if driven there by the winds.

Was it not so? Not quite a half hour later I witnessed a new tumult, at the opposite end of the street, but one that made my heart leap, as if I were seeing a miracle. What had happened was that my people from Cererê-Velho, followers of João Goanhá, had suddenly shown up behind the Hermógenes and were attacking them from the rear! In my exultation, I fired off shot after shot! The battle now had become enormous.

Taking both sides together, you can figure there were three hundred or more jagunços engaged in fierce fighting. Was there a single blunderbuss left in the whole of the gerais? There was not. And here courage would be pitted against courage, until the last of the ammunition was spent. The battle was being fought by men who were both surrounded by and surrounding others. Could they ever be untangled? Only after victory. I had no doubts. I was born to win. At that moment I saw that it was I, above all others, it was I who stood out the most, and I recognized that my real duty was not to be afraid. To have no fear whatever. And I had none! Let me have none, and all would give way before me. I was sure of it. I became puffed up. Then I thought I heard someone laughing at me, hidden laughter, sounding as close to me as if it were my own, muffled. Wereupon I became suspicious. I refused to think about what I didn't want to think it was, and assured myself it was a false notion. I was about to let out a curse: "Satan! Filthy One!" but I said only: "S—Sertão—Sertão—."

Pausing, I heard someone clearing his throat. I turned around. It was only the blind man, who moved his arms and hands, looking mean, like a Negro loading a gun. Without knowing why, I asked him:

"Are you the Sertão?"

"Yessuh, yessuh, I am the blind man, Borromeu, yessuh," he replied.

"I don't understand," I stammered.

Stammered, no; I gagged—for when I started to talk, I felt my tongue drawing back, and my whole face trembling, my cheeks, lips, even the tip of my nose and chin. But I got hold of myself. I did not experience fear. I told the blind man to sit down, and he obeyed; he was simple-minded; he did not sit on the bench but squatted on the floor instead. He laughed, and it disgusted me. But disgust is fear, is it not? Greater fearlessness

God could not have given me, and I returned to my post at the
window, from which I could oversee and command. Ah,
Mausers and Winchesters, what soft little whistles. And the
hiss of big, old blunderbusses. But, let me tell you, I did not
stand there idle; on the contrary, anyone who showed himself,
got his.

This went on for hours: cracks, bursts, and explosions under-
scored the continuous whipping about of bullets. I stayed where
I was, following out my destiny. But how can I tell you what it
was like? The telling of it turns it cold and empty. You can't
feel it, you can't see it. Shall I tell you what I did? Peering
through my gunsights, I fired endlessly. But I did not let out
yells and insults; for one thing, because I could not make my
mouth tremble in the proper way. I stomped, instead, on the
wooden floor—perhaps you can hear it. The fury of battle out
there and down below took possession of me to the point where
I almost forgot my headache, which had grown gradually worse,
risng up through the roof of my mouth, ever since the shooting
began. And I had not had a drop of water, nor smoked a cigarette. Sweating out my destiny—to my great sorrow!

How can I tell you, so that you will feel what I felt? Were you
born there? Did you undergo what we did? Did you, sir, know
Diadorim? Ah, sir, you suppose death to be a weeping and a
fallacy—deep earth and quiet bones. You should, instead, imagine someone in the dawn of love dying for one alone. You
should see men with hands upraised, killing one another, frothing in their fury! Or, one man firing and another coming at
him through the smoke, knife in hand, when the one who had
been killed, was the one who did the most killing. You sir. . . .
Give me a minute. I will tell you.

Everything was moving toward the end. My last shot was just
before I turned around to reprimand the blind man, Borromeu;
and besides, my arms were paining me. That useless, queer
blind one, squatting there. All he had done was to say, dully:
"Won't somebody give me something to eat?" I bawled him out.
Ah, let him stay there, alone, chewing tobacco and spitting
black and yellow. I started to sweat. Then, suddenly, he started
to sing: a laud.

My arms felt heavy as lead. Then I noticed something strange —the shooting in the street had stopped; it seemed a full minute since it had died down. Yes, they had ceased firing, but they were yelling, a hubbub of voices, screaming obscenities at one another. Had they used up all their ammunition? I looked at them but did not understand. Should I shoot? I think I wanted to shout, but put it off till later. I looked at the tangled scene below. And who should I see coming out of a door to join the rest —holding before him, and cocked, his two-barreled pistol—but the backlander, Teofrásio, as if he were a regular fighter! And, commanding his men, I saw Hermógenes! The hat on his head was like a big, round tray.

Then I understood—God help me.

I saw what was about to take place: Hermógenes's men and mine had issued a great and crazy challenge to each other, and were preparing to carry it out: they were gathering at opposite ends of the street—and drawing their knives. Looking, I saw Diadorim and watched his movements. I strove to shout but couldn't; I was beside myself, my head was spinning. That street was like a long pit in hell. I lost my voice.

A cramp twisted and paralyzed my arms. A thread of sweat ran down my spine. Who was disarming and shackling me, robbing me of my strength? "My honor—my honor as a brave man!" I said, groaning, to myself: a soul which had lost its body. The gun fell from my hands; I could not even hold it against my chest. I saw that my fingers were useless!

Then I became horror-stricken, as on the brink of a precipice. I saw Diadorim coming from the end of the street, advancing, with his dagger drawn—running amuck. After him all the others were rushing forward to the attack. A hundred yards. All of them, furiously, bravely. All except me! It made me want to tear my hair that I could not issue an order, shout advice. I could not even whisper to myself. My mouth filled with saliva. I drooled. But on they came, like a raging wind, roaring, rushing headlong. Then—they met and clashed. And I had to vomit, in my anguish. I tried to pray—but only one thought kept flashing through my brain. Do you know what it was? This one: "The devil in the street, in the middle of the whirlwind." If you only knew. Diadorim—I wanted to see him—hold him in my sight. I heard my teeth chattering. There was Hermógenes; inhuman, filthy—to the hairs of his beard. Diadorim went at him. He feinted and dodged. They grappled and fell to the ground, fighting.

And I just looking on! The whole place was a howling mass of bloodthirsty men, wrestling and rolling, arms and legs flying like those of a runner. "The devil in the street, in the middle of the whirlwind." Blood. They were slicing the bacon under the human rind, slashing the flesh. I saw a man's flannel shirt, then his bare back, his arms flailing as he fell, looking like the body of a butchered hog, singed and scraped. Lurching, I struggled to pray but could not. Steel, dripping red. Knife against knife, toe to toe. "The devil in the street, in the middle of the whirlwind." Now, ah, I looked and saw—clearly in a clearing—I saw Diadorim stab and bleed Hermógenes. His knife went in deep where neck and shoulder meet—the blood spurted in a high arc—he had insisted on doing a good job of killing! A sob stuck in my throat; I wanted badly to pray, if but a word, whether shouted or in silence; but the only thing I succeeded in doing, in the frenzy of the moment, was to imagine Our Lady seated in the center of the church. It was a drop of solace. But down below was the bitter gall of death, without remission. Which I swallowed alive. Cries of utter hatred. Howls. Suddenly, I could see Diadorim no longer! In the sky, a blanket of clouds. Diadorim! Now, in a paroxysm of pain, I found I was able to move; I stirred myself, I bit my hand in fury. I rose out of the abyss. I could hear firing in the distance, shots coming from great depths. Then I passed out.

I have outlasted the storms.

You, sir, knew nothing about me. Do you now know much or little? A person's life, all the paths into its past: is it a story that touches upon your own life at all, sir?

Getting back. After awhile I came to, my mind in a fog, trying to remember what had happened, trying to see, though my eyes remained closed. I heard the pleadings of the boy and the blind man, who were rubbing my arms and chest, and from what they were telling the others I learned that I had lost consciousness, fainted, but that I had not foamed at the mouth nor slavered. I continued in a daze. Then, I vaguely know, I was receiving aid from others—Jacaré, Pacamã-de-Prêsas, João Curiol, and Acauã—they were wetting my face and mouth, and I licked the water. Suddenly I was wide awake—as in that instant when you're waiting for the thunder clap, though you have seen the lightning strike.

Diadorim had died—irrevocably—and was gone from me forever. I knew it, but I did not want to hear it; tears filled my eyes.

"And the battle?" I said.

"Chief, Chief, we won, we finished them! João Goanhá and Fafafa, and some of ours, even chased a few who were left and finished them off, too," replied João Concliz. "Hermógenes is dead, stone-dead." The one who said this was João Curiol. Dead. Stone-dead. The devil's own. Hermógenes was no longer. What remained of him must look like someone whose blood had all poured out through a knife gash at the base of the neck: he would have turned yellow, the color of yellow ocher, his features twisted into a sardonic grin—a face in the grave.

From their voices, from the episodes that all were now relating, I saw how we had won, sadly enough. After the madness of the hand-to-hand fighting in the street, João Goanhá had turned against the bandits who were attacking from the rear, and had wiped them out, too. The whole thing didn't make sense. I raised my hands. I saw I was able to. My body was stiff, and my legs refused to bend, which made my steps awkward. But I got up groping, and walked; my back to the window.

It was at this point that Alaripe and Quipes showed up. They were no doubt bringing me news of Otacília; I was having a hard time remembering so many things. They were returning from a long distance, disappointed in their journey:

"It was not your betrothed, Chief," Alaripe reported. "The man's name was simply Adão Lemes, and he was accompanying his sister, a fazendeira, whose name was Aesmeralda. They were returning to their homes. So we left them at Pôrto-do-Ci, at the mouth of the Caatinga."

So many people in the world, I thought. So many lives in conflict. I thanked Alaripe, but turned to the others, and asked:

"Were many killed?"

"Too many."

João Curiol had answered me, kindly, as a friend. I sobbed without tears, openly. Now someone was telling me that the men were digging graves, taking turns at using the tools. Alaripe rolled a cigarette and offered it to me, but I refused it. "And what about Hermógenes?" Alaripe inquired.

Some of the men went to open that room and bring out Hermógenes's wife. "Go to the window, lady, and look below in the street," João Concliz told her. She wasn't a bad woman. "Take a look, lady, at a man who was possessed of the devil, but who has already begun to stink, slashed by honest steel." Would the Woman suffer? But she said no, shaking her head slightly, seriously. "I hated him," she said, and it made me shiver. Perhaps I was not yet entirely myself, from the pain that had knocked me out, and I had to sit on the bench against the wall. Half consciously I heard snatches of the talk around me. The Woman was talking. She was pleading that they bring to her the body "of that handsome young man, with the green eyes." I jumped up, and letting the tears flow, I ordered: "Bring Diadorim," for it was to him she was referring. "Let's go get him, boys. He means Reinaldo," explained Alaripe. I stayed behind, with the boy, Guirigó, and the blind man, Borromeu. "Oh my Jesus!" I heard them exclaiming.

The hot tears that burned my cheeks and salted my mouth, were now falling cold. Diadorim, Diadorim, oh, my glorious, green buriti palms. Buriti, of the golden flowers. And they brought him up the stairs and laid him on a table. I could not see him clearly through my tear-blurred eyes—it was like looking at flying white egrets. I told the men to go find candles or wax torches, and to light high bonfires of good wood around the darkening village.

I choked back a sob of pity. I heard the woman saying she would wash and dress the body. Gently, she wet the towel and wiped Diadorim's face clean of the thick crust of dry blood. His beauty was unchanged, unbelievably unchanged. Even lying there, white as powder, his face like a mask, without a drop of blood. His eyes had remained half open, so you could look into

them. The features distinct, the mouth dry. The hair looking as
if it would last forever. I do not write, I do not speak of it, not to
give it reality. It didn't happen, it couldn't be, it isn't true! Diadorim. . . .

I was telling you that the Woman was going to wash the body.
She was praying prayers of Bahia. She told everybody to leave
the room. But I stayed. The Woman shook her head gently, and
gave a sigh. She had misunderstood me. Purposely, she did not
show me the body. And she said—as Diadorim lay there, entirely nude—she said:

"She is in God's hands. The poor girl."

Then I learned what I have been keeping from you—and
please forgive me—so you would discover this bitter secret at
the same instant that I did. Diadorim's body was that of a
woman, a perfect young woman. I was dumfounded.

Pain is no greater than surprise. Like the kick of a gun.

I raised my hand to cross myself, but used it instead to stifle
a sob, and to wipe my tears. I wailed my grief aloud. Diadorim!
Diadorim had been a woman—a woman whose beauty outshone
the sunlight on the waters of the Urucúia, as I in my despair
cried out—who revealed herself in so terrible a revelation.

Don't mind me, sir. Wait a moment, I'll tell you the rest. Our
lives never come to a real end.

I reached out my hands to touch the body, then I trembled
and drew them back, as if on fire, and lowered my eyes. The
woman spread the towel and covered the body's nakedness. But
I kissed the eyes, the cheeks, the mouth. I imagined what her
hair had been like—her hair which she cut with a pair of silver
scissors—hair which if left to grow would have fallen below her
waist. I did not know by what name to call her; in anguish I exclaimed:

"My love!" I leaned against the window to shut out the sight
of the world.

The Woman washed the body and dressed it in the best garment she could find among her own belongings. Between the
hands folded across the breast she placed the cord and scapulary which had been mine, and a rosary made of small uricury
palm nuts and Job's-tears. The only thing missing—ah!—was

the much-traveled amethyst stone. Quipes came with the candles which we lit and placed at the four corners. All this took place in my presence, Others, like good Christians, had gone to open the grave. But first, out of my bitterness, I had told them: "Bury her apart from the others, in a meadow by a stream, where no one will ever find the grave nor know where it is." Having said this, I broke down completely once more. When I got hold of myself, I realized that the Woman and I were clinging to each other, weeping and sobbing together. And all my hard-bitten jagunços were crying, too. Then, we went and left the body, buried in the graveyard of Paredão, in a plain of the sertão.

She had been in love with me.

That was the last hour of the day.

The sky is falling like a curtain. I have told you all. In what I have told you, perhaps you will discover the truth for me, even better than I. That was the end.

Here the story ended.

Here, the finished story.

Here the story ends.

I galloped away from there in a frenzy. But first, I divided up the money I had, and threw away my cartridge belt—I put an end to the jagunço Riobaldo! I said goodbye to all, forever. The only ones that came away with me were the boy, the blind man, and the surviving backlanders: these I had to take back to their land, their homes. And the Woman: I said goodbye to her, too. How strange it seemed to do so—meaningless, without rhyme or reason. I also instructed João Curiol—a good Bahian in word and deed—to take her wherever she wanted to go.

I abdicated.

Where I would go, I knew quite well, even in my delirium. To one place alone: to Veredas-Mortas. Back, back—as though by seeing it all once more, repeating all, I might have again that which I had not had—Diadorim restored to life. Those were my thoughts, my poor, foolish thoughts. But it is a time that I do not recall too well, because of the blow to my health. As I went along, suddenly I would be seized by a nameless terror, and

many times I had to take hold of something to keep from falling
in a swoon; and afterwards, for a long time, I could not remember anything—who I was, my name. But Alaripe, Pacamã-de-
Prêsas, Quipes, Triol, Jesualdo, Acauã, João Concliz, and
Paspe, took care of me: they had insisted—against all my
protestations—upon coming with me, and there they were. Afterwards, Fafafa, João Nonato, and Compadre Ciril, caught up
with us. My friends. On we went.

The uplands. The oceanlike expanse died behind us.

I kept struggling forward. Almost unconsciously. How else
could I have withstood my grief? At one place—Tuim—I remember, I had to change horses. And a settler at Lambe-Mel explained that the marshy lowlands through which we were passing were more correctly called Veredas-Altas, not Veredas-
Mortas. My compadre Quelemém confirmed this to me later.
Farther on, after that, I began to quake with fever. Tertian
fever. This is only a brief sketch of a long journey but you sense
the situation. If you were to make up a song about it, it would
have to be one of woe for me.

Before long, I caved in—I could not go on. At first, they carried me in a litter. Afterwards they took me to a very poor hut. I
was beginning to rave. The last thing I remember was being
laid in a cot.

They say it was typhoid combined with malaria, virulent
malaria, of the worst kind. They say nobody had ever seen fever
go so high—Alaripe told me afterwards—and that during the
seizures I would go out of my mind. Hearing tell about it reminded me of a story about a rancher, completely evil, whom
the devil finally took possession of for his sins; and while under
the spell, in the room of his house, he would howl like a wolf,
begging relief from the heat, and he was in fact so hot the
slaves had to keep pouring buckets of water over him to keep
him from setting the room on fire and burning down the place.
Nonsense. And that he did a dance of demons, which don't even
exist. Wasn't the sickness alone enough to make him do it? I
don't know how long I stayed at that place. But when I regained consciousness, and began to get well and straightened

out in my mind, lo and behold, I was no longer in the shelter of that poor little hut, but at another place—a large fazenda—where I had been taken without knowing it.

I was on the Barbaranha, in Pé-da-Pedra, as a guest of Seo Josafá Ornelas. I took chicken broth, sitting up in bed between white sheets. And that grief which had bowed me was already more or less distant. I remember everyone there, the day and the hour. The first thing I wanted to see was the date on a wall calendar. It brought me a feeling of peace. It was as if I were waiting for myself under a cool tree. There was just one thing wrong with me. I was like a bag full of stones.

But that Seo Ornelas was a man of great kindness and courtesy. He treated me with every consideration. I was like a prince in his house. All of them—his wife, his daughters, his relatives—took care of me. But what strengthened me the most was the repeated evidence that they sincerely esteemed me as an able and upright man, and they praised the fact that I had courageously gone forward to overthrow Hermógenes and rid the gerais of outlawry.

I kept getting better, until one day I was resting in the sun light in a plaited cotton hammock. I was awakened by a feeling of happiness, a presentiment. When I looked, I saw a girl approaching. Otacília.

My heart beat rapidly. It was telling me that the old was forever new! I declare to you, sir, my Otacília looked even more beautiful. She greeted me with proper embraces, harbingers of love. She had come with her mother. And her mother, and her relatives, were all pleased, and gave me Otacília as my betrothed.

But I told everything. I declared that the love I had for her was both true and great, but that, because of a foreordained fate, I had recently lost another and cherished love. I confessed it. And that I would need time for mourning and recovery. Otacília understood and approved that I should want it that way. She remained a few days longer, keeping me company and beautifully so.

She was sure that I would return to Santa Catarina and renew our relationship; and that there would be a wedding day with me in a serge suit and a flower in my buttonhole. I did return, my heart filled with happiness, for I was deeply in love with Otacília. And so I was married—it was the best thing I have ever done—and until this day she is my companion—you have met her, you know her. But this happened months later, when the fields turned green.

I had got well again, ready to start out, when who should show up but Seo Habão—he and Seo Ornelas had made up in the meantime. He showed that he was very glad to see me, and had brought me another horse as a present—a valuable and handsome gray one. I accepted it gladly, and thanked him sincerely. But he was also the bearer of important news, which he had gone to learn and confirm out of the kindness of his heart. It was that my godfather, Selorico Mendes, had died recently, blessing and recognizing me, proud of my deeds; and had left to me in his written will his two largest fazendas. Seo Habão wanted to take me there right away—to Curralim and Corinto— to take possession. But I declined; that is, I postponed it. Later on, however, I went, and received everything without complications, without suits, as there were no other legitimate heirs, and for this I give credit to my lawyer, Dr. Meigo de Lima.

Only, this happened later, because first there was something else I had to do, to satisfy my heart's demands. I thanked everyone for everything, and said goodbye to Seo Ornelas and his folks—people who lived by the gospel. I set out with only Alaripe and Quipes. The others I left behind to await my return, lest too large a company arouse suspicion. But before leaving, I asked Dona Brazilina for a strip of black cloth which I put on my arm as a mourning band.

Where I went was a place in the gerais of Lassance: Os-Porcos. I questioned everyone there, knocked on every door— the results were pitifully meagre. I had hoped to find some old woman or some old man who knew the story, who remembered her as a child, and who could have explained to me the reasons for many things. But we did not find anyone. From there we made a big circle: Juramento, Peixe-Crú, Terra-Branca, Capela, and Capelinha-do-Chumbo. I found only one clue. This paper— a baptismal certificate—from the church at Itacambira, where so many dead are buried. There she had been taken to the font. There her birth was recorded—on September eleventh, eighteen hundred odd. Here, read it: Maria Deodorina da Fé Bettancourt Marins, who was born to wage war and never fear, and to love greatly without knowing the joy of love. Pray, sir, for this soul of mine. Does life seem sad to you?

But no one can keep me from praying, can they? Prayer is the life of the soul. When I pray I am clean of all filth, apart from all madness. Or is it the awakening of the soul?

My grief was holding me back, consuming me. I had no will to live, so listless was I—even to breathe was an effort. And, Diadorim: there were times when longing for him gave me no rest, nor could I stop thinking about him. I had denied myself that love for so long, and the friendship alone now seemed empty and bitter. And love, and her person, she too had denied me. But meanwhile, my love for Otacília was also increasing.

On the way back, as I was coming away, I picked up some unexpected news at Barra do Abaeté. About Zé Bebelo! It had to be him. I don't know why, but it gave me a big lift. Zé Bebelo was said to be a few leagues upstream, near São Gonçalo do Abaeté, at Porto-Passarinho. I headed for it. How was it that long before this I had not thought about Zé Bebelo? We pushed on at a trot, following the river. You know, sir, the Abaeté River, so beautiful it is sad; and so wide, from hill to hill.

Zé Bebelo shouted: "I be damned! I be damned!"—and embraced me cordially, very happy to see me, as if nothing had come between us. He was the same as ever, bluff and hearty.

"As I live and breathe! Riobaldo, Tatarana, Professor," he exclaimed. "Did you want peace?"

He looked me over carefully, and practically smelled me, like two steers meeting again in the corral. He said I looked good, but thinner, and my eyes somewhat sunken.

"You're late! You know? I've been dealing in cattle. I've changed my ideas. To make lots of money—that's the thing. Lots of gold dust," he said to me.

It was a pure lie. But it could have been true. Because he—for him to live—he had to swagger, to be a big shot, as he soon demonstrated:

"Good for you! So you did away with Hermógenes, eh? That's fine. You were my pupil—now weren't you?"

I let him talk, for such glories meant nothing to me. But then, not understanding me, he stopped and said:

"Well, perhaps I didn't teach you, but at least I taught you how to save your skin."

I laughed, at both of us. I spent three days with him, there at Pôrto-Passarinho.

And Zé Bebelo discussed with me in private the plans he had. Such bluster! He wanted nothing further to do with the sertão, now he was going to the capital, the big city. Get into business, study to become a lawyer. "I want to write up my exploits in the newspapers, with pictures. I'll tell about our battles, the fame that is our due." "Not mine, no, sir," I said. He wasn't going to entertain people with my name. Then he changed the subject. But during the whole of those three days he never stopped trying to buoy me up, and making plans for my future life. But he could not blot out my grief completely. However, Zé Bebelo was not a man to stop trying. For which I give thanks to God!

Because, finally, he demanded my whole attention, and said:

"Riobaldo, I know the friend you need now. Go there. But promise me, don't put it off, don't disdain it! When you leave here, go straight there. Tell him I sent you. He is different from everyone else in the world."

He even wrote a note that I was to take. And when I said goodbye, he embraced me, and I felt his affection for me. Did he still have that whistle in his pocket, I wondered? Once again he shouted: "I be damned!"

It had to be Zé Bebelo to do what he did. Only Zé Bebelo himself, to help save my future. For the note that he gave me was to my compadre, Quelemém de Góis, in Jijuã, at Vereda do Buriti Pardo. Need I say more? Go there yourself, sir. In the month of May, when the cotton is ripe. Everything white. Cotton is his main crop, all the new varieties: rasga-letras, biból, and mussulim. You will meet a person of such rare quality, that just being near him, everyone becomes calm, smiling, kind. I even ran across Vupes there.

My compadre Quelemém took me in and listened to my whole

story. I saw with what enormous patience he looked at me—calmly waiting for my pain to pass—and that he could wait still longer. Seeing this, I felt ashamed. But, finally, I took courage and asked him outright:

"Do you think I sold my soul, that I made a pact?"

Then he smiled, with ready sincerity, and gave me the answer I needed:

"Don't worry about that. It is the future that matters. To buy or to sell, sometimes, is almost the same thing."

And with this, at last, I close. I have not been relating my life to attract attention. I have told what I was and what I saw in my early days. The dawn.

I close. I have told you all. Now here I am, like a cliff above the river. I move toward old age with serenity and work. What is in store for me? I carry on. The São Francisco River—so huge it is—seems like an enormous tree, reaching to the sky. It was kind of you to have listened, and to have confirmed my belief: that the devil does not exist. Isn't that so? You are a superior, circumspect man. We are friends. It was nothing. There is no devil! What I say is, if he did . . . It is man who exists.

The passage.

Glossary of Brazilian Terms

aguardente [ah.gwar.dehn'tih], literally "fire water"—same as cachaça (*q.v.*)

burití [boo.ree.tee'], a mauritia or burity palm (*Mauritia spp.*).

caatinga [kah.teen'gah], any region of stunted vegetation, especially
that found in the drought areas of northeastern Brazil.

cabra [kah'brah], bandit, ruffian; backwoods assassin; half-breed Negro.

cachaça [kah.sha'ssah], raw, white cane alcohol; called also *pinga*
and *aguardente.*

capanga [kah.pahn'gah], thug, ruffian; hoodlum; hired assassin;
henchman; bodyguard.

caruru [kah.roo.roo'], gumbo.

chapadão [shah.pah.dahoong'], tableland, extensive plateau.

comblém [koom.blém], a type of gun of foreign make.

compadre [koom.pah'dreh], bosom friend, crony.

conto [kohn'too], one thousand *milreis*—about $250.00 at that time.

delegado [deh.leh.gah'doo], chief of police.

dona [doh'nah], lady, madam; also, a title equivalent to Miss or Mrs.
prefixed to the Christian name: as, Dona Maria.

fazenda [fah.zehn'dah], large plantation or cattle ranch; a landed
estate. (The Portuguese equivalent of Spanish *hacienda.*)

fazendeiro [fah.zehn.day'roo], owner of a *fazenda;* cattle rancher;
planter.

farofa [fah.raw'fah], a dish made of manioc meal browned in grease
or butter; sometimes mixed with bits of meat, crisp fat, chopped
eggs, etc.

faveira [fah.vay'rah], a large leguminous tree.

gerais [zheh.rise'], high open country, vast upland plains in the
backlands.

gravatá [grah.vah.tah'], any of numerous plants of the pineapple family.

jacuba [zhah.koo'bah], a drink composed of manioc meal, water, sugar or honey, and *cachaça*.

jagunço [zhah.goon'soo], in this book, a member of a lawless band of armed ruffians in the hire of rival politicos, who warred against each other and against the military, at the turn of the century, in northeastern Brazil. *Cf. cabra* and *capanga.*

januária [zhah.noo.ah'reeyah], a brand of *cachaça* (*q.v.*).

joão-congo [zhoo.ah'oong kohn'goo], a large bird of the oriole family.

liso [lee'zoo], large, flat desert. *Cf. raso.*

milreis [meel.rays'], an old Brazilian monetary unit, equal at that time to about 25 cents.

mutuca [moo.too'kah], a kind of horse fly.

noruega [noh.roo.eh'gah], a cold, sharp wind; also, cool, damp ground sloping away from the sun.

pinga [peeng'ah], same as *cachaça* (*q.v.*).

piranha [pee.rahn'yuh], a voracious fresh-water fish: the caribe.

rapadura [rah.pah.doo'rah], raw brown sugar in hard squares, eaten as food or candy.

raso [rah'zoo], extensive tract of flat, desert land. *Cf. liso.*

saci [sah.see'], in Brazilian folklore, a small, one-legged, mischievous Negro, who pesters wayfarers at night or sets traps for them.

Seo, Sêo, Seu, Sio = abbreviations of *senhor* (*q.v.*).

senhor [seh.nhor'], mister, sir; any gentleman. [Used in formal conversation as the equivalent of "you."]

serra [seh'rrah], sierra, mountain range.

sertão [sehr.tahoong'], hinterland, sparsely settled interior of the country; in particular, the backlands of the Brazilian Northeast. In this book, the term refers mainly to the northen half of the State of Minas Gerais.

sertanejo [sehr.tahn.ay.zhoo'], backlander; an inhabitant of the *sertão.*

traíra [trah.ee'rah], a voracious, fresh-water tropical fish.

vereda [veh.reh'dah], in this story, any headwaters stream smaller than a river.

zebu [zeh.boo'], humped cattle.

A Note on the Type

THE TEXT of this book was set on the Linotype in a face called PRIMER, designed by *Rudolph Ruzicka*, earlier responsible for the design of Fairfield and Fairfield Medium, Linotype faces whose virtues have for some time now been accorded wide recognition. The complete range of sizes of Primer was first made available in 1954, although the pilot size of 12 point was ready as early as 1951. The design of the face makes general reference to Linotype Century (long a serviceable type, totally lacking in manner or frills of any kind) but brilliantly corrects the characterless quality of that face.

Composed, printed, and bound by
Kingsport Press, Inc., Kingsport, Tennessee.
Typography and binding design by
VINCENT TORRE

A Note about the Author

JoÃo GuimarÃes Rosa was born in Cordisburgo, Minas Gerais, Brazil, in 1908. He studied medicine and practiced as a country doctor in the backlands and as a military doctor, taking part in the civil war of 1932. In 1934 he embarked upon a diplomatic career; from 1938 to 1942 he was the Brazilian Consul in Hamburg, Germany; from 1942 to 1944, Secretary of the Embassy in Bogotá, Colombia; from 1948 to 1951, Embassy Counselor in Paris; and then an Ambassador, head of the Frontiers Service at the Ministry of Foreign Affairs in Rio de Janeiro. Notable among his works are *Sagarana*, 1946 (English translation, 1966); *Corpo de Baile*, 1956; *Grande Sertão: Veredas*, 1956 (*The Devil to Pay in the Backlands*, 1963); and *Primeiras Estorias*, 1962 (*The Third Bank of the River and Other Stories*, 1968). Shortly before his death in 1967, Guimarães Rosa became a member of the Brazilian Academy of Letters.